Jack Spartan
Varaci Runner

K. Edward Mallory

Contents

Prologue

He would have to make a decision sometime soon, but he had a few more things to consider before committing his plan to action. There were too many variables and too many open ends at this point. He was an earthling, a Tirran as they called it, something nobody had ever seen out here in Trader Space. If they knew he was a Tirran, he wouldn't really be able to explain his being here. The only way he'd managed to get by so far was to play the charade of becoming a *Varaci,* a Varaci runner, a transporter, a smuggler. Even though Varacis weren't related by any near-term galactic standards, humans were so close to being Varaci in appearance and basic genetic structure that he could pass for one anywhere, even on their home planet.

Not that anyone even had anything against Tirrans; it's just that they were off-limits. He would be considered off-limits, deemed an "unstable," part of a "not yet ready for prime time," as in not fit for the Galactic Trading Alliance. No Tirrans in Trader Space. Tirrans were considered by the Alliance Council to be *jubutaii-atuwahx,* a somewhat culturally primitive race that had the strange and violent characteristic of fighting and warring against their own species. No other race ever allowed into the Alliance had ever exhibited this behavior. Since no other Alliance race had ever displayed this trait, the Tirrans were deliberately isolated, labeled *hodenyett,* or "forbidden," forbidden to contact and interact with. It was feared their violent nature could turn outward to others of the Galactic Trading Alliance members, or so that's what they said.

Most Alliance trader worlds knew little about the Tirrans other than they were forbidden and off-limits for contact. This, of course, did not prevent them from mining the oxygen and other plentiful and easily accessible gases from the Tirran planet or the other planets and moons in the remote Sol system if they happened to be passing by. That was the extent of the contact allowed under the Alliance regulations. Most Alliance worlds had never even heard of the planet Tirra, and few if any had any idea of what the inhabitants even looked like. Being this far out on the rim left little opportunity for Alliance contact anyway other than the occasional mining or V dredge fueling pass.

There had been a few initial viability studies done by the Alliance Authorization Commission many yenets ago, but nothing remained of a current Alliance presence other than two autonomous black stealth monitoring satellites. There had been occasional incursions by a few infrequent rogue non-Alliance bootlegger ships. These were quite rare and not worth any policing efforts by the Alliance, as the planet was too remote and the Tirrans were supposedly still too primitive to trade technology of any value to the bootlegger trade ships.

There had been plenty of conflicts in the galactic trade empire over the eons, but there was never anything like the Tirrans, a species that fights and destroys its own race. Not that the Alliance couldn't handle this situation from a military standpoint, but it was something they preferred to avoid altogether, especially since the Tirrans' actual technology level wasn't all that far behind most of the other galactic worlds.

This part was true except for the fact that the Tirrans had never discovered even basic Warp Pulse faster than light travel. The Warp Pulse Errakk drive wasn't very efficient or fast, but it did get you into the galactic traffic flow. This in itself was also a strange developmental scenario. How could a somewhat technologically advanced, though culturally primitive civilization not have discovered basic light speed travel? There were many inexplicable curiosities about this Tirran world. Earth, or Tirra, was somewhat isolated far out on the rim arm more than two hundred light-years from any other inhabited world. It wasn't too far off the Veltac 327 navigation track between Heteron and the Demic Sa system, but that was as close as it came to any other civilized worlds.

He'd done a lot of thinking about this situation and wondered about it himself. From all the evidence he'd seen, he was convinced that perhaps some potential Tirran rival or enemy had engineered this situation. Maybe this had happened over many hundreds or even thousands of years to keep Tirrans, or humans as he knew his own race, from becoming a viable force in the Alliance once they emerged from their pregalactic beginnings.

He didn't know what race might have engineered this situation, but he was sure it wasn't the Varans, or the Varaci as they were called; they were too interested in basic commerce and profits, usually of the shadier nature, to be involved in a major political venture like he envisioned. They were also halfway across the galaxy and weren't even really aware of their near-genetic twins, the Tirrans, a.k.a. humans. To him, the fact that they looked nearly identical to humans only gave them the impression that they may have a grander political venue than they actually did. There was, however, a lot of evidence that pointed to his own theory. So he only had about three hundred other Galactic Alliance races that might fit the bill as far as being the prime perpetrators. He didn't really have time to waste on this particular speculation right now; he had other more pressing matters to contend with.

There was still a lot to do before he considered taking any action on Earth's behalf even though he desperately wanted to. He still had to get his consignment of stolen Selnak energy conversion data to the Negannah system and collect his particularly nice promised payment. He'd spent a long time trying to find a run like this that would pay off like he needed to cancel his many debts and obligations throughout the galactic quadrant. His greatest concern was keeping his beautiful and capable ship *Carratta* operating in the black and paying off the various obligations against her that he'd had to incur to acquire her and get her up to full operational status.

He'd been in good shape financially until the attack by the Rahvuuna pirates that had cost so much to repair. Everything always seemed to cost more from an operational standpoint than expected. Their run in with the Rahvuuna pirates had cost him close to two million credits after the Rahvuuna's electromagnetic penetration weapon had destroyed most of *Carratta*'s electrical systems. If it hadn't been for *Carratta*'s fully independent and isolated backups systems, they would still be floating around some dead planet as a derelict ship in a derelict orbit as frozen space corpses.

When they'd finally made it back to Irradoo after two moondats of slow sub light cruise without any quantum field protection, they'd had to spend two more weneks in a low-energy state orbit getting the basic repairs that would allow reentry. They'd had to spend that time contracting multiple ferry flights from Irradoo for the parts to repair the quantum field generators and get them back online so they could make a reentry to get to the surface for a complete refit and repairs.

Their current venture was one of a critical nature both financially and survivability wise. Once he got the data to the planet Epta in the Negannah system, it could be shielded and would be untraceable; but before then, the embedded trace programs could potentially plot and disclose his position to the Selnak. The Selnak weren't overtly violent, but they did guard their ion plasma drive technology with extreme prejudice.

They were actually just a slightly above average Alliance cartel race with regard to technology and economic viability, but their ion plasma drive technology was unrivaled by any other light drive system and was the main export product of their planet. Their hyperstream magnetic containment plasma "star in a can" drive propulsion system was used by 64 percent of the Alliance's races. It is the most efficient and cost-effective system yet developed, and the Selnak guarded it's strange, actually bizarre technology, quite jealously.

Their star drive plasma quantum field reactors also powered many of the galaxies-inhabited worlds with safe, plentiful, and cheap power. All that alone should have made them a major galactic financial power, but there was a lot of competition out there. Even with the best system, they had to sell their technology with a minimum markup just to stay competitive. Many had tried to replicate the technology for a hundred or more years, but none had succeeded.

It was rumored that the Selnak plasma drive and quantum field generators were products of an alien race not even from this galaxy, perhaps something the Selnak had stumbled onto accidently. Where it came from and how it worked no one really knew, except for the Selnak, and they weren't interested in sharing other than selling fully contained and inaccessible systems. The last thing the Selnak needed was for their technology to be readily copied by multiple other worlds.

Well, he was about to find out if the Selnak's tracking programs were as good as they were rumored to be. Were they that good, or was it all a ruse they used and the threat of retaliation to keep their coveted data secret? They were about to pass through the Jotumar Delta Two open sector of the Tlilnik Null Void where his ship *Carratta* would be fully exposed to any Selnak tracking and search probes that were looking for the encoded tracking signals of the embedded trace programs in their data modules. Anyway, that's what was rumored as far as how their embedded trace programs worked.

Their electronics and communications tech hadn't been able to detect any transmissions from the Selnak data modules, but then they didn't really have the ability to detect every form of radiated transmissions at every known spectrum or encrypted subspectrum. For all they knew, the Selnak tracking program might operate with some unknown encryption and transmission technology. Supposedly, the Selnak had placed search drones in every active quadrant of the galaxy. If any of their data modules ever began transmitting a distress code because they were separated from their secure paired core field module housing, then that would trigger a search-and-destroy or search-and-report response from the drone depending on which type of drone it was. More of those rumors Jack hoped.

Well, if he did get caught, God forbid, hopefully they'd just take his ship and strand him on some less-than-desirable rock somewhere. Under the circumstances, though, they might not be so well mannered considering the potential loss they might suffer if he completed his mission. A more likely scenario is they might strand him and his crew, but it wouldn't be on a habitable rock but more likely in the void of open space. Well, he'd find out soon enough. He didn't like this contracted mission one bit, but he was desperate, and it was a last-ditch effort to keep himself and *Carratta* and her crew afloat financially. Sometimes, you did what you had to do. This was one of those times. Who would have thought, two and a half Earth years ago, that he'd be worried about these sorts of issues? Well, he'd better worry, he thought; these were now his issues, and he had his plate full.

Chapter 1: Impact

Jack Spartan had spent a major portion of his life preparing to become an astronaut. Originally from a small town near Kokomo, Indiana, where he learned to fly starting at the age of fourteen, he was now in the hot seat of the new NASA space shuttle program.

His father was a dentist who had owned his own Piper Super Cub for recreational flying, and his mother had been a high school math and science teacher before retiring to raise their family of two boys and two girls of which Jack was the oldest. When he was thirteen, he got his first dirt bike and spent a great deal of time trying to give his mother a heart attack with his crazy riding antics.

He began tinkering on a succession of motorcycles, cars, and eventually, airplanes after he started learning to fly. In addition to earning all of his pilot's licenses and ratings, he also earned an aircraft mechanic's license and, eventually, a maintenance inspection authorization endorsement. He now possessed a PhD in mechanical engineering from MIT, was an engineering graduate of the Air Force Academy, and also a graduate of the Air Force Test Pilot School. His acceptance to NASA's astronaut program was the culmination of many years of hard work and study as well as a natural talent for all things mechanical.

Sitting on the launch pad for the new ASLSS (Advanced Space Launch Shuttle System) mission, ASLSS 12, was the realization of everything he'd worked for and was now ready to accomplish. T minus four minutes and counting, auxiliary power units all online, all systems go.

Jack was officially the youngest shuttle pilot in NASA history and was now second-in-command of ASLSS Mission 12. At the age of twenty-eight, he met all the second-in-command qualifications and then some. He was also designated as the second mission payload specialist and second science officer after the two primary crew positions.

He had the same basic qualifications as the mission commander, Tony Mallory, but needed at least two actual space missions to be considered for mission commander. This would be his first actual orbital space mission. With over nine hundred hours of the older but upgraded F-22 and newer F-35 fighters as well as flight test time and 423 simulated shuttle landings, he was as qualified as any other non-command-rated shuttle pilot. Like all the NASA flight crew members, he was highly accomplished and well-rounded in many disciplines. He'd graduated number six in his class at the Air Force Academy overall and number two in science and engineering.

Fourteen years of Israeli martial arts training called Krav Maga, or Hebrew for "close combat," meant he also met all the physical requirements for NASA astronaut with ease. As far as his martial arts training, he had always said, "Hey, if you're going to do a sport for physical fitness you might as well do something practical with more than just basic fitness training on the menu." "T minus three minutes and counting. All shuttle navigation and system control modules are confirmed operational and transferred to ASLSS Shuttle *Victory,* solid rocket booster range safety devices show armed," announced the Capcom mission controller.

Shuttle Commander Tony Mallory was now flying his third ASLSS shuttle mission. He is a Navy lieutenant commander and son of a Navy admiral. His credentials were as impressive as Jack's with just a few more years of experience under his belt. He is an outstanding leader and highly regarded by his crew and fellow Navy and NASA officers. "T minus two minutes and counting. All ASLSS autonomous systems are green. Launch sequence auto abort command authority now in redundant override mode. Final launch sequence is go at T minus one minute, fifty-five and counting. Crew members close and lock your visors."

Payload Specialist Derek Chandler is a longtime NASA crew member and is flying his second ASLSS mission. Tory Jen, another seasoned NASA crew member, is the mission science officer as well as the mission flight engineer. Two additional mission crew members complete the mission roster. They are Mission Specialist John Parsons, Military Payload Technical Analyst, and Second Mission Specialist Terri Roberts also assigned as mission technical supervisor and security officer.

This is a combined military and scientific mission. "T minus one minute and counting. Orbiter transferred from ground to internal power. Ground launch sequencer is go for auto sequence start. T minus thirty one seconds and counting. Main engine hydrogen burn-off initiated. T minus sixteen seconds. Now T minus six seconds, main engine start. T minus three, two, one, zero, solid rocket booster ignition, all four SRBs verified at full output. We have liftoff, we have liftoff of Advanced Shuttle ASLSS 12 *Victory!*" announced the Capcom mission controller once again.

* * * * *

The Lokar trade ship, *Yuanjejitt,* which means roughly "bringer of far-off," completed its low V descent profile into the Tirran atmosphere to collect its needed fuel of plain condensed water and oxygen and ozone hydrates and other gases that it would later use in its somewhat primitively but massive reaction station keeping engines. Being one of the less developed and economically limited Alliance races, *Yuanjejitt* used their more primitive Errakk Star Drive and their older combination mass reactive hybrid ion maneuvering system for this routine cargo mission from their home planet Lokar to the final destination of the Voldan system.

The V dredge entry vector seemed a little off, but it was actually impossible to tell visually. The V dredge profile entry telemetry indicated all parameters normal. Still, Planetary Entry Officer Grenyu felt something was off. He conferred with Vice Entry Officer Jo-oot and Star Officer Jewatta. They weren't sure either; maybe the V trajectory was a little steep, maybe. Everything felt normal, just a slight cyclical vibration, which would be likely on a highly active weather planet like this blue ball below them.

If they had entered the system from the other side, one of the gas giants would have been closer and easier to access. As it was, the off-limit, except for cloaked fueling missions, planet known as Tirra was their best and closest fueling option. The V dredge profile showed normal on the display. Their captain, Tenemar Trolnhyett, and the prime crew were off duty and taking their feeding ritual in the ship's mess. Feeding time was a fairly complex observance for the eastern Docca Lokarans and was seldom interrupted unless something catastrophic was in the works.

A tiny, slow-moving target showed on their detection display. Jo-oot's wide, orange, catlike eyes narrowed, and his ears flattened and pulled up in the Lokar equivalent of a smile. A primitive Tirran ship was climbing through the thin upper atmosphere of the blue planet Tirra. The detection display showed a nonconverging trajectory and a dissimilar altitude convergence of almost 140 kahtaks, or a little over seventy Earth miles.

Even without the engaged cloaking shield, the Tirran ship would never see *Yuanjejitt* on their current V dredge trajectory, since *Yuanjejitt* would fall well aft of and below the Tirran ship's projected low orbit course.

Not a great deal was known about the fairly primitive inhabitants of the blue-and-green planet below, since they were, as a race, off-limits, forbidden as far as contact. Neither Jo-oot nor Grenyu had any idea of what the Tirrans actually looked like without going to the data core to do research on them. Even then, there might not have been much data available on a minor species that was unaffiliated with the Galactic Trading Alliance this far out on the galactic rim.

Jo-oot and Grenyu continued to watch the Tirran ship and the V dredge navigation readouts. The Tirran ship reminded him of pictures he'd seen of early Lokar mass thrust ships he'd seen in the academy history classes. He turned to ask Entry Officer Grenyu if she remembered ever seeing view videos of the early Lokaran mass thrust ships.

Suddenly, the amplitude of the cyclical vibrations increased substantially. They seemed to double and then triple in intensity. They were also coming at a faster rate than before, nothing too alarming, but nothing that could still be considered normal. "Jo-oot, verify V dredge entry status, state profile parameters and any deviations."

Scanning the V dredge fueling profile, Jo-oot could see nothing wrong. "All parameters and status appear normal, Grenyu." An audible high-pitched shriek suddenly filled the command deck of the Lokar trade ship. The V dredge entry angle suddenly felt and appeared much steeper than normal. Normally very shallow, they now appeared to be in a fairly steep downward pitch vector. Still, the parameters showed normal on the display. The ship lurched, and a horrifying screeching sound emanated from the hull.

"Abort V dredge profile," commanded Grenyu.

"The gas scuppers and distillation condensers now show deployed," hissed Jewatta.

"What? They shouldn't be deployed until V dredge perigee," replied Jo-oot.

The Lokar trade ship was big at 5.8 million metric Tirran tons when fully configured. When she was loaded with a complement of up to ten bulk ore hoppers, she would be an additional eight times her basic mass. The command core was large enough at three hundred thousand tons, and the modularized cargo bays added the remainder. Designed for hauling containerized cargo, the command core without the bulk ore hoppers was a large package/container transit ship with six cargo bay levels with a small crew of twenty-eight as well as a configurable modular passenger accommodation deck that could carry a small complement of up to eighteen hundred passengers plus another eighty additional crew if needed.

The passenger accommodations certainly weren't first class by any standards, but they could provide either private or shared berthing for the less discerning passengers that wanted an inexpensive way to travel the lesser known or lower economically advanced planetary trade routes. There were currently only 446 revenue passengers, as this wasn't what anyone would consider a typical holiday run to any high-traffic or desirable holiday destination. Most of the fare-paying passengers were technical workers or laborers heading to some new industrial job.

There were a few general purpose undesirables that had worn out their welcome on one of the previous planetary stops and even two aging sibling Cheemelet prostitutes that were hoping to scare up some new clientele on a different world that wasn't already bored with their wares.

In its full electromagnetic and visual spectrum cloaking shield, *Yuanjejitt* would remain invisible to any electronic sensing devices that the primitive Tirran civilization might have. There would be some magnetic flux pulses that weren't fully shielded, but this would leave little evidence of their refueling maneuver.

The full electromagnetosphere deflection shields were partially deactivated for fueling purposes, leaving only the ship's base magnetic signature and gravitational signature, which would be detectable for a short time. These were negligible in comparison to and in such close proximity to the Tirran planet. A thought passed through Grenyu's mind, Sorusites, the Sorun parasites that embedded themselves in ship's power and telemetry lines, feeding off the ship's energy. They could then replicate and feed basic stable telemetry signals to the ship's computers to hide their presence. That must be the reason all the V dredge parameters appeared normal but obviously weren't.

When they left Soru, they had deployed the Xamaniit search bots, semiorganic bot probes that could detect Sorusites, which were much like the search bots themselves. They must have missed something on the ship somewhere after their transit of Soru. Maybe they should have searched all the levels, not just the maintenance and cargo handling levels normally infected by this type of parasite. *Can't worry about that now,* thought Grenyu.

* * * * *

"All four SRBs confirmed fully separated at T plus three minutes, ten seconds," verified Flight Engineer Tory Jen as *Victory* progressed through a perfect launch sequence.

"Now T plus eight minutes, fourteen seconds. One minute, twenty seconds until MECO or main engine cut off," the Capcom mission launch announcer continued to narrate at the Cape.

"Mission profile on target, external tank separation in T minus eighty-four seconds," stated Jack.

"Roger, external tank separation in eighty-four seconds, mark," responded Commander Mallory.

"Main fuel tank ready for separation on completion of orbital verification telemetry," said Tory as a follow-up.

"Orbital maneuver commencing, maneuvering thrusters two, four, six, and eight firing," said Jack.

"Roll maneuver started, pitch to separation attitude started. Roll completed, in three, two, one, stabilization thrusters have fired.""Separation pitch maneuver now verified, launch burn complete."

"Ready for main tank separation in T minus twenty-eight, all systems go. Fuel valves confirmed closed," reported Tory.

"Commander also confirms fuel valve status secure, continue orbital entry maneuver," said Commander Mallory.

"Auto main fuel tank separation initiate in T minus four, three, two, one mark." A distant thump and a dull metallic clang were both felt and heard as the main tank separation latch dogs fired and released. A very small explosive charge fired and released the grappling dogs that secured the main fuel tank to the shuttle proper; it was still the most effective and reliable system yet designed. At the same time, the main maneuvering thrusters gave an auto-programmed three-second thrust vector away from the main fuel tank to assure positive separation.

NASA had wasted no time rebuilding the space shuttle program. A new, more advanced, more capable, larger, and greatly improved shuttle with a faster turnaround capability had been secretly in the works during the period of "NASA as a Muslim outreach organization." Three years later, the ASLSS launched its first shuttle into orbit, and the USA was soundly back in the reusable orbiter business. Five ASLSS shuttles were initially planned with five more to follow. *Victory* was on its fifth mission, while *Resolute* was being refurbished for its seventh mission. *Avenger* would be completed in two months, while *Courageous* and *Defiant* were rapidly being built by Lockheed, Boeing, ULA, and all their infinite number of subcontractors.

Tory Jen verified her display readout and confirmed visual separation on the monitor. "Initial separation verified, distance eighteen meters and increasing. Thirty meters, separation minimum distance verified. Separation of main fuel tank complete."

"Crew authorized to remove pressure helmets with main tank separation completed," stated Commander Mallory.

"OK to remove helmets," responded the shuttle crew members.

"Shuttle orbital maneuvering authorized," stated Jack.

Roger, shuttle maneuvering authorized, shuttle commander has control," replied Tony Mallory.

"Commander has control," verified Jack.

"All stations report," ordered Commander Mallory.

"At T plus fifteen minutes, twenty-two, all flight systems and navigation show normal and green," stated Jack.

"All shuttle systems normal and green, life support and pressurization normal, all maneuvering thrusters green after separation, all engineering systems green, all systems go," said Flight Engineer Tory Jen.

"Payload secure, main cargo bay and payload verified secure, subsystems and payload arm secure, mission status fully up and go," responded Payload Specialist Derek Chandler.

"Military Payload Technical green and go," said John Parsons.

"Military Payload Technical is green and go, confirmed," responded Terri Roberts.

"Roger all green and go station reports," said Commander Mallory. "Great work, crew. We have successfully completed initial launch and orbit objectives. Stand by checklist for final orbital maneuver attitude and pre-ISS docking checks to follow. We're still six hours from ISS rendezvous, but we'll need to complete the checklist early per the spec ops for our mission profile. Our attitude change and mission orders will begin in fourteen minutes. If anyone needs a quick break, now would be—"

Suddenly, there was a feeling of intense pressure and disorientation, a feeling of massiveness, of inertia, nauseating fullness, of waves of immenseness consuming smallness, like krill being consumed by a whale. It wasn't describable; it was nothing any of them or anyone else had ever experienced. It was like a massive monstrous animal, a leviathan or a mountain or a planet. It was, was . . . just there, and there was nothing to do but absorb it.

What was it? Someone shouted, muffled, "What the hell, what the . . ." Something, something in the back of Jack's mind knew what it was, a pressure wave, a pressure wave of indescribable magnitude, in space, that didn't make sense. He reached for something. Now what? What was he supposed to do automatically? Hard to think. *Yes, yes, the quick don oxygen mask. The pressure, the, the*—his head hurt—*the pressure.* But what could cause such a thing, something like that? Noise, metal, tearing, shrieking, unbearable, totally consuming noise, blackness, light, flash, pain, silence.

* * * * *

The Lokar trade ship leveled from its steeper than normal V dredge angle, nearly three times their normal approach angle for a standard fueling run and then pitched down again. Grenyu thought aloud, "It must be the Sorusites. There was no other explanation." How else could they not have accurate systems telemetry? The ship finally leveled again; the scuppers and condensers were already deployed, deployed early but not by command. They were much, much lower in the atmosphere now, much lower than planned. There was a good possibility they might be detected this low.

The sheer mass of their ship disrupting the atmosphere of the off-limit planet might be detectable by the primitive Tirrans. Well, they could worry about that later if they had to explain themselves to the Star-Nav Council. Next time, they'd make the Xamaniit search the whole ship. Demil, shog, and zemit were all Grenyu could think.

"Grenyu, at this altitude, the fueling hoppers will be full in less than a third the normal time, probably as little as seventeen hundred septus once we engage the condensers and separators," chirped Jo-oot.

"Yes, thank you, Jo-oot. We will have to calculate the time and monitor our pressures carefully. The separators will be stressed operating at this high of an input pressure, but they should be OK. We should be able to modulate them to a lower level. I will call Captain Trolnhyett and advise him of our situation. This situation meets protocol for interrupting feeding ritual. Jewatta, do you concur that this situation requires interrupting feeding ritual?"

"Yes, Grenyu, I concur this situation meets protocol for interrupting feeding ritual," replied Jewatta with a less-than-enthusiastic response. Having never interrupted a feeding ritual, they weren't sure what Captain Trolnhyett's response would be.

The partially cloaked Lokar trader leveled for the second time at thirty-two thousand mu-uts, or 105,000 Tirran feet. It had hit the shuttle in orbit when it had initially leveled at an altitude of 198 nautical miles, nearly on the same lateral trajectory and speed. In mission control, the shuttle *Victory* was there one second and gone the next. The launch from Vandenberg Air Force Base had taken *Victory* nearly twenty-four hundred nautical miles down range over the Pacific on its journey into orbit.

Some observers on Kauai got a glimpse of some debris entering and burning up in several widely and varied directions. All they knew at NASA was they probably had another Challenger or Columbia disaster. No one in Mission Control knew what had happened. Their perfect safety record for the new shuttle system had just ended. There was no adverse telemetry, no indications of any kind. Later, the

Air Force would discover a large, fast magnetic field anomaly detected by one of their supersecret antisubmarine magnetic anomaly detection satellites. What the satellite detected, though, wasn't in the ocean; it was everywhere. It was megalithic in size; it was all encompassing. It was an unexplainable anomaly. It made no sense, no sense at all.

* * * * *

Jack came to, deaf, dumb, and blind for a few moments. Nothing made sense; he was in the shuttle but not. Wires and debris were all around him. He was still in his seat, the oxygen mask clamped to his face. The seat, it was partially broken on its seat rail, tilting right and back against the cockpit storage bay and circuit breaker panel. The two-inch-thick window he was almost able to see through was shattered spiderwebs. He looked at his hands. His Nomex flight gloves that he had just donned after removing his pressure helmet and gloves were still on his hands.

He reached for the glare shield and pulled himself up and left. He reached down and released his five-way seat belt harness. His ears were pulsing with pressure—yes, pressure; there must be air if there's pressure. He took off his oxygen mask. He could breathe, but the pulses, pulses of pressure hurt everything, his ears, his lungs, even his eyes. His back and right leg hurt. He looked left. What he saw did not make sense.

There was no shuttle. *Victory* was gone from the center comm panel on to the left and back, just gone. He craned his head around and looked in all directions. All that remained of *Victory* was about fifteen feet of the front right portion of the cockpit, wires, tubing, fiber optics, and a smear of hydraulic fluid and miscellaneous debris. The ship was gone. He was in his seat, still sitting, breathing, trying to think.

Breathing, he was breathing. The ship was gone, and he was breathing and his oxygen mask was off. Yes, that's right, he had taken off his oxygen mask, and he was still breathing. He was trying to clear his head, trying to make sense of it. It didn't make sense, any sense at all. How on God's big blue Earth could he be breathing? Not a whole lot of anything was making sense. He looked at his watch. He'd set an elapsed time counter at liftoff. It was twenty-two minutes since they launched from Vandenberg. He thought he remembered T plus sixteen. He must have been out for nearly six minutes.

There was noise, loud screaming wind noise, light, wind, pressure, dark, something dark beyond the remainder of *Victory*. It was big and went in various directions. Metal beams attached to a floor of some sort. He got up and out of his seat. Carefully, he stepped over the debris of the shuttle and onto the dark surface. It was like a rough floor but tilted. In the distance was light, maybe three hundred meters away. He could see some sky, maybe a horizon. It was extremely windy outside the remains of the shuttle. It was hard to stand up from the wind. It was buffeting from all around, and pressure pulses buffeted his ears.

The half shuttle cockpit was jammed up against a vertical support of some kind that went up at least three hundred feet in the air to a ceiling above with maybe a thousand or more hex-shaped holes in it. None of this made any sense. Where was he?

There wasn't much left of *Victory*'s flight deck. A piece of structural alloy channel was wedged under the main nav system's LED display. He pulled on it, and it came free. It was about thirty inches long. His LED flashlight was still in its holder. He grabbed it but couldn't find anything else salvageable. He was having some trouble breathing and thinking. Pressure waves kept pulsing in his ears and lungs. What the hell was happening to him? Where the hell was he?

He worked his way back from the shuttle, back against the dark rough wall. He didn't know where he was, but he figured he couldn't stay there. It didn't look promising at all in the direction of the light with the horizon, just a huge gaping maw of a hole at least a thousand feet wide and three hundred or more feet high. He moved behind the shuttle debris, the remains of *Victory,* and up against the dark wall. A small ridge or ledge was on the wall running back at about the four-foot level.

He followed this back, maybe eighty feet. Farther back, maybe another three hundred feet in the dim light, was a grid of some sort on the floor and ceiling. On the ceiling, the hex holes changed to a grid. He couldn't tell for sure; it was too dark and obscured now. The pressure pulses and wind were a little less here, but it was still hard to breathe, and his breath seemed to pulse in and out of his lungs by itself. Strange thoughts kept going through his mind; wherever he was, if he survived this, he'd have hell of an after-mission report to file.

He worked his way back holding onto the protruding ridge. He was nearly out of breath but kept going. After another couple of hundred feet or so, the horizontal ridge suddenly ended at a T and turned into a vertical ridge. In another ten feet, there was another vertical ridge. Another ten feet revealed another vertical ridge, but then there was a recess of some sort. It went from the floor to about five feet above the floor and then maybe six or seven feet wide. He felt around its edges. It was about a half inch deep and seemed to have a small gap at the recess area. Could it be a door or an opening of some sort?

His ears were really starting to scream from the pressure pulses, excruciating, it seemed. Maybe the pulses weren't as bad this far back. He covered his ears with his hands, which helped for a few seconds. It was getting harder to think. He felt hypoxic, like the time he'd trained in the altitude chamber. He felt near the middle of the door; nothing, just flat, rough, metallic surface. He felt left then right; same thing. *Damn* was all he could think. He felt all the way around the frame of the, whatever it was. Nothing; it was too dark to see clearly, and cold, really cold. Now that he thought about it, he didn't feel good. He had a throbbing headache now, and he was starting to get really cold, and his ears hurt and his lungs pulsed and his eyes watered. *Crap, this is going nowhere fast* went through his mind.

He decided to move deeper into the bay or whatever this place was. He came to another door-like recess area or not a door, whatever. He felt around; it felt the same. Next was another vertical ridge. He felt it down to the floor. He tried to stand up but felt dizzy and nauseous; his ears hurt, cold. He fell against the wall with his left hand against the second recessed area. There was something there, some sort of an indent with a shallow gap, maybe an inch wide and a quarter inch deep. Even with his LED light, it was such a dark, light-absorbing surface that Jack could see little. It ran from near the bottom right corner toward the center of the door but at about a twenty-degree angle up. It was about three feet long. It didn't feel like much.

He was about to pass it by, but his head felt like it was going to implode. He felt like his life was being alternately sucked out and pumped back into his body. His hands were cold and didn't seem to be working very well now. Everything was cold. He felt the indent then ran his fingers up and down it. He pushed the gap area; nothing. He moved farther in, pushed, a slight give, maybe. He moved all the way in, pushed with his fingertips. The gap folded in, partially, like on a hinge. He pushed harder; the rest of the gap folded in. He held it there a few seconds trying to think.

He ran his fingers the length of the gap. Something was protruding from the far right end, just enough that he could get his finger behind it. He wanted to scream and curse. His head felt like a balloon that someone was blowing up and letting the air out of about every ten seconds. He pulled with his finger on the thing in the gap. It was a metal bar of some sort. It pivoted out and was attached at the left side. There was a slight bang and a loud hiss. He felt wind or air blasting at him at the edge of the recess area. The whole panel moved inward about two feet.

A wind was blasting at him from the opening. It must be at a higher pressure than where he was. It must be pressurized because where he was now was minimally pressurized and cold. There was a slight glow inside. Well, he couldn't stay where he was, couldn't take anymore; his ears, head, lungs, and eyes couldn't handle another minute of the pulsing or the cold. He fought the rushing airflow and pushed inside. There was a fifty-mile-per-hour airflow trying to suck him back out. He looked and saw a corresponding handle on the inside of the door. He pushed it flat; the door hissed and closed. The wind stopped. He collapsed on the floor against the door. He could breathe, there were no more pulses, his ears and head still hurt but not as much, and it felt much warmer now. He passed out.

* * * * *

On the control deck, Grenyu was preparing to give the order to begin fueling. First, the condensers would be brought online and then the separators wound be fired up. Then the three-stage compressors would begin compressing and then liquefying and storing the individual gases that would eventually be ionized in their reaction thrusters for orbital position maintenance. It would take them a Nishdan week to load their cargo of Burun-Rioc ore and refit and load for the return trip. It wasn't a glorious career, but it paid fairly well. Lokarans didn't care so as long as they completed the mission on time; everyone would be happy, and there would likely be bonuses involved.

Grenyu secretly wished the captain would return to the control deck so he would be relieved of some of the current responsibility, but apparently, the captain was in no hurry to get back from feeding ritual. "Hull breech, hull breech!" screamed Jewatta, pointing at the ship's pressure monitor display with his fully articulating arm swinging wildly.

"Pressure drop in fueling bay maintenance access deck. We've had a hull breech. Should I override auto mode and seal all emergency pressure bulkheads?"

"Where? Show me now!" barked Grenyu.

"Here, scauper bay access door seven lower. It's here, uh, here, was here, right here. I saw a door breech and pressure drop of 0.2 xur. I don't see it now. It was right here, a manual door, sealed. How is that possible? It's not there now. Pressure is normal. I am sorry, Grenyu. I saw it on the display, right here."

"OK, Jewatta, I believe you, what you said you saw. It must have been a transient or a false warning, maybe just a bad proximity switch on the door latch, probably caused by the rapid pressure increase and fluctuations at this low altitude. Yes, that's most likely what it was. Watch it closely and keep me advised.

"If we are still ready to begin fueling, we should commence. The captain is on his way up, and we should be fairly well into that if we don't want to earn a reprimand. If there is a problem with the door or maintenance deck seal, we will surely know it when we purge the fueling bay before we begin fueling. Jo-oot, if we are ready, please commence fueling," said Grenyu.

"Yes, Grenyu, condensers are coming online, separators ready for inflow, and compressors in auto standby. Purging inlet bays on my action at twenty-septu mark. I will monitor input for delta output differential for excessive pressure and fill rate. Inlet bay static pressure currently 0.64 of Tirran surface pressure. This is three times the normal initial fueling pressure because of our low altitude. I will initiate a slow and partial feed rate so as to not shock or overpressure the condensers."

"Yes, Jo-oot, that should work well. Do not exceed 0.24 differential pressure on initial fueling start. If all systems appear normal, there should be no need to notify Captain Trolnhyett of the transient and false hull breech. I'm sure he has more important 'captain' things to worry about."

Jo-oot entered the prefueling purge command. The secondary inlet purge doors began to open, and the flow accelerators instantly spooled to their high-pressure, high-velocity mode. When they were fully open, the fueling bay purge valves opened. In the fueling bay, a massive inrush of pressurized atmosphere blasted in through the precisely angled hex-shaped holes in the chamber ceiling. The high-pressure pulses instantly created a gigantic pressure wave and cyclonic action that scoured every bit of debris and trash from the fueling bay that might contaminate the atmospheric fuel gas inflow.

The partial remains of the Shuttle *Victory* were instantly dislodged from its spot in the fueling bay and ejected out the front of the fueling bay along with some other miscellaneous debris from the cavernous opening. On the fueling panel display, Jo-oot noted that a slightly higher than normal amount of debris was ejected from the left front fueling bay, but nothing significant. He thought it could perhaps have been some stray atmospheric condensate matter from their unusual entry profile.

* * * * *

A short while later, Jack's inert body subconsciously felt a large background vibration and a strange pulsing and thrumming sensation. As he started to awaken, a loud pulsating air rush could be heard and felt through the wall. Gaining more awareness, he started to recall the last few hours. The question was still lodged in his head, what happened and where was he? The noise from the other side of the wall was almost painfully loud. His ears still hurt, more of a dull ache now, and his back and leg felt twisted and swollen. His ears weren't pulsing now, but he could still feel a massive pressure wave though his body. It was as if the whole area or at least the corridor, or wherever he was he was, was being subjected to a huge pressure pulse, not directly but apparently on the other side of the wall.

As Jack sat up, he realized that there was a slight amount of light illuminating the entire area or corridor he was in, a very long corridor. It was sort of a pale blue-green light emanating from, well, he couldn't really tell. It was just there, a dim blue-green light, just enough to see the outline of his hand and flight suit and the shape of the corridor, which went on in both directions as far as he could see.

He remembered his LED light and found it in his front flight suit pocket. He pulled it out and pushed the switch. A beam of white light shot forth and illuminated the corridor. He shone the light around. It looked like he was in some sort of an access or maintenance tunnel. The corridor was about eight feet high by maybe five feet wide. The far side appeared to have various types of piping or conduit halfway up the wall and an occasional recessed area with flush mounted boxes in the wall about two feet square.

There were strange markings on some of the boxes and some other markings spaced periodically on hex-shaped conduit or pipes. Looking back at the door he'd come through, he could see some more indecipherable marking. They looked like instructions or warnings but in some strange cuneiform like writing. There were some marks near the writing that looked similar to arrows that pointed at the handle mechanism that matched the one on the other side of the door. He didn't know exactly what they meant, but he could probably take a pretty good guess.

He slowly stood up and braced against the wall and the door. Strangely, the floor was tilted slightly toward the outside wall by a few degrees, which made it just somewhat difficult to stand parallel to the outer wall. Whatever sort of structure or ship he was in had some peculiar characteristics. He picked up the alloy bar he'd salvaged from *Victory;* maybe it would help steady him.

The wind noise through the wall was still painfully loud, and he could still feel his body pulsing slightly from the surrounding structure. He figured it was time to try and figure out where he was and what happened to his ship and crew. He thought about his crew members for a minute. Where were they, had they made it through whatever had caused *Victory* to be destroyed? They were an amazing group of talented and capable people. He hoped and prayed that they were OK somewhere and that he'd find them soon.

He thought about what he'd seen on the other side of the very noisy wall. He had seen sky and possibly horizon. Was that forward or aft or out? Forward of "what" was the real question? Was this a ship? Somehow, instinctively and from the clues he'd seen and felt, he felt fairly sure that this must be a ship. It had to be some sort of ship that he had no knowledge of and that he'd never heard of or even imagined. There was nothing on Earth or flying above it that he was familiar with that would correlate to what he'd seen so far, but, sure hell, this had to be some sort of a ship, a really big ship. Where on God's Earth or above it was he?

From where he was, it looked like he only had two directions to travel: "possible forward," in the direction of the sky; or "possible aft," away from the sky. Possible forward it would be. As he started cautiously forward, the overwhelming wind sound suddenly stopped. Several loud thunks and a vibrating drumming sound began. Then a different, more singular wind noise began to build. A whistling and sucking sound accompanied it as well as a thrumming cycling noise. Even combined, it wasn't nearly half as loud as the previous wind noise with its associated pulsating. It was now fairly tolerable.

Chapter 2: Reconnaissance

On the control deck of the Lokar trade ship *Yuanjejitt,* Grenyu monitored the fueling sequence initiated by Jo-oot. After the fueling bays had been purged, the inlet fueling bay doors had been partially closed to regulate the total inlet pressure and differential pressure across the condensers while the gravpile was switched off to enable fueling. At this proximity to the planet, they would experience 0.92 of the planet's surface gravity for the duration of the fueling process.

The gravpile was switched off to facilitate a uniform flow density during fueling. The parameters he'd set appeared to properly control the fueling pressures in the bay and condensers. As the compressors came online to liquefy and store the separate atmospheric gases and vent overboard, any unwanted gases the compressor output temperatures began to rise about 40 percent above a normal fueling profile. It was still well within acceptable parameters, but it would bear watching. The temperatures stabilized there, and the fuel tanks began filling but filling at about three times faster than normal.

Captain Trolnhyett entered the control deck of *Yuanjejitt* directly from the express lift. "Grenyu, please report what conditions required you to summon me from the feeding ritual. Are we in a mission critical situation at this time?"

"Not at the moment, Captain Trolnhyett, but I believed we were earlier when we achieved a much higher than normal V dredge vector and ended up only thirty-five thousand mu-uts above the Tirran surface level. We are currently fueling at this altitude and will be done fueling in a very short time due to the much higher atmospheric pressure."

Grenyu explained the probable false telemetry and his theory regarding the probable infestation of the Sorusites and their supplying false telemetry data. Mulling this for a few septus, Captain Trolnhyett thought this was a likely cause based on their recent Sorun transit and the current circumstances. "That is a good theory, Grenyu. I have considerable faith in your ability to lead the nonprime crew while we are off duty. I'm not sure if this required interrupting feeding ritual, since you seem to have the situation in hand, but better safe than unsafe. I am seeing higher compressor and condenser temperatures due to the higher intake pressures. Make sure that you monitor all fueling parameters properly. When we are done, get us back on course for Nishda and proceed to search the entire ship with Xamaniit for any indication of Sorusite presence. Also dispatch some Zshrritni probes and make sure you search the main and auxiliary neural nodes for any hidden virals just in case we've been penetrated by any neural fugitives. Let me know immediately if you find any virals."

"Yes, Captain Trolnhyett. That is an excellent precaution under these circumstances. I will accomplish that as soon as we are stabilized from fueling," replied Grenyu.

"I will now return to sensar deck, as I am off duty for 8.7 more horuns," said Captain Trolnhyett, as he turned and left for the express lift.

* * * * *

Jack made his way cautiously forward, fighting the tendency to slide toward the outside wall. Visually, it was almost like walking sidewise on a slanted slope. His right leg and back protested the slope, as he had to compensate for the slightly higher floor on his right side. His head was clearing more now as his blood and brain were energized with a higher oxygen level than before. He started running various scenarios through his head trying to figure out exactly what his situation was. The only thing that kept coming back to him that made any sense, if you could call that thought as making sense, is that they had hit or been hit by some sort of huge ship. No other explanation made sense in light of the massive damage sustained by *Victory* after they had achieved initial orbit without incident. As best as he could recall, there had been no sign of any malfunctions or other problems.

He started to recall an inkling of the strange sensation of being overwhelmed by something implacable and immovable. After that, the next thing he recalled was waking up in the minuscule remains of *Victory*. Whatever had hit the shuttle had cleaved the ship cleanly through, leaving the part of the flight deck with him attached in the pilot seat wedged in some sort of cavernous bay. Although he hadn't been able to explore the entire deck where his portion of *Victory* had come to rest, based on what he'd seen, he was about 98 percent certain the remaining portion of the shuttle wasn't there. In Jack's deductive thought process, the lack of the remaining shuttle and crew members didn't bode well for their survival.

Shuttle and ISS crews and even the earliest manned space missions had seen continuous indications of various sorts of alien or UFO activity around Earth for decades. None of Earth's space-faring nations or agencies would ever acknowledge this, but most of the NASA employees, military, and probably 70 plus percent of the civilian population certainly believed in a nearby alien presence of some sort. UFOs and other strange phenomenon had been spotted, photographed, and videoed on every continent and by every nationality since the advent of the camera and well before that by artists back to biblical times.

There were even paintings of what appeared to be UFOs in dozens of medieval paintings, Egyptian hieroglyphs, and the ancient Rig Veda Sanskrit hymns of India. There was even ample evidence that civilization had risen multiple times to very great heights but that it had been, somehow, for some reason, pushed back down to near Stone Age levels, only to begin the arduous rise to an advanced technical level once again. Along the way, disease, war, and plagues had nearly wiped mankind out on numerous occasions. Still, mankind had persisted and fought its way back to its current troubled but technologically advanced level.

He certainly didn't think his situation was one of the classic alien abductions he'd scoffed at in the past, but it certainly opened up his thought process on the subject until something happened to change his currently developing viewpoint.

His exploring the corridor didn't seem to find any human or other life form activity in his immediate area, but he had no idea what he'd find as he moved forward. Wherever he was or whatever he was in felt and looked like a ship. Based on what he'd seen from a lifetime of watching sci-fi movies of various sorts, it certainly seemed like some sort of huge, strange alien ship. If it was a ship, it was a ship of titanic proportions. It did have a very alien feel to it, and the writing he'd seen was like nothing he'd ever observed anywhere else in his life.

He continued forward for another two hundred meters, but it all pretty much looked the same. On the right inboard side, he came to what looked like a sealed door opening about seven feet tall by four and a half feet wide. There was a foot square panel to the right of the door with more strange symbols that had a slight glow to them. He moved his fingers over the symbols and felt a slight relief to them. He put his ear to the door and heard only a light mechanical thrumming sound.

He pushed and rubbed on the symbols for a couple of minutes, but they didn't seem to do anything. Maybe it was a keypad of some sort, but, of course, he didn't have the proper code. He continued farther forward for another two hundred yards and came to an intersection with another corridor heading to the right or inboard at ninety degrees. From what he could see, it didn't look like the scenery changed much in the next two hundred yards in the direction he'd been heading. With that thought, he decided it was time for a change of scenery and turned down the inboard corridor. This corridor, unlike the previous one, was not tilted.

17

Fifty feet into the corridor, which looked basically the same as the first corridor, the color changed from a dark gray color to light yellowish-green, which seemed to give off a fair amount of ambient light of its own. In another ten feet, there was a bulkhead with a door in it with a slightly different panel on the right. Once again, he put his ear to the door and listened. He heard nothing but a slight electric hum. There were more strange hieroglyphic like markings and two three-inch hex-shaped markings or sensors of some type about eight inches apart on each side.

He was afraid they might be security cameras or some type of ID devices that might give away his presence. He touched and poked the markings again with no results. He moved his hand over each hex-shaped marking, and a small blue light momentarily came on in the center of each hex. Nothing else happened. Each time he moved his hand across the hex marks, he obtained the same momentary light as a result. He leaned down to get a closer look at the markings on the panel. It still looked like a cross between Chinese and hieroglyphics to him. Still baffled, he pushed himself up with both hands. As he pushed up with one hand over each hex mark, two blue lights came on at once, and a blue line illuminated the space between both hex marks. The door slid open to the left, and a bright glowing corridor opened before him.

He thought, *That must be the trick—trigger both sensors at the same time to get the door to open.* Looking down the corridor, he saw no signs of life, although he knew he had to be getting closer to some area that might be occupied by some sort of ship's crew. *Looks like forward is the only way to go from here,* he said to himself. When he was three feet inside, the door slid gently closed. The corridor went another forty feet then T'd in both directions. He approached the intersection carefully, listened, squatted low, and snuck a slow, cautious peek in each direction. The corridors curved gently inward in both directions with protruding bulkhead braces and what looked like doors at varying distances. This curved corridor also appeared to have a slightly slanted floor that sloped outward toward where he'd come from. There were still no signs of life.

In the distance, he suddenly heard a high-pitched buzzing sound. The sound was getting closer fairly fast. Years of military flight training taught him never to knee-jerk react or panic without at least briefly analyzing and thinking something through. He figured he had three options: hide in place, go back and try to hide on the other side of the door he just came through, or try to find a new place to hide. The buzzing sound was getting closer fast. He risked another concealed peek. He could see a faint glimmering shape near the top of the corridor coming his way. Some type of a small machine, maybe a small drone. He didn't think he had enough time to get through the door or find a new hide. He backed a few feet down the corridor T and flattened himself against the wall. Maybe whatever it was would be going fast enough and would keep going down the corridor it was in, and hopefully, it wouldn't notice him.

The sound got closer until it was right at the T. A two-foot-long stack of half-inch thick undulating, shimmering hex-shaped disks about five inches in diameter suddenly stopped at the corridor junction. Each disk seemed to rotate independently, randomly and change direction periodically. He thought, *Don't move. Don't breathe. Maybe they won't see you,* wishful thinking. The stack sat there for about ten seconds. Then the stack separated into two equal portions. The front half shot down the curved corridor in the same direction it had been going. The back half of the stack turned toward Jack, accelerated rapidly, and shot past him down the access corridor he'd come through. It stopped momentarily as the door opened. Then the half stack shot through, and the door closed. The buzzing sound receded into the distance, and he breathed a slow measured sigh of relief. He had no idea what those things were, but apparently, they had no interest in him, at least for now. He suddenly realized he had to pee fairly badly.

He took another slow cautious peek down both directions of the corridor. He could just barely hear the shimmering disks receding down the corridor to the left, so he decided to go down the right corridor. He cautiously advanced down the corridor and passed a slightly raised bulkhead after about twenty feet. On the left, in about twenty more feet, there appeared to be another door similar to the one he'd previously entered with the same type of entry panel. He listened with his ear against the door but didn't hear anything. Should he try to open it and see what's in it or move further down the corridor?

In the distance to his right, he heard another sound coming toward him, fast like the rotating hex disks but a different sound, like an oscillating static sound. Whatever it was, he didn't want to meet it. He put both his hands on the hex symbols by the door. The blue line flashed, and the door opened. He entered a huge room with shelves and lots of various-sized containers. It looked like a storage room of some sort, so he stepped in, moved in a few feet, and the door closed. He listened next to the door and could just barely hear the static noise. It got closer and seemed to go on by and then fade in the distance. Good, he decided. He wasn't up for any introductions quite yet. He needed more time and information to figure out what had happened and what his options were.

He didn't know if he was in a hostile environment, but he'd treat it as such until he found out otherwise. He wished he had a weapon of some sort other than the alloy bar from the shuttle he'd been carrying. He decided it was better than nothing depending on what he might run into. He turned and looked around the room. It was illuminated like the corridor. The room was large, maybe three hundred feet to the left end and two hundred to the right. It looked like it went back another six hundred feet or more from the door. It was maybe sixty feet high with multiple rows of solid-looking built-in shelving with only about eight-foot spacing between each row. All the containers appeared to be made of some sort of metal- or plastic-looking material. The shelves appeared to be very sturdy and had separate shelves at various heights. The shelves had boxlike containers of every shape and size. It looked like a cargo hold of some sort.

Maybe this ship was a cargo vessel of some sort. Maybe this was the ship's stores. A ship this large could have a large crew depending on what it was designed for or what its mission was. If it was just a cargo ship, it might not have a large crew, maybe just a maintenance crew to man and maintain it like an oil tanker or container ship. If it was a warship of some sort, it would most likely have a much larger crew contingent, like an aircraft carrier. It didn't have the feel of a warship, though. If he had to guess, it would seem more likely to be a cargo ship of some sort. Where was it from, where was it going, and what was it doing in Earth's orbit, and why had it hit *Victory?* If it was a warship of some sort, he didn't think that hitting the shuttle was a particularly effective attack strategy. It had to be an accident. Maybe they didn't even see the shuttle. He had a lot of questions but only a few guesses for answers.

He briefly thought about his crew again. He looked at his watch again; one hour eight minutes since the launch. By now, NASA, and probably the entire world, knew that *Victory* had been lost. His parents, friends, coworkers, and his girlfriend, Kerry, would all assume the worst. If there was just some way to communicate with them and let them know, but that was clearly impossible. They would already be trying to figure out what had gone wrong, what had happened to *Victory,* and what had caused it. They might never get the answer right. Only Jack knew, and he wasn't very certain. All he knew was that the shuttle had hit this massive ship or vice versa. That was about the extent of his knowledge at this point. He needed to find out more.

He listened and didn't hear anything in the room. He walked to the ends of the shelving and peered down each row. All he saw were rows of containers. Everything seems to be containerized for the most part. About halfway down one of the rows were some large machine like fixtures, maybe a dozen of them, of several different types. They looked like they might be part of something bigger, maybe to be installed onto something. They looked like they might have something to do with manufacturing or processing. No telling what they were for. He searched the cargo room for fifteen minutes. He couldn't find anything that was recognizable, that wasn't sealed, or anything he might be able to use.

He did remember that he had to pee, though, and decided to relieve himself in one of the far corners of the room. First, though, he had to get out of his ACES, or

Advanced Crew Escape Suit, the orange "pumpkin suit" that was used for launch and reentry. He wriggled out of the cumbersome orange suit and was now in his blue NASA flight suit that was worn beneath it. The ACES pressure suit wouldn't do him any good anyway without the pressure helmet and the gloves. *Oh, well, time for a pee break. No choice, no harm done,* he supposed. That certainly makes life a lot more enjoyable was his next thought.

He stashed his ACES suit behind a cargo container. He decided to go further down the curved corridor outside the door and see if there was anything more useful in that direction. He could come back here and use it as a hidey-hole if he had to, since it seemed to be unattended. He listened carefully then opened the door again on the inside panel as he had previously with the "double-hand blue light special" he had figured out. He checked in both directions then headed further down the curved corridor. The slant on this one seemed slightly less than the first one but was still somewhat annoying.

Suddenly, he felt a strange wave sensation through his body. Then he felt sort of disoriented for a second, half lost his balance then felt normal again. Looking down, he realized that he was walking level on the slanted floor now, and the walls were both slanted to the right a few degrees. It was disorienting. He tried to lean to be parallel to the wall, but then he was falling over to his left. *Just stand up straight and balance. Don't look at the walls,* he thought. Yes, he was standing level on the floor, and the walls were slightly canted to the left. It was a strange sensation.

* * * * *

On the control deck, Jewatta announced to Grenyu and Jo-oot that the gravpile was now reengaged for departure as the fueling was complete and the four fueling bays and processing machinery were secured. Jo-oot read the displays and stated that all fueling sequences were complete and *Yuanjejitt* was secure for orbital departure. "Orbital departure is ready at your command. Course to Nishda system plotted and ready to engage," said Jewatta.

"Commence orbital departure," commanded Grenyu. Jewatta fed the command to the *Yuanjejitt*'s neural command cortex, and the massive ship responded quite rapidly for an object of its size and mass. The gravpile, though less advanced than an interlaced gravfield passenger ship and more tailored for a fixed central core–type cargo ship, was still quite capable of considerable mass gravflux stabilized acceleration even without the quantum field engaged. The ship accelerated upward and began a turn toward the Ki-aja sector and the Nishda system.

Four horuns and eleven mentus after orbital departure engagement, *Yuanjejitt* had cleared the confines of the Sol system and achieved 0.05 L-vel, the minimum velocity for an Errakk drive ship to engage its light drive engines. Jewatta

21

announced the transition to engagement speed. Grenyu stated, "Verify course vector aligned and stabilized for Nishda and engage Errakk drive when the plot field is clear and locked." Jewatta verified the plot field was clear on the displays, and the nav neurals commanded the Errakk drive to initiate engagement.

The four Errakk drive engines buried in the outer quadrants of the ship started their rhythmic pulsing as the inlet and dissipation portals opened. The vacuum of space fore and aft of the portals began to bend in a visible pulsing glow as the fabric of space was compressed and expelled in massive waves of gravitational warping. The ultrastable quantum gravfield generated at the core of the ship by the gravpile generator along with the aft grav-gens on the ore hoppers, which were all encapsulated in the stabilized quantum field, allowed the massive ship to accelerate to a velocity of just under two thousand times the speed of light. As the Errakk drive came up to full power, the ship accelerated to its maximum cruise speed in just 17.4 septus. Without the quantum stasis field created by the gravpile field generators, the ship would literally turn into an ionized plasma smear spread over a tenth of a light-year sector of the galaxy.

They were now on their way and would arrive at Nishda in four daiyus. This would be the completion of the fourth leg of their eight-leg outbound run. In another sixteen daiyus and four more shorter runs, with just a simple cargo stop at Kwiikay, Trnelltroz, and Yataha, they'd be back in their own system and be ready to enjoy a couple of weneks of rest, grand feeding rituals, and time with their clanlies. The big ore loads paid a nice bonus but could take an extra two or three daiyus of loading time that none of them wanted to deal with at the end of this long out run. Sometimes, that's what it took to make a decent bonus on an otherwise average run, though.

Jo-oot checked the status of the Xamaniit and Zshrritnei probes. So far, all reports came back negative. All sixty-six of the Xamaniit probes were searching the ship's various decks and levels for Sorusites and other power and infrastructure parasites. Thirty-six Zshrritnei probes were also dispatched to various outlying neural map nodes for any hidden neural virals that might be attached and fused to the ship's multiple neural map access points.

Neural virals could be the most difficult to detect and the most destructive troublemakers, as they slowly infused their way into a ship's neural network and disrupted all the ship's control functions eventually trying to take the ship over and create their own master control neural map of the entire control cortex. They weren't really intelligent, but if they could take control of a ship, they could theoretically turn it into an autonomous life support island dedicated to the sole purpose of perpetuating their viral form. Physically, they might be the same size as your thumbnail when in their migration form, but once they were infused into a ship's power and neural network, they could eventually grow into multiple masses much larger than a person from which they could completely encapsulate whatever power source they had attached themselves to.

Until they were somewhat understood, neural virals had caused the loss of half a dozen ships from several planets. They'd only been dealing with neural virals for the last ninety yenets or so. Simple parasites like the Sorusites had been around much longer, practically forever, and were much easier to detect and eradicate. No one knew where the virals had come from, how they spread, or all the forms they could take or disguise themselves as. Fortunately, they were fairly rare in this outer sector and quadrant of the galaxy, but you could never be too careful. Their spread was slow and insidious and had to be carefully monitored and prevented. The last thing you wanted to do was lose your ship to a viral and have to abandon it and initiate a self-destruct command to destroy the infected ship and then sit in quarantine in a Lifeship while awaiting an Alliance Resqbotship for decon and rescue. That would be a very expensive tragedy any way you could envision it.

* * * * *

Jack went another four hundred feet down the curved corridor to another access door. Again, he listened and heard nothing. He opened the door and found pretty much the same cargo storage area as the previous one. A quick recon showed similar types of containers and other unrecognizable items with the only difference being the color of the containers and the markings on them. The previous ones had been mostly green, while the ones in this hold were a brownish red. There was probably some significance to that, but he didn't have any idea what it might be. *Better head farther aft and see what more there is with this strange place,* he thought to himself.

After Jack had gone another three hundred feet down the curved and slanted corridor, he came to another door, slightly wider than the previous doors he'd encountered. The curve of the corridor was not as great here. He estimated he could see maybe four but probably closer to five hundred feet before the view of the corridor disappeared around the curve. Crunching the numbers roughly in his head, he estimated that if this curved corridor continued in a complete circle that it must have a diameter of about thirty-five hundred feet, or just over a thousand meters. Just this inner cargo area, or wherever he was, was that big. His estimate didn't count the outer area he'd come from or the width of the area where the shuttle had ended up. If what he'd seen so far was the width or beam of the ship, it had to be a minimum of four thousand feet wide or more. What kind of ship was this, and what kind of power source would it need to power it? This was beyond anything even remotely imagined by NASA or any other space agency on Earth.

He put his ear against the new door and listened. This time, he heard some machine sounds, whirring and tapping or hitting sounds from somewhere deep inside the door. The whole ship had a slight low-frequency vibration, very light, more subconsciously felt than heard but just enough to be noticeable. He didn't remember noticing this earlier, but the outer area he'd come from had been so loud and inundated with pressure pulses that he wouldn't have noticed these subtle resonances anyway.

The hair stood up on the back of his neck as he imagined what he might find on the other side. He decided to bypass this for now and move farther down the corridor. As he started to move across the closed doorway, the door whooshed open, and a large shape moved toward him from inside the room. Something large like a machine moved toward him. He was ready to strike or run, but the big machine stopped and just hovered there about eight inches off the floor. It looked like a big refrigerator or something with multiple compartments and shelves with transparent doors. It looked like some sort of food in the compartments, which had somewhat of an almost decorative layout. There were maybe a dozen compartments total with what looked like multiple trays of food ready to be served in each compartment.

He could smell it now too. It smelled like food but both more acrid and sweet than anything he'd smelled before. The machine just hovered there. Then a small pair of bluish lights flashed on the front of the machine, and it made a plaintive weep, weep sound. After another fifteen seconds, it did it again. He'd only been there about thirty seconds, trying to process what he was seeing. It occurred to him that maybe he was in its way. He looked around the machine into the room. He could see a lot more movement. There was a half-dozen or more small machines moving about in the room, hovering or moving in every direction above the floor of the room. They seemed to be droids of some sort, several different types.

He didn't see any human or alien beings of any sort, just droids. There were droids maybe three feet tall with armlike appendages with fingers and articulating claws moving in various directions.

There were others that were somewhat tube shaped, four feet in length, actually slightly hexagonal shaped with various appliances sticking out along the length of its body. Another one was a circular hexagon doughnut, three feet in diameter with small pointers or probes sticking down. These two seemed to be moving between the other droids and maybe inspecting them and the food being prepped.

They all hovered and were flying freely about the room. They all appeared to be in the act of preparing food of some sort like he'd just seen on the fridge machine. The fridge "weep-weeped" at him again. He cautiously moved aside. The machine started moving again, turned to its left, and headed down the corridor at a rapid pace while slightly tilted to remain level with the floor. He could see the back side of the fridge machine, and it had another twelve compartments on the backside with the same transparent doors and food trays inside.

The door stayed open, probably because he was still in front of it. From just outside, at the edge of the door opening, he peered into the room. He still didn't see any live life forms, just droids that kept working, and they seemed to be busily preparing more food. It had to be the ship's food prep kitchen. The room was maybe sixty feet wide and went farther back like the cargo bays he'd seen. There were ten or so large tables with food items laid out on half of them that were in the process of being prepped. Eighteen or twenty more large fridge machines were against the far-right wall, lined up, sitting on the floor, apparently waiting to be loaded with the next batch of prepared food.

Everything seemed to be automated, and all the food was being completely prepped by droids. He tried to see all the way back to make sure there were no live chefs or someone that might be overseeing the droids. There were multiple rows of storage cabinets and shelving up to the ceiling about sixty feet high, with containers of every different sort on them. He decided to go in and see what he could find that might be helpful.

As he crossed into the room, the smell hit him; it was very strong, actually pungent. It was a cacophony of strange, exotic, previously unknown smells. It was food all right, food, spices, cooked, broiled, seared, whatever, but nothing quite like he'd smelled anywhere on Earth. It was so strong it was nearly nauseating. It was alien too, but not so much so that it didn't tweak his olfactory senses into reminding him that he hadn't eaten in quite a while now. He looked at his watch, T plus two hours fifty-two minutes since launch. He had eaten breakfast with *Victory*'s crew four hours before launch, so it was getting close to seven hours since he'd last had anything to eat.

He was thirsty too, very thirsty, now that he thought about it. He thought, *Funny how the baser needs still pop into our lives even with the bizarre events I've experienced today.* He thought for a minute and said to himself, *One thing for sure is all this food prep means there are plenty of food consumers here somewhere.* Whether they were all crew members or maybe there were passengers too he didn't know. Either way, there was fair amount of food prep going for a fair-sized crew.

Now the question became, should he try and eat something in here, or would it be toxic to him? Even if the food wasn't poisonous, it still might cause him some potentially painful gastronomic issues. Getting Montezuma's revenge might be a very serious issue if there was no way to treat it. Still, he would have to eat something fairly soon to keep up his strength, and it might be better to eat something "less agreeable" while he was still in pretty good shape rather than get too hungry and then ply himself with alien fare. One thing for sure was they wouldn't be pulling over at a Taco Bell anytime soon. He decided the best plan was to go for it now. Maybe just a little at first and hope for the best. If he was successful with that approach, he could experiment a little more after he passed the first taste test.

He worked his way around toward the far left side of the room and watched the droids working on the food prep. They were very quick and nimble, and apparently, there was a need for an artistic presentation. As they assembled more meals on some ornately trimmed serving platters, you could see the detail they put into each type of food that went into the meal. Each item was placed exactly the same way, and then decorative vegetable items of some sort were placed in concentric rows around a centerpiece food item.

The center items appeared to be more meat-like, and the smell confirmed that it was some sort of fricasseed delight. When the large platter was fully assembled, it was a very nice presentation even by any of Earth's finer culinary standards. That was all very interesting, but the question remained as to whether it was safe to eat. Was everything on the plate supposed to be edible, or was some of it mere decoration, like parsley was on Earth? Did people ever actually eat parsley? For some reason, the strong food smell didn't seem as strong now. Maybe he was getting used to it?

He guessed that a fully prepared meal might be the best as far as safety was concerned. Just like on Earth where some foods weren't safe to eat uncooked, so the same thing might apply here. How was he going to get a fully prepared plate? Would the droids try to stop him? They hadn't paid him any attention yet, but if he interfered with their work, would they sense that as a threat and try to stop him? Well, that probably wouldn't make sense. If some of the crew were checking up on the food prep process, it wouldn't pay to have the robotic help assaulting the crew. The other issue would be if they didn't recognize him as a crew member and sounded some sort of alert. He didn't want to take anything from a plate that might show up at its destination looking damaged, or they might send someone down to check for a malfunction.

They seemed to have about forty plates being assembled on the larger tables closest to the door. There were six or seven droids hovering around and prepping and primping the food on the table. He decided to just take a whole tray rather than pull something off a plate and have the culinary display look damaged. He worked his way to the prep table and moved toward the end with the finished platters.

There was a little less activity on the end where the platters were already completed. As he got up to the table, the droids that were there seemed to move just enough out of the way that he didn't touch them. He placed his hands on a plate and waited about fifteen seconds. No one seems to protest, so he lifted the platter up and held it above the counter for another ten seconds. He then started to back up and walk away with the platter when suddenly two of the floating fridge machines against the wall came to life, lifted a little less than a foot off the floor, and came toward the door and around to where he was backing up with the alien food platter. It stopped right where he'd been when he'd "lifted" the platter. Two of the hex tube droids came to the counter and lifted the platters on four outstretched arms.

The doors on the fridge opened, and the droids began placing the platters on the fridge machine shelves. One droid stopped for a few seconds where the empty spot was that he'd taken the platter from. It seemed hesitant for a second then grabbed the next platter and filled a fridge shelf with it. A hex doughnut droid came over and inspected the place where the platter had been. It then circled around the front half of the room and came over to where Jack was standing with the platter. *Crap, I'm busted,* he thought. He stood there holding still with the platter and waited. The doughnut droid hovered for a few more seconds then buzzed back to where it had come from and seemed to go back to its business. Hopefully, it hadn't ratted him out as a food thief to someone. Maybe it just assumed he was a live kitchen worker or inspector that was just taking a sample or meal he was entitled to as a crew member. He'd find out soon enough if it was an issue.

The droids finished loading both fridge machines with meals, and then both of them went to the door, waited a second for the door to open, and exited out the door and down the corridor to the left. Jack wondered exactly where they were going and who they were delivering the food to. *Not exactly your normal pizza delivery guy back in Indiana,* he thought.

He worked his way to the back left of the room where it was mostly storage area. He set the platter down on a shelf and inspected it. The center meat-looking piece looked somewhat like a kebob without the stick, and it weighed perhaps six or eight ounces. It was formed into a circular presentation, and there were blue, green, and orange side dishes that looked pretty much like vegetables, although not like any he'd ever seen. Some were chopped into half-inch cubes, and others were bulbous green on one end to purple tubular leaves sticking out the other end almost ten inches long. *What part is edible?* Jack wondered. There was a stringy, almost pasta-like thing that was coiled in multiple cascading layers that made an attractive little blue-and-red mountain about four inches high and wide on one side of the platter. This was probably all edible, since it looked the same all the way through.

Well, there was only one way to find out. He picked up the meat circle and tore in into two pieces to check the consistency. It wasn't too tough and tore easily

27

enough. It was pretty pungent, but he was getting used to it, and it didn't smell too bad now, especially away from the food prep area. It was very spicy smelling with maybe a bit of a burned coffee smell too. He bit off a small piece and let it sit on his tongue for a minute. In survival school, they'd taught him to hold food in his mouth for a minute, and if it didn't start an allergic reaction of some sort, it was "probably" OK to eat. Of course, they were talking about Earth food there, so did that really apply here? Well, after the "hold time" was up, he started chewing it. Still, no reaction, so he chewed it up all the way. Well, it wasn't too bad. It was definitely a bit spicy, had a pungent burnt taste to it, and had a little bit of a burning after taste, vaguely like a spicy burrito at his favorite Mex restaurant.

Next, he tried the stringy blue-and-red pasta thing, and it was fairly bitter, edible but bitter, almost like the kimchee he'd eaten once at a Korean restaurant. If he'd had some sort of sauce for it, then it might have been better. He wasn't sure about the bulbous thing with the tube leaves. He picked it up and tried to take a small bite out of the ball-like end. It was too hard, and he didn't seem to be able bite into it. The outside tasted like hot burning licorice, which he didn't like anyway, so he passed on that. Better safe than sorry. "Sorry" was what he hoped he wouldn't be, but he had to eat something.

Not knowing what the calorie content was, he figured that if he ate about half a meal, and if none of it was toxic, then this should give him enough energy to function for a while without overloading his system with the strange alien food. He didn't see any cleanup area for plate washing or anything, so he wasn't sure what to do with the platter and half-eaten meal. He decided to just leave it on one of the other counters and hope the droids would think it was just a spilled meal prep or something and possibly clean it up or dispose of it. Within ten seconds of setting the platter down, a droid came over, hovered for a few seconds, then picked up the tray and whisked it down the far end of the room and out of sight. *That was easy,* he thought. *I wonder if I could get room service.* He thought about something to drink, like maybe water, hoping that water would be the universal beverage. He didn't see anything that looked like a beverage in the kitchen area. He grabbed his alloy bar and headed to the door.

Jack once again cautiously reconned outside the door. He didn't know who or what he would eventually find but had to assume that he would sooner or later meet up with whoever was operating this huge ship. So far, all he'd seen were automated bots or droids, but after witnessing the food prep action in the kitchen, he knew there had to be an active crew or passengers somewhere on board. He just wasn't sure he was ready to meet them yet, since he didn't know who or what they were, whether he could communicate with them, whether they'd be hostile, and whether he would be able to explain what he'd believed had happened to him and how he'd gotten here. He decided to buy as much time as he could and gather as much information as he could so he'd be able to calculate the best course of action with the limited options he might have.

He went further down the curved corridor and came to another smaller door about the same size as a standard room entry door on Earth. He listened again and heard nothing. He risked giving himself away every time he opened a door and entered a new room, but he figured that was the only way he'd be able to assess what he was into here. He knew so far that he'd found a place to hide and a place to get food. So far, he hadn't been able to make heads or tails of any of the symbols or writing he'd seen anywhere on the ship. He opened the smaller door, peered in from the edge, and saw what appeared to be, well, possibly, a restroom. At the front were two identical bowl-like fixtures at a slightly higher than standard Earth height, and toward the back were two small open bays with some odd-shaped fixtures that might just be some type of a toilet.

Stepping inside, he caught a faint smell of something sweet and offal at about the same time. *Yep,* he thought, *this is definitely a restroom of some sort.* The "sink" bowls at the front were about fourteen inches in diameter with a single straight oval tube coming from the wall behind it. On the sides of the counter area, there were some half-buried cylinder-shaped objects about eighteen inches long and three inches in diameter with six holes in them facing toward the bowls that looked like sinks. Built into the wall was a dispenser with a very shiny, thin, oval container protruding out. He touched the oval container, and it slid out into his hand, while another one replaced the first one that he'd touched. *Is this supposed to be a drinking cup?* he wondered. He looked at the cup and turned it over in his hand. It was about three inches wide by about four inches deep and the same front to back. It was so thin and clear it was almost impossible to see, but it was as solid as a piece of glass but much lighter. He held it under the oval tube, and instantly, a clear fluid poured from the tube just like a public restroom at home. He smelled the fluid, hoping it was water. It smelled like water but with a bit of mustiness.

He was really thirsty and wondered if it was potable. He dipped his finger in it. It was lukewarm, and it had the same viscosity as water. He touched it to his lips and slightly to his tongue. It tasted like water but had a musty taste to it also. It could just be an issue of it being "ship's water," which had a tendency to occur on most of Earth's ocean ships and airplanes if it sat too long in storage.

Maybe if he ran it for a little while before trying it again. He ran the water by holding his hand by the spigot for a minute, and this time, the water didn't seem to have any negative issues after tasting it again. He filled the glass about half full and took a small sip. It seemed to taste better and was a bit cooler, so he swallowed another sip and waited about five minutes. He decided to go for it and drank a half of a cup. He hoped it didn't have any waterborne bacteria or other unknown parasites. Hopefully, water was water anyplace you went, although that certainly wasn't always the case on Earth. If he could find a container someplace, he would take some back to the cargo area with him. So far, he was batting three for three; he had food, water, and a place to hide and sleep.

He took a look at the toilet area. The seats were somewhat like a saddle or an old metal farm tractor seat with a wide hole in the center over a large tube heading downward. There was a slight vacuum sound that appeared to be pulling a slow airflow into the toilets. The two seats weren't the same, though. One seat was wide and deeper but more curved to the back and sides. The other was smaller and flatter overall. *Must be for momma bear and poppa bear, but no baby bears were apparently allowed in here,* he thought. *No toilet paper either.*

On the wall opposite the sinks were two large recessed doughnut-shaped fixtures about two and a half feet in diameter. They were somewhat translucent, and there were some controls and possibly directions on the wall next to each one. On each side of the doughnut fixtures were three basic hooklike fittings about five feet above the floor. Too many mysteries and not enough answers, he thought, but he supposed he wasn't doing too badly considering the circumstances. Whatever or whoever the ship's crew members were, he reasoned, at least they were comparable in size to humans and not twelve feet tall.

He didn't want to stay too long here, as there was no place to hide. He grabbed another glass and filled them both about two-thirds full. This would have to do until he found a better container. He decided to stash them in the second cargo bay for now and do a little more exploring before calling it quits for the day. He stuck his alloy beam under his arm, grabbed the two water cups, and headed back to the last cargo bay.

As he was heading back, two more fridge boys came shooting down the corridor from the kitchen. He moved against the wall, but as they got to where he was, they both slowed to a crawl and eased past him as far to the other side as possible. *Either they don't like me or they are programmed to not run over any crew members that are in the corridor,* he thought. He got back to the last cargo bay with the brownish-red labels and found a secure little niche toward the back where he could completely conceal himself behind several taller crates that were stacked next to each other. Unless they were specifically searching for him, they probably wouldn't ever see him here.

* * * * *

Later on the control deck, after Captain Trolnhyett and the prime crew returned to their duty stations, the Xamaniit probes reported three positive discoveries of Sorusites on the lower port Errakk drive engine access bay control and telemetry node. This confirmed Grenyu's earlier suspicion, which generated an "extra worthy" duty report for the trip and would result in an excellent credit bonus to his account upon arrival home at Lokar. Once the Xamaniit probes located and isolated the Sorusites, an engineering maintenance team of two specialists with Cantassdret surgical bots were sent to remove the parasites and repair any damage without further damaging the ship's telemetry and power control feeds. This was accomplished in about seven horuns without disrupting the output of the Errakk drive engine.

At the end of the third day, *Yuanjejitt* approached the Nishda system and prepared to exit Errakk star drive velocity and begin the orbital approach to Nishda. This would start outside the farthest Nishda system planet, Zoata, the eighth planet from the sun Nuutaa. Nishda was the second planet from Nuutaa and was the home planet of the system. Dimtuu was the third planet from Nuutaa, but it was primarily a mining and military outpost planet with a population of less than twenty-eight hundred Nishdan and other workers.

Captain Trolnhyett's prime crew first mate Vensutu Ne announced that *Yuanjejitt* would drop out of Errakk light drive in two mentus at the edge of the Nishda system. This would leave them approximately six horuns until Nishda orbit to prep for cargo distribution and the passenger disembarking with the required customs clearances and inspections. Their manifest estimate showed eighty-one passengers disembarking and sixty-seven expected to board in Nishda.

Chapter 3: Stowaway

For three more days, Jack hid in the cargo bay and stole food and water from the kitchen and lav. He'd found a cabinet with sealable cylindrical containers in the kitchen that held about two liters and filled two of them with water for storage in his cargo bay hide. He explored forward and aft all the way around in a large circle that came back to his starting point. There was a duplicate kitchen on the other side, but it wasn't currently being used. He decided that this must indicate that the ship's crew or passenger complement wasn't at its full capacity.

He'd discovered, with a large degree of initial adrenalin response, that while using the restroom to take care of nature's calling, that when you were finished with the seated relief variety, that if you stood in front of the sink and attempted to turn on the water flow, a large volume of somewhat chemical-smelling steam emanated from the cylinder-shaped fixtures above the sinks and a warm, moist, pulsing steam sprang from the doughnut-like fixtures in the wall behind him at the same time.

It was actually quite pleasant once you got used to it, and he could feel it tugging on his entire body in a gentle but firm sensation. When it was done after about a minute, he could feel that all of his exposed skin was clean and refreshed feeling. He hadn't found much to use in the way of toilet paper except a two-foot square sheet of cloth-like material that was nearly untearable. This had been attached to one of the many containers in the cargo bay and appeared to be some sort of instruction sheet, as it was covered in strangely printed symbols of several different types.

After a couple of rounds of the pulse/clean treatment, he decided to strip and let the process take care of his whole body. It worked quite well, and after a couple of days of intense stress and not being able to shower or even sponge bath like he would have done on *Victory,* it was a wonderful and refreshing experience. It wasn't quite a real shower, but it was darned close. Apparently, the ship's operators required a decent level of hygiene. So far, the accommodations of this ship had been quite tolerable for this unexpected guest.

The kitchen menu had varied considerably with each meal, which seemed to happen twice a day based on what Jack could tell by his Earth-based time schedule. This made it somewhat iffy as far as trying to decide what to eat that may or may not agree with him. There were some obviously bad selections he'd seen, but for the most part, everything had been fairly palatable, and he'd only had one instance of minor gut issues with something he'd eaten.

This was somewhat surprising based on his preconceived notion of what to expect and the visual appearance of some of the food. Perhaps most carbon-based life forms, assuming that's what he was dealing with, had to eat the same relatively uniform food from a chemistry perspective to obtain the energy they needed. The presentation, taste, and consistency were certainly from one end of the spectrum to the other, though. Since the ship was obviously pressurized with an oxygen-based life support system, it would stand to reason that the food energy and metabolic needs of the crew or passengers might be similar to humans. So far, this had proven to be true.

He'd again contemplated exploring further on the ship and trying to contact whoever the operators of the ship were. Instead, he decided to plead his case when he was discovered and hope for the best. Considering the circumstances, he couldn't envision too hostile of a reception, unless, of course, these beings were totally warlike or uncivilized, which didn't seem to be the case based on the accommodations he'd seen on the ship so far. He certainly couldn't stay down here forever, though.

He decided he had learned all he could from his exploration on this automated but uninhabited deck. He was planning his next move as far as meeting his unintended hosts and had decided to try to access one or more of the other decks when he felt a momentary strange sensation, and the gravity tilt of the ship suddenly shifted a few degrees. He felt momentarily nauseous and became very light for a few seconds, like he'd felt during the few minutes he'd experienced zero G weightlessness when they'd achieved orbit in *Victory*. The gravity came back on, and he was still standing on the floor, but it became instantly apparent that he was now at a fraction of the gravity he had been at a few moments ago. This was also apparent when he went to the curved corridor again and was suddenly parallel to the walls again, but he was now walking, or more appropriately hopping in long slow-motion hops on the slightly tilted floor again. He'd reasoned earlier that there must be some sort of artificial gravitational generator, and it must change or be switched on or off depending on the phase of flight they were in.

Since he'd spent three days walking level to the floor and suddenly this changed to something like it had been during the time he knew he was close to Earth, he could only reason that the ship had arrived somewhere and was now in or entering into orbit. The big question, though, was where, where was the ship, and around what was the ship about to orbit? He decided if he ever made it back to Earth, he'd have one heck of an autobiography to write, assuming they didn't lock him in the loony bin when he started talking about his, what would you call it, misadventure, disaster, what? He'd worry about that later.

A few minutes later, the gravity shifted again, and it felt more like a standard one G Earth gravity. He wondered what was happening. He went back to his little hide space and took inventory of the few things he'd been able to procure during his scouting. There wasn't much else other than the few items he'd used to try and make his stay there a little more comfortable. He had a couple of containers of water, his alloy bar, a couple of kitchen utensil items, his sheet of cloth with the strange writing on it, and not much more. At least he was well enough fed and was experiencing decent hygiene.

There was abruptly a loud distant twang followed by a low audible thud as well as a reverberation in the ship. At the distant far end of the cargo bay, a greenish bright light illuminated the center section of the wall, and a large door seam that Jack really hadn't noticed opened uniformly outward a few inches for about sixty feet wide and thirty feet high. A whooshing air sound and a pressure pulse on his ears made Jack wince for a second, and then it stabilized. "I guess it might be time to meet my hosts," said Jack aloud to himself.

* * * * *

On the control deck, Captain Trolnhyett's crew had completed the orbital approach to Nishda, and *Yuanjejitt* was now established in a 210-kahtak low-delivery orbit for four of the empty Burun-Rioc ore hoppers. These would detach shortly and start their short orbital descent to the two main mine processing facilities on the planet. Most of the planets on *Yuanjejitt*'s route were industrial planets that had their own Burun-Rioc ore processing refineries, so there would be a total of three ore hopper drops on their return run.

Nishda was the main Burun-Rioc ore provider for this half of the galaxy, but the more populated industrial planets did their own ore refining. The other refineries weren't as diversified as Nishda's, but they all had a larger processing output. All the cargo handling would take place with the gravpile generator on the low cargo handling mode, which allowed easier handling of the cargo and an easy approach to and from the ship from Nishda's cargo and passenger transfer shuttles through the center core of the cargo handling bays. The ore hoppers were fully automated, and the empty hoppers would return full on their own after a few hundred or so orbits by *Yuanjejitt*.

The cargo decks were like six large round stacked doughnuts with a central loading core for the transfer barges. This allowed for central loading and handling access to all decks. The loading barges could stack up through all six decks and load from all decks simultaneously, or they could load individually from any deck by waiting in turn.

Most of the Alliance trading planets were well enough organized and well financed that that all the barge fleets were stacked and ready to load and unload in a well-orchestrated process, but these out planets didn't usually have the resources to make it all work so seamlessly. It usually took twice as long to transfer half as much cargo on a planet like Nishda. The barge navigation and transit flights were for the most part automated, but ship-to-barge transfers were done by the barge crews and supervised by *Yuanjejitt*'s crew to make sure there were no errors or "accidental" transfers of unauthorized cargo or that no illegal contraband running occurred, at least any that *Yuanjejitt*'s crew didn't know about and make a percentage on.

There were some good side bonuses to be made by the captain and crew in smuggled contraband as long as there wasn't any truly dangerous or totally forbidden contraband being traded that could undermine the legitimate government or cause any distasteful embarrassments for the allegedly elected councils or trade officials. As long as the cargo inspectors and import officers got a fair cut, everything seemed to work smoothly and everyone came out nicely ahead. That's the way it worked out here in the outer rim, and that's how everyone liked it.

The core Alliance planets with their overblown self-importance and cumbersome trade restrictions and regulations didn't really work very well. It was different out here fortunately. There was little interest in complying with the burdensome regulations except to pay deference to them so as not to draw any attention from the annoying and usually distant Trade Alliance enforcement ships that generally patrolled the inner core worlds. Of course, there was plenty of the same graft and corruption closer into the core planets, but it generally took on more sophisticated and covert forms.

On the control deck, Captain Trolnhyett's orbital officer Shujin-ot advised him that the two ore hoppers they'd dropped at this position had cleanly separated and cleared *Yuanjejitt*'s orbital path. Two cargo barges were standing by to off-load from decks one and three as soon as they received permission. *Yuanjejitt*'s cargo supervisory crews were headed to those decks and would report in place in about five mentus.

* * * * *

Jack wasn't 100 percent sure what was happening, but he would have made a pretty good bet that since this was most likely a cargo ship, he decided they were in the midst of a cargo drop or transfer of some sort. A few seconds later, Jack heard the door to the corridor open and the sound of someone entering the cargo bay and then the door closing. He felt the hair on his arms and the back of his neck stand up, and a shiver ran down his spine.

A moment of fear of the total unknown gripped him for just a second as he realized the potentially threatening situation he was in. Still, he maintained absolute control of his thoughts and his composure. He willed himself to use every ounce of his observational skills and analyze every bit of information he was gathering. He made himself completely calm and controlled and took in everything he was hearing and seeing like the well-trained professional he was. This was pretty strange as far as experiences go, but damned if it wasn't one heck of an exciting journey at the same time. *How's this for an adrenaline rush?* he thought to himself.

He was fairly well hidden in his hiding spot, so he couldn't see much of anything from where he was. He heard several sets of footsteps and some voices that didn't sound like any earthy language he'd ever heard before. He hadn't expected to hear English or any other Earth language, but at this moment, he might have been relieved to hear a little Russian or even Swahili. The voices sounded fast and clipped as well as a little raspy and slightly melodic. There seemed to be a lot of t and j and maybe some d, r, and l sounds at the end of words in the ten to fifteen seconds he was able to listen and hear them clearly.

It sounded like four separate individuals had walked by in two groups of two. Some of it sounded vaguely similar to a few human words, but most sounded completely strange and alien. There were a few louder chirps or tweets mixed in that gave the overall impression of urgency. The voices he heard and their accompanying footsteps went down the aisle next to the one he was hiding in. He knew he would have to either be discovered or make a voluntary appearance shortly. He decided on the "Hi, my name's Jack, please take me to your leader" approach in reasonably short order but decided to wait a few minutes and try to assess the ship's crew and make a slightly better informed decision once he'd reconned a good look at them first.

He slowly and as quietly as possible worked his way from behind the containers he was hidden behind. He moved slowly and used the various containers as cover to avoid having his motion detected in case they might be looking his way, and he stayed as low as possible to the bottom of the lower level he was now on to minimize his profile. He was only about midway to the back of the cargo bay, so he only had about a thirty-foot view of the rear wall from where he was. He could still hear their voices in that direction but couldn't see any of them yet. He heard them raise their voices, and a few of the strange words seemed to be shouted. A major portion of the back wall of the cargo bay wall then began to move slowly downward into the floor accompanied by the loud metallic scraping sounds. Then he saw movement as two of the creatures moved into view from the right then moved farther into his field of view.

They were definitely not human by any stretch of the imagination. The two he could see appeared to be fairly tall, rangy, and slightly stooped at the shoulders. They were bipedal like humans, but their limbs, both legs and arms, appeared to have three sections each plus a type of hand appendage. He watched their arm and leg movements, and they seemed to be able to articulate both forward and backward at all three joints in each appendage. Although it sounded strange, it appeared to be a very fluid and graceful movement in any direction. He got the impression they could move fast and with great agility if they needed to. From what he could see, they appeared to be well but sleekly muscled on all sides of their limbs. Their skin looked to be a light pastel greenish-tan color, and they wore a tight-fitting light blue coverall with bright yellow bands near the wrists and feet.

They had some sort of footwear on that might approximate a lightweight fitted boot and strangely wide double sponson feet with an aft protruding double conjoined heel. It was hard to tell at this distance for certain. They stopped just short of going out of his field of view to the right and seemed to be watching the far wall as it slid lower into the floor.

Their heads were somewhat narrow and long with a short blunt nose about two-thirds from the top of their head. They appeared to have a fair amount of short cropped blondish-green hair over the upper and back portion of their heads as well as some longer darker tufts at their wrists just below the sleeve ends. They seemed to have a fairly prominent jaw that was slightly wider than the rest of the head as well as a slightly prominent forward protruding forehead and prominent brow with some darker eyebrows. They didn't look too unpleasant, but they were very alien looking even compared to all the imagined alien creatures in all the alien movies Jack had ever seen. They were the real deal, though, that was for sure. It gave Jack a very strange and unbalanced feeling to know he was looking at real aliens on an alien ship, yet it was somehow quite fascinating and exhilarating.

They also wore some sort of wide waist belt with various implements as well as some sort of a tactical vest garment with additional compartments and pockets. He'd thought a bit about his initial approach to whoever his hosts might be and wondered what a standard verbal announcement and a semisubmissive posture might be to show that he wasn't hostile.

Seeing these strange aliens now for the first time, he decided to stick with this plan. He moved forward to a moderate-sized container that he could use for cover if they became hostile when he announced his presence. He silently hoped these weren't some sort of common deckhand that might find it more sporting to chase and eliminate some uninvited guest and not bother reporting to whomever might be in command of the ship. *Well, there's only one way to find out,* he thought. *Maybe they don't even have ranks or positions in their societal structure.*

This is as good as any for show time, thought Jack. He stepped out about three-quarters of the way from behind the containers then raised his hands in what he hoped was a greeting gesture. Not too loudly but loud enough, he yelled, "Hello, hello, my name is Jack Spartan. Hello, I need help. I'm stranded on your ship." With the considerable background noise, it took the creatures a good five seconds to realize they were hearing something strange or new nearby. They both turned toward the sound and fixed their gaze on Jack, who was slowly moving his hands back and forth by his head and repeating his initial line to them.

They stared at Jack for a couple of more seconds, and it seemed that the one on the left turned and spoke to the other one. The one on the right bolted out of sight to the right at a very fast rate, and the remaining one took several long steps toward Jack. Jack continued to repeat himself out loud in hopes they would understand this as a possible distress call. He heard the sound of two sets of running feet heading back to the door area behind him, and then another alien appeared next to the remaining one that was looking at him. He could hear the others working their way back to the door area and back behind him. While continuing to repeat his intro line, he glanced over his shoulder and saw the two other previously unseen aliens appear at the far end of the aisle. At a quick glance, they appeared similar to the first two, except that one had on a pale orange-red outfit.

He turned halfway toward the ones at his back and crouched down on one knee while continuing to repeat himself. He hoped to God that this wasn't something that could be construed as an attack posture that might provoke a violent response. They all started making a considerable amount of spoken sounds in their alien language, and then from their belts, each took out what looked like a small three-inch oval disk-shaped object with protrusions sticking out from them and pointed it at him. *Please don't shoot,* thought Jack. They were at about thirty and fifty feet from him now, and the ones with the belt devices tossed them toward him. *Hopefully not grenades,* thought Jack. Surprisingly, both devices stayed in the air and levitated toward him. Both devices came to within about ten feet of him and hung in the air about four feet off the ground.

The alien in the orange-red outfit was speaking loudly and moving his arms all around, mostly in the direction of Jack. His arms moved fluidly, which gave them the impression of being somewhat languid. On the control deck, a minor alarm sounded and haled Captain Trolnhyett. Captain Trolnhyett answered the comm request by tapping the elongated hexahedral-shaped comm link just below his front neckline.

"Yes, Lodrenyu, what is your query?" he asked.

"Captain Trolnhyett, while we were preparing to off-load the cargo from cargo deck two, we have discovered a noncrew passenger among the shipment containers for some reason. We are transmitting it's vido to you on the security channel from two cargo inspection probes for your scrutiny. It seems to be confused and is making a strange speech that our comm links won't translate. It is most unusual, Captain. What are your orders?"

Captain Trolnhyett inquired, "Does it appear to be hostile? Possibly it is just a regular revenue passenger that is transiting to one of our planetary stops. Perhaps it somehow got past the security points on the passenger level deck and got lost. Go ahead and question it and find out what it is doing there."

"No, Captain Trolnhyett, it does not appear to be hostile. It is merely half standing with its arms raised and speaking in strange words. It looks like maybe a Varaci or possibly a Noren from what I might guess, Captain. Yes, I will report back in a few mentus," replied Lodrenyu.

"A Varaci or a Noren?" replied Captain Trolnhyett. "That's not very likely in this sector of the galactic disk, but seeing the vido you are transmitting, I can understand your belief on that assessment. Find out what it's doing there and where it's from then report back swiftly," said Captain Trolnhyett.

The four aliens spoke for a few moments then began to move closer to Jack. The one in orange-red was speaking, and it seemed to be directing itself at Jack. The language was so very strange sounding, thought Jack. The words seemed to all run together with a lot of harsh-sounding l's, r's, and t's or d's that seemed to repeat often. He could see their hands clearly now, and they were as unique as the rest of their appendages. Their hands were long and fluid looking with six fingers that were in an almost full circle. This gave them the appearance of having full opposable fingers in a complete circle. It looked very efficient and dexterous from a mechanical stand point, one of Jack's areas of engineering training. The two floating oval disks maintained their position except that they moved out of the way a bit as the aliens approached him. He hoped they weren't some automatic security weapon that might decide to fire on him.

The two closet aliens were both speaking now. Some of it was directed at him, and some seemed to be to each other. Jack stood up slowly from his crouched position and tried to listen to what they were saying. It only sounded like a series of verbal noises interspersed with some slightly familiar-sounding human sounds. Jack began speaking. "My name is Jack Spartan. I need help. I am stranded on your ship because of a crash. I am here because of an accident. Do you understand anything I am trying to say?" The aliens looked at him somewhat quizzically. Jack realized that they didn't understand him. Their reaction to his speech did seem to have a universal feel in that they didn't comprehend what he was saying. This went on for over a full minute before both parties conceded that they weren't making any headway.

Lodrenyu hailed Captain Trolnhyett again. "Captain Trolnhyett, the Varaci or Noru does not appear to be wearing any sort of comm translator, and it does not seem to understand our questions to it. It is speaking continuously, but my translator does not seem to interpret any of its words. Without a comm translator, it can't understand us, but our translators should at least be able to interpret its speech. What are your orders for us, Captain Trolnhyett?"

"Very well, Lodrenyu. I will send you two more shipment crew to take over for your loading operations. When they get there, you and Seemutii convey the Varaci to the officers briefing room by the control deck, and we will examine this further. Make certain it is not armed or carrying any forbidden articles before you bring it to the control deck. I will meet you there in a few mentus with Lucannana, the well-being seeker, and Nonaehssa, the technical engineer. We will try to communicate with it there and find out what it was doing down there in the cargo bay."

"Yes, Captain Trolnhyett, we will be at the officers briefing room shortly," replied Lodrenyu.

The aliens spoke to each other then moved closer to Jack. They were nearly a head taller than him, and they looked as if they might be very strong physically. They didn't seem to be hostile. He didn't want to provoke them, so he just stood there without trying to look too concerned. He wouldn't attempt any physical confrontation as long as they remained unthreatening. As they came closer, orange-red continued to speak to him. Even though he couldn't understand them, the tone of orange-red's voice was a little more commanding. Both the creatures reached for Jack and took his arms and hands and held them out to examine him. *Fair enough,* thought Jack, *they may not have ever seen a human before, so they need to check me out a bit.*

It was a very strange feeling being handled by aliens, and it gave him a bit of the willies. He also didn't like having his arms and hands restrained as a result of his many years of martial arts training. In Krav Maga, your arms were half of your weapon system, so you naturally avoided having them restrained if at all possible. They turned him all the way around once, then the blue-clothed one held his arms firmly, while orange-red proceeded to do a pat-down search on him.

Fair enough also, thought Jack, as he would have done the same thing in their position. Orange-red found Jack's flashlight in one of Jack's flight suit pockets. He examined it momentarily and placed it in his own vest pocket. "Make sure the trespasser isn't armed or carrying anything that could be used for a weapon," the captain had told him. As orange-red finished the pat down, it pulled something quickly from a pouch in one of its vest compartments. In half a second, Jack found his wrists crossed and pinned together in front of him by a strange double metallic band of some sort. Damn, now he'd have to fight with just his feet if things got ugly and went south for some reason.

They just stayed there for a few minutes with nothing really happening. Jack wondered what they were waiting for. The metal bands weren't painful, but they weren't exactly comfortable either. It had gone on so fast he hadn't really seen what it was or how it worked. It was on him now, though, just tight enough to fully restrain him as far as using his hands.

A few minutes later, he heard the corridor door open, and more sets of footsteps headed their way. Two more blue-dressed aliens appeared. They came toward them, and they both looked curiously at Jack and began speaking in their undecipherable language to orange-red and his partner. These two wore the same uniform and didn't appear to be much different from the others. The aliens spoke for a minute while gesturing at Jack. Then orange-red and his blue partner took his arms and led him out to the corridor door and to the left toward the elevator lift that Jack had tentatively examined previously. *I guess it's time to get the full tour of the cruise ship now,* thought Jack. As far as he was concerned, it was past time, since he'd been getting somewhat bored from the last few days of camping out on the cargo deck.

Jack and his captors—he was now thinking of them as captors, since his wrists were bound—walked the distance to the elevator, which was near the center of the ship's deck. The doors opened to the elevator, which turned out to be quite large at about six meters deep by four meters wide. Jack guessed it was used for cargo within the ship such as the food delivery bots from the kitchen. The doors closed, and the lift started to rise after orange-red opened his hand and spread his considerable finger reach across both hex marks on the panel, which caused the blue line to illuminate.

It was similar to Earth's elevators in many ways. There wasn't any recognizable lettering, but there were some controls that were similar to the door controls he'd figured out earlier. Jack felt the lift rising, and he saw a bright orange line and some characters illuminate as they apparently passed four more levels. The lift stopped when the illuminated lines were near the top of the control panel. The doors opened, and they moved into another corridor that went straight out from the lift, which also T'd left and right.

They walked forward about two hundred feet, took a slight jog to the right where the corridor T'd again, and then went left down another corridor after about four hundred feet. They passed five different crew members or possibly passengers in the process. These were dressed in both similar and also a couple of different uniforms of varying colors. Two of the aliens he saw were slighter, shorter, and definitely looked more feminine than any he'd previously seen. Maybe they were females. They weren't a great deal different from the others, but they did have a gentler feminine appearance to them. They looked at him as they walked by, and they made quite a few strange sounds after they'd passed him. *Probably commenting on the strange-looking alien they'd just seen,* he thought, *as in me, Jack Spartan, the alien.*

They'd passed half a dozen door openings along the way, but they were all closed, so he couldn't see anything as they proceeded. They came to another T and took a right turn then came to a door on their right. The door opened like the others, and they entered into a slightly darkened room. There were large inwardly scalloped table and maybe a dozen chairs that looked like they were designed to accommodate these alien creatures.

The room had an assortment of consoles around the perimeter as well as several lit displays of some sort embedded in the main table. There were attached booths with various displays and other equipment around the perimeter of the room. None of the positions were currently manned. Maybe it was a briefing room or a secondary control bridge of some sort, thought Jack. His escorts had him sit at one of the positions at the main table facing out. Orange-red said something to him, but, of course, he didn't understand it, so he just gave orange-red a slight shrug to indicate he didn't understand him. Orange-red glared at him for a second but didn't say anything else then gave a deliberate huff with a snort.

Jack looked around the room to see if there was anything he might be able to decipher. A few of the displays were lit and he could see symbols similar to the ones he'd seen on the doors as well as a mix or various graphical depictions. Two of the displays next to each other looked like two different views of a live feed to a planet that obviously wasn't Earth. He wondered if they were in orbit around another planet somewhere else in the galaxy. What an incredible realization now that he was actually seeing it. *I'm probably the first human to ever see another alien world,* he thought to himself. There was a lot more landmass and some widely spread dark green and blue areas that might be water. The landmass was various colors of gray, lighter greens, dusty browns crusted by white edges, and some dull pinks. There was a thin partial band of cloud cover over a portion of the area shown, but the striated cloud bands looked different from the familiar cloud formations he was used to on Earth. Looking back over his shoulder he saw another display with a feed showing six different frames. Each frame showed different views of a ship looking outward toward space or the planet he'd seen on the other display.

There were several smaller ships poised in space around the main ship. They looked utilitarian in purpose. He saw a large box-shaped ship drop away and another start to move into the position where the other had come from. He had to guess that since he'd seen a vast amount of cargo on a single deck that this was a major cargo transfer going on between the planet below and the ship he was on. He was trying to gauge the scale of the ship. He knew it was huge from the limited exploration he'd done, but he still didn't have anything to relate the true scale of it to what he was seeing. He thought that *Victory* would just be a speck next to this behemoth.

Suddenly, Jack heard footsteps coming down the corridor, and the blue-clothed alien jumped up toward the door. Orange-red grabbed Jack's arm and pulled him upright and facing the door. The door opened, and a larger, more weathered-looking alien dressed in a dark blue and pale green uniform came in. It was followed by two other aliens, one in a pale mustard-yellow outfit and the other in tan. The blue-and-green alien addressed orange-red, and it responded back. An exchange between them went on for over half minute.

The large alien dressed in blue and green looked at Jack. "So this is our uninvited guest. We have verified all revenue passengers and their location, and none of them match this one," said Captain Trolnhyett to the other aliens. "I am most curious as to its origin. Have you made any progress in gaining any information from it?" he asked Lodrenyu.

"No, Captain Trolnhyett. We have tried repeatedly to communicate with it, but it doesn't seem to understand anything we speak. As you can see, it has no comm translator or any other sort of equipment. We did find these two small devices when we searched it," as he held over the flashlight and Jack's watch, which they'd taken from him when they'd patted him down.

Captain Trolnhyett took the flashlight and examined it for a moment. "It appears to be some sort of a hand light, but there may be more to it." He looked at Jack and spoke to him while holding the flashlight out.

Jack assumed he wanted to know what it was, so he held his hand out and said, "It's just a flashlight. I can show you how it works," said Jack. Captain Trolnhyett pulled it back a second and waited. Jack just pointed and said, "Just push the button on the end to turn it on." He wasn't 100 percent sure, but the Varaci-looking creature didn't seem to be hostile in any way. Captain Trolnhyett handed the light to Jack, who proceeded to push the recessed button and turn the light on. Jack handed the light back to Captain Trolnhyett, who examined the light and then pushed the switch to turn it off.

To the other aliens, Captain Trolnhyett said, "Yes, it is just a light source from this initial examination." He handed the light to the alien dressed in the mustard-yellow outfit. "Nonaehssa, take these two devices to your engineering office and determine if there is anything more to them and see how they work when we are done here. This other one may possibly be a communication device of some sort. See what you can find out about both of them. Now take the comm translator you brought and configure it for the Varaci creature so we can speak with it. I want to question it and find out why it's here."

"Yes, Captain Trolnhyett, I have it right here. It is ready to fit on the Varaci," said Nonaehssa, the technical engineer.

"What do you make of it, Lucannana?" asked Captain Trolnhyett to the well-being seeker.

"I do not know, Captain Trolnhyett. It was quite a few yenets ago, but I have previously only seen two Varaci that I recall. They are a strange and somewhat reclusive race that specializes in various undesirable smuggling ventures on planets of the far five and four sectors of the rim mostly from tangen eighty and outward. I am not an expert on the Varaci, but it does look like a Varaci to me. We can run some tests on it if you'd like. It looks healthy and capable to me, but I will have to examine it more closely. It has strange clothing and little equipment of any kind other than the light. There are some symbols on its clothing, but it looks like no language form I am familiar with. I am really not sure what to make of it," replied Lucannana.

"Crat," replied Captain Trolnhyett, "maybe they are venturing further to this side of the rim in their runner ventures, or maybe this one has joined up with some of the other rogue non-Alliance bootlegger ships in this quadrant. Still, that wouldn't answer the question as to what it's doing on *Yuanjejitt* or how it got onboard without our knowledge."

The mustard-dressed alien pulled something from his vest compartment and approached Jack. It spoke several words and then unhooked the looped device, which looked like a flat metallic cloth necklace with an interesting semidiamond-shaped pendant in the center. Jack noticed that it was almost exactly like the ones they all wore around their necks except for the shape of the pendant. On the aliens, they looked like it was part of their upper garment, almost like a trim piece around the neck opening. It was about an inch wide but very thin, and it seemed to conform very closely to the uniforms of the aliens. The alien went to place it around Jack's neck, but Jack instinctively backed up. He was still bound at the wrists, and orange-red held him in place. He relaxed after a second and decided not to fight the issue. The mustard-dressed alien placed the pendant around his neck.

The pendant seemed to conform itself to his neckline and the flight suit neck opening. It was so light that he hardly felt it. Orange-red spoke several sentences to mustard-colored alien, who then spoke toward Jack. The mustard-colored alien then took a small device out of its vest and made several inputs that appeared to be an adjustment or alignment of some sort.

Orange-red then looked at Jack and spoke several sentences worth of their alien language. He then appeared to wait for some sort of response from Jack. As far as Jack could tell, it was just the same languages he'd heard previously. Orange-red said something to mustard-dressed alien, and they appeared to use the electronic gadget to apply some more adjustments. They then repeated the initial exercise of speaking to Jack and expecting a response. Jack attempted to reply several times during these exchanges with the response that he could not understand them and that he needed their help as he was marooned on their ship. Several minutes of these attempted exchanges produced no positive results.

The two aliens turned to confer with the older-looking alien with the authoritative appearance. "Captain Trolnhyett, for some reason, the translator doesn't seem to be effective with this Varaci. We have encoded it for all known possible Varaci dialects and all other languages in this half of the galactic disk. There should be at least a partial recognition of this alien's language. For some unknown reason, we have not gotten a single phrase or word that matches with anything in our data core. This is very unusual, Captain. This unit and all our translator units tested faultlessly. The sound of its language is totally unknown to any of us or to the translator algorithms. I do not have an explanation for this, Captain. Unless it is not a Varaci or is intentionally trying to mislead us, then I do not have an explanation for this strange unknown language. Captain, I also enabled tracking on the translator and set it to be nonremovable."

"Very good," said Captain Trolnhyett. The captain took an appraising look at Jack and then spoke several undecipherable sentences to him.

Again, Jack responded, "I'm sorry, I still don't understand you. I would be thrilled to be able to communicate with you and find out what my situation is here." Carefully touching the pendant on his neck, he said, "If this device is somehow supposed to help translate, then it doesn't appear to be working. I can't understand what you're saying, but if you can somehow understand what I'm saying, I am very happy to cooperate in any way I can to help enable our communications."

45

Unfortunately for both species, this entire attempt at communication between the Lokar crew and Jack still did not produce any positive results.

Turning to Nonaehssa, the technical engineer, and Lucannana, the well-being seeker, Captain Trolnhyett stated, "The issue is we still have an unauthorized alien passenger. We don't know where it came from, what it's doing here, or for that matter even where it is attempting to go. It doesn't appear to have any identification or transit documentation, and it certainly hasn't paid for its passage. At least for now we are unable to communicate with it, so I'm not even sure what jurisdiction it would fall under. Nonaehssa, if you have no other pressing matters, then keep attempting to make the translator functional with this alien's language."

The captain continued. "Lucannana, you can take the alien to well bay and run any nondestructive tests on it that you think will help us determine its origin. Lodrenyu, you and Seemutii, escort our uninvited guest to the holding suite near well bay. Bring him anywhere that Lucannana or Nonaehssa need him to facilitate their tests or technical applications. You can unbind his wrists for now, as it doesn't appear to be hostile and seems to be fairly cooperative. Leave the binders on its wrists so that it may be remotely constrained if it shows any aggressive behavior. I must get back to the control deck now and oversee our cargo and associated surface transit activities. Advise me at once if you learn anything new about our guest. I will attempt to come up with a tenable resolution for this situation."

Jack wasn't exactly sure what had transpired, but the taller authority figure turned and left. Jack assumed this one had to be an officer or other authority figure from the ship, perhaps even the captain or whatever the equivalent was that they had in their ship's hierarchy. The captain hadn't appeared to be too happy as he left, but then they hadn't accomplished much of anything during the time that he was present. Orange-red then took Jack by the arm and held some type of a control disk gadget near his wrists, which caused the restraints to release from his wrists. That was a relief and certainly a little more comfortable; however, the restraints were still attached separately to each wrist. *Well,* he thought, *if I have to fight for some reason, at least I've got my hands back now.*

The mustard-dressed guard took him by the arm, and all five of them went out the door and down the corridor to the left. After several turns and a few minutes of walking, they came to another door and entered what appeared to be a sick bay or infirmary. The room was well lit, and there appeared to be several examination tables with different sets of examination instruments and various display monitors around them. Along the edge of one of the walls, there were a dozen or more slightly reclined beds with some sort of monitoring equipment next to each one.

His captors didn't seem to be overtly hostile, but he was now concerned that this might turn into some sort of an invasive examination situation or possibly worse.

The two aliens that had initially been with the captain alien had carried on a normal conversation all the way to this sick bay area. Jack tried to weigh his options at this point and decided that if they tried to sedate him or attempt some invasive examination procedure, he might have to try to fight his way out of here, although he wasn't sure what he would do after that. Trying to find another hide might be an option, but he didn't know how long he'd be able to keep it if they sent some of the search drones he'd seen out after him. So far, the aliens had seemed fairly cordial considering that he was an uninvited interloper as far as they were concerned. Hopefully, their semicordial actions weren't geared toward the fair treatment of a condemned prisoner.

The tan-dressed alien seemed to be in charge of the sick bay area, so Jack assumed it must be some sort of a medical officer. Tan-dressed alien said something to orange-red, which caused his two guard aliens to move Jack to an examination table where they had Jack get up on it and sit. Tan-dressed alien came back with some sort of tablet device, which he then made some entries on. Then amazingly, a ring of red-and-blue lit symbols and several monitor-type screens appeared holographically in the air above the examination table.

Now that was pretty interesting, thought Jack. The tan-dressed alien stood in front of Jack and fiddled with his control module. Various readouts and symbols started to appear and move on the lighted readouts above him. The tan-dressed medical officer then took out a half round metallic and glass-looking object and placed it on Jack's inner wrist above the shackle device that was already there. It was cool and smooth and seemed to stay in place on its own. The medical officer alien looked up at the displays and studied them for a minute. Some minor ongoing conversation continued between the medical officer and Jack's guards.

The medical officer then said something to the guards, and they mildly forced him to lie down on the examination table. Jack started to resist, and the guards started to exert a little more force on him, so Jack decided to go with it for the moment unless something threatening happened. A wide pale green light appeared from an aperture in the ceiling above the examination table. Jack could feel slight electromagnetic pulses that traversed his body at the same time as the wide green light beam crossed his body. There was no pain, just a slight tingling and pulsing sensation. A full-size display appeared behind the medical officer alien, which appeared to be a full 3-D highly detailed X-ray or MRI type of image of a human body, which Jack assumed was his. The medical officer examined it for a few minutes and made various adjustments, which changed the display readouts and imagery associated with it. The display seemed to switch from musculature to skeletal, vascular, and then showed a full image of his nervous system. It also showed two different maplike images that he didn't recognize but were in the shape of his body.

It was an amazing and nearly instantaneous full medical exam, thought Jack. He wished the Air Force and NASA medical examinations had been that painless and fast. He'd spent several days every six months getting poked and prodded by each of those two institutions. One thing that the aliens didn't do that he was used to getting was a blood work exam, but maybe the wrist gadget did that without drawing blood.

The medical officer and the other mustard-dressed alien that had put the pendant around Jack's neck continued their conversation, while they examined the displays and medical images of Jack's body. Lucannana said to Nonaehssa as well as Seemutii and Lodrenyu, "Based on my examination, our guest appears to be a Varaci as we suspected. Our data on the Varaci species is not very complete, but based on the information we do have, it does seem to be a Varaci, or Varan as they call themselves. There may be some very minor differences in the organ placement as well as minor blood chemistry differences, but this could be due to inaccuracies in our data or just individual variances in this particular specimen."

"I will report this to Captain Trolnhyett. You may return him now—and, yes, the examination confirms that it is a male—to the holding room and continue your work with the translator pendant. Please advise me immediately if there is any change in his well-being either physically or mentally. If it—I mean, he should become hostile in any way, just remember to use the restraining function on your control disk."

"Yes," replied Nonaehssa, "I would like to have the translator function working so that we may communicate with him and let Captain Trolnhyett discover how he got here and what he wants aboard our ship. It is an interesting mystery that I'm sure we would all like to know the answers to."

After a few more minutes of conversation, the two guard aliens and the mustard-dressed alien took Jack down several corridors to another door entrance. Entering through the main door, Jack saw there were several smaller doors, six to be exact, which opened up into smaller rooms. There was a short central hallway and large observation windows for each room. The rooms looked to be about three by three meters. They approached one of the doors, which orange-red opened using a display pad on the outside. There was a smaller door opening at the back of the room as well as what might be a fold-down bed pinned to the wall. A small table was affixed to the wall, and there were two large chairs next to it. There was a small control panel above the table in the wall.

The main door closed behind them, and the mustard-dressed alien gestured at Jack to sit in one of the chairs. Jack sat down in one of the chairs, and the mustard-dressed alien sat in the other. The alien touched the control panel in the wall above the table. A display illuminated above the control panel in the wall, which showed various symbols like the previous writing he'd seen throughout the ship.

The alien pulled out another control module from his vest that looked surprisingly like a large iPhone. The alien made some entries on the module, and the screen on the wall changed configurations and rearranged itself with different symbols and colors. The alien spoke to Jack several times and gestured in an indication that it wanted Jack to respond and speak to him. Jack responded several times with various greetings and inquiries similar to the ones he used before. Getting a little bored with the lack of actual conversation, Jack decided to recite "Mary ad a little lamb" in a somewhat lyrical voice. The alien stared at him for a moment and looked somewhat quizzical as if to inquire what it was exactly that Jack was doing.

By now, Jack was starting to get somewhat thirsty and hungry, since it had been about six hours since his last raid on the food prep kitchen. Jack looked at the alien and asked him, "Would it be possible to have something to drink?" while at the same time using his hand to indicate that he was holding a cup while imitating a drinking motion. He made a motion like he was eating something with a utensil to indicate that he was also hungry.

The mustard-dressed alien spoke something to orange-red and the other guard. "I believe he is attempting to show us that he wishes something to drink and possibly to eat something also," said Nonaehssa, the technical engineer, to Seemutii and Lodrenyu. Mustard-dressed alien stood up and moved to the smaller door at the back of the room. It gestured to Jack to follow it. They entered the small door, which turned out to be an entrance to a small restroom facility somewhat similar to the one Jack had seen on the cargo bay deck.

There was a single sink with similar controls as well as the nearly transparent drinking cups he'd seen before. The alien took one of the cups and held it for the water to fill then started to hand it to Jack but stopped just short of handing it to him. Jack pointed at the cup and said, "Water." The alien fiddled with his control device for a moment and then spoke the word "water" back to Jack. What Jack saw was that the alien's mouth moved in what appeared to be some sort of a voice-over where the word "water" was very slightly out of sync with the alien's speech movement but close enough that it was barely discernible . Jack figured out that this was some sort of an automatic translation and had something to do with the alien's handheld device or the pendant thing around Jack's neck. "Yes," said Jack, "I would like to drink some water, drink water," as he tilted an imaginary cup to his lips. "Drink," he said as he tilted the cup then pointed to where the cup would be with his other hand while making a stirring motion with his finger and said, "Water." The alien spoke several alien words then repeated, "Drink water." The alien then handed the cup of water to Jack. Jack pointed at the cup and said, "Water," then "drink," and then he proceeded to drink the water.

Jack finished the cup of water then handed it back to the alien and said, "Thank you," which garnered a questioning look from the alien. Jack then proceeded to point at various objects in the restroom. "Sink, faucet, toilet, ceiling, floor, wall," pointing at everything possible in the small restroom. The alien stopped him for a second then fiddled with his small tablet then indicated for Jack to continue. Jack repeated everything then went back to the main room and then pointed at the table, chair, bed, and again everything that was in the minimally furnished room.

The alien listened intently then repeated each of the objects back to Jack through the translator device. Nonaehssa was fairly intrigued by this unknown alien whose language was not anywhere in the translator's data core but who easily made its language translate by associating common objects in the room. The Lokar race had used translator technology for so long that this simple association game seemed quite unfamiliar but fascinating to him. Nonaehssa contemplated this for a minute and thought that it might be fairly practical to generate a complete translator databank of this alien's language by showing it images of Lokar objects and having it speak its language into the translator when it saw items it recognized. This might take several daiyus or a wenek, but it should be sufficient to build up an adequate vocabulary that would allow them to communicate with it.

* * * * *

On the control deck, Captain Trolnhyett had been conferring with a Nishda port control officer down world by the name of Roshnil Kayshen. Captain Trolnhyett had worked with Roshnil Kayshen on several prior occasions when he'd needed some unofficial leverage to get some of *Yuanjejitt*'s undocumented contraband cargo distributed to the appropriate recipients without any Nishdan bureaucratic interference from the local import authorities who only wanted a cut of the profits for themselves anyway. There wasn't much point or much profit if you had to pay the Alliance transfer duties on every little item transported around the galaxy. He explained to Roshnil his situation with the stowaway Varaci they'd found on the ship. Nishda was an informal planet to deal with, and he didn't really want to take the Varaci on to their next transit stop of Kwiikay, where they would likely get much more scrutiny over the undocumented traveler. This could potentially delay their departure for their next leg, which would generate a penalty for the company, and his crew could possibly lose any bonuses they'd accumulated for the entire trip. He basically wanted to be rid of the problem, and since they hadn't earned any revenue from the Varaci's transit, he thought there might even be a chance to earn a few extra credits by dropping the alien off on Nishda.

Roshnil had made a tidy sum from his association with *Yuanjejitt*'s captain on several prior occasions, so he wasn't averse to helping the captain out, especially since there might be a little incentive in it for himself as well. "Yes, Captain," said Roshnil, "let me ask around a bit and see where a good destination for this stowaway might be. You say it doesn't have a language that any of your ships translators can interpret? And you say that you are fairly sure that it's a Varaci, yet the translators won't interpret it in Varaci or any of its dialects? That is quite unusual. This might make it a little more difficult as far as finding a place where it will be useful. However, there might be a chance that we have something in our main data core that will allow one of our translator units to understand it. That is most unusual and a bit of a mystery, but I think I can possibly help you out with this."

"That would be most appreciated," said Captain Trolnhyett. "If you can get me five thousand unencumbered credits for his 'employment' at the location of your choice, that would cover his missing transit revenue and cover our basic expenses for him. Anything above that that you would happen to generate would, of course, be yours to keep for this service you are providing us."

"Well, Captain Trolnhyett, then I believe we have a workable agreement. This will be beneficial to both of our causes. Give me a few horuns to see what I can do, and I will get back to you shortly with a solution to your problem," replied Roshnil.

A few mentus later, Nonaehssa called Captain Trolnhyett to give him an update on the situation with the Varaci. He explained the rudimentary translation efforts he had accomplished and explained how he thought that a few days of visual object association would very likely create a decent translator protocol that they could then use to communicate with the Varaci in whatever dialect or language it was speaking. "That's a very good initiative, Nonaehssa," said Captain Trolnhyett, "and may come in useful for where he will be going. I would be interested in knowing where it came from, where it intended on going, and how it got onto our ship undetected. However, I don't believe you will have enough time to adequately translate its language in the next few horuns before we transfer it to Nishda." He then gave Nonaehssa an abbreviated explanation of his plan to drop the Varaci on Nishda so they could be rid of their potential problem before Kwiikay or any of their other planned stops. "Perhaps in three or four moondats, when we come through Nishda again, they might have an answer to our questions about this mystery stowaway passenger." Captain Trolnhyett then directed Nonaehssa and Lucannana to make sure the Varaci was well taken care of and readied for transit to Nishda. "See to its needs if it wants food or drink then stand by to bring it to whatever transit bay I direct you to shortly," ordered the captain.

Nonaehssa acknowledged the captain's order but felt disappointed that they wouldn't get to examine the Varaci stowaway any closer. He somehow felt that there might be more to this story than just a simple stowaway issue. Nonaehssa continued the object association translating game with Jack for a while longer. After they had exhausted all the body part names, room furnishings, and the apparel they were wearing, Nonaehssa turned to the monitor above the table and began calling up pictures of various objects.

The objects were in the display, but they appeared to be three-dimensional and floated above the table outside the frame of the display. Jack recognized some of them and others he'd never seen before. An image of some sort of starship appeared, which immediately fascinated Jack. Jack pointed to the picture in the ceiling and the floor and tried to indicate the question of was this a picture of the ship they were on. After a couple of attempts, the mustard-dressed alien understood what Jack was asking and moved his hand briefly across the front of his neck in a gesture that Jack understood to mean "no."

The alien then called up an image of another ship that he then pointed to and then pointed toward the wall and ceiling. Jack leaned over and looked closely at the image. It was impossible to judge the scale of the ship by the image, but from what Jack could see, it appeared to be immense. He was trying to analyze what he was viewing and what the functions of the different sections of the ship might be. He could tell by looking at it that it was probably a cargo vessel not only by its shape but also by the sheer size of the vessel. He was trying to discern its propulsion system by looking for engines or other obvious propulsion devices. He might have been seeing what he is looking for, but he wasn't sure.

He did see two huge forward-facing openings on each side of the ship as it rotated in the displayed image. They looked like huge scoops that appeared to be retractable. *What could they possibly be for?* he wondered. Those had to be the answer to what happened to *Victory.* He looked closely at the image and then pointed at the huge scoops and said to the alien, "I think my ship *Victory* was hit by your ship, and part of it broke off and went inside this opening with me inside it. That's how I got here, that's how I got stranded on your ship." He looked at the alien and pointed to the openings several times and then pointed to himself.

Both aliens watched him but didn't seem to comprehend what he was trying to tell them. Looking at the image, Jack remembered the immense cavernous area were the remains of *Victory* were lodged. He tried to calculate the size of the opening based on the memory from the dazed state he was in at the time. With what he was coming up with, then the ship must be several thousand feet across and nearly four times that in length. The size of the ship was literally mind-boggling. What kind of propulsion system could possibly move this amount of mass at the speeds it had obviously traveled to get to another habitable system? Jack wondered where in the galaxy they might be in relation to Earth. It was hard to comprehend what the answer might be.

Jack wanted to find out more about the ship and wanted to try again to convey to the aliens what had happened to him and his ship. Suddenly, they all looked up as they heard the sound of the main door open to this area of smaller rooms. One of the hovering fridge machines that Jack had seen in the ship's big food prep kitchen came in through the door and stopped in front of the room they were in. Several words were spoken between the orange-red guard and the mustard-dressed alien.

The orange-red guard went over to the door, which opened when he held up a small electronic device. One of several small rectangular bar-shaped drones on the top of the fridge machine hovered up and went to one of the door compartments on the fridge machine, which opened as it got close to it. The bar attached itself to the end of the tray in the compartment and then proceeded to pull out the tray, which was loaded with food and various other objects.

The floating bar with the attached tray then floated into the room that Jack was in with the aliens. It placed the tray on the table then detached itself from the tray and shot back to the fridge machine. The orange-red guard then did something that caused the door to close. It appeared that they were going to feed him, which didn't sound like such a bad idea, since he'd realized it had been about six or seven hours again since he'd last eaten anything.

The thought briefly occurred to him that he hoped this wasn't the last meal of a condemned man. It didn't exactly look like the steak and lobster he would have ordered if that was really the case. Either way, it didn't look too bad, as he had kind of grown accustomed to this fare over the last several days. It smelled pretty good and had an organic meaty and somewhat spicy smell to it, although he didn't recognize the spice as anything he was familiar with. He also noted that the aliens themselves had a bit of a different smell about them, almost like a musty ginger odor, but not too strong.

Jack looked at the mustard-dressed alien then pointed at the food and then to himself in an attempt to verify that it was OK for him to eat the food. After two of those gestures, the alien said several undecipherable words to him then motioned his hand toward Jack. Jack took this to mean that it was OK to proceed. As Jack picked up one of the eating utensils, the alien briefly stopped him and spoke several words, "table," "chair," and "shoe," that had previously been translated from their little vocabulary exercise. Jack understood that the alien wanted him to say the words for the objects Jack was using as he ate.

"Fair enough," Jack said as he proceeded to name the objects that he recognized that were similar enough to human objects to give them a name. "Fork, sort of, meat, also sort of, vegetable, somewhat asparagus like, not sort of but close enough for this game," said Jack. The meal itself wasn't bad, thought Jack, but it was a little disconcerting as he proceeded to eat with the four aliens intently watching him as well as having to translate everything he touched or ate. The thought crossed Jack's mind that maybe they'd never seen an "alien" that looked quite like he did. Since they were the star-faring race, he was sure they must have seen a few others, if not many other different creatures that might be out here. He was certain of one thing, though, and that was that he'd never seen the likes of them before. *All in a day's work,* he thought.

As Jack was finishing his meal and the aliens were finishing some small talk among themselves, the tan-dressed alien detached a small palm-sized, hex-shaped object from his vest and held at about three inches from the side of his head. He proceeded to stare into space slightly then spoke several words. It appeared to Jack that it was communicating to someone using what must be their version of a cell phone or communicator.

Tan-dressed alien then said something to the other aliens, and they all got up and left Jack to himself in the room as the door closed behind them. Jack then decided to check out the restroom facility and take care of some business there as well as snoop around and see if he could discover anything else about his situation.

The image of their gigantic ship still hovered in the wall above the table. He tried to get it to enlarge or change orientation by using standard tablet gestures, but nothing seemed to work. Maybe he was locked out or needed a password or some biometric access code or something. Still, he marveled at the depicted ship's image and tried to fathom what the mass of the ship might be. He then wondered if this particular ship was even considered a large ship. Maybe it was a little bitty ship. Not likely; they probably wouldn't build a cargo ship unless it was fairly capable from a bulk cargo standpoint.

What he'd seen up until now boggled the mind. Like most humans, he'd always contemplated the possibility of extraterrestrial life, but he'd never fathomed that he would be suddenly thrust into the midst of it like this. So part of this entire situation seemed horribly cursed, while other parts of it seemed rife with infinite potential. So was he cursed or was he blessed? Only time would tell; yes, only time would tell.

Deciding that he'd had a fairly full day already, a full stomach, and had explored everything in the room that he could, he decided to rest awhile and contemplate what his next possible move might be. He examined the folded bed that was against the wall and gave it a good tug outward, which caused it to fold down into its sleeping position. In the wall cavity where the bed had been folded up were several small recessed shelves. These contained several small rectangular soft foam blocks, some sort of pillows, he guessed, as well as a lightweight blanket that was folded into a tight bundle. *I guess basic needs are basic needs whatever type of biped you might be,* thought Jack.

There appeared to be some sort of a thin foam mattress that was just a foam block attached to the bed frame that had folded down. Jack arranged the three foam blocks as pillows and unfolded the blanket and threw it across him. He lay back and started thinking about all the insane things that had transpired in the last few days. Yep, it was nap time, he thought. He dozed off and was soon napping soundly, which was what he really needed right now.

Chapter 4: Descent

It couldn't have been more than about thirty minutes when the door opened, and the orange-red guard and his partner marched back into the room. They motioned for Jack to get up while talking to him in their indecipherable language. Several English words did pop up during their dialogue, though. Apparently, a few of the words they had translated during the earlier session were now programmed into either his or their translator device. Mixed in with their alien language, Jack was sure he'd hear the words "boots," "water," and "food." As soon as Jack was up and on his feet, orange-red guard took out and operated the disk device he'd used before, which caused Jack's wrist cuffs to link back together. "Hey, why the heck did you do that?"

That isn't exactly a good sign, Jack thought. *Well, maybe they just want to move me to another room or holding cell,* he contemplated. Still, he didn't like it. It's wasn't comfortable, and he didn't like being restrained in the first place. The two guards took Jack by the arms as they had previously and walked him out the door and down the corridor. "Any chance you fellas could tell me where you're taking me?" he asked as they were walked him down corridor. They paused momentarily when he spoke, but they didn't really respond to him; they just spoke sporadically between themselves and continued walking.

They ended up in another elevator somewhere down the corridor. They entered the elevator and went down several decks to what appeared to be another cargo level. The corridor floor was slanted slightly like the other one he'd originally been on but not quite as much from what he could tell. They went quite a ways down the curved corridor past eight or so doors that looked like they could have been accesses to more cargo bays.

Finally, they came to a door that they stopped at then opened and entered. They went into another cargo bay with similar storage facilities to the previous one he had originally hidden in. This one was mostly empty, but when they got to the far end of the bay, other aliens were bringing large floating pallets of containers from another bay or perhaps ship that was directly attached to the end of this bay.

The huge pallets had an operator's position at one end, and it was manned, or in this case, "aliened," by a strange squat-looking creature with long grasshopper-like legs, two thin skeletal-like arms, and a wide triangle-shaped head with big upside-down teardrop eyes that slanted out at the bottom. Its body was short and stocky in the middle, but its appendages were quite long and thin. It had bluish-gray skin and a faded purple-and-black uniform that covered its body but not its arms or legs. Both of its hands and feet appeared to be manipulating various controls from a seated position.

This just keeps getting more bizarre and interesting by the minute, Jack thought to himself. They paused to watch for a moment and saw a dozen or more various-shaped containers levitate off the pallet and then park themselves on the tall shelving area. As the various containers would set down, disk-shaped objects detached themselves from the containers and made a beeline directly back to the pallet, where they parked themselves in an orderly row directly in front of the operator's position.

Two other pallets came from between the rows of shelving and returned to what was a cargo shuttle that was uploading its freight into the big cargo bay of the ship Jack was on. The hovering pallets were moving rapidly, and the various containers that were being loaded by the lifting disks were moving at a breakneck, coordinated pace. Jack could tell it wouldn't take long to fill the entire bay at this rate. Jack's captors prodded him along into the cargo shuttle that was disgorging its contents into the big cargo bay.

All along, Jack had been wondering where they were taking him, and now it was becoming apparent that they might be placing him on this other cargo or transfer ship that was most likely headed for the planet below. If that was the case, what did it mean? He tried to reason why they would want to transfer him off the ship and onto the planet. Were they just dropping him here for now and maybe planning to return him to Earth shortly, or was there some other reason? With his hands being shackled, he wondered if he was considered some sort of criminal or if they were just unsure of his intentions because he was perhaps a new type of alien to them. Maybe they just considered him persona non grata, since he obviously didn't belong there and couldn't communicate with them and explain his situation.

As they entered the smaller cargo ship, which actually must be quite large considering the amount of containers coming out of it, they headed down a small poorly lit corridor and passed several bulkhead-type doors. The interior of this ship was considerably less aesthetic than the big ship. From everything he was seeing, this was strictly a utilitarian setup. Nothing was too well lit, and all the interior structure and facilities looked basically like an old, well-used seagoing cargo ship back on Earth.

They went down a small flight of stairs and eventually ended up in some type of a maintenance or utility room. As they entered the room, Jack saw a bipedal creature bent over the table apparently working on some sort of machinery. It turned toward them and stood erect and then walked over to them. Jack was taken aback for a second as he realized this alien had four arms and hands that it had been using to work on whatever the project was it had on the table. It had a long head that was sloped backward from its two large round green eyes, four small nasal openings below its eyes, and a chin that sloped back into its neck.

The overall impression was that of a face that displayed intense concentration wherever it turned. Its skin had a slight yellowish-orange cast and was slightly translucent at the surface. It did have a fine covering of medium brown, tinged with almost yellow hair, mostly on the back side of its head. The hair was very soft and fine looking almost like small feathers.

The creature came up to Jack's two guards and started talking in a totally different-sounding language from what Jack had previously heard. There were a lot of distraught-sounding high-pitched vowels along with some whining sounds and quite a few clicks and hisses. It didn't really sound like a spoken language but more like a mournful bird singing about what a bad day it had just had. It was a very strange compilation of sounds, but in some ways, it was somewhat mesmerizing and almost soothing. Jack's guards spoke to it for a few moments, and he could tell they were discussing him as they made several gestures in his direction.

The guards and the new alien exchanged several articles between them, one of which was the disk that Jack had seen that controlled his wrist restraints. When they finished their conversation, they motioned Jack over to the corner of the room and sat him on a narrow bench. The new alien used the disk to release his wrist restraints for a moment. As soon as they had, though, they made him place his hands around a vertical structural member and rebound his wrists. Apparently, he wasn't going anywhere for a while. He thought, *Maybe they're just going out for a quick lunch bite and they are tying the dog up so it can't run off while there enjoying their meal.* The aliens spoke briefly for another minute, looked Jack over one more time, then orange-red and his assistant guard left, leaving Jack restrained to the cargo ship and under the watchful eye of the new four-armed alien.

The four-armed alien came over and spoke to Jack for about a minute in its strange mournful birdlike language. Jack responded to it with his standard "Hi, my name's Jack Spartan" introduction speech. After a few more moments of this, the alien decided that no progress was going to be made, and it went back to its project on the workbench. After another twenty minutes or so, the alien went over to some type of control console and made several entries of some sort. In the distance, Jack heard a strange "eeeeeeeup, eeeeeeeup" sound as an alarm siren began warbling for about half a minute. There were a couple of moderate thunks, and a slight shudder was felt in the floor of the ship.

The four-armed alien came back to another control console on this side of the workbench and punched in a couple of entries. A large holographic wall display illuminated to the left of it. From the display view, Jack could tell it was the cargo shuttle they were on, and it was dropping away from the main ship where he'd spent the last few days. The ship was so large that they fell away from it for a good half minute before he could actually see the entire shape of the ship. Yes, this was the ship that he had seen in the holding room on the wall monitor above the desk. The size and scope of it was just difficult to grasp. It had to be bigger than fifty aircraft carriers combined. The thought of a vessel this size having transited interstellar space in just a few days to another planetary system was incomprehensible. Jack marveled again at the thought that the propulsion system for a ship like this must be beyond anything the engineers on Earth could even theoretically conceive of.

As they continued their descent, Jack counted seven other smaller ships lined up beneath the big cargo ship. They were all about the same shape and size and seemed to be basically a large rectangular box design that fit into two long grooves in the belly of the big cargo ship. When they first started their descent, Jack could see three of the rectangular ships fitted flush in the groove behind them and an open space in front of where they had just left from.

Because they were flush at first, he didn't recognize them as ships that were docked, but now that he had a visual on the other ships that were lined up, he could tell how they fit into the double grooves of the cargo ship. It was hard to gauge, but if he had to estimate, he'd say each one of the cargo shuttles was the size of the U.S. Navy destroyer or larger. It appeared that the cargo shuttles were specifically designed to dock with the cargo ship, so maybe they belonged to the same government or company that was running this operation.

The cargo shuttles had what appeared to be a forward bridge on them and two large cargo doors on the left side of the ship. Since they had just undocked from the big cargo ship, he had to assume that he was in the same type of cargo shuttle as he saw on the display. If that was the case, then wherever he was inside the cargo shuttle certainly wasn't the bridge or control center, as it didn't have any forward-facing observation windows that were visible on the other cargo shuttles.

The four-armed alien was still working on the machinery on his workbench, but as they dropped farther away from the big cargo ship, the alien's bottom left hand tapped on some sort of control box on the workbench, and the view on the monitor changed to the planet below. Either the alien was watching the whole descent procedure on the display as he worked on his project or he had shifted the visual for Jack's benefit.

The whole scenario didn't bode well on Jack's mind in that here he was, some possibly new and interesting alien life form to them, yet instead of showing more interest in him, he was merely chained to a cargo shuttle maintenance room structure with some technician working on a piece of machinery while overseeing him. Well, maybe this was actually a fairly common occurrence to them, so perhaps it didn't warrant much of an enthusiastic response. Either way, it made him feel more like a piece of cargo like the containers he'd seen being unloaded from this cargo shuttle. What could they possibly have in store for him if they weren't treating him as either a potentially threatening combatant or a possible emissary of his home planet Earth?

The planet below was growing even larger now on the display. Initially, they were in a fairly low orbit from what Jack could tell when he first saw the visual switch to the planet below. They were now descending very rapidly toward the planet. He wished he knew what type of propulsion system was being used by the ships he'd seen so far. He decided he would learn as much he could about everything he was seeing and experiencing so that if he ever somehow got back to Earth, he would be able to convey as much technical data as he possibly could about his voyage.

As he looked at the display, Jack could see that the planet was a conglomeration of different hues and landforms. It also appeared to have a considerable coverage of fairly large dark blue inland seas as well as a number of large green areas from what he could see on the display. Jack had no way of knowing whether the blue areas were fresh or salt water, but it was a landlocked planet with considerable water as opposed to Earth, which is a water planet with a considerable amount of landmasses. He could see multiple bands of clouds and weather systems playing out on various areas of the planet as well as a small polar ice cap on the side of the planet he could see. It was an interesting planet, the first ever seen by human eyes outside of Earth's Sol system as far as Jack knew. It wasn't as beautiful as Earth by a large measure in Jack's opinion.

As he'd already observed, the planet appeared to be about half arid zones, while the rest of it was patchy hues of darker and lighter greens, while some of the land areas even looked more blue green. At least that's what he thought he was looking at, but he couldn't tell for sure. As they drew closer, he tried to pick out any areas that might appear to be cities or other colonized areas of civilization.

He saw one or two areas that might indicate some form of development, but he couldn't be sure. They continued their descent even further and started to pick up some light reentry turbulence as they descended into the upper atmosphere of the planet. Now he was sure that he saw some sort of small settlements or towns near two of the lighter green areas they passed over. They didn't look like much, but they did appear to have some areas of buildings or other structures. One of the settlement areas appeared to have a large open pit mining area adjacent to it in an area of desert. He couldn't tell exactly what it was, but it was a long gouge in the surface that appeared to be machine made as well as several large circles and oval cuts that went into the planet for a considerable distance.

The turbulence continued to increase until they were experiencing a continuous rhythmic vibration with lots of interspersed bumps. Watching the display, Jack could see some orange tendrils of plasma shooting past whatever type of lens they used to supply the image for the display. This also continued to increase until it fairly well blotted out the display image for about sixty seconds as the turbulence shook them, and then rapidly, both the turbulence diminished to almost nothing, and the display cleared showing an even closer view of the planet.

Jack was straining to see what detail he could see on the display as he spotted yet another small outpost of some sort. Whatever planet they were over—and he felt disappointed that he didn't at least know the name of it—didn't appear to be a heavily populated planet from what he was seeing from orbit and during reentry. He guessed now that they were descending below about a hundred thousand feet since they had reentered the atmosphere, and he could feel some amount of atmospheric buffeting on the ship despite its large size.

The four-armed alien continued to work on its project over on the bench and didn't seem interested in the entire reentry arrival procedure. Apparently, it had done this many times previously, so it must have been completely routine to the alien. This was actually Jack's first real planet reentry, which should have been in *Victory* back to Earth in another four days by his estimation. Jack imagined that he was acting like a tourist looking out an airplane window trying to take in everything he could with the arrival at a new holiday destination.

The cargo shuttle continued its descent for another ten minutes until Jack could tell from the display that they were about ten thousand feet AGL, or above ground level. He was starting to see small settlements frequently on the display with a few interconnecting surface features that looked like faint roads. He also got a look at first one and then another airborne ship out in the distance. The far one was too distant to see any details, but it did not appear to have wings like an aerodynamic vehicle of any sort.

The closer one was on a converging course and would pass behind them at a lower altitude, so he was able to get a better look at it. The ship did have wings of sorts, but it was fairly wide, at least as wide as it was long, and did look fairly aerodynamic, as if it was designed to go fast in the atmosphere. It appeared to have two or more decks and appeared as if it might function as both a passenger and cargo ship. If he had to guess he would've estimated it held perhaps one hundred passengers and ten to twenty tons of cargo. As they dropped lower still, he got a better look at one of the smaller settlements, and he could see that it had a perimeter around it of some sort, either a fence or some sort of high thin wall. It was hard to tell, but it felt like the ship was slowly decelerating. You couldn't really feel it as much as you could tell by the passage of the terrain below them on the display. Dropping below about two thousand feet, they passed above a curved perimeter zone of some sort, and now they were over an area of considerably higher population density.

They were descending over numerous larger warehouse-type buildings and some well-organized industrial-looking areas. The terrain moving below them on the display suddenly stopped, and Jack could feel a slight horizontal deceleration as the ship came to a nearly complete standstill. He didn't know what the mass of the cargo shuttle was, but it appeared to go from about 200 mph to a standstill in about ten seconds. He had just barely felt the deceleration and wondered what kind of drive and stabilization system would allow a ship this size to stop instantaneously without tearing itself apart or even feeling it.

He could see on the display now that the ship was settling vertically, and from the direction of the camera, he could see at least three more cargo shuttles, like the ones he'd seen in orbit, moored to docking bays on the ground of what was an apparently a large depot complex. He watched the display as the ship settled further. The large ship settled into its berth. As it did so, Jack could feel some slight bumps and a momentary vibration as the ship came to rest. The view of the other ships and docking complex disappeared until all he could see was the side of a building near them, which had more strange hieroglyphic-like markings on the side of it.

Nothing seemed to happen for a few minutes. Then Jack heard the sound of doors being opened and machinery moving somewhere up ahead of them in the ship. The four-armed alien set about some postlanding routine as he checked various displays and some of the equipment in the room. Perhaps he was doing a postflight check and looking for any reported damage by the ship's onboard equipment. That would seem like the normal course of things after completing even a routine flight to space based on Jack's experience.

The alien walked by Jack and said something to him in its strange language then left the room by the main door that Jack had entered from. Jack looked around to see if there was anything that might be of use to him within his reach, but he couldn't see anything. He tried pulling on the wrist restraints and even tried separating them with the structural post that his arm was wrapped around. They didn't appear to be attached by anything, and they pivoted at the joint, but nothing he did seemed to have any effect on them as far as getting them apart. He resigned himself to see what happened next on this little sightseeing adventure.

A few minutes later, he heard the sound of multiple footsteps coming his way from the entry corridor. The four-armed alien entered first followed by two yet completely different alien types that Jack had not previously seen. He thought to himself, *There's definitely no shortage of variety when it comes to alien life forms so far.* These two new ones didn't look particularly friendly. They were both about five-and-a-half-foot-tall bipeds with very long, thin arms. One was a light reddish brown, and the other had a mottled greenish-blue cast over its partially exposed body.

They appeared to be the same type of creatures, just different colors. They wore short-sleeved loose-fitting tunics and short pants of a dark-colored leatherlike material. Their heads were slightly rectangular shaped and somewhat narrow. They had high foreheads and a small flat nose with what looked like two small nasal openings that were conjoined in the middle. Their arms were thin, too long, and somewhat muscular. Their hands seemed to have three fingers and two opposable thumbs. This made them look like they would be very good at grasping things. Their mouths were almost V shaped, and they had small tight lips with little expression.

They didn't look particularly clean for some reason, and as they approached Jack with the four-armed alien, he could also tell they didn't smell very clean. They had a sharp acrid odor to them that reminded Jack of the time he'd been to the town dump with his father and smelled the burning garbage that was always smoldering at the dump. There is also a slight acidic citrus smell mixed in with it, and all mixed together, it was a bit offensive.

Overall, their appearance and smell were far from appealing. They had short cropped hair over the tops and sides of their heads that more or less matched the color of their skin, only slightly darker. For some reason, they didn't look like the types he'd strike up a conversation with in the local supermarket checkout line. Well, you could just never tell; they might be really swell guys that were representatives of the local welcoming committee. He thought he'd better hold that thought in hopes that things can only get better from here on out.

After a few moments of verbal exchange between the new aliens and the four-armed alien, the red-hued one ran off a sentence or two at Jack in a totally new and strange-sounding alien language. Of course, he didn't understand any of it, so all he did was reply in his now well-rehearsed "Hi, my name is Jack Spartan" routine. Jack thought to himself, *Either all these different aliens have extremely well-developed language skills and can converse with any other alien, or their translator pendants are highly capable of translating any type of language, except apparently human English.* He reasoned that he must be hearing their languages in their native tongue. Since his own new pendant translator only had a few words of English, it wasn't apparently capable of translating anything into something he could understand.

To Jack, their language sounded like a sharp, fast series of sh's, ch's, r's, grunts, and indecipherable expletives. He decided that their language sounded about as appealing as their looks and their smell. After another short conversation with the four-armed alien, they seemed to come to some sort of understanding. The four-armed alien handed the green-hued alien the disk that Jack knew controlled his wrist restraints. The green alien manipulated the disk for a moment, and Jack's wrist restraints released so that he could move his arm from around the structural post.

That was a major improvement, as he'd been getting pretty cramped from sitting in the same crooked position for the last hour. As soon as he'd removed his arm from around the post, though, his wrists snapped back together in their familiar restrained position. He was starting to get a little miffed about the whole scenario, but he thought, *Just hang in there and see where this leads. I'm sure I'll be able to sort this out at some point.* This was starting to remind him of the POW training he'd received at Air Force survival school, except he never expected to be a POW of some strange aliens on a different planet.

The red alien said something to him in its guttural language, which Jack took to understand that they wanted him up and moving. The alien entered something on the disk again, and the wrist restraints actually pulled him up and moved him toward the door. His previous hosts apparently hadn't felt the need to use this function of the restraints to control him. He guessed they'd always had that capability in reserve if they needed it. The green alien now had a short stick of some sort in his hand, and he gave Jack a poke with it to prod him along.

Jack was starting to dislike these two grungy charmers more each minute since he'd made their less-than-appealing acquaintance. They moved toward the exit and down the corridor toward the middle of the ship. After a couple of turns, they came to a smaller door that exited onto the docking bay. They appeared to be on the side of the cargo shuttle without any cargo doors. Jack could hear the loading activity on the other side of the ship. As they came out onto the landing platform, Jack took a deep breath of the alien planet's atmosphere, thinking that once again, he was likely the first human to ever do such a thing. He hoped there wasn't anything toxic in the air, but by now, he had to assume there wasn't. Pathogens maybe, but toxic agents probably not, he reasoned.

The air was warm and smelled somewhat dusty. It smelled like desert air with little hint of organic material in it at all. There might have been a slight smell of city and, well, not human obviously but alien activity.

From the outside, the ship appeared to be about 500 feet long, 120 feet in height, and maybe 100 feet wide. It was hard to tell this close to the ship, but it was still a good-sized vessel. They went about sixty feet and then down a darkened narrow stairway between the ship and the building they'd berthed next to. It appeared not to be used too often; maybe it was an emergency exit of some sort. When they'd gone about two stories down, it came to a long narrow level hallway that appeared to go on for several hundred feet. About fifty feet from where they'd reached the bottom of the stairs, they came to another small door. This looked like an unused door too, but it had some sort of warning sticker or instructions on. It had a mechanical latch that ran vertically from the center edge upward.

The green alien pulled the lever at the top, which caused the door to open, and they stepped through into another corridor. This corridor ran about fifty feet perpendicular to the first then came to another door with a latch that opened out to some sort of outdoor alleyway. Jack reasoned that this wasn't the standard welcoming committee routine for new foreign dignitaries coming to town.

Chapter 5: Arrival

In the alleyway was a small truck-like vehicle. It sort of looked like a pickup truck, well, sort of a ruggedized, beat-up pickup truck without wheels. It was big enough to hold the three of them in the cab, and it had a cargo area in the back with a cage over it, somewhat like a mesh camper shell. There were some containers and other items in the back inside the mesh shell. As they approached the vehicle, one door on the left side of the vehicle popped open. The door opened like a clamshell split in the middle, exposing a short front bench seat arrangement with another bench seat in the back. The green alien poked Jack in the ribs with the stick as the wrist restraints pulled him toward the opening.

He seriously thought about taking these two smelly clowns out with a couple of round kicks or snap kicks to the throat, but he didn't know how fast they were or if he could manipulate the wrist restraint disk to free himself if he took them out. He figured he'd better gather as much intel on them as he could before he decided to try anything of a tactical nature. He also didn't have the slightest clue as to where he was or what he'd do even if he gained his freedom. On the other hand, the best tactical plan could sometimes be to strike early before you were taken further into a situation you couldn't extricate yourself from.

The green alien was shoving Jack into the backseat, while the wrist restraint pulled him at the same time. The cab was about the size of a compact car with no amenities that he could see other than the seat. It did have windows and a windshield, but there was no steering wheel or stick or any other visible control device that Jack could see. The red alien slid in to the right front seat, while the green alien poked Jack a couple of more times with the stick while yelling at him in their unpleasant language.

Jack wasn't sure what the green alien was trying to tell him as he was just trying to look out to see where they would be going. The green alien continued to berate him and then said something to the red alien, which caused it to manipulate the control disk for Jack's wrist restraints. This resulted in the restraints pulling Jack's wrists to the floor and causing him to jam his body between the seat and floor. Jack now gathered that, for some reason, they wanted him lying down or out of sight. Jack was now lying on his elbows, and he pulled his knees up so that he would fit inside the width of the cab. The green alien hopped in, and the clamshell doors closed with Jack on the floor. This was quite uncomfortable and would likely get more so as they proceeded.

Jack was getting madder by the second. "Hey, let me up, let me up, you freakin' morons!" he yelled. "I get the idea that you want to me lie down, but I can't ride all the way to wherever we're going in this position." He heard and felt the vehicle come to life with a quiet humming sound and the whine of some type of cooling fans or something. He felt the vehicle rise up vertically a short distance and start moving forward. "Let me up, dammit, let me up!" Jack yelled again, adding in a few more expletives.

The vehicle was moving fairly quickly now and was jostling him around on the hard floor. He pushed up onto his knees and threw his legs onto the backseat with his knees bent and his feet up in the air so as to try and get his body onto the seat while his wrists were still pinned to the floor. He sort of half succeeded at this, but he was now twisted by having to reach over the edge the bench where his wrists were pinned. At least it was better than where he was a moment ago. The green alien saw Jack's maneuver and started yelling at him in the harsh-sounding language again. Jack yelled back at him and told him where he could go in half a dozen different ways. The alien seemed taken back somewhat that this captive was resisting and creating an issue.

Apparently, it got the message, though, as the wrist restraints released from the floor. As soon as it released, it went to the side of the vehicle in front of Jack's head where at least he didn't have to be contorted hanging off the seat. The windows were still above his head, so he couldn't see where they were going. If he twisted backward and looked over his shoulder, he could kind of get a glimpse of what was outside and where they'd been. There were a lot of larger industrial-looking structures initially, but then they started to disappear.

As they drove on for about ten minutes, he could only see the forms of a few buildings now. It definitely wasn't the congested industrial area where the cargo shuttle had landed earlier. They were definitely out of the more densely populated area where they'd started from. Jack wondered where they were going and what they had in store for him, since he apparently wasn't getting the VIP visitors welcome. If he raised his head up a little, he could see an area of the vehicles control console, which had previously been just a dark flat dash but was now lit in the center section and displayed various indications and possibly a map in a holographic-type display. The green alien periodically turned to keep an eye on him, while the red alien seemed to be concentrating on what the vehicle was doing.

Jack knew from having watched their arrival from the ship that the cargo port was fairly close to the perimeter fence he'd seen and not near the higher population center of the city. Since the buildings appeared to be getting further apart, he assumed they weren't going to the main city. A few minutes later, the vehicle slowed to a near stop. They crawled along for about a minute, while the aliens both fiddled with the controls on the console.

As they crept forward, Jack could see they were proceeding under a tall gated archway. There seemed to be an automated gate of some sort, and he could just see the edge of a small building about forty feet from the vehicle. As they went beneath it, the perimeter appeared to be a solid thin wall rather than a fence type of barrier. It wasn't very thick at all, maybe just a sheet of something about two inches thick, but it didn't look flimsy in the least, and it was about fifty feet tall. He wondered why they needed a barrier around their cities and settlements. Were they keeping something out, or were they keeping the inhabitants in?

They completed their transit through the gate then started heading away from the city perimeter. Jack tried sitting up and looking out the windows to get a better idea of where they were, but it was not really possible with the angle that his wrist restraints kept him at. "Hey, you guys, can I sit up now? This is really uncomfortable. Would you guys let me sit up now? This is killing my back." He kept repeating this and trying to sit up at the same time so they would get the idea. He thought about throwing some more vile names at them or kicking the back of their seat but thought it might be possible that they were recording his conversation for later translation. Eventually, green boy got the idea and released the restraints so that Jack could sit up. Green guy fiddled with the control disk again, and the restraints anchored itself to the back of the seat in front of Jack. Jack was still not happy, but it was a lot better than his previous position.

They didn't appear to be taking any chances with him. He thought that with them being able to control him like this that they'd at least partially release him for a bit knowing that they did have control over him. If he wasn't pinned to the back of the seat, even with his wrists pinned together, he knew he could probably strangle them both in about ten seconds before they could do anything to stop him.

So far, they weren't giving him a chance, though. He still had the dilemma of not knowing where he was or where he should go. If he could get free, he might go to the main authorities if he could figure out who that might be. He got the feeling from their behavior of whisking him away that they weren't exactly playing by the rules for some reason. He would worry about that later, but in the meantime, he would continue to do as much reconnaissance as he could and figure out anything he could about his situation.

Looking around, he could tell that he was in one of the desert areas that he'd seen during their arrival. In the far distance, he could see an island of green jungle. It was truly a strange landscape, as much of it was desert, and some of it appeared to be green dense vegetation. From the air, it had looked like it was about a 30 percent coverage of vegetation and possibly water over the desert area also. From the air, he had seen what looked like large seas or lakes.

They were now moving along at a pretty good clip at about a hundred miles per hour. The vehicle seemed to be levitated about two feet off the ground. They seemed to be following a faint-looking road, which had been cleared of any boulders or other debris that might slow their progress. It almost looked like something oily had been sprayed on the cleared area of the road bed, such as it was, to perhaps stabilize it or keep the dust down. They were going too fast for him to get a good look at anything up close, but out in the distance, there were plenty of large boulders, escarpments, small ravines, and other terrain features.

The dry areas reminded him of the pictures he'd seen of the surface of Mars from the Mars rovers NASA had sent. The color was different in that it was more tannish and brown rather than the red of Mars. In this area, there were more large boulders and low outcroppings than he'd remembered seeing on Mars. Of course, the terrain could vary considerably over distance, and he'd only seen about ten minutes of this planet outside of the city perimeter zone.

They climbed a small rise and started down the other side into a long flat valley. Far out in the distance to the right and just barely discernible was an area of blue. Hopefully, they would go near it so he could see if it was actually water as it had appeared to be from space. As they started down the shallow incline into the valley, Jack could also see an island of green vegetation about twenty miles away on the left. It looked as if they were just going to pass by the edge of it in about ten minutes. As they got closer, they were almost paralleling it but still getting closer.

At about two miles out, Jack could start to clearly make out individual trees. All the trees and bushes appeared to have a dark green almost bluish tint to the foliage. Closer still, he could tell that they were darker at the top and lighter at the bottom. He could see that it was very dense vegetation much like a heavy rain forest back on Earth. The contrast between the desert area and the jungle island was so stark that it didn't really make sense, at least by Earth standards. The barely visible road track was nearly straight, but it took a slight bend around the end of the vegetation and then straightened out ahead in the distance. They slowed to a crawl as they came around the end of the island of jungle foliage.

The aliens were looking intently at the jungle as if they were searching for something. It looked like they would pass a little less than about thirty yards from the edge of the jungle. The green alien suddenly became excited and started pointing toward the jungle. The red alien slowed the vehicle even more until they were just barely moving. Then Jack saw it, a huge tailless catlike animal nearly as large as a horse was chasing a slightly smaller herd-type animal that could've been something off the African plains. The cat creature resembled an artist's picture he'd seen of a saber-toothed tiger, but it was taller and leaner. Its head was flat across the top, and it had a longer muzzle than a regular cat but not as long as a canine. Its coloration was dark green with brown stripes vertically across most of its body, except it appeared to have a mottled area around its chest, neck, and the front of its face as best as Jack could see while it was running.

There was an open meadow area in the forest next to the road where they had a pretty good view of the drama that was unfolding. The prey animal was striped gray, brown, and black across its hind quarters and almost had a spotted Appaloosa look to it forward of that. Its head was long and narrow, and it was fast, but the cat was gaining on it in a burst of speed. The prey animal had a considerable set of antlers on it, which splayed forward over five feet in length, like fingers on a hand on both sides. It also had a backward branch on both sides that curved up with multiple pointed fingers and would have made its neck area impenetrable from any kind of an attack from above.

The prey animal took a sharp turn and tried to head back into the dense foliage, but the cat creature anticipated its move and cut the corner on it using cutoff angle just like a fighter jet to intercept it before it was able to put on speed for a dash back into the jungle. The cat made a long lunging grab as it came out of its turn and snagged the right rear hind quarter of its victim and spun it around at the same time. The momentum of the prey animal caused it to tumble and flip sideways onto its back and over onto its side. It tried to get up, but the cat was on it in an instant, lunging for its throat while staying clear of the hapless animal's thrashing feet and horns.

The struggle was over in a few seconds as the cat tore at the vital organs in the prey animal's neck. The moment the cat and its prey stopped moving, the cat became nearly invisible because of its superb camouflage. Without movement, all its colors and camouflage blended instantly into the background of the jungle.

The cat had given a colossal scream when it lunged for the throat of its prey, and the prey gave an equally garish scream as the cat had pounced on it. All the pandemonium and noise caused an explosion of other terrified creatures to erupt from the boundary of the jungle forest. A flock of several dozen flying creatures exploded from the treetops near the meadow's edge and headed in every direction before regrouping.

A pack of five or six smaller dark blue and green canine-size creatures erupted from the edge of the thick foliage and darted momentarily into the desert area. All but one of them instantly bolted back into the dense jungle but, in fear one of them, shot straight out for a short way into the barren desert area. It was moving fast and ended up three hundred feet into the barren zone. It apparently realized its error and turned to sprint back to the cover of the jungle. No sooner had it gotten turned around and aimed back toward the jungle than a shadow flashed over the vehicle, and a large raptor-like creature hit the small canine animal from above, driving it into the ground. The raptor pulled and twisted the flailing creature and killed it by stabbing it repeatedly with its short stout beak.

The cat creature now looked up from its kill and bolted for the raptor, but the raptor, which looked like a cross between a large bird and a reptile with a twelve-foot wingspan, was already aware of the cat and launched itself into the air with its prey safely grasped in its talons. Coming up short, the cat turned back toward its kill. The cat now noticed the vehicle silently sitting there. It took a couple of half-hearted bounds toward the vehicle, but the red alien did something, and they shot away from the whole scene in about half a second. Jack now had no doubt what the perimeter fencing was for around the towns and settlements.

They continued another couple of miles around the jungle zone before they headed straight out into the desert area again. Jack watched the jungle closely while they passed it, but he failed to see any other large forms of wildlife. Even if they were right there, he figured he wouldn't be able to see them unless they were moving. They were so well camouflaged and adapted to their isolated environment that they were nearly invisible unless some wild ruckus caused them to bolt from their hiding places.

A few minutes later, Jack noticed green alien reaching under the front seat where he pulled open a drawer. Reaching in, green alien took out a couple of containers and handed one to the other aliens. They each tapped the top of the rectangular-shaped containers and then began drinking from them as if they were a squarish can of soda. Jack now realized how thirsty he was, so he spoke up to try and see if he could get something from the aliens to drink. "Hey, guys, you wouldn't have another one of those or maybe just some water to spare for your best buddy here in the backseat, would you? I'm getting a little thirsty myself, and since we're all good friends now, maybe you guys can spare one of those?"

The green alien looked at Jack with what appeared to be the degree of distain. It acted as if it didn't understand or particularly care what its captive had asked. Jack knew that they'd covered some of the words associated with water, drink, and food back aboard the huge ship with the other aliens. Maybe those had been programmed into his translator pendant. He rattled off a few words that he knew they'd translated during his earlier session. "Water, drink, food, any chance you guys could spare some water, drink, food?"

The green alien looked at Jack with the realization that he knew what Jack was saying then said something to the red alien. They bantered back and forth for a few moments. Then the green alien reached into the under-seat storage bin and pulled out another container. "Water? Is that water?" asked Jack. The alien replied with several indecipherable words, and then the word "water" was interspersed twice during the sentence. Jack didn't know if this translated into a yes or no as far as it being water, but he figured he would take a chance on whatever it was.

The green alien held it up over the seat for Jack but just looked at him. Jack was still wrist restrained to the back of the seat and couldn't take it from the alien. "Well, guys, I seem to have a little problem here," said Jack. "Maybe you haven't noticed, but I can't exactly take that from you under the current circumstances." The green alien looked at the red alien for a couple of seconds, and they both burst out laughing in a kind of a strange hoff, hoff, hoffing sound. They seemed to think this was entirely hilarious and continued laughing for half a minute. Then the green alien started to put the box back in the drawer as if Jack didn't want it. "Come on, guys, I'm sure this is great entertainment for you, but I really would like a drink of water or something. Come on now, drink of water, please."

Jack nodded with his head toward his wrists, hoping to convince them to release him so he could drink. In his most pleasant and congenial voice, Jack said, "Come on now, boys, you might want to play nice on this because at some point, paybacks might be a little bit more than you bargained for." The red alien handed the control disk to the green alien, who entered some command that released Jack's left wrist from the back of the seat. It then handed the drink box to Jack, so he took it with his left hand. "Thanks, fellas," said Jack. "Now I don't have to strangle your scrawny little necks and throw your corpses to that big cat or bird back there."

Now that Jack had the box, he had to figure out how to open it. He placed it between his knees and looked at the top of the container to see what the alien had done to open it. He could see a small circular outline on one edge, so he gave it a push. Nothing seemed to happen, so he tried tapping on the box like he'd seen the aliens do. He tried this several times but couldn't open the box. He looked up at the alien who was watching him and asked, "Any chance you could give me a hint on how to open this thing?" The alien looked at Jack and then back at the other alien and said something to the other alien. Then both aliens busted out laughing again.

Jack laughed too, as he thought it was funny that these two morons were getting such a kick out of the fact that he didn't know how to use their basic technology.

Jack handed the box to the alien to see if he could get it to open it for him. The alien showed Jack the top of the box then tapped the semicircular outlined area then the far side of the box and then in the semicircle and then the far side area again. The outlined area then popped inward at the edge of the box, leaving a nice circle on the top edge of the box to drink from. The alien handed the box back to Jack.

Since he didn't know what it was, Jack decided to go slow and careful with it. He held it up to his nose and took a couple of good whiffs of it. It didn't have a lot of odor to it, but it definitely wasn't water. It smelled somewhat faintly like mild apple cider mixed with something else he couldn't identify. Whatever it was, he hoped it was compatible with his physiology.

The food on the big ship had been different but palatable, but he hadn't really had anything to drink other than water while he was there. He took a very small sip to get a taste of it. It smelled vaguely of apple cider, but it didn't taste anything at all like it. It did have a vague fruit taste but was somewhat acidic with a pretty good after bite. He wondered if it was some sort of alcoholic or other party beverage these guys were tapping into on their drive home after their hard day at work. He took a few larger sips and decided it was probably OK, but it wasn't something he would order from the officers' club bar back home.

He waited about ten minutes to see if it had any ill effects, but it seemed to be OK as far as he could tell. He drank the first half of the box then waited a while longer to make sure there weren't any cumulative effects. Though he was sure there were some variances in physiology between aliens and humans as far as food and drink consumption, he was also fairly certain now that any toxic agents would probably affect human and alien physiology in the same general way. With this basic assumption, he hoped that anything he would consume from an alien source was likely to be safe although not necessarily settling to a human's digestive system. "Well," he said aloud, "no guts, no glory."

After another ten minutes of traveling in the arid zone, they came to the top of a small rise and then stopped. The aliens spent a few moments analyzing the vehicle's display. Then they opened the door and decided to get out, perhaps to stretch their legs. As they got out, they carefully looked around in all directions both at ground level and up in the air. Apparently, they were concerned about potential animal attacks from the air as well as on the surface. Once the aliens were satisfied there was nothing nearby that might be dangerous, they decided to relieve themselves. Jack watched them as they undid part of their clothing then proceeded to relieve themselves onto the dry sand. Jack was due for the same type of break, but the aliens hadn't seemed inclined to include him on this particular undertaking. Maybe they didn't realize that he had the same physiological needs that they did after drinking, but then they didn't seem to be the brightest or most accommodating hosts either, he thought.

He yelled at them, "Hey, guys, how about a pee break for me too?" He rattled off a bunch of basic words that might be in the translation database. "Water, drink, pee, urinate, bathroom, toilet!" he repeatedly shouted at them. As they looked over at him, he tried to gesture with his free left hand what he had to do. He could see them talking for a minute then laughing in their strange-sounding language. "You guys had better let me go pee or I'll be peeing on the back floor of your truck real soon!" he yelled. He didn't know if they understood his little threat, but they did apparently understand what he was trying to convey. The red alien barked a couple of commands at him, which Jack assumed was some sort of warning. Then the green alien did something with the control disk and released him.

As he crawled out of the backseat, his wrist restraints reengaged so that he only had about half the dexterity he needed to accomplish his business. "Hey, you geek squids," he said, "it's not like I'm going to take off across this desert with all those nasty local beasties running around nearby. All I want to do is take a leak." The red alien barked a couple of more commands at him as Jack stepped by the back of the vehicle and relieved himself on the desert sand. *Well,* Jack thought, *that will certainly make the next few hours a lot more enjoyable.*

The aliens barked at him again, apparently ordering him to get back into the vehicle. He wasn't inclined to go too fast, as he was enjoying a few minutes of being up and walking around a bit. Then the alien with the control disk entered a command, and the wrist restraints pulled Jack toward the vehicle again. "OK, OK, I get the program here," Jack said. "I'm getting back in your truck now. Thanks for the break, boys. I owe you one, yeah, I really owe you one now," Jack said with a sarcastic little smile.

Back in the vehicle, they once again headed down the desolate minuscule path that passed for a road. Without his watch, Jack couldn't tell for sure, but it seemed as though they'd driven for about three more hours before they came to a barely discernible Y in the road where they took the left road and continued on. Jack knew there were outlying settlements that were fairly well dispersed from the visual display he'd seen of their arrival to the planet. He still couldn't fathom where they could possibly be taking him.

They drove on for another two hours, and he was really getting tired from this exhausting adventure. He hoped they'd get to wherever they were going soon. The only good part of this leg of the journey was they had only restrained his right wrist to the side of the vehicle so at least he could move around a little bit and sit back in the seat. They did pass another green zone, but it was still a good two miles or more from the road, so he never got to see anything associated with that one close up. An hour after they passed the green zone, he could just barely discern in the distance an area that looked like a good-sized lake or inland sea. It was faint and fairly mirage-like because of its distance, but it was definitely a body of water.

They continued to drive, and soon, it started getting dark. The red alien did something on the instrument panel, and the view in front of them switched to a daylight view for a considerable distance, while the side window view remained dark after the sun had set. *That's a neat technology,* Jack thought, *essentially a night-vision-capable windshield.* That would be a lot more comfortable than having to wear night vision goggles as long as you were inside the vehicle. There wasn't much to see, and Jack was totally exhausted from his ordeal. Without his watch and without having the benefit of Earth's day-night cycle, he didn't have an exact way to tell what time it was. He thought it was five or six days at this point, but it could have been longer.

He started thinking about his crew again and how they had worked so long and hard training for their mission all to have it come to a tragic end by this bizarre set of otherworldly circumstances. He didn't even know how or why that big ship had hit *Victory.* He wondered again if they were they just oblivious to *Victory's* presence, or did they just not care? Maybe they were having some sort of mechanical issues of their own? He would probably never know, and that part of it also caused him a great deal of melancholy. Crap, what an unbelievable ordeal he'd been through so far. He was in a bit of a letdown mode now riding along in the back of the alien vehicle, but what was next in this adventure? he wondered.

He dozed off with these thoughts running through his mind and was soon fast asleep. The vehicle was really smooth as far as the ride went. The only thing he felt while riding in it was some minor forward and aft acceleration and a minimal amount of lateral acceleration. Occasionally, he'd feel a fluid up-and-down movement as it followed the terrain, but this just tended to make the smooth ride a little bit hypnotic. The low hum of the vehicle produced a very minor vibration, which lulled him asleep even faster.

Something caused him to stir, and he woke up when the vehicle decelerated to a stop at the gated entrance of a walled town or settlement of some sort. He must've been asleep for a couple of hours, as he felt somewhat refreshed. He still felt like he could have gone back to sleep for another six or more hours, but now he was wide awake. They were still in an arid zone, but he could see some equipment and machinery dispersed around the inside of the wall as they passed under it. As they went through the gate, Jack saw another alien going back into a small building or guard shack. It was different from his personal chauffeurs, but he really didn't get a very good look at it. They started to move forward again, and Jack could see through the front window a large industrial complex of some sort. It extended for quite a ways in all directions inside the gated compound. There were warehouse-looking buildings and buildings that looked like they were used for processing something, buildings with long descending shafts with many attached side buildings with all sorts of piping, plumbing, lifts, towers, and other obviously industrial-type equipment. In the distance, he could see a large double-cylinder-shaped building with multiple tiers and adjoining multiple rows of plumbing-like fixtures.

The top of one building glowed a dull red from some internal heat source that must have been generating a tremendous amount of heat energy. Jack wondered if this was their destination or just an overnight stop along the way. He was trying to take it all in. They turned down an access alley and then descended a short inclined tunnel into the basement of some large multistory underground warehouse or factory. They came to a parking area with a hundred or so other vehicles of varying shapes and sizes. They parked the truck vehicle, and they all exited into the parking garage with Jack's wrist restraints now reengaged. Jack's drivers led him a short distance to some doors at the edge of the garage. As they left, Jack saw a small alien run up and appear to inspect the vehicle they were in just before they entered into the building through a pair of double doors.

Inside the doors, they went about fifty feet, turned down another corridor, and proceeded another hundred feet until they came to an elevator, which they boarded. The look of the entire place was low-rent industrial complex, and it had no aesthetic appeal whatsoever. The elevator was a large dirty freight elevator of some sort, and they descended in it for half a minute before it came to a stop.

All around him in the distance, even indoors, Jack could hear the sound of industrial machinery, motors, hydraulics, and other manufacturing and processing sounds of various types. They exited into a small dirty lobby manned by two guards with some sort of wands or weapons. The guards gave them a cursory once-over, and they proceeded into a larger room that was actually part of a large cavern that appeared to have been excavated out of pure bedrock. The ceiling was probably eighty feet high, and Jack could see a dozen or so tunnels leading off in various directions from the other side of the room.

The whole area was lit by a series of small but bright lamps around the perimeter and near some of the tunnel entrances. Jack could see the shapes of several aliens of different types moving on the far side of the room and in and out the tunnels. There was one that was bipedal and looked like a stooped old hunchback. There were two very thin and wiry ones walking closely and engaged in some sort of touchy-feely conversation between them. They were bipedal but appeared to have one pair of short arms with another pair of longer arms above them with a thin neck and a small oval head. Another one had a medium muscular build with short legs and long forearms that it used to walk on, somewhat like a silverback gorilla, only more graceful but less powerful. Its muscular neck and head reminded Jack somewhat of a python but with a protruding lower lip, and it sported a single row of long, dark, very heavy whiskers protruding out of the side of its face, which hung down for more than a foot and bobbed and swayed as it walked. *What a menagerie,* thought Jack.

They continued off to the right until they came to a set of doors, which they entered. They went down a short flight of stairs and into a large, dingy, poorly lit room filled with another half-dozen aliens. He'd seen several of the same types before, but now there were at least a couple of new ones that he hadn't seen.

One that they passed was quite short at about four feet tall and was thin but well-muscled with oversized legs for its body. It was hunched forward like it was designed for full-time running. It wore a pair of half pants and had bare feet and a bare upper torso. Protruding from its backside, it had a short thin tail about two-thirds the length of its legs. It had a long thin head and neck attached to a slight upper body that made it look like it was even more built for speed. Its ears were long and sleek and lay flat on the back of its head and neck. It had large oval bright green eyes on opposite sides of its head that looked like they were made to take in a lot of light. It appeared to be at least three shades of green and was covered in very short soft fur or feathers. It had a sleek and aesthetic appearance overall that kind of reminded Jack of the sleekness of a greyhound but with heavier muscled legs.

Trying to take everything in made Jack's senses reel with all the new strange sights, sounds, and smells. Besides all the bizarre-looking aliens with their unintelligible variety of languages, there was also a cacophony of strange and unidentifiable smells. The entire underground complex had its own unique humid and earthy smell that was different from anything on Earth. There was also a peculiar variety of nonhuman biological smells that taunted the olfactory senses with every odd sensation imaginable. The temperature was tolerable but just slightly on the high side, probably somewhere around eighty degrees Fahrenheit. A temperature that warm helped to enhance the already overloaded olfactory sensations Jack was experiencing.

They stopped at the far end of the room in front of a large desk cluttered with anything and everything. It appeared to be the central fixture of some sort of administrative operations area. Seated in the center of this ops area in a large mobile mechanical chair, which appeared to spin and propel itself in any direction, was a strange-looking creature with a cleaved bulbous head and a squat bug-like body. It was as far from human as anything he'd seen so far, although it looked like it may have been more deformed or injured than originally designed that way. Its body was reclined about halfway in the mobile chair, and its head came up on a short stalk of a neck, which terminated with its strange head. The body appeared to be half brownish-colored flesh and half carapace. It seemed to have four legs protruding upward from the body, but upon closer examination, it was just two legs with round padded feet and two arms with well-articulated hands and fingers at the end of the arms that were thinner than the leg appendages.

The angle that it was lying in the floating chair made it look like a huge bug, but it was in fact a bipedal creature that Jack decided appeared to probably be deformed in some way. All this was a lot to take in, thought Jack. Stranger yet was when it turned its head halfway toward Jack, he saw that it had two very large, very widely set runny or weepy eyes. The eyes were both red with yellow irises. It appeared to have a very wide mouth turned down at the ends almost at half the distance of the circumference of its head. It had a truncated inverted V of a nose with two large teardrop nostrils at its base. It seemed to have tufts of reddish-brown hair protruding from every appendage attachment on its body. The overall aura it exuded was quite revolting because of its overall alien appearance and demeanor. This creature had none of the physiologically plausible, and for the most part aesthetic, appearance of any of the aliens he'd seen so far.

The creature finished talking to the alien on the other side and spun to face Jack and his two escorts, whom Jack had now christened Dumb and Dumber in his mind. It immediately started barking at Jack's guards in a raspy snarling exchange of some sort that Jack had no inkling of understanding at all. It didn't even sound like foreign or alien words but more like the growling, gurgling, and hissing of some sick cornered animal. The guards responded to it in kind but seemed to be a little bit cowed by whatever invective they were being bombarded with.

The creature behind the desk, whose name was Cahooshek, was Sumtokan from the planet Sumtoka. He was not a happy creature, as he had not earned enough in the last fourteen yenets to return to his home planet to partake in the mating ritual that he was already two yenets overdue for. They had already held his claim for two additional yenets, but if he didn't get back and become mated in the next nine moondats, they would barter away his position, and his claim would be put off for at least another four yenets. This situation left him in a perpetual state of wanting to rip the appendages off any stray creature that got in his way. Still, he had a job to do manning and managing the lower sector mine laborers, which included conscripts, convicts, and contract miners. If he didn't perform his job correctly and efficiently, he would never get the bonuses that would allow him the trip back to Sumtoka to claim his mating rite.

Cahooshek shrieked at the two guards, whose names were Kreshku and Ruggal, "So what am I supposed to do with a Varaci stowaway that supposedly doesn't even speak its own language or anything that's translatable? Roshnil Kayshen just messaged me to expect your arrival at any time. He just so happened to mention that, for whatever reason, this creature doesn't even appear able to communicate through a translator. Based on the information from the starship captain where it was captured, this Varaci creature can't even speak. How am I supposed to recoup the four thousand credits I had to lay out this thing? If it can't communicate, it can't be taught the basic skills it needs to work the mines. About all it would be good for is for me to send it to the fight pit as practice fodder for the matches. I'd be lucky to earn back eight hundred credits if it managed to live three weneks even in the primary rounds."

"Don't try to blame your problems on us," replied Kreshku. "We did exactly as you instructed us to do and brought it back undamaged from the Wanana Wuutara cargo port."

"We performed our task, so now you owe us fifteen credits each for our services," said Ruggal. "We risked being caught with an illegal conscript that hasn't passed formal inspection or complied with possible quarantine requirements. You must pay us now as you stated when you offered us this task."

"I said I would pay you!" roared Cahooshek. "I did not say when. I will pay you in three daiyus when we get our normal distribution from the payment commission of mine operators. In the meantime, what am I supposed to do with this useless creature?"

Kreshku interrupted. "You said it does not know how to speak, but it can speak, just nothing that is translatable. It did seem to have a few words that it had gotten from somewhere, possibly aboard the cargo starship."

"Perhaps it could learn enough language if you could get someone that is good at translating languages to work with it for a while. It could be made functional enough to work the mines, at least in the lower slagging pits or something simple."

"Now who could I possibly get to willingly work with this thing and try and get its translator to work somewhat functionally?" moaned Cahooshek.

"How about that attractive—I mean, disreputable Tarcan creature Zshutana that runs the worker's brothel on the Dirga level?" asked Kreshku.

"What!" belched Cahooshek. "Hire a filthy whore runner to try and get this worthless Varaci to communicate with us? Are you crazy or just a double idiot?"

"Don't yell at me!" barked Kreshku. "You are the one that arranged this transaction. Do you have any better suggestions than Zshutana? She may be a whore runner, but she is quite astute from what I have heard, and she speaks many languages from what I have also heard. She might even know what language the Varaci speaks. Her business probably goes beyond even what the translator data cores are programmed for. If you don't like my idea, then find your own solution or take a loss on the whole deal for only eight hundred credits."

"All right, yes, yes, you've convinced me," muttered Cahooshek. "You two go to the Dirga level and tell the lovely creature Zshutana that I have a small business proposition for her and to come here now to discuss it. Tell her I will make it worth her while and that it will be interesting for her, a change of pace from her usual type of drudgery. Go now if you want to be paid for your earlier services in three daiyus like I said."

"Ha," snapped Ruggal, "you will pay us for our services in three daiyus like you said, and you will pay us three more for this errand also."

"Garazfa!" yelled Cahooshek. "Get going and do as you're told. This is part of your original services to complete this new mine worker's delivery. Now go, go!'

Cahooshek took a control disk from a side slot on his chair like the one the guards Kreshku and Ruggal had used to control Jack during their journey. He used it to maneuver Jack onto a bench at the far side of the large room and anchored him there with the wrist restraints. "You're already a horrible pain in my side and probably as worthless as the parasite suckers on a rarunet's belly," he said to Jack as he maneuvered him to the wall. Of course, Jack didn't know what he was saying only that it sounded like some strange hissing, spitting, gibberish that was totally nonsensical. Cahooshek had no idea what a very large pain in the backside that Jack would turn out to be for him in the long run. No idea at all.

Chapter 6: Zshutana

Nearly an hour passed before the two smelly guards Dumb and Dumber returned with their summoned guest in tow. Zshutana was, by any stretch of the imagination, a very interesting "female." She burst into the room with Cahooshek's two guards in tow—she also considered them smelly and dumb—and up to Cahooshek in his chair.

"So, Cahooshek, what unfortunate circumstances allow our enchanting meeting once again? It's been a considerable while since we had our little row about your workers and their unwillingness, after patronizing my humble establishment, to return to this cesspool you call a mine. But I've kept my part of the agreement faithfully, so why do you summon me here with some bizarre promise of an alleged interesting proposition? Do you actually have something that would pique my curiosity, or are you just so lonesome and bored down here that you felt you must harass one of the few honest entrepreneurs left on the Dirga level? I hope you don't expect me to fill in for your imaginary mate on your home planet Sumtoka. I doubt you will ever likely be able to return to Sumtoka, as it's apparent you are not so successful in your dismal career field. For some reason, you seem to think that my chosen career field is somehow more disreputable than yours. Why is that, Cahooshek?"

"Enough!" roared Cahooshek. "Are you always this grating and nonsensical? Can you not merely restrain yourself for a few moments to hear a simple proposition that I have for you?"

"Proposition," laughed Zshutana, "I already told you I wouldn't fill in for the imaginary mate you fantasize about on Sumtoka."

"Please, please," sighed Cahooshek, "I have a legitimate proposition for you that I think you will be interested in. I think you would find it interesting and entertaining, and I will be happy to make it worth your while. If you help me with this, I will allow my workers to frequent your establishment on a regular basis again, provided that you make provisions for them to return to work as scheduled."

Zshutana was now slightly curious. "What kind of a simple proposition? That sounds like a reasonable offer, but I do not even know what you ask of me. Tell me what it is you want, and I will think on it for a few daiyus."

"No," replied Cahooshek, "I need your answer now. All I need is a couple of daiyus of your time. I'm sure you can pull yourself away from your luxurious abode for a couple of daiyus to help me out. A couple of daiyus of your time and you can again have full access to my lower sector mine workers, well, the contract miners anyway. It will cost neither of us anything in monetary expense, but it will help you considerably in gaining more income. It is a very simple task I ask of you. I have heard that you are an expert in languages from dealing with all your clientele, is that not correct?"

"Yes," she replied, "I am quite fluent in all the languages of the lower sector mine workers and several more, and not just through the translator devices either. What does this have to do with your proposition?"

"It is quite simple. I have a new mine worker, a Varaci, that I paid a considerable sum for based on the promise that it is a very capable worker. However, it turns out that it does not speak any language known to our standard translator units. This situation makes this costly asset most useless to me, so I must figure out a way to utilize it, and I must do so fast. If I can't get it to communicate with us, then I will have to turn it over to the fight pit to try and gain some sort of compensation for my loss. Knowing that you are such an astute language expert, I thought you could help me out by spending a few daiyus with it trying to get a useful translator program working with it. Does that sound like something you might be interested in? This can get your full complement of clientele back for you."

"A simple mine worker, a Varaci? I don't believe I've ever seen one. I've only heard of them, and I did not think that they frequented this sector. Are they not runners, transporters, and smugglers of mostly inconsequential contraband? It hardly seems worth my effort, but if it will get my steady flow of customers restored, then perhaps I will consider it. It doesn't sound like too difficult a challenge," replied Zshutana. She continued. "It depends, and I suppose I will consider it if it is not too unpleasant a task. Let me see this new mine worker, and I will give it further consideration," she replied.

"Ruggal, go fetch the Varaci worker from the far edge of the room and bring it here for our esteemed Zshutana to inspect," snapped Cahooshek while pointing toward Jack in the distant corner. Jack had dozed off while the Dumber brothers had been sent on some sort of an errand. He was awake now but watching while pretending to still be asleep. One of the guards approached him from the center of the room where he could just make out the other guard.

Was it Dumb or Dumber? He couldn't remember which one, he'd decided, was which. There was another alien there talking to the strange creature in the mobile chair. From where he was, this new creature looked decidedly female, although he couldn't tell for sure what it was. The guard came up to him and said something to Jack then activated the disk, which caused Jack to be lugged toward the center of the room and the big desk. As they approached the three aliens, Jack could tell that this new alien had some definite female attributes.

She was decidedly alien yet had some very human feminine characteristics. She was bipedal and slender and dressed in a colorful and expensive-looking outfit. She was a dark tan color with some dull dark green and dark maroon symmetrical patches and lines on her arms and the area around her neck and face. Her slightly elongated face was lighter with a slight narrow heart shape to it. Yes, it was definitely female. She had high cheekbones, a feminine mouth, very large turquoise-colored eyes, and a straight but nicely proportioned nose. Her jaw bone and chin protruded slightly more than a human. Her face was quite attractive and very nicely structured. She had thick bronze-brown hair that started slightly farther back on her head and was pulled tightly back and then braided in multiple rows down to the top of her shoulders. She had feminine hips, a small waist, a fairly long upper torso, and a nicely shaped small bust under her colorful outfit. From an aesthetic standpoint, she was all-female and very attractive, but for some reason, the strangeness of her alien attributes made her a little unnerving looking. He wasn't exactly sure, but she seemed to exude a considerably tough attitude and defiance just by the way she looked. Though somewhat alien looking, she was definitely the most attractive alien creature Jack had seen since his unintentional journey had begun.

Jack was stopped just a few feet from this decidedly female alien. A few more words of conversation transpired between the female alien and the strange creature inhabiting the chair behind the counter. He didn't know what she was saying, but her voice was high, clear, and sharp. She turned in his direction, and she looked directly at him for a long few moments. She continued to stare at him and then looked him up and down while saying something to the strange chair creature. Yes, she was rather pleasant to look at, definitely the most attractive alien he'd seen since beginning this bizarre adventure however many days ago.

"This is the new mine worker, the Varaci we were just discussing?" Zshutana asked Cahooshek.

"Yes," he answered, "the one we can't communicate with that apparently doesn't speak its own language or at least is pretending not to understand us to avoid being charged with stealing passage to Nishda. Perhaps you will have some luck persuading it to begin communicating with us so that we can put it to work and recoup my investment on it. Maybe if you express my displeasure with the situation and explain to it how he could end up in the fight pit as fodder for the sporting crowd, then perhaps it might have a change of heart and become a little more cooperative with regard to his, shall we say, employment."

Zshutana asked, "Are you sure he is a Varaci? I've never seen one myself, but this creature isn't so bad actually and not at all what I expected of a race that is noted to be such devious contraband smugglers and deceitful runners. Of course, if he was a stowaway and stealing passage from wherever he came from, then perhaps he fits the reputation. I suppose we will find out shortly. Give me a few daiyus with him, and I will find out what is going on and why he was hiding and perhaps running from something in this situation that he is in. Then I can work on establishing a good language translation for you."

"Yes, that's all well and good," replied Cahooshek, "but I am not the least interested in his story, I am only interested in him being able to work and in recouping the investment that I've laid out for a worker that can't even communicate with us. I will give you two daiyus to get his communication skills up to a useful level. I need to be making some credits with him immediately, or I will have to find another way to get some sort of reimbursement for him."

"Two daiyus?" replied Zshutana. "That will be nearly impossible. I'm a highly skilled linguist, but I'm not sure we can develop a full vocabulary in that time, as it may require the programming of a full syntax decryption algorithm to make the vocabulary functional. I don't even have any idea what I'm working with yet."

"That doesn't matter," snorted Cahooshek. "I just want him communicating and working at the end of two daiyus. Now go to your task, or I may have to rethink the exceedingly generous offer I just made you and send him straight to the fight pit. This whole situation is going to give me double heart attacks if I don't get it rectified in short order."

"I will do my best," snapped Zshutana in reply, "but don't expect miracles from me when you only give me two daiyus. We have an agreement, and don't even think about trying to renege on it if the results aren't up to your standards when you're the one that is handicapping me with this ridiculous time limit."

"Go now, before I change my mind," growled Cahooshek.

"We are going," hissed Zshutana, "but don't you threaten me, and don't you forget that I have friends on other levels of this mining operation besides just the Dirga level. Now remember that, as your long-term health and retirement plans might depend on it."

"Go, go, just go, go, go. Take the command disk from Kreshku and be on your way now," snarled Cahooshek.

Zshutana took the command disk from Kreshku then said something to Jack and gently tugged him along after her. He wasn't sure what had just transpired, but it was apparent that he was now going to be under the control of the attractive but harsh female alien. He wasn't sure what this meant for his situation, but then again, he wasn't sure what was transpiring anyway in the big scheme of things.

Hopefully, he would figure out some way to communicate soon so as to get some of this confusion straightened out. He followed behind the female alien, and they proceeded out of the big room and then started through the large main area they'd come through when he first arrived here. Jack stopped a few paces into the big room and said, "Hey, how about these wrist restraints? They're uncomfortable and unnecessary. How about taking them off?" She stopped to look at him, wondering what he was saying in his strange untranslatable language.

Jack held up his crossed wrists to her while he started speaking again. In the midst of his speech, she heard the words "arm," "fingers," and "wrists." She now realized that some small portion of his language had already been programmed into the translator and that he was conveying the message that he was uncomfortable and wanted the wrist restraints released. This seemed like a reasonable appeal from what she now considered the dignified and stoic-looking alien that was alleged to be a Varaci. "OK," she said to him in her own language, "we will give that a try, but if you attempt any type of escape or attack against me, I will instantly subdue and punish you with this control," as she held up the disk and showed it to Jack.

Jack nodded his head and replied, "Yes, I understand. We have an agreement. Now please release my wrists so I can move and walk normally."

Believing that he'd understood what she'd conveyed, she released his wrists. She watched him closely for a minute as he moved his arms up and down and side to side and stretched to get the kinks out from being restrained for so long. He said, "Thanks. That's much better. I've been restrained for quite a while now, and it was getting rather uncomfortable as I hope you might imagine. Well, let's find out where we're going and get on with it," he said as he motioned his hands in the direction they were previously headed.

She watched him for another few moments and decided that he seemed to be trustworthy, at least in the interim under the conditions he was under. In the management side of her line of work she had extensive experience in judging the overall character of individuals of many races based on first impressions and initial exchanges. She was rarely if ever wrong and only by minor degrees and only at the lower end of the spectrum where it was hard to judge the degree of disreputability of a particular situation.

They went down several large corridors that were hewn out of solid bedrock and eventually into a large cavernous area at least the size of a football field. All the while, Jack was taking in as much of the strange scenery as he could. He saw numerous other aliens, some of which were familiar as well as some new types. A few seemed to be similar to his new friends back there, old Dumb and Dumber. He wondered if their type was the predominant or native species on this planet.

The big cavernous area was like a central chamber of some sort. They appeared to be in the top third of multiple levels. Entering the chamber, there was a wide path all the way around on this level with a short wall that he could look over and see the expanse of the entire cavern. He could actually see five levels above them and what looked like seven or more below them. The entire place had been warm and humid since he'd gotten here, but this central area was somewhat cooler. He could smell a myriad of odors, not only the smell of dirt and excavation but also alien odor, food, machinery and lubrication, as well as a host of alien smells that he wasn't familiar with. It wasn't the worst thing he'd ever smelled, but he didn't think they'd be bottling this and selling it in a Paris perfumery anytime soon.

They proceeded a quarter of the way around the level they were on until they came to several lifts, which they entered, and then proceeded to go down several levels. They exited the lift and went a short distance to another corridor that branched off the main cavern area. They soon entered into a smaller cavern that appeared to be some sort of a retail shopping area or maybe a food court of some sort. That's what it reminded him of, a food court in a large shopping mall, only a lot less upscale and considerably more disorganized as well as noisy and chaotic.

There were probably a hundred or more aliens eating, drinking, and congregating in the main area as well as many more in what looked like shops of various types off the main area. This smaller cavern area had three separate levels, but most of the action seemed to be on the main floor level. There were a few shops or businesses on the second level and none on the third that he could see, just some closed-off entrances. They went down a short hallway off the main level and then came to some stairs that they then went up two more levels. They then came to a locked door, which the female alien opened with a handprint. They stepped inside. They were now inside what appeared to be a nicely appointed office. A quick glance around showed the office decor as almost mimicking a wooded glen with the depiction of trees and greenery and other forest scenes and murals on the walls.

She pointed to a chair next to a large desk at the side of the room. She was obviously instructing him to sit, which he did gladly, as he was quite exhausted after a couple of days of nonstop activity with only a couple of hours of catnaps interspersed along the way. He sat down in the chair and leaned back and closed his eyes for a minute. She watched him for a moment and realized he must be tired from whatever he'd been subjected to for who knows how long. He opened his eyes and saw her staring at him. She seemed considerably less harsh looking than when she had been talking to the strange creature in the floating chair. She pointed one of her slim fingers at him and said something to him in her concise, high-toned voice. He took this to mean stay put, so he nodded his head in response and said, "Don't mind me. I'll just stay here and relax for a minute. I'm not going anywhere, so just put your mind at ease about me trying to escape. I'm not going to bolt on you."

She didn't know what he'd said, but she got the impression he understood what she'd conveyed to him. She then left the room, so Jack just sat there with his arms crossed. He leaned back and closed his eyes and drifted off for a couple of minutes.

She returned a few minutes later and sat behind the big desk opposite of him. She fiddled with something on the desktop for a moment, and a medium-sized display appeared over her desk and appeared to hover before turning in his direction. She started speaking to him in what seemed to be several different languages. An image of another different alien appeared on the display, and it also started running through various different-sounding languages. She seemed to be looking for a response from him, as if he might recognize one of the languages.

An image of yet another alien appeared, which looked remarkably human, although somehow subtly different. The alien on the display looked human, maybe slightly Asian, but not exactly, just different. It sort of gave him the impression of a used car salesman or someone that was trying to sell something to you that you didn't want. It just didn't exude a confident feeling of being reputable. This alien spoke for a short time in what seemed like several different variations of the same language. Jack didn't understand any of it, so he just looked back at the female alien and shrugged his shoulders.

"If I'm supposed to recognize any of these languages, I can tell you that they are all alien to me. Say, you wouldn't have something to eat and drink, would you? It's been a while since I've had anything, and I'm starting to get a little bit ravenous." Jack made eating and drinking motions with his hand and mouth, which she understood easily along with the two or three words that came through on her translator. She held her hand over her desk for a moment and spoke several sentences. A faint voice replied from somewhere around the desk. Then after a few more words, she turned her attention back to him. He thought she understood him about the food and drink, so maybe she had done something as far as obtaining some. *Hey, maybe she called to the nearest pizza joint for some carryout. Meat lovers with extra cheese, onions, and mushrooms would be nice.* He laughed to himself.

After a few more minutes of alien images speaking languages he didn't understand, Jack decided to try and change the methodology a little and go for the vocabulary building method that he had started earlier on the big cargo ship. He started pointing and naming body parts that he knew were already translated then moved on to other items in the room like the desk. "Arm, head, shoulders, fingers, thumb, chest, legs, feet, foot, toes, fingernails, desk, light, monitor, floor, ceiling." He went on for another minute as she watched him and figured out what he was doing. She manipulated something on the desk's surface from near wherever the speakers were. She then ran some sort of diagnostics that must have translated the words into the translator pendant she wore.

She then spoke back the words that he'd just said while pointing to the same objects they came across in English. She'd made some motions and started speaking toward her desk for about a minute, and then images started showing up in the display in front of him. Various objects began popping up on the display. As each one came up, she named it in her language and motioned for him to do the same in his. Some of the objects he recognized and made the English pronunciation for, but there were a lot of them he didn't recognize. They went through planets, suns, everyday objects and utensils, a lot of which he tried to give names to even though some of them weren't quite recognizable. They tried a few animal pictures, but none of them were creatures he recognized except for a snakelike creature and some flying bird types. *Who are you?* she thought. *You're obviously not who they think you are or we would have had this figured out by now.*

Fifteen minutes into this, there was a faint chime from the other side of the room. She motioned her hand, and a door slid open at the far end of the room. Two more obviously female aliens came in caring trays, which turned out to have a nice variety of various foods and a couple of different types of beverages. There were some cooked appetizer-looking items, some mystery meat-looking things, as well as some raw fruit and vegetable-type selections.

It all looked fairly appetizing, and it smelled pretty good too. The two new female aliens set the trays on the desk in front of them. The one female alien looked similar to his host but perhaps a bit younger with some different color variations to her skin. She was somewhat scantily dressed in a tight blue-and-red short skirt and a flimsy light blue silky blouse with deep arm cutouts that nearly exposed her breasts.

The other alien was a different race, and although definitely female, she wasn't nearly as feminine looking as the other one and his host. She was slightly taller, more muscular, and had a different-shaped head that was boxier yet still attractively female. She had a full head of gold and burnt orange hair that covered the entire back side of her head from in front of her ears. Her hairline went considerably farther down her neck, and the whole bundle came to an abrupt shaggy end nearly a foot below her head, somewhat like a lion's mane. She wore a similar outfit as the other one but in different colors of reds, oranges, and yellows. Her skin coloration was completely different in that it almost looked like a light wood grain with all the associated variegations you would expect in the grain of the wood. It was fascinating; he kind of liked it. It didn't actually look bad at all, just different from anything he'd ever seen or could have imagined.

Jack looked at the meal in front of them and then up at the female alien that had brought him here. She gestured at him and then at the food, which he immediately understood that it was OK for him to eat. He then tried sampling some of the items, and they all seemed pretty tasty with various spices, tastes, and textures. She then helped herself to some of the items, so it was apparently going to be a shared meal. She looked up at the other two female aliens and spoke a few words. They replied back to her, and after a short conversation, they hurriedly left in the direction they'd come in from.

"Thank you, girls. You can get back to work now. I think we have everything we need here." Half a mentu later, she looked up at them again and said, "Reena, Carti, you two can get back to work now. The shift change will be starting in half an horun."

"Yes, Zshutana," replied Carti, the more petite one.

"Carti, Reena, what are you girls doing just standing there staring? Get back to work now, please."

Reena replied, "Yes, well, we were, um, just wondering, um . . ."

"Girls, now get back to work. Yes, he is rather appealing, isn't he? But he is not here to play. He is here to learn to communicate. He doesn't speak any known languages, so we are programming a translator to his native language," said Zshutana.

"He looks like he could communicate quite well to me," said Carti.

"Yes, me too," said Reena.

"Girls, get back to work. I only have two daiyus to get him up to speed on languages before I have to return him to Cahooshek the Repulsive. Now go. We don't have time for this." She sighed.

The two female aliens turned and left the office, jabbering excitedly to each other, Jack noted. "I'm sure I could get him to communicate," Zshutana heard one of the girls say to the other as they left the room.

They spent the next several hours working on image-to-word associations. They covered a lot of ground and seemed to have a pretty good basic vocabulary established. There were still a lot of unknown items that Jack didn't have a description for in English, but he would eventually learn what many of them were and be able to create a close facsimile if there wasn't a direct English translation. They were able to establish a very rudimentary communication using just object names, but the speech syntax wasn't even close to being deciphered. They managed to establish that her name was Zshutana and that his name was Jack. "Zshut-ana, Zshu-tana," repeated Jack. It had a soft and pleasant sound to it, he thought; all soft vowels, no hard sound to it at all except for the *t*. She kept trying to pronounce his name, but it kept coming out as "Zsho-ahck." There must not be any sharp or hard vowels in her language, he decided.

They tried working on descriptive phrases for a while then switched to short sentences of both moving and inanimate objects displayed on the monitor. They made some minor progress on short sentences. Then things seem to get scrambled or stay scrambled if they tried anything over four or five words. Jack was waning pretty fast now and was having a hard time paying attention. This probably wasn't helping whatever computer she was using to try and compute and match their speech patterns.

Jack's head was swimming he was so exhausted so he signaled to her that he was done by putting both his hands next to one ear and closing his eyes to simulate sleep. He assumed and hoped these creatures slept and that she understood what he was conveying. She obviously did and repeated back to him what he'd said. "Tired, sleep, must sleep." She switched off the display and got up from behind the desk and said, "Walk, sleep, Zsho-ahck." They went through a door that opened into a living area. They then went through a small living room area with several pieces of fairly standard but nice-looking furniture. The decor was similar to the office area but considerably more detailed with regard to the forest and nature representations.

There was a small kitchen area off the living room that looked modern and efficient and had appliances that Jack did not recognize. At the far end of the room was an entrance to a bedroom. She took him in and pointed out some of the amenities in the partial vocabulary they'd established. "Bed, chair/seat, light, lamp," she pointed out. They'd missed some of the basic objects like pillow, covers, dresser, and closet in their initial vocabulary session, but he figured they would get to that later.

She showed him how the lighting worked; by merely holding her hand next to any light for a second, it would go on or off at its previous brightness level and could dim or brighten by moving your hand up or down once the switching signal was established. The bedroom and closets he could see were all full of female clothing and trappings. For a second, he'd thought this place was possibly a guest lodge of some sort, but seeing all the personal effects, he knew it had to be her home or apartment.

The living area basically seemed like a large, very nicely appointed apartment. Being that they were at least several stories underground, from what he could tell, in some sort of mine complex, he guessed she must live here. She must be a person of some social stature for her to have an apartment this nice, not to mention that she had what appeared to be two young servant girls bring them their dinner. From the brief foray he'd seen of the rest of the place, nothing else seemed to compare with the excellent decor of this apartment. Then again, he hadn't seen very much of the facility, so he didn't really know for sure; maybe they all lived like this.

Off the bedroom was a bathroom. It had fixtures somewhat similar to the bathroom he'd discovered on the big cargo ship. These weren't as industrial looking and made a lot more sense when you looked at them from an operating standpoint. A large curved, attractive countertop with a single sink was on one side, and next to that on a raised pedestal was a nice-looking bathtub that appeared to have some sort of whirlpool capability. Opposite that was a glass door that opened into another small nicely appointed area that turned out to be an oversized shower. It seemed to have several shower heads and controls at various levels. The thought of taking a nice hot shower suddenly seemed pretty thrilling. He managed to get clean on the ship's steam cleaning shower, or whatever you called it, but he hadn't had the satisfaction of feeling the wonderful sensation of hot water cascading over him in a shower. This one looked spectacularly inviting.

He said, "Shower, hot shower," to her, but it apparently didn't translate, as they hadn't hit upon the word "shower" yet.

She understood the "hot" part from him, but the "shower" translation was a big blank. She said the word "rain" to him and then added the word "hot" back to it. "Hot rain," she said.

"Yes, that's it," he said. "Hot rain, hot rain water," as he smiled and laughed out loud.

She was momentarily taken aback by his response. *What did that mean exactly?* she wondered. That was a strange gesture to her, more like a grimace or even a growl from an animal of some sort except for the upturned mouth. He seemed rather pleasant and happy as he did it. Most other races had various forms of laughter, but they really didn't include the facial gestures she'd just seen associated with his laughter sound.

Her version of a smile and laugh was in the eyes and the flattening of the ears with very little mouth movement to express happiness or joy. Her smile was a normal response for many of the races she was familiar with. She realized this must be his way of expressing a happy response, since she knew they just had a mutual understanding of the funny description of what he had said was a "shau-aw," and they'd agreed that it was "hot rain."

She wondered what sort of race he was from. These Varaci were certainly different and definitely more attractive than the majority of the races she was familiar with, if that was in fact what he was. It was quite strange that he didn't speak the Varan language, since he was supposed to be one. She had her doubts. From the short time she'd been acquainted with him, though, he didn't really seem to fit the overall personality profile of what she'd briefly read about the Varaci. He was also considerably more poised and confident looking than the few pictures she'd been able to find of the Varan or Varaci race.

He gestured to the shower and repeated, "Hot rain," then made a motion above his head with his fingers like the hot rain was falling on his head. He beckoned her to show him how the controls worked in the shower.

To avoid getting wet, she stood off to the side of the nearest control and showed him how it worked by placing her hand on it and sliding her hand left and right to adjust the temperature. She pointed at the different controls and said, "Rain, rain, rain," indicating that he could select any of the five or more sources for the various heads in the shower. He was seriously looking forward to jumping in to a hot shower and wondered if he should just strip down and go for it or what the protocol was here.

She touched a cabinet door next to the shower, and it slid open to reveal a stack of towels and a collection of containers that must be some sort of soap, possibly shampoo or maybe body wash. She pointed to them, and then she turned and left the room. That was good enough for him. He stripped down and grabbed a towel and threw it over the top of the shower door and grabbed a couple of containers and took them into the shower with him. He got the water turned on to two of the heads and also discovered he could regulate the pressure and pattern of the heads by moving his hand over a depiction of what looked like flowing water that was above the temperature controls. This was pure luxury, and again, he wondered who she was.

For a couple of minutes, he tried messing with the wrist restraints that were still on his wrists. They weren't uncomfortable and he could move them up and down a few inches on each arm, so they weren't really constrictive. He just wanted them off but couldn't figure out any way to accomplish that.

As well as the soap and something that must have been shampoo, he discovered a razor as well as a couple of other items he didn't recognize. His beard felt like he was at about five daiyus of growth, so he decided to take care of that while he was at it. After a long luxurious shower that totally heat soaked his body, he called it quits and grabbed a towel to dry off. He poked his head out of the shower door and looked around and saw that his grimy flight suit and underwear were no longer on the floor but were now cleaned, dry, and folded on the counter. He hadn't heard anyone while he was in the shower, and he wondered if she had done this, and how on Earth, or wherever they were, had she cleaned, dried, and folded his clothing so fast? Well, that was an interesting question, but he was too tired worry about it now.

He got dressed and went from the bedroom into the living room where he saw her in the kitchen area. He went over to her and told her, "Thank you," and that he appreciated her hospitality and especially the warm shower hot rain and the decent food. He didn't know if she understood more than just a few words of what he'd said, but she seemed to comprehend what he was saying by the tone of his voice and the gestures he made. She stared at him for a few moments then touched his now cleanly shaved face. Her eyes narrowed, and the skin around them pulled back a bit, and her ears flattened somewhat against her head. Her large turquoise eyes seemed to sparkle when this happened. Altogether, the individual features might be misconstrued, but combined, they gave a rather warm and engaging feeling. Jack wasn't exactly sure what this gesture meant, or even if it was voluntary or involuntary, but he could tell it was some sort of positive response.

She turned away and gestured toward the kitchen appliances. She said a couple of words in her language he didn't understand, but then she slid the door to a recessed cabinet open by touching it then pointed into it, showing him a collection of food items. She then said, "Zsho-ahck, food, eat, drink, water."

He shook his head and smiled and said, "No, I, Jack, sleep."

She understood and said, "Yes, Zsho-ahck sleep." She walked him back to the bedroom and pointed to the bed and said, "Zsho-ahck sleep." He wasn't sure of the protocol at this point and vaguely wondered if this might be a sleepover of some sort. He didn't think so, but being in a totally alien environment with no idea whatsoever about their customs, he didn't really know what to expect.

Not wanting to look like a total idiot but wondering what the right protocol was, he asked, "Where does Zshutana sleep?"

She looked at him curiously for second, wondering exactly what he was asking. She then looked at him then pointed to the bed and said, "Zshutana bed." She then pointed behind her to the outer rooms or beyond and said, "Zshutana sleep." He felt relieved now knowing that this was in fact her home as well as her bedroom and that she was planning on sleeping in another room. She was certainly attractive enough in an alien way, but he was glad that the subject hadn't actually come up. She pointed at the bed again and said, "Zsho-ahck sleep." Then she left the apartment altogether and went back to her office. From there, she locked Jack in the apartment and armed the monitoring system so she could keep an eye on him and know if he needed anything at the same time. They both knew he was essentially a prisoner, and she didn't want to risk having him escape and incurring the wrath of that vile bottom scavenger Cahooshek.

She would let him sleep for seven horuns and then get him back on the translator program. She would catch a little sleep herself in a spare room of her business area. They still had much to do, and she didn't want to give Cahooshek any excuse for reneging on their agreement. Well, she thought to herself, this was certainly turning out to be a much more agreeable venture than she had anticipated considering the initial source of the task. She actually liked this alien considerably. Not only was he striking in appearance but he seemed to have a high degree of good character. He just seemed to have an aura of trustworthiness about him. These were characteristics she hadn't really experienced since being forced to leave her home planet of Tarca when she was just fifteen, nearly thirty yenets earlier.

She awoke at the fifth horun that she had set her alarm for. She performed her morning bathing and other rituals where she'd slept in her business area and then checked on her language student, Zsho-ahck, with her monitoring vido. Only she had the capability to see her own residence with the carefully concealed security system she used to monitor her home and business operation. She could see that he was still soundly sleeping in her bed and that his light blue one-piece outfit was draped over the nearby chair. The sight of him gave her a feeling of cheerfulness and also made her feel serene. These were feelings that were rare in the hectic and sometimes dangerous environment she lived in. She was looking forward to today's language and communication session. She made a brief foray down to her business office and checked in on her number-one assistant, Chiima.

Business had been moderate last night with no disturbances other than one mildly intoxicated Lumien client that had been gently removed by her security bot she affectionately called Zana. She went back to her apartment and checked for any important messages. There were a couple from some of the other mine interests, but she could answer those later. Fortunately, there was nothing from the worm Cahooshek, so it looked like she might have a full daiyus with Zsho-ahck with hopefully no interference. She left the office and went to the apartment and to her open bedroom door. He was still sleeping, now on his side with his arm wrapped around one of her pillows. She watched him for a couple of minutes as he lay there sleeping and breathing. His skin tone was such a uniform very light brown, not gray or white. It was unique and so undisturbed by variegations like most others. His hair was dark and full on his head, but he seemed to have some small amounts of smooth dark hair on his upper chest next to her pillow. "Zsho-ahck, it is time to wake up and continue our language programming and lesson."

Jack awoke to the sound of her pleasant, clear feminine voice, although he didn't know what she was saying except for his name. He rolled over and sat up and saw her standing in the doorway. He stared at her for a moment and looked around to make sure that everything he'd seen yesterday was still real. He'd slept the sleep of the dead last night and had no recollection of waking or stirring all night long. "Good morning," he said to her. "I slept well last night. I had a good sleep. Jack sleep good, and I hope you had the same."

She only understood a couple of the words he said, but she figured by the end of the daiyus, they would be doing a lot better. Trying to use some of the words she knew he understood, she said, "Come now, walk, eat, drink, words, display, Zsho-ahck."

He understood what she was trying to convey to him, but he wasn't sure about the urgency of it. Perhaps she was busy and had a limited amount of time for him to learn and program the language into their translators. Whatever the reason, he knew she'd been kind and generous with him, so he wanted to help her out by complying with her request. "OK," he said, pointing to his flight suit he said. "Jack, clothes, dressed. Give me a couple of minutes, and I'll be right out." She understood "Jack and clothes," so she left him in the bedroom as she went out to the kitchen to see what she could find for a morning meal.

He hurried and got dressed and joined her a couple of minutes later in the kitchen. "So what are we having for breakfast this morning? Food, eat, drink?"

She looked at him, and her eyes did the smiling gesture again. She started pulling a variety of items out of the food cooling unit and laid them all out on the counter for him to see. "Zsho-ahck, food, eat, drink, fast, words, words, words." She shook her head yes and gestured. After the last week of chaos, he was just enjoying himself for a while and didn't feel the desire to hurry himself. Apparently, she wanted to get right to it this morning with the words and programming, so he picked at a couple of food items and had a drink that was like a thin fruit smoothie of some unknown variety. The good part was he hoped that the better the communications got, the better he could understand her, and her him, and he would be able to explain his situation and maybe start to figure out some sort of resolution to his dilemma.

As soon as he had finished his meal, he looked at her and smiled then pointed to his teeth. He said, "Teeth, dirty, brush, clean, wash." He didn't think they'd covered any of those words, but he thought he'd give them a try anyway. He hadn't brushed his teeth in over a week, and though he was sort of getting used to it, it was still way past time, so he was hoping she had some sort of oral hygiene technique he could use. He then made a brushing motion, indicating how he might brush his teeth. He hadn't seen her smile like a human, per se, but he did get an occasional glimpse and could tell that she had a nice row of white teeth hiding in her very slightly elongated mouth. He pointed at her face and said, "Zshutana teeth," then said, "Jack see," then pointing at his eyes and back at her mouth. She looked at him cautiously for a second then took a half step toward him. He said again, "Jack teeth," then made a big exaggerated smile at her while showing her his teeth, while he tapped on his front teeth with his fingernail. "Zshutana teeth?" he said. She understood now what he wanted, but it was kind of an unnatural gesture for her.

She thought for a second and decided it was just interest of learning from a biological standpoint. She moved a little closer to him and started to imitate the strange smile gesture that he'd been showing her so that he could see her teeth. He naturally put his left hand on her left shoulder to draw her slightly closer so he could get a better look. He didn't even think about it until he felt her stiffen up for a second, but then she relaxed and let him move her a little closer. He made another exaggerated smile at her to get her to do the same. She hesitantly bared her teeth, and he gazed intently at her teeth and mouth structure.

It was fascinating to be looking at an alien's mouth structure to him. The basic design of her teeth was somewhat similar to humans but with slightly smaller teeth. Instead of one set of canines, she had two sets, top and bottom, separated by one incisor between them. The canines were somewhat prominent, leaving no doubt that whatever her race was, they were definitely on the higher end of the carnivore food chain. He opened his mouth while smiling so she would imitate him, while he used his other hand to gently move her jaw back and forth for a better look. He let her go so she wouldn't become uncomfortable then looked at her and said, "Zshutana's teeth good, strong, nice, pretty," hoping that even though they might not have touched on those words yet that she would understand what he was conveying. He knew for sure that his father, the dentist, would be wildly intrigued to examine her alien mouth structure.

She said, "Zsho-ahck, walk, come, teeth." She took him to her bathroom where she found her version of a toothbrush in one of the cabinets. She gave him some sort of powder that apparently went with it, and he proceeded to luxuriously brush his teeth for five minutes.

The shower and shave last night and the good tooth brushing this morning made him feel like a whole new person, practically human again, he thought. He also thought, *It's funny how the little things in life can make bizarre situations so much more bearable.*

When he was done, he gestured what should he do with the toothbrush. She replied by pointing at him and saying, "Zsho-ahck, teeth."

He nodded his head and said, "Thank you," as he slipped the toothbrush into one of his zippered flight suit pockets. It would be nice to keep it if he couldn't find one anywhere else.

He looked at her again then pointed in the direction of her office and said, "Words, words, words." Her eyes smiled at him again, and they headed for the office to beat themselves senseless with another day of word games, vocabulary exercises, and syntax programming. He was really starting to like the way her eyes smiled, as he now thought of it. It was a very warm and congenial gesture. Unlike a human smile, which could be somewhat faked, he didn't think there was any way to fake those large, beautiful, smiling turquoise eyes. They worked hard at it all morning then took a little break for mid meal and to allow their brains to cool off from the nonstop verbal and mental work. They were making considerable progress now and were able to carry on a basic conversation as long as the vocabulary and sentence structure wasn't too complex.

They started again right after mid meal, and Jack wanted to start asking her questions about who she was and where they were as well as trying to explain to her who he was and how he got here. He desperately wanted to know what his future situation here was, but he could kind of sense that she didn't want to go in that direction at least right away. Well, the more speech structure and vocabulary they had, the better they would be able to communicate later. It was kind of a catch-22—try to articulate more complex ideas with less speech now, or wait until later and have a better chance at better comprehending the whole situation.

They continued on for a long time, probably five or six hours with only a couple of short breaks. He tried talking to her to get some of the answers he wanted, but she shied away from them when he tried, so he didn't push her. She was definitely in a rush to try and make as much progress with the language and the translator program as possible. He wasn't sure why, and she didn't seem to want to talk about it. Whatever the reason, she obviously wasn't getting paid by the hour for this venture, which brought to his mind another question, which was, why was she doing this in the first place?

Jack was starting to get hungry again and guessed that it must be getting to be about 5:00 or 6:00 p.m. Then he realized he didn't even know what the length of the day was on this planet in hours. Well, either way, he was starting to get hungry. Just as he was thinking about that, she called out again, and in a short while, two servants or perhaps delivery girls showed up with a couple of trays of food for them again. These two females were different from the first two, so either Zshutana had more servants or these were some sort of food delivery girls.

These two girls were the same as each other but were different from the other two that had been there previously. They both had lovely bronze-colored skin with lighter striations of tan and thin medium blue lines. They were of a light feminine build, and they weren't nearly as muscular as the one with the wood grain skin. Their heads were slightly narrower with a slightly more protruding forehead compared to the others. One had thick brown hair, which was cut fairly short, while the other had medium-length hair that seemed to fan out around the whole back and top of her bare shoulders. Again, they were both scantily clad, and they appeared to be totally comfortable like that in their surroundings. Apparently, they just weren't too modest here or the warmth of the environment just made them want to wear less clothing. Again, they lingered for a minute, and then he heard Zshutana call them by name, Jahaqa and Sulaweii. He thought that's what he heard her call them anyway. He didn't catch every word, but he thought he heard her tell them to get back to work. Maybe they were employees of some sort, he wondered.

They started to eat their shared meal again, which he was beginning to enjoy sharing even more with her company. He asked her, "Who are the, these girls that bring food that we eat?"

She looked at him and stared for a moment and replied, "They work, they are workers, mine. Not working, then walk, comes now food, no, comes bring food, we eat."

"Your workers," he said. "How work? What work for Zshutana they work?"

"They work, my, mine, they workers mine," she said.

"They work in mine, dig, cut rock, they work as miners in mine?" he asked.

"No, not in work mine, my workers," she said in a slightly defensive tone.

"OK, OK, your workers," he said, pointing at her.

"Yes." She nodded her head. "Workers my."

"What work, how work, your, these workers?" he asked. This was so frustrating, he thought. They could communicate, but the translator couldn't get a concise thought across in a fluid manner whatsoever. Well, it was a great improvement over what they had yesterday, so they would just have to keep working at it.

"My work, workers," she said, "go with miners or some others. The sleeping room, no sleep, not sleep. They jump, um, no, with miners, no sleep in sleep room. In sleep room with miners, workers work, workers, jump play, no, make more." He could tell she was getting frustrated, and he wasn't quite sure what she was trying to express. Then she said, "Work." Then she made a gesture with both her hands that left no doubt. Did she really just do that? There wasn't much room for interpretation on that. Yes, he was certain that's what she meant. These young scantily dressed girls were working girls. Well, he was in no position to either judge them or even worry about it for that matter. She stared blankly at him for a half minute as if she were waiting for him to comment or possibly to deride her in some way. He was trying to think of a way to convey that it was OK by him without sounding contrite.

Since he didn't know any of their customs or how their society was structured, he didn't have the slightest clue as to whether this was perfectly normal or not. The thought of working girls on an alien planet had never occurred to him. In as casual a conversational tone as he could muster, he said, "OK, girls work, workers with miners in sleeping room, no sleep." He gave a small smile and a short laugh just because it was funny trying to convey this potentially delicate subject matter through an electronic translator that couldn't translate more than about a tenth of a percent of the English language. He said to her, "Girls work miners, Zshutana work miners?"

"No, Zshutana no work miners. My, I, Zshutana, no, I mother girls, mother like, keep girls not hurt. Zshutana make work, house, sleep, food give girls. Lost girls, home no, food no, safe no, Zshutana make home, food, safe. Twenty girls, eight girls work miners, twelve girls work, eat, clothes, buy, sell, more. Eight girls choose miners, more credits. I try them get work no miners, them make work other work. They not want other so now only help them best able."

He thought it sounded more like she was running an orphanage than a sporting house. He wasn't too worried about it either way; for all he knew, this was a perfectly legitimate occupation here. The good part was he now had her talking. If he could get her away from the strict vocabulary training, he might be able to learn more about his situation as well as improve the translator programming at the same time. He plied her with more questions about her situation. As best as he could understand, she was taking care of twenty females of different races, apparently from several different planets. She seemed to convey that there were some other businesses or interests that were helping her with food, clothing, and other support. Also, the rest of the girls were either employed somewhere nearby or helped out in general with their group. He wasn't sure of the origins of the girls, but it sounded like they might be orphans or homeless for one reason or another.

He brought the conversation back to this planet to see what information she could give him on it. "Here, this planet, Zshutana home?" She looked at him a moment but wasn't sure of his question. Was he asking her if this was her home or home planet, or did he mean something else? she wondered. He said, "Child, baby Zshutana, here, this planet?"

Oh, she thought, *he wants to know if I was an infant on this planet or am I from here, was I born here.* "No," she said, "Zshutana no baby, child, this planet Nishda. Zshutana, baby, child, Tarca. Zshutana here come fifteen yenets, mother no, father no. No easy, hard yes."

If he understood her correctly, she came here from another planet at fifteen with no mother or father or any family. He couldn't begin to imagine what that must have been like for her at that age or how she got here or how she survived. "So this planet is called Nishda," he pointed down and said, "This planet is Nishda."

She shook her head in the affirmative and gave a small wave of her hand while she said, "Nishda, planet Nishda. Planet Nishda hard, rocks, hot, plants no, animals no, rocks, dirt, water no, races no, people no."

"This planet, Nishda, had no plants or animals. It was just rocks. Is that what you are saying?" he asked. "I've seen vast areas of jungle, trees and plants, with many animals."

"Yes," she replied, "all dead planet, they make, bring animals, plants, make breathing. Want dig, make mines and dig. Make Nishda planet for animals, breathing, mining."

That's utterly amazing, thought Jack. The entire planet is terraformed so that they can live on it and mine. "When, how long, how many years ago did they do this," he asked.

"Still now, doing," she replied, "make, no start sixty-eight yenets age. Start fastest kinds, plants, animals that bind with plants for planet Nishda. All same from different planets, work best with same, breathe air, make more breathe air."

He said, "But I've seen much water from orbit and on the ground. They couldn't have brought all the water here."

"Not bring water," she said, "water deep low, under, down, many kahtak, twenty kahtak, much water, big, bigger, water under. Bring up water. Big, push, water push water up. Make water areas, seas. Much water, must make slow water coming up. Too much under, too much water, make twenty mu-uts, deep, on the,

the Nishda, if all water up. Must be caution. Keep water under or much too water, much too water."

Jack could hardly believe what he was hearing. There was a vast underground ocean under the surface, way under the surface, like twenty kilometers deep is what it sounded like. And they had to be careful because it was too much water, so much that it could cover the planet to, what did she say, twenty mu-uts deep? They have terraformed and are terraforming the entire planet using a vast under-surface sea. *Amazing, completely amazing,* he thought. Well, he'd think about that for a while and try to consider the implications of such a vast enterprise. The resources it would take would be astronomical.

If they were putting that much energy, time, and expense into terraforming and mining this planet, this previously dead planet, then whatever they are mining must be extremely valuable. He asked her, "Then the mining is why they brought plants and animals here? What are they mining that makes them come here and do all this?"

She thought for a second. "The metal, in ground metal, Burun-Rioc, mining this and some other. Mostly Burun-Rioc, metal. Metal in the ground, dirt, then take. Take metal from ground, make the metal, strong, very strong. Burun-Rioc metal, make ship, starship metal. They get metal, very, very strong metal. Mix Burun-Rioc with other ground metal, uh, um, added other, make very strong metals."

"So is this the only place for this Burun-Rioc, dirt metal, we say ore, is it just here?"

"No," she replied, "but, no, not just here, most here big, best, easier here is the ground metal, Burun-Rioc, metal."

So, he said to himself, *here is where they mine the metal to build starships because it has the most high-grade ore and easier to mine this Burun-Rioc metal.* If terraforming a planet is easier than other places, it must be rare and valuable. An entire planet terraformed so they could mine a high-strength ore for the metal to build starships. *That must somehow make sense from their economic standpoint,* he thought. It must be easier to terraform the planet than to try and run an operation of this size in a hostile environment that wouldn't support life. Maybe this Burun-Rioc ore is only found in asteroid fields or planets like Mercury that are too close to a star. *Wouldn't the "want to terraform Mars" scientist crowd back on Earth be amazed by the scope of this scenario,* he thought.

So he now had enough background information on what was going on here. It was time to ask her what his involvement was in all this. "So why are we in such a big hurry to get the translator programmed and my language up to a good communication level?"

She looked at him for a long time trying to think how she should answer him. She wasn't really sure of his circumstances herself, and she certainly didn't take the word of the miserable Cahooshek. She had to word this correctly and hope the translator would convey the correct meaning. "You must make communicate with others. The disgusting worm Cahooshek, must work for Cahooshek you. He pay, you owed many credits for crime, your, your, you cheating. Your passage steal on, *Yuanjejitt* ship, your come here, not pay credits." He thought he understood her to say he was a stowaway, stealing passage. He kept listening.

Her translation was still scrambled, but it came across as "You passage take, pay not, you work now, off pay debt. Cahooshek your pay debt, passage debt, work now must. Work mine pay Cahooshek. Not good work inside mine. Why you take, steal passage, here? Why you come here Nishda, why passage steal?"

"Wait, wait," Jack said. "This Cahooshek told you I am stowaway. That I stole passage on the big starship? They must have thought they found me on that ship as a stowaway. They sold me to a mine operator and they thought I was a stowaway and now I must work my off my debt? That must be what they believe."

"Yes," she said, "this what tell me they. Correct not, they lie about what you do. What you do? Why you steal passage, not steal why you on *Yuanjejitt*, come here? You not on *Yuanjejitt*? How here? How Zsho-ahck here?"

"*Yuanjejitt*," he attempted to say. "That's the name ship, I guess. No, yes, I was on *Yuanjejitt*, the ship, but not stowaway. They probably believe this, since I couldn't explain my presence to them," answered Jack.

Jack attempted to explain he was there by an accident, a very horrible accident. "I was in another ship, my ship, *Victory*. We were entering orbit around my planet, my planet Earth. We were just establishing our orbit, and we were hit, hit by another ship, a huge ship, the huge ship you call *Yuanjejitt*. It destroyed my ship *Victory* and killed all the other crew members. I don't know how I survived. The part of the ship I was in was broken off and wedged in some big bay or opening, part of the big cargo ship. I was able to get inside before I died. I was in the cargo hold for several days. I didn't really know where I was. They found me when the ship got to this planet's orbit. Then they brought me down here. That's all I know. My ship was destroyed and the crew killed, and they brought me here. Now I know why, but apparently, they don't know how I got on their ship. They think I stowed away, that I was stealing passage. Do you believe me?" he asked her. She couldn't understand all his explanation, but she was able to understand enough. What a strange question, she thought, no one would ever ask you if you believed them if they were trying to fabricate something false, a lie. She stared at him for half a minute studying his face. She didn't really know his species, but she could read character better than the next twenty-nine Nishdans put together.

Yes, she believed him, absolutely, but he said his planet Earth; he was on a ship from a planet called Earth. She had never heard of this planet. "What planet Earth, I not of Earth know? You Varaci not? They say me you Varaci, you are a Varaci not?"

"No," said Jack, "I'm not a Varaci. What is a Varaci? I've never heard of a Varaci. Six daiyus ago, I'd never even heard of any other inhabitable planets or inhabitants of other planets."

"What you mean heard not other planets? You say you, your ship hit, *Yuanjejitt* destroyed by, how you know not planets and races other?"

"Our planet, our race of people," Jack said, "we are just barely able to go to orbit and to our moon. All we have ever done, the most we've done is go to our moon. No space travel between stars. We've just recently learned how to get to orbit and around our solar system with some probes, explorer machines."

"This hard, this believe not. They say me Varaci you. Search Varaci on core my. Core data Varaci show. You look Varaci. Very like Varaci. More big, tall, more, no less, me not right say. Varaci I see, look false heart, true not, so not straight in my face. You know words my, my understand?"

"Yes," Jack replied, "I look very much like these Varaci but maybe a little different. Maybe they are more devious or something like that."

He wasn't sure if she was getting the full meaning of his response, but she seemed to be responding to his words the way he hoped. Maybe the English translation to her language was better than the other way around, he hoped so. He could tell that the translation was beginning to improve. It still needed a lot of work to actually become fluent, but at least they were getting the basic message across. It sure beat actually having to learn a new language. "Now reason makes, Zsho-ahck know not Varaci. Translator know not Zsho-ahck language. Now make translate language all new. What name language you is Earthun, Eartha?"

"English," he replied, "is my native language."

She said, "Eartha, Earth language not know translator. Earth language many different, not same, backward words. Translator, core thinking, uh, reason, no, hard making work. More hard others."

"Words backward, mixed," she said.

"Yes," he said, "English is a different language, different from most other languages on Earth in that way."

"Other, more languages this Earth planet? What meaning other languages? Zshutana understand not."

"There are many languages on my planet Earth," said Jack. "I would guess maybe five thousand—no, probably more, maybe more than six thousand languages on my planet Earth from what I've heard. Most speak the main twenty or so, but there are many thousands more."

"Six thousand on Earth planet languages?" she said. She wasn't sure she understood that correctly. "How possible six thousand? This right not," she asked.

"Yes," he said, "more than six thousand languages on Earth. I only know one, which is English, and a few words of some others."

"How this?" she said. "How talk, communicate, translators?" she asked again, tapping her translator.

"No translators," he said. "We must learn other languages to communicate. Some computer programs will translate written languages, and some will almost translate spoken words, but not very well, about like what we are doing here. Communication is very difficult at times," he said.

"Zshutana, eight languages speak," she said. "More languages here Nishda planet, less others. One language on other planets, most planets. Some three four planets only one language. Earth planet has six more thousand languages, this strange. Zshutana not know of a like planet Earth planet. Where the Earth planet?" she asked.

"Well," Jack said, "I couldn't really say from here because I don't know where we are. I don't know where this planet Nishda is from Earth. On Earth, we don't know where any other planets capable of supporting life are. We don't know of any actual other beings than us, although many people speculate and believe there are others, like yourself, out in the galaxy."

She was completely surprised. "You say not know of others, other person beings except Earth race. To my, Zshutana, strange very Earth planet, thousands speak languages this Earth and no other race you aware know. Sound strange very most amount highest strange, my know of, told of. No planet like your Earth, anywhere my of know."

"Now must we more make words, translate language. Order fix, words mixed," she said.

"Yes, yes," he said, contemplating everything she'd just said. Earth circumstances were apparently unique, possible outright bizarre to her; this would make Earth a strange and inexplicable planet by her standards. How or why was Earth so different and most likely isolated from everything else, every other civilization out in the galaxy? Apparently, there were dozens or maybe even hundreds based on what she'd told him.

So why was Earth so isolated? Wouldn't the other space-faring races attempt to contact them? There were many answers he didn't know and many questions he would have to ask. He felt as if he had barely, just imperceptibly, scratched the surface of a huge puzzle that he didn't even have the pieces to assemble. So Earth was an enigma that was apparently different from other inhabited planets in the galaxy. He would have to try to figure out why. How was Earth different, and why was it different? There had to be a reason, and there had to be answers out there. How he would get those answers he wasn't sure, but he felt that for some reason, it was very important, yes, very, very important to find out everything he could about this enigma.

"Zsho-ahck, words more now," said Zshutana.

"Yes, sorry, of course," said Jack, coming out of his thoughts. He'd never gotten the answer to his previous question. "Why are we in such a hurry for the words and translator?" he asked again. She looked at him again. He'd gotten her off subject the previous time he'd asked her that. She thought about that for a second and realized he was very smart. Yes, he was apparently quite astute at leading you in the direction he wanted to take you. She'd not met anyone with the ability to distract her from the subject at hand so easily. He could apparently easily do that even though they were barely communicating now.

How very fascinating, she thought. Her eyes smiled for a second and he caught it, and she knew he'd seen it.

"You smiled for a second," he said. "What were you thinking?"

She smiled again. "Thinking I, this our time here spent, is a time of knowledge good, also enjoyment. Zshutana appreciate time, learning good here."

"Yes," replied Jack, "for me too. Everything here is new and enjoyable for me, all new experiences. I've enjoyed your company too. You are a good teacher and translator. Thank you for helping me as well as helping me to understand much of what has happened to me. You are good to work with. I have enjoyed it considerably." She smiled again, and he added, "But you still haven't answered my question, why the hurry, why the fast speed on the word lessons?"

Her smile instantly faded. "Cahooshek, the Sumtokan stench. This creature despise I him. You now work must him for. Only he gives my daiyus two, two daiyus to make you, your language communicate with translator. He soon come will. Not certain when soon. Soon, though, to you make work. Zshutana need Zsho-ahck be good language for to work. This language better more than before but must better be for Zsho-ahck. The Cahooshek could be here, be here you anytime for, here for Zsho-ahck."

Chapter 7: Internment

Jack thought for a minute; he would have to wait and see how this panned out with this Cahooshek character that Zshutana obviously detested. He'd briefly thought again of trying to escape, but the same dilemma still existed as far as where he would go and what he would do. He had little knowledge of this planet and its environment. He also didn't think it would fare well for Zshutana if he managed to escape while in her care or custody, depending on how you phrased it. He'd have to ride this one out and see where it ended up. She thought for another minute then said to him, "I think now work more words meaning to pictures this display. Let core see, no more understand core make we talking we have made. Now have we much talked. More words we make core to process to make words fit, not mixed words so much so."

"OK," he said, "we will make more word associations and let the core—this is a computer I would guess—try to assemble my English words and make them fit your word patterns, your speech syntax, we would call it." They spent the next two hours refining and adding to the basic vocabulary.

They concentrated on descriptive words and action words. Though he'd never had much interest in the structure of the English language, Jack knew that without the adjectives and verbs of any language, you basically ended up with a jumble of objects or nouns that really didn't do anything but just sit there and look pretty. You also needed those pesky but necessary adverbs like "the" to pull it all together. Once they'd built a good base of all these and she'd fed them to the core for input to the translator program, it all started to come together pretty well. They ran multiple phrases and complete paragraphs multiple times until it started to sound fairly fluid. It wasn't perfect, but it would get better once they had a fuller vocabulary base and added a few more refinements. The closer they stayed to Zshutana's native tongue for the translator, which he learned was Tarcan, the better it seemed to work. Tarcan, he'd learned, or dialects of it, was spoken widely on four planets in three systems and had originated in one of the local sector systems as a prime language. If they could get a one-language-to-one-language translation, then the translator would be able to decipher the others.

"So we've put in quite a lot of time and we seem to be making some nice progress now," Jack said to her.

"Yes, we are doing well now, and it is well to have good communication with you then," she replied. "The first part of our journey was frustrating and challenged for me, I am now glad that I had this chance to help you. Either now soon, maybe tonight or tomorrow morning, the miserable thing Cahooshek will come to collect you for and make you work. If there was something I could do to stop this, I would, but I do not know of anything that would be of helpful. This story you have told me of the big ship *Yuanjejitt* hitting your ship sad is. This would not be a good thing and would be likely investigated by the Galactic Trade Alliance, even out here on the rim worlds. You but must be careful for this reason. The Cahooshek slime would not want to be involved in an investigation. If we tried to make this come to be known, they may try and harm you, to stop you. Do you make this sense?" she asked him.

"Yes," he said, "I understand. Don't worry, I will use caution in everything I do here. I must learn what it takes to get along here, how to function, and I will learn. Now that you've helped me with your language, I will be much better able to do this. Listen, though, I know how well you've done and how well the translator is working for me now, but I must do something to help myself. I must try to gain some advantage. I have to ask you if you will help me and pretend that our language translation is not working so well, that it is only as good or maybe worse than we were before this last round of programming."

This didn't seem to make sense to her. "Why?" she asked. "Why would you wish to not have good communication? Would that not hurt you?"

"Yes," he said, "it might hurt me a little, but it could help me even more some. If this Cahooshek friend of yours, that you are so fond of, doesn't know that I can understand him and his associates very well, they may talk more freely among themselves while I am nearby, and I may be able to learn things that I otherwise might not be able to. Is there any way that they would know or could tell that the translator is actually working so well? Can I hide how well it now works from them?"

She contemplated all that for a few moments. "No, they could not tell. Translators only translate what you say. If you don't say so much, then they won't know that you are understanding. You can say your words backward and confuse translator. Cahooshek not my friend. I have huge disgust for this miserable creature. Why do you say this?" She seemed somewhat confused.

"Never mind that part," he said. "That was kind of a joke. I was just being facetious, sort of teasing you."

"Facetious, joke?" she asked.

"It's OK," he said. "I know you don't like him. I was just teasing you to make a jest, sort of amusing," he said.

"OK," she replied, "I will gladly help you with this like you ask. The Cahooshek thing may be angry with me, maybe he yell at me, but I don't care. I will just yell back and tell him he did not give me enough time for such a difficult task with such a stunted student. It will be his fault that the translator does not function well, not mine," as she smiled with her eyes and made a little tittering sound.

He smiled back at her and said, "Thank you. Again, I appreciate your help very much. Such a slow and stunted student," he said and laughed out loud. She smiled back at him again, and her eyes radiated their approval. "I'm not sure what my situation would be if you hadn't helped me with all this. I appreciate your hospitality and time and really relished the hot shower, you know, the hot rain and good food. Maybe if this Cahooshek doesn't come tonight, I could have another one if that's OK with you. I had been without a shower for over a wenek, seven daiyus, before yesterday."

"Yes, yes," she responded, "that would be most, what do you say, 'OK by me.'"

Jack asked her more about the planet and the mining operation. The planet, as she'd partly explained earlier, had been terraformed so that it could be more easily mined by using an imported and then ultimately permanent population. The mine was established by the Galactic Trading Alliance along with several of the separate planet alliances that were nearest to Nishda in this quadrant. The vast underground seas, much like those initially discovered on Earth in late 2015, had been tapped as a source of both liquid water and energy. This had allowed the terraforming of vast regions of the planet in the areas that were most conducive to establishing a viable habitat. They had imported the fastest-growing and most aggressive jungle forest environments and the symbiotic animal life necessary to balance the rapidly terraforming ecological niches. Other areas were turned into inland seas and lakes to help establish self-sustaining weather systems and fairly predictable precipitation patterns that would eventually provide consistent precipitation for the entire planet.

The mining operation, like most mines, was established for multiple minerals, ores, and their derivative compounds. The primary high value ore that made it economically feasible and required the terraforming of the planet is called Burun-Rioc. The Burun-Rioc ore is unique in that it is a natural element found only on a few planets and asteroids in limited amounts except for Nishda, where it is somewhat plentiful. The Burun-Rioc has never been duplicated in any laboratory, and it is not known under what conditions it naturally forms. This Burun-Rioc is unique in that it fuses at the subatomic level with other elements and creates unique physical properties while super-enhancing the properties of the other elements and the molecular properties of the derived engineered metallurgic compounds.

It creates essentially unique elemental compounds that possess astounding physical properties that are unlike any of the base elements or other standard alloys of metals. Additional elements can also be added to these unique compounded elements, giving them additional enhanced properties, while the unique base elements always retain their specific properties without being corrupted but only enhanced by the addition of the other elements. Extremely high strength as well as near total abrasion resistance and impervious corrosion qualities make it the most highly prized alloy in the galaxy. Unique magnetic and conductive properties and also semiconductor properties were also derived from the super-enhanced qualities of the Burun-Rioc alloys. The primary alloy compounded elements are used for the hulls and structures of starships that are fitted with interstellar drive engines. By introducing synthetically produced pure diamond and also adding to the Burun-Rioc ore titanium, beryllium, erbium, and vanadium, they were able to produce a metallurgical alloy so hard that it was nearly impenetrable from any ballistic attacks and plasma or light beam weapons even when not protected by a quantum field. All this was funded and sanctioned by an organization of planets called the Galactic Trading Alliance.

Zshutana's own knowledge of the overall infrastructure of the planet and its operation plus some quick research on her core neural cortex gave Jack a pretty good understanding of the new environment he was now about to be immersed in. "Thank you again," he said to her. "This will help me figure out some sort of a plan as far as what I need to do to get out of this situation that I'm about to be subjected to."

"What do you think you will do?" she asked him.

"I'm not sure yet," he replied. "I still need to find out exactly what they intend to do with me and what, if any, options I might have to get out of this fraudulent indentured work scenario. If there is a chance that I can access Nishda's core system or if I can somehow stay in contact with you, I might have a better chance of researching my way out of this."

"Yes," she said, "more information may help you some, but you must be careful about what you do. Before you came here, the disgusting Cahooshek said that if I couldn't make you communicating well enough for you to work, then he would have to take a loss on you by putting you in the fight pit as fodder for the sporting crowds in the pit matches."

"Pit matches, fight pits, what are those?" he asked.

Her eyes darkened, and instead of the bright luminous smile, a different look manifested itself; it was not only a frown but also a look of revulsion crossed her face. "For diversion, um, for sport," she began, "they have an arena on one of the lowest mine levels, the Kiraga level, where there are certain illegal things that occur. The arena is where they have fighting combat. Some are for combat of the regular miners against other miners. Some are combat fighting between the hybrid mine laborers, some of which they have bred illegally and without oversight or the required restrictions. Everything is illegal there, but the mine bosses do not go there. They know it would not be safe for them, and also they ignore it because they make many credits by allowing it."

"Well, thanks for that information. It doesn't sound like a place where you would want to go to if you can avoid it," he said.

He started to ask her about how the planet and mining operation was managed. He wanted to know how the government was structured and who the bosses were, but as he started to ask, a rapid chime sounded from her desk. She looked at it and half growled. "Cahooshek, that miserable vermin. I will answer it now, so you must be silent." Jack nodded at her in compliance. She touched the surface of the desk, and Cahooshek's rasping voice filled the air.

"Zshutana, are you there?" he rasped. Jack could now understand him too.

"Yes, Cahooshek, what do you want? Checking up on your latest investment? We are making some progress, but this strange unknown language is giving me great difficulty. I will need at least another wenek to get decent communication abilities programmed into the core and his translator. This is extremely difficult, which you did not advise me of beforehand. He is also not overly bright or particularly responsive with regard to my language training. I highly recommend leaving him here at least another wenek."

"Enough!" Cahooshek barked at her. "We will be there in fifteen mentus, so have him ready for us."

She started to reply that this was a ridiculous request, but Cahooshek terminated the connection. "They will be here shortly," she said to Jack. "There is nothing I can do to slow them down now."

"That's OK," he said. "You did all you could do so I'll just deal with it as it occurs. Now remember, when they get here, I will only be fluent enough to take basic instructions. You may have to repeat things to me for me to comprehend them. Do you understand what I'm saying?"

"Yes, I understand," as she realized and marveled at his fast reasoning ability. "Do not worry, I will play my role, and we will fool the disgusting worm."

"Very good," replied Jack, "and I can't thank you enough for helping me try to figure this whole mess out. Since we don't know what Cahooshek plans on doing with me, and I may not be able to contact you, you may have to do a little detective work to try and find out where I am and see if it's possible to contact me."

"Detective work?" she asked. "What is detective work?"

"Like research," he said, "you will have to try to find out what they've done with me and how to get in touch with me if you can."

"Yes, yes, I will search for you as soon as I am able, and I will try to find out if there's any way that I can help you," she responded.

"Do not be too worried," she said. "I have many eyes and ears throughout the mine to tell me what things are happening. I should be able to find out something very soon about you."

"OK, that's fine. Just do the best that you can, but be careful yourself. I don't want you to get in trouble or possibly hurt trying to help me," he said.

"Do not worry," she replied. "I am used to taking care of myself and fending for all the younger ones that are under my care."

"OK, then," he replied, "and, uh, what did you mean I'm not too bright or overly cooperative?" he asked as he smiled at her.

Her eyes smiled back, and she replied, "I am just doing as you asked and already playing my part in our plan against the hideous vermin Cahooshek."

"Oh, well, thank goodness," he replied. "I wouldn't want you to think I was a sluggish student and not working up to my potential this whole time." She looked at him for a long time until he broke into a laugh and a huge grin. She wasn't sure for a second, but she thought he was chiding her. Now she knew for sure, and her eyes returned a very bright and delightful smile.

A high-pitched tone emanated from behind her desk. Her smile instantly faded, and her mood changed to one of dejection. "He is here." She groaned. "I would just as soon feed him to the smelting furnace on the Numarar level than let him in the door."

"Don't worry about it for now," said Jack. "Just play your part for now, and maybe later, we can figure out how to deal with him."

"Yes, OK," she replied. "Just stay seated there as if we are still working on words while I let the parasite stench in." Jack watched her as she moved toward the main office door as he momentarily pondered the posture and attitude he should assume for his reunion with this Cahooshek.

She opened the door to find Cahooshek and his two dullard subordinates with him. Cahooshek, still in his chair, glided into the room with Dumb and Dumber in tow. "I hope you've managed to keep your end of our bargain and decipher and program enough of this creature's bizarre language that we can put him to work in some useful capacity," he rasped. "If you've failed, I will have no alternative but to break our agreement, and I will end up having to give this ignorant Varaci creature to the mine bosses to use as exhibition fodder for their games."

She replied, "I told you at the beginning how much time I needed to do the level of programming and training he required, but as usual, you are too senseless to understand the basic requirements needed for this level of achievement."

"Stop your silly female bantering." He groaned. "Did you successfully complete my demands, or did you fail me?"

"Demands," she replied, "you can demand that it rain gold-coated credits, but your ignorance will not make it happen." She looked at him with all the disgust she could muster. "But to answer your question, yes, I have successfully reached a level of passable communication with your Varaci mine worker. The translator output is very basic and marginal, but you should be able to instruct him to do anything he would need to do as a mine worker. You may have to repeat things or use simpler words, but you should be able to sufficiently communicate with him, and it should improve some over time. He seems to at least be smart enough to understand what you want him to do as long as the translator can find the words that he can understand. I think if you use this method and go slow and be sure to show him what you want him to do, you should be able to get whatever work out of him you want."

"I will be the judge of that," Cahooshek replied. "I hope, for all our sakes, that this is the case, as the only way I will recoup my misguided investment will be to get an ample amount of labor out of him. Now if you will kindly give me the command disk, we will be on our way."

She reluctantly handed over the command disk they'd given her when she'd first taken Jack at Cahooshek's mine level. "Here is your command disk," she replied, "but I don't believe it will be necessary, as I have not had to control him with it here. He seems like a docile enough creature and has shown no signs of aggression."

Cahooshek replied, "Your job is completed, let us hope successfully. I will let you know as to whether or not I believe you've done an adequate job with this task."

Cahooshek took the command disk, and once again, Jack found his wrists bound as he was pulled to his feet and maneuvered toward the door. Jack, having listened to both sides of the complete conversation between Cahooshek and Zshutana, knew what an admirable job she'd done convincing them of his "lack of fluency ability." As they headed toward the door, he was able to get one brief last look at her and see the anguish on her face as he was herded out of her office and back toward Cahooshek's domain and the mining operation.

They returned through the labyrinth that Jack had seen on his way to Zshutana's the daiyus before. On the return, Cahooshek groused and berated continuously to his minions about both Jack and Zshutana and their lack of language skills. Several times, he berated Jack with derogatory terms trying to elicit a response or possibly just out of general vindictiveness. Jack had to weigh and measure his responses to try and establish a minimal degree of communication ability to keep himself viable for whatever the purported employment opportunity was that awaited him. With some mixed responses of his "name, good, see, look, rock," and a few nonsensical words thrown in, Jack was able to demonstrate his verbal aptitude. He tried to show a little bit of cooperation and not appear belligerent. He reasoned that it wouldn't do him any good and might only serve to incur greater restraints on his ability to alter any situation in his favor.

They went past the main area that led to Cahooshek's control area and into a larger passage that led to an industrial-size elevator lift that only went down from their current level. Cahooshek continued to grumble about Jack and Zshutana's uselessness as well as everything else under Nishda's surface. Jack was beginning to appreciate Zshutana's considerable disdain for this disagreeable creature. Jack didn't know what time it was, but he knew it was at the end of a fairly long daiyus. If he had to guess, he'd say that the daiyus here on Nishda were slightly longer than Earth's twenty-four hours, and it felt like the gravity was slightly higher also. They boarded the lift along with a dozen other alien types like Jack had seen previously. These were apparently all miners judging from their clothing and safety gear that was somewhat similar to what miners would wear on Earth.

They passed an intermediate level and continued to descend another three hundred feet before they reached the bottom. Exiting the lift, they came to a side room staffed by an old alien with a lot of miles on him. He was a dull blue and dusty gray color with short splotchy bluish-gray hair on most of his exposed skin. His face was thin with large black eyes with multiple horizontal wrinkles and large drooping ears. His arms were spindly and wrinkled with a left hand that had three very short amputated fingers and two normal ones as well as a thumb. His right hand was missing, but it had a six-fingered mechanical prosthesis in its place. Cahooshek said to the alien, "Jattar, here is a new mine worker that you can put on the twenty-five to zero nine shift as a drill operator. He should be capable of running a zibur drill or a hactra hammer rig. He will need training and mining gear and clothing. Use caution with him, as I have a large sum invested in him. Make sure he knows the safety protocols so that he hopefully avoids being damaged or getting himself killed."

The old alien replied in a wheezing breathless voice, "Yes, Cahooshek, I see that you bring me another new conscript. I hope it lasts longer than the last one that ended up collapsing the mine tunnel on itself and ending its short career. What kind is this one? It looks unfamiliar to me."

"This one is a Varaci from the planet Vara," replied Cahooshek, "but its language skills are limited. I've just spent two daiyus having its language decoded and programmed to its translator, but the results are less than adequate. Give it a few daiyus of training, and if it doesn't work out, I will have to find an alternative way to try to recoup my investment. And, yes," Cahooshek replied to the ancient alien, "the last recruit did not fare well, but fortunately, it was not mine, so I lost no investment in it. This one is mine, however, so you must take the utmost care with him. The only way I can earn enough credits to get off this rock and back to my beloved Sumtoka will be to make enough credits off these indentured conscripts, bank my profits, and then sell them without significant loss. If they are injured or killed before I at least break even on my investment, then I will take a loss.

"I am holding you responsible for the safety of my investment, Jattar. Contract labor costs out here are too expensive to hire outside labor. I only make a tiny pittance by supplying contract labor. The only way for me to reap any decent profit is by using conscripts or indentured criminals and recouping more than my initial investment. If you want to keep your easy management position here, then make sure nothing happens to this conscript for at least long enough that I make back my investment and a decent profit. Here is his command disk. Contact me if you have any problems with him. I am skeptical of his abilities, but he does look strong and healthy enough to perform any of the basic tasks under your control."

"Yes, Cahooshek, I will do my best and ensure that he remains viable for as long as possible," replied Jattar.

Overhearing the entire conversation but trying to remain disinterested as if he didn't understand, Jack now had a good understanding of his circumstances with regard to being shanghaied into his new career field as a mine laborer. Cahooshek and his two grunt assistants exited, leaving Jack with the old alien. The old alien made a cackling rasping sound that was somewhat like laughter. Then it took the command disk and pulled Jack toward him. "Well, now, conscript," rasped the old alien whose name Jack now knew was Jattar, "you're not supposed to be too good with talking or understanding. We'll have to work on that some so I can get some decent work out of you. In the meantime, come with me and I will get you some clothes and gear that's better for your job than what you are wearing now. You understand anything about what I'm saying to you?" rasped the old alien as he gave Jack a couple of jerks with the command disk.

Jack carefully thought about his response and how much he wanted the alien to know about how much he could understand and speak. He needed to learn more about his surroundings and further consider his options, but he didn't want word getting back to Cahooshek that he was more fluent than Cahooshek realized. The longer he could maintain his language charade, the more he could learn and the more they would divulge in his presence. He wondered who the previous conscripts, as Cahooshek had called them, were and whether they were still alive. He was convinced that none of them were human or even this Varaci race, since none of the local aliens had recognized him as one of these Varaci that he apparently looked like.

Jack replied to the old alien with a mixture of nonsense words as well as a few that he knew would translate properly along with a couple in proper sequence that made it sound like he might be trying to make a sentence or convey some concept or thought. He threw in his name a few times, hoping to convey to the alien that this was his name on the premise that if the alien could recognize him by name, he might start to develop enough personal recognition that he could gain a small amount of trust and get the old alien to release his wrist restraints.

"Well, at least it looks like you're trying to be a little bit cooperative," groaned the old alien, "but I didn't catch but about half dozen of those words you just flung at me. What's that word 'joak,' 'jwok'? What's that all about? What is it you trying to say? You said that four times, that 'jwok,' 'jwak.' What is that?" Jack realized he'd connected slightly with the old alien and used his thumbs to point at himself while saying his name several times again for the alien. "That your name, you trying to tell me that's what you go by for a name, that it's Jwak, Jwaka, something like that?" Jack repeated the gesture and his name again several times but more slowly so that the alien could pick up on it properly. "OK, Ja-ak, that's what we'll call you, then, if you say that's your name. Sounds pretty strange to me. Can't imagine what language that would have come from. Don't really sound like nothing I ever heard anywhere before." The old alien Jattar started to ramble on.

The area they were in now was mostly hewn directly out of bedrock. The doors and corridors were all framed out at the ends, but they were basically in a cave that was fairly dank and only halfway lit by occasional fixtures along the way. They went down a hallway and into another room that was apparently a supply room for miners' clothing and equipment. The old alien picked Jack out some previously used heavy-duty work coveralls that looked like they might fit. He also got Jack a strap-on helmet with a light attached to the top of it. The light was pretty straightforward with an on-off switch, an intensity control, and a beam width adjustment. It was compact and bright, but Jack couldn't tell what the power source was for it.

The helmet didn't fit too well, but it was functional. It was apparently made for something with a head that was shaped differently than a human's. It was a little too long in the back and too narrow in the front, but it would do. He tried the coveralls on over his blue NASA flight suit. They were a little baggy and also a bit short in length coming just to the top of his flight boots. The old alien released Jack's wrist restraints while Jack put on his coveralls but reengaged them as soon as Jack was suited up. Jack started making noises of protest and thought it worth throwing in a couple of intelligible words to convey the logic of how was he supposed to work with his wrists restrained. "Work, no, how," with a few mystery words included seemed to convince the old alien that it didn't make much sense to have a worker constrained.

"All right, OK," grumbled the old alien, "but if you go and try something, I'll slap 'em back on faster than you can blink your funny-looking round eyes." So they reached an agreement on the wrist restraints for now, and Jack was happy to be able to move his arms freely again.

Jack appreciated the fact that Zshutana had all his clothing cleaned, but he didn't know how long it would last in this environment. Jack spent a few minutes getting the old alien to help him learn the names of his issued equipment. Whenever the alien told him what the items were, Jack would throw back a few fabricated words and then slowly "catch on" to what Jattar was telling him, and then he would "learn" what the item was called. This kept the old alien entertained for half an hour, or horun, while Jack tried to recon all the different things in the room in case there was something that he might use later for whatever plan he came up with. He didn't see any weapons, but there were numerous tools and other items that he could possibly utilize if you had to.

Grabbing a helmet and dark vision goggles for himself, the old alien said, "Come on now, you Ja-ak, we need to get you down on a zibur drill rig and see if I can teach you how to not kill yourself on it. It is pretty simple as long as you don't undercut yourself into a loose fracture zone. Even those stupid Zumarans can run them, but they're just not smart enough to keep from burying themselves."

Old Jattar rattled on as they headed down a wider corridor toward the operating section of the mine.

Jack could hear heavy machinery working around them in several different directions. They passed dozens of other various aliens going in the opposite direction, all of which Jack could tell were obviously miners by their similar outfits. They came to a central cavern about eight hundred feet across. The far side of it had a conveyor with ore hoppers that were carrying bucket loads of grayish-green ore diagonally then upward toward the surface. The conveyor with its hoppers originated in a two-hundred-foot wide pit, which was being continuously filled by loaders that periodically appeared from eight different tunnel entrances around the cavern perimeter. "Those are the donda loaders," Jattar said to Jack. "They'll bring the ore you mine to the conveyor pit, where it will then be brought to the surface for processing and refining or shipping. You have to be careful and keep your light on anytime you're in this loading pit area or any of the mine pit tunnels. The donda loaders don't use drivers and are self-piloted. When your light is on, it sends a signal that they can usually recognize, and they will avoid you. But you have to be careful because now and then, their sensors get dirty and they can't pick up on you real good. Do you know what I speak of? Do you know any of this that I'm saying to you?" the old alien asked.

Again, Jack was cautious with his answer. "Light, on, yes," then some gibberish words, "danger, watch things," then some more incoherent words to simulate a poorly functioning translator.

That seemed to convince Jattar that Jack had some fair level of understanding of what he was trying to explain to him. "Good, then. Now follow me," said Jattar. "Make sure your light is on and stay watchful. The light is more so others can see you. You may have to wear the dark vision goggles where the mine is not lit. The side corridors are not lit, but the zibur rigs will have their own lighting. There are plenty of things that'll get you killed down here. The most likely would be your own stupidity." Jack was sure that was close to the truth, as he was sure that was probably the case in any mine or other hazardous occupation.

They worked their way around the perimeter of the loading area then back toward one of the mining tunnels. Jattar said, "There may be several active side drifts in any one of these main shafts, but there will only be one donda loader working each main shaft. Wait till you see the donda loader enter or leave the shaft so you know where it is and can get out of the way just in case it doesn't spot you. You understanding any of this?" asked the old alien again.

"This one, one shaft, one donda, watch for," replied Jack with the necessary babble thrown in for effect.

"That's right," replied Jattar. "I think you're starting to get it some. We'll go down this second shaft because there is no active drilling and no donda hauling the ore out right now." As they entered the dark mine shaft, the old alien said, "Your dark vision will adjust automatically to maintain the brightness level that it's set on so it will look like daylight for you." The night vision goggles, when Jack tried them, were excellent. They showed everything in high-res color with a very slight pinkish glow with excellent contrast and visual acuity. They were much better and weighed less than the ones he'd used in the military back on Earth.

"Right up here is the first side drift in this shaft where the zibur drill you'll be riding is staged." They went about two hundred feet down a smaller side shaft to where a large industrial machine was parked. It was about the size of a fairly large bulldozer and looked similar in that it had tracks on both sides and an overhead hard canopy above the driver's seat. It had a push blade on the back that was parked in an up position and some type of tubular rotary gears between the treads. Jattar pointed at the blade and the gears between the tracks and explained that after the sonic drills on the front of the machine excavated the ore, it would feed to the back of the machine until it piled up, and then you pushed it with the blade to the main shaft where the donda loader would take it to the hopper pit. Jattar showed Jack how to board the machine between the blade and the driver's seat.

They climbed up on the zibur drill machine, and Jattar sat down in the driver's seat and motioned Jack to sit on the frame next to him. "Put your hand on this spot here, and we will program all the zibur drills for your access so that you can use any that you might be assigned to." The console in front of Jattar came to life in various colors, and Jack put his hand on a red-and-blue-lit circle where the old alien pointed. "Now just hold it there for a few seconds until I tell you good, and we will have these zibur drills programmed for you," said Jattar.

The old alien then spent about twenty minutes going over all the controls of the zibur drill rig. Jack wasn't sure how it was powered, but when the old alien switched the main power on, the machine came to life and had a continuous light vibration and a loud hum. A large 3-D holo display came to life in front of the driver, which showed an enhanced view of the area in front of the drill rig. Playing along with the language issues, Jack threw in what he thought was the right amount of proper responses along with the requisite nonsensical babble. The zibur drill was essentially a targetable sonic drilling rig that used fourteen very high-frequency, high-powered sonic wave emitters to break the rock in front of the machine into fairly consistent-sized ore pieces that then fed out the back of the machine as it worked its way forward. Once a mass of ore about half the size of the zibur drill rig was amassed behind the machine, the operator would then push the ore out the side drift to the main shaft, where the donda loader would then scoop it up and transport it to the hopper pit.

Jattar explained to Jack, "What we are looking here for is the blue and gray veins. That is the Burun-Rioc ore. There's quite a bit of it spread around in this area, but it's mostly small spindly veins. Through the display, you can see how the veins stand out against the background rock. So we're always looking for a heavier vein, but if you can't find none, then the smaller ones will do. Both the zibur and the donda will measure pretty good estimates of how much Burun-Rioc ore you dig by the density of the ore to its volume ratio.

"The more Burun-Rioc you can mine, the higher bonus you should get at the end of the moondat. But, well, you're a conscript, so you won't actually get the bonus you tally up, but Cahooshek will get it for you. You gotta be extra careful when you're digging because there can be fracture lines in the rock above that can break off and fall down on the zibur rig. Mostly they're small and won't hurt you, but some can be big enough to crush your whole rig. That's what happened to the last conscript 'cause he wasn't paying enough attention and he got his self too far into a fracture zone, and it collapsed down on him. If you find a fracture zone, just back off and hit it with the zibur waves from a distance until it comes down, and then you can break it up with your rig then. The display will show you the fracture zones ahead of you with the red line showing their location. The problem is it won't really show you anything overhead too good, so you have to watch for those yourself.

"Now hold on and I'll show you how it's done. Then you can take a try at it. Are you getting what I'm telling you here?" asked Jattar.

"Yes," Jack replied, "rock, drive, fall, back push, rock, crack rock, fall, blue rock, thick good," with a fair amount of good gibberish thrown in just keep up the pretense. He was actually looking forward to operating this alien piece of machinery for various reasons. Being a machine operator and basically a mechanical gearhead, it was always fun to get a hold of a new piece of machinery. It would also help him start to learn the basic functions of these alien vehicles. Having gone from the highly complex space shuttle launch to doing nothing but being in custody or hiding for a week, he was itching to get his hands on something that he could control and manipulate again.

"OK, then, I think you are getting it at least from an understanding point," said Jattar. "Whether you can actually run this rig, we'll find out in a few mentus. One thing you got to do every time is engage this sonic barrier switch. This gives you an active counter-frequency barrier to the sonic pulses of the zibur drill. Just make sure your arms and legs and stuff are all inside before you engage it, or you'll get a real nasty deep abrasion on anything it touches. The sonic waves will distort your view outside the cab of the rig, but you'll still be able to see using the display because it's stabilized. You gotta stop about every four or five mentus and check for overhead fracture zones. OK, I'm engaging the sonic barrier and then the zibur rig, so hold on. Oh, and the sonic drills shouldn't start if the barrier isn't on, but you never know when the safety cutout could fail. You don't want to operate the rig with the sonic barrier off. If the waves reflected back just at the wrong angle without the barrier on, it could do some serious damage to your body, like basically scrambling it."

Jattar switched on the sonic barrier, and immediately, a hazy semiopaque wall appeared all around the cab of the drill rig. It gave off a high-pitched, undulating buzz that seemed to penetrate the whole body from every direction. It wasn't painful, but it put your whole body into a tense feeling of slight sensory overload. Jattar said, "It's not real pleasant when you run the barrier, but it would be a whole lot more unpleasant if you didn't turn it on. Like I said, there's a lockout to prevent you from running the zibur rig before you engage the barrier, but it might not always work, and you wouldn't know until you got hit by the zibur waves and had your ears, eyes, and everything else blown out. So just don't do that," said Jattar. Jack thought that if you had to spend the whole day wired up like this, you would feel more than just totally wiped by the end of the day. Jattar said, "Use the two foot pedals to advance and reverse as well as to turn in either direction. Use this guidance control stick to target the ore-bearing rock with the zibur waves. You can vary the power output of the rig and control how big the ore pieces end up by how long and how wide you hit them with the zibur waves. You don't want 'em too small or you'll just be pushing dust, and if they're too big, they won't go under the zibur rig.

"I think you're gettin' this better than you're letting on or the translator's being able to decode. I can tell by the way you are takin' it all in," said the old alien. Jattar did a series of demonstrations and showed Jack the various ways to approach and mine the ore as well as push it out to the donda loaders. It was pretty simple, so in short order, Jattar let Jack have a try at it. Jack pretty much mastered it in a few minutes. It wasn't a very fast process. It mined the ore-bearing rock at about one foot per minute. It was fast enough, though, that you had to push a load out about every six to eight minutes. "You seem to have a pretty good understanding of it," Jattar said to Jack. "Just make sure you watch for those overhead fracture lines. You might come across one or maybe two a daiyus. Just back up and hit them from a distance until they drop and then bust 'em up and push them out. I'll hop off now and check back in a couple of horuns. That'll be the end of this shift, and I'll take you back to the conzone, then. Just be careful and don't hurt yourself."

Jack let Jattar off the rig and went back to mining as soon as he left. It was a far cry from flying *Victory* or an F-35, but at least he wasn't sitting around twiddling his thumbs. The sonic barrier was unpleasant, but you could somewhat tune it out if you kept busy working. Jack plugged away for most of two horuns. This was better than being incarcerated, but he was certain he wasn't planning on making a career out of mining.

He was also certain that he wouldn't be making any escape attempt on the zibur mining rig with a travel speed of one to two feet per minute while excavating ore. Still, he was grateful, since things could have been worse. He survived *Victory's* crash and the rest of the crew's fate, and he was sure he'd have some valid options sometime soon as far as altering his current fate. It was just a matter of time, planning, and maybe a little luck. Jattar returned a short while later to let Jack know that he was at the end of the shift. Jattar said, "You tallied up a good ore tonnage for this short period, especially for a novice operator. Cahooshek will be pleased that his prospects for you to earn back your conscript price will be good. Come with me now and we will get you signed in with the rest of the mining conscripts."

Jack replied with the requisite babble thrown in, "Go, now, food, eat, sleep."

"Yes, I guess you may be hungry. We will go get some food for you, and I will check you into the conscript detention zone. You will be living there with the other conscripts and the inmate convicts."

As they left the side drift and then the main shaft and entered the hopper cavern, Jack saw about eighty or so miners heading to the main entrance tunnel. It was hard to tell, but it looked like there were maybe six or eight types of aliens all dressed in some sort of mining outfits. They soon passed an equal number of miners heading back into the active mine area. Jack noticed a few of both groups looking at him and commenting to their fellow miners. He realized he was a bit unique in overall appearance compared to all the other aliens and wondered if maybe they had never seen anyone that looked quite like him. He was starting to realize what it might be like to be a standalone minority in a crowd that had never seen his kind before. He wasn't uncomfortable, but it did make him conscious of the fact that he might have some issues with this part of the equation.

Jack and Jattar followed the main group a couple of hundred mu-uts through three different tunnels where the group split about 60 percent to the left and the rest with Jack and Jattar to the right. Jattar said, "Those are the contract miners that are going to their own quarters, and you and the rest of the cons must stay inside the conscript and convict detention zone that we call the conzone. This part of the mine is inside of the conzone, but some contract operators work here."

Just past where the two groups split on the contract side, there was a security gate that was manned by some sort of guards in black-and-blue uniforms. They were carrying some type of metal wand about three feet in length that appeared to have some type of mechanical or electrical controls on one end along with a handle. They mostly just stood there and held the wands in front of them and briefly scanned each contract miner as they exited the gated area. Farther down the corridor, at a small guard shack, Jattar checked in with a guard attendant and said, "This is Cahooshek's new conscript number 2641. You should have already got the required handling data for him with the selected restrictions that are set for him. I will take him in and get him set up in the conzone. Do you have a room for him yet?"

"Yes," replied the guard. "Here is his meal badge, and he is assigned to berthing room four. You can pick up his bedding and other supplies at the supply room on the way in."

"Well, we will go on in, then. Come with me now," the old alien said to Jack.

They proceeded past another security gate where the guards decided to stop Jack and give him a little more scrutiny with a more thorough ten-second wand screening. Jack returned the favor by evaluating them against the typical rent-a-cop Earth standard and gave them about a four out of ten on the potential competency scale.

Having listened to the whole exchange between Jattar and the attendant guard, Jack was trying to estimate what his situation would be like in here in this conscript and potentially criminal population area. They stopped at a small room on the way where he was issued some bedding, toiletries, and a set of work clothes that weren't too unlike his NASA flight suit except they were a drab brownish green. He was able to get a handheld razor as well as other common items like a small brush with a handle on it that approximated a toothbrush as well as a container that could possibly be some sort of tooth powder or maybe just general purpose soap. Zshutana had a razor in her shower, and a lot, if not most, of the aliens appeared to have various degrees of bodily hair of varying textures and colors. Many appeared to be fairly well groomed, while a few others were somewhat unkept and scruffy looking. He guessed that shaving and grooming must be a standard practice in many of the alien cultures. Jack then made the obligatory noises to Jattar as he queried him about his situation. "Food, eat, sleep?" Jack asked, as if his chief concerns were simply food and sleep.

After gathering the bedding and toiletries, Jack and Jattar then proceeded through a common area with several various aliens sitting around or gathered in small groups. They went down another corridor and then into the second room on the right of the main corridor. The room had twelve elevated beds around the perimeter against the wall. Next to the beds were a type of storage cabinet or dresser and another short vertical cabinet. In the center of the room were four small tables and some chairs. There was one alien by one of the bed and dresser combinations that was just finishing changing its clothes. Jattar said to Jack, "This will be your berthing quarters where you will sleep. All the miners in here will be on your same mining shift. This way, all that are in this room can work, eat, and sleep at the same time. Other shifts will be in the other berthing quarters. The fifth berth over there will be yours. The others probably went to eat while we were getting your bed makings. Put your things by your berth, and I will take you to the conzone miner's rations hall. Take this conscript meal badge because you will need it anytime you get food at the rations hall."

Jack replied, "Card, eat, things here, stay."

Jattar then said to the other alien that was about to leave the room, "Who are you, and where are the others? Have they already left to eat?"

The alien, which had a slight build and was about five and a half feet tall with very light bluish-colored skin and a narrow head with a slightly wider jaw structure, replied, "I am Junot of Riina, 1397. The others have gone to eat their night meal, and I am going there now. Aren't you Jattar, the equipment overseer?"

Jattar replied, "Yes, and this is the new Varaci conscript that goes by Jua-ak, number 2641. If you are going to the rations hall now, please proceed and we will follow you."

"Yes, I was leaving now, but I, uh, wasn't going to the rations hall. I was going . . ." The alien conscript started to reply.

"I want to go the rations hall," said Jattar. "You will take us."

"Uh, well, yes, I will take you to the rations hall if you wish," replied Junot. Jack dropped his things off at his assigned berth, and they proceeded to follow this Junot alien to the rations hall where Jack hoped that his meal badge would get him something palatable to eat.

As they left the berth room, Jattar said to Jack, "There are five other berthing rooms in this section and four other sections. There are two berth rooms for each ten-horun shift. The toilet and washing chamber is at the far end of the corridor."

They went back the way they originally came from the berthing chambers and then down another corridor past some other rooms and facilities until they finally came to the entrance of the rations hall. The rations hall consisted of a large cafeteria-style facility not unlike something you might find on Earth where they served institutionalized food. There were about two hundred or more patrons sitting and eating at about thirty long tables or waiting in line to be served. Jattar said to the conscript Junot, "I will leave now. You will take this new conscript, Jua-ak, 2641, and explain to him the ways and the rules of living in the conscript zone and help him get through the eating and other procedures here. You must be diligent because his translator does not work well with his Varaci language for some reason. He is fairly limited in his communication abilities, so you may have to explain how things work while using more than just speaking."

Junot replied, "I am not sure. I am very busy, and I don't believe I will have time for this."

"You will make time," replied Jattar, "or I will report to Cahooshek that you were uncooperative and not helpful to Cahooshek's valuable new conscript. I'm sure he would be able to find a reason to have another six moondats added to your conscription period for your lack of cooperation. So now, Junot, 1397, do you think will be able to find time in your real busy schedule to help out our good Cahooshek?"

"Yes, yes, absolutely yes," replied Junot. "I didn't realize this was one of Cahooshek's conscripts. I would be more than happy, qua-quite thrilled to help in whatever way I can to, uh, help this Ja-ak get adjusted to the conscript system."

"Good," said Jattar. "I knew you'd be a good choice to leave Cahooshek's new conscript with. Now don't disappoint me none and take real good care of Jua-ak, 2641. I will be back later to check on him."

"Yes, yes, I will take good care of him," replied Junot. "When will you be back to check on him?"

Jattar replied, "I'll be back when I get back. In the meantime, you will take extra good care of Cahooshek's prized new conscript."

"Yes, yes, I will," replied Junot.

Jattar left Jack with his new companion and left the rations hall for his own domain. Junot started in. "Well, I guess I'm in charge of you from now on. You'll have to do what I tell you or Cahooshek won't be pleased."

Jack already didn't like this little weasel of an alien and was fairly certain that the reason it wasn't with the rest of the miners was that they didn't want its company. He thought about reading this little wiener the riot act, but he knew it would probably get back to the others how much he actually understood through his translator, thanks to Zshutana's help. Instead, he just looked down at the pathetic little conscript and said in an intimidating voice, "Jack food now, you take."

With Jack still staring him down, the little alien stammered, "Uh, ye-yes, uh, the food is, uh, served over here in the food line. We can, uh, go, uh, get some now. Uh, you'll, uh, of course, need your meal badge, OK?"

They both grabbed some trays at the front of the line after showing their meal badges to an attendant. The serving line wasn't too long. There wasn't much variety, although what was there didn't look too bad and smelled halfway decent.

They were handed platefuls of an assortment of different fare that probably could have passed for the food at some of the institutionalized cafeterias on Earth. Jack said to Junot, "Only food, this?" with a couple of stray nonsense words thrown in.

"Uh, yes," replied Junot, "this rations hall food is for conscripts and the convicts that are indentured or incarcerated. The conscripts and the convicts can only eat here, but the contract miners and other workers can eat anywhere they want. They have other places around the mines where you can buy other food and a lot of other things too. I've never been there, but some other conscripts have told me about it. The contract miners can eat here if they want, but I've never really see them here much. Every once in a while, some new ones might come by just see what they serve here, but that's about it. Is your translator working? Do you understand what I just answered you?" Junot asked Jack.

Jack replied, "Hmmmfp, conscripts, convicts only here."

"Yes, that's it," replied Junot.

They sat down to eat their institutional meals at one of the tables with a couple of other conscripts, or possibly convicts, thought Jack. Jack could tell that Junot wasn't very comfortable as he watched the little alien's eyes dart around the room with nervous anxiety. From a few tables away, three of the resident miners got up and approached Jack's table.

"Who's your new friend there, Junot?" said one of the trio.

"Yeah, who's your new friend, Junot? We didn't think you had any friends. Maybe you bought yourself a mail-order friend so you'd have someone to talk to," said one of the other miners.

Junot stammered, "Th-this is, is Cahoo-Cahooshek's, Jattar the overseer—I mean, it's his, Cahooshek's, new conscript. They put me in charge of him. It's my job to get him trained to the conscript system so he knows what he's doing. Uh, uh, his translator doesn't work too well, so he can't speak very good," said Junot, while wondering if he should have mentioned that.

The first miner said, "So he can't speak too good. Why is that? Maybe he's not too smart, or maybe he got stuck in orbit for a while without air."

They all laughed for half a minute like it was the funniest thing they'd ever heard. Jack just took it all in as if he didn't understand much of what they were saying. He actually had to stifle a smile because they didn't know how close to the truth they'd actually come as far as their lack-of-air-in-orbit joke.

The alien miners were a type that Jack had previously seen, but the third one that hadn't spoken was considerably different. It had a bluish and red tint to its skin and was covered in short black hair with two bare stripes about two inches wide on either side of a four-inch Mohawk. It was short bodied and barrel chested but had excessively long arms and legs for its body dimensions. It looked like it could be fairly strong and fairly fast at the same time. It almost looked like it was designed by a committee that was trying to get too many positive attributes out of a single design but failed overall in the aesthetics department.

"It, he, doesn't speak good b-because he's, it's a Varaci," blurted Junot.

The third alien now spoke up. "I've spoken to a Varaci before, once a long time ago. I didn't have any trouble speaking to it. They aren't common around here in this sector, but their language is in the core neural cortex. It should be able to speak unless it translator is broken. How do you know it's a Varaci?" the miner probed.

"That's, that's what Jattar told me," stammered Junot. "It's—I mean, he's Cahooshek's conscript. Cahooshek told Jattar that he's a Varaci. I guess that's what—I mean, I guess that would mean that he's a Varaci."

"Well, it does look like the several Varaci I've seen, but it doesn't quite appear to be nearly as devious looking. Its eyes are different, and it's a bit larger. Maybe it's a defective Varaci of some sort," the third miner said while watching Jack to see if it could get a response. Jack just looked at the third miner and gave it a half smile without any other reaction. Jack thought he would have to be a little more wary of this one, as he could tell it was feeling him out.

The first miner said, "Well, Junot, we have to be going, but maybe we'll see you around the common area later. We're sure you're going to do a really good job training this conscript for Cahooshek. We just hope nothing bad happens to him while he's in your care. I'm sure old Cahooshek wouldn't be too pleased if something bad happened to his new conscript while you were in charge of him."

The three miners busted out snorting and laughing and headed out the entrance to the rations hall. Little Junot seemed fairly relieved as they left, although his eyes continued to dart around the hall as if there might be more anxiety issues lurking nearby. Just for fun, Jack prodded him a bit. "Friends of yours, Junot?" he asked.

"No, no, uh, yes, no, miners, they are convicts, but they are on parole. They are working off the rest their debt now that they are out of prison. They don't, they don't treat me nice. They were prisoners for robbing and beating someone."

As he said that, Junot realized that he didn't know why Jack was a conscript. He knew Jack wasn't a convict, but he also knew you could get conscripted for just about any reason. "What are, what, why are you a conscript?" stammered Junot.

"Relax," said Jack. "I haven't beaten anybody since my last stand-up sparring match, and that was a couple of yenets ago." A slight look of fear flashed across Junot's face. "Seriously," said Jack, "I was conscripted because I supposedly stole passage on a star freighter to get to this lovely planet Nishda."

"What do you mean *supposedly*?" asked Junot.

"Forget it," said Jack. "Just assume I was a stowaway and got caught. Maybe I'll tell you more about it some other time. So now, what do we do after we've finished our gourmet dinner, or night meal as you call it? Are there any other mandatory formations we're required to attend?" he asked Junot.

"Mandatory formations?" queried Junot.

Jack replied, "Is there anything else we have to do? Are we free to wander around? What time does our next shift start? I'm about ready to call it quits. I've been up for probably twenty-four horuns. Can I go back to my berth bunk and hit the rack?" said Jack tiredly.

"Uh, yes, there's no other requirements, but most of the others go to the gaming room in the common area or maybe the, uh, well, I'll tell you later about that," said Junot.

"OK," said Jack. "So what do you normally do after the rations hall?"

"I, uh, try to go someplace where it's mostly quiet, maybe not too many others around. I kind of like it mostly quiet, you know," replied Junot.

"Well, not really," replied Jack, "but I think I understand what you're trying to tell me." He was starting to have a little pity on this strange little conscript of an alien who was obviously a bit of an outcast and probably spent most of his time hiding in fear from the other conscripts and convicts in the mining operation.

"Wait, wait," gasped Junot. "You are speaking good to me now. How are you speaking good now?" he said, somewhat baffled.

Oh, crap, thought Jack, he'd just blown his own cover. It was a lot harder to maintain than he'd thought, especially if you're totally exhausted from lack of sleep and forgot for a second that your translator isn't supposed to work. *I guess that's why I'm just a science geek and airplane driver instead of some secret espionage agent,* thought Jack.

"All right," he said to Junot in a low voice, "I can speak and understand quite well through my translator now, but I couldn't before. I don't want Jattar or Cahooshek to know that I can, though. It wouldn't matter much as far as I'm concerned, but it might cause problems for someone else I know that I don't want to get hurt. Do you understand what I mean?" said Jack.

"What? No, I don't exactly. What, what do you mean?" stammered Junot.

"What I mean," said Jack, "is that you are the only one that knows how well I can speak, and I don't want anyone else to know that unless I decide so. What I'm saying is if my friend got hurt because someone let it be known that I'm fairly fluent that it wouldn't be a very good thing for that person that divulged my secret. Now do you understand what I'm saying?" asked Jack.

"I, I, yes, I, I und-understand," croaked Junot.

"Now, relax," said Jack. "I have no desire to harm you in any way. In fact, I think you might be helpful to me because I think you see a lot of what's going on around here in the mine operations. So maybe you can be helpful to me when I need to know things but don't want to have to ask others because, well, you know, I can't speak very well because my translator doesn't work with my mystery language. Do you think we could be friends and that you could be helpful to me?" he said to Junot.

"Yes, I, yes," replied Junot in a relieved voice, "I could help you with that, and I'm really good at keeping secrets—I mean, who would I tell anyway?" replied Junot. Then Junot thought to himself, *He said friends. I've never had a friend down here before. It would be good to have a friend.*

Jack didn't like having it be this harsh with him, but his own life and possibly Zshutana's might be at risk, so he had to make sure there wasn't any possible consequences of his own blunder that he'd just made by revealing his actual fluency capability. "All right," said Jack, "I'll trust you on this, but please don't let me down. Now let's go somewhere more private." They left the rations hall and headed back toward the berthing chamber. They went back to the berthing quarters, and no one else was back yet.

They sat at a table, and Jack thought about how to proceed. Jack said, "So tell me, why are you a conscript here, Junot? What did you do to earn your place among our fellow conscript miners?"

"Well, I'm, I am not. Well, I didn't do anything, really. I'm not—"

"Stop," said Jack, "don't try to lie or hide anything. Just tell me the truth and we'll get along just fine. But lie to me or do something that gets my friend hurt, and you won't like the payback."

Junot was silent for a minute and then thought, *There was that word again, "friend," That sure sounded uplifting. Imagine having a friend.* He hadn't even thought about that; the concept of having a friend in the mine just hadn't occurred to him. "I, I," he said, "I'm not, not really a conscript. I'm a, I'm a, actually, I'm a convict," he tried to say with a little bit of bravado to make himself sound more important.

"A convict," said Jack with a bit of skepticism. "For some reason, you just don't seem the type. Come on, Junot, now level with me and tell me the truth."

"It's true. I am a convict, and I'm working off my debt. I have five more yenets before I'm eligible for parole and maybe two years of work parole to get back to any sort of job outside," said Junot with a dejected look.

"OK," said Jack. "So tell me how you ended up as a convict in a mining operation paying off your debt."

"Well, I, uh," stammered Junot.

"Come on," said Jack, "just tell me."

"I was working for the Wanana import inspector's office as an electronics and security programming technician."

"Now, wait," said Jack. "What's Wanana?"

Junot replied, "Well, you know, Wanana is the main city on this side of the planet. It's where you or anyone had to come in from when you came from orbit, unless you came from Se-ahlaalu. Wanana and Se-ahlaalu are the two main cities on the planet. Se-ahlaalu is almost halfway around the planet on the other side. Well, uh, anyway, I was maintaining and updating all their security monitoring systems. That's what I trained to do. I was really quite good at it too. I found out that they were bypassing most of the monitoring protocols on certain companies' inspection requirements and reports. They told me not to worry about it. Then they started making me change the automatic reporting protocols to report that all the bypassed companies were actually in compliance and inspected. I didn't want to do it, but they told me I had to, and if I didn't, they might hurt me or have me arrested. Well, what they were doing was too obvious and too much. They got caught by the Alliance inspectors team on a routine inspection. That only happens maybe about once every five yenets, if even that often. They pointed to me like I was the one that was running the whole thing. I was just doing what they made me do. The only proof of things they had were my inputs and bypass protocols that had been changed from the original ones.

"They said I was working with some off Nishda smugglers that I never even heard of and had done it all on my own. I tried to tell the Alliance inspectors, but they just left it in the hands of the local trade enforcement division, and they convicted me of import rule violations and tampering with government monitoring systems and sent me here for seven yenets. I wouldn't have done any of that stuff if they hadn't made me. I didn't want to get in trouble for anything like that. You don't think I would have done that, do you?" the little alien whined.

"I don't know," said Jack. "It doesn't sound like it by the way you've explained it, so I guess I'll have to take your word for it."

"You will," said Junot, "you would believe me about what I've told you?"

"Well, yes," said Jack. "Is there any reason that I shouldn't?"

"No," said Junot, "no, it's just that people don't believe me much since I've been down here. They used to before. There was never any problem before, but not now."

"OK," said Jack, "I believe you. It all sounds plausible and logical. Now tell me how you ended up in the mining operation. What's a little guy like you doing running a zibur rig in this sort of operation?"

"Oh, I don't run the zibur rigs—I mean, I can, and I have some, but mostly I keep them running, especially the electrics and programming, updates, reboots, and that sort of thing. I'm a lot cheaper and probably better than a contract tech repair specialist, so that's where I ended up after they found out what I do. I think the ones that sent me here hoped I might get killed running the rigs down here, but the mine bosses found out how good I was with electrics and programming, so here I am. The less downtime there is, the more credits they can pocket in production bonuses, so I'm helpful to them in that way. That's kind of one of the reasons that some of the miners don't like me, though. They don't get any downtime because of mechanical failures because I keep the rigs running so well. The ones that don't like to work too much don't like that because there's hardly any maintenance downtime.

"Well, uh, well, what about you, Jack? You said you supposedly stole passage here. Did you do that or didn't you?" asked Junot.

"No," said Jack, "I didn't, but it's a long story, and I'll tell you about it another time. Right now, I'm going to call it quits and hit the hay. It's been a long wenek and a long daiyus, and tomorrow, I guess I'll be banging away on a zibur rig all daiyus, so I'd better catch up on some z's."

"What do you mean *hay* and z's?" asked Junot.

"I'll tell you about that later also," said Jack. "Now, how do we know when it's time to get up and get going for the next shift? What's the routine here in the morning?"

Junot replied, "The horn will sound at 2100 horun. Then we have two horuns to be ready and eat and then report for our mine shift at 2300 horun."

Junot continued to explain to Jack how the mine shift operation worked and how the schedule was set up. Jack learned that the Nishdan daiyus were twenty-eight horuns with eight-daiyus weneks and eighty-eight weneks in a yenet but only eleven moondats with sixty-four daiyus. There's a total of 704 daiyus in a yenet, or Nishdan year. For some reason, Jack's translator wouldn't convert time units into the correct English translation. Maybe it was because the units weren't the same, so it couldn't convert them into a unit that didn't exist in English. If this was correct, then the Nishdan yenet was almost two Earth years long. That would mean that his conscript time, or Junot's Nishda convict time, was nearly double that in Earth years. The thought of that didn't sit too well with him.

Zshutana had said she had been here nearly thirty yenets, or Nishdan years, and had come here when she was fifteen. That would make her forty-five yenets old or not quite double that in Earth years. So she had to be somewhere around ninety Earth years old. That was impossible, thought Jack, or maybe some sort of miracle. If he would've had to guess, he would've said that she didn't look a daiyus over twenty-five, at least by Earth appearances. That was a bit mind-boggling; he'd have to come back to that later. He also learned that the labor week consisted of seven days, or daiyus, on and then one daiyus off. Running one of those zibur rigs for seven long daiyus straight was going to be a pretty serious beating even for somebody in as good of physical condition as Jack. Jack lay there trying to compute the vagaries of all the new information he'd gathered, but he couldn't stay awake, so he finally gave up and drifted off to sleep. He woke up a couple of times when he heard others come in and go to bed, but no one bothered him, so he fell right back into a hard sleep.

The next thing he knew, Jack woke to the short repeating wail of an ascending horn. Fortunately, it wasn't too loud and only lasted about twenty seconds. He rolled over and noticed the room was dimly lit. He could just make out that others were starting to stir in their bunks. He watched for a few minutes to see what the routine was going to be in the mornings. Within a few minutes, about half the miners had wandered out, and the remaining ones were in the process of starting to do the same. Jack dressed in the mine worker's outfit he had been issued. This would keep his NASA flight suit from getting worn out so fast and also keep him from standing out in the crowd so much. Junot was suddenly there ready to help Jack with his mining operation familiarization.

"So what's the morning routine here?" Jack whispered to Junot.

Junot replied, "Some of the miners will go get their morning food first and then come back here and clean up, while some will do this in the opposite order. I prefer to eat first then come back. There will be less workers that way. But we can do it whichever way you want," the little alien said to Jack.

"We'll just do it whichever way you prefer," Jack said to him.

With a look of relief, Junot said, "Oh, good, I think that's the best choice." Jack kind of got the feeling that there might be some miners or others that Junot wished to avoid. He was all right with that, since he wished to maintain a low profile anyway, at least for now.

First one and then another of the other miners came over to where Jack and Junot were talking. The first one was a big bruiser about six feet four of a type Jack might have seen in the mine previously. It held out his hand to Jack and said, "I am Cherga, now a mine convict from Zanaii. I am hactra operator. Who are you, new berther?"

This miner seemed straightforward and honest, thought Jack, at least on the surface. He shook the big miners hand and replied, "Jack Spartan, Jack zibur drive," wondering how long he should keep up the bad translator charade. He decided to hold on to that for a while so as to protect Zshutana. Since he didn't actually have to learn the language, he could always feign that the translator became fully functional at any time.

Junot piped up, "His translator doesn't function very well, so I have been assigned to help him learn his work duties and get adapted to the mining operations."

The second miner, who was shorter and slighter than Cherga, said, "What? You, our little mine snirt, is in charge of helping out a new conscript, or is it convict? We must give all credit where it is worthy."

"Go easy on our little insect friend," said Cherga. "If it weren't for him, our poor bosses would never get any bonuses, and we would have to take an extra daiyus off once in a while. What would we do with all our spare time down here in this hole of a mine? It's not like I would be out spending a daiyus on the water catching fish with my brother's son. I haven't seen the sun in over two yenets since coming here. So we might as well work and get it over with. Who knows, maybe they will reduce our sentences if we make so much good ore every day," he said with a huge snorting laugh.

"I only do what I have to do to survive here too," griped Junot. "What else would you have me do? They tell me to fix and maintain the rigs, so that is what I do, just like you mine the ore because that is your job."

"Well, maybe you could just not be such an expert maintainer all the time," snorted Cherga. "Maybe we would all get a half extra daiyus off every now and then. Do not worry, it will all work out in the end. Our only goal is to get out of here someday. Well, we are going for food now. See you there, new convict Jack—I mean, conscript," huffed Cherga.

Jack and Junot left for the rations hall a few mentus later. At the rations hall, they had a breakfast of some new mystery items Jack hadn't seen before. It wasn't anything he'd actually order at a restaurant, but it was edible. *Maybe they'll have biscuits and gravy with hash browns and grits tomorrow,* he mused. They sat at a table with several other inmates that were either conscripts or convicts. Jack wasn't really sure how or why it mattered one way or the other how you were designated unless it was some sort of a status issue.

The conversation was sparse, especially with Jack's "translator-induced" speech impediment. He did manage to allow them to deduce that he was a Varaci conscript assigned to a zibur rig and that Junot was assisting with his indoctrination as a mine worker. As they left, Junot had them go through a second line near the exit that was piled with boxed meals to go. He explained to Jack that he could take this with him on his shift and eat whenever he wanted. As long as he met the basic quota of 120 tons per daiyus, he wouldn't be penalized. The bad part was you didn't have an actual tally of your ore load until the donda loaders tallied it at the end of the daiyus. You could estimate it, though, by using two tons a push to the donda or one ton per drill run. The zibur had its own estimate, but that could be off by as much as 20 or 30 percent from the donda, which was the official reading. For some reason, the zibur drill rigs always read higher than the donda loaders at the end of the daiyus.

They headed back to the berth zone and cleaned up a bit before heading out. Junot told Jack they could clean up in the washing room either in the morning or at night as long as you started and ended your shift on time. Jack headed out when the other miners did, and Junot headed to his assigned rounds maintaining and repairing any rigs that were in need from the last shift. Jack found his rig and had it up and running in a few minutes. About five hours or halfway through his shift, Jack added up his pushes and estimated that he was a good 20 percent ahead of schedule. He took a break and wolfed down his mid meal of mystery box food, which consisted of some sort of small blue fruits and a red-and-green stalk-shaped vegetable item and a lump of meat stuff. It wasn't exactly a burger, as it was salty and slightly bitter, but it seemed to be protein. He decided to hop down and do a little workout next to the rig. It felt good to stretch and get the kinks out as well as lift some larger ore pieces to get his muscles working and pumped up pretty good. He'd have to ask around and see if there was any sort of gym facilities for the conscripts when he got back later. He wished he had his watch or something to tell time with. He would ask about that possibility also. He jumped back on the rig and banged away for another couple of hours, always remembering to check his overhead every few mentus for vertical fracture lines.

Eventually, he found one and backed off to attack it from a distance. It slowed him down a little, but the resultant ore from its crash ended up making up the difference. A couple of horuns later, he saw a flashing light signaling him and turned to find Jattar watching him from behind. He stopped the rig and waited to see what the old alien wanted. Jattar climbed up on the rig and said he just wanted to check on Jack and see how things were going with Cahooshek's newest conscript.

"Jack good. Dig, push, dig, push," said Jack, giving him the short version. That satisfied, Jattar and he left Jack to his work, since he'd checked the donda tally on the way in and knew that Jack had already met his goal. Everything else was just extra credits in Cahooshek's pocket and eventually a small bonus for Jattar. Yes, it looked like Cahooshek's gamble on this conscript was going to pay off as long as it didn't get killed by an overhead fracture line or other mining mishap.

About a half horun later, a loud bang sounded as a rock thrown by the next shift operator hit the rig. Jack stopped the rig and turned to see the miner slap his chest and yell at him. "Shift up five mentus ago. You stop working now. It's my shift."

Jack replied, "OK, you shift now, sorry," said Jack. The miner gave him a bit of a huff as they swapped places. Jack exited the side drift and the main shaft. He had to watch out, as the next round of donda loaders were already starting to move for the new shift.

Back at the berth chamber, Jack saw one other miner getting ready to head out. They exchanged a brief half-hearted greeting, and the miner left. Jack grabbed his toiletries and headed to the restroom and showers. In the shower and restroom chamber, there were sinks up front with toilet stalls in the next area and then six shower rooms at the very back. Two of the showers appeared to be in use with closed doors. They weren't anything fancy, but they would work as far as getting the daiyus dust and grime off. He decided to grab a shave first and experiment with his various toiletry items to figure out what they all were. He managed to get the one powder to suds up some, but the other one turned to a viscous jell. *Maybe that's supposed to be a shave cream of some sort,* he wondered, since there weren't any labels on the toiletries for some reason.

As he was getting ready to try it, he thought he heard a bit of a commotion with some laughter farther back in the shower chamber. A second round along with a muffled cry got his attention. He set his razor down and cautiously walked toward the back. Not knowing the customs of this alien culture, he didn't have the slightest idea of what he might find. As he approached the rearmost room on the right, he could just see into the now open shower room. There were three aliens surrounding a smaller alien, and they were holding its face under a stream of running water. All three laughed, and he heard one of them say, "Maybe he just needs a little cleaner soap to go with the water to help him remember not to be such a good rig repairer."

"That might do the trick," said one of the others. The smaller creature being tormented began to convulse, and suddenly, Jack could see that it was Junot that they were abusing.

Jack took four fast quiet steps and hit the closest one with a palm strike to the side of the head. The next closest one, which Jack now recognized as the ring leader from last night's rations hall confrontation, pulled back far enough in surprise that Jack hit him with a hard left straight. The last one stepped back and let go of Junot at the same time. Jack grabbed Junot before he hit the floor then sidestepped as the alien lunged at him. A quick hammer fist to the side of the head and a snap kick to the kidney area sent him headfirst into the opposite wall. He was only half stunned and tried to take another lunge at Jack, but Jack just sidestepped him again and caught the alien with a short right palm strike to the left jaw.

It wasn't all that hard, but it dropped him cold. The first two aliens were trying to get to their feet but were only about half coherent. The second one he'd hit with the left jab was bleeding a nice dark maroon fluid from its nose and upper lip. The ring leader alien mumbled something about "Kill, get, be sorry," but Jack's translator wasn't picking much of it up from the floor of the shower room with the water running where the alien was trying to get up.

Jack jammed his foot down on the alien, smashing his face into the floor. "I don't think so," said Jack, thinking, *Damn, I gotta tone this down some.* "Junot if hurt, I find you, hurt you," he said to the alien under his boot. *That should be succinct enough,* he thought. *Crap, so much for keeping a low profile. I hope there's a plan B out there somewhere,* he said to himself as he dragged Junot out of the shower.

He stopped by the sink area and propped Junot up on the counter. He seemed to be uninjured other than he was woozy and completely incoherent as well as soaked. "Junot, Junot, are you OK? Talk to me." Jack shook him gently.

Junot pitched forward slightly and coughed out a mouthful of water. Jack caught him before he went all the way over and held them for a minute while he coughed out more water. "I'm, think, I'm," cough, cough, sputtered Junot. "Where, what," cough, as he spit up some more.

"Come on," said Jack, "let's get you out of here and back to the berth chamber." Jack grabbed his toiletry things and pulled Junot to his feet and half carried him back to their bunk room. When they got there, Cherga and two other aliens were there getting ready to head out to the rations hall.

"What happened to this one?" said the big alien Cherga while pointing at Junot.

Jack responded, "Fall, slip, shower, good, OK, now."

"Well, he has looked better," replied Cherga.

"Yes," replied Jack, "good, soon." After the others had left, Jack began trying to get Junot to talk.

"Junot, are you OK? Can you talk to me? Speak to me, Junot," said Jack. Junot sputtered a couple of times and then seemed to come out of it somewhat. "What happened?" Jack asked. "Why were they abusing you like that? Did you do something to set them off? What happened?"

"No, ahcugh, I don't, I don't know," coughed Junot. "I didn't do anything. I was just trying to avoid them. They followed me to the toilet then grabbed me and took me back, ack hackch, to the shower room. They said they were going to hurt me, maybe kill me, if I didn't do what they wanted."

"Well, what did they want?" asked Jack.

"I don't know. They never said. They just started slamming me around and tilting my head back and running water onto my face. They never said anything about what they wanted. I don't know," replied Junot.

"Well, I think you're all right now," said Jack. "It doesn't look like they had a chance to beat on you or anything. I think you're just shook up and about half drowned. If you're OK, why don't you put on some dry clothes and we'll go to the rations hall and get some food?"

"OK, I OK, I think I could eat something," replied Junot as Jack helped him over to his berth and storage area.

Junot managed to get himself cleaned up and dried off without too much of a problem, so they headed over to the rations hall to check out the evening menu. They grabbed their meals from the line and found a table with just a couple of other miners. The meal looked about the same as last night's meal to Jack, just slightly rearranged. They ate quickly without saying much so that Jack could maintain his fluency cover for now. Jack did notice that several of the miners stared at him for a bit longer than normal. He wondered if it was just because he was still slightly different from the rest of the miners or if word had already leaked out about the butt whoopin he'd just delivered. After they finished their meal, they headed back to the berthing room. When they got there, no one else was there again.

Jack thought there must be some other activities the other miners were involved in, since the only time they seemed to be there was to sleep. He asked Junot, "Where are all the other miners when they're not working their shift or sleeping here?"

Junot replied, "They could be in several different places. Of course, the contract miners could be anywhere in the mine that has food and other things to do. There are lots of different diversions that could be had in the mines depending on what your wants are. They have gambling and different kinds of shows you can watch. There are stores where you can buy clothing and stores with all kinds of gadgets you could buy. They even have a place where you can spend some time with a female if you want to."

"Yes, I've heard of that," Jack said. "What about the conscripts and convicts that can't go to the open side of the mine? Where are all the miners that normally sleep in these berthing chambers?"

Junot answered, "Well, there are the common areas you came through on the way to the conscript side. They have games and different events to watch on the large displays there. There is a place for physical training and working the body."

"There is? Tell me about that place, a gym is what I call it. Where is that?" asked Jack. "Can you take me there?"

"Yes, I can take you there, but I don't like to go in. They will make fun of me there," said Junot.

"That's OK. You can just get me close or tell me how to get there. I need to get some exercise," said Jack. "I've had too much inactivity in the last wenek, or whatever it's been since I've been in this ordeal. By the way, how do you know when your shift is up or it's time to go to eat or whatever? I had a watch, a timekeeper, but I, ah, lost it," Jack said to Junot.

"You mean to know what horun it is?" asked Junot. "That's easy. You just look at your translator. It always has the horun if you want it."

"What do you mean look at the translator?" Jack asked.

"You just speak, 'Display horun,' and you will see the current horun," said Junot. "You did not know this? How is that? Most all translators have the same basic functions. The horun display is one of them."

"I've never had a translator until a few daiyus ago," said Jack. "I didn't know they had that function. All I have to do is say, 'Show horun'?" As he said those words, a small display, almost like a small heads-up display, popped into the upper left field of Jack's vision showing the digits H1126.48. "Hey, that's neat. I didn't know it could do that. No one bothered to tell me," said Jack.

"You may want to turn it off for sleeping," said Junot. "Just say, 'Hide horun,' and it will vanish."

"Can it do more than show time? What else can it do?" asked Jack.

"Well, yes, there are several other basic functions," said Junot. "It will display for you current date, temperature, heading, elevation above standard surface level, and velocity. It also has horun alarm functions so that you can wake up. These can be displayed individually or in any desired group. You can also arrange them where you wish or choose the desired brightness and color of the display. Your language should be pretty well decoded by now, but there may be some errors or voids for some things that have not been translated yet. Tell it to display menu, and it will give you a list of commands to arrange the functions that can be displayed."

"OK. Thanks, Junot," said Jack. "I wasn't aware of these functions, since all we had done previously was try to get it to translate my language."

"That is understandable," said Junot, "since if it could not translate to your language, it would not be able to display anything that was not translatable. It is strange that you never had a translator until now and that your language was not in the core data."

Jack said, "So back to the other subject, do you know of anything else that the other conscripts do besides what you told me? There is usually more going on than meets the eye as far as local entertainment is concerned based on my experience."

"What do you mean by 'meets the eye'?" said Junot.

Jack replied, "That means readily apparent or what is obviously seen."

"Oh, yes," said Junot, "meets the eye, I know what you mean now. There is a thing they call the fight pits, but I have not been to them because I don't think it would be a safe place for me."

"Yes, I've heard a little bit about those from my friend," said Jack. "Maybe we'll have to check those out, at least to see what they're all about sometime soon," said Jack.

"No, I, uh, don't want to go there," replied Junot.

"OK, no problem," said Jack. "So in the meantime, why don't you get me headed toward that gym you told me about?"

"Oh, well, all right, I will take you there," said Junot, "but I'm not going in. I'll just leave you at the entrance."

"Fair enough," said Jack. "I am looking forward to some decent workout action." Junot took Jack through several tunnels to the entrance of the mine's version of a fitness center. As soon as he pointed out the entrance to Jack, Junot hurried out of there as quickly as he could. *Strange little guy,* thought Jack, *but I don't blame him if they've been tormenting him the whole time he's been here. He really doesn't seem like too bad of a little alien. He's been pretty helpful to me so far.*

The gym was a decent-size space. It looked to be about 100 feet by 150 feet in size with a fair amount of basic workout equipment. There were various forms of free weights as well as some simple generic-looking workout machines. It was all fairly conventional but somewhat primitive looking, but then Jack wasn't expecting all that much in the mining conscript zone. There were about a dozen miners working out in the gym. There were some types of equipment he hadn't seen before, but they kind of made sense when you analyzed them. There was one where you could take your feet and hands and both pull and push against variable amounts of resistance that could be set by a large friction dial.

He decided to just jump into it and try and replicate his standard home routine with the equipment that he had here. It looked like he could easily accomplish that, so he started in with some free weights and then experimented with some of the machines. He had some minor conversations with a couple of the aliens but nothing too in-depth, as they were all interested in getting through their own workouts. He met one that was named Nunashaj and another named Covranah-en. The second one, Covranah-en, said he had heard of the new conscript from Vara named Ja-ack. Jack kept the conversation very basic, as he still wasn't sure if he wanted to reveal his real identity, and he was also afraid he might run into a miner or someone that was more familiar with actual Varacis who were apparently from Vara. Jack, of course, knew absolutely nothing about Vara other than it wasn't near this quadrant of the galaxy.

The good news was he was able to bang out a decent workout, and he felt pretty good after not having been able to do much for the last eight or more daiyus. The other good news was he could now tell the time as well as the date and other information on his translator. He would play around with the translator functions later and see what options he had available as far as setting various parameters and formats that would be useful to him. The clock readout was straightforward as it read out six digits of the twenty-eight-hour Nishdan daiyus. The date made no sense to him, though, as it showed thirteen digits. He had no idea what it was referenced to. Was it referenced to Nishda's calendar, or was it referenced to a Galactic standard, or maybe it was actually showing both? He'd have to get more information from Junot if he couldn't figure it out himself.

The next daiyus, Jack asked Junot if he knew of any way to search or contact anyone outside the mine conzone. If there was, he wanted to know if it could be done secretly. Junot said he thought that he could access an outside neural cortex point through his tech access connection that he used for researching the electrical and other maintenance troubleshooting. He said he hadn't tried it before, but he thought he could piggyback on a maintenance access line in a way that would make it discreet and untraceable. He said that some of his security systems programs had built-in encryption capability that might allow him to piggyback in the encrypted data mode on the general maintenance stream without being detected. Junot also said, "Even if it is detected, they won't be able to easily decode it because it is encrypted." Junot said it would be unlikely that they could even find it at all, but if they did, they would have to decrypt it and then put it back together to make any sense out of it.

Jack said, "That sounds like a plan that might work for me. How long do you think it would take to get that set up so that I could use it?"

Junot replied that he thought he could have it set up in a couple of daiyus. He told Jack not to tell any of the other miners that he had access to the maintenance depot area where he had the tools and diagnostic equipment he used for repairing the mining equipment. He admitted that he spent as much time there as he could unless he was in the field repairing a piece of equipment. He could avoid the miners that might want to harm him as much as possible that way. Jack said not to worry, that he would never tell anyone and that he understood why Junot tried to avoid them.

"Just tell me where and when to meet you after tomorrow's shift so we can try to figure out how to make it all work. The most important thing, though, is I don't want you to get in any kind of trouble or hurt in any way for trying to help me," said Jack.

Junot said, "Don't worry about that too much because I think I am too valuable to them to get in much trouble for a small infraction like that."

Jack replied, "OK, but still be careful because we don't know exactly what their response would be if you got caught." Junot wasn't sure what Jack had in mind, but it was really quite exciting thinking of covert things like this, and he wanted to help his new friend Jack in any way he could.

The next two daiyus were basically workaday routines repeated by Jack as he ran the zibur rig all daiyus. He finished about 20 percent above the standard quota, so he thought that should be enough to keep Jattar and Cahooshek off his back for any reasons. He hit the conscript version of the gym each daiyus after work then grabbed a quick shower before meeting Junot for the evening meal at the rations hall. On the second daiyus, Junot said he had tapped a maintenance access line and put together the encrypted and piggybacked comm program.

They headed to the maintenance depot where Junot had access to the outside comm lines. Junot said he had the place to himself most of the time, but occasionally, another maintenance technician would come in from the other side of the mine complex looking for something they didn't have over there. He asked Jack who it was he wanted to contact outside the conzone, but Jack said it would be better if Junot didn't know so that he couldn't tell anyone if they tried to force him. Junot thought that made sense, but it did sound a little forbidding the way Jack was talking about it.

Jack said to Junot, "It's just better for us if you show me how to trace someone on the outside and then contact them without anyone hacking into it from either end."

"Hacking?" asked Junot. "Is that hitting or cutting somehow?"

"Well, sort of, yes, but not exactly," said Jack. "It's like snooping, like when the Alliance inspectors team caught you falsifying those reports that the inspectors made you do. We just don't want to get caught because obviously it would just be a lot better if we didn't."

"Well, then, let me show you how to trace someone," said Junot. "If they are here in the Corodune mine complex, it will be easier and much less noticeable than if we try to go outside."

"Yes, it will be someone here in the mine complex. I just need to make contact with them and see if they are all right."

"OK," said Junot. "Let me show you how to run the program, and I will let you enter the name and search when we get to that point."

Junot ran Jack through the initial part of the search setup. When they got to the name entry part, Junot let Jack enter that on his own. Jack entered Zshutana's name and hit the trace function. In about a second, it came up with two probable individuals. Only one of them was within the mine complex, so that pretty much narrowed it to one possibility. Jack keyed the connect function that Junot had shown him, and he heard a faint beeping sound that indicated a secure transmit signal was pinging the comm link he wanted.

After about twenty seconds, Jack was wondering if it was pinging the correct address when he heard the comm pick up on the far end. "Yes, who is this?" He heard Zshutana's slightly altered voice ask.

"Hello, it's your language student, but don't say my name from your end. Just call me, ummmm, call me Duunda, and I'll call you Teela for security reasons," said Jack.

"Ja-a . . ." she almost shouted before it registered what he'd said. She knew his unique-sounding voice instantly and almost couldn't stop from saying his name several times. "Where, where are you, uh . . . Duunda? I've been trying everything to find out where they've taken you. Are you all right? What have they done to you?"

"Yes, Teela," said Jack, "I am fine. I am still in the mine complex. They have me working a zibur drill, and I'm being held in the conscript section of the mine.

I'm talking to you through a secure comm link that a friend set up for me. They shouldn't be able to trace it, as it's well concealed, but just in case, from now on, I don't want to use real names. Does this make sense to you?" he asked her.

"Yes, yes, of course," she said. "Anything we can do to make it harder for anyone to trace us is a good idea."

Smart girl, thought Jack, but then he already knew that. "OK," he said. "I can't talk long right now, but I just wanted to establish a comm link with you if I could and make sure you were all right. Are you OK? They haven't harassed you or anything since they took me out of there?"

"No, yes," she said, "I mean, I'm fine, and they haven't bothered me since you've been gone. They must've decided that I did a good enough job for them, so they haven't bothered me about anything," she said.

"Good, that's good," said Jack. "I didn't want you to take any heat because of me, and I appreciate your going along with my situation here. I just wanted to check on you and also let you know that I'm OK. I'm just working in the mine, and I'm reasonably sure that they're happy with my work, since I'm meeting all my quotas here. Unfortunately, you can't contact me here, since I only have access to this link from one location and at restricted times. I will try to contact you again soon, but I don't know when or how often that will be. We haven't been able to work that out yet."

"That's OK," she replied. "I'm just very pleased to hear that you are OK and to know where you are. I will see if there is anything I can do on my end to help matters, but I don't know what that would be right now."

"That's fine," said Jack. "I appreciate that, but make sure you don't draw any attention to yourself or do anything that would jeopardize your situation."

"No, no, I won't," she said. "I'll be careful, but I'll do a little bit of searching around to see how things work around there. Maybe I can find something that can help you in some way."

"OK, then," he replied. "I need to get going now so we don't draw any attention to ourselves here. I'll contact you as soon as I can and let you know what else is going on. When is the best time for you so that I can try and plan it?"

"Anytime is good for me," she said. "I'll just make sure I have my comm link with me at all times. And I am just curious, who is this Teela and Duunda that we speak of?"

"No one in particular," said Jack, "just the name of a miner I briefly met down here and the name of some conscript's wife or girlfriend that I overheard. I'm guessing they must be somewhat common names, so it shouldn't draw any attention if this link is traced."

"Yes," she said, "those are just common names, so I think that is a good plan."

"All right, then," he said. "I'll contact you again as soon as I can. Just be careful and keep a watch out for anything unusual that might indicate they might be monitoring our link. Be careful and take care. It was good to hear your voice, and I hope to hear it again soon. Thanks again for all your help," he said to her.

"Yes, it was good to hear your voice also, and I hope to hear it again soon," she said to him. "You also take great caution down in the mine. That can be a very unsafe place, especially for someone that has not been around it much before."

"OK, I will. Good-bye. I will contact you again soon," he said. She returned the good-bye, and he reluctantly broke the comm link connection. He hated to break the connection to the last pleasant and civilized person and experience he'd had. It seemed funny how he was starting to think of these aliens as people in general. A little over a week ago, he'd never even seen any definitive proof that aliens actually existed.

Since the disaster with *Victory,* the only exposure he'd had with other sentient beings were with beings he would have classified as aliens from outer space. It certainly wasn't all good experiences, but it was certainly interesting and educational. He had encountered both good and bad individuals, but he was now totally immersed in a completely alien culture, and all the aliens around him were now his sole contact with sentient technology-oriented beings. This whole set of strange circumstances was one heck of an astonishing adventure. He couldn't imagine anything even remotely as unusual and bizarre as this situation he'd been thrust into. He had read a fair amount of sci-fi novels since his youth, but he'd never read or heard of any story that was similar to this bizarre adventure. I guess you have to roll with the punches, just as he'd always done, he thought to himself.

He found Junot in the next room keeping an eye out for possible interlopers. He let Junot know he was done, and Junot went back to secure the comm link and delete the access history for the link. "All is well with your friend?" Junot asked Jack.

"Yes, and thank you for helping me so that I could check on the situation with her," Jack said.

"Ah, so your friend is a female," said Junot.

Damn, I did it again, thought Jack. *I need to think through every word that is going to come out of my mouth. I'm not really geared for this clandestine stuff,* he thought. *I'm pretty sure Junot is going to be trustworthy, but that's not going to be the case with everyone here. I've got to adjust my mind-set to be totally aware that anything I say can give away something about my situation.*

"Yes, Junot," Jack said, "my friend is a female, and she helped me greatly before I got here, but you can't say anything about this to anyone even if you're questioned."

"Yes, I understand," said Junot. "I believe you saved my life, so I will never intentionally do anything to betray you. I consider you my friend, and I wouldn't want any harm to come to you or any of your other friends."

"Thanks, Junot. I appreciate that, and I consider you my friend also," Jack said to Junot. "I'm glad you got stuck with my mining orientation and that it has worked out for both of us," added Jack.

"So am I," said Junot, truly thrilled to have someone down in the mine that wasn't picking on him and who respected his abilities and opinion and called him friend.

Jack and Junot left the maintenance depot and headed back to the common areas. Jack asked Junot how often he thought he could contact his friend and still remain undetected. Junot replied that he couldn't really say for sure but that he didn't think that any more often than every five to six daiyus would be a good idea. Even a little more would be better, and alternating time intervals would be the least detectable. "That should be good," said Jack. "I want to keep her informed about what I'm doing and make sure that she isn't taking any heat for anything I'm involved in."

"What do you mean *taking heat?*" asked Junot.

"Well, that means someone might be questioning her or causing her some sort of problems because of me or what I'm doing."

"What could you be doing that could cause her any problems on the outside?" replied Junot.

"I'm not sure yet other than checking in on her," replied Jack, "but you never know how things might pan out around here."

"Pan out?" said Junot. "What does this mean? All we do is drill for ore, break and fix zibur rigs, eat, sleep, and sit around," said Junot.

"Well, for now, that's all we do," said Jack, "but that doesn't mean that's all we are going to be doing."

"Like what? What do you mean?" said Junot.

"I don't know. I haven't figured that out yet. I've only been here a few days, so I'm just beginning to work on it, but I'll come up with something entertaining. I hope you're up for a little excitement."

"Like what? I still don't know what you mean," said Junot.

"Trust me," said Jack, "just trust me and you will."

Chapter 8: Gladiator

Jack spent the next couple of daiyus prodding Junot about the structure of the economic system, government and legal system, law enforcement, and other aspects of the planet as well as how these systems carried over into the galactic system. After repeated questions by Junot as to why Jack was asking him all these questions, Jack finally told him he was just interested in how the average citizen would function in Nishda's economic infrastructure. There was an official state-sponsored economy as well as a large underground economy that functioned as a result of the heavily bureaucratized and inefficient official state economic system.

The state system was rife with graft and corruption on its own but had a fairly well-balanced and symbiotic working relationship with the underground economy. To Jack, it sounded a lot like many of the socialist economies of Europe and to some degree even the United States. The danger of this type of system was you could never tell who you could work with and who you couldn't trust except by word of mouth. Loyalties of the participants usually lay with which side of the street they were dealing with at the moment. This had its advantages and disadvantages but was sometimes less predictable than the purely ideological players even though it would seem in theory to be the other way around.

The law enforcement situation was another precarious scenario. The two large Nishdan cities, Wanana and Se-ahlaalu, had their own official police forces, but the corporate entities also had their own private enforcement firms to police their own interests. Sometimes, these two police forces worked together, and at other times, they were more rivals. Again, the ability to know who worked for or with or against the opposition would be a challenging equation to compute, thought Jack, especially in an alien environment where he didn't know the spoken or unspoken protocols.

There was a semi-planetwide police force called Provosts, but because there was a whole lot of nothing but jungle and desert to police, they stayed primarily near

Wanana and showed little interest in faraway Se-ahlaalu. The entire population base of the planet was concentrated in the two main cities and the outlying mining complexes and a few agriculture centers. The Corodune mine complex used their own rent-a-cops to monitor and control the entire mine complex including the conscript and convict workforce that Jack was part of. Jack guessed that the incentive for the slave labor operation was that it was cheaper to hire fifty or so rent-a-cops to oversee the several hundred plus conscripts and convicts than it would have otherwise been for costly contract workers. It was just too far away from the main galactic economy way out here in the mine, way out here on Nishda. That apparently was what made it possible for the mine bosses to come out ahead so well economically.

From what Jack could tell, the rent-a-cops were like most corporate police forces; they were understaffed for economic reasons and relied heavily on electronic monitoring systems. From what Junot told him, there were large gaps in the monitoring system simply because there wasn't the manpower to monitor every area of the mine. They relied instead on monitoring choke points and other areas where it might be likely that potential inmate troubles might occur. Jack didn't want to get too specific with Junot about what he was contemplating because he actually didn't know himself. He was really just gathering as much intel as he could so that he would know as much about his options as possible.

One thing he'd made up his mind about, though, was that he wasn't going to spend the next five or ten Nishda yenets here operating a zibur rig paying off a debt that he didn't owe. He had no idea yet what he would do to change this situation, but you had to start somewhere with any kind of a plan.

On the eighth daiyus, Jack and Junot got a daiyus off, since they were both on or ahead of schedule in their respective "career field." Jack was getting restless to contact Zshutana again. Not that he had anything especially exciting or important to tell her, but he just wanted to hear another friendly voice and stay connected to some degree of civilization, such as it was at Zshutana's. He'd been hitting the conscript gym daily and was feeling pretty good about his physical condition. His back and leg no longer hurt from his ordeal aboard *Victory*.

When he thought about how close, in mere inches, he'd come to suffering the same fate as the rest of his crew, all he could do was thank God that he'd somehow survived the collision and ended up here. Sometimes, where you ended up wasn't where you wanted to be, but it was exponentially better than where you could have been. At least here in the mine, he had the ability to possibly influence his future if he could just get a handle on what he would have to do to get out of this situation.

The food here agreed with him well enough even though it wasn't anything to write home about, but it certainly wasn't reason enough to stick around here as a conscript, as he laughed to himself at that thought. The real question was, even if he could get out, which he was sure he eventually could, what would he do once he did? The options on the outside were limited by the daunting fact that he didn't have the slightest idea how to survive and support himself on the outside. There probably weren't many ads in the local paper for space shuttle pilots. Zshutana would more than likely be willing to help him, but he didn't even know what resources she had available in that respect, and he had no intention of getting her visibly involved in anything that could harm her.

The thought of staying at the mine and eventually becoming a paid contract worker was a zero option as far as he was concerned because he didn't think his conscript sentence was realistic with respect to his alleged crime of stealing passage. He was fairly certain that he might suffer some sort of mining accident once his usefulness was finished or he might be forced to stay on in perpetuity. He just didn't know.

Jack was still playing it careful with the translator fluency issue around his fellow inmates, as he now thought of them. He was giving them a little bit of improvement in his speaking ability as would be expected. After the other berthing inmates got going on their daiyus off, the big gruff hactra operator Cherga came up to him. "So Varaci Ja-ak, you speak now a little better than before."

"Yes, hello to you now, Cherga. I get better some with more practice talking. My trainer Junot, he makes me learn much, very hard make he me work."

"Then he seems to do a good job. It is good he is helpful for you, then," replied Cherga.

"Yes," acknowledged Jack, "Junot good trainer."

"Now, what do you do today, since you have no work?" asked the big alien from Zanaii.

"Not sure," said Jack. "May get working body at physical room, gym room. Maybe entertainments see on displays at common area. Don't know, ask why, Cherga?"

"Perhaps later after the night meal, big night at fight pits. You know of these, probably not, only talking to Junot snirt all the time? He never goes there. We try once to get him to come. We even promised him we will not feed him to kruztwox this time, but he still not go," laughed Cherga.

"Now," said Jack, "you not before feed him to kruztwox since only he goes not, so how Junot know you not feed him this time to kruztwox?"

Cherga looked at Jack for a couple of seconds. Then he burst out laughing in a series of big huffing gasps. "Shoka," he said, "you are right, how would he know if we have never fed him to kruztwox before? That makes me laugh," retorted Cherga.

"Hear of fight, fight pit, yes, from Junot," said Jack, "sound curious to me. Wanted to know more of fight pit watching. You go after meal, Jack would go and too. You Cherga show this to Jack?" Jack asked the big alien.

"Yes," said Cherga. "One horun after end of night meal, I will meet you here. I will take you, and I have a good seats to see fights. I have good seats in seat area, no standing. Bring the little Junot if you can get him. The ones I go with usually, Sobul and Lenjaii, will not be there. They must go to yenet end parole hearing. You will like this, I'm sure. It will be an amusing time."

"Yes, good, then here I be one horun after food eat," Jack replied.

A while later, Jack found Junot and asked when it would be OK to talk to his outside friend again. "Today would not be good," said Junot. "I don't usually go to the maintenance depot on a daiyus off. If I went there with another miner, it might seem suspicious to any of the other repair techs that might show up if they realized it was my daiyus off. Tomorrow might be the best daiyus, as there is only one other tech from the other sector on duty tomorrow, and it is also a different shift."

"OK," said Jack, "that sounds like a better plan. We'll wait until tomorrow. I talked to our friend Cherga a little while ago, and he offered to take us to the fight pit tonight and has some good seats that we are welcome to use. Why don't we go check out the fights so that I have a better idea about what's going on around here? Cherga said you're welcome to go if you want."

"Oh, well, I'm not sure I want to go and see that. I don't think that would be a very good thing for us to go to," replied a fidgeting Junot.

"Come on, Junot, you might even like it," said Jack. "I'll be there, and I won't let anything happen to you. We could just go for a while. If you don't like it, we can leave. It would be something different from the usual, and it might be somewhat entertaining."

Junot replied, "I'm not really sure. How could you make sure that nothing happened? What if they, uh, want to, uh . . ."

"What if they what?" said Jack. "What if they tried to feed you to a kruztwox?"

"Yes, that," stammered Junot in fearful tone, "or what if the others try to . . ."

"Wait, relax, Junot," said Jack. "I can't imagine anyone would try to hurt you in a crowded place, and those idiots from the other daiyus should know better after their little attitude adjustment. Cherga seems like a decent-enough sort. He may be a little gruff and gregarious, but he's probably OK. I don't think he would let anyone mess with his personal guests either. It's OK if you don't want to go. I understand. I just thought it might be something different and a little adventurous for you."

"No, OK, I guess I could go if you think that nothing could happen to us. If you want me to go, I would go," said Junot.

"Well, yes, I want you to go," replied Jack, "but only if you're comfortable with it and if you're not going to worry too much. We'll watch out for you. Both Cherga and I will make sure all is well."

"OK, OK, I guess I'll go, then," said Junot.

Jack and Junot showed up at the appointed time followed shortly by Cherga. "Ah, Varaci Ja-ak, it is good to see you here with your little trainer friend Junot," said the big miner from Zanaii. "Little Junot, I hope you have decided to join us at the fight pits tonight. I still promise we will not feed you to the kruztwox," said Cherga with a hearty hafaff. "Do not worry, we will not let anything happen to our newest zibur miner and our best repair tech. If it were not for you, Junot, all the zibur rigs and hactra hammers might be broken, and they would make us mine the Burun-Rioc ore by hand. The ones that whine about having to work too much do not know what real work is. You should let all the machines break for a while and see how they like mining with a pick and hammer. Now, do not worry, we will have an amusing time tonight. All will be well, you will see," snorted Cherga.

"See, Junot, everything will be fine, and we'll have a good time," said Jack.

"Well, I hope so," said Junot with not too much enthusiasm.

"Come, let us go now and see what entertainment they will have for us at the pits tonight," said Cherga as he led them off toward the fight pits that were hidden deep within the mine complex.

As they headed down, Jack said to Cherga, "Who fights at pits, tell us about?"

Cherga replied, "Miners fight most often, both cons and contract miners. There are different matches at different times of the moondat and yenet. At the beginning of the moondat, just the miners or maybe other workers from Corodune mine will fight. Usually, there are four, but sometimes up to six matches depending on how many enter. It depends also on how many from each shift can get to the pit that want to fight. Sometimes those that want to fight will have others fill in for their work shift so that their work does not go unfilled. On the third wenek of the moondat of the second and fourth parts of the yenet, they will bring in the best fighters from other mines."

"Wait," said Jack, "other mines send fighter?"

"Yes," said Cherga. "Fighting is not supposed to be allowed by the mine. They are afraid those injured cannot work, and the mine will lose credits. But the mine bosses allow this because they, the local mine bosses, will broker the bets and make credits. They will set the betting odds, and they will take a portion of the winnings. It is said that if they broker enough of the bets, they can make more than their regular status pays, but who knows for sure? So there is much incentive for them to allow the fights without the Alliance and their GTA mine controller's knowledge. I also believe that the mine controllers must get a portion for themselves even though they supposedly do not allow the fights. That is how things work. Everything seems to flow uphill. At the specified times, they will hold final matches that will lead to the end-of-yenet champion matches."

"This sounds to be good diversion," said Jack. "Do fighters make credits?" asked Jack.

"No," said Cherga, "but injuries will be treated as if they were mine work injuries. They will be treated so that the fighter will not lose pay credits if they are from the contract side. The conscript side will also have injuries treated, but the mine bosses have agreed to not punish fighters by adding extra time to their sentences for time that they would miss if injured and they could not work."

Jack wanted to make some snide remark about the generosity of the mine bosses, but he didn't know how well it would come across in his "feeble vocabulary." All he decided to say was "Generous bosses," and he left it at that.

"Yes," replied Cherga, "very generous of them when they make many credits from the pits."

"Why, then, miners fight if no credits?" asked Jack.

"Miners will bet on themselves to win the match," said Cherga. "They cannot bet on their rival. This would make them to not want to win the match. So only winning will make the fighter to earn credits."

"Yes, understand now," said Jack.

That was a little different, thought Jack, but if there wasn't any wage incentive for the fights, then the only way for a fighter to come out ahead would be to bet on himself. Of course, if he didn't bet at all or only made a small bet, because he didn't think he would win the fight, then that might have some implications also. Well, he would see how it all went soon enough.

Cherga, Jack, and Junot, along with a couple of hundred others, continued down several corridors then down several roughly hewn inclines until they were at the lowest mine level. "We are now at the Kirago level where the fight pits are found," said Cherga. There were multiple old exploratory shafts in various directions, but the main corridor ended up in a large arena not unlike something you'd find on Earth. The lower portion held the match ring, which was surrounded by a low wire cage about four feet in height. The area directly around the ring was at the same level and had concentric benches of hewn bedrock all the way around. The area behind the seated bench area was tiered and sloped upward toward the back but had no benches for sitting. The bench area looked like it might hold two hundred or so spectators, while the standing area behind the benches would hold another two or three hundred spectators.

Both areas looked like they were about one-third filled, but more spectators were coming in behind them to add to that. "Come," said Cherga, "we have good seats on the far side in the second row."

"Good place for us," said Jack.

"Are you sure this will be a safe place for us to sit that close to the ring?" asked Junot.

"Yes, no reason for worries," said Cherga. "If fighters fall from the ring, it will just be straight over the edge. Hardly ever do they hit the watchers." He laughed. Cherga then added, "Hardly ever do the kruztwox grab the watchers when those matches are going." Again, he laughed.

"Kruztwox, what are?" asked Jack. He thought it was some imaginary creature that Cherga was just using to jerk Junot's chain, but maybe not. Maybe there was such a thing as a kruztwox, or maybe Cherga was just jerking both of their chains. It was always fun being the new guy in town because you never knew what the locals were going to pull on you in the fun sport of practical joking and baiting the new guy.

"Kruztwox," said Cherga, "gorroks, and drugas are the hybrid mine laborers. Gorroks and drugas are the less hybridized mine workers," said Cherga. "They are like clones, but they were engineered to work in the mines before Nishda was well terraformed. They are very tough and can survive in the very harsh conditions that were originally on Nishda. But they did not work well as miners. They were too primitive and did not take well to running any sort of machines. They are more likely to go berserk than to put in a daiyus of work in the mine. Most of them were terminated, but they kept some for breeding purposes and further research in case they wanted to try this method again.

"After they began the fight pit matches, they discovered that it was easy to get them provoked enough so that they would battle each other. So, usually, on the eighth wenek or fourth period of the moondat, they will bring out a pair of gorroks or a pair of drugas to do battle. They will usually stop when one has dominated the other like many other species that fight for dominance. A couple of times, they have fought the drugas against the gorroks, but they will not stop fighting, and it is a death match every time.

"The kruztwox, though, they are different. They were designed after the gorroks and drugas. They have a partial helix from both the gorroks and drugas, and they were designed specifically to battle each other as well as the gorroks and drugas. They were designed illegally without regulations or oversight from the Alliance Helix Control directors. They will only rarely fight them, as they are difficult to control even in a fully enclosed cage. They can destroy a gorrok or druga in less than half of a mentu. Even against two gorroks or drugas that are fighting for their life, they will win in a matter of mentus.

"The gorroks and drugas are omnivores, so they are less difficult to maintain. The kruztwox, though, are strictly carnivores—they will only eat meat. They must have all meat every daiyus. So they, the kruztwox keepers, must go to the grenzons every few weneks, the forest zones that are terraformed, and hunt some large creatures to supply the meat to maintain the kruztwox."

"Ah, then, is good stay away kruztwox. Not friendly, then, kruztwox," replied Jack.

The arena was about half filled now, and the arriving spectators seemed to be tapering off. Cherga added, "This will be a good fight tonight. This is the second quarter fight, so the beginners will be already excluded out. The better fighters will be battling tonight. Probably there will only be four rounds, but they will be better than six or more beginner rounds. It will all start in just a few mentus. How are you doing little Junot? Everything is good with you so far?" Cherga asked.

"Yes, yes, I am OK, just as long as nothing comes from the ring that can hurt us."

"Relax easily, little machine tech," replied Cherga. "I have been coming here every wenek for nearly three yenets now. Nothing has ever happened of a dangerous nature. Well, except for that one time a crazed kruztwox got halfway out of the enclosed cage, and they had to hit it a dozen times with lightning sticks before it's neural system shut down, and it collapsed halfway out of the cage. Harrafff," laughed Cherga, "but do not worry, there will be no kruztwox in tonight's events."

Jack thought Junot looked a bit pale, but maybe it was just that he was sitting in the shadow of an overhead beam that was supporting a floodlight for the ring. "Tell me now, Varaci Ja-ak, why does your translator work not so well? Isn't your Vara or Varaci language in the core? You should talk better, but it is not so bad now."

"Not sure for reason," said Jack. "Might possible translator bad. Not work, words mix. Possible Junot fix translator, for me hope this," said Jack.

"Tell me of your home, Vara. What is it like? Maybe it is like my planet Zanaii, which is very nice planet. There are many good quiet places to live."

Crap, thought Jack, *I haven't the slightest idea what Vara or Varaci is like. Can I fake it, or does he know more than he's saying?* wondered Jack. "Yes," replied Jack, "good planet to those from there, not probably nice planet as Zanaii. Later can compare home planets soon," said Jack. "Fight show now starting."

Saved by the soon-to-be-rung bell, Jack thought to himself. Just then, two aliens came down the walkway and bounded into the ring. One was tall and lanky with medium green skin and a bald head except for short bluish ponytail coming out of the base of his head. He was dressed somewhat formally in a dark blue and off-white jacket with black trousers and some sort of athletic-like shoes covering his large feet. The other was similar in design to one of Cahooshek's minions but with lighter skin and different markings. He was also shorter and more athletic with a quickness about him that let you know he was no slouch in the physical department. The lanky one took front and center and started with an introduction speech. "You all know me. My name is Sha-aga, your exceptionally charming, talented, and most handsome fight announcer. And here, our friendly zibur miner, former conscript, and this evening's referee is Ulzaka, as you should also know." A small applause went up from the crowd.

"This evening's first fight will start in just a few mentus. Standard fight match rules will be in effect as usual, which means, of course, that there are no rules." A good-size assortment of hooting, hollering, and laughing erupted with that statement. It took a few seconds for it to die down. "Of course, there are a few rules that can disqualify a fighter, and they are, of course, no eye gouging, no eye gouging, as well as no eye gouging."

More laughter followed from the audience. "Other than those three rules, there are essentially no rules, well, except, of course, no bringing in outside weapons of any sort as long as you don't get caught bringing them in. Fighters caught bringing in an outside weapon, you will be disqualified, or possibly not, if we really want to see the match. So, fighters, don't get caught bringing in an outside weapon. We will now bring in our first match fighters for introduction, and the match will begin. Matches will consist of three, six-mentu rounds with two-mentu rests between rounds, or perhaps more rounds if no clear winner is apparent."

A cheer and hollering arose as two aliens, one from each side of the arena, converged on the ring. The first one had a medium build with a strong upper torso and arms. It had a small squarish head with small facial features, short blondish-orange hair with long sideburns that continued all the way down into a short goatee. It was wearing some grungy grey shorts that looked like cutoff sweats and a dirty brown V-cut T-shirt that looked like it hadn't been washed in a few moondats. Jack surmised that this wasn't a middleweight MMA championship fight in Vegas, so they didn't put much stock in their fighting apparel.

The announcer introduced him as Tajdra of Havora to a half-hearted spectator response. The second fighter had a heavier, boxier build with a large round head and a squared-off jaw. His head sprouted multiple individual tufts of brown and black hair about three inches long that were all combed backward but which stuck up more than staying down. His body had virtually no taper to it and was fairly thick but with shorter arms than his opponent that were more heavily muscled overall. He wore a pair of dark red knee-length shorts and a faded armless T-shirt that might have once been a striped blue and gold color.

The announcer introduced him as Krekka from Dimmatua. Showing its favor, the crowd gave a much more rousing response when the announcer Sha-aga introduced him. The favorite for this match was obviously Krekka. Sizing up both fighters, Jack thought that it was probably a fairly evenly matched fight. Krekka definitely looked more solid and dangerous, but the other fighter, Tajdra, had a wariness and a more fluid stance that could give him a slight advantage.

Without knowing their fight histories, it would be hard to place a bet on either one of them, thought Jack. Krekka definitely looked like more of a brawler. You wouldn't want to get hit by him if he connected with the weight of his solid body behind it. Tajdra, on the other hand, looked like he could move quite deftly, and though he may not have the power that Krekka did, Jack thought that if he kept moving and hammering away, that could make the difference in this fight. On the other hand, the crowd's reaction to Krekka was more favorable. Jack didn't know if that was based on popularity or ability. Trying to gauge a fight like this completely cold left too many unanswered variables if you didn't have some background history on the fighters.

"Don't forget to place your bets before the match starts in one mentu and forty-four septus," chided the announcer. "Only one mentu and thirty-three septus now. Hurry before you're locked out. You can see the odds are 1.8 to 1 for your favorite Krekka. If I could bet, I know who I'd be betting on," harangued Sha-aga. "Don't wail to us if you miss your chance to rake in some easy credits on this first match. Now one mentu and eight septus to fight time!"

Jack prodded Cherga. "How bet, where odds?"

"On your translator menu, should be," replied Cherga. "Go to menu, other, fight pit, enter match code for fights, three thirty-seven, select current, this will show you time to bet on current match. Your win, loss, and credit record will display in the normal side view as long as you're logged in."

"OK, good. Thanks," said Jack as he ran through the entry setup as Cherga had just explained. There it was, just as Cherga had said. Also displayed were the fighters' names, win-loss records, and a small image as well as the other data he'd told Jack. Next to a Bet Now icon was a countdown timer, and next to the menus was a timer that said Round Time.

Cherga added, "You can only see the fight pit menu while we are down here. This keeps any of the Alliance inspector teams from seeing or monitoring the fight pit data should they ever show up and inspect the mine. They would have to be in here during a match to see the menu."

"Good, that idea good," replied Jack.

The match started with the sound of a loud obnoxious buzzer. Krekka came out swinging and trying to bulldoze his opponent Tajdra. Tajdra moved deftly out of Krekka's reach. Krekka kept coming at him and trying to force him onto the wire fence of the ring, but the ring was round, so there was no corner that he could force Tajdra into. Krekka figured out Tajdra's tactics and realized that he was burning a lot more energy chasing Tajdra than Tajdra was burning evading him. Krekka decided to switch tactics and force Tajdra to come to him.

If Tajdra wouldn't come to him for the fight, then he would win by default. Tajdra knew this too, but he was just trying to wear down Krekka so that he would have a chance at Krekka when he got tired and started to leave some openings. Krekka wasn't tired yet with only two mentus into the round, so it would now have to become a battle of hit and move and hit and move for Tajdra. This might work for Tajdra as long as he kept moving and didn't let Krekka run over him while he was attacking and retreating.

Tajdra made three fast attacks and retreats. In and out, he moved, each time trying to land a right straight and a left hook combo then a right straight, right hook, left hook combo. Krekka was covering pretty well, but Tajdra managed to land a solid blow with a double right hook that connected on the second swing. This stunned Krekka for just a split second, but then he came out blazing with a blitzkrieg of haymakers designed to take out anything in their path. Tajdra ducked the first three swings while trying to make an escape by getting off-line from Krekka's drive.

Krekka's left swing glanced off Tajdra's shoulder and caught the top of his head with a decent glancing blow. This knocked Tajdra off balance just hard enough to knock him about halfway off his feet. It looked more serious than it was, but it was definitely a point score for the judge Sha-aga and the crowd. The crowd was revved now that it looked like it was going to be a nicely matched fight. They were all yelling and hollering and cheering on their favorite fighter.

Tajdra reeled a bit but was back on his feet in half a septu. He knew he had to stay out of the way of those power blows while he recovered somewhat until the round ended. The initial success caused Krekka to forget about his strategy, and he started chasing Tajdra in the hopes of landing another connecting blow and winning the match. Tajdra realized his opponent's error and let him chase him for the next thirty septus until the round ended with the sound of the buzzer.

"So how you like fighting so far, Varaci Ja-ak?" said Cherga.

"Good, good fight, good fighters," replied Jack.

"How about you, little Junot, not so bad, yes?" Cherga prodded Junot.

"Well, I'm glad it's them beating each other senseless and not me. It's not really my sort of sport. I'd rather play a good game of farakal where I can put my brain to a better use than using it as punching bag," replied Junot.

"Ah, you play farakal. I have not found anyone here that knows the game. I have played since I was boy," said Cherga.

"Yes, I play, and rather well," said Junot. "I didn't think there was anyone here that plays. I have only had the comp bots in the maintenance depot to play."

"Really? You have a game set there?" asked Cherga.

"No, just the sim on the maint-ref computer. It's better than nothing. It's OK but obviously not the real thing. It does help your strategy skills and forces your moves if you play in a timed mode," said Junot.

"Yes, that would be interesting, but I have never used a sim. Only the real game is what I know," replied Cherga.

"Do you just play standard high ridge, or have you ever gone into long war?" asked Junot.

"Either one," said Cherga, "I have been playing since I was weaned from mother's milk."

"Really? Oh, you play long war," said Junot excitedly.

"Of course," retorted Cherga, "all in my family played, taught from my grand pat. Most in our village played. In the cold months, we had to entertain ourselves."

"Now, wait, there's one thing I would have to know," said Junot most seriously. "Do you, do you cheat?"

"Why, yes, of course, absolutely. How else would you play?" asked Cherga.

"I have never cheated," said Junot.

"Why not?" asked Cherga.

"Well, I, ah, I never played with anyone that knew how, so I never had anyone that could teach me, even though I know how in theory," replied Junot.

"Ahh," said Cherga, "I can teach you to cheat and cheat well. It's like another game within a game. It doubles—no, quadruples your strategy and your options. Think of the unlimited options in a game of farakal long war with unlimited cheating."

"That sounds incredible. I can't even imagine the endless options you could play," replied Junot. "Would you really teach me how to play like that?" asked Junot.

"Yes, yes, of course," replied Cherga. "Who else would I have to play with here? I've tried to get others interested to learn, but no one seems enticed, so I have never gone as far as trying to get a game set."

Junot replied excitedly, "Well, if we could get a game set, that would be excellent. We will have to come up with a game set, maybe from the outside somehow. I'll have to figure out how." Jack didn't know what farakal or long war was, but it sounded interesting, and it was apparent that a new friendship had just been formed. All it took was a little effort on the part of those involved, and something new and good would come of it.

At the end of the two-mentu rest, the buzzer sounded again. Both fighters were pretty well recovered, and each decided to keep with their previous strategy. Krekka came out more reserved but tried to slowly work Tajdra against the ring. Tajdra let himself be pushed back then suddenly attacked Krekka with a double straight, a right hook, and left uppercut combo. He was out then back in before Krekka could fully realize what was coming or react to the attack. Tajdra tried two quick left jabs, then a right overhand when Krekka dropped his hands to fend off the jabs and a right hook. Recoiling and moving out, Tajdra tried a fast right straight, and Krekka wasn't quite fast enough to cover. The punch caught Krekka square in the face. It lacked power because Tajdra was moving back, but it was enough to stun Krekka and send him stumbling backward. Tajdra moved in and tried two more attacks in succession, and all Krekka could do was fend off the blows.

Krekka, starting to tire, lunged at Tajdra, trying to grab him and take the lighter opponent to the ground. Tajdra sidestepped and threw a quick left-right double that just barely connected then moved out. Krekka tried grappling with Tajdra two more times but couldn't move fast enough to catch Tajdra for a takedown. On the third try by Krekka, Tajdra feigned another left feint and then moved fast to the right with a left straight and a right hook that caught Krekka with his guard down. The hook landed squarely on the left back side of Krekka's head and sent him sprawling into the ring fence.

Krekka went down for a second, and Tajdra went in to try and finish Krekka with a quick combo, but Krekka wasn't out of it yet as he recovered somewhat and put a foot up to block Tajdra's advance. His foot caught Tajdra in the abs, but from Krekka's low position, it didn't have enough power to do any damage. It did drive Tajdra back long enough for Krekka to regain his fight stance and launch a weak counterattack. Krekka managed a couple of half quick swings as he lunged at Tajdra, and one of them even landed well on Tajdra's sternum. It was a painful hit but not one that would add any damage in the short term of the fight. As they squared up for another go after a couple of more mentus of this, the buzzer sounded, and the ref Ulzaka sent them back to their respective side to recoup for another two mentus.

"Very good fight for first match," said Cherga to Jack and Junot. "Usually, first one or two are average, but the fighting is almost even. Miners' favorite is Krekka, but new contract miner from 1900 horun shift is good with movement."

"Yes," said Jack, "moves good but not careful."

"I see that too," replied Cherga. "You know fight methods, you have seen before?" asked Cherga.

"Uh, yes, have matches where from I," replied Jack, not wanting to get too specific.

"Ahh, good," said Cherga, "so you understand this and know how fighting is done. There are no rules here like some other places, though. Just no blinding of eyes so miners aren't useless to work in the mine afterward. Too many rules, padding, helmets, padded gloves in other fight places make outcome more about rules than fighter skill. This arena best thing about being conscript or convict, real fighting based on fighter's skill. You probably have never seen anything like this before."

"Yes," said Jack, "my place fighting real, no rules except no eye blind, same like this. Skill more than here fighters."

"Harrafff," laughed Cherga, "I've never heard of such a place, never heard of anything about Vara or Varaci like that. This I would like to see but does not exist."

"Not Varaci, not Vara, but does exist," replied Jack. As a somewhat puzzled Cherga started to inquire further, the buzzer sounded again for round three.

The two fighters came off their respective ring side. Both appeared tired but still alert and functional. Krekka, now realizing the danger he was in and that Tajdra wasn't a weak opponent, moved cautiously toward the other fighter. Tajdra appeared more tired than the previous round, and his guard was about half down from the start of the round.

Krekka moved in as close as he could then made a fast lunge at Tajdra with a double straight combo and then threw a couple of wide haymakers trying to connect with Tajdra. One of the first unguarded straights took a slight glance off the side of Tajdra's head but was otherwise deflected. Tajdra ducked the first wide swing then moved out of range for the second. Once again, Krekka was chasing him and taking some wild swings as Tajdra weaved and ducked with hidden energy that he hadn't shown when coming off the ring side. Krekka was getting more tired by the septu in his effort to catch Tajdra. Again, he dove to try and lock up Tajdra and take him to the ground, but he only got half a hand on Tajdra as Tajdra moved off-line again and avoided Krekka's grasp.

It was apparent to Jack where this was going and that it wouldn't last much longer. Tajdra was just too fast and nimble to allow the heavier, more powerful opponent to take him down like that. Unless Tajdra tripped or Krekka got very lucky, that just wasn't going to happen. Krekka tried to regain his composure and get his energy wasting lunges under control, but he'd already burned too much of his reserves to keep his finer motor skills under control. He tried to bait Tajdra a couple of more times with some faked attacks, but Tajdra just shrugged them off and let Krekka burn that much more of his reserves.

When Krekka made a third advance, Tajdra made another move to back off-line, but instead, the instant Krekka thought he was moving out of range, he dropped his guard, and Tajdra moved forward with a quick left jab that brought Krekka's hand to center guard and allowed Tajdra to follow up with an instant right hook that caught Krekka square and hard on the jaw. Jack could tell that it was solid and connected perfectly by the sound. Krekka went down on the hard floor in a heap and didn't move. A loud but smaller cheer went up from the portion of the spectators that had bet on Tajdra, while the rest cursed and threw a fit over their wrong choice for backing the losing fighter Krekka. Jack knew he'd called this one right in his mind and deliberated in his head if all the variables that applied to this fight, which were basically the same as human fight matches, were the same across the board for all the alien matches.

The fight announcer Sha-aga started. "Amazing, astounding, what an incredible fight! Can you believe it? What an upset. Your favored fighter Krekka has fallen to the new Corodune challenger Tajdra of Havora. Who would have thought?" With that, he grabbed Tajdra's arm and raised it in victory. "Great job, Tajdra of Havora, an outstanding fight. Congratulations on your win. What do you have to say about the fight?"

Tajdra began answering, "I, I am just glad to have won. Krekka was a good opponent, but I beat him fair. I will go onto more rounds and beat more opponents."

"That's great, just great," replied Sha-aga. "We will see you again in the ring soon. Once again, great job, great job."

In the meantime, several of the miners had come into the ring and gathered up Krekka and helped him to his feet while starting to revive him. Another couple of miners helped Tajdra exit the ring. Then Sha-aga started announcing for the next match. Sha-aga announced, "Now that was a great match, although some of you are disappointed with the outcome. You just never know what's going to happen down here in the Corodune fight pit. One minute, you're a favorite fighter, and the next moment, you can be knocked out by a new challenger."

Jack thought about Sha-aga's statement in his pitch for the first match when he said that he knew who he would bet on, but he hadn't actually said who it was. He could also easily tell that the new challenger Tajdra had considerably more experience than he was being billed for. Jack wondered how much if any manipulation was going on behind the scenes with whoever was organizing the matches. That's something to consider, Jack thought to himself, if he ever seriously decided to place any bets on these matches.

"Our next match," the announcer began, "will be between two excellent fighters that you've seen before, Garwan of Nishda and Dedoowa of Tarca." Jack listened to the announcer's pitch and looked at his translator's display to see what was coming up. It looked like another fairly even match based on what was shown. The one fighter, Dedoowa of Tarca, was from the same planet as Zshutana. As the two fighters were brought out and introduced, Jack could see the similarity of the more humanoid form in the Tarcan fighter Dedoowa. He had similar facial features as Zshutana, only more obviously masculine. His coloration was similar but varied as well as being slightly darker and more vivid than Zshutana's. The other fighter, Garwan of Nishda, was taller than Dedoowa by a good half a foot, but he was very thin although fairly muscular. Since Nishda was terraformed and had no native population, Jack wondered why this Garwan was announced as being from Nishda. Maybe he had been born and raised here in the last twenty-five yenets, but that didn't seem likely.

Across the fight ring in the standing area were three aliens that Jack had briefly met before, if you count kicking someone's butt as a formal introduction. The three aliens from the Junot shower episode saw Jack and Junot sitting with Cherga in the bench area. The one alien said to the leader of their group, "Rigya, look, over there across the ring in the bench area, that little bug Junot, and isn't that the Varaci trash that ambushed us in the showering chamber when we were trying to teach the little bug a lesson?"

161

"Well, that's the bug Junot for sure," replied Rigya. "I'm not sure about the other, I didn't get a very good look at him. But I think it is. Who else would be with that little insect bug?" he said.

"I think it looks like him," said the second alien whose name was Leeto. "I didn't see him too good either, but it probably is."

To the first alien, Rigya said, "Seguu, go over to the other side of the ring and get your friend Cuwuc and his two other friends and come back over here."

"Why? What are you going to do?" asked Seguu.

"Just shut up and get over there," replied Rigya. "I'll tell you in a few mentus, and be silent about it."

The next match started off well with both fighters fairly well matched. It went almost to the end of the second round when Dedoowa of Tarca managed to get inside the longer reach of Garwan's swings and deliver a quick one-two combo that sent the lighter alien fighter to the ground. Both punches landed hard, and the stunned but mostly uninjured Garwan wasn't able to get back on his feet without assistance from the referee Ulzaka and Sha-aga, the announcer.

Two other aliens then helped Garwan out of the ring, while Dedoowa received his accolades and applause from the crowd of spectators. Cherga pointed out to Jack the 2.6 to 1 odds in favor of Dedoowa. Cherga said he'd thought the fight went pretty well considering the high odds in favor of Dedoowa. Cherga asked Jack if he'd decided to bet on any fights yet. "Well, Jack not bet. Jack no have credits," he replied.

"Ah, Cherga so sorry," he replied. "The mine will pay you twenty credits at the end of wenek. Not so much, but it will be good for betting or some extra rations of different kinds if you want. Every two weneks, they pay conscripts and convicts twenty credits. Practically, that is free labor for mine. Contract labor makes many times more than conscripts. Contracts make two hundred or more credits every two weneks plus bonus if they mine more ore or have extra high-grade Burun-Rioc. It is still cheaper for mine to use conscripts, but there are not enough, so some areas outside conzone must use contract workers. I, Cherga, wouldn't be surprised if they convicted those not guilty just to work in mine."

"You think this?" Jack asked Cherga.

"Oh, yes," he replied, "Cherga would not doubt this for a mentu."

"Jack this think too," responded Jack.

Sha-aga announced the next two fighters, and the spectators hit a higher degree of excitement than he'd seen in the two previous matches. "Ah, very good," said

Cherga. "These fighters large and rough. This will be a good match, you will see. Too bad you don't have credits to bet with. This will be a good match to bet on. Maybe you get Junot to bet. He could win some credits tonight. Narnov will be my favorite, but Szetsalu will give him a good run. Narnov bigger and quick, but Szetsalu maneuvers well." Jack sized up the two fighters who were both as big as Cherga and even a little more solid looking. Watching the way they carried themselves, he'd guess that this was going to be more of a brawl and less of a stand-up match.

The match started with the both fighters charging each other and colliding in a momentous crash. That should have stunned either one of them, but they grappled and fought for position over the other fighter. Using pure strength and little technique, they battled while trying to get an advantage using their fists and legs. Trying to throw the other one to the ground, the bigger one, Narnov, spun halfway and managed to get his hip under Szetsalu and pulled him over and down to the ground. From there, the match turned into a fray of grappling, slugging, and wrestling.

"See, I told you this would be a good fight," said Cherga. "This is more to my liking," as he stood up and yelled for his fighter to destroy the other.

"Exciting but little skill here!" yelled Jack over the noise of the spectators.

"Ha, you not like match. This is best one so far," railed Cherga.

"No, it good match but only brawl. No skilled fighting," replied Jack.

"Perhaps, but still great fight," responded Cherga.

The buzzer rang, and when the time-out ended, the next round began with little change in the strategy of the fighters. Narnov seemed to be getting a little advantage, but Szetsalu was good at staying out of the bigger fighter's grasp or wresting free before Narnov could gain a decisive advantage. By the third round, both the fighters were exhausted and slowing, but Szetsalu seemed to have the advantage in energy reserves.

Junot, who didn't seem too thrilled by the whole event, asked Jack if they could go after this round was over. "Well, yes, Junot, you can take off anytime you want if you're not liking this," said Jack.

"Um, OK, well, I'm just a little tired from the other thing that happened, and I'd stay, but I'm really drained. You, uh, said that you wouldn't let anything happen to me down here. I was just nervous that, well, maybe it would be better if you could get me back to the main mine area by the berth chamber. You could just come right back then if you wanted to. I was just sort—"

"No, it's OK," said Jack. "I'll take you up right now," Jack said to Junot. "Cherga, you can tell me about the outcome of the match later." Jack told Cherga that he was going to take Junot back to the berth area and he'd be back to see the rest of the matches in a little while.

"Is Junot OK?" asked Cherga.

"Only tired some, not feel so good," replied Jack.

Jack and Junot went out toward the entrance to the fight pit and out the corridor leading to the inclines up to the other main mine levels. There wasn't anyone else in the corridor, as everyone was already at the fight pit. As they passed a side corridor, Jack heard someone yell, "Hey, there they are now. Grab them and drag them back down here. We'll show them a few things about ambushing and messing with us!"

A gang of a half-dozen alien miners converged on Jack and Junot from the side corridor. The first one lurched at Jack in an effort to grab him. Jack put a defensive front kick squarely in his solar plexus. This sent the attacker reeling backward with a painful "umpff" that knocked the wind out of him. Two more attackers dodged around their stunned comrade and tried to jump on Jack and pull him down the corridor. The first one was met with a side step and a round kick that connected with its back and sent it flailing forward. The second alien tried to wrap Jack up in a bear hug. Jack based and hit it with a right knee, left elbow to the head, and a right palm strike to the alien's head as he slammed it away, which caused it to crumble sideways onto the ground.

At the same time, a larger alien grabbed Jack by the throat in an attempt to choke him. Jack responded by plucking down and away on the attempted stranglehold then countered with a simultaneous groin kick. As the alien bent forward as a response to the kick, Jack grabbed his head to control him and brought his right knee into the alien's face, sending it careening backward in a spray of blood. Jack based again as another alien tried a frontal attack and another one circled behind him. The alien that attacked from the front received a one-two straight combo that sent it sprawling, while the one that attacked from the back was checked by a defensive back kick. The alien came at him again as Jack turned and based. A quick left jab to the throat and a hard right elbow to the face ended the alien's attack.

The first attacker that took the kick to the solar plexus was on its feet now and trying to advance on Jack, while another was advancing from the side. The alien from the side had a bar or something in his hand and swung at Jack with an overhand strike. Jack was too close to move outside the arc of the weapon, so he dove forward with his arm outstretched to get inside the swing. Jack deflected the strike to the outside then locked the attacker up by grasping its elbow. Two right knee strikes to the stomach and another to the head as the alien collapsed forward from the first knee strikes finished the attacker as Jack stripped the weapon, some sort of a metal bar, from its grasp.

The first attacker was now on Jack trying to grab and strike him from behind. Jack whirled inside its grip, bringing his right elbow solidly onto the alien's neck with a wicked thud. The alien went down hard and stayed down while it grabbed its throat and gasped for air. Jack then heard the sound of Junot yelling from the corridor. The lighting wasn't great, but he could see another miner dragging a flailing Junot down the corridor. The alien that had Junot wasn't aware that all his comrades were lying in the dirt, some of them seriously injured.

The alien looked up just in time and saw Jack coming toward him and tried to pull Junot up to block Jack's attack. It wasn't fast enough, and Jack caught it with a straight palm strike to the side of its face. Jack didn't want to risk injuring Junot, so he limited his attack to something that would only cause the kidnapper to drop his victim. The alien dropped Junot to the ground, and Jack stepped around him to confront the alien. The alien had been knocked back and was half down on its knee. Jack could tell it was going to lunge at him, so he hit him with a solid right round kick to the side of the head. This sent the alien sprawling a good six feet down the corridor where it lay in a heap without moving.

Jack turned to make sure there were no more attackers then to check on Junot. "Junot, Junot, are you OK?" asked Jack.

"Jack, yes. What happened, what, what?" was all that Junot could get out.

"You're OK. Come on, let's get out of here," said Jack as he quickly recovered his breath from the fight. As they got to the main corridor, there were several other passing miners that had heard the confrontation, and they were looking at the carnage that Jack had wrought on the attackers.

Junot looked around and couldn't believe what he was seeing. There were five utterly destroyed attackers plus the one down the corridor. "What in the Creator's rim happened here to these miners?" asked one of the bystanders as Jack worked his way around the carnage with Junot.

"Not know, just see now," replied Jack. "Should get medical," said Jack to the alien. "Come on, Junot, let's get out of here," ordered Jack as he half carried the small alien out of the corridor.

Jack got Junot back to the berthing chamber and checked him over again. "Well, it doesn't appear that you were hurt, Junot," said Jack, "just jerked around a little. I'm sure you'll be fine in a little while after you settle down. I'm going to go back and see if Cherga knew anything about this, just to be sure. That would seriously piss me off."

"But what, what if they, those miners, come back here now?" whined Junot.

"I don't think that's much of a possibility, Junot. They won't be doing much of anything for a while."

"Are you sure?" asked Junot. "How did you, how did you do that? How did you fight all those miners? How did—are you a soldier of some kind? What did you do to them? What was all that?" Junot asked in a stuttering voice.

"Nothing," said Jack, "just a hobby I do that I'm pretty good at."

"A hobby?" asked Junot. "What exactly does that mean, a *hobby*?"

"Umm, well, like a sport or a pastime, something I do for fun and to stay in good shape," said Jack.

"You have a sport for attacking many miners?" asked Junot.

"No, not exactly," replied Jack. "Remember, they attacked us. My sport is more about defending against being attacked, even by a bunch of miners. It's a form of martial arts called Krav Maga. It means 'close combat' in Hebrew."

"Hebrew?" said Junot with a quizzical look on his face. "You said *combat,* so you are a soldier of some kind. This makes the most sense to me," said Junot, looking more shaken than before.

"No, I'm not a soldier, but soldiers do use it in one nation's army," said Jack.

"But you do it, this Krahavmagavka, for a sport? Is this what you mean?" asked Junot.

"K-R-A-V M-A-G-A," Jack pronounced it slowly. "Yes, that's what I do for a sport."

"Well, if you're not a soldier, what are you—I mean, before they sent you to the mine?" asked Junot.

"Well, I'm a fighter pilot and a space shuttle pilot," responded Jack.

"You mean you fly starships, starships that are for fighting?" asked Junot.

"Yes, except they are airplanes for fighting battles and spaceships for doing research, mostly. We don't go to the stars, just into orbit," said Jack.

"Airplanes?" said Junot.

"Ships that don't fly in space, just in the atmosphere," said Jack.

Junot puzzled over this for a few seconds. It really didn't make any sense to him based on his knowledge of starship pilots. *Starships or spaceships that don't go to the stars? That sounded strange, almost primitive,* thought Junot. "Why would they put a starship pilot down here in the mines?" asked Junot. "I thought you were conscripted because you stole passage on a starship. Isn't that what you said?" he asked.

"No," replied Jack, "I said that's what they sent me here for, but I said I'd explain it to you later, which I will. But right now, you're going to stay here while I go check up on Cherga and find out what's going on with that. Unless you want to go back to the fight pit with me now?" said Jack.

"No, no, no, you go. I'll stay here," said Junot.

"OK," said Jack, "you'll be fine here. No one will be coming here except the miners that live here. I'll be back in a little while."

"OK," replied Junot, "but be careful. There could be more miners down there, the ones that want to hurt us."

"Don't worry," replied Jack, "I'm always careful. It's one of my specialties."

Jack borrowed someone's hat that was lying nearby and his own coat to use as a disguise in case there was still any excitement near the side corridor where the miners had attacked them. Junot sat there and pondered the events that had happened and wondered what it was like to be a starship pilot or a space pilot or fighter pilot, whatever it was that Jack had been trying to explain to him. He'd never met a starship pilot before. He'd only been on a starship once before, and that was when he'd come to Nishda as a young Riinan from his home planet of Riina.

Jack put his jacket and the hat on as he got close to the area where they'd been attacked. He could hear a lot of talking and saw a group of miners milling around. There was a fair-size crowd, and it looked like they were in the process of hauling off the last of the injured. There were four mine guards like he'd seen when he first arrived, and they appeared to be asking the miners what they knew about the incident. He hid as much as he could under his hat and jacket as he walked by the far side of the corridor.

One of guards summoned him over. "You miner, you Ja-ak, 2641, stop. What do you know about the attack incident here?"

Jack, realizing they must have something that could read the data in his translator, stopped and responded to the guard. "2641 just going fight pit. Go now not miss matches. What this attack? Not know me," Jack replied.

"You know nothing of this, then?" the guard replied.

"No," said Jack. "Going fight pit now."

"Why do you speak strangely? What's wrong with you?" responded the guard.

"Translator bad, not, work good, no," he replied, realizing that his "bad translator" act might draw some degree of suspicion from someone like the guard. "Translator fix soon," added Jack.

"All right, go on, then, 2641. Stay out of our way here now," snapped the guard.

"2641 go now yes," said Jack.

Jack made it back to the fight pit without any further harassment. Now he wanted to find out if Cherga had anything to do with this. He would be able to tell by Cherga's initial reaction to his presence as long as he didn't see Jack from a distance and have time to fake his reaction. If this had been some sort of a setup, Jack wouldn't be able to do anything about it now, but at least he'd know what the score was. Jack warily entered the pit area in his disguise and spotted Cherga with his back to the entrance watching the match and rooting for one of the fighters.

To stay out of Cherga's field of vision, Jack avoided the aisle and instead worked his way through the standing crowd to directly behind where Cherga was seated. When the spectators all jumped to their feet to cheer on their fighters, Jack hopped across a couple of the bench rows until he was directly behind Cherga's bench. As soon as the excitement dropped off and the crowd fell into their seats, Jack jumped over Cherga's bench and dropped down beside him. Cherga started to notice his presence, so Jack loudly piped up and said, "Jack is back now, how are matches?"

"Ah, Jack, good. You have missed two good matches. Too bad, but still there is one to go, which should be the best one of tonight's fight pit matches. What took so long?" replied Cherga. "I think maybe you fall asleep and not come back for the finish of the night's matches."

"Oh, we held up some. Take longer as all things always do. I'm sure I not miss the best match," Jack replied as he chuckled to himself.

They watched the last few mentus of this match between two agile and muscular opponents. The fighters were on their feet for twenty more septus then ended up grappling each other to the ground. After another twenty seconds, one of them managed to get the other in a sort of a convoluted headlock. Instead of a ten count, the referee just waited until it was apparent that the headlocked fighter would not be able to free himself then slapped the winner on the shoulder while yelling, "Match over!" The next match was similar with regard to the fighters' physical attributes, as they all appeared to be fit and capable. They all seemed to have a natural degree of fighting ability, but Jack didn't detect any type of formal fight training.

The last match started upright but soon ended up on the ground as a rolling, kicking, gouging wrestling match. The last match seemed to draw the greatest enthusiasm from Cherga as well as the spectators. The matches were all out fighting until submission, injury, or inability to continue. The matches got the spectators pumped into a near frenzy until it almost looked like a free-for-all was going in the audience. Jack could easily see why the fight pit matches would be the prime means of relaxation and entertainment for the miners and conscripts trapped in the perpetually dreary underground environment of the mining operation.

The last fight ended when the loser took an inadvertent knee to the groin, which caused him to gasp and grab himself in pain, leaving him open for a punching attack to the head. He tried to turn away and attempted to cover and hide from the assault but not in time. The ref pulled the miner off his overwhelmed opponent and called the match. The crowd was already on its feet, and a great deal of pandemonium broke out as the fight pit matches ended for the night.

Sha-aga, the announcer, started in with the canned promo and recap of the match and beckoned everyone not to forget to come to next week's match and "Don't forget to bring a big bucket of credits so you can have the chance to win big on next week's finals matches where the chances of striking it rich are practically astronomical." The crowd was still on their feet talking, yelling, and slap fighting among themselves. *Just a bunch of rowdy good old boy miners doing what they could to ease the reality of their boredom and captivity situation,* Jack thought to himself.

"Come, Jack, we will go to the common area and get some xula if you want or just see if there is anything to watch on the vido displays."

"Xula?" said Jack. "What that? I not heard of."

"Ah, you know, a drink, a sweet-taste drink. They do not have it at the rations hall, only at the common area. Sadly, there is no qalalé here on the conscript side, so we must do with xula. The xula is OK, but I would probably give all my left and right toenails for a large tank of qalalé," replied Cherga.

"Qalalé? I do not know also," queried Jack.

"You do not know what qalalé is either?" asked Cherga with the surprised look.

"Perhaps," said Jack, "but just not know by this word."

"Ah, OK," replied Cherga. "Qalalé is drink that they make of grains. It is fermented, and it turns to alcohol. Most excellent in every variety it is. There are many variable tastes to it. My favored qalalé is dark gold brown and which is full with much taste. There are many others, but most are lighter than what I relish."

"Ah, know what qalalé is," said Jack. "I say qalalé, must be beer, ale, also lager, different names. Cherga's qalalé probably be stout or dark porter," said Jack.

"Qalalé is then Jack's beer or also ale, and also the others," replied Cherga, "and Cherga beer is called qalalé stout. Ah, this is good then."

"No, this bad," replied Jack.

"Bad? Not bad. Why you say bad?" quizzed Cherga.

"Bad, very bad, bad, bad, bad, no beer, no qalalé, that bad," Jack said in his most serious manner.

"Achhaff," wailed Cherga, "yes, that is bad, very, very bad to have no qalalé for Cherga and no ale beer for Jack."

Cherga and Jack both had a good laugh at that as the headed out of the pit. They passed the spot where he and Junot had been ambushed, and there were still two guards at the entrance to the side corridor. They seemed to be finishing whatever type of investigation they were doing and just giving all the miners the once-over as they poured out of the pit and down the corridor. *Maybe they were looking for someone with injuries as a possible suspect,* thought Jack. If that was the case, their prime suspects would have to be the fighters that had just fought their matches in the pit. Jack's lower right shin was a little bruised from the round kick he'd delivered, and he'd taken a slight hit on his left shoulder, but these minor injuries weren't painful enough that he would give any indication that he'd been in a clash.

"Ha, see those two sludge slugs looking at us over there?" said Cherga as he looked over at the mine guards. "What meddling are those two parasites doing down here? I can count on one finger the number of times I have seen the spineless vermin down here before in last two yenets. Ah, I know, they have gotten lost again far from their safe secure shack and they are now afraid to ask for directions back to their home," he added.

"Yes, I see," replied Jack, "only when I arrive mine have I seen them before."

As they neared the common area, Jack said to Cherga, "Cherga go common. Jack go to berth chamber. Jack come back meet Cherga in short mentus."

"Yes, OK. Jack is OK?" asked Cherga.

"Yes, Jack good, short mentus," replied Jack. Jack found Junot sitting by his berth looking at something on a small tablet monitor. Jack hadn't really been gone that long from when he'd left Junot earlier, but he wanted to make sure that Junot hadn't become nervous and run off to hide somewhere. Another conscript was doing something at his bunk area on the other side of the room. Jack thought he remembered its name being Neseta or Seseta, something like that. Jack discreetly returned the borrowed hat to the other bunk when no one was looking.

Jack said in a low-tone voice, "Junot, how are you holding up? Is everything OK?"

"Yes, Jack. I still just can't believe what you did. How did that happen? I've just never heard of anything like that," Junot rambled in a slightly too loud and excited voice.

"Quiet, shhh, not so loud," Jack admonished him. "This is our secret, at least for now until or if we hear something about it from anyone. Remember, you've got to keep this just between us and not talk loudly about it if others are around," whisper Jack.

"Yes, yes, I know," said Junot, "but I was thinking what an amazing thing it was like I'd never seen before."

"Yes, yes, but not a big deal," replied Jack, "but it's just probably best that others don't know about this, OK? So let's just keep it quiet."

"I will, I will," said Junot. "I'll just have to be careful, but I will."

"OK, just remember that," said Jack. "I'm going to go back to the common area and try some xula drink with Cherga. Do you want to go with me?"

"No, no, thanks, it's been a long daiyus, and I'm really tired," replied Junot.

"Ok," said Jack. "What I'm going to do is tell Cherga that you just now made a fix for my translator that repaired the programming so that I can talk to him normally. I've checked him out, and I'm sure he's OK, but I'm going to tell him that I'm only going to speak normally around him and you for now so that I can keep a slight advantage over these guards and the mine bosses. Can you keep that straight and remember it?" he asked Junot.

"Yes, no problem with that. I can do that," replied Junot.

"OK, great, and thanks for fixing my translator, Junot," said Jack.

"But I, you, I didn't really, you said that you, I," stammered Junot.

"Yes, you did," said Jack. "You really fixed it, OK?" said Jack.

"Oh, yes, right, I get it," said Junot. "I really did fix it. OK, OK."

"OK, I'll see you after a while," said Jack as he headed out the berthing chamber door to go meet Cherga.

"Hi, Cherga, did you order one of those xula drinks for me to try?" Jack casually asked Cherga as he came in and sat down by the big miner.

"Yes, right here for you I have gotten one," said Cherga as he stared at Jack for a moment, trying to figure out if something had changed. "You are, uh, something, oh, yes, ha, you are talking like a normal person now. What has happened!" exclaimed Cherga.

"Junot, it is Junot. He has fixed the programming in my translator. He has been working on it for a while and thought he finally had it figured out. Something to do with the way the programming searches for the correct syntax order sequence, I think is what he told me," replied Jack.

"Ahh, yes," replied Cherga, "whatever that might be. Either way, it seems to work. This should be much easier to carry on a discussion now. This is very good and will help you in your work and everywhere else," added Cherga.

"Yes, it probably will," said Jack, "but I was thinking about it and thought that it might be to my advantage if the bosses and the guards still think that my translator is not working correctly. They may think I don't hear them properly and they may speak more freely than otherwise, and I may be able to hear some of their secrets or plans they talk about between themselves. So if you don't mind, I just want to use the good translator function with you and Junot while pretending not to hear or speak too well because of a poor translator with all the others. Would it be a problem if you played along with this?" he asked Cherga.

Thinking about it for a second, Cherga responded, "This is very clever and sounds like a good idea. Yes, completely I would be willing to go along with this. Perhaps you could learn of some secret way to screw up the vermin that run this mine operation who are the real criminals and should be incarcerated in the mines."

"Great, and I appreciate your help," said Jack. "Thank you for accepting my idea on this issue, but tell me, why do you consider the mine bosses to be the criminals?" said Jack.

Cherga wondered for a second if he could trust Jack and realized that Jack had already asked for his confidence on his own plan. "Well, there is this small story," said Cherga. "I have a brother, Rugao, who has a wife and also his son. He, Rugao, was involved in a loading accident at the spaceport in Wanana where he works. He did not cause it, but he was there, and they assigned some blame to him as well as three others. Much equipment was damaged, and one worker was highly injured, and another died. For some reason, well, I do know the reason, my brother and the three men were blamed for this accident when it was actually the fault of the operator as well as some old worn equipment. How can I say this? To punish someone for their higher bosses and take the blame from off of themselves as well as recoup the credits lost from the accident, they decided to sell my brother and these men to the mines as convict labor."

"My brother's wife—her name is Tanarrah—had no one else to turn to for help if my brother went to the mines. Without Rugao, she and the boy, Tagga-ki, could possibly not survive. Well, since I had no wife at the moment and I wasn't doing much other than working sometimes as a driver and sometimes as a cargo worker, I thought it would not hurt me to go to the mines for a few yenets, but it would certainly do considerable harm to Rugao and his family if Rugao had to go. So at the last moments before his confinement here, I told them we wished to switch. They will allow you to do this under some circumstances, especially if it benefits them, which it does, since I am somewhat bigger and more stronger than my brother. The lower bosses that conspired for this were quite fine with this change."

"That's, that's a very noble thing for you to do for your brother," said Jack. "How many brothers would do that for the other? You are an honorable person to do such a thing."

"Yes, well, perhaps," replied Cherga, "but there was really no other way to make this bad situation work out. It is sad though that we must endure this treachery that will ruin persons' lives only because some boss wants to go on another holiday to Guieena or some other resort planet. I will easily endure this short sentence and I will merely return to whatever I was doing before this, and my brother and his family will continue with their lives. Perhaps I will even become a contract miner, though I can't say I care for the underground life."

"What of the other three workers that were sentenced with your brother?" asked Jack.

Cherga replied, "They were also convicted to mines but not to this Corodune mine complex. There are a number of other mines that mine a variety of minerals all around Wanana, but they did not tell us where the others were sent, as they just sent us right out after each of our sentencings."

"Well, it seems that everyone I've come across so far has an interesting tale to tell," said Jack as he continued. "From what I can tell, the mine seems to be making a large portion of its profits by using slave labor."

Cherga replied, "There are many conscripts and convicts here because they committed a crime or other infraction, but it is true that they will fill needed miner's slots by any means they can get away with. So you say others have tales to tell such as my own? Are you speaking of our little friend Junot?"

"Yes," said Jack, "but you will have to ask him yourself or let him tell you at his own time."

"And what of you, Varaci Ja-ak?" said Cherga.

Jack replied, "Yes, something similar but a bit more complex. I will tell you another daiyus soon when we have more time. For now, let us enjoy the xula, and you can show me what else there is to do in the common area here, maybe that vido you told me about."

Jack and Cherga spent the remainder of the evening checking out the various attributes of the common area. One thing Jack was able to see was various entertainment vidos from both Nishda as well as imported from some other planets. The vido programming seemed to consist mostly of news shows as well as some sporting events that he had never obviously seen before. There were some team sports as well as solo sports of various types. Some were outdoor activities similar to what you'd see on Earth as well as a few types of motorsports involving types of riding machines similar to a dirt bike or quad types. The riding machines were called zinah-vas.

They had two, three, or four wheels, but the wheels rarely touch the ground. They could also launch themselves vertically up to a height of about twenty feet as they raced across the terrain from what Jack could see on the vido display. If the wheels touched the ground at all, it was usually just when the machine was coming off a high airborne jump, and the wheels mostly just absorbed the descent shock and kept the machine from crashing. They looked quite fun, and Jack thought he would like to take a shot at them some time. Jack also spent a little time probing Cherga about what he knew as far as the mining company's infrastructure as well as the cities of Wanana and Se-ahlaalu.

He also asked Junot as much as he could about the planet Vara, which he, Jack, was supposed to be a native of. From what information he could garner from Junot, Vara was a semiarid planet with a small equatorial greenbelt. The reputation of the planet's natives known as the Varaci or Varans was that of somewhat backhanded petty wheelers and dealers and smugglers of medium to occasionally high-value contraband that was generally blacklisted by the Galactic Trading Alliance, unless, of course, the Alliance itself was controlling it. Generally, if there is a Varaci ship involved, the manifest would be more than likely to contain illicit trade goods or contraband. Without actual further core research, that's about all the information Jack could get out of Junot as far as his knowledge of Vara and its native population.

Things seemed to settle into their normal workaday routine for a couple of daiyus. Jack spent as much time running scenarios through his head as far as possible ways to escape this nightmare situation of being conscripted for something he hadn't done. Of the three miners he knew, including himself, none were there for infractions they'd actually committed. How many other miners were in the same situation? He didn't really know. Would a general insurrection work or just rain destruction down on them? Theoretically, it seemed like it would be fairly easy to accomplish for the insurrection phase, since all that seemed to control the mine was rent-a-cops. The question would be, what sort of fallout would follow?

Was the whole planet's infrastructure this corrupt in a big collaborative effort against the citizens, or was it just the local mining operation? What about the Galactic Trading Alliance? Was it also corrupt, or maybe was it actually the policing entity that tried to combat the corruption? If that were the case, was it just the issue that Nishda was too remote from the core governing body of the Alliance for them to bother with the more remote worlds? He had too many questions and not much in the way of answers.

From what he'd seen so far, there were maybe just pockets of corruption and there were probably areas of the infrastructure that were run legitimately. It seemed too much like Earth in many ways with regard to graft and corruption. He had sort of hoped that the rest of the galaxy, now that he actually knew it was out there and populated, would have matured beyond the general conditions of Earth with regard to corruption into a more altruistic civilization. Maybe it had to do with the fact that this far out on the rim, it was more of a frontier zone where the standard rules of the galactic civilization didn't apply. Also, why was Earth not known to be involved in the Trading Alliance? Was Earth still just too primitive, or were there other factors involved? All he knew for sure was that being stuck in a mine running an ore-smashing rig wasn't going to get him anywhere fast. He definitely wasn't taking to this involuntary career change in any positive ways.

On the third daiyus after the fight pit matches, Jack was met by four guards when he came off his shift of running the zibur rig. "2641, you are instructed to come with us," said the slightly smaller of the four identically dressed guards.

"Food, now, eat," replied Jack, hoping they would possibly come back after the mealtime so that he could find Junot and coach him about what to say if they questioned him also.

"You must come now with us, 2641," said the alien guard with an emphasis on now.

"Now, yes, 2641," responded Jack. Jack decided he would just have to go along with the situation and see what transpired. He followed the guards through the main entrance to the conzone and eventually up the elevator to what was possibly the ground level of the mining complex.

He was brought to a waiting area outside of some type of operations area for the guard detachment. It wasn't big or fancy, just a general purpose waiting area. He was instructed to sit on a bench along the wall where he waited for several mentus until another four guards came in escorting Junot. Junot looked considerably frightened, but his eyes lit up, and he looked greatly relieved when he saw Jack sitting on the bench. Junot was also instructed to sit on the bench next to Jack. He still looked very worried and looked like he wanted to start asking Jack every question he could think of about what was happening and what he was supposed to do. Jack wasn't sure either, but he just whispered quietly to Junot, "Shhhh, they may be listening. Just tell the truth about the cleaning shower attack and then the attack by the fight pit when we were leaving, but nothing more. Truth is the easiest, no false memories required. Now, shhhh. All will be OK." Junot nodded his understanding and proceeded to sit there quietly as Jack had told him.

A few mentus later, the guards escorted Junot through the double doors on the other side of the room. He hoped whatever kind of questioning they were going to do with Junot wouldn't be too hard on him. The first rule of interrogation, thought Jack, is never let those being questioned collaborate beforehand; always keep them separate so you can compare any differences in their answers. Even if they had been listening, all they would've heard Jack say was to tell the truth.

It wasn't much, but that little bit of coaching probably helped Junot considerably as far as what to say and how to say it. It would give Junot something to focus on and help keep him on track and hopefully prevent him from divulging anything more than the basic information they probably wanted to know regarding the attack and injured miners near the fight pit. Junot was only in there about fifteen mentus before they brought him out and led him away, presumably back to the conzone. Junot didn't look too flustered, so hopefully, they hadn't been too harsh on him. Jack's two guards now signaled him to come with them through the doors where Junot had entered just a few mentus earlier.

Upon entering the room, Jack saw four aliens seated at a long table facing an empty chair about ten feet in front of them. Off to the side was another alien in a floating chair that he recognized as Cahooshek, the alien that had conscripted him and consigned him to the mining operation. "2641, you will sit and answer questions regarding injured mine workers near the main corridor to the fight pit arena," said one of the aliens to Jack.

"Two"—and then gibberish—"one, sit," replied Jack with a quizzical tone.

"What's wrong with your conscript, Cahooshek?" snapped one of the alien interrogators.

"It is something to do with a bad translator. Somehow, its language does not translate properly. I, we, don't really know why," grunted Cahooshek defensively.

"Well, how are we supposed to properly question your conscript if it can't communicate with us?" responded the alien.

"Well, it can understand well enough to take instructions and run a zibur rig, actually quite well."

"Well, I hope it can answer our questions to our satisfaction, as we have six injured mine workers, four that will be out of the mine working force for a considerable time, if not permanently."

Jack thought, *Good, they are already talking around me. Hopefully, I can make this work to my benefit.*

"Well, let us proceed, then," grumbled the alien. Slowing down its speech some and attempting to enunciate clearly, the alien asked Jack, "Six miners were severely injured in an assault near the main corridor of the fight pit. Many miners were questioned as to what they saw. One miner questioned answered that he saw a conscript that resembled you, a unique-looking Varaci conscript, accompanied by the smaller repair tech convict known to him and recognized as Junot, 1397. What do you know about this assault and the injury to the miners?" asked the alien sternly.

Here, Jack had to play a fine line between feigning comprehension and giving them the answers they wanted while taking the onus for the attacks off of him and Junot and placing them on the miners where it belonged. "Miners attack, miners"—gibberish—"Junot, miners attack Jack, 2641."

The lead alien responded, "You are telling us that the miners attacked you and the tech Junot?"

Jack paused as if trying to comprehend. "Miners, yes, attack Junot now also before now," replied Jack.

"Can you tell us why these miners would want to attack Junot as well as you?" The alien already knew the answer because he had gotten it from Junot himself. He wanted to see if he would get the same answer from Jack.

"Fix, Junot, machine fix, mine dig zibur machine. Miners bad, not"—gibberish— "want work. Want hurt Junot. No work miners then," Jack replied in what he hoped was his best Academy award-winning performance.

That seemed to satisfy the alien tribunal as far as Jack could tell at least for the moment. The four of them put their alien heads together and bantered between themselves for a few moments. Jack could tell they were working up to something as he heard them arguing about what to ask him next. "These miners that were injured in the assault," said the lead alien, "are known for their bad nature and attitude. How is it that they came to be so injured when they attacked you and the small Junot? You said that they all attacked you, yet you are uninjured as far as we see, and yet they that attacked you were no longer standing," queried the alien in a somewhat excited state.

"Miners attack, Jack stop miners," replied Jack.

"So you are the one that stopped the miners that attacked you and the tech Junot?" asked the alien trying to qualify Jack's answer.

"Jack attack back miners, miners stop, yes," replied Jack again.

"How did you stop these miners that attacked you?" asked another one of the aliens at the table.

"Hit, hits, attack stop," replied Jack. His confirmation seemed to excite the aliens even further.

"You are a Varaci, or are you are a soldier of some type that fights with hands?" asked the second alien.

"Soldier not," replied Jack. "Varaci," pausing for a second, "Jack Varaci," he said, deciding to stick with what little bit of cover story he had and hoping that they wouldn't question him further about his alleged home planet that he knew virtually nothing about. The aliens went through another thirty seconds of bantering among themselves. They seemed to be even more excited than previously.

The head alien started to speak to Jack. "The miners you have injured, we are not sure how, this is very costly to the mine. You must make restitution for the mining income lost because of the loss of the miners' labor. We will have to add additional time to your conscription obligation to reimburse the mine for the losses you have caused."

Jack replied, "Jack save keep Junot. Junot fix machines. Jack Junot save mine much credits, yes?" The interrogators hadn't expected this level of logic in a response from the mining conscript.

They jabbered among themselves for a few moments and then responded to Jack. "This does not matter as far as the rules that state that you must make amends for the losses you have caused, but we may take this into consideration as far as the amount of penalty required to reimburse the mine. We must deliberate for a short time to calculate the correct compensation that must be rendered to the mine." As the members of the inquisition put their heads together again, Jack had a pretty good sense that they had already come up with some plan to help them with their decision of supposed options of punishment they might bestow on him. The lead alien began to speak again, "It has been decided that an additional three yenets of conscription would be the suitable compensation for the loss caused to the mine by this event."

Jack stared at them blankly while thinking how completely typical this was for this kind of corrupt operation. He also decided that it wouldn't matter anyway, since he wasn't planning on sticking around and would use whatever means necessary to escape the situation. Still, he was waiting for the other shoe to fall, as he was sure there was more to this scenario. "But, of course," began the head alien, "if there was some manner in which you could repay the mine faster than the normal rate of zibur operator, then we would certainly consider reducing the additional conscription time by an appropriate amount."

Here it comes, thought Jack, as he just continued to stare at them to see what they were going to propose and how they were going to propose it.

"That is, what we mean is if you could provide some service to us that would help repay the mine faster, we would certainly consider reducing your conscription time," said the alien. Jack continued to stare at them. "Surely, you could provide some service to us to help yourself, could you not?" asked the alien as it started to get irritated.

"What?" asked Jack as he thought about how much fun it would be to jump up and ring their necks, but then there was the issue of the wrist restraints.

They were taken aback for a second by Jack's direct question. Then they regained their composure. "You must fight for us, fight for the mine, in the fight pits. We believe you must have a type of superior fighting skills, such as a soldier, to defend against and defeat six of these dangerous miners. You would fight the challengers from the Corodune mine first. Then if you are effective, you would fight the challengers from the other mine operations," added the head alien.

"Yes," said Jack.

"Yes?" replied the head alien in a surprised questioning tone. "Yes, you agree to fight for us, for the mine?"

"Yes," replied Jack, "only."

"Yes, only, uh, what do you mean only?" replied the alien.

"Hold wrist off," responded Jack, holding up his wrist restraints for them to see.

The aliens looked each other and jabbered for a few moments then replied, "That would not be allowed. Our miners must know that they can be corrected at any time. The restraints are very important to our discipline for convicts here."

Besides his long-term plans, Jack knew he had to get the restraints removed, as it would be possible for them to control the outcome of any fight if they could constrain his wrists and fighting ability. "No, Jack convict no, conscript Jack. Conscripts no restraints have, some few convicts only," he replied. Jack knew they were more interested in getting him to fight than they were about the loss of labor from the miners or anything else. He wouldn't budge until he got his way because he knew what they wanted even if they didn't. If not now, then in short order, he knew they'd come around to his demand.

"No, I don't believe this would be a wise choice or acceptable under our regulations," replied the head alien, thinking this was a minor issue and that he could dissuade Jack from his request by threatening more conscription time. "Surely you must not wish to have additional time added to your conscription sentence, do you?" said the alien.

"No," replied Jack sternly.

The aliens seemed momentarily relieved. "No," replied Jack, "no fight wrist holders on." The alien tribunal, who'd thought for a moment that they had won the argument, was suddenly forced to realize they were back at square one. "Jack fight no wrist hold," Jack said firmly to reiterate his position.

The aliens began arguing loudly between themselves and then seemed to come to a consensus. The lead alien spoke. "We have decided that it would not cause harm to have your wrist restraints removed during the fights, so we will grant your request." The alien started to speak again.

"No," said Jack, "off wrist hold now always. Jack work good, fight good, you like much."

Once again, the aliens stared incredulously at Jack then started arguing between themselves. They settled down and addressed Jack again. "We will grant your request, but do not attempt any sort of forbidden actions. We will monitor you to assure us that you are complying with our demands and the rules of the mine conscripts. Do you understand this?" they head alien asked Jack.

Jack replied, "Jack obeyed always good rules, good work. Only defend from miners." This seemed to satisfy the mine bosses, or whatever their positions were, from what Jack could tell. The important part was they believed they'd gotten what they'd wanted, and Jack knew he'd gotten what he wanted. This was the first positive step in his plan to blow this pop stand, and it had the potential to work out for him in more ways than one.

Well, might as well go for broke, thought Jack. *All they can do is throw a fit and tell me no.* "More," said Jack.

"More, what more, more what?" responded the head alien in a belligerent voice. "What do you talk about *more?*"

Jack responded, "Mine, you, get credits large Jack win, yes?"

The aliens conferred briefly between themselves. "We may perhaps make some profit but only if you were to be victorious in your matches," the head alien said cautiously. "Why do you want to know?"

Jack replied, "No credits Jack. Mine, you, pay Jack credits to fight win. Thousand credits now give, two hundred credits Jack win each," said Jack, hoping that conveyed that he wanted a thousand credits upfront and two hundred for each match that he won.

"What? That's absurd. Who do you think you are demanding that kind of payment to fight for us?" exploded the head alien.

Well, maybe it was a little high, thought Jack, so he could always come down a little. What he'd established by their response was that they would at least be somewhat open to the idea. "Large too much?" replied Jack, giving them a chance to counteroffer.

"Yes, too much!" yelled the alien. "Cahooshek, what sort of rebellious conscript do you have here!" yelled the alien to Cahooshek. Cahooshek himself thought it was somewhat funny, since he would probably get screwed on the deal somehow and not get any of the mine's profit even though it was his conscript.

Still, if this conscript was as skilled as they thought, then Cahooshek would have the chance to make some good profits just by betting on the matches. Cahooshek replied to the head interrogator, "This is your enterprise, not mine. I am merely here as a consultant regarding my conscript. You must make any decisions regarding this matter." *There,* thought Cahooshek, *that should take the issue from my back. If the stingy bastards want him to fight badly enough, then let them pay him something. It is of no concern of mine.*

Jack could tell they were steamed because they'd never had to negotiate about anything with a conscript or convict. "What gives you, conscript, the right to ask us for this kind of credits just to fight? We should send you back to the mine and add ten yenets to your conscript time for asking such an outlandish thing," the alien howled.

"Understand," Jack responded, "fair, pay fair. You, mine large credits get. Jack no credits got. Must got credits Jack, like others all. Fair ask for Jack," he added. The inquisitors were starting to calm down a bit and contemplate the logic of Jack's argument. They convened in a huddle once again and came back to Jack a few moments later.

"We have decided that your argument has a very slight degree of merit. However, you are an unproven risk and you value yourself too highly for this request," said the alien. "We agree to pay you three hundred credits initially with fifty credits

181

for every winning match. We will pay you the upfront part, but we will put a hold on it, and you will return it if you fail to win the first five matches," said the lead alien. Jack thought about holding out for more and bargaining for better terms, but he didn't think he could get much more out of them until he was a proven commodity. He decided to agree to their terms.

"Fair, fair, good," said Jack. Jack smiled to himself without giving anything away. *There's nothing like showing up for an interrogation and walking out with your first MMA fight contract and your wrist restraints removed,* thought Jack satisfyingly to himself.

The alien interrogators seemed satisfied and appeared to be finished with their agenda. The head alien spoke to Jack one more time. "The guards will escort you to the security post where you first came in, and they will remove the wrist restraints there. Remember what we told you about attempting any forbidden actions."

"Yes," said Jack, holding up his wrists. "Good for Jack, good for mine good." The guards then escorted Jack out of the room and back to the main conzone all the way to the security shack that he'd passed through when he'd entered the mine's conzone area.

Apparently, the guards on duty there had already received some sort of order to remove his wrist restraints. One of them programmed something into a control disk, and his wrist restraint wraps uncurled and fell off his wrists. *Now that's a great feeling,* Jack thought to himself as he contemplated the full implications of his new situation while rubbing his now naked wrists. One of the guards escorted him past the main entrance gate and toward the common area, and Jack was now on his own again. He wished they had some good ale or some of Cherga's qalalé, as this would certainly be an occasion to celebrate.

Instead, he went back toward the berthing chamber to see if he could find Junot and find out what had transpired during Junot's questioning. He found Junot waiting for him, and Junot was worried about what he'd told the mine bosses that had questioned him. "Jack, you told me to tell the truth, but I was worried that I'd tell them more than you wanted me to. I hope I didn't tell them anything I wasn't supposed to," moaned Junot with an anxious expression.

"If you were worried, then you probably didn't," said Jack. "What did you tell them?" he asked Junot.

"I told them about how they attacked me in the cleaning shower room and then how they attacked us coming out of the fight pit arena. I told them everything I could remember about what happened and how they tried to drag me away down the side corridor and how you stopped the miner that was dragging me. I hope that's OK, That's what you told me. I'm really sorry if—"

"Stop," said Jack, "that's fine, absolutely perfect. That's what you were supposed to tell them. Did you say anything about my female friend outside and our communications or any other plans we'd talked about?" Jack asked.

"No, no, never, nothing about any of that. I wouldn't say—"

"OK, OK," said Jack. "I was just checking and making sure you hadn't gotten carried away in there. You did fine, just perfectly fine. We both did fine, and everything seems to have worked for the better, at least in the interim."

"Well, what did they ask you about, Jack? What did they want?" said Junot.

"They just asked me about the fight and the attacks," said Jack. "What they really wanted was for me to agree to fight for them in the fight pit. Now, you can't tell anyone about this, not Cherga or any other friends you may have. I may need your help with some things," said Jack.

"Yes, I understand," said Junot. "I will not talk about this with anyone, and I'll do whatever you want me to, to help you."

"Thanks. That's good," said Jack. "For now, all I need to do is check in with my friend on the outside if you think this might be a good time to contact her."

"Yes," said Junot, "I think that would be OK, since it's Foursday, and I never see anyone else at the maintenance depot on Foursdays."

"Good," said Jack. "Since they grabbed us for questioning right after our shift, let's swing through the rations hall and grab a bite. Then we'll quietly sneak over to the maintenance depot and see if we can contact my friend."

They grabbed a quick bite of institutionalized mystery food at the rations hall and headed to the maintenance depot. When they got there, they confirmed that no one else was there, and Junot got Jack set up on the clandestine comm link so he could call his female friend. The connection clicked, and Jack heard the line pick up at the other end. "Yes, who is it?" he heard her voice say from the other end.

"Teela, hello, it's Duunda. How are you?" said Jack.

"Oh, J—Duunda, hello, it's so good to hear from you. Are you OK? How are you doing? I was beginning to worry, since I hadn't heard from you for a while," Zshutana said excitedly from her end.

"I am fine. I'm sorry I couldn't get back to you sooner. We have been working a lot, and I could not get to where I could contact you."

"That's OK," she replied. "I'm just glad to hear from you and to hear that you are OK. Are there any changes to your status there? Is there any possibility of you taking a holiday, anything new to tell me?" she asked.

"No and yes," he said to her. "Do you think you might be able to do us a small favor?" he asked her.

"Well, yes, of course, anything," she said without hesitation.

He was trying to figure out how to explain his new situation to her both covertly and from a positive aspect so she wouldn't be too upset. "Do you remember the fight pits and the matches we discussed briefly?" he asked her.

"Yes, well, why?" she asked. "What does that have to do with anything?"

Jack replied, "Well, I knew you knew of them from our previous conversation. What I was wondering is, do you have access to or any way to place bets on them?"

"Well, yes, I suppose so. I know many of the miners and other workers will wager on them and usually lose their pay credits every time they do. Why would you want to know this?" she asked.

"Well, I have to ask you a question," he said to her.

"What is it, uh, Duunda? Just ask," she said.

"OK," he replied. "Do you trust me?" he asked her.

She paused for a second to think about the question, and the only answer she could come up with was he had to be the most trustworthy person she'd ever met. Her pause worried him for a second, but then she answered him. "I just had to think for a second how to answer that. To me, you seem like the most trustworthy person I have yet known. Does that answer your question?" she said to him.

"Yes, it does, and thank you," he said. "Then I have a small business proposition I would like you to consider. Would you mind hearing me out on it for a minute?"

She wasn't sure what she had expected, but she didn't think that was it, so she said, "Well, yes, I suppose, of course. A business proposition, what is it?"

Jack replied, "I have some inside information on some of the matches as to who is very likely to win. If you would like to take a slight betting chance, I'm very certain I could help you make a fair amount of extra credits if you have some spare credits you wouldn't mind wagering."

Jack knew she was an astute businessperson but didn't know what her attitude about gambling would be especially for something she'd expressed a dislike for.

"Well, I've never done anything like that," she replied. "I'm not sure that wagering on something like that would be a very good investment choice. How can you be sure or know what the outcome of a particular match might be?" she asked skeptically.

"Well, the reason I know the likely outcome of a particular match," he said, "is it will be the matches that I am fighting in, so I will have a pretty good idea of what the outcome will be."

"What, what?" she said. "Did you say you are going to be fighting in the matches, you yourself, fighting in the matches?" She gasped.

"Yes," he said. "They want me to fight in their fight pit arena in their fight matches."

"No, no, that's probably not a good idea. You could get really hurt or worse doing that. I've heard of some of the injuries that have happened to the fighters in those matches. Some have gotten killed. You shouldn't do that, Ja—Duunda. You could get very seriously injured," she said in a very apprehensive voice.

"No, it's OK," he said, "and I really don't have a choice. They are basically forcing me to fight, but I've arranged it so it's on my terms."

"No, but still you could get really hurt, and I wouldn't want that," she said.

"I know and appreciate that you don't want me to get hurt," he replied, "but one of the very many things you don't know about me is that I did this sort of thing for many yenets before I ended up here. I've watched their matches, and they are very unskilled, so there is little risk of me getting seriously hurt. Either way, I've got to do it, and I thought it would be very lucrative for you if you wanted to make some good credits by betting on the matches I'm in."

"Why? Why would they want you to fight in the pit matches?" she asked. "You have only been down there for a short time. How did this happen?"

He thought, now he would have to explain the attack issue. "Well," he began, "a friend of mine here, the one that set up this comm link for me, was attacked by some miners, and I jumped in and stopped their attack and kept him from getting hurt."

"Why did they attack him? How many miners attacked him?" she asked.

Crap, he thought, *how much more of a hole can I dig for myself here?* "Well, they are just sort of not very nice miners that like to pick on him because he's somewhat small," Jack said.

"That's terrible," she said. "How many were there?"

Explaining some things to women is challenging, thought Jack. "Well, I believe there were six of them that attacked us. That's what the mine bosses said, the mine bosses that want me to fight for them now," he explained.

"Attacked us?" she asked. "I thought you said they attacked your friend."

"Yes, yes, they did attack him, but I was with him, so they actually attacked us, both of us," he tried to clarify.

"Ja—Duunda," she said, "this doesn't sound very good. Now I'm really troubled about you being down there. I've got to try and figure out some way to try and help you, maybe, if there was just some way to get you out of there. I'm just really . . ."

"Stop, wait," said Jack, "that's what I'm working on, and this is part of the plan that I have come up with so far. There's a lot more to it, but I can't explain it to you over this comm line even though it's probably secure. What I need for us to do is try and make a whole lot of credits, and you could help us do this by wagering on the matches that I'm going to be in. Do you kind of understand where I'm going with this?" he asked her.

She processed this for a few septus and decided she had at least a partial idea of what he was thinking. "Yes, I think I do understand what you're trying to do. I still don't like it. I don't have to like it, but it does make sense as far as what you're saying. You were attacked by six miners?" She suddenly thought to ask, "Did you get hurt? What happened?" she added.

"No, I didn't get hurt, and neither did my friend. But the miners got hurt and will be out of work for a while, which was the pretext the mine bosses used to get me to fight for them. That's all I should say about it for now. I don't know how much you have, how many credits you can spare to wager on my matches. It would be better to wager more on the first matches because the odds won't be in my favor then. You'll get the best returns on the earliest matches, but even after that, you'll still do good," Jack explained.

"All right," she said. "Just tell me which matches to bet on, and I will do as you ask, but I won't like the fact that you are fighting in the matches. How will you let me know which ones you are in?" she asked.

Jack replied, "I should know a daiyus or two in advance of when I'll be fighting. I will let you know as soon as I can so you can have time to get your wager in. We will just have to play it by ear a bit until we figure out the best way to do this."

"Well, OK, I'll be waiting to hear from you then," she said.

"OK, I will get back to you as soon as I can, Teela," he said to Zshutana. "I think we should cut this off for now," he said. "I'll get back to you as soon as I can and let you know how this works out." They finished their good-byes, and Jack signed off using Junot's instructions. *That's good,* Jack thought. *That's one side of the equation to start putting this all together.*

Jack and Junot left the maintenance depot and headed back toward the common area. Jack explained to Junot what he was planning on doing as far as the wagering situation. He told Junot that he should bet whatever credits he had available on Jack's fights. Junot asked Jack if he thought he could actually win all the matches. Jack said he wasn't sure, but he had a pretty good chance, since he hadn't seen any particularly well-trained fighters, although the competition would get stiffer as he moved up the ladder. Jack pointed out to Junot that the betting odds would be against him initially, since he was unknown, so the best returns would come in his first few matches. Junot told Jack he had about two hundred credits saved up and asked Jack if he should wager them all. "Yes," said Jack. "You'll make your biggest returns when the odds are against me, so wager heavily on the first few matches. I'll explain it to you a little better when you get ready to wager for the first time," Jack said to Junot.

* * * * *

Things settled back into their regular routine of mining for a few daiyus. Jack let Cherga in on the situation and swore him to secrecy regarding the mine bosses' requirement that he fight for them.

He also encouraged Cherga to wager on his matches if he wanted to make some sure returns on his "investments." Cherga chided him, "Are you sure you're up for such a strenuous activity, Varaci Ja-ak? You appear to be a little more aligned with the executive class to me. I am not so sure that mixing it up with these convict miners will be the best thing for your overall health."

Jack replied, "Don't worry about me. Just put your money where your mouth is if you want to make some fast and easy credits. Just remember, as a new challenger in the pit arena, the odds will be highly against me, maybe ten or more to one for the first few matches, so your best returns will be on my first showings. Pay attention now and I will show you how these matches should be fought."

"OK, my friend," said Cherga. "If you are so convinced of your ability, I will risk some credits on your efforts. Hopefully, you will not go crashing down and I will make some outrageous returns on my gamble." They both laughed chiding each other over the prospects of Jack fighting in the pit arena. Cherga wasn't entirely convinced of Jack's prowess based on his claims, but there was a solid confidence in Jack's attitude toward the task. The Varaci had proven himself worthy in every other aspect so far. Perhaps there was even more to this Varaci with the unique outspoken and honest personality than the normally cryptic Varan race warranted.

The next daiyus after his shift, Jack received a message through his translator telling him to proceed to the guard post at the mine conscript entrance to register for this week's upcoming fight pit match. Jack wasn't aware that the translator unit had any comm or messaging capability, as he had never heard anyone mention anything about it before. It made sense, though, since he'd been able to see information on the participants in the prior week's pit matches as well as other information since he'd learned of the heads-up capability on the translator. Well, he thought, if it can receive, it can most likely reply and transmit. That means that the mine bosses might have the capability to eavesdrop on anyone's conversation or other activities linked to the translator.

Now that he was a "party of interest" to the bosses, he would have to be very cautious about what he said and did. Unless he could figure out a way to circumvent what the translator could see or hear, there was a pretty fair chance that anything he said or did could be monitored by the mine bosses. This now concerned him considerably, and he reasoned it was probably why there was a minimal guard presence in most of the conzone areas. The mine bosses probably have the ability to know anything that might be going on without a heavy physical presence among the conscript population.

If this was the case, he wondered why they'd sent him the message to register for the fight match. Were they just so anxious to get their protégé into action that they blew their protocol and messaged him directly, or was his language charade effective enough that he convinced them that he didn't have the capacity to deduce the other implications of an electronic device that had the capacity to deliver a message directly to him? He might never know the answer, but he would certainly proceed accordingly based on what he now knew.

Jack was able to complete his registration for the upcoming match simply by looking at the display and having it spell out the conditions and the few rules of the match, which he basically already knew. There were images and the standard strangely written dialogue accompanying it, which he didn't yet have the ability to translate. He guessed that even though the translator did a good job of translating his oral language and displayed some basic information somewhat like a heads-up display that it still couldn't translate written English, since it didn't have anything in its data core to reference. Though it would probably have that capability, he was guessing that the English translating ability of the translator was strictly a verbal association algorithm.

When he got back to the berthing chamber—*that's such a strange translation,* thought Jack —he found Junot and had him scrounge up an old-fashioned writing instrument, which looked a lot like a pen, and something to write on, which looked a lot like some sort of packaging paper. He then blocked the view of his writing material from the translator by wrapping a spare miner's shirt around his neck. He then wrote out in English that the mine bosses could listen in on their conversation through the translators. He then wrote out the English alphabet along with about two hundred common words. He then had Junot sit down while he covered up Junot's translator. Then he proceeded to read all the words to Junot but not the part about the eavesdropping capabilities of the bosses. He then instructed Junot, in as few words as possible, to translate the writing out of view of the translator.

Junot got the basic idea of what Jack was conveying. Jack then led him off to the maintenance depot where they proceeded to hammer out an English language written translation algorithm. The computational power of the core was quite substantial, and in no time, Jack and Junot were communicating through a written dialogue derived by a phonetic conversion algorithm of the English language all out of the view of the translator. Jack explained how he had received the message to register for the upcoming match and how that also meant the translators probably had both a listening and transmitting capability that the bosses could use to spy on the conscripts. Junot immediately understood the implications of the situation and set about trying to find out exactly what the capabilities of the translators were by searching the more covert areas of the core database.

It wasn't long before he discovered quite a bit about the capabilities of the translators above and beyond what he'd already known. Not only did they have the ability to spy on the wearer but they also had a coded tracking ability as well as a hard encrypted identification stamp. Jack wrote silently to Junot with the translator blocked, "Would it be possible to turn off the listening and transmitting ability of the translator as well as the identification stamp and tracking capability?"

Junot wrote back, "I am not sure. I have never investigated this before or even thought about it."

"Maybe not," said Jack. "But as an electronics technician and security monitoring systems specialist, this is kind of right up your alley."

"My alley?" wrote Junot.

"Yes, your alley," replied Jack, "your area of expertise, your specialty, your area of special knowledge, that's what I mean by alley."

"Oh, OK, I wasn't sure what you meant," wrote Junot.

Jack wrote back, "Don't get in any trouble. I want you to stay covert. Find out exactly how these things work and what we can do to subvert them. Switching them off may not work. We may have to work around them, even trick them into thinking they're still working, but instead, they're really working for us. Does that make sense?"

"Yes," wrote Junot, "kind of like what they were making me do when they got caught and put the blame on me."

"Yes," wrote Jack, "but at an even more covert level. In fact, with the capabilities of these translators, if you or your former employers weren't aware of it, it might be how the Alliance found out about what they were doing when they sent in their audit team."

A look of astonishment crossed Junot's face. He wrote, "I never thought of that. I always wondered how they found out what we were doing, since they never told us. I warned them that I didn't think it was totally secure, but I didn't realize they had the ability to see what we were doing all along."

"I would almost bet that that's what happened," wrote Jack. "If we can control what they see and hear and keep our own communications hidden and maybe even scrambled, then we will be way ahead of the game as far as knowing what they might be trying to do to us."

"Yes," wrote Junot, "that would be so, so, enjoyable."

"Exactly," replied Jack. "Now we must thoroughly destroy this written conversation, and then in the next few daiyus, you can get working on the translator issue," wrote Jack as he pointed at all their scribblings on the old-fashioned communications method.

Junot eliminated their written conversation record by tearing it up and feeding it into incineration chute used to eliminate the mine's burnable waste materials. They then took a couple of mentus to contact Zshutana and let her know that Jack's first match was scheduled in two daiyus. Keeping the conversation to about fifteen words and using their covert names, Jack was able to convey to her the information and sign off immediately so that it would be virtually impossible for them to know who was contacted or what was said. Zshutana was able to grasp the reason for the brevity of the exchange, but she was still disappointed that it only lasted for about sixty septus.

The next two daiyus, they all went through their normal work routines, and Jack hit the gym both nights to get toned up and tuned up for his first match. He wasn't too worried about any of the first several matches, but he wished he had a good sparring partner so that he could hone his skills back to a reasonable competition level. That night, Jack checked his credits account through his translator. Sure enough, there were the three hundred credits plus twenty more for his two weeks on the job as a zibur rig operator. There was a subnote on the three hundred credits that said they were restricted for possible collection but that the account holder had full access to them otherwise. On the night of Jack's first match, both he and

Junot and Cherga went to the fight pit arena about an horun early to make sure Jack was properly checked in and briefed for his first match.

They were in another medium-sized room off the far side of the fight pit arena opposite the main entrance. All the contenders and their associates as well as several arena assistants were present. Both Sha-aga, the announcer, and the referee Ulzaka were there to recite the rules and give them an alleged pep talk. The rules basically consisted of what Jack had heard previously, which was no eye gouging, don't get caught taking a weapon into the arena, and be sure to beat your opponent into uncontested submission. No gloves, no helmets, and no shin guards or other safety equipment was the name of the game. The only thing Jack didn't like about the entire scenario so far was that there were no mats in the arena, so takedowns would mean you wanted your opponent on the bottom and not you. That was simple enough in a commonsense way, but it also made sense that the best way to fight in this arena would be a stand-up fight. Jack knew that wasn't always possible, but he knew he would be less likely to sustain any serious injuries by staying on his feet. The pep talk from the announcer Sha-aga basically consisted of him telling the new contenders not to feel too bad when they got beat and telling the experienced contenders not to beat the novices so badly that they couldn't work or fight again.

About twenty mentus before the first match, Jack learned that he would fight in the second match, and his opponent would be a convict miner named Sulok of Havora with a four and five record. Not too great of an opponent as far as his fight record, but it seemed strange that they would pit a first-time fighter with someone that had at least nine fights under his belt. That didn't make sense based on what Jack thought the mine bosses were planning with regard to running the matches in their favor and trying to string them out as long as possible.

From what Jack understood about bookies and odds making, he knew that if the most money is gambled on the favorites, then it's when the favorites fail to win that the bookmakers make the most money. This could be what the bosses were trying to do, but placing him against a nine-time contender still seemed way outside the envelope for that strategy. When they posted the fight odds, Jack was even more surprised because with Sulok's poor win record, the odds were thirty to one over Jack, the new contestant. Those were pretty horrific odds for Jack, so there probably wouldn't be too many people betting on him except for him, Junot, Cherga, Zshutana, and maybe even the mine bosses. Jack didn't know who had set the odds, but he'd bet the mine bosses had their hands in it somehow.

The fact that he was a new unknown entity, as well as supposedly being a Varaci, who were generally known for their devious propensities and not their hand-to-hand fighting abilities, probably helped push the odds far out against him for his first fight pit match. The first match started after the requisite promotional pandering by Sha-aga and the introduction of the first contenders, Rolak of Nishda versus Narnov of Debanna, who had lost in a previous match last wenek. Just as soon as the first match started, the betting closed for it as expected. Jack's match against Sulok of Havora then opened for betting.

Jack had gone over the betting process with Cherga beforehand as well as verifying it beforehand with Cherga's help that he would be able to use the restricted funds to wager on the pit matches. He decided to go for broke and wagered his full 320 credits on himself for the match. He crunched the numbers and figured out that with those thirty to one odds that he would net 9,600 credits if he won. *Well, don't count your chickens,* he said to himself. He hoped the others had gotten their bets in on time and weren't afraid to bet more than just a few credits on the first go with these impressively bad odds.

Cherga and Junot had left a couple of mentus earlier after Jack had assured them that everything was set for the match on his side. Jack saw his upcoming opponent, so he went over to introduce himself as well as get a feel for his opponent's attitude and demeanor. "Sulok of Havora, I, Jack of Vara, good luck you on this night," said Jack as an introduction.

Sulok of Havora, who was about three inches taller than Jack, looked at Jack with a condescending smirk. "Luck, ha, fool of Vara, Sulok will chew you and spit you to the ground. What kind of fool Varaci, a sneaking scheming Varaci, thinks he can challenge a champion of Havora in the fight pit?"

"Ah, Sulok, a champion of Havora, should Jack concede match now?" said Jack.

"That would be a wise choice for a fool Varaci," growled Sulok.

"Ah, then no glory for champion Sulok," chided Jack.

"I will take my winning glory on the fool Varaci, but it is hardly worth the effort," countered Sulok.

"Yes," said Jack. "Sulok win four of five, this champion record?" Jack chided further.

"You are fool, Varaci. I should kill you here and now," threatened Sulok.

Jack backed off to give himself a little room just in case. "Save it for pit, Sulok. You'll need it," said Jack.

"You are fool and will run away," snarled Sulok of Havora.

I'm seriously looking forward to this now, thought Jack. Jack had a pretty good feel for this brawler now. He was big and strong and probably fairly fast, but it was apparent to Jack that this venom-spewing brawler had no discipline at all. Still, he would have to be careful not to get caught up in the kind of free-for-all clash that this type of adversary may be somewhat good at.

Besides winning the match, one of Jack's important goals would be to not end it too fast or too decisively so that he could keep the odds marginally against him for the next several matches. This would keep the mine bosses happy as well as maximizing his and his friends' winnings on the next few matches.

In the third round of the first match, Narnov of Delanna managed to come out ahead by taking his opponent Rolak to the ground and getting a few good punches and couple of elbow strikes that took the will out of the challenger. The match was called in the favor of Narnov, and then it was time for Jack and Sulok's match.

The announcer Sha-aga went into his routine about the previous match and how exciting and spectacular it was. Then he announced the next match, which was Jack's, "We now have a new challenger for the next match of the night." A few half-hearted cheers for the new challenger arose along with a fair share of heckling and groaning at the announcement for Jack the Varaci as the new contestant. "All the way from Vara, we bring you Varaci Ja-ak, who is matched against a well-known contender, our nearly insane arena veteran, Sulok of Havora."

Sulok came into the arena jumping and howling in a grand attempt to garner the admiration of what followers he had. A better cheer went up for Sulok but only because he was a known quantity and most would be betting on him. His four and five fight record wasn't anything to brag about, but it was better than the new contender, which made Sulok the likely sure bet. It seemed to Jack that if Sulok would have been a little better-rated fighter, then he wouldn't have been expected to fight a new contender. Jack still wondered why they had put him with a ranked fighter for his first match, since that would have been unheard of back on Earth.

Some in the crowd probably thought it would be entertaining because of the fact that they'd never seen a Varaci before and definitely not in a fight. Either way, it would be fun to see the newbie get a sound thrashing like the new ones always did. "Come on, all you dangerous and heartless conscripts and convicts, let's make some noise for our veteran fighter Sulok and the daring new challenger Varaci Ja-ak. We're sure this will be a great fight, and even if it isn't, the next one coming up will surely be amazing. Just wait and see, because we always aim to please!" bellowed Sha-aga. "Let the match begin." The buzzer sounded, and the match was on.

Jack came out about a third of the way to give himself some maneuvering room. Sulok charged hard directly at Jack, half lunging and taking three huge swings while trying to overrun and intimidate Jack at the same time. Sulok's first swing was not even in range, and the second swing Jack easily ducked while moving deftly to the left. Sulok's third swing found nothing in the vicinity to connect with. Jack wanted to get a good feel for any technique his opponent might actually have before he engaged him and at the same time let his opponent tire a bit. The spectators came alive a little with a few hoots and yells when they realized it wasn't going to be an instant route. Sulok charged Jack again with basically the same three-swing attack.

This time, he anticipated Jack trying to duck and move left, so halfway into his attack, he tried to counter Jack's move by turning right to face and attack Jack. The problem was Jack wasn't there. As Sulok started his second attack, Jack ducked then feigned the same move to the left, but instead, he bobbed right. Just as Sulok thought he was going to find Jack where he wanted him, Jack let loose with an easy right hook from Sulok's eight o'clock position. He popped Sulok on the back left side of his head just hard enough to send the Havoran tripping into the wire. Sulok had been wide open, and Jack could have put him down, but he had to try and make the match go three rounds to keep the odds against himself as much as possible.

Sulok was slightly shaken for an instant but turned and pushed himself off the wire and rushed Jack in an attempt to tackle him. Jack dodged then sidestepped just slightly and straight-armed Sulok with his right arm while at the same time grabbing his opponent and propelling him past and into the center of the fight ring where Sulok stumbled and nearly crashed into a heap. Jumping up, Sulok was enraged but held his position for a minute trying to figure out some sort of attack plan.

He seethed at Jack. "You are not fighting me. Fight me like a real fighter. You fight like a female!"

"Well, then if that's the case, it seems to be working against you pretty well, wouldn't you say?" chided Jack. Sulok had enough sense to realize that what he'd been trying wasn't going to work, so he decided to try and slowly work Jack to the wire where he could trap and pummel him. What he didn't expect was that Jack just stood his ground in the middle of the arena and didn't back away.

He came at Jack slowly looking for an opening, but Jack was completely covered in his fight stance, leaving no openings. Now Sulok had his hands up and his elbows splayed wide in an amateurish stance that left him wide open in multiple areas. After a fair amount of time spent moving around the ring, Jack let him come in and figured he could take a couple of Sulok's hits if he blocked them effectively just so that it looked like Sulok was getting some points on him. Sulok moved in and threw a couple of his wide swings connecting with Jack's arms as Jack blocked each swing then moved out of range.

As Sulok wound up for a third swing, Jack deftly popped him in the face with a quick left jab just hard enough to get his opponent's attention, which resulted in Sulok moving both his hands back in an attempt to block Jack's punches. When he did this, Jack moved in low and fast and delivered a quick, light liver shot while at the same time wondering if Sulok had a liver and if it was located in the normal place. Jack then followed up with a fast but easy left hook that sent his opponent stumbling off to his left and into the wire again. Just as Sulok was trying to regain his composure, the buzzer sounded, and they went to a time-out.

The crowd of spectators, including Junot and Cherga, were now in a fairly frenzied state as they grew more excited by the unexpected quality of the match. Cherga and Junot ran over to the wire during the time-out. Cherga bellowed, "Well, my Varaci Ja-ak friend, it appears you speak some truth about your knowledge and skills in the fight pit."

"Yes, I've had some experience in the ring before, but it's not over yet," countered Jack. "My experience is more in combat-type training, but we did a fair amount of sparring along with it. My opponent, Sulok, has no training, discipline, or patience. Still, I wouldn't want to get hit by one of his wild swings. It looks like the second round will be starting shortly. I'll see you shortly after the match," said Jack. "I hope you put a decent wager on this before the match started," added Jack.

"Yes, I wagered one hundred credits," said Cherga.

"And I wagered 150 credits," chimed Junot.

"That's great," said Jack. "I'll do the best I can to make sure you come out ahead on your wagers."

With only about twenty seconds left until the time-out was over, Jack went back to his spot in the ring. Zshutana sat watching at her big desk on the display that was linked to the closed-loop mine channels. The first round was very nerve-racking for her, but she felt better now after watching Jack adeptly avoid being injured by his larger opponent. Still, she would keep asking that nothing would happen to him that would end up with him being hurt. That's about all she could think of to do from where she was.

The buzzer sounded for the second round, and both fighters came off their spots toward the center of the ring. Sulok was considerably more cautious now that he discovered how useless his brawling attacks were against this new Varaci opponent. He had anticipated obliterating this new fighter in the first mentu of the match just to show the crowd how good of a fighter he really was. It seemed sort of strange to him that the match had even gone this long, since what little he'd heard about Varacis wasn't anything good, especially concerning their supposed nonexistent fighting ability. He just knew that he had to be more careful and pay attention to what he was doing in this round.

Sulok advanced cautiously toward Jack with his hands up then lunged at Jack while swinging as fast and wildly as he could, hoping to connect with one of his swings. Jack dodged just out of range for the first couple of swings then redirected Sulok's next swing and moved off-line. As Sulok started to turn back to face his opponent, Jack dropped slightly and put two fast mid body strikes on Sulok's midsection then moved back out of Sulok's range. Sulok swung wildly while he tried to absorb the pain of the punches and having the wind half knocked out of him.

The pain only made Sulok madder, so he charged Jack again, hoping to overrun the Varaci and take him down. Instead of avoiding Sulok, Jack let him overrun him until he was inside Sulok's effective range. Sulok swung brutally at Jack but was too close to connect with anything, while Jack just covered as Sulok tried to land multiple punches on him. It looked like Jack was getting hit repeatedly, but the only effect that Sulok was having on Jack was pointless flailing on Jack's arms and shoulders. Jack waited for Sulok to start to back off and try to see what effect his punches had on Jack. As soon as Sulok started back, he left himself wide open, and Jack hit him with an easy right uppercut palm strike followed by a light left straight. Jack didn't want to hit him hard enough to put him down yet, but he wanted Sulok to know he'd been hit.

Sulok stumbled back as Jack's punches connected and stunned him enough to replace the rage in him with a small degree of fear. Sulok had fought nine other opponents in the ring, and he believed he had only lost to any of them because he was overmatched in size and strength.

The last two punches that had connected he'd never even seen and still didn't know where they'd come from. He suddenly realized that he'd never fought anyone like this Varaci before and couldn't even remember having ever seen anyone that fought this way before. Sulok wasn't sure what he was thinking, but he did realize that he was now on the defensive and that he wasn't taking the fight to the Varaci, but rather the fight was coming to him and not in a good way. As they came to the middle of the ring again, Sulok said to Jack, "Where have you learned this fighting, Varaci?"

"Here and there," replied Jack.

"I will have learned some new things today," said Sulok.

"Then I won't hurt you so that you can't remember them," said Jack.

"Good, that is good. Now let us finish the match," replied Sulok, realizing that the whole demeanor of the match had changed.

Jack moved in on his opponent and pushed him back with several left jabs and let his guard down just enough so that Sulok would see the opening and attack. Sulok lunged with both hands to grab Jack around the neck. Jack let him connect so they could get a few seconds of close-in grappling before the round ended. Jack plucked his opponent's grip from his neck and locked him up so that all that Sulok could do was struggle for some sort of advantage. The buzzer sounded, and Jack disengaged and pushed Sulok back and said, "Time."

"Yes, yes," replied Sulok. "I almost had you that time. That is what I'll do again next time."

"Yes, I think you did," said Jack. "And thanks for the warning," he chided Sulok.

As Jack went back to his spot, he wondered how they, whoever they were, scored the fights. He knew it was apparent that Sulok was now on the defensive, but he didn't know if that was enough to have the match called in his favor. He didn't really want to hurt the miner, since his adversary had actually shown a little bit of deference and had acknowledged the defensive position he was now in. Still, Jack needed a decisive win for this match for several reasons. Primarily, he didn't want the match going to Sulok just because he was the known fighter homeboy. He was going to have to put his opponent down during the third round.

The third round started with Sulok charging to the center of the ring, while Jack held back to see what he was going to do. "I still must do my best whatever the outcome," said Sulok as he came at Jack.

"Yes, you must, and so must I," replied Jack. Sulok dove for Jack's legs in an attempt to take him down, but Jack just sprawled out and dropped his weight onto Sulok, pulled himself up, and pushed off Sulok's shoulder and up into a fight stance, while Sulok still lay spread-eagled on the ground. Jack could have kneed him or even put him in an arm bar, but he wanted the round to go on for a while longer.

Sulok got back up and came at Jack in a fake attempt to take him down again but instead tried a punching attack with a wild assortment of flailing swings and punches. Jack ducked, deflected, or covered everything his opponent threw at him. Jack let this go on for another couple of minutes until he knew they were far enough into the round that he knew it was time to end the match. He still didn't want it to look too one-sided, so he moved in when Sulok started another attack and waited for a nice clear opening, which didn't take long.

Sulok took four arbitrary swings at Jack, while Jack just covered and blocked his opponent's punches. Sulok dropped his left hand as he was attempting to wind up for a right swing, Jack let go with a quick but easy right hook that connected firmly enough to send Sulok stumbling to the right and onto one knee. Sulok stood up and tried to shake it off and regain his composure. Once he was up again, Sulok came charging at Jack with a look of rage and desperate confusion. He took a long wind up and swing at Jack with his right fist, which Jack ducked and deflected to Sulok's left while he moved off-line to Sulok's right. As Sulok tried to turn to face Jack, he was completely open with no defense at all. Jack popped him with a quick left straight and sent the already off-balance Sulok tripping backward into the ground. Jack didn't want to hit him hard enough that he would be unconscious during his fall, and he hoped that Sulok would try to cover and keep from hitting the hard ground with his head.

Instinct seemed to take over as Sulok fell backward, and he did manage to bring his arms up and protect his head during the fall. Still, it looked like a pretty good crash to Jack, and it sounded painful as Sulok literally bit the dust and the rock floor. Sulok lay there in a heap for about five septus without moving. He managed to sit about halfway up while trying to gather enough strength to sit all the way up but then collapsed back onto his elbows where he lay there panting. It was apparent to the referee and to Sha-aga, the announcer, that the match was over and the winner was Jack.

Sha-aga jumped into the ring and grabbed Jack's arms and raised them in victory. The spectators let loose with a loud and excited cheer. They hadn't expected the match to be anywhere near this entertaining. Jack took a quick victory circuit then went back to where Sulok was trying to sit up again and helped his vanquished opponent get to his feet. "You are OK, Sulok," said Jack.

"Yes, yes, I probably, I think, yes, so," muttered Sulok. "You have, you have much, much skill in this, this," slurred Sulok.

"Yes, some," said Jack, "that is why I did not wish to really hurt you. You should be OK shortly. Remember, don't get angry and always think about what you are doing. Keep your head and your senses about you at all times. Never let your guard down. Perhaps you'll do better against your next opponent," cautioned Jack.

"Yes, I, I will hope so," stammered Sulok as some of the arena workers took over and helped him out of the fight pit arena.

"Amazing, amazing!" barked Sha-aga. "Who would have guessed that this new fight pit challenger would have done even half this well against such a seasoned veteran? This was a great match, yes, really a splendid match," continued Sha-aga. "Can he do it again? That will yet to be seen, as, as, as in seen here next wenek for all you magnificent fight pit fans and spectators!" The crowd was still excited and jabbering their approval of the match. Jack exited the ring through the rear entrance and went around to the spectators' bench where Cherga and Junot were waiting for him impatiently.

"You did it, you did it!" exclaimed Junot excitedly.

"Yes, outstanding," said Cherga, "very, very good, my Varaci friend. You are most deft moving about the pit arena. This I would not have guessed from a such common conscript such as yourself," chided Cherga.

Junot piped up, "Jack, I couldn't believe it. I don't know much about this fight pit sport, but it is a lot more interesting when your friend is one of the fighters. I was worried at first because the other fighter was so large and formidable. I didn't know what was going to happen."

Jack replied, "Well, just remember that if I tell you to bet on a match, there's a very good chance that you're going to come out ahead. I believe you two did very well on your wagers tonight, but the odds won't be that far against me on the next match, since I just won this one."

"That's right," said Junot. "I bet 150 credits. How much did I win? Did I get to double my money?"

"No," replied Jack, "you didn't double your money. You bet 150 credits, but the odds against me winning were thirty to one. To figure out how much you will win, just take the amount you wagered and multiply the first number of the odds, divide that by the second number, and then add your bet back in. So you, Junot, will get your 150 credits plus 4,500 credits."

"Oh my, my, oh, hiyet iyee!" yelped Junot. "I can't believe it. I just can't believe it. That's amazing."

"Now don't get carried away," replied Jack. "You could have just as easily lost your bet and you'd be out your 150 credits."

"Yes, but you won, and I made all this money," countered Junot.

"Well, the odds won't be thirty to one next time," said Jack. "We'll be lucky if there are still as high as ten to one against me. So using that little formula, you can figure out how much it'll take with the winning wager to make the same amount. It'll take a lot more than your 150 credits to return 4500. And the same for you, Cherga, to make another return like the three thousand credits you got this time."

"Yes, Varaci Jack, I know the odds, and from what I've seen tonight, I think I will make another healthy bet on your next match," replied Cherga. "But you are correct that the odds will be much changed toward your favor. We will only have two or three more matches with the odds against you if you continue to win. Maybe you should not win so much."

"Well," said Jack, "that idea did cross my mind, but I'm going to bet the maximum on every fight. If we only bet on the matches that I will win, then they would know what I was doing and probably stop me from betting. So, no, I think the only way to proceed is to just win every match that I can. Our returns based on the odds will diminish, but if we wager large amounts, we will still make considerable profits."

"Yes, I suppose you are correct," said Cherga.

"I don't care about the mine bosses," said Jack, "but if a lot of miners start betting on me, I don't want to do anything to hurt their returns either."

Both Cherga and Junot agreed that that would be the only honest thing to do. "So how much did you bet on the match?" Junot asked Jack.

"Now keep this quiet, just between us," Jack said to Junot and Cherga. "I had 320 credits, and I bet it all on my match. That gave me a winning return of—"

"No, wait, wait," said Junot, "let me figure it out. That's, that's, umm, that's, oh my, that's, that's 9600, 9600 credits, oh my, I, oh, oh my."

"Yes, that's correct," said Jack, "and on my next match, I am going to bet every penny of it again."

"All that will be a lot," said Junot. "Umm, don't you think you might want to save a little of it out, and, uh, what's a penny?"

"No," replied Jack, "and a penny is just a small denomination of credits on my planet, and I'm going for broke, as that is part of my plan on how to get out of this place. If I do get out somehow, I will need considerable funds to live and function on the outside."

"How will your plan do that?" asked Cherga. "They may or may not let you pay off your debt in exchange for your freedom. If you think you might try to escape, I would not recommend it, as they will work hard to find you. They will confiscate your winnings if you escape as well as add sizable time to your sentence."

"Yes, I would have guessed as much," replied Jack, "so I'm working it through right now and trying to figure out what options I have. Right now, the best thing to do is try to make as many credits as I can gambling on myself and then see what opportunities might present themselves as far as ending my indenturehood here. We will just have to wait and see what turns up."

"Well, I wish you the best of luck in your attempt," said Cherga.

While Zshutana watched the match, she practically held her breath until the end of the match. She was most grateful that Jack was so capable of avoiding injury and defeating his opponent. She could tell by his adept movements that he knew what he was doing, or so it seemed to her. She was surprised several times when Jack seemed to let his adversary move in on him and attack him, although Jack didn't seem to be injured in any way when the other fighter attacked.

She didn't like the pit fighting, but it certainly held her attention when she knew Jack was down there fighting in the ring. *Why did males always do these kinds of things?* she wondered. She thought about the match and how it had scared her but was also somewhat stimulating. Then she remembered she had bet on the match like Jack had asked her. She wondered how much she would get back after wagering 1,200 credits. Since she'd never wagered on anything before, she wasn't quite sure how that odds thing worked in betting.

The next daiyus, it was back to the old grind of running the zibur drill for Jack, and the same for the others in their respective jobs. Midway through the wenek, Cherga caught up with Jack and said that he was going to visit a friend of his over at the foundry section of the mine. Cherga wanted to know if Jack would be interested in meeting his friend and seeing the forge and foundry plant. "Yes, absolutely," replied Jack. "What exactly do they have over there?" he asked Cherga.

"Ahh, there is much to see of an interesting nature. After they extract and smelt the Burun-Rioc ore, some of it is smelted and drawn right here at the mine complex into a very high purity state for use in special applications. I'm sure you will find it most interesting, Varaci Jack," replied Cherga.

"Yes, it sounds interesting in many ways, so I'm sure I will," said Jack.

They headed off in a different direction where Jack had never been in the mine complex. They came to a security stand, and Cherga explained that the foundry area was technically outside of the conzone but that they allowed conscripts that were approved to travel in the foundry area because they needed the labor of the conscripts in the foundry periodically. "But I'm not approved for that as far as I know," said Jack. "How will they let me past the checkpoint?"

"It will be OK because my friend already put in an approval for your visit," explained Cherga. "You can go with me because I am taking you over to supposedly interview for a position in the foundry. As long as you are back to the checkpoint before the close of the daiyus, it will not raise any concerns."

"OK," said Jack. "I wasn't aware that conscripts could venture anywhere outside the conzone. This should be very interesting."

They passed through the checkpoint without trouble with Cherga vouching for Jack and Jack receiving a quick scan by the guard. "Back by close of daiyus," the guard admonished them as a reminder as they passed through.

"Yes, always," replied Cherga. Out of hearing reach of the guard, Cherga said, "If it weren't for the scanning, the fool guards would never know who came and went. They would probably sleep through most of the daiyus if they could get away with it."

"Something to remember," said Jack.

They went a considerable distance and up several levels from where they'd started until they ended up in a large foundry complex that could have been above ground but could have been partially below ground for all Jack knew. Jack couldn't tell by the interior of the building. There were more than a dozen aliens working at various tasks throughout the complex. Cherga gave Jack a basic tour of the facility as they proceeded to the far end of the complex. There was a type of centrifugal separators, Cherga explained, as he pointed out three large structures fed by some type of conveyor system.

There were also three large thermal ionization ejection smelters used for the preliminary smelting of the Burun-Rioc ore. Cherga also explained that an alloying plant was located next to this operation. He told Jack they would probably see that after they met his friend Za-arvak. "Za-arvak is the head of the operation and a production metallurgist who manufacturers much of the specialty alloys requested by many manufacturing operations in this sector of the disk. Za-arvak is also from my home planet of Zanaii, although from the industrial city Kukiba, in the southern hemisphere many zones from my family home."

When they'd gone all the way through the main smelting complex, they came to a slightly smaller separate area that was the alloying plant. Cherga explained that there were six separate combinant fusing alloying stations. Each station could infuse the Burun-Rioc ore with a variety of different alloying components. "We will meet Za-arvak in a minute, and he can explain it to you better than I," said Cherga.

About halfway through the alloying plant, they came upon a tall, strange-looking, vaguely reptilian-like alien that was directing two other aliens regarding some sort of task. His skin was slightly greenish and leathery-like, and he rasped slightly as he talked to the other aliens while his back was toward Jack in Cherga. Jack got the impression that he was fairly old for some reason; perhaps it was just his posture because his movements still seem fluid and concise as he talked to the other aliens. He was obviously not the same alien race as Cherga even though he was from the same planet Zanaii. "Gah, Cherga," the alien Za-arvak said in

202

agreeing, "how are you Zanaii friend? I have not seen you for a while since you last worked for us in the plant 6.5 moondats ago."

"Good to see you also, Za-arvak. I am well, but I have been busy and working much. I should come here for a visit more often."

"This is my friend I was telling you about, Varaci Ja-ak. I thought he would be interested in seeing your foundry and the alloying operation, since he, too, toils in the mine but as a zibur operator. It is most interesting for those of us with good curiosity to see what the outcome of our labors are."

"Ah, yes," said Za-arvak to Jack, "you are one of the fight pit contenders that I watched this last wenek. I believe your match was a little more one-sided than they initially expected as well as a different outcome from what was anticipated. You appear to have some natural skills for that endeavor."

"Yes, thank you," said Jack being polite, "but I'm sure it was just a fair amount of luck is all."

"Thank you and fair luck, shatzak," said Za-arvak. "I lost fifty credits on that match. The least you could do is lose for your first match," laughed Za-arvak out loud with a unique roiling laugh.

"Well, I tried, I really tried," said Jack, "but for some reason, my opponent just wouldn't stay on his feet, and he kept running into my punches frequently. Perhaps you will consider rethinking your wager if I fight again next wenek," added Jack.

"Hafk, no doubt I will," replied Za-arvak, "but I don't believe the odds will be as greatly against you next wenek."

"No, they won't," replied Jack, "but you can make your lost fifty credits back easily and considerably more if you carefully consider your next wager."

"Well, if you are so certain of the next match, then I believe I will, yes, I believe I definitely will," said Za-arvak. "I believe I like this new conscript," Za-arvak said to Cherga.

"Yes, he is a good one in many ways," said Cherga.

"Well, good, very good," said Za-arvak. "You have come all this way for a pleasant social visit. Would your friend Varaci Ja-ak like to have a tour of our foundry operation?"

"Yes, absolutely," replied Jack, "I would find that extremely interesting. I would like to learn as much as possible about the Burun-Rioc ore that we mine and what it becomes as an end product and how that happens."

"Very well," said Za-arvak. "I enjoy explaining our operation to those that show an interest in it. Do you have any knowledge of metallurgical concepts or of foundries or how metals are alloyed?" Za-arvak asked Jack.

"Not a great deal," replied Jack. "It is not my area of specialty. I do understand the basics of alloys and the benefits derived from the various elemental materials that can be added to different metals to enhance their capabilities."

"Very good, then," replied Za-arvak. "That's probably a greater amount than the average worker here. The area we are in now is the alloying plant. The larger area you came through first is the Burun-Rioc processing and smelting plant. After the ore is initially mechanically crushed, it is pulverized to sand-size particles by sonic wave processors and then transported by conveyor to the large density isolation centrifugal separators." Za-arvak went on to explain how the isolation centrifugal separators broke down the ore components even finer by using an extreme velocity vortex to pulverize and separate all the materials by molecular density and then siphon them off at various levels much like an old-style distillation tower.

He explained that this left the various raw materials at a better than 99.9 percent purity state with very little byproduct contamination. "That is very interesting," said Jack. "I wasn't aware that you could distillate solid mineral compounds simply by using purely mechanical means."

"Oh, yes, absolutely," replied Za-arvak. "It is one of the most efficient methods available because it requires less energy, since no heating is involved until later on in the process."

Za-arvak went on to explain that once the Burun-Rioc ore was separated and isolated, it was then processed in the thermal ionization ejection smelters where it was turned into ingots of pure Burun-Rioc metal ready to have the desired alloying metals, compounds, and other alloys infused with it. The Burun-Rioc exhibited little beneficial properties of its own, but when added to other elements and alloys, it would enhance them exponentially. The new resulting alloys were then ready to be hot-rolled into bars, round stock, or coils depending on their future use.

Jack asked why they called it Burun-Rioc and why its properties were so unique as an alloying agent. Za-arvak answered that the Burun-Rioc ore was named after the metallurgy engineer that initially discovered the unique properties of the rare metal and how to combine it with other elements to create subatomically bonded enhanced super alloys. Za-arvak explained that unlike other standard alloys of steel, aluminum, or titanium, the Burun-Rioc didn't give up atoms to create alloy mixtures but retained its atomic structure while enhancing the alloying elements structure.

Burun-Rioc is a unique natural element only found on a few planets, and it could not be duplicated in the laboratory. It will allow other elements to fuse at the subatomic level yet maintain their unique physical properties while at the same time enhancing the properties of the other elements. They are essentially elemental compounds that possess astounding physical properties unlike any of the base elements or other standard alloys of metals. Burun-Rioc remains malleable while in its initial heated phase and prior to cryogenic quenching. A unique property of the Burun-Rioc is that when it cools through cryogenic quenching, it permanently bonds or sets to the other elements that are present and creates bonds with strengths and properties like no other alloy.

Jack didn't fully understand all the metallurgical chemistry of it but did have a pretty good grasp as to what Za-arvak was explaining. Instead of just creating an improved metal alloy by the addition of enhancing elements, they were actually creating various types of unique super alloys that were impossible to create with any other primary element other than the Burun-Rioc because of its unique properties and the unique way it combined the other elements. Za-arvak went on to explain what some of the most popular alloying elements were that were used to create Burun-Rioc enhanced super alloys. These consisted of iron, nickel, titanium, aluminum, magnesium, beryllium, and even the noble metals, nonmetals, and ferrous and some nonferrous alloy metals.

The Burun-Rioc was unique in that it didn't require elements in the same periodic range or family to combine with it because the elements never actually combined but only enhanced each other's presence. Jack asked Za-arvak about the various alloying elements that were added to the Burun-Rioc and what their super alloy properties were once they were created. "It sounds like it would be interesting to experiment with every type of potential alloying element just to see what types of super alloys and their properties you could come up with," stated Jack. "Although I'm sure they've probably discovered just about everything imaginable so far," he added.

"Well, no, actually not," said Za-arvak. "They've probably only discovered perhaps half or less of the potential Burun-Rioc alloys, if even that many, because of the vast variety and combinations of elements as well as existing alloys it will bind with it," replied Za-arvak.

"That's simply amazing," said Jack. "Think of the potential possibilities of the various alloys that have yet to be discovered. There might be super alloy properties that no one has even imagined yet."

"Undoubtedly," replied Za-arvak, "but there are not enough researchers trying out new combinations. You seem to have a very good grasp of the concepts involved in metal alloying research, apparently much better than you indicated when I first inquired about your interest," said Za-arvak.

Jack replied, "I do have some background in science and engineering research, though not in the field of metallurgy."

"Still, your understanding seems better than most others around the mine complex. It is difficult to get knowledgeable and capable help this far from the large cities on a remote planet that was recently terraformed and that is still underpopulated. Science-trained people do not wish to come to a location this remote far from the interests of the city or to a planet less civilized than they are comfortable with."

"Yes, that has always been a problem for remote postings in any type of situation," replied Jack.

"Cherga," said Za-arvak, "did you not tell me that your friend here was conscripted for stealing passage on a starship freighter here to Nishda? That is most unusual, as many travelers come to Nishda reluctantly and must be offered enticement for employment and paid passage to come here. Why would you wish to come to Nishda badly enough to steal passage here?"

"I didn't," replied Jack, "but it's a long and nearly unbelievable story. Suffice to say for now, I awoke on a starship, which I'd never seen or heard of before, and they found me in a cargo hold where I had been trying to survive for several daiyus, and they assumed that I had stowed away. Then from what I've learned about how this mine operates, I was sold as a conscript to pay off the passage that I had allegedly stolen to become a stowaway."

"That is a most remarkable story," replied Za-arvak, "but how did you get aboard the starship?"

"That is the remarkable and complex part that I cannot tell at this time, but I assure you it's like no other story you've ever heard before."

"Hmmm, all right, I'm sure you must have your reasons, so we will not go into it further. Cherga vouches for your character, so that will suffice for now."

"Suffice now for what exactly?" asked Jack.

Za-arvak replied, "Cherga asked you here because he thought you'd be interested in the foundry, and he thought I would be interested in meeting his friend whom I'd lost the wager on. As it turns out, I am most impressed with your knowledge and understanding of what I've explained to you about the metallurgy and what we do here. If you would be interested, I could request that you be allowed to work some of your conscript time here at the foundry. I believe it may be more interesting and to your liking than operating the mining equipment. Of course, if you prefer operating the zibur drill every daiyus, then that is fine also. I believe this may be more to your liking, though, and it would help me considerably to have someone knowledgeable in the sciences fields to help me oversee our operation. Of course, I could not pay you the going wages for a contract employee because you're a conscript, but I believe you would still find the working conditions much more gratifying than in the bowels of the mine."

"Well, thank you for the generous offer," replied Jack. "I would certainly be interested in improving my current station in life. I'm not really sure how it would work as far as me being able to come here to work, but if there is a way to arrange it, I'd certainly give it a try. I have to tell you, though, that the mine bosses are the ones that compelled me to fight. I would still have to leave work here to attend the matches even if I was in the middle of work here."

"That would be no problem," said Za-arvak. "I am curious, though. Why would the mine bosses wish to compel you to fight?"

"I believe they want me to fight against the other mines or other operations that have their own contestants—that is, if I go far enough up the winning ladder."

"I see," said Za-arvak. "Wasn't this your first match? How did they know you would be able to do so well in the fight pit arena?"

"Another strange story," replied Jack, "which I will tell you if you promise that it will stay here and go no further."

"Yes, I give you my word on that," replied Za-arvak.

"Some miners attacked Cherga's and my friend Junot," said Jack, as he told them the whole story.

"Because I was there, they attacked me also. When they attacked, I fought them off, and then the mine bosses found out about it and basically told me I would fight in the matches for them."

"Who attacked you and Junot?" asked Cherga in an angry tone. "When was this? When did this happen? Who did this!" he angrily exclaimed.

Jack told him, "When I took Junot back to the berthing chamber during the first match we attended. I don't know who they were except for one I had seen in the rations hall before. That doesn't matter now anyway."

"It surely does," blurted Cherga. "I will find them and make them wish they had not tried such a thing."

"Don't worry, Cherga, they won't be doing anything for a while except recovering from their learning experience."

"Are you sure?" asked Cherga. "How many were there? What happened?"

"I believe there were six," said Jack. "They just attacked us from the side tunnel, and I fought them off."

"You fought off six miners?" asked Za-arvak.

"Yes," replied Jack, "that is what the mine bosses told me, and that is the reason they wanted me to fight in the matches for them. But you must tell no one else because if the word gets out, it will change the wagering odds considerably, and the mine bosses will not be happy about that."

"Yes, I understand now how this came about," said Za-arvak. "That does sound like something the bosses would do, without a doubt."

"Do not worry," said Cherga, "we will keep this to ourselves so that there are no further issues for you with the bosses."

"Yes, thank you," said Jack, "I believe that is best for now as far as this situation is concerned."

"Well, enough of that for now," said Za-arvak. "If you agree, I will put in a request for your assistance here. I can see no reason why the bosses would object as long as you meet their requirement to fight in the pit matches."

"OK," said Jack, "that sounds interesting to me, so I will be happy to give it a try. Cherga, you will have to help me watch over Junot a bit if I'm not going to be in the conzone as much. I don't think he will have any more trouble with the miners, but it might further dissuade them if they knew they would also have to deal with you."

"Yes, surely," replied Cherga. "If any of these vermin attempt to harm him, they will answer to me, and they will surely wish they hadn't."

Za-arvak continued showing Jack and Cherga around the foundry and mill operation. Jack asked Za-arvak what Cherga's tasks had been when he'd worked there. Za-arvak told Jack it was a little bit of everything but mostly organizing preproduction and postproduction materials for delivery when they needed extra help during periods of high demand. Za-arvak said that Cherga was very good at keeping the production flow organized when they were busy, which allowed Za-arvak the ability to deal with other administrative issues. "Yes," said Cherga, "I know little of the engineering of alloys, but I can keep all the pieces and steps that need to be done for the process organized and going in the proper direction."

Za-arvak said, "That is a very important skill for when we are more busy. Without it, we would not be able to produce but a portion of what is called for. Cherga has been very helpful to us during the times we were tasked to produce our alloys at a higher rate.

Jack replied, "Cherga seems to be a person of many talents, a good person to have around for every situation."

"Yes, he is," replied Za-arvak. If our production goes up in a moondat or two like it usually does, I will surely be requesting his help again."

"That's good," said Jack. "Maybe I will get to work alongside him here if it works out that way."

"Perhaps it will," said Za-arvak.

"I would look greatly forward to that myself," said Cherga.

Jack and Cherga finished their foundry tour a while later and headed back to the conzone. They talked about the possibility of being able to work at the foundry for Za-arvak and what a great improvement it would be over the mundane work of a machinery operator in the mine. Jack said his only misgiving would be not being able to watch out for Junot. He thought that Junot was fairly valuable to the mine bosses and he wondered if he could suggest to them that it might be in their interest to keep him protected from the miners that had tried to hurt and kidnap him.

Cherga suggested, "Perhaps Za-arvak might have a position for Junot also. Then we wouldn't have to worry about him being on his own at the mine."

"That would be a great idea if they would let him out of the mine maintenance work," replied Jack. "Surely there's something of a technical nature that Junot could do around the foundry operation. I'm not sure if Za-arvak even knows there's someone with his technical skills conscripted to the mine. The problem will be that the mine bosses might not want to let him go because it's more valuable for them to have him working in the mine than working in the foundry."

"We will have to see what is possible," said Cherga. "There are often more ways to get something done than there initially appears to be," added Cherga.

"Yes, that's true," replied Jack. "As they say, there's more than one way to skin a cat."

"Skin a ca-at?" said Cherga. "What is a ca-at, and why would you want to skin it?"

"Never mind," replied Jack, "it's just a saying that means the same thing."

Two daiyus later, Cherga told Jack that Za-arvak had contacted him through the mine comm system at the security checkpoint and they had told him that Za-arvak's request to have Jack transferred to the foundry had been approved. Jack was to report the next day for the zero seven shift. "Well, that's good news," said Jack. "I'm sure I'll find foundry operations more interesting than the zibur rig, not that it wasn't somewhat entertaining for a daiyus or two. I told Junot about the possibility of me working there, and he wasn't too happy about it, but I told him you'd be watching over him in the meantime and there was nothing to worry about. I didn't say anything to him about the possibility of him working at the foundry because we don't know if that's an option yet, and I didn't want to get his hopes up."

"Yes, yes," said Cherga, "that makes sense, and I won't give him anything about that either. It is best that we take this one step at a time for now, since we do not know what will happen."

Jack thought about something that came to his mind then said to Cherga, "You said Za-arvak contacted you through the mine comm system. How does that work? I haven't heard of that."

"Oh, the mine comm system," replied Cherga, "is just a communication system within the mine. The conscripts and the convicts don't have free access to any comm system either to the outside or even within the mine. When the bosses or someone wants to contact you, they send a guard with a message for you to go to the security shed and find out what the message is. Then you can contact whoever sent you the message."

"That seems like a bit too much security for conscripts and convicts not being able to communicate within the mine or to the outside without permission."

"Yes," said Cherga, "it is. I believe it is just a part of the punishment phase of our confinement for being a conscript or convict in the first place." Jack would have liked to have told Cherga about Junot's encrypted comm system that they were using to call outside to Zshutana, but he'd hold that back for a while and let Junot decide on it.

The next daiyus after their work shift, Junot told Jack that he'd been doing some more research on the translator capabilities and that he'd found some interesting information on them deep in the core database. Junot motioned that they needed to go to the maintenance depot where they could communicate in writing without being spied upon by the bosses in case they were listening. Good, thought Jack, maybe Junot could figure out a way to send a text message to Zshutana and let her know what was going on. He wanted to talk to her, but he didn't think it would be safe with the possibility of the bosses listening in even with Zshutana's and his coded names and encrypted comm.

They went to the maintenance depot and set up the written message system they'd used before. Junot seemed somewhat excited about what he'd learned about the translator system. He wrote to Jack that it was possible that their translators had a spying capability like Jack had already deduced. They also had an encoded tracking capability, which all worked from an encrypted unique identification stamp. This didn't surprise Jack at all, and it made sense based on what he figured out from the translator's comm capability and probable eavesdropping ability. Each unit would have an individual ID so that it could be monitored and tracked individually if necessary.

Well, it's possible that two could play this game, thought Jack. In writing, Jack asked Junot if he thought it would it be possible to turn off the listening and transmitting capability of the translator as well as the identification stamp that would halt the tracking capability. Jack even went one step further and asked Junot if it might be possible for a translator to be reprogrammed to have a different or fake ID or even multiple fake IDs to choose from. It all sounded kind of dangerous and forbidden to Junot, but it also sounded intriguing that he might be able to outsmart the mine bosses somehow.

Junot answered Jack, "I'm not really sure because I've never thought about that or ever heard of anything like that before. I didn't even realize that the translators had this capability. That seems pretty devious of them to do that without people knowing about it," answered Junot.

"Well," wrote Jack, "you just think about it for a couple of daiyus and do some more research. Dig as deep as you can and find out everything you can about these translators and their capabilities. Find out how they are programmed and encrypted and how the ID system works. Be careful, though. There might be some alert system that warns the GTA if anyone ever starts looking for this kind of information. Stay as far off the main cortex grid as you can."

"I will," replied Junot. "Not only will I be in the subcortex dark zone where this is sometimes talked about but I will be fully encrypted and piggybacked on the rest of the mine system dataflow."

"OK," wrote Jack, "that sounds good. We just don't want any trouble coming out of this."

Jack asked Junot if there was any way they could send an encrypted text to his friend to let her know what's going on. "Yes," wrote Junot, "we could run it through the same encryption process as the voice system. She may or may not respond right away if she doesn't see it, but if she set up an alert ping, she would probably see it and respond. If she responds later when we are not online, then we may not get her message or know that she replied."

"OK," wrote Jack, "that makes sense, but it's worth a try. Also I had another thought. It would be a longshot, maybe not secure, but if the bosses can communicate through the translator system, would it be possible for us to also do that? Maybe there is a way we could encrypt or scramble it so that no one could spy on us. They wouldn't expect anyone to be using their comm system, so they might not ever think to look there. Add that to your list of things to look into when you start digging into the translator system capabilities."

"OK, I will get to it as soon as possible," replied Junot.

Junot then set up an encrypted text-only comm link. Jack typed a fairly short message telling "Teela" that the translators are probably compromised and used to spy, track, and watch people. "No voice comm until further notice." He would be back with more info shortly. "Back with you soon, your friend D." Jack just used the D to see if she would respond with the correct codename to verify that their line wasn't compromised. Jack sat there for a few mentus waiting to see if there would be any response.

Just when he was ready to give up, he got a response. "Good to hear from you, Duunda. It took me a couple of mentus to figure out how to reply. I understand your message, and I will wait to hear from you via text soon. It is sad that we can't speak for now, but we will sometime soon. Hope to hear from you again shortly, T."

Smart girl, thought Jack. He replied, "OK for now, then. Good-bye, and I will get back to you soon."

"I will be waiting to hear from you. Bye for now, T," she wrote.

Jack went over to Junot, who was waiting patiently and wrote, "All is OK. Let's destroy all this written evidence, and then we can go back to the common area or berthing chamber."

Back at the common area, they both got some xula to drink. Jack didn't think it was too bad, although Junot only tolerated it. "So tomorrow, I have to report to the foundry to start my new 'career' as a metallurgist's assistant," Jack said to Junot.

"Yes, I know," said Junot. "I'm not so happy about that, but it will probably be better for you to work there than in the mine. I will be OK as long as Cherga will watch out for me like he says he will. I don't think the miners that attacked us will be too keen on trying to come after me especially if they know Cherga will also be watching out for me. They probably don't know that you'll be working in the foundry anyway."

"Good," said Jack. "I'm glad you're OK with that. If I hear from the bosses again or I can contact them, I will let them know that it's in their best interest to make sure that nothing happens to you also. Hopefully, I will hear in a daiyus or two about the next fight schedule coming up for this wenek. As soon as I do, we will have to do a little strategic planning with all of our parties that are involved. In the meantime, just work on the other project we talked about earlier today, and I'll see how I fit into my new job position at the foundry."

"Yes, I will," said Junot. "I'm looking forward to that. It should be interesting and challenging."

Later that night, Jack saw Cherga in the berthing chamber. "Cherga," said Jack, "I am going to the foundry tomorrow to work for Za-arvak. What should I know about working for him—I mean, Za-arvak as a person? What will be helpful based on your experience?"

Cherga replied, "Za-arvak is a good boss to work for. He is fair but will expect much out of you. With your knowledge, you will be very helpful to him."

"Yes," said Jack, "I will try to be as helpful as I can to him but also to myself and you and Junot. Do you know how he feels about the conscripts and the mine operation in general?"

Cherga replied, "I do not know for sure, but I do not believe that he likes the way the conscripts are treated. Still, Za-arvak is an upper-level contract employee of the mine, so his loyalty will be with the mine operation more than anywhere else. I suspect that he earns good credits in his position, so anything you can do to make his work easier and more productive will be beneficial to him as well as you."

"Good, that's as it should be," said Jack. "I will try to repay him for the chance to work there with good results. Thanks for the helpful information. This will help me get off to a good start with Za-arvak tomorrow."

The next daiyus, after passing through mine security where he was now authorized to pass, Jack reported to Za-arvak at the foundry alloying plant. "Ah, I am glad that you are able to come to the foundry and help me with our operation here," said Za-arvak.

"I am very happy to be here. I'm looking forward to doing and learning much at your foundry operation," said Jack.

Za-arvak said, "Good. Let's get started. There is much to do today, and we might as well get into it as much as we can. First, we will look at the production scheduling so you can figure out how to be helpful with the logistics of the operation. Then later, I will instruct you on the basics of the alloying metallurgy, which will tie in with the production schedule with regard to the correct sequence and the methods for producing the various alloys that we create here."

"That sounds good," said Jack. "I am very ready to learn about everything that you do here," as they headed to the production and processing side of the plant. Za-arvak then took Jack to the production office where he authorized him access to the foundry's data core and computing operation.

With Junot's written text algorithm, Jack was now able to read the data that was displayed on all the consoles and have it translated into English for him by his translator. The text-to-speech program learned rapidly as he read out loud while reading it. It wasn't long before he had a pretty good grasp on the way the production facility ran. It would take some skill and planning to learn to coordinate the production orders versus the plant's ability to meet the orders based on the raw materials available, the timeline involved in production, and the availability and quantity of the various alloying components needed to complete the production. It was all pretty cut and dried to some extent and just a function of juggling all the variables needed to keep the production going without any downtime because of lack of materials or timing.

By the end of Jack's second daiyus, Za-arvak could see that Jack had a very high capacity to comprehend, plan, and properly react to the continuous onslaught of information and variables thrown at him by the endlessly changing production requirements of the foundry. It wasn't a large production foundry, but it produced a large variety of specialty alloys for many different customers. Za-arvak could tell that it would only be a short time before he could turn Jack loose to run the production scheduling side of the operation on his own.

After his third daiyus on his new job, Jack was summoned for a message at the security shed. He was informed that he would be scheduled for the third fight match at the pit in three daiyus time. He'd missed one daiyus, but he'd still been trying to get in a minimum of a thirty-minute workout each daiyus after he got off his work shift from the foundry. He checked in with Junot and Cherga, and everything seemed to be progressing nicely on their end. Junot signaled to Jack that he was working on the translator questions, but he didn't indicate that he'd come up with anything new.

Jack asked Junot if he thought it would be possible if he himself or Junot could alert his friend about the upcoming match. "My friend can probably figure out the schedule without help, but I just want to make sure that they are aware of it."

"Yes, we can do that right after you get off your shift at the foundry. I will stay up late from my shift and will go right to the maintenance depot," said Junot.

"Great," said Jack. "I appreciate that and will make it up to you somehow."

"Make it up?" snorted Junot. "I would have to pay you back many times for your help against those ones that tried to hurt me. Do not even say that. It is unnecessary."

"OK, but thanks anyhow. I do appreciate your help," said Jack. Jack wondered, since he was working outside of the conzone now, if he would have any freedom of movement around the rest of the mine complex.

By the fourth daiyus, Za-arvak was quite pleased at the very rapid progress that Jack displayed. If everything continued to run as smoothly as it was under Jack's watchful eye, then in another wenek, he could start to teach Jack some of the complexities of the metallurgy alloying methods. Jack was also finding the whole operation very interesting, as he was learning quite a bit about new forms of alloying associated with the Burun-Rioc that he knew no other earthling had ever heard of before.

Jack wondered if he was prohibited from going anywhere else but the actual mine and foundry. He also wondered if they could or would actually track him by his translator. Later when he found Cherga, he asked him if there were any rules about where he could or couldn't go outside of the conzone. Cherga said he really wasn't sure, since that issue had never come up when he was working at the foundry. He said he just assumed that since he was on loan to the foundry as a special conscript worker that he was probably supposed to stay at the foundry site and nowhere else, although he really didn't know the answer to that question. "Why do you want to know?" asked Cherga.

Jack replied, "I thought it would be nice to get away for an horun and maybe find some food that wasn't from the rations hall."

"Ahhhh, yes, the thought of that does sound tempting," mused Cherga. "If you go, perhaps you could bring me back a sample of something other than the dreary fare that we must eat every daiyus." Cherga wondered why he'd never thought of that himself. Perhaps he would have to make a side excursion at some point if he went to visit Za-arvak again sometime soon. "Better yet," said Cherga, "perhaps we can make a short side trip some time if I should go back to the foundry in the near future."

"Now that is a great idea," said Jack. "I will ask Za-arvak about it shortly just to make sure that we don't get a dose of grief for our efforts."

The next daiyus at the foundry, Jack and Za-arvak went over all of Jack's assigned duties for the pre-and postproduction alloy operation. Za-arvak helped Jack fine-tune a few details, but from what he could see, it appeared that Jack had a very good understanding of the foundry in both theory and operation. Za-arvak was slightly skeptical before he'd met Jack, but now it was apparent that Cherga's conscript friend was more than capable, even much more than capable. Za-arvak explained to Jack once again how it was difficult to get qualified help this far from the larger cities on this remote planet. Jack said he understood and that he was glad that he could help Za-arvak especially in light of the fact that this was much more interesting than running the zibur drill. Jack then mentioned the fact that it was a ten-horun shift for him and wondered if there was any opportunity for him to get some food or if there was a mid-meal break allowed. Perhaps he could find something nearby.

"Oh my, I didn't think, I simply, I simply forgot about that," said Za-arvak. "I usually don't eat throughout the daiyus myself, or if I do, it will be just something I have hidden in my office. My apologies for not thinking of this sooner."

"That's OK, no problem at all," replied Jack. "I just didn't know what the status of that was, so I had to ask. Do I need to bring something with me, or is there a place nearby where I can get something to eat during the mid-daiyus meal?"

"Well, I hadn't really thought about it," said Za-arvak. "I suppose you could do either one. It wouldn't matter to me as long as you were up to speed on everything in the production operation."

"That would bring up another question for me," said Jack. "If I wanted to go somewhere nearby in the mine, would I actually be allowed to do that, since I'm a conscript, or am I required to stay in the foundry area?"

Za-arvak said, "Hmmm, well, now, I'm not actually sure about that either, as the question has never come up before. Let me see if there is anything written down about it, or I could ask the mine security offices to see if they have an opinion on it."

"That's fine," replied Jack. "I just didn't want to do anything questionable that might cause a problem, so I thought it would be better to ask first."

Jack thought to himself that if he could get out for an horun every two or three daiyus, he might be able to set up short rendezvous with Zshutana and minimize their security risk of communicating on the mine comm system. But then there was the potential issue of the translators actually being used as spy devices by the mine bosses. They would have to come up with something to counter that before he could have a clandestine meeting with anyone. This potentially being spied on was a new situation for Jack, and he had to admit that he really didn't like it. He would have to put some serious thought into thinking about how to counter the situation and also hope that Junot would come up with some information on how to crack the capabilities of their translators.

Three more daiyus had passed, and everything was pretty much status quo. Junot had indicated that he hadn't figured out anything on the translators yet, but he was developing a lot of information about their operation, programming, and encrypted security access. He indicated that what he really needed was access to a deactivated translator so that he could tear it apart and analyze the individual components that made up the unit. Jack passed this information onto Cherga and asked him if he knew where they issued translators and where they might have access to a deactivated or inoperative translator unit.

Cherga said he wasn't sure, but he had to guess it would have something to do with the security offices of the mine, which were located on the surface level near the mine entrance where they had all initially arrived. Since most persons already had their own translator, it wasn't very often that they ever had to get a new one or have one repaired, although it did occasionally happen. Later that week, they would find out that two contract miners had been killed in another section of the mine. Cherga had a convict friend with some medical background training who was usually called in to help the minimally staffed well-being office when they had an issue like that.

It was now the daiyus of Jack's next fight pit match. He had managed to get in a couple of daiyus of decent training at the gym and felt pretty good going into it overall. The schedule showed him going up against another zibur operator named Kobekka from Nishda, another apparently semi-anonymous transplant. Cherga said Kobekka was actually a native of Diakk and that he was big and mean. Cherga said he would not wish to fight him but would if he had to. His record was at nine and two, and Jack tried to speculate why they were pitting him against a much higher-ranked fighter this early in his own brief career.

When the odds posted at eighteen to one against Jack, he knew it was because the bosses were trying to keep them against him as long as they could. Good, he thought, that would give his tight little circle of friends the best return odds on him for as long as possible. The trick would be to keep the word from spreading and having the odds turn in his favor too soon. He would try to milk this for all it was worth as long as he could. Junot had gotten the word to Zshutana, and Jack was going for broke with his full 9,600 credits. Whoever was brokering the fights would be unhappy with that and the other high wagers from his corner, but they should be able to sufficiently offset that with their own winnings to keep them placated. Jack wondered if the bosses were trying to keep the odds against him high as he had thought earlier or if they had some other devious agenda that he wasn't aware of.

They got to the pit arena about an hour early, and Cherga helped Jack warm up with some light sparring that Jack coached him through, while Junot paced nervously nearby. Jack hadn't used any footwork or groundwork yet and didn't know if he would need to for this match, but he ran as many scenarios through his head as he could to refresh his short-term memory. Even with years of practice, it always helped to be mentally prepared for any situation you might encounter in a match.

The announcer Sha-aga and the referee Ulzaka went through their usual prefight routine, and then the matches started. Jack stayed out of sight and paced himself lightly and stretched every muscle he could think of, while Junot gave him an amateur assessment of the first two matches. Shortly after the third round started, Jack said, "OK, enough," and they went to watch the remainder of the match, while he got his head into fight mode by watching the two contestants beat each other into submission with continuous head and body blows.

While it wasn't an efficient or decisive way to fight, the spectators enjoyed it as they yelled and cajoled for or against the fighters. Toward the end of the third round, the smaller of the two fighters, a miner named Yudolu from a planet called Shihaya, gave up against his larger opponent named Reemoq from Bangara. A quick cleanup of the ring followed to remove the two mixed colors of purple-and-orange-hued blood that fairly well covered the center portion of the ring.

The next match was called, and Jack and his opponent Kobekka entered the fight pit ring. After the preliminary announcements, the buzzer sounded, and the fight was on. Kobekka charged from his side of the ring and attempted to steamroll his smaller challenger. Jack deftly sidestepped as Kobekka's momentum carried him past as he tried to spin and change his direction. Jack was tempted to put a round kick in Kobekka's side or lower calf but decided to hold off on any footwork until he needed it.

Kobekka charged Jack again but checked his momentum to see which way Jack would try to evade him. Jack could tell that Kobekka's initial plan was now to get close and tackle him and try to take him to the ground for a beating or prolonged wrestling match. Jack didn't want to go to the ground with this miner, at least not too early, as he appeared very strong and he didn't want to burn a lot of his own reserves getting out of it in case Kobekka had any decent ground moves.

Kobekka stopped short of Jack, took a couple of half-hearted or feigned swings, and then lunged at Jack again, trying to trap him in a bear hug and take him down. Jack stood his ground and based against Kobekka's charge, blocking him with his forearm and stopping his drive. The miner was big and probably outweighed Jack by a good thirty-five pounds, and it was all muscle. Kobekka tried several times to wrap Jack up, but Jack was able to maneuver away from all of Kobekka's lunges. Frustrated, Kobekka tried a few more swings in an attempt to either connect or throw Jack off balance so that he could try another takedown on his smaller opponent.

Kobekka's first swing connected with Jack's left arm. Jack blocked it, but it knocked him slightly off balance as he ducked the second swing from Kobekka's left while backing off-line and out of range. Kobekka charged again, trying to take Jack down, but Jack stopped him again by basing and halting the attack with a series of fast combination punches. Kobekka was wide open for a knee to the midsection, but Jack held off again on the knees or kicks. As Kobekka backed off the attack slightly, Jack popped with a left jab followed by a quick right hook that half connected with Kobekka's jaw.

The two light punches didn't do much to stun the miner, but they were hard and fast enough to make him think twice about lunging at Jack while leaving himself open. So far, nothing Kobekka had tried had had any effect on this new Varaci contender. Kobekka had a good fight record, and he'd expected this smaller Varaci opponent to be an easy and quick victory, especially in light of what he'd been told about the demeanor of the Varan race. Whoever this Varaci was he wasn't an easy pushover.

Kobekka thought he might try pushing the Varaci to the wire by either trapping him or pummeling him against the side of the ring. As he started to try to push Jack back, the buzzer sounded, and the first round ended with a draw. Kobekka had been more aggressive, but Jack had the only points for connecting with any punches.

Zshutana watched the fight on her office display with several of the girls that worked for her. She thought it might be less stressful if she didn't have to watch it alone, but now she wasn't so sure. She knew Jack was very capable based on what she'd seen during the last match, but she could also see how strong and fast the big miner was in this second match. She had also wagered thirty-three thousand of the thirty-six thousand credits she had won on the last match. Although she had set aside three thousand credits from the original wager plus a little extra, it would still be nice to win this wager rather than lose it. Jack not getting hurt was the main issue of the match, but she could do a lot to help her girls if she won this current match with the odds still set this high against Jack. Whatever the outcome was, it didn't matter that much as long as Jack wasn't injured. Now she wasn't so sure that having company for watching the match was the best idea, since the other girls seemed more interested in commenting on the fighter's physical attributes rather than the aspects of the actual fight. They were right, though, as she listened to their commentary that the Varaci Jack was quite attractive.

The second round started more cautiously as Kobekka came out actually trying to evaluate Jack's strategy and see if he could find some opening or weakness in his opponent's technique. He knew he couldn't simply tackle and beat the Varaci like he had the other unschooled opponents in the past. He had already tried that several times and had been stopped every time. The blast attack of rapid punches while charging also hadn't worked, since all he'd gotten out of that was a fast and accurate return of the same.

He thought again that if he could push the Varaci to the wire, then he might be able to take him down or pummel him while he had him against the wire. He made several attempts to maneuver Jack to the wire, but Jack just kept moving off-line and circling Kobekka. Even more frustrated, Kobekka tried a couple of more feigns and lunged at Jack while swinging and trying to tackle him at the same time. Jack ducked and dove under the attack and turned fast and gave Kobekka a good fully weighted left jab to the midsection. It didn't knock the air out of Kobekka, but it did give him a pretty good taste of the power Jack could deliver with his punches.

The crowd of miners was getting loud and screaming for more action and blood. Jack needed to win the match, but he wanted to keep the odds against him as much as possible. He came at Kobekka and threw a few unguided swings to keep the fight momentum up then moved in close so that any swings by Kobekka that might connect wouldn't do any damage while at the same time staying ready for any lunge that Kobekka might try to take him to the ground with. Kobekka tried pummeling Jack on the head then tried moving lower to the body where he could then try and tackle the smaller zibur operator to the ground.

Jack concentrated on his defense and let Kobekka swing and hit him as much as he wanted while blocking all the head shots and all but one of the body shots that the miner threw at him. That one hurt a bit, but it was a glancing blow just below his left arm. It looked to the crowd like Jack was taking a pretty good beating, but all the blows inflicted by Kobekka were effectively blocked or deflected. That went on like this for the remainder of the round, and it looked like a very even match when the buzzer sounded again.

The third round opened with Kobekka more emboldened from his perceived gains at the end of the last round. He once again charged Jack with a series of wide hard swings and an attempted tackle. Jack ducked and blocked the punches and based against Kobekka's tackle. Kobekka had enough momentum that he managed to get Jack close to the wire, but Jack stopped Kobekka's drive by locking up Kobekka's left arm and using his momentum to pull Kobekka through the arc of his own charge as he pulled him past and into the wire with a huge crash followed by the yell of the spectators.

Kobekka went down against the wire cage fence with his back and his arms up as he tried to catch himself. Jack was tempted to close in with a full knee drive but checked himself and backed off to let Kobekka regain his balance and footing. Kobekka got to his feet and drove at Jack in another high-energy attack, this time with the intent of taking Jack to the ground. Jack feigned left then went right and moved out of Kobekka's line of momentum and turned to face his attacker as Kobekka again turned and charged. With a shorter drive and less momentum, Jack let him drive into him again and try to take him down. Jack based against Kobekka's lunge then blocked a couple of Kobekka's ill-placed, too-close swings.

As Kobekka went to pull back for another lunge, Jack caught him with a light right hook to the side of the head followed by an instantaneous medium straight jab to the left side of Kobekka's face. This sent Kobekka stumbling backward, but he managed to stay on his feet. Kobekka hadn't said anything to Jack so far in the match, but now he was mad and hissed at Jack. "Is that the best you have, Varaci? Because now I will show you what happens to a lowlife Varan runner when they mess with a real warrior of Diakk."

"No," replied Jack.

Kobekka looked confused for half a second. "No? What you mean no, you devious Varan worm?" growled Kobekka.

"No, that's not the best I have. I'm saving that for another day." Jack taunted his arrogant opponent.

"Now you pay!" howled Kobekka as he charged Jack while swinging wildly and trying again to tackle Jack and take him to the ground. Jack made a slight move to the right then he ducked Kobekka's right wide swing at his head while he dodged left.

As Kobekka started to turn back toward his adversary, Jack connected with a hard right palm strike to Kobekka's temple then recoiled and hit him with a hard right body shot and a fast left hook to the jaw. Each hit was cumulative, but Jack still didn't want to put his opponent down. Jack wanted him madder and more careless, which would actually make him easier to control and make the fight more dramatic. Jack knew he was far enough ahead in points to win the match at this point, but he knew he didn't want to lose any ground if things went south. He'd already developed a healthy dislike for this arrogant miner from Diakk and wouldn't feel too bad about taking him out. Still, he didn't want to put Kobekka down so hard that he ended up with some sort of permanent damage.

Kobekka had seriously felt that last round of blows, but it hadn't taken any of the fight out of him. As Jack had predicted, it just made this hothead from Diakk even madder to the point that he was completely incensed. Kobekka rushed Jack and dove for his legs, trying one last time to take Jack off his feet. Jack jumped and sidestepped Kobekka's desperate lunge as Kobekka crashed heavily to the hard fight pit floor. Jack wasn't sure if he would stay down or get up, but Kobekka made a surprisingly fast jump up and lunged toward Jack, surprising him just enough that Kobekka was able to get one arm wrapped around Jack. Jack braced with a quick defensive wall using his forearm to stop Kobekka from totally wrapping him up.

Jack could feel the power of his opponent as Kobekka continued to lunge against him, trying to get him in a bear hug where he could try to take Jack to the ground. After a nearly all-stand-up fight, the spectators were screaming wildly at the prospect of a good knockdown ground match. Jack didn't really want to go to the ground with Kobekka and thought for a moment he might have to deliver a few good knee strikes to stop that possibility. Just as Jack was putting a little too much thought into it, Kobekka lowered his stance and rushed Jack at the midsection. Jack's instinct was to counter with the full knee strike to the head, but he held off a split second too long and let Kobekka get a firm hold on him.

To keep from going over backward with Kobekka's weight on top of him, Jack shot his legs back and dropped his weight on top of Kobekka. They were a little off kilter, and Jack realized they were going down sideways with Jack just slightly on top of Kobekka and off to the side. Jack started to roll away from his opponent even before they hit the ground, but Kobekka was fast and made a quick recovery and lunged at Jack to get to his feet. Jack knew he was going over this time but managed to get a knee between him and his opponent. Jack rolled with Kobekka's momentum then managed to shove his adversary a good six feet onto his back, giving Jack enough time to scramble to his feet.

As Kobekka crashed then rolled over and staggered to his own feet, Jack taunted him again. "Hey, Kobekka, that was fun. You want to do it again?" Now fairly winded, Kobekka just grunted and gathered himself for another charge at Jack. Jack knew he didn't have much time left in the last round and decided he had to finish it as soon as possible. Kobekka rushed at Jack surprisingly fast. Jack let Kobekka partially wrap him up again. As Kobekka tried to grab him again, Jack brought up a quick right uppercut palm strike to Kobekka's chin. This caused Kobekka's head to snap back slightly while causing Kobekka to drop his arms and leave himself wide open. Jack took a half step in to put himself in perfect range and dropped a solid left elbow onto Kobekka's neck. Kobekka let out a big yelp as he toppled sideways onto the pit floor.

He lay there for about three seconds then started to crawl back to his feet. Before Kobekka could get fully to his feet, the buzzer sounded and ended the match. Kobekka tried to get up and continue the fight, but Ulzaka, the referee, stopped him as he got to his feet and tried to make another lunge at Jack. The crowd of spectators roared their combined approval and disapproval. *Damn,* thought Jack, *that didn't go quite as planned, but I guess it'll do.*

Sha-aga, the announcer, and Ulzaka, the referee, conferred for a few seconds. Then Sha-aga loudly and ceremoniously announced Jack as the winner of the match. The crowd roared again, and Cherga and Junot rushed into the fight pit to congratulate Jack and help him out of the fight pit. They were both exuberant at Jack's win. "You did it, Jack. You did it again. You won another match," said Junot excitedly.

"Yes, a truly outstanding performance, my friend," added Cherga. "For a few moments, though, you had us worried. I thought, 'Well, there goes all of my previous winnings, but I hope that Jack does not get too injured even if he does not fare well.' But happily, my thoughts were faulty as you came out on top, and we have all fared well at your expense. Good ending, yes, a very good ending, Varaci Jack," as they all laughed out loud.

Jack, Cherga, and Junot headed back to the common area after the match where they celebrated with some xula, while Junot and Cherga relived the match as Jack relaxed and unwound. Jack wished he had a nice pint of real amber ale or some of Cherga's qalalé to celebrate with. Several of the other mine workers congratulated Jack on his match victory. A couple of them drifted by and made snide remarks about losing their wager on Jack's match. Cherga responded by goading them with an admonishment that they had bet on the wrong fighter. "Yes, perhaps a wiser choice might help you next time," Cherga further goaded them.

There was little rest for the wicked, though, as they were all back to their assigned jobs the next daiyus. They were completely astounded when their calculated winnings showed up in their accounts. Jack was up to 172,800 credits, Cherga was up to 45,000 credits, Junot was up to 81,000 credits, and Za-arvak had decided to wager on Jack and was up to 5,400 credits on his first go. Zshutana, however, was up to a phenomenal 594,000 credits. The odds against Jack winning would be falling dramatically after his two wins with the large payouts to several of the gamblers. All that Zshutana knew was that she could probably get the rest of her girls out of the trade and into something legitimate with her winnings.

Jack was back at work with Za-arvak in the foundry the next morning. Za-arvak regaled Jack with highlights of the match and let Jack know how elated he was that he had come out ahead with 5,400 credits on his wager. "I guess that makes up for the fifty credits you lost the first time around," chided Jack.

"Yes, it does and quite a bit more," replied Za-arvak. "I'm surprised the posted odds were that much against you, but I don't think they will stay that way for long," said Za-arvak.

"No, I don't think they will either," replied Jack. "I'm not sure why the odds were still against me to that degree, and I'm wondering that maybe as a Varaci, they didn't expect me to fare so well against these supposedly much more experienced opponents. Also, I'm just guessing, but maybe they are matching me against opponents that they think are considerably better than me to keep the odds higher against me than they might otherwise be."

"Yes," replied Za-arvak, "they may be doing that on purpose, but apparently, you have sabotaged their plans a bit. Just be careful that they don't try to figure out a way to try and take you down in some shady manner if that is their goal."

"Thanks," replied Jack, "good advice, and I'll keep it in mind from now on." Jack knew one thing for sure, and it was that the mine bosses would do whatever they could to maximize their profit at his expense. *Well, we will see who comes out ahead in this venture,* thought Jack.

After Jack was sure that everything was running smoothly in the alloy production area, he went over to the metallurgy lab and started getting more familiar with the core data on the Burun-Rioc ore and the methods to combine it as an alloy to various other compounds and elements. Over the next week, he started tinkering with a small lab smelter to see what properties he could get out of both the standard known alloys with the Burun-Rioc ore as well as some exotic unknown ingredients he started adding and cooking up. Some of the alloys didn't seem to gain much in the way of improved properties, while others seemed to respond well to the additional elemental properties that were added and combined with the Burun-Rioc ore. He continued to experiment in small controlled batches throughout the week.

Three daiyus later, when he was checking on Junot, he discovered Junot to be in a very excited state. "Jack, Jack, I have discovered some really interesting things about the translator and its functions that will allow us to either bypass, override, or even control any of the functions of the translator." Jack tried signaling to Junot not to say anything about this out loud and pointed at the translator to indicate that the mine bosses might be eavesdropping on them.

Junot put his fingers to his lips then pointed at Jack to indicate to Jack not to speak anything out loud, but then he said, "That's just it, Jack. I figured out how to prevent any transmission to the coded frequencies that they could listen in on. What I'm saying to you now is not going anywhere except to you. They can't hear me or anything I'm saying through my translator. Everything that goes through the translator is digitized data bits and not actual aural or analog signals. They can't hear what is transmitted, and they can't hear what you are receiving."

Junot continued. "I was able to dissect the translator I got from a friend who got one off a miner that wouldn't be needing his any longer. The translators are quite advanced technology as far as what they can do. They are similar in a lot of ways to the equipment, hardware, and programming I worked on previously but with some different access and security issues from what I was familiar with. I was able to find some buried material on the cortex that had detailed a theory on how to crack the access protocols built into the translator security nodes. We need to go to the maintenance depot so I can modify your translator, and then we could fix Cherga's translator too. I think there are some other modifications we could perform also like we talked about before, but I haven't worked those out yet. The first thing we need to do is to make sure the mine bosses or anyone else can't be listening in on what we're talking about."

Jack just nodded his head and said, "That sounds like a good idea," as they headed off toward the maintenance depot.

When they got there, Junot attached a cabled programming module to the back of Jack's translator and set to work with a small programming controller box. Junot started talking. "The first thing we need to do is decode your translator's unique identification protocol codes. Once we do that, I can gain access to the translator programming command processes by using a backdoor access to the routing and execute commands. Once we have full access to the selectable security functions, we can set any level of transmit or bypass commands that we want. I was able to set up a menu of selectable commands in the heads-up display area of my translator, and now I'll do that to your translator too. This will allow you to turn off or on the transmit mode that the mine bosses could listen in on. It will also have other functions that we may want once I'm able to develop those.

"I was able to color code the display readout green with your word 'Safe' so that you know when it's OK to talk freely without being overheard. If you leave the transmitter on, it will show in red the word 'Caution' in the corner of your display so that you'll know you might be overheard by the mine bosses. I think it's important to leave the transmitter on most of the time unless we are talking about something in private. Otherwise, they might figure out that we've blocked the transmitter somehow if there is a continuous total lack of conversation on our part."

Jack just nodded at Junot and gave him a thumbs-up and replied, "I understand."

A few more mentus of tinkering, and Junot announced that he'd finished. A small red word illuminated in the corner of Jack's heads-up display showing the word "Caution." Junot said, "Look above the caution warning and select the menu item Transmitter Off, and the warning should turn to a green 'Safe' indication." Jack did as Junot instructed him, and he now saw the green word "Safe" indication.

"I see it now. I've got a green 'Safe' indication," said Jack. "Are you absolutely sure that this works? Are you sure there isn't some way they can override it?" asked Jack in somewhat of a whisper.

"Yes, I'm sure it works," said Junot, "and no need to whisper. I was able to test the transmitter output on my translator with and without the transmitter activated. It stopped the transmission cold, and I'll test yours here in just a minute. The great part is I was able to interrupt the transmitter output after their monitoring circuit."

"There's a monitoring circuit?" asked Jack.

"Yes," said Junot, "there's a monitoring circuit that provides a short verification pulse about every one hundred septus to confirm that the system is still continuously operational. I don't think they monitor this continuously, more likely just when they want to check it. The way I have bypassed this is to allow this monitoring system to broadcast that the transmitter is active, but I have interrupted the transmit capability only on the output side of the transmitter, and they will have no way of knowing that there is no signal generated other than the lack of a voice signal they would receive. The monitoring signal will still be transmitting as it's supposed to be."

"That's brilliant," said Jack, "absolutely brilliant. This will allow us to talk privately and plan anything we want without the rotten mine bosses listening in on us."

"Yes," said Junot. "I don't like the thought of them spying on us anytime they want to either. What exactly are we planning anyway?" asked Junot.

"Well, I'm not really sure yet," replied Jack, "but whatever it is, we won't have to worry about anyone listening in on us, thanks to you. Great work, Junot. I would buy you a big jar of qalalé if they had any here. I guess I'll have to give you a rain check until we can arrange that."

"Oh, that sounds wonderful," said Junot. "I haven't had a taste of qalalé in quite a long time now. I'll take you up on that as soon as you figure out how to get us some. And what's a rain check exactly?"

"I think you've already figured that out," said Jack.

"Now that we can talk openly between us," said Jack, "tell me what else you've learned about these translators and what they can or can't do."

"Well, they can do a lot of different things from what I've discovered," said Junot. "So far, all we've done is turn off their eavesdropping capability so they can't hear us. They also have a coded tracking ability with an encrypted identification stamp like we talked about before. I think there should be a way to turn this off also, but it would be different than the voice transmitter monitoring system because you would basically disappear from their monitoring system, which might set off some sort of an alarm. We wouldn't want to do that."

Jack pondered that for a mentu then said, "What we would really need to do is decode their encryption program and put that into a decoy transmitter of some sort. That would make it look like you are located where the decoy is while you turned your tracking monitor off to allow you to go anywhere without being tracked. The problem may be is if you pass a monitoring checkpoint without any identification stamp that may also set off an alarm."

Junot said, "I'm not sure how they are monitored yet. In that case, you would need a fake identification stamp to pretend to be somebody else. I don't know to what level the system is fully utilized outside of the conzone. I wouldn't think it would be necessary to monitor every worker in every location. It would be too data intensive and serve little purpose. They would probably only monitor people entering or leaving main areas of the complex and maybe only if there is a security issue of some sort. I will try to do some more research on this and see what I can find out. I should be able to come up with some sort of a decoy that is programmed to mimic your specific identification code."

Jack asked, "If their monitoring system has some sort of readers or decoders, could we also make our own reader or even hijack one of theirs for our own use? If we had that ability, we could read anyone's identification code and then program that into a decoy and essentially be anyone we wanted to be. Don't the guards at the entrance checkpoints have some sort of reader device? If we can't figure out how to make one of our own, maybe we could 'borrow' one of theirs," said Jack.

"Well, uh, I guess that would be possible, but how would we borrow a reader?" said Junot.

"I don't know exactly," said Jack, "but it's just an idea to keep on the shelf in case we come across an opportunity of some sort. The 'rent-a-cop' guards aren't too cautious about most things from what I've seen," said Jack. "It wouldn't be inconceivable that they might misplace one somewhere and just go get another one to replace it if they couldn't find it. It would depend on how tightly the readers are controlled, but since it's probably just a passive device for reading identification codes, I wouldn't think it would be that well monitored. It wouldn't be likely that they would expect anyone to steal a code reader anyway. Who would want to other than us? My biggest concern would be is if the reader has some sort of tracking device in it itself. We wouldn't want to get caught with a missing reader. Maybe if we could depower it somehow, then we wouldn't have to worry about it being tracked," added Jack.

"Junot, how exactly are all these small devices like translators and readers powered?" asked Jack.

"Oh, they have a standard power seed module in them like any other small powered device," replied Junot.

"How does that work exactly?" asked Jack.

"Well, you know," said Junot, "just an everyday PSM."

"Explain to me how that works," asked Jack.

"What do you mean explain to you how that works? A PSM, everyone knows how those work," replied Junot.

"Well, I'm just trying to figure out the best way to go about this and utilize a reader," said Jack, "so humor me and explain to me how this PSM works."

"Well, OK, I guess," said Junot. "A standard PSM is just an encapsulated and shielded pelletized tritium granule that emits beta ray electrons through beta decay, which are converted to an 18.6-electron-volt output through a receptor converter and current amplifier. Everyone knows that," said Junot.

"Yes, I know," replied Jack. "Trying to hide his ignorance of this technology. What's the final voltage and amperage output of a PSM, and how long do they last?" asked Jack.

"Well, it varies, as you probably know," said Junot, "from 0.3 volts up to 18.6, which can be amplified up to 48 volts without losing all the miniscule current output to parasitic induction loss. The biggest ones are 48 volts from a single PSM seed, and they'll last up to about twelve yenets with average use. Their output amperage is anywhere from point zero five milliamps to 1.2 amps. Of course, the higher the continuous average current draw, the shorter their life span is. Shouldn't you know this if you're a fighter pilot?" asked Junot.

"Yes," said Jack, "I do know it in theory, but it's a little bit different where I come from, on, uhh, you know, Vara." Junot gave Jack a strange look and wondered what it was his friend was alluding to or maybe even trying to hide. Well, he'd ask Jack more about it later. In the meantime, they would just continue to try and figure out how to override and outsmart the mine bosses with their translator tracking and monitoring systems.

Back at work the following daiyus at the foundry, Jack was glad to find out that Za-arvak was even more elated about his winnings. Jack said, "I'm sure the odds against me won't be quite as high next time even though they seem to keep ramping up my opponents to a level that they think will defeat me or at least keep the odds high against me."

"Yes, I've noticed that," said Za-arvak. "They seem to be matching you against contenders considerably above your entry-level position with the odds considerably higher against you compared to anyone else I've seen in the fight pit matches. It makes me wonder what their reasoning is behind the strategy."

"Me too," said Jack. "I'm not 100 percent sure how all those gambling odds and winnings are derived other than the basic math, but I'm glad you came out with some nice winnings on this match. Don't forget to bet on me again next time if you want to win some more."

"Well, I very likely will," replied Za-arvak, "that is, as long as they don't match you up against some outright monster."

"Well, don't worry too much," said Jack. "I've got a few tricks left up my sleeve for the matches ahead."

They got on well the next couple of daiyus, and Jack was way ahead on his production schedule and was looking forward to some more alloy tinkerings in the afternoon. He asked Za-arvak if he'd thought any more about allowing Jack to go to the main concession areas of the mine operation for some sort of food other than what he'd been having to eat at the rations hall or bringing with him.

"I did do a little research on it," said Za-arvak, "and I couldn't find anything prohibiting it, but that might just be because this situation has never been anticipated. I don't see a problem with it as long as you don't go talking about it to your friends in the conzone and won't be taking any food or other items back there that they wouldn't be able to get in the conzone area. Remember, if you don't make it back through the checkpoint at the required time, they might put out an alert on you. That wouldn't do any of us any good, as you'd be back in the mine on a zibur rig and I'd be without my new best production manager I've ever had."

"Don't worry," replied Jack. "I'm just going to see what kind of interesting cuisine I might find for mid meal, and if you need me to run any errands for you while I'm out, I can do that too. In fact, if you wanted to give me some sort of a permission pass saying that I'm on an errand for you, that might save us both some trouble later if I was stopped or questioned by any of the mine guards."

"That's a good idea," said Za-arvak. "I'll generate a foundry ID card for you with an embedded access code that will allow you to come and go freely between the foundry and the rest of the mine operation. Essentially, it will show that you are a worker for the foundry, which has a higher access level and is restricted to only foundry workers."

The next daiyus, Za-arvak had a foundry ID pass for Jack, which would allow him to access the general mine area as well as an authorization programmed into the card's ID chip showing that Jack was on an authorized errand for the head of the foundry operation. "You shouldn't have any trouble with this," said Za-arvak, "but I think you should leave it at the foundry when you go back to the conzone so that none of the others there will be able to know that you have this ability. That might just cause some problems of a different nature, which we might want to avoid."

"I agree," said Jack. "It wouldn't do for any of the other conscripts or convicts to know that one of them had the ability to travel freely outside the conzone. I'll just leave it here every night locked in my desk."

"Yes, that should be fine," replied Za-arvak.

Yes, thought Jack, *this is working out better than I would have imagined.* "Well, if you don't mind," asked Jack, "I wouldn't mind taking an horun now. The production schedule for today is complete and all set for tomorrow as well. I'll be back in a little while and start playing with some alloy combinations until it's time to head back to the conzone, if that's all OK with you."

"Yes, that's fine," said Za-arvak. "Just don't get lost or be late. I'd better show you how to get to the main concession area of the mine from here. It will take you a good fifteen mentus even if you don't get turned around. We are kind of on the far side from the conzone and the general mine production output area and from the main concession and contract mine workers' area."

Za-arvak pulled up a map of the mine operation and sent it to Jack's translator. Jack received a small alert message at the bottom of his heads-up display. Apparently, Za-arvak also had the ability to access the mine's translator-based comm system. When he directed it to open from the menu, the map appeared with his current position on. "That will be helpful," said Jack. "I haven't seen this function before," he said to Za-arvak."

"No, probably not," said Za-arvak. "Now that I think of it, I believe the conscripts and convicts are restricted from this function because of security and all, of course."

"I'm probably not supposed to authorize you for this, but it would be silly of me to have my errand runner running errands without the ability to find his way around or his way back. I don't believe I will be too worried about it, but like the other things, just don't allow your conscript associates to know about it."

"This is great," said Jack. "It will help considerably for my errands."

Za-arvak said, "To get where you want to go, just look in the menu section of the map mode and select destination. Then tell it where you want to go, and it will direct you there with turn-by-turn instructions as you progress."

"This is excellent," said Jack. "I would probably get lost and spend half my time just figuring out where I was. Well, I guess I'll give it a go and try and find something much more palatable than the conscript food. I'm really looking forward to it. I will be back in a short while. Thanks again," he said to Za-arvak.

Jack commanded the concession area where Zshutana's apartment was located. He wasn't sure that she would be there, but since she ran her business from there, then there was a pretty good chance she would be. If not, he would just make sure to try and find some decent food, since all he'd eaten in nearly two moondats was the delectable rations hall food. Come to think of it, he was going to get something anyway whether she was there because, first of all, he wanted something, and he also needed to explain to Za-arvak what culinary delight he'd encountered on his adventure. It sounded like a win-win to him either way.

Jack followed the small green arrows and the commands that showed up on his heads-up display directing him to the concessions area and Zshutana's apartment. It was a bit of a jaunt, and he hurried as fast as he could without being conspicuous. He passed many other various workers along the way, and none of them seemed to give him too much more than a passing glance. As the only actual human or possibly a somewhat rare Varaci in this sector, he was afraid he might have stood out a little too much. His status as a conscript allegedly on an errand for his boss made him a bit nervous too, but he had a fair justification and legitimate documentation for being where he was on the orders of his boss.

It took him twenty-one mentus to find his way to the mall-like shopping and concessions area where Zshutana's apartment was located on the second floor. As he headed for the stairs to her apartment, he glanced in one of the shops he passed and happened to see a face and a form he recognized. She was there in the middle of the store looking at some clothing items that were stacked in piles. She was holding up what looked like a blouse as if to judge if it was the correct size. He watched her for a moment then slowly moved to the next row of merchandise and worked his way toward her while staying out of her sight behind her. When she had worked her way toward the end of the row, he was just behind her and said, "Might I help you find something, miss?" She froze in place for a second, afraid to turn around. She recognized his voice but was afraid to turn around, but she couldn't stop herself.

She stared at him for a moment, dropped what she was holding, and threw her arms around him and said in a hushed but highly excited voice, "Jack, Jack, I couldn't believe my ears and now my eyes. Is it really you? What are you doing here? Are you OK? Did you escape? Oh, please tell me what's going on. What on Nishda are—" Suddenly feeling self-conscience at her overexuberance, she backed away a few inches but couldn't take her eyes off of him. Yes, it really was him, and her eyes took in the wonderful sight of him standing there before her. He looked even better in person than he did in the fight vidos, even better than she remembered when he'd been in her apartment as her language student.

What was she thinking? A lot of confusing thoughts went through her head. A dozen thoughts and questions popped into her head at once, but all she wanted to do was look at him for a few more moments and not say anything to break the moment. "Shh . . . don't say anything more," he said. "Yes, it's me, but let me talk but don't say anything. Can we go up to your apartment, and I can explain what's going on? Now you must not talk right now. They, the mine bosses, can possibly listen in to us, but they can't hear my transmission because it's blocked," as he glanced once again to the corner of his heads-up display to verify the green word "'Safe" was displayed.

"Come on, let's go," he said, as he took her hand and guided her out of the shop and up to her apartment. She palmed the access code at her door, and they slipped into her office. She looked outside briefly and closed the door behind them as they went inside. She turned to face him and gazed at him for a second then could no longer resist her need to touch him as she threw her arms around him and pulled him as close as she possibly could. She wanted to say a hundred things to him but kept silent as he'd directed her. He felt her warm lithe body against his, and after months of confusion, horror, and incarceration, it was the most inviting thing he'd ever felt in his life.

They held each other for what seemed like an hour, but it was only for a mentu. He suddenly knew he wanted to kiss her more than anyone he'd ever wanted to kiss before. He knew where that would lead and knew he would be powerless to stop if he didn't stop now. She had no reservations and clung to him like a lost puppy. She felt warm and willing in his arms, and he wanted nothing more in the world than to hold her and touch her and feel her body against him. *How on Earth did we get this far this fast? I barely know her, but she feels like everything that exists in this world to me right now.* Her amazing turquoise eyes were looking into his eyes only inches away. He'd never seen anything like them in his life. Her body clung eagerly to his, and her breathing was heavy and steady. She stared at him both waiting and wanting, afraid herself of the next moment and what it may or may not bring. Her thoughts were being overwhelmed by his touch and the feel of his body as they clung to each other, anticipating and experiencing every nuance and sensation.

Her lips parted slightly, and she smelled like warm cinnamon and exotic perfume. There was no stopping himself. He slowly drew closer to her until their lips lightly touched, then the closeness and passion overwhelmed them both. Suddenly they were like two ravenous animals with insatiable appetites. He kissed her hard and passionately, and she returned his kisses with every ounce of energy and strength in her body. She let him taste her and kiss her and feel her. He picked her up and took her to her bedroom, where he laid her gently on the bed all the while kissing her, touching her, and breathing in her delicious scent. She lay beneath him and gazed into his eyes, utterly and completely vulnerable and impatiently willing and waiting.

He wasn't sure what to expect, but she was so beautiful and feminine, and it felt so perfect. It must have been meant to be. She reached down and unfastened her top and pulled it off in one quick motion. He gazed at her for a moment hungrily then ran his hands over her body, feeling the firmness of her lithe muscles as she breathed harder and faster. Her small breasts were firm with large brown nipples, and her body was colored like her face and arms. Her eyes were afire with light and warmth, while her whole body begged to be fulfilled. His mouth found one of her breasts, and she moaned with pleasure as he felt her body quiver.

She pulled at his shirt until it was off, and then he pulled off her slacks. He took a moment to look at her perfect petite form, perfect and perfectly female in every aspect. Her eyes begged for his attention, and he began kissing her again. Their bodies embraced, and he felt her sweet breasts against his chest while her body was pushing against him as she grasped for him with her arms and mouth. He was out of his clothes and naked against her. She wrapped herself around him and opened herself to him. They made love for the next horun nonstop until they were both exhausted and totally fulfilled. He wanted to stay there in her bed nonstop for the next four daiyus, but he came out of his sexual haze long enough to remember why he was there.

"I didn't mean for this to happen. I didn't come here for this. Just to see you is what I thought. I mean it was wonderful, perfect. I couldn't help myself. I suddenly needed you like I've never needed anyone before," he said.

"I needed you too, desperately," she whispered. "Could it not have been more apparent? It seems strange, but it was meant to be. I could just feel it, could not you?"

"Yes, completely, totally in every way," he said. "Nothing could have been more perfect. But I'm afraid for you. I don't want to cause you any harm. Now, no more talking on your part, just listen for a few minutes."

She nodded affirmatively and listened while he held her and then got up and started to dress as he explained to her about the translators and how they worked as well as how only his translator was able to block out any eavesdropping. He explained all the capabilities of the translator devices as far as what they knew about them and that they were working on how to override them and even possibly make them work for them instead of against them.

He desperately wanted to stay there with her and start it all over again. He explained his time constraint and how he could explain it off as his being lost this first time. Another ten mentus passed, and he decided he had to pull himself out of there. "I wish I could stay, but it's too dangerous, too dangerous for you. I will figure out how to get back soon, and we will figure out a way to modify all of our translators. That will be the first step in fixing this whole situation," he said.

She nodded her understanding and smiled at him. His kissed her again, and it was all he could humanely do to pull himself away from her. "Stay here," he said. "I'll let myself out. I have to get a quick bite of food on the way and take some back to my new boss, Za-arvak."

She laughed a quick little twitter of a laugh, and her eyes smiled spectacularly at him as she jumped out of bed and followed him to the door completely at ease in her nakedness. "I must see you for every septu I can," she whispered. When they made it to the door, she slid her arms around him again. They looked into each other's eyes, and he kissed her again. It was all he could do to stop himself as he let her go.

"I'll see you as soon as I can," he said to her. She hugged him and kissed him quickly and pushed him out the door.

His mind was spinning now. He couldn't believe what had just happened. He'd known he already cared about her but hadn't expected anything like what had just happened. He was usually exceptionally good at keeping everything on track and the mission priority as the main agenda, but this had thrown him a real curve ball. *OK,* he thought, *you've already blown your timeline, but you can explain that away as a navigation error and getting lost and not knowing the navigation function of the translator very well or just losing track of time while exploring.*

Yes, he'd lost track of time, all right, definitely the best way possible too. Maybe Za-arvak wouldn't even say anything, as all Jack was doing for the rest of the daiyus was experimenting on alloy combinations. Either way, he'd better get his rear in gear. He swung through the first promising food shop and grabbed two orders of something called gennupa and trafila. It looked something like oriental food, although he didn't know exactly what it was. The trafila was a side dish of some sort, and he'd been able to pay for it with his credit account like Junot had explained to him. With some disposable utensils he found in the bag, he was able to eat the trafila. The gennupa was some sort of meat shaped like a curved stick he could just pick up. The gennupa was pretty good, but the trafila was pretty bland and didn't taste at all like it looked. He'd pass on that next time.

It only took him seventeen mentus to get back to the foundry. He had to pass a checkpoint on the way that was staffed by a less-than-official-looking guard who merely wanded him to determine if he was allowed to enter. He'd barely noticed the guard on the way out, but he was in a hurry and distracted with following the directions to the concessions area. He'd have to pay closer attention and start cataloging these details in the future. He got back to the metallurgy lab and decided it would be prudent to check in with Za-arvak and fess up rather than try to sneak in. Besides, he had a food offering for Za-arvak, and that might tide things over a bit. He remembered to switch his translator from the green safe to the red caution mode now that he was back in the foundry area.

Stopping in at Za-arvak's office, Jack popped his head in and said he was back and had brought Za-arvak a little snack to try. "Oh, good, you're back," said Za-arvak. "I was starting to worry that you had become lost."

"Well, I did get a little turned around on the way out," said Jack, "and I also got sidetracked a little investigating all the attractions around the concession area. I hope that's not a problem, but I really enjoyed myself being out for the first time in a while. I'll try not to let it happen again, and I don't know if you'll like it, but I brought you back a little snack like I had," Jack said, trying to lessen the impact on his indiscretion.

"Not to worry," said Za-arvak, "as long as you made it back in time to get back to the conzone before the nightly curfew, and since you've got us ahead in production and scheduling, then all is well." Jack felt a great sense of relief knowing he hadn't blown his first daiyus out. If Za-arvak only knew what Jack's real adventure had been, Jack was sure he wouldn't approve of it for a conscript serving time for an infraction.

Jack handed Za-arvak the bag with the food he gotten at the concession area. "It's just some gennupa and trafila," said Jack. "I don't know if you like it or not," he added.

"Oh, well, thank you, then," said Za-arvak. "I do like the trafila quite well," he replied, "but I don't really care for the gennupa so much, as it's a bit hard to chew."

"OK, well, don't eat anything you don't care for," replied Jack.

"Oh, I'll give it a try," said Za-arvak. "It's sure to be better than what I sometimes bring from home."

Well, he'd just have to be more careful in the future and not let his emotions overpower him. He hoped that Zshutana didn't have any misgivings about their little "meeting" today, but it certainly didn't seem like she'd had any regrets about their unexpected get-together. Jack went back to work for a couple of horuns experimenting with different alloy combinations, but he was a having a hard time concentrating on anything he was doing as he kept replaying the time he'd spent with Zshutana over and over in his head. She was a remarkable and beautiful woman, person, Nishdan, Tarcan? He wasn't sure how to exactly classify her or any of the other aliens he'd seen or met based on his earthborn upbringing. He'd also been thinking of all these different races of beings as aliens.

Was there even such a term as "alien" out here in this multirace galaxy? If there was such a term, was he the one that was considered an alien, or was anyone not from your own planet considered an alien? On a terraformed planet like Nishda where everyone was from another planet, was everyone considered an alien? *Probably not,* he laughed to himself. What about the etiquette of inter-planetary-race sex relations? he wondered. Did he break any taboos today? It certainly didn't feel like it. It was as wonderful and natural as any encounter he could ever imagine. It just seemed to happen like it was supposed to, and everything was fine, but what if they'd gotten involved to a certain point and suddenly discovered that the hardware wasn't compatible? Thank God everything had worked out perfectly, but there were a lot of strange possibilities floating around in his head.

The one thing that he kept coming back to was that he wanted to see Zshutana again and soon. Not just because of the amazing intimacy they'd just shared but because he'd never met anyone as captivating, alluring, and desirable. Not only was she all of those but she was just enjoyable to be with. While thinking of her, he also wondered how many of the other races were so closely similar in biological design.

Was it normal and acceptable for them to interbreed, or were there limits or prohibitions? Considering Zshutana's trade and the variety of miners and other mine workers around, there must be some degree of inter-race relationships allowed. Well, who knows, maybe it was just a free-for-all and none of the race restrictions he envisioned even existed. Imagine those taboos and prohibitions compared to the racial and religious bias and other injustices that were so prevalent on Earth for so many centuries. Hopefully, everything that was swirling through his mind was a total nonissue. It was a nonissue to him, but he didn't know how it would be in the galactic community that he now found himself immersed in.

Back in her apartment office, Zshutana sat at her desk trying to keep her mind on some basic credit accounting and payment schedules as well as keeping track of all her charges. She wasn't having much success, as her thoughts went continuously back to Jack and their encounter. She couldn't help replaying everything in her mind from the instant she'd heard his voice behind her and turned around to see his beautiful features and his lovely but different kind of smile. Of course, she'd been thinking about him continuously and worrying about him from the time the miserable Cahooshek and his thugs had carted him off to the mine.

The surprise of his sudden appearance in the shop downstairs and their unbelievable mutual attraction from the second they were alone was more than she could even comprehend at the moment. She couldn't have fathomed the instantaneous and overwhelming need she had for him the second she found herself in his arms.

It was much, yes, much more than just a physical attraction. Yes, he was an incredibly beautiful person in every respect, but there was much more to it than that. She'd never experienced anything like that before, and she knew that there was probably nothing else out there like she had just experienced. She liked it, and she liked it a lot, yes, quite a lot, more than she could think of the words to describe it. Good Great One of Creation, what was she going to do? She felt depressed for a minute because she didn't know and because he wasn't there now, but then she thought about him, and it seemed to blunt the obvious negative side of the situation for a while.

Jack found Junot that evening and gave him a very watered-down version of his visit with Zshutana and his excursion outside of the conzone, making sure that Junot was to keep it to himself and that no one should know that he Jack, a conscript, was allowed outside the conzone to wander around freely. He explained that he thought it would be a good idea if they could find a way to modify her translator like theirs, since there was always a possibility that the mine bosses might listen in on her as well, since they possibly learned from Cahooshek of her language training involvement with him.

Jack said, "Junot, it's probably a good plan to have someone on the outside of the conzone that we can trust, and it wouldn't be good if they could tap into her translator. Is there any way that I could take your equipment with me and try to modify her translator if I'm able to see her again?"

"Possibly," replied Junot. "The programming module is compact enough to be portable, but it is a complex and somewhat lengthy process that would be hard to teach someone that isn't familiar with security protocols and the other programming requirements to set it up correctly. It would take me at least a half an horun to program it myself. It's not automated in any way. I have to go through it step by step to install, set up, and bypass all the required security hardware and protocols. It would probably take me a week or more to train you how to do that, and then I'd have to teach you how to run the test validation side of the modification.

"There's even more to it because I'm trying to figure out how to piggyback through the intercom system so that we can use the translators as a comm device for us. I am fairly sure I have that figured out. It's basically much the same as the main mining operation comm system that I tapped into before. I was able to piggyback on the hard lines of the mine's comm system and then just use a standard security encryption program to keep our communications secure. I haven't figured out yet how to do that on this nano-wave modulated comm system. There really is no way to piggyback on it, and the encryption codes I have access to won't work with this type of system environment. This nano-wave system is just a huge jumble of individual nano frequencies that are used to transmit and receive within a given frequency block. Trying to piggyback on any one of these would just leave our comms wide open for anyone to intercept. I really have no idea on how to get around this, so maybe it's not possible even though the basic mechanics of it is simple enough."

Jack asked, "You say there's a whole jumble of different frequencies within a main block. How many are there, and how far are they separated?"

"I am not sure," replied Junot, "but I think there's around two thousand separate frequencies per block, and there are ten main frequency blocks. Each bandwidth block is separated at 0.5 nano-mu-uts. Why do you want to know?"

"Have you ever heard of frequency hopping encryption?" asked Jack.

"No, I've never heard of that. What is it?" replied Junot.

"It's where they write a program where paired transmitters and receivers jump from frequency to frequency with every few data bits or at given time intervals that are transmitted."

"Well, that wouldn't work," said Junot. "How would the receiver ever capture all those transmissions across two thousand different frequency shifts and ten blocks?"

"Well, that's the beauty of the system," said Jack. "No one will know what frequency you are transmitting on, so they could never listen in on you. But if the transmitter and receiver are coordinated or paired and have the ability to match frequency shifts both simultaneously and instantaneously, then you have the ability to carry on a normal conversation that is fully encrypted because it's never in the same place, frequency-wise, for more than a few septus. No one has the ability to figure out where your next frequency shift is going to be. The transmitter and receiver must be paired and synchronized to each other. This could possibly be done within multiple channels of the translator, which would allow discreet communication between given pairs of translators as well as having a common channel where all the translators can go for centralized communication. All you have to do is come up with a predetermined, nonrepetitive frequency hopping algorithm that each paired set of translators is synchronized to and then you can have an unbreakable encryption capability."

Jack continued. "As long as no one else has access to the pairing protocol while the units are being paired, then there is no way for them to attain the key that would allow them to find the frequency hopping order. The transmitter and receiver are permanently paired and synced until they are changed by the operators. Do you think you can come up with something like that?" asked Jack. "It's more programming than hardware, but you have to have both to make it work."

Junot sat and pondered the question for a few mentus, just saying to himself over and over, "I don't know, I don't know. I think I might be able to come up with something like that." Junot then started talking to himself out loud about what piece of hardware he could use for this and what programming protocol he could use for that.

"Just think on it for a couple of daiyus and see if it makes sense and see what you come up with," said Jack.

"OK, I will," said Junot. "I've never heard of anything like this Jack. Where did you get an idea for something like this? It sounds really very cryptic."

"Well, remember I told you I was a fighter pilot," said Jack. "Our aircraft, our fighters, as well as our transports and bombers all had systems like this for both their communications and radar systems so that they couldn't be overheard or jammed. An enemy can't really jam or monitor the entire frequency spectrum because it's too vast, and they would lose access to the same frequency spectrum themselves if they tried to blanket jam the entire spectrum."

"That's just, that's, that's crazy," said Junot. "I don't think anyone has ever imagined anything like this, but I think I can come up with it in a few daiyus or maybe a wenek, since it's really just a programming issue."

Jack added, "The way our systems worked was that in addition to all the frequency hopping encryption, we also had to encode everything that went through the encryption system. It was unbreakable as far as we knew, but someone was always trying."

"Well, that sounds really interesting," said Junot, "but I would really need to have physical access to someone's translator to modify it and reprogram it to make it work even if I can figure out how to do it."

"OK," said Jack, "I'll work on that end of it and see what I can come up with. While you're designing this, also think if there is a way to protect a translator so that it can't be tampered with or they can't reverse engineer what you've come up with in case they get a hold of something you've modified. Maybe a special destruct command or software wipe, a three- or four-word command or something that will cause the software to wipe and maybe fry the circuitry of any hardware you install. That way, they could never use this against us if they should inadvertently get access to it."

"Well, OK, I think," said Junot, "there may be some type of programs out there already like that, like they use to protect company's secrets and program software. Maybe I can find something like that to use."

"OK, great," said Jack. "We can't be too careful. So have at it, and I'll see what I can do on my end."

The next daiyus at the foundry, while going over some production scheduling with Za-arvak, Jack mentioned to him that he noticed that he, Za-arvak, spent a lot time addressing, monitoring, and fixing the support equipment used in the foundry and alloy production facility. "Yes," said Za-arvak, "I have to spend an inordinate amount of time just keeping everything running around here. It's helped greatly having you running the operational and scheduling time, and you seem to be very good at keeping your systems up and operational. It's the same story again, as there is a lot more infrastructure to maintain here, and I just can't find the type of well-trained technicians I need this far out on the rim away from the big city. No amount of pay seems to attract the type of help we need out here, so I end up doing much of everything myself," Za-arvak complained.

This was just the scenario Jack was hoping for, so he instantly but casually replied, "Well, I have another good friend on the conscript side that is very skilled in both electronic and mechanical maintenance," he told Za-arvak. "The bosses use him as a repair tech for all the mine equipment, and it saves them a lot of credits compared to a contract technician, which is what he tells me."

"Really?" queried Za-arvak. "Because I've asked numerous times if they had anyone over there with those skills, and they always tell me no, but supposedly they'll let me know if someone shows up."

"Yes, he's quite good," replied Jack. "Some of the miners were even mad at him because he kept the equipment working so well that they never got any downtime because of equipment failures and had to work all the time. I'm guessing the bosses wouldn't want to let you have him because they don't have anyone to replace him, certainly not anyone that wouldn't cost them a lot to replace."

"Well, that's really not surprising," said Za-arvak. "Those rotten crooks, and, yes, I mean crooks," he replied, "they know quite well I could really use someone like that, but they're keeping him for themselves so they don't have to spend any credits on contract labor. I would also wager that they are pocketing all the savings they are gaining from that scenario also."

"Yes, that's what it is, that's exactly what it is," Jack further added. "Well, if you thought you might have some use for him over here, I'm sure he would love to come over here and put his talents to better use than the mine equipment repair. Is there some way you can request him if you want him?"

"Well, yes, of course," replied Za-arvak. "The foundry takes precedence over the mining operation. All I have to do is request him. I'm sure they won't be happy, since hiring an outside contract tech will cost them a decent amount of credits, which will come right out of their pockets. I'm really glad you mentioned this," said Za-arvak. "I never would have known, and they never would have told me. This might make the difference of meeting all our quotas and adding more to our own bonuses on the production side of the foundry."

"Well, I'm glad I mentioned it to you, then," replied Jack.

"You tell your friend—what is his name?" asked Za-arvak.

"Junot, Junot Saranuna of Riina, 1397," replied Jack.

Za-arvak smiled wryly at Jack. "You can tell your friend Junot that he can expect to be here tomorrow or the next daiyus at the latest. I am going to put in a request for a transfer for him right now. I will let you know as soon as I hear back, and it will be soon because I will put a priority order on it too."

"That's great," replied Jack. "I am absolutely certain that he will be thrilled with this opportunity. He's a very conscientious person and a hard worker. I'm sure you'll be pleased to have him."

"Yes, I will, oh, yes, indeed, I will," replied Za-arvak.

Wow, thought Jack, *I'd been trying to think of a way to get Junot out of the mine and over here. This couldn't have worked out any better.* Jack could hardly wait to finish his shift at the foundry so he could spring this new surprise on Junot. *I know he'll be glad to get out of the mine equipment repair business and away from the potential retaliation from the miners,* thought Jack.

Later when Jack found Junot and verified his translator was switched to safe mode, he said, "Hey, Junot, have you had a chance to come up with any ideas on the translator issue?"

"No, nothing specific, but I'm researching on how to generate a frequency hopping program. It's going to take me a few daiyus or more to figure out what kind of hardware or software it will take to accommodate that degree of switched synchronization. There may be some type of commercial program out there that can be modified into something that will work for us, probably some sort of an industrial timing and synchronization system. I'm sure I can do the research here, but I don't know how I would get access to anything like that here in the conzone. It's not like I can look it up in a catalog and just order a dual or multifrequency synchronized phase shift modulation unit or whatever it will take to generate the frequency hopping technology we'll need."

Jack replied, "Well, what if I could get you access to that catalog as well as the means to obtain the hardware you need?"

"Yeah, well, not much chance of that in here," said Junot, "unless you can figure out how to get something like that over in your foundry job and also get it to me here to experiment with."

Jack said, "What if I could get you over to the foundry and let you experiment over there in their lab with all sorts of goodies at your disposal?"

"That would be just great, but I can't imagine any way of sneaking me over there without getting caught. I could end up back on the rock pile in the mine and lose my repair job or worse."

"Well," said Jack, "I've got little surprise for you. Tomorrow or the daiyus after, you're going with me to the foundry where you're going to be employed as their new repair tech and electronics specialist. You can have access to all kinds of good tech stuff to play with, more than you have at the maintenance depot down here."

Junot just stared at Jack for about ten seconds. His mouth was open, but nothing was coming out. Then he finally managed to say something. "Oh, come on, that's mean to play a trick like that on me. You know I'd like nothing better than to get out of this place, even just for a little while. That's just not . . ."

"No trick," said Jack. "I told Za-arvak about your type of skills, and he decided he needed you right now. He even said he'd been asking the mine ops for anyone like you forever, but they claimed there weren't any skilled maintenance techs. He was not happy that they'd been keeping you to themselves when the foundry operation has preference over the mine operation."

"Are you serious? Are you really serious?" said Junot somewhat hesitantly?

"Yes, I'm totally serious," said Jack. "I wouldn't joke with you on something like that. Za-arvak said he had to get it cleared but that he would put a priority request on it and that he thought you would be up there by tomorrow or the next daiyus at the latest."

"Oh, oh, oh, heeeeah!" shrieked Junot as he literally jumped for joy as he comprehended the news.

"Now, remember," said Jack, "and this could blow it for both of us if you don't keep your cool about what we are doing to any other mine workers. They would

242

be really jealous and could possibly cause trouble if they knew you and I were getting to go outside the conzone every daiyus."

"OK, OK," replied Junot, "I won't tell anyone, but I just can't believe it. This is so great, I just can't believe it. What about Cherga, though? Won't he need to know?"

"Yes," replied Jack, "but I'll tell him and make sure he knows about keeping quiet. He's worked at the foundry before and knows about keeping quiet about a good deal like this." Jack added, "While you're at it, think about a way to get your translator-modifying equipment to the foundry so we can modify Zshutana's translator like ours for privacy. Our boss, Za-arvak, is quite smart, so you'll either have to hide it completely or disguise it as something else, some other type of test equipment or something."

"OK, I will," said Junot. "I can probably hide it alongside or inside some standard test equipment that I might use on a regular basis over there. I'll come up with something."

The next morning, Junot was told by a guard to report to the guard shack for a message where he was informed that he was being assigned to the foundry as a repair technician and he was to accompany Jack the Varaci to the foundry where he would meet his new boss Za-arvak and learn about his new assignment. As Junot and Jack passed though the security checkpoint on the way to the foundry, Junot couldn't believe he was outside the conzone area for the first time in many long moondats. Jack gave him a brief tour of the foundry like Cherga had done with him recently. Even though Junot had somewhat of an interesting job repairing the mining equipment at the mine, he was looking forward to doing more technical troubleshooting and repairs on the kind of electronics and other technical equipment that he preferred.

When they finally got to the office complex of the alloy lab, Jack took Junot in and introduced him to Za-arvak. Za-arvak introduced himself to Junot and said, "I was quite glad to learn from your friend Jack that there was a technician with your skills in the mine that I could conscript for the work here in the alloy lab and foundry. This will take a great load off of me and help our overall production capability greatly. The mine bosses tried to give me a hard time and said you couldn't be conscripted to me because you were actually a convict and not a conscript. I looked at your record and the circumstances that got you sentenced down there. I am actually somewhat skeptical of the circumstances. Like many of the conscripts and other workers down here, you may be here under a dubious sentence. Hopefully, that is the case with you. Otherwise, I don't think Jack would have recommended you."

Za-arvak continued. "Unfortunately, there is nothing I can do about the sentence and your conviction. However, if you are willing to work for me here and do a good job, I can certainly put in a good word for you at any upcoming parole hearing you might have."

Junot replied, Oh, thank you. I would very much appreciate that. I am very happy to come up here and work at something challenging and interesting. This is much more preferable than working in the mine even though the repair job I had was considerably better than operating machinery down in the actual mine tunnels. I will do the best work I can, and I am sure I will be able to help you in many ways."

Jack said, "Well, I must get to my own work now."

"Yes, very good," said Za-arvak. "I will take Junot here and introduce him to his duties as well as show him around the foundry and the alloy lab. I will bring him by your station later at the mid-meal horun. We will see you later, then," said Za-arvak.

Jack spent the first half of the daiyus checking on the production schedules and had to modify a few of the materials lists to produce the right alloys for the orders that had come in at the end of the previous daiyus. Once everything was in order and the day's production schedule was going well, he headed over to the alloy lab and started tinkering with some of his new experimental alloys.

The unique atomic structure of the Burun-Rioc ore was like nothing Jack had ever heard of on Earth. Its strange ability to enhance but not combine with so many other elements, minerals, and compounds and turn them all into a cohesive new alloy with unique new properties was simply amazing. It seemed like there was literally an unlimited amount of new combinations of Burun-Rioc alloys possible. In small batches, Jack tried various combinations of Burun-Rioc ore with separate and combined mixtures of titanium, chromium, nickel, cobalt, molybdenum, carbon, tungsten, and manganese.

Most of the time, the properties of the individual components showed through and were often greatly enhanced by the presence of the other elements, but sometimes the properties were less prevalent depending on what other elements were included or left out and in what concentrations. Either way, it was an interesting exercise, and Jack was thoroughly enjoying himself. He wouldn't know what all the properties of the new alloys were until he could test them for all the various properties such as hardness, corrosion resistance, tensile strength, as well as bending, flexibility, and sheer strength. He had some very good test equipment he was learning to use, but it was a pretty steep learning curve because of the alien nature of the equipment.

Time must have been flying because he was having fun. In short order, Za-arvak and Junot showed up for mid meal after completing most of Junot's orientation to the facility. They went to a small room not far from the alloy lab that appeared to be something like a small employee break room. When they got there, they discovered there were three orders of some sort of takeout-looking mid-meal food. Za-arvak said, "I somehow managed to take the initiative and so ordered some food from the concessions area and had it delivered for Junot's first daiyus here, since I didn't think he would know what else to do for mid meal around here. Don't get used to it, though, since I hardly ever eat mid meal myself, but today is a good daiyus, since I'll be able to incorporate two good support specialists that will help me considerably with my work here."

"As I've noted previously, you both have no idea how difficult it is to get qualified help this far out from the main population centers of this planet or anywhere in this remote quadrant of the rim. Sometimes, I think it would be easier in a black hole."

"Well, we are both just glad to be here and out of the mine," said Jack. "This is much more challenging and interesting than anything down there, well, except maybe the fight pit matches, but then, that's a whole different situation," Jack said with a chuckle.

"Yes, I can imagine," responded Za-arvak. "Speaking of the fight pit, do you know if you'll be fighting this Senesday as expected?"

Jack replied, "The bosses haven't told anyone to notify me yet, so I'm not sure, but I would guess that they would put me up for another match. If they do say anything to me, I will be sure to let you know."

"Yes, I would hate to miss my chance to make another small fortune on the wagering like I did last time," said Za-arvak.

"Well, don't get too carried away on the wagers," Jack said to Za-arvak. "I may have just gotten lucky the first couple of times, and they seem to be matching me up with fighters that are much better than my previous match. I think they are trying to keep the odds as high against me as they can, but they could put me up against someone that is very good, and I could end up losing. I just don't want you to lose a good sum of credits if my luck runs out," said Jack, thinking that he'd at least given Za-arvak a fair warning as to the vagaries of wagering on sporting events.

"Ummmm, well, perhaps," said Za-arvak, "but you seem to have a natural talent for the fight pit matches. I think your supposed luck may hold."

"Well, OK, then I guess you to will have to wager whatever you can afford to lose," said Jack, "but whatever you wager, you can be sure I'll give it my best shot regardless of who I'm up against. They may try and overmatch me again, but I may have a few tricks up my sleeve."

"Tricks up your sleeve? What is that exactly?" said Za-arvak with a somewhat quizzical look.

"Oh, it's just a saying," said Jack. "It means I might have a few tricks or skills that they are not even aware of that I've been saving that I can use to my benefit."

"Not to worry, I will wager what I'm comfortable with, and perhaps I may even make another large sum like I did last time."

"Well, I hope so too," replied Jack, "but remember, it's still a wager and not a sure thing."

Za-arvak spent the next couple of daiyus getting Junot up to speed on what needed to be maintained and monitored on a daily basis in and around the foundry. Junot was glad to be working on something new and more interesting than mining equipment, and he especially liked his free-roaming ability around the foundry, especially without the fear of the miners that had harassed him previously. It was almost like being back in his old job except for the fact that he knew he had to return to the conzone every night. That and the fact that he wasn't getting paid for his services by his employer were the only real differences. Either way, it was still a huge improvement over his previous situation.

That evening, Jack was told that he would be fighting in the next pit match on this upcoming Senesday. The only information they gave him when he was summoned to the guard shack was that his would be the third match and would be fighting a miner named Chartak Sula of Raranah. Well, he'd have access to the core tomorrow at the foundry and he could look up Raranah, and he'd ask Cherga what he knew about his upcoming opponent.

He and Junot met Cherga for the night meal at the rations hall. It wasn't exactly the concessions food Jack had enjoyed recently, but it would do. The conversation discreetly bantered around Jack and Junot's assignment at the foundry. Jack mentioned that it was going to get busier because of increased demand and the fact that they would be able to help Za-arvak increase his production rate. Maybe there would be another opening for an experienced foundry worker again if Cherga was interested. "That would be good with me," said Cherga. "That place gives me a bit of a headache, but it would be a good break from the mine operation, which gets boring daiyus after daiyus."

"I'll put a bug in Za-arvak's ear as soon as I get a chance, then," said Jack.

"A bug? What kind of bug? In his ear? I'm not sure I understand," replied Cherga.

"Me neither. You speak some strange things. Why would you put a bug in someone's ear?" said Junot.

"Not a real bug," replied Jack. "It's a saying. It means I will try to convince him or make him think it's a good idea," said Jack.

"But a bug? I'm not sure that would work or that he would appreciate that," said Cherga.

"Hmm, OK, I won't put a bug in his ear," said Jack. "I'll just make a discreet suggestion to him."

"OK, good, that might work better," said Cherga, as he thought that Jack came up with some very strange ideas occasionally.

"So, Cherga, I found out today that my next fight is scheduled this Senesday. I will be in the third match, and my opponent will be a miner named Chartak Sula of Raranah. Have you heard of him or seen him fight?" asked Jack.

"Chartak Sula of Raranah? You are joking with me, is that not correct?" replied Cherga.

"No," said Jack, "that's what they told me at the guard shack earlier when they informed me of the fight schedule."

Cherga replied, "Well, my friend, this is not so good news. They must consider you a very good fighter, or they wish to see you taken out very early in your fight pit career."

"Tell me more," replied Jack.

Cherga went on. "Chartak Sula was last year's second-place champion in the fight pit. He is a contract miner now, and he barely lost to another very good fighter named Fuundar Daak of Gennakah. The match was really a draw, and many think Chartak Sula was the winner, but the ref and Sha-aga said that Fuundar Daak won by two technical points.

"I do not understand why they would be matching you, a new fighter, against someone so experienced as Chartak Sula. Yes, yes, I know you have won two matches now, but Chartak Sula is at least eight or ten levels above where you are in the overall rankings. This makes no sense to me at all."

"It does to me now," said Jack. "They have already lost considerable credits by my winning against such heavy odds in the last two fights. This is not what they had planned even though they knew I probably had some pretty good fighting skills. They have tried to match me against fighters that would give me a good fight but end up winning in the end so they could reap their biggest returns. I am just guessing that was what they had planned. By me winning the last two matches, they have seriously miscalculated and lost a lot of credits because of our small group that is betting on me. So now they have chosen one of their best fighters to keep the odds higher against me so they can recover their losses. That's the only reason I can think of that they would be overmatching me so drastically. I am pretty sure they must be playing the back side of the matches. That is the only thing that makes sense for the way they are rigging this. I'm almost surprised they didn't match me against the champion, Fuundar Daak, to push the odds even higher against me."

"Perhaps they would have," replied Cherga, "but that is not possible, since Fuundar Daak was killed in his next match when he volunteered to fight a gorroks to prove that he was indeed the best fighter. Unfortunately, the gorroks hit him with a huge blow in the second round of the match. The gorroks was able to get a hold of Daak and tore him to pieces."

"Literally or figuratively?" asked Jack.

"Literally," replied Cherga. "The gorroks broke Fuundar Daak's arm and then slammed him to the ground and stomped on his head then twisted his head until his neck was broken and his head was nearly ripped from his body."

"That's horrid," said Junot. "I heard about that, but I'm glad I missed it. How terrible."

"That does sound a little gruesome," said Jack. "We're not going to worry about that too much right now. We're just going to concentrate on Senesday's match with Chartak Sula. Tell me more about how he fights and anything else you know about him," asked Jack.

They finished their meal, and as they got up to go back to the common area, Jack said, "Cherga, if you're not doing anything at the moment, why don't you come with Junot and me, and we'll show you something you haven't seen before?"

"Show me something I haven't seen before?" replied Cherga. "What would that be?"

Junot said, "Well, it's kind of a surprise and something we think you'll like, but you have to be quiet and can't say anything on the way there."

"A surprise and something I will like and I can't speak on the way there? This sounds very mysterious and intriguing, just the sort of thing I like," said Cherga. "Well, I am up for something of a surprise, so we shall go."

Junot and Jack took Cherga to the maintenance depot. When they got there, they blocked his translator visually like they had Jack's and explained to him what they were going to do to his translator. He sat silently, while Junot modified and tweaked his translator for thirty mentus. When he was done, Junot said to him, "From your menu on the left, select the safe command. Do you see the word 'safe' illuminated in green?" Cherga nodded his head in the affirmative. "OK, you may now talk freely, and the mine bosses or whoever may be monitoring us won't be able to hear you. Your transmissions are blocked, but you always have to make sure that it is in safe mode if you want a private conversation."

Junot went on to explain the rest of the operation of the modified translator as well as the other modifications they were working on. Cherga was incensed when he found out that the mine bosses had the ability to listen in and eavesdrop on their conversations at will. "Those despicable Rudagon dung heaps. This doesn't surprise me one bit, though," he lamented angrily. "But your modification will allow us to talk secretly as long as it is in safe mode?" confirmed Cherga.

"Yes," replied Junot, "but you must remember to put it back in the red caution mode when you don't need to speak privately, or they may think their spying equipment isn't working if they don't hear anything for a long time. Then they may try to find out what is wrong with it and attempt to fix it and find out what we've done to it."

"Yes," said Cherga, "I won't forget this. You have done a good thing here with these translators. So useful they are but also a vile tool of these despicable mine boss jobakta worms," said Cherga.

"Junot, while we are here at the maintenance depot, let me contact Zshutana and let her know about the upcoming fight," said Jack.

"OK, we can do that. Give me a few mentus to get it set up. Also use your translator in the safe mode, as it will give us an extra layer of security," said Junot.

"Zshutana? Who is this Zshutana person?" Cherga asked Jack.

"Oh, a friend of mine on the outside that may be helping me with some of my plans," replied Jack, "but please don't mention her name anywhere else in the mine, as I want to keep her name out of anything we may be involved in."

"Yes, not to worry," replied Cherga. "It is good to know that we have a contact and possible help on the outside. I was not aware of this."

"I'm trying to be cautious and only let those that have a need to know in on our information and plans," replied Jack.

"A very good strategy," replied Cherga.

Junot yelled over to Jack from where he was working on the comms on the other side of the room, "It's all set to go, Jack! All you have to do is initiate the call."

"That's great, Junot, and thanks," he replied as he sat down to initiate the call to Zshutana. He wasn't sure exactly what to say to her, but he figured it would come naturally enough on its own. He heard the phone chirping on her end as it buzzed to get her attention.

"Hello, who is calling?" she said cautiously?

"Teela, hi, it's Duunda."

She paused for a second, wanting to say his name but knew not to. "Duunda, how are you? I've been hoping I would hear from you. It's so good to hear your voice."

"Yes, it's so good to hear your voice too. I've really wanted to contact you, but this is the first time I've been able to."

"I know, I understand," she replied. "This is terribly frustrating for me. Do you think I might be able to see you anytime soon? I mean that would be a really nice thing. If that were possible, I would really like to see you," she said.

"Yes, there's nothing I'd like better," he answered. "I'm trying to figure out how to free up some time and do just that. Also, my next event will be on Senesday, and I just wanted to make sure you were up on that."

"Yes, yes, I saw the schedule, which was just posted. I hope it will be a safe or an easy one," she said.

"Well, I'm not so sure on this one," he said, "so be careful with what you want to risk. It's up to you, of course, but I just wanted to let you know, since we didn't get to talk much about that during our last meeting."

"No, we did not, did we?" she replied as her eyes smiled and radiated with delight. "I believe we had other more pressing matters to attend to, did we not?" she added.

He gave a little chuckle and replied, "Indeed, we did, most pressing and urgent matters it seemed to me. Did it seem that way to you?" he gently chided back as it was suddenly getting difficult to concentrate on the conversation at hand.

"Oh, yes, truly urgent and utterly vital and pressing matters," she responded back. How unbelievably frustrating; he felt like a teenager and could barely stand it. What he wouldn't give to crawl through the comm line and see her right now.

"Well, after my next event, I'm going to try and come see you, but I will have my friend with me," he said.

She was immediately elated when he said this but wasn't sure what he meant by his friend being with him. "Oh, that would be wonderful, really wonderful. But I'm not sure what you mean about your friend being with you."

"Yes, I know," he said, "but my friend, the one who helped me with my other speech problem, I think he could help you with your speech issue also. He is making some great improvements in our ability to communicate, and the first step would be to help you with your speech problem as soon as we can."

"OK, yes, I understand. That would be a very important thing to get help with, but when do you think this might be?"

"I'm not sure, but maybe, well, hopefully soon," he replied. "There is nothing I would like better."

"Me too," she said back to him.

"Well, I think I need to get going now," he said reluctantly to her.

"OK, all right," she said. "Do well and be careful in your next event. I'll think about what you said regarding that."

"OK, I'll get back to you as soon as I can and let you know what I am planning. I'll see you soon." He ended his call with her with a few more longing words and then cut the connection. He sat there for a mentu before he realized how hard he was breathing. He tried to clear his head of the frustrating thoughts that were controlling his emotions, then he headed back to the common area with Junot and Cherga.

The next daiyus at the foundry, after everything was scheduled and set for the daiyus, Jack went to the alloy lab and started experimenting with some variations and different concentrations of tungsten, cobalt, carbon, iron, vanadium, and nickel all combined with the v. He could only imagine the types of super alloys the real metallurgists and engineers on Earth could up with if they had access to this amazing elemental Burun-Rioc ore as they called it here. He had a hard time not thinking about Zshutana knowing that she wasn't that far away. He had plenty of other things to attend to and didn't think he could press for another concession area visit between now and the next one that he was planning to try and get Junot out with him on. He didn't know how agreeable to that Za-arvak would be, but he'd been OK with everything else so far.

After combining his newest alloy mixture in the small magnetic containment plasma-fired research furnace, he set it to extrude a short six-inch bar stock to test the characteristics of his alloy mixture. He let it cool slowly without quenching it for about ten mentus. Then he started testing the properties of this new alloy. He drilled and machined a section then worked it down to a basic knife shape. It worked well and machined fairly easily. It was slightly harder to work than mild steel, and it had a beautiful rippling, almost iridescent sheen to it. At least in the annealed state, it was attractive and easy enough to work. The next step would be to heat it above the crystallization temperature of any of the combine elements then quickly cryogenically quench it to set the Burun-Rioc process and then retest the end product alloy. He had tried this with several other combinations but not at the current percentage levels of the various elements. He'd had some decent results but nothing exceptional. Some of the ones he'd created were too soft, too brittle, or too ductile.

After verifying that he had correctly recorded the alloy content, Jack set up the heating and quenching process that would fully transform the alloy properties. Heating the new alloy to the proper temperature resulted in a beautiful, shiny, large crystalline grained ingot that audibly pinged, actually almost sang when quenched in the cryo vat. After it had returned to room temperature, Jack put it through the series of materials tests. Everything about the alloy was spectacular. It seemed to be impervious to all the destructive hardness and thermal tests. It wouldn't scratch or melt with the plasma pin torch and showed no measureable elasticity. It was almost like a metal diamond. Unfortunately, on the compression test, the sample broke at an estimated pressure of 49,700 pounds per square inch converted from Nishda's galactic standard reading of 6,788.3 gautons.

Everything about this alloy is amazing, thought Jack, *but it can't take a compressive load.* Looking at the broken sample, Jack could see that it had sheared along the crystalline line forms in the large metallic crystals of the ingot, which had formed during the quenching phase. Apparently, it was so hard that it gave up considerable structural strength because of the shear zones in the crystalline structure. He thought about it for a while trying to think of a way to overcome this property that was making the nearly perfect alloy nearly useless for his purpose, since impact force could likely cause the same structural failure as compression force. What was it that made the Japanese samurai swords, their katanas, which were so outstanding, so flexible and so resilient?

He knew the basic components of their katanas was carbon steel, but his alloy was so much superior, yet it was too weak under compression and would break. Then he remembered seeing a YouTube video once on how they were made. It wasn't so much the ingredients in the alloy but the fact that they folded the steel over and over on itself, making a strong but brittle steel extremely strong by the mechanical bonding of the alloyed carbon steel. That would make sense; as the crystalline structure of the metal was folded over and over, then the shear zone in the structure would disappear, leaving only the strength and flexibility of the steel. They also tempered the edge with clay somehow to make it extremely hard, which allowed it to be sharpened to a razor's edge while retaining the strong and flexible main shaft of the blade.

He ran the alloy mixture again and reproduced the annealed ingot from the first attempt. This time, though, he kept the ingot at a semiductile temperature and flattened it to about an eighth inch on a press in the test production room adjacent to the alloy lab. He folded the metal onto itself using a forming brake in the room, reheated it, pressed it, then repeated it. Heat, press, heat, fold, heat, press, repeat. Eight times he did this, calculating that this gave him 256 mechanically bonded layers. He heated it the last time then let it cool to room temperature. He machined it and drilled it like before. Everything seemed to repeat as far as workability of the alloy. He then reheated the new folded metal ingot to a bright orange color then cryo-quenched it.

When the new folded alloy ingot finished the cryo process, Jack pulled it out, warmed it to room temp, and cleaned off the slag residue. It looked similar to the previous rendition, but the single direction large crystalline structure was gone and in its place was a beautiful multifaceted microcrystalline, multidirectional metal structure. Jack handled it for a minute then decided to run it through the standard metallurgical test.

When he ran the tests, it quickly became apparent that nothing he'd created or tested before was like this new alloy sample. The hardness was unprecedented and was literally off the scale. It wouldn't even deform from compression under the severest test conditions. Like the previous unfolded sample, it wouldn't scratch or melt with the plasma pin torch at what converted to 4,500 degrees Celsius. It did, however, show some small degree of flexibility, but when he tried to shatter it or cleave it like the prior sample, it remained unscathed. He tried machining it and drilling it, and it was totally impervious to any mechanical destructive testing he tried on it.

Whatever combination of alloys he'd created, it didn't appear to be like anything else in the previously known metallurgical database that he'd referenced in the foundry's records. Even the Burun-Rioc starship structural alloys didn't have the resilience of what he'd come up with, at least based on what he'd read and the initial testing of his sample. He thought, *Whatever I've created here may be a big boost to help Za-arvak in some way.* He wasn't sure that there would be a way to mass produce folded alloys but figured if the alloy was good enough, they would find a way. This would be good for one thing, though, and that would be to make what would likely be the best katana blade the galaxy has ever seen. The way it would have to be done is to completely machine, sharpen, and polish the katana blade in the pre-cryo state while it could still be shaped. Once the cryo-quenching process was done, there would be no modifying the blade unless there was some machining process he was unaware of.

Jack decided to write up a short report for Za-arvak on the properties and composition of the alloy. He wondered if he would get to name it, him being a conscript of Nishda. If not, it wouldn't really matter; maybe they would let Za-arvak name it or even name it after Za-arvak. That would be just fine with Jack too. On Earth, it would be called Tamahagane steel or Damascus, but since it really wasn't steel, that wouldn't apply either. Jack laughed to himself. *I guess if I was going to name it, I would call it Spartan steel.*

A little while later, Jack brought the sample and the report to Za-arvak in his office. "I think I've come up with something you might be interested in while I was experimenting with some new alloys," he said to Za-arvak. Jack went on to explain his findings and the report while showing Za-arvak the sample alloy. "I've looked at all the alloys shown in the foundry database, but I haven't seen anything like this, at least not with these attributes or characteristics. It would be hard to manufacture in large quantities because of the process involved, but it might be useful for small articles that need exceptional strength and durability."

Za-arvak read the report and the properties in the report. "This is really quite fascinating. The mechanical properties are simply amazing. I've never seen this combination of elements in an alloy before, and I've never heard of this folding process. Where did you come up with such an unusual process?" Jack went on to explain it but without going into the Earth origins of katanas. He told about the broken sample that had fractured along the crystalline structure line and said he'd remembered hearing somewhere about some ancient metal folding and forging technique using steel, so he thought he would try it on his new alloy.

"This seems like a very promising alloy," said Za-arvak. "We will have to send the sample and the report to the Nishda research lab in Wanana where they can run a full series of tests on it and see what the complete properties analysis breakdown is. Very well done," Za-arvak said as he congratulated Jack on his excellent work. They discussed the properties of the alloy for a few more minutes then Za-arvak said he had an appointment for a vido meeting he had to attend to in just a short while. "Perhaps tomorrow when I have more time, I can come down to the lab and see what you are working on," said Za-arvak.

"I'd like that," replied Jack, thinking to himself that he now had some time right now that he could work on his own project without interruption.

Jack met with Junot when it was time to go back to the conzone and told him to go on back alone, as Za-arvak had some after-hours work he wanted Jack to attend to. "I'll see you later when I get back," he told Junot. "Keep working on the translator issue if you've got some time," he added.

"Yes, that's what I was planning on doing," said Junot. "I think I may have some new data available that will help me figure out how to crack some of the access protocols in the translator."

"Great," said Jack. "The sooner we can figure out all the secrets of those convoluted things, the better." Jack then headed back to the alloy lab to try and figure out some of his own metallurgy mysteries.

Jack was glad that he'd been able to come up with something to potentially help Za-arvak, especially since Za-arvak had been so helpful to him in his situation. Hopefully, this would also buy Jack some additional leeway as far as access to the concession area with Junot as well as for other reasons. In the meantime, he would start working on his own little project. If his long-term plan was going to work, he would likely need one or more types of weapons. He hadn't seen much in the way of firearms or other weapons, but he knew the mine bosses or crew on the ship could control you with a control disk and wrist restraints that they had used on him previously. The object would be to keep them from ever applying the wrist or any other restraints in the future. To do that, he might need some type of weapon. The only thing he could think of right now is to make a katana or samurai sword as well as a *tanto* or short sword and maybe a basic knife or two out of this amazing Burun-Rioc -based Spartan alloy he had created. He set to work re-creating the previous alloy configuration and programmed the plasma research furnace for an extrusion length for his blade blanks at the equivalent of forty-six inches, twenty-three inches, and at eleven inches.

In just over an horun, he had his six raw blade blanks. He started with one of the two shorter ones to see if it would turn out like his initial sample. Heat, press, fold, press, heat, press, repeat. In another horun, he had his first folded alloy knife blank. Even in a rough unpolished state, it had a unique, almost iridescent look to it. He then set about programming the computer-guided milling machine to generate the actual knife blank. When it was complete, he held a fabulous Burun-Rioc super alloy knife blade just short of twelve inches long now. The metallurgical aspects of it were amazing, and it had a stunningly bright silver iridescent appearance. It had multiple layers that he could see shimmering in the light while moving it back and forth across the entire blade and handle section. The machining had produced a multifaceted, multilayered work of art.

Jack could hardly wait to sharpen it and polish, but the latter would have to wait for a while as he applied himself to the practical aspect of the project. He checked the time and decided he didn't have enough time to complete any more raw blanks into finished blanks ready for milling. He had to be back on the conscript side shortly or it might arouse some sort or automated alarm. He hid the raw blanks and one finished blank in a small storage room near the back of lab supply room under some other old stock that looked like it hadn't been moved for years. Later, he could machine, sharpen, and harden his first finished blank before he finished the remaining ones. Tomorrow was his daiyus off and his third fight pit match, so he wouldn't be able to get back to his project until after that anyway.

The next daiyus, Jack was up early and decided to go to the gym and get a light workout in, in preparation for this evening's fight. After he'd gotten a decent warm-up and felt like he was up to par, he headed back to the berthing chamber to find out if Junot had any more luck on his quest to reprogram the translators. Junot was already gone, and he found both Cherga and Junot in the rations hall having their breakfast. "Hi, guys, how's it going?" asked Jack as he sat down to have some breakfast with his friends.

"It's good for us," replied Cherga, "but then neither of us has to fight Chartak Sula of Raranah. I hope you are up for this match, my friend. I don't mind a good fight myself, but I think I would have to pass on this one."

"OK, so tell me more about how he fights so I can have an idea of what I'm up against. I've never seen him fight, so it would be helpful if I knew his techniques."

Cherga replied, "He seems to have skills and experience above any of the common miners. With some of the lesser-skilled fighters, he only seemed to be toying with them, just delaying and taking his time, as if he were enjoying their systematic demise."

"OK, that's good info," said Jack, "but how does he attack his opponents? Does he lunge at them and try to take them down, or does he stay on his feet and try to fight them with his hands, or maybe a combination of both? Does he use his feet or knees to kick his opponents, and if he takes them to the ground, does he try to beat them or put them in some type of a hold?"

"I don't remember too much specifically, since it's been a while since I've seen him fight," replied Cherga, "but it seemed like he spent a lot of time on his feet attacking his opponents with punches, lots of combinations of different punches that he would attack them with. At first, he would go easy on them, but then he would start to work all around them and wear them down until he could do whatever he wanted with them. I do remember one match where his opponent was standing up to him fairly well, and Chartak Sula did dive in and take him to the ground. He seems to control his opponent very well and continue to wear him down with both punches and holds until his opponent—it was Ummandu that time—was completely subdued."

"OK, good," said Jack, "that's the kind of information I want to know. That will help me form a strategy on how to conduct this fight."

"So how about you, Junot? Have you been making any progress on your project?" said Jack as he mouthed "safe mode" to his friends. They nodded and gave him a thumbs-up gesture that he'd taught them earlier when they discussed their safety protocols for dealing with the translator issue. Cherga wasn't so sure, as he'd explained that it meant a derogatory gesture on his home planet. Here in the conzone, though, it didn't matter, so they went with it.

"Very great," replied Junot. "I have found a great deal of information on the construction and programming of the translators, all very hard to access, underplanet-type stuff in the dark part of the core where most people don't access. If it wasn't for the open access routing in the maintenance depot, I wouldn't be able to find any of this. Hopefully, they won't try to block me from the maintenance depot now that I'm working over in the foundry for Za-arvak. If they tried to, I will just tell them I need access there to help Za-arvak in the foundry, and I think they would leave me alone."

"Well, just keep a low profile if you can," said Jack. "So what did you learn about the translators?"

Junot replied, "A lot about what we already suspected and sort of talked about. The translators have spying capability, coded tracking ability, and an encrypted identification stamp. I've learned that there may be some way to break the security encryption so that you can enter the programming functions of the translators. I will have to do some more research. A lot of what I've come across is just posted as theories, but some of it looks feasible. I don't think that anyone has actually ever figured out how to do this yet, but it gives me a direction to start exploring in," said Junot.

"OK, good," said Jack, "just be extra careful."

"I will," said Junot. "If I can gain full access to the programming functions of the translator, I will be able to do like we talked about before. I'll be able to turn the tracking off and on, and I'll be able to program in any identification code so that the translator will read as any ID of anyone that you want."

"That's excellent, Junot," said Jack. "What else? Any luck with the comm functions of the translators being coopted by our merry little band of bandits here?"

"I haven't gotten that far into it yet, but if the mine bosses or others are able to use it for that, then we should certainly be able to piggyback on their system somehow. We'll just have to learn how to make it completely secret, probably using your frequency-jumping system if I can figure out how to make that work."

"Have you thought any more about what it is you're actually planning?" asked Cherga.

"Not exactly," replied Jack, "but anything that gives us an advantage over these contemptible mine bosses will certainly help us in the long run and help determine what it is we can do to thwart them somehow."

"I would agree, and perhaps there's a way to cause them great loss without getting ourselves accused of it," said Cherga. "Would not that be enjoyable?"

"Yes," said Jack, "but we have to be careful not to entrap ourselves along with our potential quarry."

Jack, Cherga, and Junot showed up for the match an hour early as usual, and they went through the usual preliminaries and sales pitch by Sha-aga, the announcer. Jack talked to two of that night's other contenders, and they were fairly baffled by his match up against the infamous Chartak Sula also. The general consensus was that whoever was responsible for the lineup was trying to take Jack out and keep the odds stacked against him. There was no sign of Chartak Sula yet, so Jack just waited it out until the match start time and warmed up a little by shadowboxing and some easy sparring with Cherga. Cherga said, "Come on, Junot, it's your turn to spar with Jack. I'm getting tired, and my arm hurts."

"Oh, do you think I should? Would it help?" replied Junot. "Oh, you are just teasing me. That would not be very smart for me to do. I would probably get my nose and everything else broken. No, that wouldn't be very smart at all."

"You could spar with me," said Jack. "I wouldn't hit you, and I might be able to teach you a few interesting and useful things."

"Well, maybe some other time, but right now probably isn't the best time for fighting lessons," said Junot.

"Yes, you're right about that," said Jack, "but maybe another time for sure. You might like it. I know a lot of dirty tricks to use against attackers. I might have to use some of them tonight."

The first match started right on schedule after Sha-aga introduced the contenders Sudow of Benacra and Roandar from Uknalah. It was a somewhat one-sided match with Roandar dominating Sudow from the first few moments of the opening-round. Sudow put up a valiant effort, but it was purely defensive from the beginning of the match. A little past the halfway point of the second round, Roandar caught Sudow with his hands down and no defenses in place, so he pummeled him with four or five good hits that put Sudow on the ground with Roandar on top of him continuing the attack. The ref let it continue for a few septus then jumped in to save Sudow from a serious pounding that might have ended with permanent injuries. The match was called with Roandar as the easy victor.

The second match was between Hushna Ro of Tuballa and Dunu ata Mar of Cherga's home planet, Zanaii. This looked to be more evenly matched fight and a lot more interesting, thought Jack as he assessed both fighters to be capable, fast, and experienced based on their looks and ranking. The first round had little give and take by either contender as they felt each other out and probed for weaknesses. There were a few good jabs and combos and one takedown lunge attempt, but neither fighter scored any serious points. Toward the end of the first round, Hushna Ro made several attempts to work Dunu ata Mar onto the wire rope of the ring, but Dunu skillfully managed to keep moving and avoided being trapped by his slightly bigger opponent. They both had just started throwing a few more aggressive attacks when the first round buzzer sounded.

When the buzzer sounded for the second round, Dunu ata Mar charged from his edge of the ring, faded back, then charged again. The first charge was rebuffed, but the second one came so fast that Hushna Ro wasn't quite ready and caught a glancing straight punch to the face followed by a sloppy but fairly well-landed left hook. It was a solid hit, but Hushna Ro was a very solid contender, so it didn't faze him too badly. The rest of the second round went pretty much the same with each fighter getting in a few good licks but with neither side showing a decisive advantage. Each attack grew a little more vicious, and each response to each attack matched it in kind. The spectators were getting more excited and agitated as the tempo of the match increased. There was still no sign of Chartak Sula as far as Jack could tell. Jack wondered if he was going to be a no-show, but based on his reputation, this was probably just part of his usual routine.

The third round started with Dunu ata Mar charging out for a full frontal assault on Hushna Ro, but there was no feigned backing off this time. The rest of the match turned into a give-it-and-take-it slug fest. Right at the halfway point of the round, Hushna Ro dove in on Dunu ata Mar and grabbed him squarely at the waist, plowed his shoulders under Dunu ata Mar, and lifted him all the way off the ground to his shoulders where he dumped him over backward into a crashing heap that landed hard on the ground. Swinging around and maneuvering fast, Hushna Ro dove onto Dunu ata Mar and began to pummel him mercilessly.

Dunu ata Mar was able to block a lot the pounding fists that assailed him, but a few of them got through and scored some good hits. Hushna Ro jumped on Dunu ata Mar's back and got him in a stranglehold, then Dunu ata Mar tried to roll away. Hushna Ro now had total control and a good chokehold on Dunu ata Mar. Hushna Ro continued to beat on Dunu ata Mar, and all Dunu ata Mar could do at this point was try to cover and keep his head out of the reach of Hushna Ro's continued bashing. Just as the ref was ready to tap them out and pull them off to call the match, the buzzer sounded, and the match was over. The clear victor was Hushna Ro. The spectators had been in a continuous uproar for the entire last round, and they jumped and screamed even louder as the ref pulled the contestants to their feet and raised Hushna Ro's arms in victory.

The excitement went on for another three mentus as the victor paraded around the ring. Jack was still searching, and then at the back of the crowd, he saw a large, strong different-looking alien accompanied by two other miners. From what Jack could see at this distance, it looked like he might have a good six inches on Jack. He was broad and muscular with dark burnt-orange skin coloring and what looked like close-cropped dark yellow-blond hair tinged with dark tips. *Quite a unique look,* Jack thought to himself.

As he got closer, Jack could see deep wide-set eyes with some degree of downward slant at the outside as well as large flat double-pointed ears that looked like they'd been cut that way on purpose. They were plastered to the side of his head pointing straight backward with a little downward slant at the tips. His head was actually somewhat narrow compared to the rest of his body, which was fairly wide but not all that thick front to back in comparison. The crowd gave way to him as he worked his way down toward the ring, while at the same time, Sha-aga began to announce the third and final match of the night.

Sha-aga bellowed in his announcer's voice, "Our third and final match for tonight will be an, um, interesting and probably exciting match. One of our newest challengers, Ja-ak of Vara, after two consecutive wins but with a record of only two and zero, will fight last year's fight pit champion, Chartak Sula of Raranah."

A loud roar went up as the champion Chartak Sula worked his way to the front of the crowd and deftly hopped the fight pit ring fence. He held his hands above his head and spun in circles while he shouted, "I am Chartak Sula, Chartak Sula of Raranah, and I'm here for you. I am Chartak Sula, and I am here to win all the matches, so wager on me, and I will fill your pockets with credits."

The crowd let loose with a huge roar as Chartak Sula paraded around the ring. He neither acknowledged Jack nor showed him any animosity but seemed totally self-absorbed in his own personal show. Sha-aga let this go on for several mentus, while he admonished the spectators to not forget to wager for their favorite contestant. Sha-aga came back to Jack and reintroduced him to the crowd, while he reminded them of Jack's excellent two-and-zero record. Jack hoped his friends had held a little back in their wager so they wouldn't lose all their winnings just in case he didn't win this match.

He'd placed his bet just before the end of the second match, and he'd even held back two thousand credits from his own winnings just in case he had to pay back the mine bosses in case he lost everything. Well, he wasn't planning on losing, but there would be a little leftover if he didn't fare so well tonight. The odds are still eight to one against him, which actually seemed a little low considering his meager winning streak versus Chartak Sula's reputation as last year's fight pit champion.

Sha-aga had drawn out the introduction long enough that hopefully every spectator both here and throughout the Corodune mine complex had placed a wager. Sha-aga then announced that the match was ready to begin. Jack looked at his opponent again and wondered what his weaknesses might be. He looked strong and agile but slightly out of proportion to anything Jack had previously seen. With his wide but not very thick body and downturned eyes and ears, as well as his slightly short legs, he almost looked ever so slightly insect-like. Jack wondered if Chartak Sula was better at forward and backward movement but not lateral or turning movement. *Well, I'll find out in about twenty septus,* he thought. At Sha-aga's instruction, the fighters each took their side of the ring, and the buzzer sounded.

Jack came off the edge of his ring side moving deftly in a quick left then quick right feint. Chartak Sula came straight at Jack with a moderate charge. Jack's quick left then right feint caused Chartak Sula to shift right then left to match Jack's movement. Chartak Sula was quick, but Jack noticed just the slightest fraction of a septus hesitation as he turned back to match Jack's move. Chartak moved very fluidly as he moved toward Jack, but Jack could tell he was just a little less nimble in his sideways movement as he'd guessed earlier. They squared up, and each threw a few probing shots. Jack looked for openings in Chartak Sula's defense and found it to be fairly tight unlike any of his previous opponent's.

Chartak Sula threw a three-punch combo then lunged at Jack, trying to get him in a front hold while he simultaneously threw a well-aimed head butt at Jack's face. Jack had seen very little other than basic punching and brawling used in any of the matches, but obviously, Chartak Sula had some other tricks. Chartak Sula's head butt was fast, and Jack just barely had enough time to move his hands up and block it and move out of range.

Chartak Sula kept coming with a one-two combo that Jack ducked and moved off-line. Jack had to give him credit for his speed and his continuous drive with one attack followed by another. Jack continued to duck and weave. He kept watching and analyzing his opponent's footwork and cataloging his attacks and types of punch combos. For every attack that Chartak made, Jack moved back and sideways. Chartak could follow him and then attack superbly in a straight line, but each time Jack moved off-line, there was a slight delay on Chartak Sula's part.

The farther off-line Jack moved and the closer in Jack was, the harder it was for his opponent to stay with him. On one of the attacks, Chartak tried a dive for Jack's legs to take him down, but he dropped his arms and torso onto Chartak and pushed off and thwarted the attempt. Chartak had yet to acknowledge Jack and seemed to be concentrating on developing his strategy against the newcomer. After multiple attacks on this Varaci, he'd yet to connect or find a weakness in Jack's defense. He wasn't getting tired, but he was getting tired of not connecting or doing any damage to the Varan. This was a new situation for Chartak Sula in this respect.

Other than a few probing jabs, Jack had yet to counter any of Chartak's attacks. He was hoping that Chartak would get tired or careless and leave his guard down for an instant so Jack could deliver a nice welcoming thump. Chartak tried a quick attack and fade followed by another hard drive. Instead of backing out of it, Jack moved in for a fast right straight followed by a wide outside left hook. The straight barely connected as it was mostly deflected by Chartak, but the wide hook landed solidly enough to get Chartak's attention. Now surprised and suddenly angered, Chartak lunged after Jack to exact a quick revenge, but Jack backed off again and turned Chartak's effort into wasted energy.

Chartak attacked again, but Jack held his ground this time and let himself get into a close-quarters scuffle long enough to trade a few body shots. Jack wanted to see what type of close-in moves his opponent might try to use. After a half-dozen close-in swings, Chartak tried to dive down for Jack's legs again. Jack stopped his attack by moving forward, while he threw a short left knee strike to check Chartak's attack. That connected nicely, and the pain to his chest from Jack's knee strike and the strange defense his opponent used surprised Chartak.

Chartak would usually give little deference to an unexperienced challenger like this Varan that was here only as exhibition fight fodder. Strangely, though, he'd scored little and actually been hit a few times by this novice. Perhaps he would have to turn up the heat a little and teach this neophyte a new lesson or two. He'd already been wondering why he was called to fight this novice, but perhaps the bosses had known the Varan was a little better than average and thought that he, Chartak, could make an interesting time of the match.

The spectators were now starting to show some serious enthusiasm for a fight they thought would originally be an easy and quick exhibition fight. They wouldn't get much return on their wagers at eight-to-one betting on Chartak, who was a given, but if they made a big-enough bet, they could get some fair winnings. There were a couple of them, though, that had seen the Varan fight before and were starting to appreciate the skills he was showing. A couple of them had even made some small wagers on "Jack of Vara" just for fun while at the same time betting on Chartak Sula. Chartak was a sure bet, but there wouldn't be much payout; whereas a small bet on the Varaci wouldn't cost them much and would be a good payout if for some reason this Varaci actually won.

Now that the novice had stayed in the match for a few mentus, Chartak chided the novice for fun, "So are you having fun, Varaci beginner? Have you learned anything new today yet?"

Jack replied, "Just studying your technique and looking for your weaknesses, Chartak."

"Perhaps I should charge you a training fee for the lessons you will learn here today," added Chartak.

"Perhaps, or perhaps I should charge you a fee for the lessons you will learn today, oh, great Chartak, champion of Corodune mine," chided Jack.

Chartak half laughed and half snarled back at Jack. "Insane, you are insane, I like that. Ha, an arrogant or stupid beginner with, what, two wins to his record? The utter ignorance and brashness of a mindless youngster that is about to learn some very hard lessons."

"Perhaps or perhaps not, and it will be three wins after today," replied Jack, smiling wryly at Chartak to further provoke him.

"I was going to be gentle with you today, but I find it difficult to be generous with such a brazen and haughty young delinquent such as yourself."

"That is funny," replied Jack.

"What is funny?" said Chartak.

"I was going to say the same thing to you, Chartak," chided Jack again.

Chartak lunged at Jack, taking three wide swings and carefully aiming to connect with a high-low-high combination, but Jack ducked the first two and moved off-line right, and there was no target for Chartak on the third swing. He turned back to move in on the Varaci, but Jack moved faster in the opposite direction. Before Chartak could turn back again, Jack let fly with an outside swing that half connected an open palm strike with the back of Chartak's head. Jack ducked and came in with a left body shot that fully connected with his opponent's torso with a solid thud.

Quickly backing out then coming back in, Jack set up for a left, right, left hook, right straight combo. Two of the punches half connected, and the other two were blocked, but Jack was back out of range before Chartak could find a target to attack. Not hurt but now considerably madder, Chartak growled, "Perhaps you are not such the total novice that I was led to believe. It does not matter. I will soon make you pay for your overconfidence."

"Perhaps, perhaps not," replied Jack again.

Chartak made a lunge, a stop, and a lunge that threw off Jack's planned attack and put him on the defensive. Chartak came in with another three-swing attack. Jack easily blocked the two high swings, but the middle lower swing caught him on the rib cage and knocked him back at the same time he was trying to back out. The extra momentum caused him to trip slightly on the uneven pit floor just enough to give Chartak a chance to come in on him again with a two-swing attack and a lunge that almost got Jack wrapped up in a front bear hug. Jack was just able to base and get his right arm up between himself and Chartak and his left arm up to block the repeated right swings that Chartak was trying to drop on him.

Chartak was strong and outweighed Jack by a good thirty plus pounds, but Jack had fought many larger men in his years of martial arts training. As Chartak tried to run over Jack, he hesitated for an instant, and Jack hit him with two hard, fast right knee strikes to the lower and mid torso. The second one connected nicely and knocked the wind out of Chartak, giving Jack the chance to separate and move off-line left. As Chartak was starting to come up and turn toward his challenger, Jack let fly a nice, solid left round kick to Chartak's midsection. The kick sent Chartak stumbling to his left, and he just barely stayed on his feet as he tried to recover from the kick and turned to face Jack again. Just as Jack was ready to press the attack, the buzzer sounded, and the round ended. Chartak Sula regained his footing and stood, with an incredulous look on his face, and stared at Jack. The spectators screamed and roared. The pandemonium was like a wildfire. The mine bosses sat stunned in their darkened lair watching the match in disbelief.

Jack went to his side, stretched, checked a couple of the areas that were sure to bruise up, and gathered his thoughts on the match. There were no fight managers, cold water, or medics in these matches between rounds. It was all or nothing, win or lose, but no draw. Chartak Sula now thoroughly realized that this was no novice brawler to be taken lightly. He would likely have to draw on every bit of skill and cunning he held in reserve. Surely, the mine bosses would have warned him, their champion, of this Varan and his skills. He supposed that as the reigning champion, he should be the one actually responsible for determining his opponent's skills. *Damn the parasite mine bosses,* he thought. He had one very good move that would surely work. He would wait for the right timing.

The buzzer sounded for the second round, and both fighters moved cautiously to the center of the ring. They probed and tested each other's defenses even further. "You are right, I have learned something today," said Chartak Sula.

"And what is that?" replied Jack, watching cautiously for any sudden moves by Chartak.

"Never underestimate the abilities of your enemy, at least until you see what his capabilities are," replied Chartak Sula.

"Yes, that is a wise philosophy," replied Jack, "one I have always tried to set in my mind, one that has been drilled into me by many yenets of training."

"I do not doubt that now," replied Chartak Sula.

Jack added, "But I do not consider you an enemy, just an adversary to be challenged."

"Perhaps, perhaps not," replied Chartak with a strange wry smile of his own. "Either way, this must go on until it is over."

Jack nodded in agreement, and Chartak attacked with a series of short feints and retreats. Like the one in the first round, Jack recognized how confusing it was because of his ability to shoot forward and retreat at such great speed. There was no human equivalent to this tactic, and Jack was forced to develop countertactics to deal with it on the fly. So far, his best strategy had been to outmaneuver his opponent to the left or right, but Chartak's actions were so fast it pushed the limits of Jack's ability to change directions in his maneuvering.

Chartak's next charge was a feint followed by an immediate attack. Jack didn't have time to move off-line, so he popped a quick defensive front kick into Chartak Sula's torso as Chartak made his bid to start his multiple-punch attack. Chartak attacked again, and Jack feigned another front kick, which Chartak had anticipated but not the feigned part. He attempted to block Jack's front kick, which wasn't there, and as he did, Jack moved off-line to the left and delivered two quick left jabs then moved left again before Chartak could follow him. Jack dropped another quick jab and moved right at the same time Chartak was moving left to try and match Jack's maneuvering.

As Jack crossed in front of him, Chartak sprang forward with astonishing speed and hit Jack with a two- and three-punch combos before Jack could move to the right out of range. Two of the five swings landed, glancing blows to his cheek and forehead, but he'd managed to block or deflect the majority of the power behind the attack. Jack wished he'd been able to see Chartak fight in a decent match before having to come up against him for the first time. *New rule,* he said to himself, *never change directions and cross in front of Chartak Sula unless you're well out of range. His forward movement was just too fast. Unless . . .* he'd come back to that shortly.

Jack moved further right then in and then out, but allowed Chartak enough time to counter Jack's side movement. As Jack came in, Chartak sprung forward to attack, and Jack had to jump left to avoid another head-on collision with his opponent. Jack threw a quick one-two combo and moved far back and off-line to assess his situation. Both fighters were gaining some insight to the others skills. Jack decided this would have to be strictly a hit-and-move fight; no slugging it out with this opponent. He probably didn't want to get in a ground contest with Chartak either, but he didn't really know what Chartak's ground skills might be.

Move in, feign right early, go left fast, go more left, hit, try to make him stumble and drop a round kick, keep moving left, outpace him. Low right body shot, quick left inside hook, move out left. Chartak shot forward again just as Jack moved out and left. It was straight on, but it was close enough that Chartak tried a long haymaker from the right. Jack ducked, and Chartak's momentum carried him past Jack, exposing his side and back. Jack sent a mid left round kick toward the back of Chartak's thigh but was slightly off balance and too high and caught him solidly in the lower back. He'd lost some of his power, but the round kick was still solid and added to Chartak's momentum, tripping him as he dropped his hands to the ground to catch himself from crashing.

Jack moved in to try and catch Chartak with his defenses down, but somehow, miraculously, Chartak had landed facing Jack and managed to lunge toward Jack in another quick attack. Too quick swings by Chartak caused Jack to duck and move, but the directions of the swings forced Jack to move in the wrong direction directly into Chartak's line. Chartak shot forward, catching Jack at the waist level before he could base and stop from being run over. Both fighters went down with Chartak on top in Jack's guard. Chartak started swinging at Jack in an attempt to overwhelm him and pummel him into submission. Jack covered for the blows and waited an instant for an opening then delivered a quick, solid right palm strike to Chartak's chin. In the split second that Chartak took to recover from the hit, Jack trapped his opponent's left leg while he shot up with his right arm, grabbing the back side of Chartak's arm while his right knee jammed into Chartak's torso. Jack shot up and rolled Chartak onto his back and delivered two good strikes to Chartak's face before Chartak could start to block them. As soon as Chartak went to block the punches, Jack dropped two more solid strikes to Chartak's torso before pushing himself up and off of his opponent.

Jack was hurting from having Chartak land on top of, but he figured he'd repaid him fairly well with the multiple hits he landed on Chartak's face during the brawl. Backing off, Jack watched as Chartak coiled his wide narrow body into a half circle then snapped forward and upward, landing on his feet. Jack was amazed at the ability of his opponent's anatomy as if he was a coiled spring shooting in the forward direction. Just barely audible over the din of the crowd's roar, Jack was able to hear, "Very impressive," from Chartak. "No one has ever been able to escape that move once I was able to take them down. You have some very capable and different skills. We are both learning much today."

"Yes," panted Jack, "and I have never seen anyone with the ability to move like you do."

Chartak replied, "It is just the natural ability of the people on my mountainous home planet, Havora. From birth, we learn to jump up, down, and across on every hill, rock, and trail. Only in the larger cities have they carved out flat places where you can take more level steps than vertical steps."

"I can certainly see how that would give you these abilities," replied Jack. They took a few more probing shots at each other. Then once again, the buzzer sounded, ending the round.

They both went to their respective sides of the ring where they each had to spend the next two mentus recovering from the previous brawl of a round. Damn, he was thirsty, thought Jack. He would have to check the rules of the fight see if there is any way he could bring some water the next time he had to fight. As the two-minute time-out was nearing the end, the crowd started to chant. Many chanted for Chartak Sula, as they had their money riding on him, but quite a few were cheering for Varaci Jack, the novice underdog. The buzzer sounded, and third and final round of the match began. Jack was going to have to work hard to figure out a strategy to try and take his opponent out. Chartak's physical adeptness and unique capabilities were different from anything or anyone he'd ever fought before.

The third round started with Chartak moving toward Jack while jostling left and right but without turning as he came forward. Jack guessed that he was trying to confuse Jack and keep him from deciding which way to move. *Two can play that game,* thought Jack. Instead of waiting for Chartak to get within striking distance, Jack moved left just as Chartak reached his attack range and sprung. Jack dodged right as fast as he could manage to get outside of Chartak's range as Chartak's momentum carried him too far forward before he could turn on Jack. Jack came in with his own feign as he set up for an obvious combo but instead popped a fast left snap kick to Chartak's torso followed by an instantaneous high right round kick to Chartak's shoulder. The first kick hurt a little, and the second hurt a lot as Jack's shin connected solidly with Chartak's upper arm.

Neither Chartak nor the spectators had ever seen anyone fight with their feet like this. The spectators were going crazy over this new type of fighting, but Chartak was seriously worried. He'd never seen anything like it and had little idea of how to defend against it, and he had a bad feeling that this purportedly novice Varan opponent hadn't even begun to show what he knew. Somewhere, somehow, this Varaci, a race normally known for slinking away from any type of confrontations and slinking around the galaxy smuggling contraband cargo, had spent a great deal of time perfecting these unusual skills. How and where, he didn't know; his only concern now was not catching one of those foot missiles to the head.

Jack continued to work his way around on Chartak's left. He could keep ahead of Chartak's turning rate but had to move very fast to get some sort of an attack in before Chartak was able to turn to fully meet him. This was burning too much energy and would burn Jack out before he was able to get in enough decent hits to do any damage. Chartak just had too much stamina to keep up this strategy continuously. Jack backed off a second and kept a decent distance while he caught his breath. Chartak thought Jack was wearing down and advanced for another attack. Chartak sprung, and Jack dove forward under his swinging assault, hoping that Chartak had never seen this tactic. As Chartak sprung, the Varaci dove under his swings and went straight past him and turned and flung his right leg hard at Chartak's side before he could turn to meet him. The kick connected solidly with Chartak's side and knocked the wind out of him again.

Instead of pressing the attack, Jack backed off just enough to put himself in Chartak's ideal attack range. Just as he thought, Chartak realized this and started to spring; Jack did the same. As Chartak sprung forward, Jack dove in on Chartak and let loose a quick one-two combo while ducking and dodging Chartak's swings. He then leaped halfway up to Chartak's head and brought his right knee up in a high knee strike that hit Chartak squarely on the left side of his sternum, which followed through partly to his face. Jack came down in a half-assed landing that might have sprained his ankle if he hadn't broken his fall with his outstretched arms.

Chartak was knocked back hard against the ring wire and crashed sideways onto the floor. Jack wasn't sure what Chartak's condition was, but he couldn't afford to stay there in his own off-balance position long enough to find out. Jack got his footing and just started to back away when Chartak sprawled on his belly on all fours then sprung forward with amazing speed like a predatory cat from a crouch. That was the image Jack saw in his head when he saw Chartak spring toward him, a predatory cat, a leopard, or the likes launching directly at him.

Jack knew he was still too close for Chartak to miss him, so he had to go with the situation. Chartak hit Jack mid height just as Jack was fully gaining his footing to back up. The force of the hit carried Jack over backward, but instead of crashing onto his back, he grabbed Chartak's shirt at the shoulders and continued to roll all the way over and back with Chartak. Chartak's momentum had been too great for him to stop. Jack added his own rolling momentum to the two grappling fighters, which brought him all the way over into the mount position on top of Chartak. In the mount position, Jack quickly delivered multiple strikes in a barrage of hammer fist and overhead palm strikes whenever there was an opening.

Chartak tried to spring up using his legs, but Jack shifted his weight every time and neutralized Chartak's momentum. As Chartak tried to counter with a right punch, Jack stuffed Chartak's right arm, hooked Chartak's left arm, and pulled him up, while at the same time, he threw his left leg over Chartak's head, conveniently hitting him in the side of the head with his heel. Jack then pulled Chartak in close with both his heels as he pulled Chartak's arm back in an arm bar hold that prevented Chartak from escaping. Chartak tried to roll into Jack, and Jack pummeled him with his free hand. The pandemonium of the crowd was insane. They were all howling and screaming at the top of their lungs. It was likely as dangerous outside the ring as inside, Jack quickly noted.

Jack had a good hold on him and started perching his pelvis up to push Chartak's shoulder joint away from his arm. He could feel Chartak's tendons start to stretch and twitch. Chartak tried to use his powerful legs to shoot all the way back over, but all it did was cause him more extreme pain. Chartak tried a few off-balance far arm punches and even tried to bite at Jack's calf. The punches from the opposite arm were useless, as they had no target, and Chartak's biting attempt was thwarted with a quick heel from Jack to the side of Chartak's head. Chartak was cursing Jack in every possible way. "You're pinned, Chartak!" screamed Jack at his opponent. "I can break your arm and dislocate your shoulder. Yield the match, or I'll have to hurt you."

"No, ahhh, shondaa you!" screamed Chartak.

"Ref, call the match, or I'll have to hurt him!" screamed Jack.

"No, only he can yield!" screamed the ref back.

Jack applied more pressure; he could feel the tendon starting to give way. Chartak screamed, "Yield, yield, ahhhheaaah, shondaa, I yield, Chartak Sula yield!" Jack let up some of the pressure to ease the pain to his opponent's shoulder but not enough that Chartak would be able to break the hold.

The ref raised his hands. "Chartak yields, Chartak yields the match! Match goes to Ja-ak of Vara, match goes to Ja-ak of Vara!" yelled the ref in confirmation.

Jack unwound his hold and carefully got up while keeping a close watch on Chartak in case he decided to retaliate. Both fighters were exhausted, but Jack wasn't sure how the great Chartak Sula would react to being bested by the alleged rookie. "Chartak, are you ok? I'm going to let you up now." asked Jack.

"Yes, yes," moaned Chartak. "For sure, there is one thing, and that is that you are no beginner here."

"Here on Nishda, yes," said Jack, "but not in the ring and fighting."

"Where then? On your home planet, Vara?" said Chartak.

"No, not Vara or anywhere else you've ever heard of," replied Jack.

"Well, that is a mystery, then. You have bested me fairly. I don't know how, but surely you did," groaned Chartak. The postfight ritual was chaotic and exciting. Chartak, being more professional than the other fighters, took the loss graciously but was definitely dejected. He realized, though, that this Varan Jack was no novice and not even any type of ordinary fighter like he had always fought. Jack was declared the winner, and the crowd knew they had a new champion in their midst that could compete against any of the other mines' fighters.

* * * * *

The mine bosses sat silently in their compound. They were incensed at losing so much and paying out against the odds they'd set. "How could this have happened?" said the head boss. "We wanted him to do well initially but not win every match. We kept his opponents matched well above him to prevent this. We should have been able to string this out for moondats with wins and losses of our choosing."

The lesser mine boss with the large bulbous bald head said, "Apparently, we underestimated his capabilities."

Another lesser boss asked, "Who exactly is he? What do we know of him other than he is Cahooshek's conscript that was sentenced for stealing passage?"

"Well, just that he is a Varaci and is serving his conscript time here at the mine, and now he works for Za-arvak, the metallurgist at the foundry."

"We know very little, then," replied the second alien boss.

"Well, how much do we need to know other than he's a conscript paying off his debt?" piped up a fourth alien mine boss.

"Well, it would have been wise of us to know enough about him to prevent our losses in this venture," said the head boss.

The third boss said, "Surely, we could use him against the other mines and the city matches and recover our losses."

The head boss said, "Yes, we will do that, but the matches are too far apart to recover our current losses quickly. The largest following is right here in the inner mine and all those that watch from outside. They prefer our rules, or lack of. We will have to continue to fight him right here at Corodune if we want to recover our losses soon."

"How will we do that?" asked the second boss. "He has already defeated the champion, and the odds will be reversed on anyone we send to fight him."

"We will have to change our strategy. I have an idea for both," said the head boss. "We will do both and come out well ahead," he added.

* * * * *

Zshutana had watched the match with two of her girls again. It was all she could do to get through to the end. She had been certain for a few mentus that Jack was outmatched and that he would end up getting hurt, but the situation was what it was, so she stuck it out to the end. She would have felt much better if she could have been there in person and seen him afterward. She was just grateful that he'd prevailed and wasn't seriously hurt. In fact, she suddenly realized that his victory over the dangerous opponent was very exhilarating in more ways than one. She really wished she could see him right now. Maybe, just maybe, he would be able to get out shortly and see her soon. Yes, she really had something urgent she would like to see him about.

At the common area, there was a big celebration for Jack's victory over the champion, Chartak Sula; Jack, Junot, Cherga, and some of his friends as well as a fair group of hangers-on all congratulating Jack and his friends. There were even a few that had bet on Jack and made a decent return on their wagers. Even the ones that had lost their bets weren't too upset and were just thrilled to be hanging out with the new champion. There wasn't much entertainment for the cons in the mine, so the pit matches and a new champion was a thrilling event to many of the workers. The conscript and convict conzone side hadn't had the championship on their side for four yenets, so Jack's victory made it doubly exhilarating.

They all drank their xula soft drinks and got a certain degree of euphoria just from the excitement of the event and the party. Jack said to Junot, "Come on, let's take this on the road. I'll explain it to you as we go." Jack grabbed Cherga and told him to come along and beckoned all the others involved. Soon, they had a grand parade going in the conzone as everyone marched and sang and yelled together. "Stay friendly and be extra nice to any guards we encounter," Jack said to Junot, Cherga, and the others.

They paraded around, picking up new celebrants, and marched around, having a good old time. Soon, they had a crowd of eighty or so conzone miners as they careened throughout the conzone singing, yelling, celebrating, and just generally having a good time. When Jack led them near the entry checkpoint to the conzone, he told Cherga, "Take them all right up to the entrance, but don't do anything dangerous. You're just having fun and not causing any problems. Don't get into any kind of head-butting contest with the guards. In fact, try to get them involved. Be extra nice, like they're your best old friends. Keep them distracted and away from the guard shack. Does that make sense?" Jack asked.

"Yes," said Cherga, "but that will be a stretch to pretend that I am friendly with these miserable guard vermin."

"I know," said Jack, "but I know you can do it for the cause. And make sure Junot doesn't get run over because he's the key to the future success of our plans."

"Yes, I will do everything you request," replied Cherga. "Here we go now."

The group of revelers careened in and near the checkpoint and guard shack. The guards were initially confused and somewhat distressed as they yelled orders at the cons to stay back or be reprimanded. The partygoers were so friendly, congenial, and engaging, though, that the guards couldn't do anything but return their congeniality.

Jack worked his way behind the group of revelers and over to the back of the guard shack. A quick peek showed no guards in the shack. He ducked in and looked around and saw two wands in one corner and another two at the end of the shack. He grabbed one of the first two and slid it down his pants leg and prayed it didn't have an active tracking device embedded in it. He peeked outside and then snuck back out and melted into the crowd of happy miners. He signaled to Cherga, and they moved the group away from the checkpoint and back toward the conzone proper. The party eventually made its way back to the common area, but with no qalalé to sustain it like a real party, it died out after a short time.

When they were alone, Cherga and Junot couldn't wait to ask Jack how the snatch had gone off. Jack signaled to them, "Verify safe mode," for the translators. "Perfect," said Jack. "There were four of them, so I only grabbed one to keep the confusion factor going. I just hope it doesn't have a tracking device in it."

"Let's take it to the to the maintenance depot and check it out," said Junot, "and I can deactivate it if it does. This should allow me to fully analyze all the ID tracking and encryption capabilities it has. We'll finally know what they can and can't do as far as tracking and identifying anyone that has a translator, which, of course, is everyone."

"Do you think they will miss it and start a search for it?" asked Cherga.

"I don't think so," said Jack. "If they do miss it, they're more likely to keep it quiet, so none of them takes any heat for losing it. It would be better to not report it if you're a guard and hope the issue never comes up rather than report it lost or stolen and get fired or have to pay for it. They were just lying around in the shack, so I'm guessing they're not even assigned to a specific guard. If no one is missing their own assigned wand, then the chances of it being reported are fairly unlikely."

"All right, then," said Junot, "let's get this to the depot and tear into it so I can see what makes it work. This is almost like a gift from the technology gods."

"OK," said Jack, "I'm not really sure what I can do to help you with that, but Cherga and I will both do whatever we can."

An horun and a half after, Junot had dissected the security wand, and he was making some real headway into the security system protocols of the translator ID system. "This is pretty fascinating," he said. "I think I have most of the security parameters mapped and logged into my decryption program. It's a pretty sophisticated system as far as its capabilities. It's essentially a transponder system that allows their core-based monitoring system to ID and track anyone's translator, which is assigned a unique address code. We kind of guessed that already, but we didn't really know how it worked and exactly what the capabilities are. Now that I know exactly what it's reading and what data is being transmitted, I can either shut it off, block it, or replicate it. I'm sure I could also generate either a random or programmed code for another translator and essentially create a disguised translator so that it is reporting someone else's code and not your real code. By leaving the normally locked programming mode open, you could change the unique or discrete code whenever you wanted to for whatever you wanted simply by accessing the setup initialization code. I could add a simple menu item to take you back into the setup function anytime you needed to get in there."

"That's outstanding, Junot," said Jack. "If we can control all the tracking, reporting, and programming aspects of a translator, then we can basically create new identities at random."

Junot added, "I may also be able to replicate the wand function and maybe make a mini wand reader that will allow any of us to read anyone else's translator and know who they are without asking or talking to them. Sort of, uhh, like almost reading their mind or, well, at least their identity anyway."

"That would be a handy gadget, very handy," said Jack.

"As far as making a random fake ID, I think that might be a little harder," said Junot. "There is a fair amount of data with each discrete ID, so you would have to replicate all that to make a new fake ID without any missing data blocks. It would be doable but time consuming and prone to errors. If we can read other IDs, we can probably capture and store them and maybe modify them later. The best way to project a fake ID is to use someone else's that already exists. We would just change the ID functions but leave all the other extraneous data intact."

Jack asked, "So for how long have people worn translators like this?"

Junot replied, "Well, I'm not really sure. As long as I can remember, they've always had them."

Cherga added, "I did not have one on when I was a younget, but I remember my parents putting one on when we went to the bigger city of Nunnatak. I remember them telling me it was because there were many people from other places or planets that spoke other languages, and it would allow us to talk to anyone."

"So you or your parents didn't wear one all the time—just when you went somewhere where you would need the translator capabilities? You could take them off or on by yourself—they weren't permanent?"

"Yes," replied Cherga, "not like now where everyone has one, at least like here in the mine or the big cities like Wanana and Se-ahlaalú."

"It sounds like they are mostly interested in monitoring people in the higher-population areas and, of course, definitely the population of the mine and conzone," said Jack. "Well, back to my other question, how about decoys?" asked Jack.

"What do you mean decoys?" asked Cherga.

"What I mean is, could you take either your ID code or even someone else's and put it on a little chip or something and make it generate their ID code for at least a little while? You could then send whoever might be trying to track you on a wild goose chase going after some chip instead of really tracking you."

"What do you mean wild gooshe chase?" asked Junot.

"Yes, what is that?" added Cherga.

"Uh, well, just another saying," said Jack. "It sort of means running around looking for something even though you know it may not be there."

"Why would you do that?" asked Cherga.

I guess I should to try to keep my idiom sayings to myself, thought Jack. "Well, just in case it might be out there even though there isn't a good chance you would still want to try."

"Hmmmm, I suppose," said Cherga, "although I would prefer that there is a good chance or you would most likely be wasting your time."

"Exactly," said Jack, "exactly. We'll leave it at that."

"What about the decoys, Junot," asked Jack.

"Yes, I think I know what you mean. I could program an open blank code, self-powered chip with a replicated ID code but without any of the nonimportant translator data. It would transmit your ID, or really anyone's ID that you programmed into it, and it would register as that person in the core's tracking system," said Junot.

"This is very devious thinking to imagine these sorts of things," said Cherga.

"Well, I'll take that as a compliment," replied Jack. "The Galactic Trading Alliance, I'm guessing that they are the overseers of this technology, has set these translators and the entire system up and basically advertised them as purely a translator device when in reality they are more of a tracking and eavesdropping unit that they can use to monitor the majority of a planet's citizens with. I'm not sure I like the thought of being monitored by some faceless entity all the time everywhere I go. I don't know about you, but I find it very intrusive, and I don't think they should have the right to do that to ordinary citizens."

"I don't either," said Junot. "That's just kind of rude or something now that I think about it."

"I guess I would have to agree," said Cherga, "now that I think about it like Junot. I think that they must have added these capabilities over many years. The translators certainly have been improved, if that's what you would call it, over the yenets with new features and many new capabilities. I'm not sure, but when I was very young, it seems like all they would do is translate and not much else, at least as far as we knew."

"Yes, well, I guess this isn't your father's translator, is it?" said Jack. "Metaphorically, I meant that metaphorically, it's a saying," added Jack.

"Metaphorically, yes, of course," replied Cherga with a laugh. "No, it certainly isn't our father's same translator."

Jack wanted to make a quick call to Zshutana while they were there, but he was afraid that without her translator being modified and the fact that the mine bosses were probably even more unhappy with his winning streak, in spite of how they had tried to rig the match, that they might be watching him or even her, and it was probably better to lie low for a while. He would try to work in a visit to her later with Junot and have him modify her translator so they could finally communicate without worrying about the mine bosses or anyone else eavesdropping. As much as he wanted to hear her voice and talk to her, there was no point in risking everything for a few words on a comm link. They decided there wasn't much more they could do that night with the security wand, so they hid it in the maintenance depot shop, and they all headed back to the berthing area. It had been a long daiyus for everyone.

The next daiyus at work, Za-arvak was glad to let Jack know that he'd won a considerable sum on the match wagering the night before. "I'm just glad that I got lucky and won and that you came out ahead," said Jack. "Otherwise, you might have me scrubbing toilets this morning instead of running the production shop and playing with new alloys."

"Certainly not," laughed Za-arvak. "You are much too valuable to me here running this operation to be used in any other capacity. Yes, and Junot is most capable also. He is turning out to be quite valuable with regard to maintaining and repairing much of our equipment here. The mine bosses complained bitterly when I stole him from them, but the foundry takes precedence over their mining operation. With everything running so smoothly, we should be able to increase our production rates and take on some new work. We would probably be able to bring Cherga back, as you suggested earlier, once we get some new orders set up."

"That would be great," said Jack. "I'm sure he would enjoy the change of pace from the mine as much as Junot and I have."

"Yes, and with those ideas in mind, I am going to have to meet with some potential customers in Wanana for the next two or three daiyus," said Za-arvak. "They are requesting my consultation on the best ways to set up an additional manufacturing plant using some of our truillium and zernuriun alloys to produce smaller, more efficient drive engine components for surface transport vehicles. So I would like to have you run the operation for a few daiyus for me. This will be a big relief for me, as I know you will be able to take care of any issues that arise while I'm gone. I will leave orders to that effect authorizing you to deal with any changes or modifications of the operations of the foundry. If anything truly major comes up, you can always contact me through the core comm system. I will authorize you on that today, but I'm sure you'll be fine on your own."

Jack replied, "Well, I appreciate your confidence in me. I'm sure I can handle things for you for a few daiyus. Umm, there is a small favor I was going to ask also," said Jack. "Would you mind if Junot and I went out to the concessions area for a bite of real food one daiyus while you're not here? That would be a nice little treat for both of us."

"Well, yes, that should not pose a problem," replied Za-arvak. "As long as everything is working properly and the schedule is up to speed, I don't see a problem with that."

"Great," said Jack, "that is much appreciated. We will be really looking forward to some nonconzone food for our lunch."

On the way back to the conzone, Junot said, "Do you want me to have my tools and parts ready for your friend's translator modification if we are allowed out for lunch at the concessions area like you said earlier?"

"Yes, Junot, we'll go get some real food tomorrow and make a little side trip to modify Zshutana's translator so she can talk in the safe mode like ours. Do you have everything you need to make that happen while we're out for a lunch break?"

"Yes," replied Junot, "I can get everything in my maintenance pack, and it should only take me about twenty mentus now that I know how to access everything inside the translator."

"OK, good. Let's stop by the maintenance depot and set up a comm link, and I'll let her know to expect us."

They stopped by the maintenance depot, and Junot set up the link for Jack. He really wanted to say a lot more to her, but he had to play it safe and keep it very short. She picked up the comm on the fourth buzz. "Yes, hello," she said.

He liked hearing her voice. "Hello, Teela, it's Duunda," he said, using their phony names.

She was instantly excited to hear his voice too but knew to play along. "Duunda, hello, yes, this is Teela."

Jack replied, "I can't really talk now and neither can you, but I just wanted to tell you that tomorrow we, my friend Kolo and I, will be in your area, and we could come by at middaiyus horun for a short visit. Is that convenient for you?"

"Oh, yes, yes, that would fine, very fine," she said.

"OK, then," said Jack, "we will see you tomorrow barring any work issues or other problems. I have to go now, so I will see you tomorrow, Teela. Good-bye," he said, hating to have to drop the comm link.

"OK, I'll see you tomorrow, Duunda. Good-bye," Zshutana replied. She suddenly felt very elated. She wondered what exactly was on the agenda but didn't really care as long as she could see him. He did say he was bringing his friend, so that probably meant they had a way to fix her translator so that she could talk freely without having to worry about the mine bosses eavesdropping. Thinking back to last time they'd met, it was really quite interesting when she couldn't talk or say anything during their time together.

Everything was running properly, and the production and machine and processing workers in the foundry section had reported they were on schedule for all their tasks, and some had already been completed for the daiyus. Junot appeared in Jack's office and reported that he had completed the repairs on the broken alloy analyzer he'd been working on and that the separator injection pump in the feed housing control for the number two foundry line feed synchronizer was also back in service. "Great work, Junot. Do you have everything you need to complete the fix on my friend's T unit?" Jack asked.

"Yes, I'm all set for that," said Junot.

"OK, then, let's go get us a little bite of real food for a change, and, hey, I'm buying."

"OK, that sounds great to me. I haven't had anything but ration hall food for a long, long time," replied Junot.

Jack was able to lead them to the concession and shopping area in just over ten mentus, since he knew his way this time and had the translator mapping to back him up. He slowed down and circled the shopping area and then split up with Junot and met him back on the other side. He stopped and watched and made sure that they weren't being followed. Of course, if the mine bosses were tracking them somehow, they'd know where they were anyway. It was a risk he was willing to take, since he was allegedly running errands for his boss Za-arvak.

They got back to the far side, and Jack led them up the entrance and stairs to Zshutana's office door. Jack pushed the door button, and in just a few moments, Zshutana opened the door. She'd seen them coming up the stairs on the security display, and it was all she could do to keep from running out to meet them. Jack stared at her, and she stared back at him. "Hi, we made it," he said while feeling somewhat foolish for not quite knowing what to say for the one-way conversation that was required while he held his finger to his lips to keep her from talking. Her eyes were like turquoise fire the way they radiated so much energy and emotion. She just nodded as she waved them in.

"This is my good friend Junot," he said to her as they came into her office. "He's very good with many types of electronics, especially translators. He is going to make a few helpful modifications to your translator." Zshutana held out her hands to greet Junot, and she nodded at him and smiled with her eyes, ears, and everything else.

Junot had never seen eyes like that before, at least not up close where he was looking right into them. "Oh, my, oh, she's so beautiful. Jack, she's just really beautiful. I mean, I just meant to say, I mean . . ." said Junot, not quite knowing what to say now.

Jack said, "Yes, she is very beautiful and very, very nice, so just relax and let's get her translator, uh, um, adjusted, and then we'll all be able to have a nice conversation." Zshutana blushed a little from the two compliments and just from being this close to Jack again. Her whole body just radiated with anticipation and delight. Jack could feel it or sense it or something; it was, well, he wasn't really sure. He wondered if Junot could sense it or if it was only him. It was almost as if the air around them was charged somehow. It wasn't like anything he'd ever experienced in the presence of a beautiful woman before. Maybe she could explain it to him sometime soon. Maybe it was some amazing aura given off by aliens from her planet. Whatever it was, it was quite marvelous.

She ushered them into her office area, and Junot set to work tinkering on her translator as she leaned back in her desk chair so he could easily access the translator. Jack was pretty sure Junot could sense it; there was a euphoria in the air as he sat there working on her translator. He was very lively and animated as he described what he was doing to the translator and how it would work after he modified it. Zshutana listed intently as they both described the operation of the caution and safe modes and how she should always verify the green safe mode before discussing anything private. It took Junot just at twenty mentus to complete the mods, and then he said, "Well, I'm all done, but we'll run a few tests and verify there are no transmissions in the safe mode and that all the outputs are completely blocked."

Junot had Zshutana turn the translator from the caution to safe mode and verified the total absence of any transmissions other than the background carrier wave that told any monitoring points that the translator was still working. "It all checks good. There is no detectable output when it's running in safe mode," he said. "Wait a minute, though, I want to check something." Junot got up and took the signal detector and went around the entire room as well as Zshutana's apartment area. Jack and Zshutana watched him as he traced all the corners of the rooms. "It appears to be clean at least for now. No stray transmissions of any sort that I can detect. We should be able to talk freely now," said Junot.

Jack said to Zshutana, "Meet Junot Saranuna of Riina, my good mining friend and resident security and translator expert."

"It's very nice to meet you, Junot. Jack has told me a little about you in the limited time we've been able to communicate, and thank you for the compliment about me being attractive," as she glanced at Jack with her amazing turquoise eyes that continued to smile radiantly at both of them. That's amazing, thought Jack, he'd never seen so much emotion revealed in someone's eyes before.

"Oh, yes, and, well, it's a nice to meet you too, and Jack has told me a little about you too, like how you helped him to learn his language for the translator and all," as Junot blushed from her attention.

"Well, not all, I hope," she said as she smiled and went on. "I hope you are both hungry, and I hope you can stay awhile. Since I knew you were coming, I had some of my girls prepare a nice mid-daiyus meal for us."

Junot began speaking before Jack could get a word in. "Oh, yes, we are starved. We haven't had anything. At least I haven't had anything other than ration hall food for many moondats, yenets actually. Do you really have some real food for us? I couldn't believe we were actually going to get to eat some real food today. You really don't know how much—"

"Yes, yes, I have a nice treat for you. Just hang on and we will be eating in a few mentus," she replied. Jack looked at her, and she smiled at him knowing what a great treat this would be for both of them, especially Junot by his reaction. With that, Zshutana said something into her desk comm, and in less than a mentu, three of her girls arrived with several platters of various varieties of meats, greens, and other different delicacies.

When the food was set in place, Junot could hardly keep his eyes off of it, and the smell was simply intoxicating. Before they began, Zshutana said, "Girls, this is Jack of Vara and his friend Junot of Riina. This is Celiah, Zinsai, and Li-ialah."

"It's very nice to meet you, ladies. Thank you for preparing this wonderful meal for us. We will be forever grateful," said Jack.

Junot piped in, "Yes, oh, yes, thank you. I, we, really, very appreciate. I think I'm getting dizzy from the smell of this. It really smells wonderful," stammered Junot.

"Thank you, girls. I'll call you in a little while when we're done," said Zshutana. "Well, go ahead, Junot, jump in and help yourself," said Zshutana. With that, Junot, Jack, and Zshutana enjoyed the very nice mid meal that Zshutana had prepared. This was certainly better than anything Jack had eaten since this whole adventure had started. It was even much better than the food he'd had on the big transport ship on the way here and much, much better than anything he'd had since arriving on Nishda. It was even better than what he'd had with Zshutana the couple of daiyus he had been here with her during his translator language training.

Over their meal, they talked about their new ability to talk freely without anyone eavesdropping on them. Jack told Zshutana that Junot was working on more mods for them, but they still didn't know all the possibilities of what they may be able to accomplish. Zshutana was both thrilled and relieved that Jack's last fight had come out in his favor. "It was a lot closer than I wanted," said Jack. "Chartak was a good fighter with considerable natural skills. He just didn't have the training and the experience of fighting someone like me that has had a lot more training."

"How did you learn to fight like that?" Zshutana wanted to know. Jack explained that it was just a form of martial arts fighting and exercise discipline he'd been doing since he started as a boy at fourteen; he liked to call it a "highly useful hobby."

Junot said, "That seems like something soldiers would learn in their training. Had Jack planned on being a soldier or something?"

"Well, no, not really," replied Jack, "but it's good to have some type of martial arts skills just for self-defense."

"I believe you are right on that," said Junot. "It's sure been needed since you've been here at the mine. Would it be possible for someone like me to learn those type of fighting skills? I mean, I'm just wondering. I'm not, I wouldn't want to go in the fight pit or anything. I mean, just for my own protection and that sort of thing."

"Sure, Junot," replied Jack. "You could learn some basic skills that would be very helpful to you. I'd be happy to teach you sometime. We'll plan on it in the near future."

"Really? I'd really like that if I could learn to do some of those things you do in fighting."

"Yes, of course, Junot, but just know that it takes a lot of work and lots of repetition and practice. Like every daiyus, practice for quite a while before you get good at it," said Jack.

"I understand. I'm sure I could do it if you would teach me," said Junot.

"OK, then, we'll start tomorrow," said Jack, "right after work and on our daiyus off from work."

"OK, I really want to start. Can we start today, maybe?" asked Junot.

"Well, maybe," said Jack, "and also know that you have to exercise a lot and learn to be flexible and gain strength too."

"You have to exercise?" said Junot.

"Yes, almost every daiyus, like I've been doing in the workout gym in the conzone," replied Jack.

"Oh, I didn't know that," said Junot, "but, yes, I'm sure I can do that."

"OK, just be ready for some sore muscles because you're going to have them," said Jack. Junot just smiled at Jack and shook his head yes. He could hardly wait.

"How much time do you have before you have to go back?" asked Zshutana with her eyes sparkling radiantly.

"Well, we lucked out today because Za-arvak had to go to Wanana for a couple of daiyus for a business meeting. Everything is caught up at the foundry, so we could probably stretch our visit a little while longer," said Jack cautiously. "Why? What did you have in mind?" he asked.

Her eyes lit up like fireworks as she gave him an incredibly alluring smile. Zshutana pressed her intercom button and called her girls in to take away the remnants of their meal. "Thank you, girls, for bringing us such a nice lunch," Zshutana said to them. "If you can clear our places so we can talk about some business things. And, Celiah and Li-ialah, would you come back when you're done, please?"

The girls took the remainder of the nice lunch away, and the two pretty girls named Celiah and Li-ialah returned as requested. "Yes, Zshutana, what can we do for you?" asked the one named Celiah.

Zshutana replied, "Would you two sweet ones please take this nice young Junot here for a little tour of our facility here? He's been incarcerated in the conzone for quite a while and hasn't had anything good to eat until today or anything else nice for quite a long while either. Do you think you could show him around for an horun while I discuss some business with Jack here?"

"Oh, yes, we'd love to," said Celiah. "Come on, Junot, we'll show you around for a while."

"Come on with us," said Li-ialah. "We'll have some fun, and we'll show you some fun things."

Junot wasn't quite sure, but it sounded OK. He looked at Jack for approval. "Go on, Junot. I'm sure everything will be fine, and I'm sure you'll be perfectly safe in the care of these talented young ladies," said Jack. With that, the girls grabbed Junot by the arms and practically carried him out of Zshutana's apartment while they squealed and giggled all the way out.

"That was a very good idea," said Jack.

She just stared at him as her eyes became more radiant and inviting by the moment. She got up before he could and came over to him. "I've missed you and thought about you every daiyus since you were here. I hope you don't mind me telling you that," she said as she touched him and ran her hands over him and pulled herself close to him.

"I've thought about you nonstop since I was here too," said Jack, trying to get the words out while totally consumed by her closeness. "I can't describe it. There's something about you, about us. There's just no words for it. I just want to be with you and touch you," he said to her. He wrapped his arms around her and felt her warm lean body pressing up against his, so inviting and eager. Her eyes were radiant like dark turquoise fire, and her ears were happy and smiling like all of the rest of her. He held her and gently kissed her. She kissed him back, and her body seemed to quiver with an electric radiance and anticipation. He could hardly contain himself as he kissed her face and neck and ran his hands across her perfect small breasts and firm body.

She pulled him closer. "Yes, yes, yes," she whispered imploringly in his ear. With that, he picked her up and carried her to her bedroom and laid her gently on the bed. He kissed her slowly and deliberately from her head to her feet. She moaned softly as he caressed her and massaged her in all the right places. He gently undressed her as he worked his way down then back up until she lay naked on the bed beneath him. He looked at her beautiful lithe body and wondered at its amazing allure.

"Now, now, Jack, please, I want you now. I need you, Jack. I've been wanting you, needing you every daiyus. I've never needed anything like I need you right now," she whispered with such sweet abandon and honesty.

"Shhh . . ." he whispered to her. "I need you too like I've never needed or wanted anyone before." He kissed her, and she wrapped herself around him.

"Love me, Jack. all of me is for you. Just love me and make me feel loved." They loved and grasped and held to each other for the next full hour. It was love and lust and uncontrolled passion. They couldn't get enough of each other. They couldn't get close enough to the other. All they wanted was each other and more and more of the same.

It was the most amazing hour either of them had ever had, even more remarkable than their last short time together. It went by too quickly, and they knew he would have to get back to the foundry and then later the mine. They were just both grateful that they'd been able to have the time together and further cement the bond and knowledge of their unique attraction and appreciation of each other. Neither had ever known anyone like the other or felt the unrestrained and open need to be with anyone like this. This was something exceptional that Jack had never experienced, and neither had Zshutana.

"I want to just stay here with you and not leave, ever," he said to her as they lay next to each other.

"Yes, me too," she replied, "but I'm afraid Celiah and Li-ialah will be back with Junot shortly, and you will have to go back to your work and the conzone as always. Still, I am so pleased that you were able to come today and stay for a while. I hope you enjoyed the meal and everything else."

"Yes, the meal was fabulous and greatly appreciated, but I especially enjoyed the 'everything else' part."

She smiled at him with her radiant eyes and pulled herself closer, as close as she could get so that she could feel every part of her body touching his. "I wish you could stay too, but you must get dressed now, as the girls will have your friend back shortly.

"OK, all right," he said as he kissed her and held her for a few moments more.

They got up and dressed, taking a few moments here and there to show their affection to each other. "I will try to see you again as soon as the opportunity allows. I'm just not sure how soon that will be. Za-arvak is a good boss to work for, but I'm not sure how often he will let me out, and there may be issues with him letting me be out that the mine bosses could interfere with if they knew. It's not a very stable situation, and I don't like being under the watchful eye of the bosses and their fraudulent incarceration system here."

"I understand," she said, "but what can you do? We are all under the jurisdiction of this rotten and corrupt system. We can only make the best of what we have."

"Well, I've never settled for what other people have tried to tell me I can do or not do. I'm not sure what I'm going to do yet, but I can say that I won't submit to the authority of these corrupt bosses and their corrupt system."

"Oh, Jack, I'm afraid what you're saying sounds dangerous. You could be hurt or worse if you go against the forces that run this system."

"Maybe," he said, "but better to risk something to gain something than to submit as a servant or a slave to this tyranny and injustice. It's just not in my nature to allow anyone to try and control me like this. That and the fact that they've already been trying to hurt me or worse by overmatching me in the fight pit so they could reap an illicit profit. Now they are really unhappy with me because I've cost them a ton of credits on these matches that they've forced me to fight. As an investment, I'm not panning out for them like they'd calculated. I wouldn't be surprised if they were planning some sort of retribution."

She didn't know what else to say, but she'd never met anyone like him before. Most people didn't like the benign-sounding but ever-intrusive Galactic Trading Alliance, but few if any ever challenged the authority of the Trading Alliance or its minions. Their ever-pervasive tentacles were in every aspect of everyone's lives except for a few outlaw traders and runners that lived on the fringe of the economic system.

He didn't seem to be too concerned with this. Was it just his nature? Or maybe he just wasn't aware of the reach and unlimited resources and power of the GTA. Maybe it was both. Either way, she was afraid for what might happen to him if he tried to stand against the powers that controlled everything. She finally said,

"Jack, you have to be very careful. You don't know the extent of the Galactic Trading Alliance and everything they control. This mine, the bosses, the city bureaucrats, everything is either directly controlled by the GTA or part of the Alliance, or they at least must answer to the Alliance. Even if they don't like it, they still fall under the Alliance's jurisdiction, even out here on the rim on this remote terraformed planet."

"OK, thanks, I appreciate the info and the warning," he replied. "Like I said, I don't know what I'm going to do yet, but I need to get as much information and do as much reconnaissance as I can so that I have some idea of what I'm up against. I have access to the core data computers at the foundry, but I'm not even sure what a lot of the subject matter is that I should be researching. I mean, I have a pretty good idea, but I honestly don't know much about the government infrastructure or anything about the Alliance. I suppose that will be my next research area."

"Well, that will help, I'm sure, but you probably won't like what you will find out about the Alliance and all it controls. They keep the peace but at the expense of individual planets, systems, and people that don't even count as individuals. They are really less of a Trading Alliance and more of a totalitarian overseer whose only goal is the perpetuation of the Alliance at the expense of anything or anyone that gets in their way. They may seem somewhat benign on the surface, but they're not. That is really what happened to my home planet of Tarca and how I ended up here," replied Zshutana.

"I'm sorry about that, but it makes me even more determined to find out everything I can about my situation here as well as whatever I can about the Alliance and how it runs the planets under its control."

As she was thinking about how to explain the overall structure of the Alliance as far as she understood it, the buzzer sounded on her comm link. "We're back with our new friend Junot," said one of the girls over the comm link.

Zshutana replied to her, "Good, come back in and drop him off. He and Jack must get back to their work at the foundry." Junot came in with the two pretty girls with a curious and quiet look on his face.

"Hi, Junot, is everything OK? Did you have fun on your tour?" said Jack.

"Uh-huh," he replied, shaking his head in the affirmative.

"OK, girls, off with you two. Junot has to get back to work now. Thank you for watching over him for us for a while," said Zshutana. Both the girls gave Junot a kiss on the head and ran out the door jabbering and giggling.

"I guess you had a good time. Everyone seems to be happy," said Jack.

"Uh-huh," said Junot with a smile and a smirk on his face.

"Is everything OK?" said Jack. "The cat sort of has your tongue?"

"Uh-huh, fine, cat, what, has my tongue?" replied Junot.

"Another saying of mine. It means you're not saying very much," answered Jack.

"Uh-huh," replied Junot.

"OK," said Jack, "we'll leave it at that for now."

"Uh-huh," answered Junot.

"Well, sadly we must be on our way," said Jack, "but we do appreciate the wonderful meal. That was the best meal I've had in a couple of moondats and a lot longer for Junot."

Junot managed, "Uh, uh-huh, really, really I thank you very much for, uh, the meal and, uh, uh-huh."

They stood to leave. "Go ahead, Junot. I'll be right behind you," said Jack.

As Junot stepped out the door and down the steps, Zshutana grabbed him one last time and gave him a long hug and a kiss. "I miss you already," she said.

"I miss you too already. I'll be back as soon as I can. See you soon," he said as he kissed her quickly and left the office and went to catch up with Junot.

As Jack and Junot left the concession area, they looked around briefly at the shops. Junot could hardly contain himself. "Are you going to say something finally?" asked Jack.

"Jack, Jack, you wouldn't believe it. I couldn't believe it. They took me back to where they live, and they started poking me and tickling me. They were so nice and so funny. Then they, uh, started to, uh, kiss, kissing me, and, ah, grabbing me, both of them. I, I, what was I supposed to do?"

"Well, what did you do?" asked Jack with a barely suppressed smile on his lips.

"I, uh, I, um, started kissing them back, and then the next thing I knew, they were like rubbing all up against me and then . . ."

"Stop, that's good enough. You can spare me the details," said Jack. "Suffice to say, you had a really good time today, is that correct?"

Junot replied, "Oh, oh yes, I've never had anything like that happen to me before, I've never, I've really never."

"Well, good. I'm glad everything went well and we had a great little break from our incarceration scenario. Breaks don't get any better than this, do they? Junot, listen, now you can't tell anyone, not anyone, not even Cherga about this. If word got out about our little adventure, they'd put a stop to it instantly. We probably wouldn't even be able to work at the foundry. Even Za-arvak might get into some sort of trouble over this. Junot, OK? Junot, this is just between us, no one else. Not a word. Don't even dream about it in case you talk in your sleep. Understand, top secret, OK?" admonished Jack.

"Yes, OK, I understand," said Junot. "I won't tell anyone anything. Do you think we can come back sometime? I don't mean like right now but maybe some time, sometime soon," asked an imploring Junot.

"Well, I sure hope so," said Jack, "but the only way that is going to happen is if no one else ever finds out about this."

"I understand, I really understand. Don't worry," said Junot adamantly.

"OK," said Jack, "let's get back to work and make sure everything is working well for Za-arvak at the foundry. We can't let him down in any way. The hard part will be to keep your mind on the work and not on our wonderful meal adventure at Zshutana's today. As hard as that will be, we still have to keep our act together and make sure we meet our obligations for Za-arvak because he's the one that is basically making this possible."

Junot replied, "I will. I'll do a super job todaiyus and every daiyus."

"Don't say anything to anyone," said Jack, "not even about the food or the concession area or being let out to explore. We just work at the foundry and we always stay there."

"Right, yes, I understand, don't worry," said Junot.

Jack went on, "Now don't forget, if you can figure out a way to camouflage our translator transponder's code and make decoys that will imitate where we are supposed to be, then we could move around a lot more autonomously with less risk. We would still have to use discretion and be careful, but we could conceivably gain a little bit of unauthorized freedom."

"Yes, that would help us a lot, wouldn't it?" said Junot half to himself and half out loud as he contemplated the ramifications of that possibility.

"And," said Jack with a pause to emphasize his point, "we wouldn't want to get caught, or they might add ten yenets to our conscript time or worse. This is a dangerous game we are playing, Junot."

"Wait, what, what could be worse?" asked Junot.

"Just use your imagination," replied Jack.

They finished their shift at the foundry, and Junot could hardly keep his mind off the daiyus events, and for that matter, neither could Jack. "Junot, I'm going to stay after a while and catch up on some technical stuff on the production issues. You'll have to go back to the conzone, and I'll be along in a couple of horuns when I'm caught up. We'll have to start your training in martial arts tomorrow. I don't want to get behind on anything here. Besides, I think you've had enough excitement and, uh, training for one daiyus already."

"Oh, OK, but I'm all right. Is there anything I can help you with to help you get caught up on?"

"No, you just go on back and maybe get something done on the translator issue while I wrap things up here. Then we won't have to worry about being behind tomorrow," said Jack.

"All right," said Junot as he headed out to go back to the conzone.

"And remember," said Jack, "not a word to anyone."

"OK, OK," said Junot, "I know, not a word."

As soon as Junot had gone, Jack went to the storage area and grabbed his katana and tanto blade blanks. He set to work machining and polishing them. Each stage produced an even more amazing-looking, iridescent metallic finish unlike anything he'd ever seen before. He polished them and sharpened them to an amazing edge. Even unhardened, they were quite strong and spectacularly sharp. They just weren't hardened into his incredible Spartan alloy at this stage. They were probably a little better than a good-quality tool steel strength at this stage, but that would change shortly. The blades made of the Burun-Rioc ore and the other alloyed elements were still workable at this point. When he was done, he would heat treat them and then cryo quench them.

The Burun-Rioc would turn them into the incredible alloy he'd discovered with his many hours of experimentation. Once it was hardened like his final test blade, it would be one of the most resilient and strongest alloys ever developed. The machining and polishing was going fast with the incredible manufacturing capabilities he had at his command.

He fired up the plasma research furnace and got it ready for his heat treatment process. He set the controls to bring the blades to the proper bright orange temperature and set them in the furnace using the special handling tongs that were there for handing hot samples. He got the cryo quench bath ready and had everything laid out ready to go. When the blades had been in the furnace for about twenty mentus and had achieved a uniform temperature, he began pulling them out one at a time and quenching them in the cryo bath to set the new Burun-Rioc alloy into its permanent hardened state. The sound they made as he quenched them was somewhat strange and frightening.

The Burun-Rioc alloy squealed, groaned, and popped and sounded as if it was being tortured relentlessly somewhere in the depths of hell. He couldn't fathom the structural forces that the alloy was going through when it was instantaneously quenched from orange hot to somewhere close to minus two hundred degrees Celsius. He didn't know what was happening physically at the atomic structural level, but it must have been an amazing transformation of the alloy elements. Whatever was happening to the metal, it was truly astounding.

Though he was handling them with tongs when he quenched them, he could still somehow feel the amazing physical changes to the blades as he quenched each on in the cryo bath. Twenty mentus later, he had four hardened Burun-Rioc blades that he'd pulled out of the ultracold cryo bath. He ended up with two full-length katanas at forty-five inches and two shorter tanto blades and two combat knives with overall lengths of twenty-six inches and twelve-inches. He might make some others later, but for now, this would be a good start.

All he had to do now was fashion some braided wraps for the handles and he would be nearly done, except for the *sayas,* or scabbards. Jack hoped the alloy mix had turned out like his final experimental blade and that nothing had gone wrong and that he'd successfully duplicated his earlier experiment. He examined the shorter tanto blade and wiped it down with a rag. It shone brightly and radiated strength in the way it felt. He very gently felt the cutting edge. It felt even sharper than previously if that were possible. It was as if the quenching had somehow tightened the metallic crystalline structure even more. He laid the first blade down and inspected and cleaned the next three.

When all four blades were clean, he took them back to his hidden storage area. Once in the privacy of the storage area, he tried banging the back side one of the long katanas on the hard metal edge of the building structure. The blade made a beautiful metallic ringing sound with each strike. He checked the side of the blade where he'd hit the metal edge of the building. There was no indication of any damage or even scuffing to the blade. The building, though, had some dents in it where the dull side of the blade had hit it. He hit the metal again with a considerably harder blow. The blade resonated in his hands as it struck and bounced back into the air. No damage to the blade at all.

He hated to do it for fear it would dull the blade, but he wanted to see how well it would hold its edge. He took another swing at the corner of the building with the cutting edge. The blade struck, and it cut through and buried itself a good four inches into the solid metal. "Wow, amazing, just wow," he said to himself as he pulled the blade free from the solid material. He wiped it off then inspected the blade. There was some minor external surface scuffing, but it wiped off and he could see no damage to the edge of the blade. He gently touched the edge of the blade, and it felt just as sharp as it had before. He smiled to himself. "I think I got it right," he said aloud to himself.

One more thing, Jack thought to himself. He took the katana and the two tantos out and quickly measured the blades with the 3D mapping analyzer in the lab and plugged the parameters into the processing computer. In a few mentus, he had the dimensions logged for a precise thin-walled saya, or scabbard, for each of the blades. He found some lightweight titanium alloy and programmed the saya dimension into the sonic and laser milling machine. He stored the file and would come back and finish it tomorrow or the next daiyus. He then hid the blades back in the store room and called it a daiyus as he headed back to the conzone before he ran into a curfew issue.

* * * * *

Cahooshek sat indignantly as the mine bosses grilled him about his conscript. "I've told you everything I know about the Varaci. I told you this before you chose to fight him in the fight pit. All I know is what I was told by Roshnil Kayshen and what he was told by the captain of the star freighter *Yuanjejitt*. The crew of *Yuanjejitt* found him on the ship having stowed away. He was brought here to work off his debt for the passage. They probably assumed he was running from something, and that would be my guess too," said Cahooshek to the head boss. He was tired and tired of this inquisition. He didn't really know any more, so what was the point of their incessant questioning?

"There is nothing else you know about this Varan stowaway, then?" the head boss said to Cahooshek.

"No, nothing at all. If there was, I would surely tell you so I could be done with this harassment and go back to my own interests," replied Cahooshek.

"All right, you may go, but if we find out you've been hiding anything from us, you will be held accountable," said the head boss. The other bosses just looked at Cahooshek as if he was to blame for their less-than-fortunate situation.

"Thank you, Oh Venerable Ones. I will return to my very humble abode now if my presence is no longer required," replied Cahooshek with more than enough sarcasm to make them doubt his sincerity.

After Cahooshek had been dismissed, the head boss said to the others, "This is what we will do. I have a way to make this come out well for us." They all sat with rapt attention as he began to explain his plan.

* * * * *

"When do you think we might be able to visit your friend Zshutana again?" asked Junot quietly on their way to the foundry the next daiyus.

"Do you mean my friend Zshutana or your friends Celiah and Li-ialah?" Jack asked while stifling a smile.

"Uh, well, uh," stammered Junot, "uh, I guess if they happened to be there, that would, um, be OK. I was just thinking about what a great meal that was. I haven't had anything like that in a long time, you know. It was really good, wasn't it?"

"Yes, it was very good, Junot," said Jack. "I'm sure that's what you were thinking about—the nice gourmet meal we had. Maybe we could call Zshutana and tell her we'd like to come over for another mid-daiyus meal, which I call lunch by the way, but not to worry about having the girls there."

"Oh, no, you don't have to do that," said Junot. "We wouldn't want to, uh, uh, offend them or anything."

"Relax, Junot, I was kidding. I wouldn't do that. We'll see how everything is going at the foundry today, and if it looks good, maybe we can sneak away for a quick bite, if you know what I mean." Junot just nodded and smiled a huge grin that he couldn't hide as they made their way to the foundry.

Things didn't go quite as planned, and they weren't able to sneak out like they'd wanted. An entire production run was ruined in the morning when a batch of Burun-Rioc alloy was contaminated by some unknown quantities of foreign compounds that were added to the alloy batch when the processing mix control hoppers malfunctioned and started randomly dumping every sort of compound into the alloy mix, whether it was compatible or not. Whatever it was coming out the end of the alloying process, it wasn't what was specified in the alloy production order, and they would have to fix the problem and start over on the production run. "Crap," said Jack to Junot as he was explaining it. "I hope this isn't something I did to cause this, and I hope Za-arvak isn't too upset when he gets back. I think if we can get everything back on track and get the run going again, he won't be too unhappy."

A few mentus later when they got into the mixing hopper control console, they discovered a strange thing—a nest of several small furry black and green creatures about the size of and somewhat reminiscent of a mouse were all clustered in and around one of the larger power feeds of the optical wiring. They were flatter and without any tails like a mouse, and all they had for a head was a small bump with several sets of small clamping jaws that were attached to the optical wiring. "What the heck are those things?" Jack said to Junot.

"Wenlits, I think," replied Junot. "I've never seen one before, but I've read about them and seen some pictures. They're parasitic power feeders that will attach themselves to any low-voltage power feed and suck the energy out while they corrupt any associated data that is transmitted in the line. This must be what screwed up the auto command sequences for the alloy hopper mix orders when the foundry crew set up your production order."

Junot added, "They're not very sophisticated parasites, though, because they disrupt the data flow and therefore give themselves away when things start going wrong."

"That's just great," said Jack. "What are we supposed to do about them? Do you know of any way to get rid of them?"

Junot replied, "Well, I know they can use some small autonomous drones to hunt them down and kill and remove them, but I don't know if we have anything like that here. Maybe you should call Za-arvak and see what he says. I don't think it's too bad, though. These things just disrupt the data stream and suck a little power from the system. Some other kinds of power parasites can do a lot of damage, a lot more. If they haven't scrambled the stored data protocols and memory in the processing core of the control modules, then we may be able to get the system right back online once they're removed."

"OK, let's go back to the office and give Za-arvak a call and see what he says," responded Jack.

"Are you sure they are wenlits?" asked Za-arvak somewhat skeptically.

Jack replied, "That's what Junot says. He's never seen one, but he's seen images of them and read up on them a little. We are sending you some images now."

"Yes, I think you may be right. They do look like wenlits," said Za-arvak, "but they look somewhat different from the ones I saw on Markuva a few yenets ago. Those were probably bigger, and they were more lightly colored with a longer-shaped head and only two sets of jaws instead of four or five smaller ones. Oh, well, it doesn't matter. We still need to deal with them. It looks like I may have to stay here another daiyus or two to finalize the requirements for this contract. We don't have anything to handle this problem at the foundry. I will contact the mine headquarters and have them address this. They will want to be in on it and probably want to find out where they came from if possible and ensure they are all eradicated so they don't spread to any other operations. You'd better stay close at hand and try to get the alloy order back in production when you can. I'll let you know what I come up with from here."

292

"All right," said Jack, "I will try to get everything straightened out, but we won't be able to get the order going on that alloy unit until we get those things out of the control system and make sure the alloy protocols haven't been damaged."

"Yes, I understand that," said Za-arvak. "This was totally outside of your control, so don't worry about that. Just make sure everything is on track that you can, and I'm sure the mine operators will want to take rapid action on this. I'm guessing we'll hear something back within an horun after I contact them."

"OK," said Jack, "we will be standing by here."

Za-arvak was right; within forty mentus of their call, he had called back and informed Jack that the headquarters bosses had called in a crew from Wanana to investigate and eradicate the vermin wenlits. They would be there in a couple of horuns, and Jack and Junot needed to stay there and give them any assistance they needed. After Za-arvak was off the comm link, Jack said to Junot that they must be flying in if they were going to be here in a couple of horuns from Wanana because it was a lot longer trip by ground vehicle."

"That would make sense," replied Junot. "They must want to get right on this before the wenlits multiply and infect the whole mine operation. Those wenlits don't look like much, but if they start multiplying and spreading, they can take out the electrical and control infrastructure of an entire city from what I've heard."

"Well, so much for our chances of visiting our mutual friends for now. I didn't promise you anything, so you can't be too mad at me," said Jack.

"Oh, I know. It just seemed like for one little septu, we were going to be like normal people for a little while instead of the cons that we've been made out to be."

"Don't worry, Junot, sometime soon, we may get our lives back or at least some new and more rewarding lives. Keep the faith. We can only go uphill from here," said Jack.

"Do you really think so?" asked Junot.

"Oh, absolutely," said Jack. "It's already gotten way better than it was a moondat or two ago, don't you think?"

"You're right, Jack. A couple of moondats ago, I was hiding from the miners that wanted to hurt me. Now I've got a way better job and had some good food, and, uh, I, uh, well, got to, you know, get a girlfriend."

"Girlfriends, plural, I think would be the correct term," said Jack.

Junot smiled at him and said, "Yes, you're right again, it was girlfriends," said Junot.

The wenlit eradication team arrived as advertised. They were actually only two aliens and some floating cargo containers similar to what Jack had seen being off-loaded on the big ship *Yuanjejitt*. The two aliens were both small and very dark orange-skinned with dark hair and eyes and long protruding noses and chins and long thin fragile-looking swept-back ears. They sort of reminded Jack of some sort of vermin themselves. "Zilrhanis," whispered Junot to Jack when he first saw them coming with an escort of two mine guards provided by the mine.

"Is that good or bad?" asked Jack before they got into earshot.

"Not always so good, but if they can get rid of the wenlits, I suppose it is good," replied Junot.

The two Zilrhani aliens approached Jack and Junot. "We are here from Nishda Quarantine Service because of a report of possible wenlits or other noxious parasite infestation. We are seeking the person Ja-ak of Vara as our contact," said the first dark orange creature.

"I'm Jack of Vara," replied Jack. "How can we help you?"

The first orange alien replied, "Please lead us to the possible infestation site for us to examine and evaluate the findings."

"Sure," said Jack, "come this way and we'll show you the area that is infested," while he thought to himself, *Some of these aliens seem totally alien and others like Junot, Zshutana, Cherga, and Za-arvak seem pretty normal to me even though they're different and obviously alien to humans.* He got a somewhat creepy feeling of alienness from these two Zilrhanis. They were just sort of strange, like they were on some sort of a different wavelength or something. Junot certainly hadn't seemed too enamored by them when he saw them.

After examining the alleged wenlits and even capturing one and subjecting it to some sort of biological exam in what turned out to be a small portable lab, the aliens from the Nishda Quarantine Service announced, "These are not wenlits. They are geminutes, very similar, and they employ the same method of feeding for them. They reproduce differently, more in mass waves that coordinate across their genome through translational biogenic auras, which, of course, is a form of radiant biomolecular communication. They are most destructive, and their hormonal levels indicate that they are only one or two daiyus from propagating another wave. It is fortunate that you discovered these before further infestation. They can multiply at a logarithmic propagation rate. They have not been seen on Nishda prior to this. How they arrived is a mystery, but that will be researched. They are not native to Nishda, as, of course, nothing is native here. They somehow have imported from elsewhere. We must commence a control and eradication process at once, with your permission, of course."

"Yes, please do. I am merely a representative of Za-arvak of the foundry for the Corodune mine. Please proceed and do whatever is necessary. What exactly is your plan for them?" said Jack.

The second orange alien replied, "We have analyzed and charted their specific genetic signature. We will program this to the search-and-destroy drones. The drones will search for any biologics with this signature. When they find a matching biologic signature, they will ask for verification, and the geminutes will be targeted for eradication."

"That's very interesting," said Jack. "How do they detect a matching biologic signature?"

"Most biologic signatures of all species are already cataloged and can be loaded into the search sensor of the drones. They will then search for trace biological signatures of the known DNA structure, which will be present in or around any object or area frequented by the targeted biologic."

"I see, that's very fascinating," said Jack. "Can they track larger biologicals such a Nishdans or Tarcans or others?"

"Well, yes, I suppose," answered the second orange Zilrhani, "but we do not do that, as this is not in our drone or database capability. There are provosts or other government organizations that can do that with criminals or fugitives from what we have heard."

"That's interesting," said Jack. "Thanks for the information."

"Yes, we will proceed now with the mission to eradicate these vermin," said the first Zilrhani.

Jack and Junot watched them as they opened the second floating container after securing it in place near the site where the geminute infestation was. The container appeared to be a small self-contained control center, whereas the first and smaller container had been a small bioresearch lab. They worked for a few mentus programming data. Then they opened the end panel and slid out a rack with several stacks of small round disks stacked horizontally on them. After a few more mentus of inputs, one of the stacks lifted off its storage rack and separated into about twenty separate small disks and flew to the site where they had seen the geminutes. The disks formed into a line and separated themselves by about thirty inches and started rotating in a counterclockwise orbit about a mu-ut off the ground. After about thirty septus, they all halted and held their position. "The search disks have located their first geminute biologic," said the first Zilrhani. "It is now waiting authorization to terminate its target."

The Zilrhani tapped an execute code, and a bright green flash of light shot from the third drone from the inside of the line, and a small puff of smoke rose from where it had fried the first geminute. The line of drones completed the first search circle then moved out to the next larger radius not previously covered. It found another geminute, and the Zilrhani operator typed a few commands before hitting execute. "The search biologic protocol appears to be working properly for these geminutes. I will now authorize them to full autonomous operation mode, and they will search and destroy all geminutes in the predetermined search area. Then we will program another drone swarm to begin searching in other areas and see if we can find a trail of infestation that will eventually lead us back to the source. If we can do that, we may be able to eradicate them all before they spread further. If hopefully we found them early enough, they may not have had a chance to branch out in other directions. Fortunately, they do not travel greatly from their source unless they are expanding their territory because of a large population increase. Hopefully they are isolated to this area in or near the mine. These drones are small and flexible enough to get into any place the geminutes can. After we have cleared the local area, we will send in another swarm of slightly larger drones to clean up the debris left from the hunter drones."

Jack and Junot watched as the swarm of hunter drones made a larger and larger circular search pattern. They barely paused as they shot and destroyed dozens of hiding geminutes. The drones went in, under, and around anything and everything that was located in the area. It was interesting and somewhat entertaining to watch as they went about the methodical business of hunting and killing the dozens of parasitic geminutes in the area. At one point, they all converged on a point near a junction box with a large number of wires entering it. Two of the probes entered the box through cooling louvers on the side, while a half dozen floated outside as if waiting for the others. A moment later, a dozen of more geminutes came shooting out of the cooling louvers where the drones had entered. The waiting drones all fired and killed every geminute that emerged from the cabinet.

"The drones are very careful not to damage any wiring, electronics, or other fragile hardware," said the Zilrhani operating the controls. "It would not be good to kill the parasites and then damage the infrastructure we are trying to save," he added.

"That's quite good," said Jack. "You seem to have your system well perfected."

The two drones inside the junction box emerged, and the swarm of small drone disks returned to its search-and-destroy mission. In another ten mentus, the entire area was cleared. As they were finishing, the entire swarm split up and went on a random search pattern over the entire area again. "This area is most likely cleared," said the Zilrhani. "We will broaden our search area and see if we can determine the direction of the origin for the geminutes. We will come back and search again for any signs of the geminutes once the entire area is cleared." Jack and Junot watched the Zilrhanis as they headed off in another direction in search of more geminutes.

"That's fascinating to watch," Jack said to Junot.

"Yes, but I don't like the Zilrhanis," said Junot. "They are very strange creatures. They give me the shivers just watching them."

"Yes," replied Jack, "they are certainly different, but they seem to know what they're doing with the infestation of geminutes." He went on, "When I was on the ship where I was allegedly a stowaway, I saw swarms of these drones going through the deck level that I was on and beyond. I thought they would stop and investigate me or maybe even attack me, but they didn't pay any attention to me. I wondered what they were doing or what they were looking for, but apparently, it wasn't me."

Junot replied, "I would guess they were looking for some sort of parasites like these drones were. Ships can become infested with different types of parasites too. They can hide and wreak havoc with the ship's systems if they're not discovered. They might have had some sort of problem with them on the ship, or maybe they were just doing a routine search. A big cargo ship can have a huge amount of area for them to hide. They are supposed to search for parasites before leaving a system, but I guess they sometimes get lazy, and that is how the parasites can make it to another planet and cause all sorts of problems. They can hide in the cargo containers and come down to the planet that way too."

"Well, it looks like Nishda has a problem with them now," said Jack. "I hope they can find all these things and wipe them out before they destroy the economy here."

Jack sent Za-arvak a message that the geminutes were being eradicated and that he thought they would be able to resume production tomorrow. Za-arvak replied that Jack and Junot had done a good job finding and handling the parasite problem. He said he would notify Jack when he would be returning as it could now be another two or three daiyus getting all the details hammered out. Jack said to Junot, "Well, Junot, if we can get the production back up to speed, maybe we can sneak in another visit with Zshutana and her girls. Let's run some quick tests of the production machinery and the control systems so we will know if we will be able to get back into production tomorrow or if we will have to do more repairs." A short while later, they decided that everything checked out and only some minor recalibration would be required to get things back on track.

"Junot, I wanted to start teaching you some of martial arts tonight, but with this geminute situation, we will have to hold off a daiyus or two. Do you want to go back to the conzone and get some food while I finish up here and check on the Zilrhanis? You can grab me something from the rations hall too because it will be closed when I get back."

"All right," said Junot, "I'm kind of tired and hungry, and I'll grab you something to eat too. Just watch out for those Zilrhanis. I just don't trust them. You never know what they might try to do."

"OK, thanks," replied Jack. "I'll be along in just a little while, and I'll be hungry when I get there too, so I will see you in while."

Jack made a quick check on the Zilrhanis. They were still working and said they would be stopping for the night in about an horun. Jack went back to the lab and checked on the equipment there. Everything seemed to work as advertised, so he ran the stored milling program for his katana and tanto sayas, or scabbards. In about forty-five mentus, he had perfectly fitting computer-generated and milled titanium sayas. All he had to do now is come up with some sort of a cording or leather wrap for the *tsuka,* or handle of the katana. Jack's katanas wouldn't be quite as decorative as some of the katanas he'd seen, but they would be every bit as functional and at least ten times harder and probably every bit as sharp.

The spectacular part of these katanas and tantos was the amazing Burun-Rioc alloy that was so uniquely iridescent. What they lacked in sophistication more than made up by their functionality and the beauty of the alloy metal. He admired the blades and their sayas for a few more mentus then carefully hid them back in the storage room. He even checked for the possibility of geminutes because he didn't want the Zilrhanis and their probes snooping around in there for any reason. When he was satisfied that everything was secure, he closed up the storage area and the lab and headed back to the conzone.

When he got back to the conzone, he found Cherga but not Junot. Cherga said, "Junot left this food for you here and said he was going to work on the . . ." then pointed at the translator around his neck. Jack checked his translator display and switched to safe mode and announced safe mode to Cherga. Cherga replied "Safe," and said Junot had some ideas he wanted to work on and wanted to go to the maintenance depot as soon as he'd finished the evening rations.

Jack replied, "He must have something good he wants to look into because he said he was tired. He must've really thought of something interesting that he had to investigate right now. As soon as I finish this snack, I think I'll run up there and see what he's doing. You can come along if you want and see what kind of progress he's making on our little venture."

"Yes, this sounds more interesting than lounging about in the common area here. I will go along also," said Cherga.

They found Junot hard at work over a disassembled translator. He had a tiny micro data cable attached to the tiny input connector and was working on the data that the translator was displaying on his computer display. When he saw them coming, he motioned them over and excitedly pointed to his translator and mouthed "safe mode" then began to explain what he was doing. "I think I found the secret to fully controlling the translator functions. They are designed to be quite impervious to any sort of tampering. All their access protocols are protected by both physical and programmed shielding that prohibits access to all their protocol programming functions. This would prevent most anyone from accessing their setup and programming functions. There really is no way to directly access or even backdoor your way into the programming module near the core of the processor. The problem is the security node or guard processor that filters everything that goes in or out of the translator core. Strangely, the security node is the weak point itself. Because it must allow all data to or from the core processor to pass through it, it is mounted on an isolated subplatform outside of the core housing. So I thought, why can't I just bypass it and access the core without the security node filtering it?"

Junot continued while Jack and Cherga listened. "Well, they actually designed the security node so that you can't do that. If you try to pass data directly to the core by bypassing it, then it will shut down the core and send the tampering alert that this specific unit has been accessed by an unauthorized person."

"How did you figure all this out?" asked Jack.

Junot replied, "Well, I noticed a tiny security node antenna trace coming out of the security node. Not many people would see this or recognize it for what it is. So I clipped the antenna lead and grounded the output side so it couldn't transmit the data feed stream it was trying to transmit into my maintenance computer. The security node transmitter output isn't protected. The security node itself and the core are both protected by the security node. When I triggered the security node tampering alert and watched it shut down the translator core, I was able to capture the encrypted access protocols to both the security node and the translator core. Once I had those, I was able to create a duplicate security node that was capable of accessing the actual security node as well as the translator core and all its command and control functions. The real security node then gave me full access to itself and the translator core as well as all the data that was processed into or out of both of them. Um, basically, I tricked it is what I was trying to explain."

"That's truly amazing, Junot," said Jack. "Now that you have all this unlimited access, what does it actually allow us to do?"

Junot replied, "Well, I'm just figuring that out now, but from what I can figure out so far, I would have to say everything."

"What do you mean by everything?" asked Jack.

"Well, from what I've seen, I guess I mean everything," said Junot. "I should be able to access all of the communication functions of the translator as well as the transponder output and ID codes programmed into the translator. I can turn off or on the tracking output of the translator and reprogram the transponder or other encrypted identification software at will. Also, like you asked before, all I have to do is program any transponder ID code into a small blank self-powered processor chip, and you would have one of those, what did you call it, uh, um, oh, yes, you would have one of those decoys."

"Junot, are you serious? You figured out all that, what, like just tonight?" asked Jack.

"Well, no, not tonight but over the last few daiyus," replied Junot.

"You are an absolute genius, a real true genius. This is just fantastic, Junot. I wouldn't have believed anyone could figure that out, and you've unraveled it all in just a few nights. An absolute genius, that's what you are, Junot."

Junot blushed and turned a nice bright reddish blue under his normal skin tone. "Well, I don't, I'm not, I'm just glad I was able to figure it out, and it's what you wanted me to do."

"You did great, Junot, and, yes, it would take a true genius to figure out all of that, that's all there is to it," said Jack. "So how long do you think it will take before you're able to implement all this on our translators?" asked Jack.

"Well, I would say give me a couple of daiyus to test everything and make sure it's behaving the way we want it to. I want to fully integrate it with the internal visual display and control system of the translators so that we can completely control all the functions on demand. I will have to incorporate both safe and caution modes as well as on and off transponder codes so that we can operate in, um, um, what would you call it? Where they think they know where we are or what we're doing, but we might really be somewhere else?"

"Stealth mode, I think we could call that stealth mode," said Jack.

"What is it exactly you are thinking?" asked Cherga. "What are you planning to do with all this capability our little genius friend Junot is coming up with?"

"I'm still not exactly sure," replied Jack, "but I know that we've all been shanghaied into our situation here and forced to work for years without pay or amenities for convictions of charges we haven't done. We won't really know what we can try to do until we know what our capabilities are with regard to the translator issues."

"Yes, I would agree completely," said Cherga, "but what can we possibly do while we are incarcerated in the mine operation? There is no way I know to fight the powers who put us here. They are faceless bureaucrats, and I don't even know who it is that I would fight so that there would be justice."

"Well, it's a big galaxy," said Jack, "and I don't know what I'll do or what any of us will do, but I sure don't plan on spending the next three to five or more yenets here working as a slave so that these mine bosses or the GTA or whoever can get rich off my blood and sweat while we get nothing in return. In my case, they are also trying to make money off of my fighting, and I'm not sure what they may try and pull next because of the losses they incurred because they didn't think I would win all the matches or maybe I wasn't somehow controllable. Things could get considerably more dangerous for me, and I don't know what form of retribution they have in mind or what they are capable of. I know they're not happy with me even though I'm doing exactly what they forced me to do."

"I understand what it is you're saying," said Cherga, "but I still don't know what it is we can do to make things right for us."

"I'm not sure either," said Jack, "but we are learning quite a bit about what they do to control us with the translators, thanks to Junot's brilliant work. With the information capabilities he's giving us, we might stand a chance against the faceless enemy. We might have a chance that we didn't have before, maybe one that we didn't even know existed. So now we can start thinking about ways to counter what they've done to us."

"Jack, Jack," said Junot, "I almost forgot the other part."

"What's that, Junot? What other part?" said Jack.

"The translator, the part about the comm and the control capability."

"OK, well, tell us about it, then," replied Jack.

"Right," said Junot, "um, the comm part is sort of like what we were talking about before. The mine bosses or maybe the provosts or government higher-ups have the ability to use the translators as a clandestine-type comm link like we knew and talked about before. We ordinary people don't get to use it or even know about it. They can use their translator and talk to anyone just about anywhere on the planet or the planet's system. They don't have to use the normal comm system like we do. They kind of piggyback on a lot of the main comm systems, but a lot of their comm capability is separate and encrypted to deny access to everyday people that might try to listen in on them."

"That's also very interesting too, Junot. How did you find out about that?" Said Jack.

"Well, some of it I found in the dark core but nothing specific. Then I also found the comm link circuitry when I gained full access control of the translator core. All the circuitry and protocol applications are all there. We wouldn't normally have access to it or be able to control it anyway because it is remotely controlled by the authorities or mine bosses or whoever. This is how they would spy on us. I was able to turn the spying function off and block it so we could have our safe and caution mode, but I didn't know how they were capable of capturing or receiving our conversations. It only makes sense that they would use the comm infrastructure that is in place to spy on us."

"Yes, that does make perfect sense," said Jack. "No sense reinventing the wheel if you don't have to."

Junot replied, "Well, um, yeah, uh, I think I know what you mean, one of those saying things again."

"Yes," laughed Jack, "one of those sayings things again. What was the other thing about the translators you wanted to tell us?" asked Jack.

"Oh, yes," said Junot, "when I took the guard's security wand apart and examined it, I also discovered that it's got a control capability that can only be turned on or authorized remotely and not from the wand itself."

"Well, we somewhat expected something like that," said Jack. "What exactly does it do?"

"Well, the commands in the wand, once authorized, are 'warn,' 'stun,' and 'incapacitate.' The wands can be both universal and directional and programmable to a specific person's translator. What I mean is they can point them at a crowd and incapacitate, stun, or warn everyone, or they can program them for an individual or group of people."

"That is a very despicable thing," said Cherga.

"Yes, indeed, it is," said Jack. "How does it do those things? What do they use to incapacitate people?"

"Well, they don't have a lot of information actually in the wand, just the controls and the authorization receiver, but the information I searched on the dark core says they can use straight electrical current to shock, sound waves to cause pain, or brain wave frequency disruption to scramble your thoughts, or any combination of the three, which are all generated directly from anyone's translator. The wand is just the control," replied Junot.

"That's not very nice of them, now is it? Can you turn that capability off?" asked Jack.

"Yes, but I would want to only remove the direct output side of the system—what would we call that, the control system inside the translator to control people?" asked Junot.

"That's fine, call it whatever you want," said Jack.

"OK," said Junot, "the control part. Anyway, from what I can tell, it's a monitored parameter of the translator capabilities, so I would leave the monitored portion of it intact and only cut the final output side so they won't think that something is defective in our translators."

"That would be the way to go, then," replied Jack. "Let's get this all done as soon as you can. We don't know how long it might be before we might need all these capabilities."

They all discussed the probabilities of what they could or couldn't do if their abilities to control the translators worked out like Junot thought they would. Cherga decided to call it a daiyus, since he didn't have much to add from a technical standpoint, and he headed back to the common area. Jack said, "So, Junot, tell me more about the monetary system here. What happens to any credits of those miners that were killed? Like these translators you're tinkering on, what happens to their credits or other possessions?"

Junot replied, "Um, I'm not sure about everything, like possessions and stuff, but I know that most of the credits would go to the mine bosses. Supposedly, whatever debts we convicts or conscripts still owe can be confiscated from our accounts and paid to whomever we allegedly owe them to—that is, after the Galactic Trading Alliance takes their 50 percent death tax."

Jack said, "That's a nice cut. I suppose it's for administrative fees and such. What or who has access to a person's account? Can the mine bosses just go in and take whatever they want whenever they want?"

"No, no," said Junot, "the monetary system is controlled centrally by the GTA. It didn't used to be, but now they get first shot at everything, and no one else can access anyone's account without first submitting the requests and documentation to the central GTA accounts system. I guess that's one good thing about the system—the local mine bosses can't see or raid our individual accounts without going through the GTA accounts system. Since we are just cons, though, they will get half of what we have as soon as the GTA reviews the supporting documents and makes a determination on our final status. You can probably guess how they would judge any findings between the mine bosses and a con."

"Well, I guess there's some good news and bad news in that," said Jack. "What about transfers and tracking of transfers—say, for instance, if I was to get killed in a foundry accident or something but I had transferred some of my credits over to a friend's account, like for example you? Now that I am dead and they say that I owe them some sort of reparations, can they come after what I've transferred to someone else's account?"

Junot replied, "No, well, I'm not really sure about that. I do know that they would have to go to the GTA Central Monetary Committee for a ruling on that. They just can't go from one person's account to another and arbitrarily start confiscating credits."

"So how would they go about doing that, and how long would it take?" asked Jack.

"Oh, gersht, I think that could take moondats to sort out," replied Junot. "They would have to get documented permission all the way back from the GTA Central."

"So how exactly is that accomplished?" asked Jack.

"Well, they would have to send the request by a starship by whatever the most direct routing to the GTA Central would be and then wait for the message to come back after whatever length of time it took the GTA Central Monetary Committee to make a determination. The GTA could even ask for additional documentation or evidence, and that could take four times as long or more."

Jack said, "Well, why couldn't they just contact this Central Monetary Committee directly and get an answer right away? Why would they have to send the message on a starship?"

"Well, because it would take thirty thousand yenets for the message to make it in one direction from here to near the galactic core via any sort of comm link—that is, if the message didn't get lost or garbled in all the interstellar radio frequency noise. That's kind of a silly question coming from a fighter pilot, don't you think?"

"Yes, I suppose," said Jack. "So they send it by starships so it won't get lost and because it's faster that way?"

"Well, of course, that's silly," said Junot. "Everyone knows the only way to make communications go faster than light is to send them on starships that can go faster than light. There is no such thing as radio waves or comm links that can go faster than light. Sometimes I wonder about you, Jack. Some of the crazy things you say or ask are pretty nonsensical when you think about it."

"You can't even begin to imagine," retorted Jack. "I can't wait to give you all the details someday, but for right now, you're better off not knowing all my issues."

"OK, if you say so," said Junot. "It's almost like if you were living in some sort of time warp or something."

"Yes, or something," said Jack. "OK, Junot, here's what I want to do if you are willing to help me out on this. I am certain that the mine bosses want some sort of retribution against me, since I've cost them so much. If they can get half of my credits simply because I get killed here in the mine, what would prevent them from helping to expedite my demise? It would be a win-win situation for them. Also from what you've said, they may not even know who else is betting on me to win, so they wouldn't know who else to go after even if they could legally. They would know that I was betting on myself, though, since they are the ones that funded me, and any fighter would likely be betting on themselves anyway. They were probably hoping I would lose and would have to pay them back their three hundred credits too. Does that make sense to you?" asked Jack.

"Yes, of course," replied Junot, "and I wouldn't put it past them if they thought they could get away with it."

"Well, I can't think of anything that would stop them, can you?" asked Jack.

"No, no, I can't think of anything at all that would stop them," replied Junot somberly.

"What I would like to do, Junot, is transfer about half my credits to your account and half to Zshutana's or maybe some to Cherga's. If something were to happen to me, which is somewhat possible under the circumstances, I would rather you and she have my credits than have the mine bosses get them. There's always the possibility that they would come back to you and try and collect my 'alleged debt,' but with the delay factor of the GTA, it might give you a chance to do something else, like buy your way out of here or something. If nothing does happen to me, then you can transfer them back to me in the future. I'm guessing I can trust you not to abscond with my portion and run off to Tahiti or some other exotic place."

"Why, yes, well, of course," replied Junot, "but I'm not sure about that Tahiti, where is that?"

"Well, just take my word for it, you would like it. It's kind of like being at Zshutana's only on a tropical beach with all the qalalé you can drink," laughed Jack.

"That does sound nice," said Junot. "Are there, are there . . . ?"

"Girls? Oh, yes," replied Jack. "OK, here's what I want you to do," said Jack. "I will transfer half of my funds over to your account and the other half to Zshutana's for now. I'm not sure if I can just do that on my own or if you have to authorize it or allow me to do that. It sounds like they can't tell where my credits went or where yours came from for a while, so you should be OK for a moondat or more before they could even start snooping around our accounts. Mine, though, would be much more available if I were to die, and they would try to confiscate it."

"I really hope that doesn't happen," said Junot.

"Yes, me too," replied Jack. "In the meantime, you just keep working on all the translator issues and see how many of them we can get implemented as soon as we can. We'll want to get Zshutana's fixed up too so if you can then figure out how to do the mods from a portable maintenance kit if you can."

"Yes, I should be able to do that," replied Junot. "It's mostly small micro level hardware mods and some reprograming once I access the core of the translator and the security node. The kit I used before will just need a few things added to it."

"OK, that sounds good," said Jack. "Do you want me to stay and help with anything right now, or do you want me to leave you alone so you can think about all this stuff?"

"No, you can stay. You can help keep me on track and maybe give me some suggestions when I get stumped on something."

"Great," replied Jack. "I'll be happy to do anything I can to help you figure this out and get it working for us."

The next daiyus at work, Jack and Junot were kind of dragging, as they had stayed up late trying to figure out all the parameters that would need to be added to the heads-up display commands to fully control all the functions of the translator. When they got to the foundry lab, the Zilrhanis were setting up their portable control station for the daiyus. The first Zilrhani reported to Jack and said, "We are going to continue on yesterday's search. We believe that we found and eliminated all the geminutes in your area. We will search again to be certain and then follow the indications of the directions they came from."

"Where did they appear to come from?" said Jack.

The second Zilrhani replied, "We are not certain yet, of course, but it appears that they came from the general direction of the ground transportation depot. We would estimate that they came in from somewhere else on a ground vehicle. If we can find a ground vehicle that is highly contaminated, we will then check its map logs. We may be able to find where they came from originally."

"That would be some good detective work, then," said Jack. "Would you mind if I come along and watch you work? Perhaps I would learn something and maybe be better at spotting these types of infestations in the future."

"Yes, this would be good. We see no reason to dissuade you from this," replied the first Zilrhani.

"Great," said Jack. "Let me go check on a few things here regarding our production schedule, and I will be ready to accompany you very shortly."

"That will be good," replied the second Zilrhani. "We will be thirty mentus or maybe more verifying that all the geminute parasites have been eradicated from your area."

Jack hurried back to the lab where Junot was working on getting the production schedule back up to speed. "Junot," said Jack, "I'm going to follow the Zilrhanis over to the vehicle depot where they think the geminutes came from and see how they track them down. I shouldn't be too long. Do you think you can get the production up and running and back on schedule on your own?"

"Yes, I, um, can do that," replied Junot. "Why would you want to go over there and watch the Zilrhanis again? That wouldn't be interesting enough to watch for two daiyus at least as far as I would think," said Junot.

"Yes, I know," said Jack. "I just want to get a look around over there and see what's going on and learn as much about their tracking technologies as I can."

"OK, well, it still doesn't sound all that interesting to me," said Junot.

A short while later, Jack accompanied the Zilrhanis in the direction they believed the geminutes had come from. They eventually came to a large underground parking depot with perhaps three hundred or more vehicles of various shapes and sizes parked all around. There were several that looked like the one that Jack had arrived at the mine in just a few months ago. The Zilrhani probe drones began picking up geminute hits as they got to within fifty mu-uts of the parking depot. By the time they actually got into the parking depot, the drones were rooting out small nests and individual geminutes at a fairly steady pace.

"Yes, they definitely came from here. It is very likely they came from another location on a ground vehicle, perhaps a supply shipment. It will be hard to track the source prior to here other than to wait for reports of infestation from other locations. Most all traffic is from Wanana, so it is likely the geminutes came from there and from a space freighter cargo shipment prior to that. They would likely be in a dormant stage when they arrived, so it is not always easy to find where they came from, since they don't become active until they've been somewhere for a while," said one of the Zilrhanis to Jack. Jack thought he wouldn't be surprised if they came in on the starship he was on, as he'd seen no indication of caution or checking for parasites during the cargo transfer he witnessed. Not that he knew what checking for parasites on a starship cargo transfer actually consisted of, but since he'd seen similar drones working on the freighter, he thought it possible that the ship had been infested.

While the Zilrhanis worked the area and hunted down more geminutes, Jack wandered around the parking depot and inspected the various types of ground vehicles. Eventually, a small, rather placid-looking alien approached him. It was thin and had languid, somewhat reptilian-looking eyes and features, and it wore a loose-fitting jumpsuit over its brown and purplish leatherlike skin. "May I help you?" It somewhat hissed in a breathless-sounding voice as it approached him.

"Well, perhaps," replied Jack. "I am here observing the Zilrhanis as they are searching for the geminute parasites. As you may be aware, they believe that these parasites most likely came to the Corodune mine on a ground vehicle that most probably arrived from Wanana. I am wondering if you keep logs of all vehicle movements and how closely you monitor arrivals and departures and whether you inspect all vehicles for possible parasite infestation upon their arrival," said Jack in a slightly authoritative voice without trying to actually intimidate the small alien.

The small alien hesitated for a few seconds then carefully formulated a cautious answer. "I am only an attendant here. We have not had any parasite infestations previously. I do not know of any requirements to inspect arriving vehicles for parasites."

"No, no, of course not," replied Jack. "We are just trying to formulate possible policies to combat this infestation because of the circumstances we are experiencing. You can't be too cautious with so much at stake here."

"Yes, of course," replied the attendant alien in a relieved tone.

Jack continued. "It is likely that the government in Wanana may want to implement more stringent monitoring policies due to the infestation. So I am just interested in your current policies as far as monitoring vehicle usage. Perhaps you can tell me how that works here."

The small alien replied somewhat less guardedly, "Well, as I stated, I am just an attendant here to help with any problems or concerns. There are only two of us, myself and Tegu, who come in at the 1400 horun time. We only provide assistance when it is requested for the mine vehicles. They are scheduled by whatever department needs them through the scheduling department."

"I see," said Jack, acting somewhat concerned at the attendant's lack of oversight. "What about any maintenance or fueling that may be required? Do you have any oversight with regard to that? It seems as if that may be a good time to inspect a vehicle for infestation—that is, when it arrives from a trip to Wanana or elsewhere."

"Yes, I think, yes, that would be a good time to inspect the vehicles. When they arrive, they go to the maintenance area for a quick inspection and fueling. That would be a function of the maintenance department," said the small alien, relieved that it would be someone else's responsibility to inspect for parasites.

"Now, do all these vehicles go to the maintenance department upon their arrival?" asked Jack.

"No, well, of course not, just the mine company vehicles," replied the small alien. "The private vehicles would only go there if they are contracted for maintenance or fuel."

"I see," said Jack. "That may pose an issue if some of the vehicles did not receive an inspection upon arrival. That would certainly pose more of an opportunity for parasites to arrive undetected."

"Oh, yes, of course," replied the alien, further relieved that the issue would be outside his area of responsibility.

"So just to clarify," said Jack, "you are not required to check anyone in or out when they are using the vehicles, and they are not required to show authorization papers for vehicle acquisition?"

"Papers?" asked the alien. "What do you mean papers?"

"Uh, oh, sorry," replied Jack, "an old military term used to indicate a certain action or authorization has been approved." *Oops, I guess I'm living in the past, technology-wise,* thought Jack.

"No, we are not required to check anything. That is authorized through the scheduling department for company vehicles," replied the little alien.

"Yes, of course," said Jack. "What about any private vehicles? How are they designated and authorized for entry and exit to this complex?"

"I am not sure what you are asking," replied the alien. "They enter or leave whenever they get here or when they leave."

"Yes, I understand that now," said Jack, "but they must pass the security perimeter at the mine entrance and entering or leaving Wanana, but once they're inside, then they pass no further, uh, inspection points."

"Well, yes, that about describes it," said the alien. "Why do you ask?"

Jack didn't want to press the little alien about things that might be apparent to a normal inhabitant of Nishda. He definitely didn't want to draw any suspicion to himself. Jack started laying on the BS layers to help cover his questioning. "I am just trying to get a good feel for the vehicle traffic flow in and out of the mine and what may be the best places for a parasite inspection point to help prevent

309

the spread of these noxious and destructive creatures. As a professional full-time vehicle parking attendant, what is your opinion as far as the best place to inspect arriving or departing vehicles for parasites?"

The little alien was now relieved to divulge himself of any involvement with vehicles inspections. "Oh, I would, uh, definitely say the best place for that would be in the maintenance depot when the vehicles arrive. I'm sure they are much more capable and equipped to perform any sort of inspection like that."

"Yes, that would make the most sense, wouldn't it?" said Jack. "That's a very good idea, and I'll be sure to pass that on to the Zilrhani inspectors with your name as the recommending agent."

The little alien suddenly looked pleased with himself and relieved at the same time. "Oh, yes, thank you. My name is Skenek Ipto Eh, Corodune vehicle parking area three attendant."

"Very good, then, Skenek Ipto Eh, I will pass on your suggestion with full approval, and I thank you for your help today."

Jack said he must go observe the Zilrhanis and their progress, so he excused himself and then wound his way through the parking depot while observing every type of vehicle. He had no idea if any of the vehicles, either company or private, had any sort of security devices, a kill switch, or tracking system or what they were equipped with. He didn't even know exactly how they operated. They were probably somewhat similar to the zibur drill rig in the respect that they were just a machine. He would have more research to do before he could contemplate any sort of plan. Tactical reconnaissance and planning, the key to any successful military mission—how many times had he had that drilled into his head? Somehow, though, he felt as if he were still winging the whole situation.

Jack watched the Zilrhanis for a while, taking in as much of that tactical reconnaissance as he could gather. After he'd observed about all he could that might be useful to him, he thanked the Zilrhanis and headed back to the foundry to make sure everything was getting back on track there.

He found Junot in the production office arguing with one of the production workers from the production plasma furnace crew. "Hey, Junot, how is the schedule coming after our little geminute setback?"

"Good mostly," said Junot. "We are only half a daiyus from being back on track, but the furnace crew wants to go home for the daiyus, and I've asked them to stay for a couple of extra horuns and finish the production run we started late this afternoon. They said they never have to stay and aren't interested in getting back on schedule."

Jack thought for a mentu and then asked the plasma furnace worker, "You have never had to stay after horuns to make up for some production delay?"

"No, why would we do that?" replied the rough-looking alien who was apparently acting as the voice for the entire shift of fifteen furnace crew operators.

Jack stated, "Well, it would be important to Za-arvak and the operation as a whole if we could get back on schedule after yesterday's production delay."

"Well, it would be important for us to go home at the end of today's shift. That is what we do every daiyus," replied the furnace worker.

"I understand completely, but, um, what type of incentive would it take to have your crew stay for an additional few hours and complete today's run?" asked Jack.

"What do you mean incentive?" asked the worker.

"You work for horun rates, is that correct?" asked Jack.

"Yes, that's right, we receive four credits for every horun we work," replied the worker.

"I can offer you six credits per horun for the additional horuns you work tonight," said Jack. "That is called time and half overtime."

"You will pay us extra six credits for each horun past our normal time?" asked the worker. The concept seemed foreign to the alien worker, but apparently, it seemed as if it had some appeal. "Yes, we would do that," replied the worker after a few more seconds of thought.

"Do you mean all of your crew? Will they accept that too?" asked Jack.

"Yes, I am speaking for them," replied the worker.

"OK, great," replied Jack. "Back to work and you will receive time and a half for working overtime tonight."

Jack thought, *Here I am on a foreign world and I've just negotiated what is probably their first organized labor contract for time and half overtime.* He laughed to himself.

"Can we do that?" asked Junot.

"Oh, absolutely," replied Jack. "Whatever it takes to get this production back on schedule is good with Za-arvak, I'm sure."

Jack sent Junot back to the conzone to work on the translator project at the maintenance depot, while he stayed there and supervised the plasma furnace crew to make sure they were still making headway on getting back on their production schedule.

Later, he found some type of good cording material in one of the work areas in the foundry and took that back to the lab storage room and took out the katanas and tantos he'd made. After admiring them for a mentu, he began carefully wrapping the handles in the cording material. It took several tries to get it looking right as well as good and tight like it needed to be. It wasn't as pretty as a ray skin and cord wrap on a real Japanese katana, but it would do and didn't look half bad.

The iridescent, almost luminescent shimmer of the blades of the Burun-Rioc alloy made them as unique and beautiful as anything he'd ever seen. Actually, while thinking about it, Jack realized these were truly the only katanas and tantos as well as his knife blade made of his Spartan alloy anywhere in existence as far as he knew. He finished wrapping the second blade, a tanto, then hid them again and went to check on the furnace crew. They'd been at it for another two and a half horuns and were almost up to their projected production level.

"Great job, guys. We are pretty close to where we need to be. You can call it quits for the daiyus and finish the rest of the catchup tomorrow," Jack told them. They were almost reluctant to quit, since they were making time and a half, but Jack promised them more in the future, as he was sure there would be plenty of extra work with the new production contracts that Za-arvak was currently negotiating. That seemed to appease them, and they were now all happy to quit for the daiyus.

When Jack made it back to the conzone, Junot was still not back yet, so Jack went to check on him at the maintenance depot. Junot was still there working diligently on the translator. "I'm pretty sure I've got it all figured out," Junot told Jack. "I've run all the output tests on every circuit and everything that is supposed to be transmitting, like the pulsed monitor output of the security node and the core, which are still simulating their monitoring functions while they no longer have the ability to carry out any remote commands from any mine or other security forces. The translator wearer is now in full control of all functions of the translator and not the other way around. I did leave the control receiver circuit functional and keyed them to a warning on the HUD so you'll know if anyone is trying to control us and to what degree. We'll get a warning on the HUD that shows 'control warning,' and it will show what they are trying to do to any of us."

Junot had even figured out how to remove the translator units from the person themselves without causing any malfunction or security alert to the authorities. "That's the way it should be," said Jack. "We, or any citizen, should control the translator functions and not some faceless government or corporate functionary. See, I told you that you were a genius, and I was right," he said to Junot. Jack then added, "And we're basically back on schedule at the foundry, and if Za-arvak is still gone tomorrow, then maybe we can escape for a couple of horuns and go see Zshutana and her lovely girls. Our first priority will be to get her translator modified, but then, who knows what might transpire?" he said encouragingly to Junot.

"OK," said Junot, "OK, OK, oh, OK. The only thing I haven't completely figured out is how to fully encrypt and tap into the comm link system with the translator. The system is there, and I know how to access it, but the frequency hopping encryption is turning out to be a little harder to put together than I thought, and I haven't really had time to get into it that much. It's so much more complex and requires so many data control variables. I'll get it, but it may take a little time."

"That's OK, "said Jack. "That will be a bonus feature. If you can get everything else figured out first that will make us impervious to any electronic control or retribution they may try, then we're in really good shape."

Junot replied, "Let me take your translator off and modify it right now. I have that part figured out, so there is no sense in waiting." Junot was able remove Jack's translator and start modifying the control functions of the unit. In an horun, he had it finished, and Jack put it back on. While it was off, Jack could talk to Junot, and Junot's translator would translate Jack's language, but Jack could not understand a word of Junot's. It was truly a strange and indecipherable series of sounds and strange tones but not like any foreign language Jack had ever heard. The translators were obviously a remarkably handy device as far as their translating function, but everything else the GTA, or whoever, had tacked on was truly a sinister scenario.

All Jack could do was shrug when Junot tried to say something. It served to remind him of what a strange and alien situation he was in. He felt like he instantly went from a situation he was comfortably immersed in to one where he was a complete and total outsider from a place that didn't even exist to the people here. When he had the translator back on, Jack said, "Wow, that's better. I felt utterly lost for a while when I couldn't understand what you were saying. What did you say when I had my translator off?"

Junot replied, "I said I'll bet you don't have the slightest idea what I'm saying to you right now. I can tell by the look on your face that you don't understand anything at all." They both had a good laugh at that. "Now let me show you how to use the new functions and controls I set up for the translator. It's got a lot more selectable options and operating parameters than were previously there," said Junot.

The next daiyus at the foundry, they were able to get completely back on the production schedule. Just before the mid horun, Jack contacted Za-arvak and gave him a brief update and let him know everything was back on track. "That is amazing," replied Za-arvak. "How on Nishda did you get caught up? I thought it would be daiyus or possible a wenek before we ever got caught up."

"Very simple," said Jack. "I'll explain it when you get back, if that's OK?"

"Yes, that's fine. We will need some of that production ability with these new contracts I'm working on. I should be back by tomorrow if all goes well," said Za-arvak.

"If it's OK with you, since we are all up to speed, would you mind if Junot and I took a long noon meal today at the concession area?" Jack asked.

"Yes, by all means. That is the least bit of reward I could offer you for such a good job," replied Za-arvak.

"OK, great," said Jack. "We will see you tomorrow night, then."

"Oh, yes," Jack said to Junot a few mentus later, "we are on for a little rendezvous action today, and it's fully approved by the boss!"

"Oh, yes, oh, yes!" screeched Junot, hardly able to contain himself.

"Remember," said Jack, "first things first. We have to get Zshutana's translator mods done first. Then we will be free to, uh, relax a bit."

"Yes, OK. I'll get all the things I need to get the mods done, and I'll be ready by the mid meal—I mean, noon lunch as you call it," Junot said to Jack.

They headed to Zshutana's at 1400 horun, or right at midday. When they got there, Jack buzzed her door, and in less than three septus, the door flew open, and she threw herself around Jack in a big smothering bear hug. "I saw you on the monitor, so I got to the door as fast as I could," Zshutana said breathlessly. "Junot, hello. You both come in right now," as she grabbed them both and pulled them in and closed the door.

"Wait, everybody check safe mode before we go on," said Jack. They all gave each other a thumbs-up. "Sorry for the unannounced visit, but we just now got a little parole reprieve from the boss. You can't believe the crazy stuff we've been dealing with for the last couple of daiyus, parasitic power rodents that eat power supplies and terminals and labor issues. Just crazy," said Jack.

"Well, I'm glad you are here now so you can relax and take a nice break from the foundry," she said. "Are you hungry? Do you want something to eat?" she asked.

"Oh, yes!" exclaimed Junot in a very eager voice.

"OK, yes, we sure could go for some of that great food, as in real food again," said Jack.

Zshutana spoke into her intercom and then said, "Give us a few mentus, and the girls will round something up. In the meantime, tell me what's going on. Is everything OK? I'm sure glad all the fight pit craziness is over. That was making me insane."

"Well, it was kind of fun, but, yes, I'm glad it's over because of the way the mine bosses were controlling it. I don't like being forced into something against my will. It's just more of the same situation as everything else here," replied Jack. "First things first, though. One of the main reasons for coming here today, besides just wanting to see you, is to make some more mods your translator." Junot gave Zshutana a brief rundown of the modifications he'd come up with. She was stunned by all the capabilities of the translators and how the Alliance used the device to control and spy on anybody they wanted.

Junot took her translator off and began working on it again. Jack said a few words to her while her translator was off. She looked at him quizzically and said, "What? What? I can't understand. What are you saying? All I hear are strange words." Jack looked at her and pointed at her and gave her a thumbs-up. He then pointed to himself and then her and gave her a thumbs-down. She said, "Oh, of course, you can understand me, but I can't understand you without my translator. I should have realized that after helping you with your translator, but I haven't been without one for as long as I can remember." He gave her a thumbs-up. She smiled at him slyly and licked her lips discreetly. "After mid meal," she whispered so quietly he could barely hear her.

It's going to be damn near impossible to stay on task here, he thought to himself. She ran her hand up his arm and back down his side then across his leg.

Junot, somewhat oblivious in his concentration, said, "This should only take me about twenty mentus or maybe less. Her translator doesn't have all the restricted access blocks like ours did. There are some basic ones in place but not as many layers, and the access codes are only just barely encrypted."

"That's great, Junot, just keep working on it," said Jack as she wrapped her feet around his leg and pulled gently at first, then a little more insistently while she looked at him unabashedly with her incredible eyes, her eyes that were nearly on fire, turquoise blue fire. He really, really liked looking into her amazing eyes. He couldn't even describe how much he liked looking into those amazing eyes. He thought he was going to grab her right there and . . . "Junot, do you just about have that translator mod figured out?" he said huskily.

"Well, yes, I, uh, should have it done here in about, oh, maybe five more mentus at the most. Why? Are you OK, Jack? You sound sort of fuzzy or something," said Junot.

A few mentus later, Junot announced, "I, uh, think I'm just about done with the translator mods. All I have to do is repower it and run a few tests, and I think we will be ready to go."

"Great," said Jack. "Can you keep working on it while we eat, or do you need to set it aside?"

"No, no," replied Junot, "I'm done with the delicate stuff, and it's all closed up. I just need to put it back on Zshutana and turn it on and initialize it, and we can run the tests on all the upgrades I just installed."

"OK, well, go ahead," said Zshutana. "I would sort of like to hear Jack's voice again and have it make sense instead of the strange words I have been hearing him speak." A few mentus later, Junot had her translator back on her and working.

A small chime sounded and brought them back to the present. She smiled at Jack and said, "Mid meal is served."

"Oh, yes, great," said Junot. "I'm really hungry for some of your great food like last time," he added.

"Hmm, what else are you hungry for like last time, Junot?" she said. He looked at her and turned a dark crimson and blue. He started to try to say something, and she said, "It's OK, Junot. We wouldn't want to skip the most important part of the meal. There will be plenty on the desert menu, I promise." It was hard to imagine, but Junot turned an even darker shade of crimson and then broke out in an ear-to-ear grin.

"I think you've piqued his interest," said Jack.

"I believe I have," she replied.

Two girls came in with another nice array of very appetizing and wonderful-smelling food. "You both remember Li-ialah from last time. I'm sure you do, don't you, Junot?" Zshutana asked in a pleasant conversational tone.

"Oh, yes, of course, I, of course, uh, certainly do," Junot replied.

"Yes, I'm sure," replied Zshutana, "and this is Carti. Celiah is off today, so Carti is helping around here today."

Carti spoke up excitedly. "Hi, Junot, it's really nice to meet you. Li-ialah and Celiah told me so much about you. I hope you have some time after mid meal so we can visit for a while and get to know each other, if that's OK?"

Zshutana interjected, "Yes, Junot, Carti has been wanting to meet you both since she'd heard about your last visit. Thank you, girls. I'll give you a call when we're done eating. We have a little work to do while we're all here."

Both girls replied OK, and as they left, the new girl Carti said, "Well, I almost got to meet Jack before when you first met him and were training him on language, Zshutana."

"Yes, yes, that's correct," replied Zshutana. "Now, go on and I'll call you in a little while. We'll see you both shortly," Zshutana said as she shooed them out of the room.

Junot and Jack watched them go. Junot could hardly take his eyes off them from the time they entered the room. They had a great mid meal and conversation about all the new capabilities of the translators that Junot had discovered and had implemented for them. Zshutana called the girls back to clean up the spoils of their meal. "That was most lovely as expected," she said to the girls as they cleared away the meal. "Do you two girls think you could entertain Junot for an horun or so while Jack and I discuss some very important and urgent business?" Zshutana said to the girls.

"Oh, yes, we'd really love to," said Carti enthusiastically.

"Yes, we'll take very good care of him," added Li-ialah.

"Thank you, girls. We'll see you after a while," said Zshutana.

With that, she grabbed Jack by the hand and said, "Why don't we go do something that doesn't require any translation—that is, if you're interested?" she added.

"That sounds astonishingly good to me," said Jack. "Let's go, beautiful woman."

"Woman? What is woman?" she asked.

"Oh, that is the female of my race—man is male and woman is female," he replied.

"I like the sound of that," she said as every part of her face and body seemed to light up and smile at him like nothing he'd ever seen. He took her hand, and they raced each other to her bedroom.

"Now this is what I call a perfect daiyus," he said to her breathlessly as they threw themselves on the bed.

She rolled on top of him and stared at him seductively with her indescribably spectacular eyes. "It's going to get a whole lot more perfect in the next few mentus," she said to him in a heavy panting voice.

"Yes, I believe it will," he said to her as he pulled her close and began to kiss her.

* * * * *

"Well, Junot, how did you like what was on the dessert menu for today?" Zshutana asked when they all met up again in her office two horuns later.

"I, well, what, uh, what am I supposed to, uh, wow, I don't, uh, really know how to answer except these have sure been the best mid meals I've ever had. A person sure could get used to this kind of treatment," replied Junot.

"We love you, Junot. You're such a sweetheart," said Li-ialah.

"Yes," said Carti, "I'm sure glad Celiah was off today and I got to meet you. I really like you. You're so cute and nice and enthusiastic about everything. You should come by again very soon and as much as you want. I'll always be available anytime you want to see me."

"Really? That would be great," said Junot. "I'd really like that too."

Jack piped in, "Well, remember, Junot, as much as we'd like to, we can't just wander around outside the conzone anytime we like. Don't be making any promises you can't keep."

"Well, maybe we could get out more now that we've done such a good job at the foundry," replied Junot. "Maybe Za-arvak will let us go out to lunch more often."

"Maybe," said Jack, "but we still can't make any promises as much as we'd like to. We'll have to see what happens after Za-arvak gets back from his meetings and what that new production contract will require. It all hinges on what happens at the foundry."

"OK, I know, but we can always hope for the best," said Junot.

"Yes," said Jack, "but the real problem is I think you're just a bad boy, Junot, and that's all there is to it. Don't you think so, Zshutana?"

"Yes, definitely," replied Zshutana. "That's most definitely the main problem, Junot is a bad boy, and he's going to get us all in trouble."

"What? I'm not sure what, ah, what do you mean?" said Junot, somewhat confused and worried.

"Nothing," said Zshutana. "We're just teasing you, Junot. We're just giving you a hard time because you're so sweet and naive, that's all."

"Oh, OK, I thought I did something wrong," replied Junot.

"No, no, not at all," said Zshutana. "The girls and I are just glad you had a good time and everyone is happy. You're absolutely fine."

"Zshutana, can you have the girls entertain Junot for a little while longer? There's something I want to ask you about in private that I didn't mention earlier," said Jack.

"Of course. Girls, can you please take care of Junot for a little while longer while I go talk to Jack?" said Zshutana. "What is it?" she asked when they were back in her room behind the closed door. "Did you want to add something to our last little discussion?" as she reached up and kissed his face and ran her fingers through his dark hair.

"Ummm, I'd surely love to," replied Jack, "but unfortunately, I don't think we have enough time for that now. No, I wanted to ask you something else. Would you be willing to take my winnings from the fight pit matches and hold them until some future time for me?" He explained to her how he thought the mine bosses might be trying to get some of their lost earnings back from the matches he'd won against their attempted rigged fights. He told how Junot had explained that if he were to be accidently killed in a mine accident that since he was a conscript owing reparations that they would take everything he'd earned if he were to somehow meet his demise.

"That's horrible, Jack. How could they do that?" she responded.

"That's just how their system is rigged," said Jack. "You know how disreputable these boss cretins are. They'd do anything to anyone just to get whatever they can out of the situation. That's how I ended up here in the first place as well as Junot and Cherga."

Zshutana replied, "I know how they are, and I'd do anything, whatever you want, to help you out, but I still can't believe how horrible those disgusting creatures are. I don't think even that miserable slime thing Cahooshek would stoop that low."

"Well, maybe not, I don't know," he replied, "but I'll set up a transfer from my end and put it through in short order. Just take care of my investment and do with it whatever is safe while it's in your care."

"Yes, OK, I will. Just let me know what you want me to do, and I'll take care of it for you," she replied.

"Well, Junot, did you have a good lunch and a good time with the girls today?" asked Zshutana when they'd returned from their little financial meeting.

"Well, oh, yes, you certainly know it," replied Junot. "What better time could anyone have than what we've had here? I just hope we get to come back soon and, uh, visit over lunch again."

"Yes, I'll second that," said Jack.

"Mmmm, me too, I hope you can make it on a regular basis," said Zshutana as she cuddled up to Jack, not afraid to show her affection for him now. "The girls really like you, Junot. I'm sure they'd like to see you very soon again too."

"Well, I'm going to do everything I can to visit here as much as possible," he replied.

"Well, it's time for us to get back to the foundry and make sure everything is in order before Za-arvak gets back. It was nice that he let us out to play today. As long as we do a good job for him, he'll probably let us out as much as he can without jeopardizing his own position."

A few mentus later, they were ready to leave. Zshutana hugged Jack and held him for a long time. "You be very careful, Jack," she said. "Watch all around and don't let anything happen. The bosses and their minions like Cahooshek are capable of anything. If you really think they are out to try and hurt you or worse, you're going to have to do something to stop them. I don't know what—they control everything and everyone here to some degree. You'll have to use all your skills to stop them somehow. They are just so devious, and you don't know what they'll try to come up with."

"I know," said Jack. "I'm already being careful, and I have some ideas already too. The first one is to divest myself of my winnings in case something does happen to me. At least I can stop them from profiting from anything they try to do. All the things we've learned about the translators and how to use them to our advantage will help immensely. They can no longer use them against us, but we can use what we've figured out against them in ways they haven't thought about. We're in a precarious situation, but we have a fair upper hand with a lot of the things we've—and by that I mean mostly what Junot has—figured out. Thank God for Junot or I'm not sure where we'd be at this point."

When Junot and Jack had made it back to the foundry, they found everything in order. The new incentives of overtime pay seemed to keep the foundry workers motivated and more prone to take responsibility for their work areas from what Jack could tell. When Za-arvak returned and Jack explained what he'd done with the pay and other incentives to get the foundry back up to speed after the infestation shutdown, Za-arvak was impressed with the reasoning and the results. Being primarily a technical manager and operator, he'd never envisioned such tactics to motivate the workers and increase their productivity. He told Jack how fortunate he was to have found someone like Jack to help with all the workings of the foundry. He was certain things wouldn't be half as well organized and efficient if Jack hadn't been there to help.

It had been a full two weneks since Jack's last fight against the former champion Chartak Sula, and as far as he knew, he wouldn't have to fight this week, since he had beaten the previous champion in the last match. He didn't know if he would have to fight again, maybe not for this yenet unless some up-and-coming challenger wanted a go at him or maybe an exhibition fight against some other former champion or against another mine; he just didn't know. He knew some sort of trouble had to be brewing against him, but he didn't know what. Just to keep his edge, he made sure he hit the conzone gym and worked out at every opportunity and sparred when he could get a partner. He started teaching Junot some basic defense moves and got him working out in the gym too.

After their little martial arts training session, Jack was going to go over to the maintenance depot with Junot and see if he could be of any help with the last phase of Junot's modifications to the translators where Junot was trying to tap into the comm system of the mine bosses and piggyback on it with their own encrypted comm system. As they left the common area and headed toward the maintenance depot, they were met by six mine guards.

"Ja-ak of Vara is to come with us by order of the mine bosses," said the guard's apparent leader. Jack was immediately on the defensive and ready to fight if he had to, but the guards didn't seem to be interested in a physical confrontation. They didn't appear to be too eager to confront the mine pit champion anyway. Jack thought he could probably take them out, especially since he knew they had no way to implement any of their electronic or sonic restraints or controls against him. He quickly gauged the situation and decided to let it ride and see what their intentions were. He didn't want to get Junot hurt either, and he didn't want to have to go into a fugitive mode without better preparation.

"OK, fellas, where are we going, and what's this about?" asked Jack, trying to engage the guards and gather any intel on the situation that he could.

"We were told to find and escort you," responded the guard.

"Yes, I understand that, and I am, of course, happily complying, but it would be kind of nice to at least know where we are headed," said Jack.

"I was not instructed to tell you where, only to escort you to the—" The guard stopped short.

"Yes, well, I think I'll find out where we're going soon enough when we get there, so it's probably not going to be a big secret for a whole lot longer," said Jack, trying to reason with the guard. Jack went on. "So did they tell you specifically not to tell me, or did the bosses just not give any specific instructions regarding that?"

"Well, they just didn't give me any instructions about telling you anything," replied the guard.

"So what is your name anyway, Mr. Guard?" asked Jack.

"Me, I, um, I did, uh, not receive instructions to give you my name," said the guard, somewhat unsure of himself.

"But you didn't receive instruction not to, did you?" asked Jack.

"No, uh, I did not," said the guard.

"So, see, then it's OK. It's just your name, not a big deal," replied Jack.

"I guess not," said the guard.

"So your name is what?" said Jack.

"My name is Wojar," said the guard.

"See now, Wojar, that was easy enough. We're getting along great now," said Jack.

"So, Wojar, now that we know it's OK to talk about stuff that the bosses haven't specifically said not to, where do you suppose it is that they want you to escort me to?" Jack said reassuringly.

"Well, uh, I guess since we'll be there in a few mentus, uh, it's OK. We're to escort you to the fight pit arena," replied the guard.

"Oh, OK, see, that wasn't so bad," said Jack. "The fight pit, huh? That should be fun, although I wasn't planning on going tonight. The fights might be pretty entertaining tonight. Did they say why you were supposed to escort us to the fight pit? That seems a little odd, don't you think?"

"No, they did not say, just to escort you there," said the guard.

"Oh, OK, that's fine," said Jack. *No point in pressing the issue,* he thought, *if they don't know any more than that anyway.*

When they arrived at the entrance to the arena, they went past it and around to another corridor and toward another smaller entrance. "I hate to be the one to break this to you, but I think we missed the entrance to the arena back there," said Jack.

"Yes, we are instructed to take you to the entrance at the back of the arena area," replied Wojar, the guard. They entered into a room Jack hadn't seen before, and they were brought to a sitting area with another door.

Jack could hear the crowd on the other side cheering for the contestants of a fight that he could tell was already under way in the pit arena. "Now what are you supposed to do with us?" Jack asked Wojar, the guard.

"We are to wait here with you under escort until we hear your name called in the arena," replied Wojar.

"Ah, yes, that's a good idea. Do you suppose they want to give me an award for my last fight victory or something like that? Wouldn't that be a nice surprise?" Jack asked Wojar.

"I do not know," said Wojar. "I am only to escort you to the pit when I hear your name announced," he said.

"What about Junot here? Do you have instructions regarding him?" asked Jack.

"No," replied Wojar, "only for you."

"Would it be OK with you and your friends here if he could go, then? I'm sure he'd like to watch the fights out there in the arena. In fact, I would guess that Cherga is out there, and he would like to go sit with Cherga."

"Yes, OK, we have no orders against that," said the guard.

"Great," replied Jack, "just let me tell him something for Cherga and he can be on his way."

"Yes, OK," said the guard, watching Jack closely.

Jack said to Junot as quietly as possible, "All right, Junot, they've cooked up something here. It appears that I'll be fighting again tonight. I might even be fighting more than one, I don't know. I'm sure the mine bosses have something cooked up for me that they're sure I can't win. See if you can find Cherga and take my credits and bet everything on me to win. You do with your credits whatever you feel right about, OK?"

Junot hadn't said anything, since they were intercepted by the guards. He was scared and wasn't sure what Jack was planning on doing and was just trying to stay alert and be ready to use the couple of hours of martial arts training that Jack had given him if he had to. "What? Are you sh-sure?" as he tried to assimilate what Jack was saying to him.

"Yes," said Jack. "They brought me here for some sort of fight, probably something I wouldn't agree to, to try and make their money back on me. Just relax and take it easy and see if you can find Cherga. Don't forget to bet my credits before the closeout time and enjoy the match. Everything will be OK, OK?"

"Yes, OK," said Junot.

"OK, go," said Jack as he turned his attention back to the guards to try and garner any other information they might have. Junot hightailed it out of there as fast as he could, while Jack started probing he guards.

Jack pulled up the fight schedule on his translator display, but all it showed was four normally scheduled matches. It looked like the third match was just about to begin. He recognized three of the eight fighters, but there didn't seem to be anything unusual about the overall lineup. "So have you seen the fight roster for tonight?" he asked the head guard Wojar.

"Yes, it is in my translator," replied the guard.

"So wouldn't it be nice to see the last match from the stands instead of being locked in this room?" Jack said in slightly imploring voice.

"Yes," replied Wojar, "but we are ordered to stay with you here until we hear your name announced, then we are to take you to the pit."

"So I am probably getting some sort of an award or something, wouldn't you guess?" Jack said to the guards.

"I am not thinking that, no," replied Wojar.

"Well, darn," responded Jack, "I was really hoping I might be getting some type of an award, maybe a ribbon or trophy and maybe even a gift certificate to Taco Bell."

"I—tagobale, what is this? What is this you talk of?" said the guard confusedly.

"Oh, nothing," replied Jack, "I was just thinking about some really good gourmet junk food, if you know what I mean."

"Junk and food, no, I'm not sure. I know nothing of what you are speaking," said Wojar.

"That's OK," replied Jack. "I'm guessing they don't have a Taco Bell anywhere nearby, but then you never know, they seem to be just about everywhere."

Jack could tell by the sounds that the third fight went on for the full three rounds. The crowd sounded pretty enthusiastic, so the fight must have been pretty good. Another match soon started, but it sounded like it only went about a round and a half. The crowd seemed somewhat disappointed in the quality of the match by the sound of it.

Sha-aga, the announcer, could be heard announcing the winner and the loser, but Jack couldn't make out the names of the fighters. He'd seen their names in his translator HUD already anyhow; he just couldn't tell who the victor was from the announcer's banter. After a few mentus, Jack could hear Sha-aga start in on one of his prefight promotions again. He started revving the crowd up, and Jack could hear them excitedly cheering. Then they started chanting, and he could hear them chant a name, his name . . . "Ja-ak Varaci, Ja-ak Varaci, Ja-ak Varaci, Ja-ak Varaci," the crowd chanted enthusiastically.

"I guess that's our cue," Jack said to Wojar.

"Yes, we will go to the pit now as ordered," replied Wojar as he and the other guards escorted Jack to the pit arena. As they entered the arena, the crowd grew more erratic and excited. They continued to chant his name and yell wildly.

I didn't realize I had gained such a popular following, he thought to himself as they entered. The guards stood behind Jack for a minute then turned and marched partially out as if they'd been given a cue. "Hey, thanks for the safe escort, guys, much appreciated," Jack said to the guards as they marched off.

Sha-aga started in with a brief bio on Jack and his short but illustrious fight record. The crowd already knew his stats, but Sha-aga had to deliver as much hype as possible. Sha-aga spent a good couple of mentus of promoting Jack as Jack hammed it up a little to play along with whatever stunt they were trying to sell. Then Sha-aga got down to the actual details. "Now this is the most exciting and incredible attraction we've had in a considerable while," Sha-aga stated. "Nothing like what we have tonight has been seen since our last pit champion met his demise in a truly gruesome way at the hands of a truly fearsome opponent when he challenged a gorroks to, well, what turned out to be a death match, his death match actually." The crowd rallied and went crazy with cheering and the remembrance of Fuundar Daak's death at the hands of the gorroks.

Sha-aga continued. "Well, tonight, we don't have a gorroks. We have, we have . . . something even better. That's right, that's right. Tonight, we have a match between our Varan champion and . . . you won't believe it, one of the few remaining drugas in captivity, or anywhere else, right here in our own Corodune fight pit."

The crowd went wild. They screamed and stomped and even slugged it out among themselves in a few spots in the stands. Jack didn't like it, but he wasn't surprised that the bosses would try something like this. Anything to get their losses back and deliver some retribution to the Varaci that had cost them so much. He'd heard of the drugas, gorroks, and the even more dreadful kruztwox from Cherga and a little from Junot. He'd never seen one, but he was positive he didn't want to see any of them for the first time as an opponent in the fit pit. He wondered for a second which side Junot would bet on, and Cherga too if he were out there watching. He hoped Zshutana wasn't aware of the fight. She wouldn't have any reason to watch it unless she knew he was fighting, which she probably didn't for this allegedly "impromptu" match that he wasn't scheduled to fight in.

As Jack watched, what previously looked like a canvas ceiling cover above the pit unfolded, and a tall, stout fence enclosure was lowered around the outside of the fight pit and him. After the perimeter was secured, another octagonal dome section draped down and was lowered onto the perimeter section and secured by several workers. Jack's escorts now backed further away and left through the door opening at the edge of the new pit enclosure. He thought about taking out the guards and making a run for it, but again, without a clandestine exit, he'd have every guard and mine employee looking for him within two mentus with probably some sort of price on his head for an incentive. He'd just have to deal with the situation, whatever it was going to be.

The spectators continued to chant and yell as Sha-aga bantered on about the match. From the far edge of the room, a pair of large double doors opened, and a wheeled cage emerged from the other side. The cage was covered with more canvas, but the crowd yelled even louder as the cage was rolled toward the far edge of the pit enclosure. The cage shook with a strange guttural wail that emanated from inside the canvas covering. Now a deep shrieking banshee scream came from under the covering followed again by the bizarre wailing and a loud huffing sound. The spectators wailed and screamed to match the sound from the covered cage. This seemed to infuriate whatever was under the canvas and caused it to scream and shake the entire cage and cover. *Maybe I should have fought my way out earlier and taken a chance against the entire mine security force,* thought Jack, *well, too late now.*

Sha-aga looked down at Jack from his announcer's stand and said to Jack something like "Sorry, friend, I did not know. Bosses. Good luck." Jack couldn't make it all out, but he kind of caught the message that Sha-aga didn't know anything about this fight set up either. *Well, that's somewhat encouraging,* Jack thought. At least the people down here hadn't helped set him up. Well, he had bigger problems to worry about at the moment.

The shrouded cage shook, and the terrifying sounds continued to emanate from under the covering. The attendants placed the cage against the pit enclosure door and secured it in place with some heavy-duty shackles of some sort. The animal, or whatever was inside, was getting madder and more irate by the moment. Sha-aga, the announcer, yelled above the noise of the caged creature, "Now, fight pit lovers, we bring you something you haven't seen before in the fight pit. We give you a real living druga!" As Sha-aga announced that, the shroud was pulled back from the cage. The noise stopped as the creature came into the light. The spectators went nearly silent except for a few murmurs and gasps at the creature's appearance. The druga looked around and took in its surrounding.

Jack could see a level of intelligence in it that looked more capable than the sounds of what was under the shroud only moment s ago. It wasn't as big as he'd anticipated, but it still stood a good six feet seven or eight. It was powerfully built with lean sinewy muscle over heavy bone. It was rangy and powerful looking at the same time. Its skin was the color of a ripe avocado with areas of dark tan and possibly a dark blue or gray outline between the striations of color. It also had long tendrils of thin blood-red-lined markings covering its body in meandering spiderweb-like directions. The lines met at central nexus points at various points on its body. The nexus points were behind the eyes, on the tops of the shoulders, and at the back of the wrists, all four of them—all four of the wrists, that is. There were also points above the knees and near its ankles.

These didn't look like what would be a natural placement location to Jack for some reason. For some reason, they almost appeared engineered, as if they provided some sort of sensory organ or, well, who knows? The creature, which looked very alien, continued to look around. It looked at Jack for an instant and then continued to take in its new surroundings. Maybe it had never been here before and was momentarily absorbed by its new surroundings. Its face was a muscular contorted triangle shape that reminded Jack vaguely of a praying mantis except its eyes were much smaller and were more slit-like about midway up its head. There were two elongated raised tubal bumps that must be a nose, as they ended in two fairly large holes that pulsed open and closed as the creature breathed. The mouth was a shallow upside-down U shape near the bottom of its head with a few scraggly-looking teeth protruding outside the taught lips.

The creature suddenly yawned, shook its head, and stretched its limbs for a few seconds. Jack had seen some other four-armed creature somewhat like this when he'd first entered the mine as well as the one on the orbital cargo vessel he had arrived on. Those two four-armed creatures had been different from each other, and this one was totally different. The one that had been a mine worker was much smaller and docile looking. He wondered if that was one of the aliens that this large creature had been hybridized from.

Looking at it closely, Jack could see a thin sheen of what appeared to be short, fine silky hair over much of it body. The color of the hair matched its skin coloring except where the red blood lines were and where the hair was in two lighter patches on its sides. It was wearing some primitive-looking work pants that were short and well-worn along with sandals and an open, heavy sleeveless shirt that looked something like a vest. Looking at its head, Jack saw that it wore a translator collar that appeared to be adhered directly to its skin.

The spectator crowd was near silent now as they watched it and waited to see what it would do. It seemed to have settled down considerably now that it was no longer hidden under the cage shroud. The attendants pulled a chain, and a door slid open between the creature cage and the pit cage that Jack was in. Jack had no idea what its fight capabilities were, but he'd have to guess that it was mostly pure brute force and little if any skill level. From its expression and actions, it did possess a certain level of intelligence and must be somewhat intelligent if it was genetically engineered to work in the mine. But then again, that experiment supposedly hadn't worked out too well.

Jack now thought the real problem is, how do you fight a four-armed opponent? Maybe it would be like fighting two opponents but from the same location. The difference would be that two separate opponents weren't neurologically connected, so their coordination wasn't perfectly timed. Well, he'd find out shortly. He was trying to analyze the creature's behavior. So far, the only aggression it had shown was when it was shrouded in the cage. Right now, it seemed more interested in taking in its surroundings.

The crowd was starting to make some noise and throw some taunts at it. Jack knew one thing, though, and it was that he was going to stay out of its grip and try to wear it down somehow and wait for some very strategic hits if he was going to have a chance against it. Somehow, looking at it, it didn't look like it would be short on stamina. "Junot . . . bet!" Jack yelled as loud as he could in case his friend was too mesmerized by this spectacle to remember to wager.

The creature made a grunt and a growl and shook its head. It spun around and moved across its smaller cage. Then it did it again and moved toward the door but stopped. It grunted again and swatted at its head and jumped back to the other side of its cage. Now Jack knew what they were doing. The creature's translator must have the same or similar functions that Junot had discovered in their own.

The translator must have some sort or electrical or sonic punishment system in it that the mine bosses or the GTA could use for citizen control. The creature was getting more agitated as it appeared to be tormented several more times. By the sixth or seventh time, it was thoroughly unhappy, and it dove through the cage door into the pit arena. It stopped on the far side and looked around seemingly relieved that the torture had stopped. The attendants closed the cage door, and the crowd let out a decent cheer. Jack thought, *Maybe these druga creatures weren't inherently aggressive unless they were provoked or unless something sets them off.*

The druga looked around again. It looked at Jack but didn't seem overconcerned about his presence. Suddenly, the creature let out loud scream and a long mournful wail while it grabbed its head with its top hands and the cage wire with its slightly longer lower hands. Jack didn't like what they were doing to it, but he was in no position to protest.

The creature stopped its wailing and looked around. Then it suddenly jumped and flung its arms all around itself in the air and against the cage. It was really starting to look angry and desperate. Again, it jumped and screamed and swatted and flailed. Then it gazed off into space for a mentu as if it were listening to something. When it recovered, it looked at Jack in a not very friendly manner. "Hey, buddy, I didn't have anything to do with that, but I'd be happy to introduce you to the dirt bags that did," Jack said to it in as calm and soothing voice as he could. The druga turned away from him and looked around, possibly trying to figure out if there was a way out of the cage it was in. The druga grabbed its head again and let out a half roar, half scream. It was now seriously mad, and it didn't seem like it could take much more.

The creature looked at Jack and launched itself from the other side of the cage straight at him. Jack waited a half second for the timing then shot himself away from the creature's intended aim point at a forty-five-degree angle. Its speed was so great that Jack knew it couldn't change course as it rocketed toward him. The crowd went crazy and let out a huge cheer. The druga crashed into the side of the pit cage where Jack had been only second ago. Jack was now two-thirds of the way around the pit facing the creature and moving away. The screams of the crowd caused the druga to spin around and look at the source of the noise. It let out a huge scream of its own, and the crowd yelled and screamed back at it. The drugas grabbed its head again in obvious pain and spun around, snarling and screaming in agony. It saw Jack and charged again and fairly well flung itself at him from halfway across the cage. Jack went to the left again as the creature crashed on by him, this time reaching with all its arms in the direction that Jack had dodged it. Its fingers just barely grazed Jack's shoulder as he bolted away from its trajectory to the other side of the cage again.

It's already learning fast that I'm dodging its attack and where I'm going, thought Jack. With the crowd screaming, the angry creature launched itself at Jack again, but this time, it slowed itself somewhat in its attack. Jack caught the momentum change and switched tactics as the enraged druga hurled toward him. For just a split second, Jack feigned another dodge to the left then went forty-five right. The druga had anticipated another left dodge by Jack and had altered its charge in mid stride to try and intercept him. Coming up empty, it spun looking for its intended victim. Now it seemed to be more enraged, but now it was directed at Jack for outmaneuvering it. It snorted and shook its head in anger. It crouched down and screamed at Jack a loud, terrifying high-pitched roar.

"Yeah, I know what you're thinking," Jack said to it. It looked at him for a second as if trying to guess which way Jack might try to evade it. It started moving toward Jack without charging, trying to close the distance before it attacked. Jack tried moving to the side, but it just turned to follow him, which helped close the gap. Jack knew he was going to have to use everything he had to survive this situation. With four powerful arms, he didn't know how he would escape it if it ever got a hold of him.

It crept closer and started to crouch. It looked a little to each side of Jack as if trying to decide which way Jack might try to escape. It lunged at Jack, but before it could gather very much momentum, Jack lunged at it and met it with a full-force frontal defensive kick to the chest. He wanted to aim higher and try for a head shot, but as tall as it was, he was afraid if he lost his balance, he could end up on the floor and be in worse trouble. It wasn't worth the chance. The creature was stunned, as it hadn't expected to be attacked. It stumbled back about three steps as Jack moved off-line to its left side. Before the druga could fully recover and turn toward him, Jack moved in and hit it hard with a round kick just above the calf. The creature screamed and half turned, and Jack hit it with another hard round kick to its lower left arm just above the elbow. The druga screamed and clutched its lower left arm with its other lower arm. It spun toward Jack, but it half stumbled from the pain of its left leg. *Good, maybe I've slowed it down a bit,* thought Jack.

As soon as his second round kick had connected, Jack moved back and out of range. He didn't know if he'd inflicted any damage to the druga, but he didn't want to be anywhere close to the deadly trap of those four arms. The druga took a couple of faltering steps toward him then seemed to recover from the leg pain. *No serious damage,* thought Jack. He didn't bear the creature any ill; he just wanted to survive against it. He wished he could pull a rabbit out of a hat and come up with some miracle save for this situation; better yet, one of his katanas that were safely stored at the foundry would have been nice.

The druga came toward him again. It was swaying its head back and forth slightly and making guttural chanting like sounds. What was it doing? Was it trying to distract him? wondered Jack. That would be a higher thought-processing scenario than he would have guessed it capable of. *Never underestimate your opponent,* he thought. *Watch it, don't take your eyes off it,* he reminded himself. It seemed to be trying to lull him, even outsmart him at the tactical level.

It charged him and lunged for him with its upper arms, and Jack moved left as fast as he could. The druga swung with its right hand and got a half-decent grip on Jack's right arm, but Jack was just barely able to twist completely around, and it lost its grasp. It was too close now, and it took a quick lunge at him, while Jack was still backing away from the last evasive maneuver. The creature managed to grab Jack's left arm and pull him in where it then grabbed his other arm. The creature made a satisfied grunt as it pulled him closer. It had Jack's left arm with both of its right hands now and let go with it upper right arm and attempted to go for Jack's neck.

Jack was now so close to it that he brought his right knee up to its groin as hard as he could. He didn't know what it had for genitals or even if it was male of female, but he figured there had to be something of a tender nature there that would cause it to loosen its grip on him. Whatever he hit had the desired effect, although maybe not to the extent he'd hoped for. The druga grunted and stumbled and half released Jack but not enough that he could break away.

It seemed to recover almost instantly and pulled Jack toward it while screeching loudly in his face. It was mad and hurting now, and there was retribution in it eyes. As it pulled Jack roughly to it, Jack pulled toward it and helped accelerate the creature's pull. He lowered his head and connected a full-on head butt between the creature's upper jaw and nasal area. A good solid hit with a nice satisfying crunch caused the druga to release Jack with its upper arms and grab its face. Its lower hands still held him but not nearly as tightly as he was a few moments ago. The maddened and now bleeding druga recovered and went on the offensive.

It pulled back for a strike with its right fist. Jack pulled himself closer and popped a hard left knee into the druga in what would be a liver shot to a human. The first one just slightly stunned the druga, but two more connected with enough underlying organ tissue to cause the creature some more serious pain. The druga swung with its right arm, but Jack was in too close, and the druga was in such pain from the head butt that it couldn't get a good fix on where Jack was to hit him.

The creature was trying to position Jack so it could hit him with one set of hands while holding him with the other. It grabbed Jack by the shoulders then shifted its lower hands to his mid torso and swung at Jack's head. Jack arched backward as far and hard as he could, and both swings of the powerful arms missed. As soon as he felt the second swing pass and then recoil, he swung forward and hit the druga with a right straight to the throat as hard as he could. The druga hacked and coughed and grabbed its throat as it tried to recover from the throat strike. It was temporarily out of the fight even though it still held Jack firmly with its lower arms. Jacks hands were free, and he decided he had to get out of the creature's grasp before it killed him. He straightened the fingers of his right hand and jabbed at the creature's eyes three times as fast as he could.

He couldn't tell exactly how many times he'd connected, but it must have been enough because the druga dropped him as it reached for its eyes. Jack hit the ground and rolled away as far and as fast as he could then got to his feet and started to back to the far side of the pit. The druga appeared to be holding its upper right hand over its right eye while moving its head all around trying to find its opponent. It let out a low loud gruff as it swung around looking for Jack. It was extremely mad, and it wanted some payback on Jack. Jack tried to determine how badly it was hurt, but he couldn't tell for sure. Except for the eye, it seemed to be pretty much OK. It started working its way toward Jack but with greater caution and respect for its smaller opponent. It kept its upper right hand over its right eye. *Three arms and one eye, the odds are getting a little better in my favor,* Jack thought to himself.

* * * * *

The smaller, younger mine boss said to its superior, "What will we do if the Varaci continues to dominate the fight? The druga seems to be injured. What if the druga loses to the Varaci?"

"We will not allow the Varaci to win the fight," replied the senior mine boss.

"You are suggesting that we will use the punishment device in the Varaci's translator to allow the druga to win?" asked the junior mine boss.

"We will do what is necessary. We have too much at stake to allow a random outcome for this match," replied the main boss.

"But is that not forbidden against Galactic citizens without prior permission from the Governance Bureau?" inquired the junior boss again.

"The Varaci is a conscript, therefore we have prior permission for anytime that any convict or conscript causes a threat to the security of the mine operation. That is already established. Ruuntah, why do you persist on asking distracting questions regarding our position toward the Varaci? Do you have some concern as to the legality of our position with regard to this conscript?" replied the senior boss.

"No, I, not at all," replied the junior boss, "I am only curious about learning the correct ways of dealing with these criminals and how we should go about, uh, protecting our interests here in the mine," replied the junior boss Ruuntah.

"Ah, well, good, then. Pay attention and learn how we must deal with these low vermin that are in our charge," said the senior boss.

"Yes, of course," replied Ruuntah, "I will learn all I can from this situation. So now I know that we can use extraordinary measures against the conscripts and the convicts because they are already deemed a threat."

"We must use discretion. It is important that we only use those methods to protect the mine and our, um, interests related to the mine," replied the senior boss.

"Oh, that is very good to know, then," replied the junior boss again.

* * * * *

The druga closed toward Jack cautiously. "What is your name, druga? Do you speak, or are you some sort of simple drone?" Jack prodded the creature.

The druga stopped and looked at Jack for a few seconds. "I speak when so I wish" came a quiet guttural voice from the creature's mouth.

"Very good," said Jack. "I was afraid you could not understand or speak. Why do you fight me, druga?" asked Jack, trying to garner any information about his opponent that he could. He was quite surprised that it could speak based on what he'd heard about these hybrids from the others.

"Pain stop when I fight. More, better food when fight was promised," replied the druga. The druga added, "Why you come all here and fight a druga, me?" it asked.

"I am forced to fight too," said Jack. "I do not wish to."

The druga thought for a mentu as it circled toward Jack. "We do what our masters force us to. We must do this," replied the druga.

"Yes, I understand," replied Jack, "that is all we can do for now."

Trying to learn as much about his opponent as possible, Jack added, "What do gorroks and kruztwox say about fighting?"

The druga looked at him somewhat funny like it wasn't sure if Jack was asking a real question. Then it replied, "What question is this? Gorroks and kruztwox not say anything. They are animals, not talk. What you mean that?" The druga sounded somewhat more irate than it already was.

"I don't mean anything at all. I've never seen one of them or even a druga until today," replied Jack.

The druga snorted, and it somewhat sounded like a laugh. "And you are here to fight a druga and never have you seen one before." The druga snorted again somewhat like a laugh. "What you think of drugas now?" it said.

Jack replied, "I still don't know much about them except that I don't have any desire to fight one. That much I know."

"Too late now, must fight," said the druga.

"Yes," said Jack, "we must fight, but you still didn't tell me your name. You do have a name, I would guess?"

"Name of mine is Qrolqar," said the druga.

"OK," replied Jack, "at least I know who I'm fighting now."

"Yes, you fight Qrolqar, the druga. You may have luck with you today. I will not kill you, but you might be wishing so."

"OK, I'll take what I can get in that respect," replied Jack, "but don't count your chickens."

"Count chickens? What count chickens?" growled Qrolqar the druga.

The spectators were getting slightly restless in the short time that Jack had bantered with the druga—Qrolqar, the druga, now that it had a name. At least he's learned that the druga could speak, was intelligent, and probably had pretty good reasoning skills. This was a very dangerous creature by any standards, thought Jack. Time to press the fight. The druga then went into another spasm and grabbed its head then shook violently and came around seething with anger.

Someone else watching must have noticed the slight lull in the action and decided to move things along.

Just as Jack was thinking how nice it would be to wrap his hands around the neck of a few mine bosses and choke the life out of them, the druga screamed and launched itself at Jack. It dove headlong straight at Jack from halfway across the pit. Jack dove and rolled away at a forty-five-degree angle as fast as he could. He hoped the druga would pile itself up from the forthcoming dive crash and that he could launch a good kicking assault while it was down and hopefully keep it down, but the druga used its four arms to stop like a dog and whirl around and charge again. Jack had barely made it to his feet when the druga was on him again. Jack feigned right and then moved left. The druga was fast and turned back to attack him just as Jack threw a low round kick to the back of the creature's right calf. It was a little higher than he'd planned, so it didn't take the druga's leg out from under him, but it was a very painful strike with a lot of force. The creature screamed and tried to finish its turn toward Jack but stumbled slightly then tried to regain its footing.

The druga backed off a little and took a few moments to recover from the solid hit it had just taken. It came back at Jack slowly and closed to within about four feet before it attacked again. This time, it tried to use Jack's feigned move and made a quick left then stopped and made a right lunge toward Jack. Jack had it figured out but was about a quarter of a second behind the move and just managed to bob below the druga's double-armed strike. He almost got away unscathed, but the lower arm of the druga caught a glancing blow off of Jack's shoulder and barely grazed his lower jaw as he was maneuvering out of the way. He could feel the power of the druga in that glancing blow, and it nearly knocked him off his feet, but he kept upright and moving to stay away from the rampaging druga.

The fight must have been going on for what felt like fifteen or more mentus now, thought Jack. Apparently, there were no rounds in this match. It looked like a fight to the finish; last man, druga, Varaci, whatever, standing. He was starting to get a little winded, but the druga didn't seem to be losing any momentum at all. The druga now had it figured out that it had a much better chance of catching this Varaci creature if it could work its way in close before it attacked.

Jack decided he would have to go on the full offensive, since trying to wear the druga down didn't seem to be working. Jack moved fast toward the druga and feigned a right, a left, then attacked with a short left front kick to distract then followed with a double right round kick to the lower and upper arms followed by a quick withdrawal as the druga tried to retaliate and overrun him. Jack figured correctly that the druga wouldn't know how to defend that attack, and both of his kicks landed solidly above each of the left elbows. There wasn't any crippling damage, but both kicks were solid, and Jack hoped that this would cost the druga about a 20 percent loss of its arm usage in strength and speed, at least for a few mentus. Jack now had a weak side to work on, he hoped.

Qrolqar thought, *The Varaci creature is quite fast, and it hurts when it hits you with its feet and its hands.* It had never fought anything like this that was so effective with all its arms and legs, and it only had two arms. The druga was used to having a big advantage over any of its adversaries with its four arms, but this foot-fighting creature was different and dangerous. The druga didn't feel fear like other creatures, but it did feel concern. Perhaps he would be punished if he didn't perform well enough against this Varaci creature. Move up on it slowly then attack. Trick it and capture it that way. This seemed to be working the best so far. Watch out for its feet that can cause such hurt. Be careful now, this enemy is tricky itself. Closer now, closer.

Jack watched the druga move in on him. The druga attacked, and Jack faked a front kick and dropped to the ground just in front of the druga. Qrolqar hesitated for a split second as he thought the Varaci had attacked with his feet again but instead fell to the ground. Qrolqar couldn't believe this situation, and it took another half septu before he decided to attack again.

Never go to the ground in a fight unless you're forced to, Jack heard in his head from his years of training, but this was a unique situation. The druga had more upper body strength and options than Jack could safely deal with, but it also had no ground or foot-fighting skills that it had demonstrated. Jack hit the ground in front of the druga and let his momentum carry himself into the druga's legs. He plowed his shoulder into the druga's knee and grabbed the back of its foot and pulled toward himself at the same time. The druga tried to reach down for him, but the fulcrum lever pushed the druga over backward hard. Jack thought the druga looked top heavy with its four arms and muscular upper body. He had to find a way to get this thing off its feet. This was a little bit of a long shot, but it worked.

The druga crashed heavily to the hard ground, knocking the wind out of it and hitting its head at the same time. Jack was up and around to its head in a half second and got in two solid kicks to the head before the druga came out of its daze and rolled to attack him. As Jack tried to maneuver, he saw a warning flash in his HUD for a second that some sort of punishment or incapacitation signal had been sent. It distracted him for just a second.

The druga grabbed Jack's foot as he attempted to press one more kick to the downed opponent. It pulled Jack hard, and Jack went down but did a fair job of breaking his own fall. The druga grabbed Jack's left leg with both hands and started to pull him in. Jack was still out of reach of the druga's lower arms but not for long. He rolled to his left and brought first one then two more quick heel kicks to the druga's hands. It would either have to let go to try and catch Jack's kicks or take serious punishment on its hands and have to let go anyway. The druga let go, and Jack rolled out of range and up on his feet. The spectators were now yelling and screaming at levels they'd never hit before.

The druga was still fast. With four arms to push itself up, it was up and charging Jack almost instantly. The more Jack watched it, the more convinced he was that it wasn't great at maneuvering even though it was fast. As it came at him, he feigned right then left then back right again. The druga anticipated a feign and compensated for it by going to its right to head Jack off, but not the second feign in the first direction. Jack moved left and popped the druga on the side of the leg just below the knee with a fast solid side kick. This would have taken any human off their feet and left them on the ground at least temporarily if not permanently disabled. It almost had that effect on the druga but not quite.

Qrolqar, the druga, went down but not without twisting around fast enough to take a swing at Jack with both right arms. The upper fist missed Jack by a fraction of an inch, but the lower one caught him solidly in the ribs on his right side. This sent Jack sprawling, and he hit hard on the ground. Again, he did a fair job of breaking his fall, but the pain on his right rib cage was severe. He was down for a couple of seconds and could barely breathe before he could force his way back up. Fortunately, the druga was still down also, but it was trying to get to its feet but with some difficulty. Jack's side kick to the knee had done some viable damage, and the druga wasn't moving nearly as fast now.

* * * * *

"Now, now, hit the Varaci again with the sonic wave and keep it debilitated long enough for the druga to capture it," said the senior mine boss to Zshogoteh, the one that had the control panel for the translator.

"Yes, Yuramah," as he engaged the remote relay in the Varaci's translator that would trigger the sonic incapacitation signal that would temporarily disable the Varaci that was the source of all their financial troubles. All six of the mine bosses watched intently to see the reaction to the signal and to see how subtle it would be. "It should just lightly stun and mesmerize the Varan but not be too obvious to any of the nearby casual observers that something had happened to the victim of the signal," said the senior boss.

They all watched closely trying to see any changes or indications that something had happened. "We may not even be able to notice anything ourselves that is overt that affects the Varaci. He will be unresponsive for a short while, and this will allow the druga to take care of him once and for all," added the senior boss. "I had the guard promise the druga extra rations and that it would receive preferences if it did a good job and severely punished the arrogant Varaci," the senior mine boss added.

The druga got up and moved toward Jack with a definite hobble. Jack was up and started circling right to make the druga endure as much pain and lose as much of its concentration as possible. Jack saw the warning flash in his HUD. The bosses were trying to incapacitate him again. This time, he ignored the warning. The biggest problem now would be to ignore the pain in his ribs long enough to finish this fight. *God, how long had this been going on?* he thought, *twenty mentus or more it felt like.* It was impossible to tell, as time seemed to dilate in these circumstances. *Don't show your pain or injury to the druga or it might try to take advantage of it.* The druga tried to close in as much as possible like before, but Jack was outmaneuvering it now.

"Stand and fight me now, Varaci," said Qrolqar. "Where you are going now, Varaci?"

"Anywhere I want," replied Jack. The crowd was nearly silent now as they focused on the combatants.

"Why do you run? Let's finish fight," said the druga.

"Don't worry, we'll finish it soon enough," responded Jack.

The druga wasn't sure how to attack now. When it tried to trick the Varaci, it outtricked him each time. When he simply attacked it, then it outmaneuvered him. How should he attack this tricky creature? thought Qrolqar. He decided to just keep pressing toward the small tricky opponent until he got the right chance to catch it. Qrolqar pushed Jack toward the pit edge and bracketed each way as Jack made a slight move in the direction he might bolt.

Jack let the druga get closer and closer. The druga lunged, and Jack moved his leg for a front kick that the druga anticipated incorrectly. The druga tried to grab the kick, but it wasn't there. The kick was a feign that dropped the druga's hands, and Jack leapt in with a left right combo followed by a left hook and an incredibly fast right straight as he moved left when the druga's arms came back up to defend the left right punches. Three of the four punches landed solidly before the druga could even see them. They stunned him appreciably, and he stumbled back and tried to gather himself back to the present.

This infuriated the druga. He charged blindly at the Varaci and was screaming and swinging wildly as he charged. Jack ducked right and down as the furious Qrolqar came swinging and screaming past him. He sidestepped as the angry druga flew past him, and as the druga tried to turn to follow his movement, Jack leapt high and came down with a high-low sweeping round kick that landed squarely on the druga's neck with a terrific *slwack*. The druga grunted loudly and grabbed his neck with all four of its hands as he crashed to his knees and just barely caught himself from going over and down. Still, he didn't go down and managed to get back to his feet.

Jack had jumped away and spun with his momentum to keep from losing his balance and put some distance between him and the druga. He'd been lucky so far and had managed to keep the murderous creature from grabbing him again where its shear strength and multiple arms would overwhelm him. The druga still wasn't out of the fight yet. It came again, although somewhat worse for wear. Its anger was palpable, and it had murder in its eyes. It pushed toward him again and kept pushing him toward the fence. Jack decided no feign this time and hoped that the druga would think it was a feign and go the other way trying to stop him. The combination of feigns was now totally random, so Jack hoped no feign would be a feign. The druga was too beat and tired, though, to think it through and just lunged at Jack when he moved, catching him by the waist and pulling him in. The crowd was now screaming and jumping completely out of its collective mind.

As the druga yanked him in, Jack pulled himself in and tried to drive his elbow into the head of the druga. But the upper right arm of the druga caught his elbow and pinned it down to his chest. The druga's two left arms were already working at pinning his other arm, and the druga's lower right arm was scrambling for his left leg. Jack knew he didn't have much time and he couldn't match strength against this creature with four strong arms.

Jack arched himself backward as far as he could in the druga's grasp. It was just enough to jam his right knee on the druga's chest and push. It gave him just enough extra leverage and space to get his right leg up for a side knee strike to the druga's face, maybe. Jack strained with all his remaining strength to get more space, but the druga had him tight and was pulling him in. Jack didn't have the space or time for the face strike but just enough, barely enough, space for a short head butt at the druga's open throat. It wasn't hard, but it was hard enough. The druga gurgled and gasped and let Jack just loose enough that he now had about double the space. It still wasn't a lot, but it was enough to deliver a decent throat strike with his now free left hand.

The druga let go with it upper right hand but still held him with the other, just barely. The same space was now almost totally open, so Jack pushed back and slightly free then let go with a close-in knife edge kick to the druga's neck. The heel of his foot landed squarely on the druga's throat with a sickening thud. The druga involuntarily lurched, gagged, and dropped Jack as it grabbed its throat. It crashed to the ground and was flailing and gasping for air. Guttural grunting noise escaped from its mouth as it continued to flail and writhe. Jack was up on his feet moving in to attack while the druga was still down. He moved around toward its head so he could add some more head shots if he needed to. The druga's whole body was spasming and lurching up and down and side to side. He wanted to head kick it and finish it off, but its wild gyrations were starting to slow. In another ten septus, it was mostly just lying there twitching and trying to breathe still clutching its throat.

Jack approached cautiously in case it was doing a little faking of its own, but he could tell from the rasping breathing that its trachea, or whatever similar passage it has, was crushed. It was still breathing but not enough to sustain itself with enough oxygen to function. He had no doubt from the throat kicks he delivered and the rasping sounds it was making that it would be staying down. The din from the spectators started low then rose to a full screaming roar. The Varaci had defeated the druga. This had never happened before, and the crowd was crazy. The guards and attendants weren't too keen on approaching or entering the pit cage, but the fight announcer Sha-aga was certain the druga was finished. He'd seen and called enough fights to know when a contestant was finished. Sha-aga entered the cage and briefly checked the druga then grabbed Jack's arms and raised them in victory.

"We have a victor. The victor of the match is the Varan, the Varaci Ja-ak!" yelled Sha-aga. The crowd roared even more. Few in the crowd expected the Varaci to survive let alone win. They were stunned yet utterly electrified by the outcome even though most had lost a fair amount of credits on the match. Somehow, in some way, it gave legitimacy to their own plight against the corrupt mine operation and its disreputable bosses. They, the crowd collectively, had gotten the upper hand against the disreputable bosses and the notorious system they were oppressed by. What a new and amazing feeling of power and even freedom it gave them. Even if it was for just a few mentus and they didn't fully comprehend it, they now felt the power, the power of knowing that they weren't totally subservient to the supremacy and whims of the rotten system that ran the mine and penal system that enslaved so many of them unjustly. It was a euphoric feeling, a feeling that many of them had not experienced in a long time or maybe never had.

For some reason, the fight pit was now no longer just a form of entertainment; it somehow felt like it held some sort of symbolism. They didn't know what it was, but somehow, something had changed, and it was something good. It was some sort of a premonition, maybe a feeling of their future. There was a feeling of, of what, hope? This was something new that they as a whole didn't recognize or know exactly what it was. It felt real and palpable, and it somehow welled up in them from a place they'd never known. Something had happened right here in this sinister little fight pit, and they didn't quite comprehend what it was or how to quantify it. But it was there and it was real, and nothing or no one would ever be able to change it or stop it or put it back in a bottle or wherever it had come from.

* * * * *

"Why did you not engage the sonic waves on the Varaci when I ordered you to!" screamed the chief mine boss to the subordinate one at the control console.

"I did, I did exactly as you ordered, Yuramah," said the junior boss Zshogoteh at the console. "It must not have worked or the signal did not go through or something. I did engage the sonic signal just as you ordered," said Zshogoteh in a fearful voice.

"You must be a fool, and you probably screwed it up or hit the wrong command," railed Yuramah.

"No, see here, it shows the command was engaged here on the console," whined Zshogoteh. "Something went wrong. It didn't work. Maybe it won't work that far down in the fight pit."

Yuramah steamed. "Nonsense, the punishment signal worked on the gorroks to make it fight. Do you all have any idea how much this has cost us? Well, do you?" They all cowered under his wrath.

"What will we do?" asked one of the midlevel bosses named Shheenu.

* * * * *

The spectators were wild and ecstatic like they'd never been before. The attendants came in and examined the druga they were required to look after. It was still breathing, but that was about it. They opened the pit cage and, the fight spectators rushed in and hoisted the victor to their shoulders. They proceeded to parade Jack through the corridors and all through the conzone. This had been the biggest fight they'd ever held, and none had missed it either in person or in the common area on the vido displays or anywhere else in the mine complex. Junot and Cherga were in the crowd, and when they could get close enough, they yelled up that they were both so glad that Jack had survived and won. No one could believe it, and all the mine cons were euphoric with the victory, a victory that was an awakening that had somehow given them a new sense of pride about their existence as cons consigned in a corrupt penal system.

The celebration went on for several horuns until the miners were all exhausted. Jack begged out after an horun with Junot and Cherga when he truthfully complained that his injuries from the fight were taking their toll and he needed to get a hot shower and some food. Cherga and Junot helped him through both.

He decided he probably had one or more slightly cracked ribs as well as a fair collection of other scrapes and contusions. "I think I need something to wrap my rib cage with. Do you suppose there is some sort of medical office or clinic here at the mine that could maybe wrap me up a little?" asked Jack to Junot and Cherga when they'd made it back to the berthing area.

"I'll see what I can find here," said Cherga. "There is a small well-being office at the surface from what I've heard, but I don't think they pay much attention to us conzone types. I've never heard of them seeing anyone down here, and I don't know how we would get you up there to be seen."

"Somehow, that doesn't surprise me," replied Jack as he winced from the pain.

They were able to come up with a long piece of cloth from another con that was nearby, and they got Jack wrapped up well enough that the pain became more tolerable. "Check safe mode on your translator," said Jack.

"Safe, yes," Cherga and Junot both replied.

"You know this doesn't bode well here tonight. The way they came and forced Junot and I into the fight pit complex and made me fight the druga," said Jack, "I'm sure they are trying to put me down one way or the other, and they have to be seriously pissed by my win tonight. What do you two think?"

"I think so too," said Junot. "I'm sure they weren't happy with you before this match, and now they are even more unhappy."

"Yes, I would agree," said Cherga, "but what are you thinking? What are you going to do?"

"Well, this is what it comes down to," replied Jack. "One way or the other, they have to take me out. They have got to be desperate at this point to try and get some of their credits back. By the way, Junot, did you remember to bet like I asked you to before the match? I almost forgot to ask with all this other excitement."

"Uh, um, I, uh," stammered Junot.

"You forgot to bet?" asked Jack, staring at him expectantly.

"No, no, I remembered to bet, and I even told Cherga to bet," replied Junot. "Well, I, um, I, um . . ."

"What, then?" said Jack.

Junot replied, "Well, I, uh, um, I was worried that you, uh, wouldn't, uh, maybe do so well, so I, uh, I only bet half your credits on the match."

"Only half?" asked Jack.

"Um, yes, only half," replied Junot.

"OK, then, that's OK," said Jack. "I wish you would have bet them all like I asked, and here's why. This is an all-or-nothing game I—or we, actually, are playing against these corrupt mine bosses. If I had lost and been killed, then they would have claimed my winnings, although it may have taken them a while to get them from you and probably Zshutana, who is also holding some of my winnings. Either way, it doesn't make any sense to make it easier for them to get any portion of any of our winnings."

"I'm really sorry, Jack. I should have done like you asked. I just wasn't thinking, and I was terrified about the druga. I was just trying to play it a little bit safe just, well, in case, you know. But, Jack, we still won a lot. I'm actually rich, really rich now. I have 1.9 million credits, and Cherga has six hundred thousand, so we still did really good. Who would have ever thought we'd get rich by going to the mines as a convict or conscript?" Junot added enthusiastically.

"That's true, Junot, and I'm really happy about that part for everyone involved. I just hope the thieving mine bosses don't try to figure out a way to steal it back from us. They will first have to figure out it's us that have done the bulk of the winning, but you never know what those cretins will try to pull. How about you, Cherga? What did you bet?" asked Jack.

"Well, I, uh, too bet half when Junot said that was what he was going to do. It sounded as if it made good logic at the time."

"OK, I understand, and it kind of did," said Jack. "It's one of those looks-good-on-paper situations until you actually think it through. Hell, the mine bosses probably wouldn't have had enough credits left to cover that size of a bet anyway. Maybe you guys actually saved my bacon by doing that. We may never know."

"What is ba-conah?" asked Junot.

"Just another one of my sayings," replied Jack, "and bacon is a really good breakfast meat. Something they unfortunately don't serve in the rations hall." He laughed. "So anyway, how's it looking on the translator mods, Junot? I know I just asked you a little while ago, but time may be getting critical," said Jack. "The bosses are seriously unhappy and will want to do something to me, maybe outright kill me if they think they can get a sizeable portion of their losses back that way. I'm going to have to do something, and I'll need as much of your super tech mods as I can get to help me out. I'll go without if I have to, but the reader mod and the decoys would be a huge help."

"You will go?" asked Cherga. "What do you mean you will go?"

Jack replied, "Look, they are trying to kill me, and eventually, they will succeed. They have the time, resources, and they'll make the opportunity. I'm going to have to bail on this situation and figure out how to get along on my own somewhere else. I don't see any other way around it."

"I would agree with all you say," said Cherga, "but I do not see how you could ever accomplish this. I have never heard of anyone escaping the conzone or any other penal system. How would that be possible? I am not sure that I've ever heard of anyone even trying," he added.

"Maybe that's my ticket out, then," replied Jack. "They may not expect anyone to try, and they may not even have much in the way of countermeasures in place to stop someone. Maybe they just aren't equipped to handle that situation if no one bothers to try. But think about this. We now have the ability to change or disguise our identity. That was their sole means of controlling us as far as we know. With the wand, we can read anyone else's ID, and maybe with a comm capability, we can communicate over an encrypted network, and with the decoys, we can lead anyone astray that is trying to hunt us, as in this case me."

"I don't know, I just don't know," replied Junot, "it just sounds very dangerous. What will you do if you get caught?"

"Well, I'll do my best not to get caught, and if I do, at least I'll have been free for a little while. One thing for sure is they aren't ever going to let me leave here alive, so if you think about it, it's the only choice I have unless I want to live and die here as a slave."

"What about us?" asked Cherga. "What do you think will happen if you escape and they know we are friends with you?"

"I'm not sure," replied Jack. "They may try and take your credits or use some sort of torture to see if you know where I went. I don't know how they operate, so I can't really say specifically. On the other hand, they may not do anything. They may not think you know or had anything to do with it. The only thing I can say is just go about your everyday business, and if they ask you, just deny, deny, deny. But here is my promise to you both and to Zshutana. If I make it out and have the ability, I will do everything in my power to come back here and set things right. That may mean getting you all out of here somehow or burning this operation to the ground if I have to, but I will do anything and everything to make that happen, of that I promise you."

Cherga replied, "Well, I have seen you do many things that I would not have dreamed of. You seem to think of things that none of us has thought about. Your word is good enough for me. You may not succeed, and I somehow don't see any way that you could, but I know that you will do whatever you can to help our cause. Certainly, that is good enough for me."

"Well, thanks for the vote of confidence at least on the honor system part," said Jack. "I still have a few of those tricks up my sleeve that I told you about, and I've been planning this for quite a while. I won't give you any details that you don't need to know. If you're questioned or worse by the mine bosses, you can't tell what you don't know. How about you, Junot? How do you feel about this whole plan?" asked Jack.

"Yes, OK. I don't like it, but I know what you are saying about the mine bosses, and them trying to kill you is true. Anyone could see that now. You have to do what you can to get out of here. It scares me to think of them hunting you like the geminute parasites. What if they catch you?"

"Like I said before," replied Jack, "I'll do my best not to get caught, and if they do and try to kill me, then I'll take as many of them with me as I can, and I guarantee that will be quite a few."

"OK," replied Junot, "I can't even fathom that much, that much, what do you call it, braveness—is that a word? But then I can't imagine going into the pit against a druga either."

"It's nothing," said Jack, "not courage or bravery or anything. It's just doing something, anything when you don't have another choice. You just go. You just do it. You just go and do everything in your ability to stack the odds in your favor and then you go. That's all there is to it."

"OK, then," said Junot, "but I'm still glad it's you and not me. Well, also, I think I figured out the reader part of the wand. I can't duplicate the circuitry for it or replicate it in any way with what I have here, but its small, and I can pull it out of the wand and incorporate it in your translator. It's just a matter of routing power to it and then feeding the output side to your translator, and the desired translator commands back to the reader," he said to Jack. "I'd like to be able to add it to everyone's, but I don't have any of the types of chips with receivers in them that they use to make the reader. The input and controls are pretty simple. I'll add that to your translator as soon as we can get away to do it. The decoys are different, though, much easier in that all I have to do is take a standard blank storage chip and couple it to an also standard maintenance telemetry transmit chip, and you'll have yourself a decoy. You'll program a transponder ID into it simply by using the modified programming control functions in your own translator. You can program yours or anyone else's ID that you've read into a decoy chip, and then there will be a false transponder ID of that person showing their position. The power seed is a very small one, but it should last a good three to four weneks."

"That sounds good," said Jack. "What if, what if . . . on the decoys, I didn't want it to last that long? What if I only wanted it to last, say, ten or twenty mentus for some reason?"

"Well, that would be easy," said Junot. "I would just add a programmable timer to the power circuit so that it would turn off in the amount of time you wanted it to."

"That would be great," said Jack. "Add a timer to them if you can. If they switch off after a while without being found, then they won't know that they are being tricked, and we can lead them on a wild goose chase—and, yes, there's that saying again—for as long as we can."

"OK, I'll do it, I'll get right to it," said Junot.

"Now, both of you tell me even more about the two big cities of Nishda," prodded Jack. He listened to what they had to tell him of the cities and the planet. He spent the next two days researching as much as he could about the planets infrastructure as well as the workings of the transportation system and how various ground vehicles worked. He added this information to the previous information he'd gathered from the neural core and other sources.

The second daiyus after Jack's druga fight, when he was back at the foundry, Za-arvak called him in and told him the mine bosses had just told him that they were canceling Jack's authorization to work at the foundry for "unspecified security reasons." Za-arvak was livid and was going to go over their heads to get Jack reinstated, but he said it could take several weneks or maybe even a moondat or more to get him reinstated. "Our foundry operation has much greater precedence over their mine operation," said Za-arvak, "but I may have to go all the way to the Galactic Trading Alliance mining headquarters to get what I want on this."

"That may be a problem," replied Jack, "since it appears that the goal of the bosses is to get rid of me, and I mean in a permanent way. They are not happy with my continuous winning streak. They have tried to rig the odds and fights against me on every fight."

"Yes, that has become apparent by the last two matches," said Za-arvak, "and the last thing I want is for my star manager to get injured or killed because of these greedy mine bosses and their grievous plans. Unfortunately, there is nothing I can do to protect you at this point until I get approval from higher authority to put an end to these absurdities."

"Well, I certainly appreciate your intervention on my behalf," said Jack.

"Well, I wish there was more that I could do," replied Za-arvak, "but at the moment, I can do nothing and I literally have no recourse on your behalf."

"That's OK, I still appreciate it," said Jack. "Just be careful yourself that you're not interrupting their plans to the point that they might take some action against you yourself."

"Why, they wouldn't dare," groused Za-arvak angrily. "Who do these rotten mine boss cretins think they are?"

"Just be careful anyway," replied Jack. "They are getting desperate, and I wouldn't put anything past them. Check your six and make sure they aren't trying to pull something on you."

"Check my six?" asked Za-arvak.

"That means watch your back or keep an eye on what they may be trying to pull."

"Oh, well, OK, yes, I will," replied Za-arvak.

The next two daiyus, Jack spent keeping a low profile. The mine bosses had revoked his authorization outside the conzone to the foundry, yet he hadn't been assigned to any work assignment or back to his zibur drill rig or anything. He knew they were tracking him and watching him as much as possible within the mine and conzone. He went from seriously mad to completely bored in half a daiyu. He kept his translator off of safe mode for the most part so that they wouldn't realize he could go off-line. He tried to act as normal as possible. The next evening when Junot got off of his work shift, he checked in with Jack.

"Go safe, Jack," he signaled. "I got it, I got it," whispered Junot in case the bosses had listening devices planted anywhere in the conzone.

"Got what?" Jack said, thinking he knew at least part of the answer.

"The decoys, I got the decoys working. Here, I have one for you and me. We can turn them on, and we will appear to stay right here in the berthing room, and we can turn off our own transponder and we can leave and go anywhere we want."

"That's great, Junot," replied Jack, "that's absolutely great. Are you sure it works? Have you been able to test it?"

"Yes, yes," said Junot, "I checked it with the wand, and it reads perfectly, and then with my transponder off, it can't see me or anything. As long as we are not spotted visually, we are free to roam where we want. We need to go to the maintenance depot, and I can modify your translator with the wand reader circuitry. Then you'll know everyone you're near and can copy anyone's ID and put it into a decoy if you want."

"Perfect, absolutely perfect, my genius friend," replied Jack as they headed out the door while leaving their fake electronic personas behind in the berthing area.

In the maintenance depot, Junot took Jack's translator and started working on the mod to add the wand reader and install the new software in it. Junot made a few comments about what he was doing but knew Jack couldn't understand him without his translator on, so he kept it to a minimum. When he was done, he put the translator back on Jack and said, "There you go, Jack. You can now read anyone's transponder ID simply by selecting the small icon that looks like an eye and then placing the red circle over that person and selecting the read transponder button below the eye icon. It'll show you their transponder ID number, name, planet of origin, sex, legal status if other than normal, job title, and any government status they might hold. I'd tell you to try it on me, but since my transponder is off right now, it won't work."

"That's amazing," replied Jack. "All that is extremely helpful information right at a glance. That doesn't give the average guy much of a chance against anyone with a reader wand or similar technology. I guess that may be why no one tries to escape this mine operation. If anyone can ID you instantly just by wanding you or maybe by using other scanning methods, then you wouldn't have any chance at all of evading the goons from the government."

"No, no chance at all," responded Junot. "Now that we have that mod completed, let's get some of the decoys made up for you. I was able to scrounge up eleven blank chip disks plus the two we left in the berthing room. Maybe I can find some more later, but that's all I could find for now," said Junot.

"A few more might be helpful, but I'll take what I can get right now," replied Jack.

Junot added, "They are normally used as replacement chips for monitoring equipment for sending telemetry from different types of machinery and other monitoring devices. They can be programmed to transmit just about anything because they are used in a variety of devices. Like right now, we are sending fake transponder IDs, so they think we are in the berthing room. This is kind of fun in a lot of ways."

"Yes," said Jack, "unless we get caught. I'm sure the mine bosses and the Alliance wouldn't appreciate us tampering with their secret ID and security system. I'm sure there's one or more laws that we are breaking somewhere in this operation, which could add yenets or a dakun to our sentences."

"What else can we work on while I'm here?" asked Jack. "As long as I haven't been assigned any job and I can't get back to the foundry 'officially,' I might as well be doing something constructive."

Junot replied, "OK, well, uh, let me open the comm program I've been working on. I've got it pretty well figured out as far as how to access the mine comm system from just about any location in the mine and maybe even on the planet. I have that great encryption program like I used before, but I can't figure out how to make it jump around to different channels because it's different from the standard system. Without a master code algorithm that we can establish at each end user site, I don't know how to make it shift to a channel that the receiver will be expecting. Basically, the transmission just gets lost because the receiver and the sender don't know where to go."

Jack replied, "Hmmm, well, let me think about that for a little while and see if I can remember how the tech wienies set that up. That isn't my area of expertise, but I have read a little bit about it. I think random frequency hopping is one of the hardest encryption methods to break and to generate."

Jack pondered how to address this but couldn't think of or remember anything that could generate a random frequency and match or capture it without knowing the algorithm in advance. "I don't think what you're trying to do is possible, Junot. The sender and receiver have to have a known set of frequency coordinates to go to, in order to match both parties. I think the only thing you can do is set up a known, as in preset, but randomly generated set of synchronized hopping frequencies. What you can do is make a different randomly generated set for each daiyus or wenek in advance and use the set that's been set for that daiyus. That way, even if they accidently find us on one set of frequencies on a given daiyus, it would only be for that daiyus. I doubt that they will ever find us, but I'm sure we'd be safe if they did by the next daiyus."

"OK, then, I guess I was trying to make something happen that isn't really possible," said Junot. "I can do what you just said, though, and make up a schedule of preprogrammed random hops."

"OK, do that first and give them to me for at least . . . let's say, at least a yenet out. Even if you don't have the system up and running and if I have to vanish, I'll know where you'll be at any given time in the future when you do get your program running because I will already be synced to your frequencies in advance."

"I'll do that right now," replied Junot. "It should only take a little while. We would only be hopping around 60 frequencies and maybe 120 subfrequencies. We would only hop maybe ten or twelve in any given horun, but we can pic those out for a yenet in advance in a random order. Thanks, Jack. I was getting kind of lost in all the different ways that didn't seem to work as far as trying to make the random part work without a predetermined key. This will be a lot easier, and I'll have it done in a short while." Junot set to work and came up with the random frequency hopping schedule for the next yenet and plugged them into both his and Jack's translators.

"This is great Junot," said Jack. "Even if I have to make my great escape in the next daiyus or two, I will know where to find you in the future. I don't want to have to leave you guys, but I don't see any alternative at this point. I need some breathing room on the outside to be able to fight these tyrants, and the only way I'm going to be able to do that is to make my move and blow this pop stand."

"Pop stand? What's a pop stand?" asked Junot. "Oh, and also what's a tech weenie?"

Jack laughed out loud. "Just more sayings as usual. Pop stand is a euphemism for a crappy situation, and, uh, tech weenie means guys that are really smart with electronics and computers and programming and those sorts of things."

"You mean like me?" asked Junot.

"Yes, very much like you, Junot. You are very much a tech weenie, a very, very good one too. I don't think I've ever met a smarter one than you."

Junot smiled and replied, "Oh, OK, thanks, Jack. I'm a good tech weenie, then, and I'm glad I've been able to help you out with all this really interesting stuff."

"Me too, yes, me too," replied Jack. "I wouldn't be able to do any of what I'm doing without you. Thanks for all your great help."

"I'm glad I can help, and I'm glad I'm doing something I'm good at. I like trying to figure out all this stuff. I think that's about all I can do for today, though. I'll get back on it tomorrow," said Junot.

* * * * *

"What is the Varaci doing?" asked the senior mine boss.

"Nothing, just staying in the conzone berthing area in his assigned room. He has been there for the last two horuns. He has shown little activity today and has spoken little to the other cons," replied a junior boss that was monitoring the translator tracking system. "Surely there must be something more important for me to be doing than monitoring the whereabouts of this low vermin of a Varan conscript," complained the junior boss.

"Do as you are instructed," said the senior boss. "It is important for us to keep track of this conscript so that we will know where he is when we execute our final plan against him. We can't have him wandering off to some remote part of the mine when we wish to use him."

"Why not just throw him in a holding cell like any other conscript that might be causing trouble?" asked the junior boss. "Then we will know exactly where he is at all times and we won't have to waste—I mean, spend all this time monitoring him."

"Because," growled the senior boss, "that is what you're instructed to do, and he is too popular among the other cons. Locking him up would make it too apparent that we are planning something special for this troublemaker. We need to keep up the façade that he is just a trouble-causing, arrogant conscript that wants to fight anything he can to prove himself some sort of champion. If we locked him up, it might cause problems among the other cons if we are not careful. This entire operation must be run as a balancing act. We don't want a rebellion on our hands, as we would not have enough resources to stop a full-blown rebellion. Now do as you're told and monitor the Varan's location at all times. We've already put a stop to his wandering around outside the conzone and working for that softheaded scientist Za-arvak at the foundry. He'll probably try to go over our heads to get his worker back, but by then, it will be too late. Why the Alliance mine directorate gives the foundry precedence over our mine operation, I will never know."

* * * * *

Junot retrieved the two decoy chips in the berthing room and made sure that he and Jack then turned their translator transponders back on. "Well, that all seems to have worked exactly as advertised," said Jack. "At least there's no overt indication that they're on to us," replied Junot. He handed Jack the two decoys they'd used that daiyus. "Here are these two decoys to add to the others. I was able to get timer programs added onto the other eleven decoys, but these two don't have timers."

"That's OK," replied Jack. "I'm guessing that I'll only need the timers on maybe half of them, so I should have plenty, unless you happen to scrounge up a few more on your rounds."

"I'll keep looking," said Junot.

Jack spent the next two daiyus planning and researching as much as he could about the mine, the planet, and the cities. His resources were limited, but he managed to get to the maintenance depot with Junot again using the decoys as they had previously. They worked on the comm frequency hopping issue, and Jack did more research on the neural core access from the computers there.

"What is it you're looking for?" Junot asked him.

"Everything," replied Jack. "I'm trying to find out as much about the planet, the cities and the infrastructure, the monetary system as it's controlled by the Galactic Alliance, as well as all of the types of transportation available on the planet. The more I can educate myself about how everything works here, the better the chances are that I won't get tripped up by some simple, mundane, everydaiyus technical or cultural issue. Stranger in a strange land is the role I'm playing here. I need to become one of the natives."

"OK, I think I understand what you're saying. Although I'm not sure why you wouldn't mostly know all that stuff anyway," replied Junot.

"Well, you will someday when I explain all of it to you," said Jack. "In the meantime, just trust me that I need to learn as much about the systems and culture here as I can. Let's just say I'm a babe in the woods."

"Well, uh, OK, you're a baby in the forest, but I don't know why," said Junot, "but you sure do say a lot of strange things," he added.

The next daiyus, they were able to get back to the maintenance depot again and put together a rudimentary version of a secure encrypted comm system working through their translators. If they both turned on their comm link to the prearranged random frequency hopping schedule, they were able to communicate successfully. Junot hadn't yet figured out how to add a dialing or paging function to it. They didn't want to leave it on or open all the time for fear that someone might eventually catch on to their system and try to hack into it. Junot wasn't sure that it was secure enough yet, and they didn't want to risk being found out. "About all we can do at this point is, when I make a run for it, to check in at a predetermined time. Let's say 0700 and 1900, before your shift and after the night meal," said Jack.

"OK, that would be good for now until I figure out a way to make the system be able to page another translator," said Junot. He then continued. "I'm sure the bosses have some sort of calling or paging system, and I would bet that it uses their individual transponder code. They may have to register it to some type of discrete account for mine bosses or something, which is obviously something we don't have access to. I guess we'll just have to come up with something of our own. We would probably have to have a fake ID of some sort. Otherwise, they might be able to recognize our IDs on the comm net, especially if they set some sort of alert for our IDs. It may take me a few daiyus or maybe even a wenek to figure out."

"I'm sure you'll come up with something. You always do," said Jack.

Jack thought to himself and was quiet for a minute then said, "Junot, I wanted to try and call Zshutana on the mine landline system, but I'm not sure if her office or apartment comm links are secure. I wanted to let her know what I was planning, but I don't think that would be a good move about now. There's too much of a chance that they might be monitoring her comm link now that I'm such a hot commodity. If I can't figure out a way to contact her, I'd like you to try and contact her if you can get the secure comm link up and running or even pay her a lunch visit from the foundry now that I can't do that either. When I leave, I could try and stop there briefly and let her know, but that might be too dangerous too."

"All right, Jack, I'll try and do whatever I can to let her know. I may have a better chance than you. I'll do what I can."

"Thanks I appreciate it," said Jack.

They met with Cherga later and gave him a short rundown of what was going to transpire. "Yes, it seems you have little choice at this point, but you will need much luck and great caution."

"More like something on the scale of divine intervention," said Jack.

"Hmmm, yes, help from the Great Above would be the most beneficial, but I have yet to experience any of that in my own struggles. Perhaps he is too busy to spare me any time with my insignificant little matters. Perhaps some daiyus, you never know."

"Well, yes, you never know," replied Jack, "you just never know." *Funny,* thought Jack, *I've been here for months and never thought to ask anyone about their deities and what they believe, if anything. I'll have to remember to do some research on that when I get a chance. That would be a very interesting research subject. How many people have ever gotten to ask an alien or even many aliens from different worlds about their belief systems?*

The next daiyus, Jack stuck close to the common area and the general conzone habitation areas after they noticed a couple of guards wandering around in the areas that they normally didn't bother patrolling. *Better keep a presence here in case they are keeping an eye on me,* thought Jack. It wouldn't be good to disappear using a decoy when they are obviously making themselves known and doing some reconning themselves.

It was hard to move about or go unnoticed without someone congratulating him on last wenek's fight pit victory. They all seemed to have a greater reverence for him and an appreciation for his victory against the druga. It was different from any of his other fights; it was more like he had achieved somewhat of a pop culture status but maybe somewhat more serious. He wasn't sure what it was and couldn't really put a name to it. It was almost as if there was a feeling of expectation or anticipation or even, even, he wasn't sure; it just wasn't quite making sense to him.

Chapter 9: Fugitive

He was getting tired and bored of being restricted to the conzone and not having anything constructive to do other than hitting the gym, which he'd done gingerly every day with his ribs still hurting. He'd exhausted about everything he had access to or could think of to do as far as researching the alien planet or preparing for his escape. The biggest question now was when. He knew it had to be soon. He'd run various options through his head as far as when the best time to bolt would be.

He was trying to figure the best time, the best route, and the best way to avoid drawing any attention to himself so that he would have the most time to disappear before his absence was noticed. It was going to be a little dicey with his somewhat celebrity status and the bosses and their guards keeping a closer watch on him than usual. It would have been a lot easier if he could have left from the foundry from an early lunch and not have been counted late until the curfew time. Even then it might have been another full daiyus before they realized he was actually missing and gotten a full-blown posse after him. *Woulda, coulda, shoulda,* he said to himself.

He headed over to the gym and decided to try another light workout if he could manage it with his ribs still hurting. He was now convinced that they were just bruised and not broken. He'd promised Junot some more martial arts training when Junot got back from his shift at the foundry. He saw a couple of the gym regulars and exchanged a few pleasantries. He'd even had a few other miners causally approach him about doing some martial arts training like he was doing with Junot. This actually wasn't a half-bad idea, and he would have seriously considered it if he didn't have more urgent plans. He told the several inquirers that he would consider it after his injuries were healed and let them know shortly.

"Hi, Jack, you're already here and waiting," said Junot as he popped into the gym.

"Oh, hi, Junot. I ran out of other ways to entertain myself, so I came down to get in a workout before our lesson."

Junot replied, "OK, well, let's go to it. I'm all ready. The rations hall opens in an horun, and I'm hungry, so we can head over there when we're done if you want."

"Yeah, that sounds good," replied Jack, "well, not actually 'good,' but it'll have to do, I guess."

Junot laughed. "It is not quite as good as Zshutana's lunch specials I'd have to say," he added in a guarded whisper.

They both laughed hilariously when Jack added, "Yes, and the desserts are positively dismal by comparison."

Jack had them go through a warm-up routine then went over the basics that he had started previously with Junot. Jack led him through a fair beginner's lesson in Krav Maga demonstrating how to break chokeholds and deflect your opponent's punches and other combatives. It was fun teaching his friend some basics, but his heart wasn't fully in it today because his mind was preoccupied with the other aspects of the situation. "OK, that's enough for today," said Jack.

"Oh, but I was just getting going," complained Junot.

"Yes, I know," said Jack, "but my mind is kind of wandering away, and I'm getting really hungry too. Let's head over to the rations hall and get some of that dessertless cuisine they're so famous for. Let's stop by the berthing room for a minute and let me grab some stuff," Jack added.

In the berthing room, Jack grabbed his miner's jacket and the little secret stash of transponder decoys, which, except for a few other clothing articles, was about the extent of his personal belongings. He didn't really have a feeling or anything, but he just wanted to be prepared at all times in case he had to bug out. He knew it was getting down to the wire, and he didn't know what might be the trigger that would cause his escape plans to be put into motion. After the fine night meal at the rations hall, Jack decided to hit the showers early before the off-shift miners started filing in after whatever the evenings activities ended. Junot said he would go find Cherga and see what he was doing. "OK, I'll see you in a while," he said to Junot as he headed toward the shower room.

As Jack headed down the main corridor and into the showers, a figure stepped out from the back shower area then two others from behind him. Jack recognized one of them as one of the guards that he'd recently seen patrolling though the conzone where there weren't normally any guards. "Pretty strange place to be patrolling. Do you patrol here often?" he said to the guard in a sarcastic voice. The guard only looked at Jack without saying anything. Jack quickly reconned his situation and started to back out of the part of the room where the showers were located. As he glanced behind him, three more guards moved into the main room from the corridor and blocked his exit.

"OK, hit him with the stun wand, and we'll get the wrist binders on him. I don't want to have to deal with this druga killer without having him subdued. Then we'll take him to the fight pit as instructed," said the lead guard to the closest one next to him.

"So the druga from my last fight died?" Jack piped up, trying to gain some time and analyze his situation.

"No," replied the guard, "but it will be a long time mending and might not fight again, so it might as well be dead."

"And you're supposed to take me to the fight pit for what? Another match? Against who or what?" asked Jack.

The second guard with the wand raised the wand and pointed it at Jack. Jack hoped that Junot was right and that whatever personnel control capabilities the wand possessed wouldn't work because the receiver in his translator had been deactivated. The second guard made several gestures at Jack with the wand, but nothing happened except the warning that flashed in Jack's HUD.

"It's not working," said the guard with the wand. "Something is wrong with it."

"Xardof, use your wand!" the lead guard yelled at another guard with a wand. Jack made a grasping motion to his head and ears as the second guard aimed his wand at him as the warning flashed in his translator display. The security wand waved up and down, and the warning flashed in Jack's HUD. "There he goes. Now subdue him," barked the lead guard as Jack pretended to falter and collapse. Four of the guards made a move to either catch or attack Jack, he couldn't tell and it didn't matter.

As the first one closed in, Jack, half leaning over and pretending to be in anguish from the security wand, did a supremely fast-stepping side kick and caught the guard at the base of the chin. He heard the jaw snap and got a glimpse of the first attacker falling as he spun quickly and brought a hard rear elbow to the neck of the guard that had moved in to grab him from behind. His right elbow connected hard with the guard's neck, and the sudden impact caused the guard to scream and then pass out from the instantaneous extreme pain and shock to his main artery at the same time he hit the floor. The third and fourth guard backed off briefly, but the lead guard was screaming, "Take him down, take him down now!" As the two guards readied themselves to pounce, the last guard from the doorway rushed as fast as he could directly at Jack.

Jack sidestepped the overspeed attack of the guard, and there was enough distraction for a second that he launched himself at one of the guards that had been preparing to attack him. *Take the fight to the enemy, don't let them bring their fight to you,* Jack heard in his head from his old and wise instructor from many years ago. A snap side kick to the guard's knee brought him toppling down as Jack zipped by him and came straight on to the other of the pair of guards. He leapt straight at the guard and brought his right knee hard into the lower abdomen of the guard. The unprepared guard took a massive hit to his diaphragm and other internal organs. The guard let out a huge grunt of a yelp and dropped to the ground on both knees just as Jack caught him with a left knee to the side of the head. The previously overzealous guard that had tried to rush him had now spun around and launched himself into another attack. Out of the corner of his eye, Jack caught the lead guard moving toward him with something in his hands.

* * * * *

Junot came into the common area as a dozen or so of the cons bolted out of the room. He went over to where he saw Cherga getting up from a table with a couple of other miners. "Hi, Cherga, I was just wondering what your plans were for this evening," said Junot as he approached the table.

"Junot, there you are," said Cherga excitedly. "Where is Jack? Where is Jack? Do you know?"

"Well, yes," said Junot, "I just left him a few mentus ago by the berthing room. Hey, what's all the excitement about? Where's everyone going?" as they watched most of the rest of the miners in the room leave at a hurried pace.

"You just left him a few mentus ago, you say? We must go find him right now," said Cherga.

"Well, OK. He was just heading to the showers a little while ago, and I thought I'd come see if I could find you. What's going on here now?" said Junot.

Cherga replied, "They just made an announcement in the common area here that there was going to be a special exhibition fight tonight at the pit and that the Varan champion Ja-ak was going to be challenging the kruztwox, and it would likely be a fight to the death. Everyone got up to go to the fight pit nearly as fast as they could. They probably wanted a good seat, I would guess."

"What? That's crazy," said Junot. "I just, I just left Jack a few mentus ago, and he was going to the showers. There was nothing about the fight pit or a kruztwox or anything," said Junot shakily.

"Of course not," said Cherga, "they are trying to force him to fight again, this time against a kruztwox. Come on, we must go to the showers and find him before they can grab him. Be ready to fight with some of your new fighting skills that Jack has been teaching you."

"I, uh, I, all right, OK," said Junot, feeling like he was going to pass out or throw up.

"Come on, come on, we must go now," prodded Cherga as he headed toward the showers as fast as he could go.

Jack moved toward the overzealous guard and popped a short targeted round kick to the abdomen as the guard tried to grab him. The guard went down halfway, and Jack grabbed him and spun toward the lead guard with something in his hands. It looked like the security wand the other guard had been holding a few moments ago. The lead guard tried pointing it at Jack then gave up and held it like a club as he advanced on Jack. Jack held the partially incapacitated guard between the advancing guard and himself. As the lead guard tried to rush him while swinging the wand, Jack pushed the other guard toward his assailant. It didn't stop him, but it slowed the guard for a moment and messed up his timing when he tried to swing at Jack with the wand.

The guard swung and missed as Jack dodged the swing. As the lead guard pulled back and wound up for a another swing, Jack dove deep inside the arc of the swing and slammed the guard with his right forearm on the left shoulder, while he grabbed the guard's right arm behind the elbow with his left hand and pulled the lead guard into him. As he pulled the guard in, he hit the guard's groin and abdomen with two hard right knee strikes. The guard doubled over, and Jack brought his knee up to the guard's face and snapped a light knee to the guard's face, just enough to knock him out but not enough to kill him or do serious permanent damage.

The first guard that had taken a hit to the knee was trying to get up and trying to say something, possibly trying to call for backup on his translator or report to the mine bosses. "Sorry, guy, ain't happening," Jack said mostly to himself as he moved quickly and hit the guard on the side of the head with a quick round kick and put him down. Two more guards were trying to pull themselves up, and he dispatched them with another round kick and a snap kick to the side of the head.

Suddenly, Jack heard running coming toward him outside of the shower area. "Crap," he cursed and decided he'd have to try and put them down before he could run or they would just follow him and report his position. He half hid behind the sink array and was ready to attack when they came through the door. Suddenly, they burst into the room, and to his relief, it was Cherga followed immediately by Junot.

"Jack, Jack, are you all right?" Junot yelped as he was trying to catch his breath.

"What happened here?" said Cherga as he took a quick survey of the carnage of the guards on the floor that Jack had demolished.

"They were trying to take me down and immobilize me," replied Jack slightly out of breath yet still very pumped up on adrenalin. "One of them said they were going to take me to the fight pit when they got me wrist cuffed, but that didn't happen."

"Yes," said Cherga, "we just heard an announcement in the common area that there was going to be a special exhibition fight tonight at the pit and that the Varan champion Ja-ak was going to be challenging the kruztwox."

"Challenging a kruztwox? This proves they are completely deranged," replied Jack. "I guess that would be the next logical step in their plans, though. I guess if they wanted to take me out, that would be one good way to do it. They could get whatever winnings they could from the match plus any of my own banked winnings if I were to end up dead."

"Now what will you do?" asked Cherga. "They won't have anything good for you now that you've assaulted their guards, some of them quite severely perhaps from the looks of them."

"Come to the outside of the room here," said Jack, "I don't want any of them to possibly hear me. Junot, do you think you could take one of the decoy transponders to the mine entrance and plant it on some miner that is headed into the mine for his shift?"

"Yes, uh, yes, I suppose I could do that. What are you trying to do?" asked Junot.

"All right," said Jack, "it's time for me to make my move and get out of the mine. The mine bosses have made the timing decision for me. I want you to take a decoy with a timer and set it for twenty mentus just before you plant it on someone. They'll carry it into the mine where the signal will make it look like I'm running in that direction and trying to hide. After the twenty mentus, the timer will shut the transponder off, and they won't be able to find it and know that it's a decoy. They'll just keep looking for me down in the mine shafts for a while. If they find the decoy, they'll know that I have the ability to mislead them, and they'll start looking elsewhere for me. Those twenty mentus will buy me a good head start in the opposite direction while they concentrate all of their man—I mean, guard power down in the bowels of the mine."

"OK, OK, I can do that," said Junot.

"Then what are you going to do?" asked Cherga.

"Just escape for now, but I don't have time to explain it all," said Jack, "but I've got it pretty well worked out on how to get out of here. Here, take this decoy with a timer and head on out," Jack said to Junot. "Cherga, maybe you can hang around here when the guards start to show up and tell them you saw me heading toward the direction of the mine. Now it's time for me to hit the road before any more of these goons show up. Hey, thanks for all your help, guys. I'll be in touch with you somehow, sometime soon. I'm not sure how or where or when, but if I make it out of here, I'll do whatever I have to, to make this right," said Jack.

"OK, I guess, well, all I can, uh, say is good journey to you, Jack," said Junot as it seemed as if he was about to cry.

"Yes, we will be all right here," said Cherga. "Let the Great Above watch over you like he should. You will have a dangerous but in the end safe journey, I can sense this. You should go now, and, Junot, you go plant the decoy. We will do our part to make your escape from this dismal place go well. We will see you sometime soon, our Varaci friend." Cherga clasped Jack's wrist and arm, and Junot clasped them both. Then he turned and sprinted off in the direction of the mine tunnels.

Jack said, "See you both soon," as he headed the opposite direction toward the berthing area and then the conzone exit he normally used when going to the foundry. He stopped at the berthing area and grabbed his miner's jacket and the few other clothing items he had and bundled them securely in a cloth bag.

Jack put his miner's jacket on and pulled the hood up over his head and slouched to try and make himself look shorter and less humanlike. He headed cautiously toward the conzone exit to the foundry, trying to look as much like a tired off-duty contract miner as possible. Nearing the exit, he heard a commotion up ahead that sounded like miners being harassed or questioned. He ducked down a side corridor before he came to the checkpoint and listened and waited.

From what he could tell without getting too close, there was apparently enough of a general alarm in place that they were doing a cursory check of anyone near an exit point. Since anyone attempting to exit would have to be authorized, he guessed it might just be an ID check. He had already turned off his transponder ID on his translator so that he couldn't be automatically tracked, but he hadn't uploaded a new fake ID. None of the conzone miner's ID's that he passed would work as a bootlegged ID because they wouldn't be allowed past the checkpoint. He needed a management or guard ID or maybe a contract worker that had normal access outside the conzone; otherwise, he'd just be starting another battle.

* * * * *

Junot got to the mine entrance and saw a couple of small groups heading into the mining area. He had switched the decoy on and off several times on the way down. He wanted to leave a little bit of a trail in case they were tracking Jack's ID, but he didn't want to get caught with the fake transponder ID on him. He got up close to the last group of miners heading into their shifts. He could easily tell what they did by the clothing they wore. The zibur drivers deep in the long mine shafts would be wearing heavier clothing or coats because it would be colder and damp deep in the shafts.

He saw a likely candidate and moved in closer. He set the timer for twenty mentus and managed to get the timer into an open pocket of a zibur driver. "Hey, what are you doing there?" said the miner as he'd felt someone brush up against him lightly.

"Oh, uh, mine maintenance. I'm just checking to see if anyone has any issues with their mining equipment. I need to make a report to the maintenance office about any inoperative equipment. Does anyone have broken equipment that needs repair?" Junot asked the group in general.

"No, no" came an assortment of grumbles and negative replies back to him. One operator said that the seat was loose on his machine because of a broken weld.

"OK," replied Junot. "Give me your name and machine ID, and I will get it scheduled for repair. Just trying to make sure everyone's equipment is up and working the way it's supposed to be." A general lack of response and enthusiasm followed, but Junot wasn't concerned about it, since he'd managed to get the decoy planted. He turned and hightailed it out of there.

Cherga waited around for a while until more miners showed up and wondered what happened. He told them that he'd seen the Varaci Jack come out from where all the injured or unconscious guards were and head in the general direction of the mine. "Don't you know him? Aren't you a friend of his?" asked one of the miners.

"An acquaintance, yes," replied Cherga, "but I don't think he saw me when he came running out. He was in a hurry, and it looked like he might have been beaten a bit and perhaps wasn't too aware." After he'd gotten the rumor going about Jack's alleged direction of flight, he thought it would be better if any investigating guards got the info from third-party types rather than him, so he headed back toward the common area to check and see if Junot had returned.

Jack knew he needed an ID of some sort other than his own. As he got closer to the main corridor again, he saw two miners walking past. They were talking and speculating about what all the excitement and ID checking might be about. As they got to within about fifteen feet, he was able to read their IDs with the reader mod that Junot had added to his translator. One was from Narrona, a planet he hadn't heard of, and the other was from Lokar originally. They were both hactra hammer operators. One of them was somewhat tall and rangy looking, and the other was shorter and stockier with a wide placid-looking face and orange catlike eyes. The taller one was named Nemel Je, and the other was Tineelmar.

He decided to capture a copy of the taller one, as it was somewhat built like a human. If any of the guards tapped his ID, he didn't want to look too far out of character from whatever type of alien he was trying to emulate. The miner's ID captured perfectly, and an option came up to store it. He selected save, and the ID profile jumped to a currently empty list of stored profiles and then showed as ID number one. *Junot, what a super job you did setting up this security wand mod into the translator. I've got to hand it to you, this is likely going to save my bacon. I hope you were able to get that decoy placed, and I'm betting you did.* Jack then selected the stored ID profile, and again several options came up; they were Use in Translator, Modify, and Delete. Jack selected Use in Translator, and the display now showed "Active: Profile ID #01 Nemel Je, Narrona." *It would be a good idea to know your name and place of origin,* thought Jack, *just in case you're asked. Yep, you're definitely a genius, Junot,* thought Jack.

Jack went back down the main corridor away from the security checkpoint in an effort to find some more potential bootleg IDs that might be useful. Maybe he would find a guard or other company official that he could borrow an ID from to make his exit through the checkpoint. He made several trips up and down the main corridor and back to the previous side corridor and then back again. He captured a couple of more potentially useful IDs, but none from any officials or contract employees that would allow him to exit through the checkpoint unmolested. He thought about running it, but even though he knew he could make it through, that would immediately focus all the guards' attention on his own location. *Be patient,* he thought.

As he neared the side corridor for the fourth time, he heard some more commotion from the direction of the checkpoint. He ducked into the side corridor and tried to hear what was going on. He could just barely make out something about additional off-duty guards being called up and told to report to the mine entrance. Then he heard the sound of running footsteps, and it sounded as if four or five bodies were running toward him from the checkpoint. He turned and headed down the side corridor as fast as he could then hunched down somewhat and slowed to a leisurely pace. It sounded as if one of the runners had turned down the side corridor.

The footsteps came closer as he continued to stroll slowly down the corridor. "All workers must stop and be scanned for ID check," a voice sounded behind him. Jack ignored the order and kept walking further down the corridor as far out of view from the main corridor as possible. "You, miner or worker, stop for an ID scan by order of the Corodune Mine Authority." Jack ignored the order one more time, trying to get just a little further from the main corridor. "You, worker, stop now or I will punish you," said the voice somewhat hesitantly.

"Wha-what are you saying? Are you saying something to me? I can't hear so good, too much noisy equipment operating for too many yenets. Can you speak louder, please?" Jack said in a somewhat feeble voice.

The guard looked somewhat confused for a second then regained his guard demeanor. "Stop there and face me so that I may check your ID and status."

"Yes, what, yes," said Jack, feigning confusion and misunderstanding, "I think. Did you say stop, or I'm not sure really actually?"

"Yes, stop, stop now!" yelled the exasperated guard.

"Oh, yes, of course, of course," replied Jack.

"You are a hactra operator, Nemel Je of Narrona, is that correct?" queried the guard after reading Jack's translator ID.

"Yes, yes, I am Nemel Je. I have operated a hactra unit for many yenets here. What is it you want?" said Jack in as helpful a tone as he could muster.

"I'll ask the questions," said the guard, trying to get back as much of his guard bravado as possible. The thought briefly crossed the guard's mind about who the guards were all looking for, and the thought that he was alone in a dark corridor might not be the best move he'd ever made. Well, he'd worry about that later. The fugitive was last tracked in the mine core area heading further into the mine, and here he was a good kahtak away from there having fun harassing some old hactra operator. He relaxed a little and looked at the old hactra operator as he came closer. Now that he could sort of see the old hactra operator, the guard didn't think he looked all that old and didn't look like someone that would walk that slow and rambling.

Jack hit him with an open hand between the thumb and first finger just above the translator in the throat. The guard was fairly large and stocky, but the throat punch instantly paralyzed him from doing anything but grabbing his throat and gasping for air. The guard's thoughts were scrambled somewhere between none of this making sense and gasping for air. The guard stumbled and fell backward, unable to make any noise or call for help. As he fell against the wall, the guard's instinct made him want to stand up and fight, but he was dazed and was losing awareness rapidly. Jack was behind him in an instant and had a choke hold on him as the guard now struggled to gain his feet or any kind of control. Jack knew the throat punch was only temporary and he had to put the guard out before he could call for help or sound some type of alarm.

362

The guard struggled by instinct alone, but Jack had him securely in a rear choke hold and applied as much leverage as he could to cut off the big guard's air and blood supply as fast as he could. The guard struggled and pushed up with his feet, pushing Jack against the wall, but Jack held firm and kept the pressure on. The guard flailed for a few more septus then went limp. Jack held the choke on for another few seconds to make sure the guard was completely out.

Jack had to work fast, since he didn't know how long the alien guard would be out. A human could be choked out for as long as five mentus, but the norm was usually only for a few seconds if the carotid artery was only closed for a moment. He had no idea how long this unknown alien would be out. It could snap back in ten septus for all he knew. He pulled the guard's slightly shabby uniform jacket off and grabbed a quick ID scan from the guard's translator. "Drellac Ne-ahtag, Corodune mine guard. Access level 2BeFF1. H56-LT1K. Tian Vota authorized." Jack wasn't sure what all of this meant, but he was fairly certain the guard had just come in from the outside of the security checkpoint, so he should be authorized to go back.

The guard started to stir, and Jack jumped on him again and put him out with another choke hold. He put the guard's jacket on over his own mine jacket and left the hood up. Maybe they didn't go together, but it was all he had for concealment. He dragged the guard a little further down the corridor and into a dark recessed niche. He pulled the guard's uniform pants down and after a few seconds of tugging was able to tear them off. He bound the guard's wrists behind his back then tied one of the guard's legs to the bound wrists. He tore off a piece of cloth then stuffed it in the guard's mouth and tied the remaining piece of material around the guard's mouth.

Now he had to figure out how to disable the guard's translator so he couldn't somehow signal for help. He didn't have the tools Junot had to remove the translator. The translator was slightly loose around the guard's neck, so he tried to get the heel of his boot onto the pendant transmitter unit. He couldn't get enough space to get the thing on the ground where he could try and stomp on it. He tried working his toe onto it, but that didn't work either.

The guard was immobilized, but if he came to, he could still call for help through whatever comm links the guards had on their translators. Jack took a quick dash down the corridor and looked around. There was another side corridor with a door. Inside he found some stuff that might be cleaning and maintenance tools and other assorted hardware. There was a metal rod about three feet long and about three-quarters of an inch in diameter. From the height and wear marks on the door, it looked like it was used to prop the door open. Jack grabbed the bar and looked around again. There was a heavy-looking block about four inches square that looked like a door stop for the other door. He grabbed that and ran back to where the guard was again. Once again, the guard was just starting to groan and come around a little.

Jack wedged the guard onto his side and pushed the metal rod onto the guard's translator pedant and pushed the pedant against the rock floor. He lifted the heavy block and struck the metal rod against the guard's translator. Once, twice, he hit it. On the third try, he saw the guard's translator crush, and a small flash and a puff of smoke spewed out from the translator. He must have smashed the power source and shorted out the translator. He gave it a couple of extra whacks just to be sure. The translator was now in numerous smashed pieces. He figured that was probably all he could do to it and hoped the comm part of the guard's translator was thoroughly smashed. The guard was too heavy to drag all the way to the second side corridor room where he'd found the metal bar, so he'd have to leave him here. He hoped no one that had any interest in helping a guard would come by for at least a few mentus. *Damn, that was quite a workout for the last few minutes. Now get yourself together and get going,* he thought.

Now the goal would be to act as casually as possible. Jack pulled the hood up over his head and approached the checkpoint. He put his head down and started mumbling aloud and bitching to himself about the company and how they never wanted to pay for his extra time. As he approached the checkpoint, the guard stationed there challenged him. "Who passes there? All workers must identify themselves before exiting."

"Yeah, yeah, just me, Drellac Ne-ahtag, Corodune mine guard. Crepit company, never wants to pay for your time. Can't believe they called us out and now they don't want us, cheap vermin." Jack kept yammering as he approached and kept walking past.

The checkpoint guard scanned this grumbling guard's ID. "Didn't you just come in a few mentus ago when all the off-duty guards were called?" he asked as the grumbling guard lumbered past.

"Yeah, yeah, they called everyone out then said they didn't need everyone once we got there. Told some of us to go back, and we weren't getting any pay for getting called out either. Typical crepit company. Same dumb stuff all the time. Doesn't surprise me one bit." Jack bitched and moaned and just kept walking through the checkpoint.

The checkpoint guard replied, "Doesn't surprise me either," just to agree with the disgruntled guard that sauntered on down the exit corridor.

Jack passed a couple of other workers coming into the mine, but everything seemed to be pretty normal on this side of the mine away from the conzone. He kept his hood up but picked up his pace when he was around the corner and out of sight of the checkpoint. He knew where he had to go first and headed on the familiar trek he'd made many times for the last couple of moondats direct for the foundry. So far, they didn't seem to be searching for him outside the conzone, but that could change at any time. Junot must have gotten the decoy planted, or they would have already broadened their search. How long the decoy would keep them busy in the mine shafts, he could only guess, but probably for not more than and horun or two. He had to work fast.

He took his usual route into the foundry, as this would be the most routine and would probably look normal unless they knew he was being hunted out here, which, for the most part, he didn't think they would. He did take a couple of less populated back ways into the inner offices and finally to the storage rooms where he'd hidden his little katana project. He didn't want any confrontation with management if he could avoid it. This also took him in where he knew he could bypass the security doors, since he didn't have his foundry ID anymore. Yep, there they were. He'd had been worried a bit that someone might have come across them after they'd stopped his access to the foundry. He took a quick look at his handiwork then bundled them up to disguise them. Just as he was coming out of the storage room and was ready to backtrack his way out of the foundry, he heard someone heading his way. *Maybe just a worker or something,* he thought.

They were definitely coming toward the room. He could dive into the storage room, but they'd probably hear that anyway. Well, he would just wait it out. It just sounded like a single person, so probably not a search party. He could pull his katana out quickly if they were a threat or just put them down. The door opened, and Za-arvak stepped in. "Jack, well, how on Nishda did you get in here? I thought I heard something, and I didn't think anyone was here. Did they let you come back to the foundry? I didn't hear anything about that. In fact, I saw what they tried to do to you on that last pit fight. How terrible that was, and how amazing that you came through that so well. I thought you were in serious trouble for a while. Well, it's just good to see you again after a long wenek of having to fend for myself here without your help."

Jack replied, "Thanks, Za-arvak, but I did get beat up quite a bit in that match. The druga was a serious opponent, and the match could have gone either way at any point if it would have landed a solid hit."

"Well, I'm just glad that's over with," replied Za-arvak. "Maybe they'll let you get back to work here now where you're really needed, and you can be done with the whole fight pit situation."

"It's not done," said Jack. "Do you know what's going on right now?"

"No," said Za-arvak, "other than you are back here at the foundry for the moment."

"Well," replied Jack, "about a half horun ago, several guards sent by the mine bosses tried to capture me and take me to the pit for an impromptu match against a kruztwox, which I supposedly challenged. The announcement was made throughout the conzone and is probably on all the mine vido channels by now. The only problem, though, is their star attraction has failed to show up for the match. They are currently searching for me in the mine complex, but I don't think it will be long before they figure out I'm not there and move their search to the rest of the mine complex."

Za-arvak was silent for a moment then said, "This is much like your fight with the druga, then, only even more dangerous."

"Yes," as Jack nodded his head to concur.

Za-arvak began. "I knew the mine bosses were corrupt and greedy, but I didn't think they'd stoop to this level of deviancy. I'm going to report this to the Trading Alliance tomorrow morning and try to bring an end to this corruption."

"No," said Jack, "all you will do is endanger yourself or worse. I'll handle this in my own way."

Za-arvak asked, "Well, what are you going to do? What can I do to help you?"

"Nothing really," said Jack. "Anything you do may be a problem for you. I recommend just complying with them in whatever way you can to a minimal extent. Otherwise, just sit back and watch the show."

"All right, then. Tell me why you came back here, then." said Za-arvak.

"I have it pretty well planned out," said Jack, "to the best of my ability with the information and resources I have, but I needed these," as he patted the wrapped-up katanas and tantos.

"The edge weapons you've stored here," replied Za-arvak.

"Yes," replied Jack, "you obviously found them, then. Thanks for not removing them or reporting them to the mine bosses."

"Yes, I found them after they made you stop work here. I looked around at all your work, trying to figure out how to try to replicate some of your considerable efforts here. They are quite amazing. I've never seen anything like them," replied Za-arvak.

"Some of the older inhabited planets have some primitive edge weapon history, but I've never seen anything that elegant and apparently functional, especially considering the alloy you created them with. They are indeed things of deadly beauty. And to think you created these on the side while you were accomplishing everything else here. Truly amazing, but what are you going to do with a few edge weapons against the forces and technology of the mine and their Trading Alliance allies?"

"I have a few things planned," said Jack, "but it would be better if you didn't know any details just in case they should question you. If you don't know, you can't tell them anything. That is safer for both of us."

Za-arvak thought for a few moments but didn't know what else to add. "Well, all I can do is wish you a safe and successful journey for whatever it is you are going to try. If they come here and ask if I've seen you, what do you wish me to say?"

"The truth will be the easiest thing to remember. Then you don't have to make up anything. Just tell them that I came here briefly, didn't say where I was going or what I was doing. Then I left. Feel free to omit the part about the edge weapons, though. It would probably be better if they didn't know I was armed even with a primitive edge weapon."

"Then consider it so done," Za-arvak said to Jack. "You have been a tremendous help and an honorable person your entire time here. You did much to help me and my position here, for that I thank you. I am curious, though. What do you call these beautiful edge weapons?"

Jack smiled, sensing Za-arvak's interest in his extraordinary creations. "The longer ones are called katanas, and the shorter mid-length ones are tantos. The short hand knives are called *kaiken*."

Za-arvak replied, "Hmmm, yes, interesting names for interesting weapons. I hope they will serve you well, then. Be careful out there, as the so-called Galactic Trading Alliance and its minions can be dangerous and devious and they have unlimited resources at their bidding. Safe journey to you, my friend," said Za-arvak as he clasped Jack's forearm.

"Thanks and thanks for all your help and support," said Jack, "but now I must be on my way. I feel it will only be a short time before they are looking for me in every corner of the Corodune mine. Strangely, I feel that I want to disappoint them and not comply with their desires. I will have my work cut out for me," said Jack as he said good-bye to Za-arvak and headed out the door.

Next stop, Budget Rent a Car, said Jack to himself as he headed out of the foundry to where he'd encountered the surface vehicle attendant a few weneks ago during the geminute parasite infestation. He wasn't sure how long the guard he'd temporarily disabled or the guard's status would remain safe to use. As he made his way to the surface and toward the garage depot area, he stopped and examined a few more transponder IDs from various passersby. He found a couple of potentially useful ones from what were contract workers with mid-level jobs from the looks of them. They didn't look like mine workers but probably some sort of clerical or other nonlabor position.

He went into a public restroom he passed and ditched the guard's jacket just in case someone might put out a search description for someone with half of a guard's uniform. He changed his appearance as best as he could with what he had. He rearranged his hair somewhat and turned his jacket inside out, which gave it some color variance and a different look. He tried to stay in the shadows or at least out of the more brightly lit areas where there might be more potential to be spotted visually. He wasn't worried about electronic checkpoints, since he had already changed his electronic footprint by changing his translator ID twice. He was now Timitu Arcootah, supply shipping manager from Taratuu, another planet he hadn't heard of. His biggest concern right now was a visual ID. He didn't know what sort of recognition surveillance capability they might have if any.

He was basically on the same route he would have taken if he was going to Zshutana's except that he would turn before he got to the central core where he would have to take the lift system to the Dirga level where the food and shopping court area was along with her place of business. He had run this situation through his head for several daiyus now and still hadn't made up his mind as to whether he should try to let her know what he was doing. It was still really a matter of what the situation was as far as whether they were looking for him outside the conzone yet.

He didn't think the chances were good that they were looking here yet, but if they knew he was running, it would certainly be smart for them to monitor any of his former haunts. Did they even know that he'd been here since his initial language lesson with Zshutana? He didn't know that either. It was a pretty significant risk, and he knew he'd have only a fair chance of escape if they were waiting there for him. He knew he couldn't go to her office or apartment but wondered what the chance might be that she would be nearby in one of the shops again. He wished that Junot had been able to get the secure comm system fully operational including the call capability, but that wasn't the case, so he was stuck with what they had for now.

He decided on a compromise. He would take a quick pass through the food court and shopping area in the off chance that she might be there where he'd found her before. He could also check to see if there was any presence of surveillance of Zshutana's apartment, which would let him know if they had her in the equation of being involved with him. He watched the approach to the food court area and fell in behind a group of half-a-dozen miners that were heading in for some food or entertainment.

With his hood up and a fake transponder ID in among the group, he would be nearly impossible to recognize. When they got closer to the large central gathering area, he ducked into one of the shops along the side of the courtyard. The shop was nearly empty except for a couple of females and another couple. From here, he could watch the opposite side of the courtyard where anyone surveilling Zshutana's place would most likely have positioned themselves. He pretended to be shopping and looking at various items in the store but scanned the shops and tables on the other side of the courtyard.

Sitting at one of the tables on the far side was someone he recognized. It was one of Cahooshek's not too brilliant flunkies. *What was his name? Rugga, Ruggal, yes,* he thought, *that was it.* He was with someone else sitting and drinking something at a table. They were trying to be nonchalant, but they kept looking around and then up to the second story where Zshutana's apartment entrance was. *Yes, that answered that question,* Jack thought to himself. They definitely had some surveillance going. Was it preemptive on their part knowing that they were going to try to force him to fight tonight, or did they have some other plans in store, possibly for Zshutana?

"Jack, is that you, is that you Jack?" said a female voice. He turned to look, and it was one of the two females he'd seen shopping when he came in the story. He looked at her, trying to place her. Yes, she was one of Zshutana's girls. "It is you. I didn't recognize you. You are somehow different," she said. "It's me Li-ialah, and this is Inseenai," she said, gesturing to the other girl. "We work at Zshutana's upstairs."

"Yes, of course," said Jack as he took her arm and guided her toward the back of the store. "I didn't recognize you either because I was busy looking outside."

"Well, I got a new hair style and colored darker for the time of yenet. Oh, this is really great. Zshutana will be so glad to see you. She's been worried not knowing what's been going on for a while. Is Junot here too? I'd really like to see him if he's here." She started to ramble on.

"No, sorry, he's not here, but we have to be very careful. Some of Cahooshek's fools are watching Zshutana's apartment from out in the courtyard."

"What?" she said. "Those scurzards are watching Zshutana's?" as she tried to head over for a look.

Jack stopped her. "Wait, you can't just go stare at them. You have to be very discreet."

"Is there a way for Zshutana to get down here without coming through her normal office door?" he asked.

"Well, uh, yes, she could come through her back entrance through our area and around the back."

"OK," said Jack, "I want you to go up that back way quietly and discreetly and then go see Zshutana and tell her I'm down here. But you can't just say it out loud. You have to write it down or whisper it very quietly in her ear. Tell her she is being watched from the courtyard and to come down here the back way. They may have her apartment bugged with listening devices, so you can't talk about this out loud. You can only whisper or write it down. Can you do that?"

"Yes, I can do that. I'll be very quiet. I sure wish Junot was here too."

"I'm sure he wishes he were here too," he said to her. "And, Li-ialah," said Jack, "after you tell Zshutana, I want you to go gather as big a carry bag of nonperishable food as you can quickly gather and bring it back down here to me. Just bring stuff that keeps and doesn't spoil, OK?"

"Yes, OK," she said. "Come on, Inseenai," she said, "and don't say anything about this to any of the other girls or anyone. Let's go."

Jack watched them go then carefully worked his way back to where he could see the courtyard. The two super sleuth wannabes were still there eyeballing Zshutana's apartment and any of the attractive alien females that happened to walk past. A few mentus later, he heard his name called quietly from the back of the store. He took a last glance at the bozos in the courtyard and turned and moved to the back of the store. She was half hidden behind a table at a display piled high with goods. She waited for him to come to her. Then when he was close enough, she jumped into his arms, and they just held each other for a mentu.

"I'm so glad to see you," she said as she held him and reached up to kiss him.

He kissed her back and said, "I'm so glad to see you too. You just can't imagine how much. I just wanted to try and let you know what's going on, but we don't have much time. There are two of Cahooshek's goons watching your place, and I've just escaped from the conzone."

He went on to explain how they tried to make him fight the kruztwox and how they were basically trying to kill him. He told her he had to escape, but he didn't want to tell her how in case they came to question her.

"That's horrible, Jack. I wouldn't put anything past those despicable mine boss vermin and their disgusting partner Cahooshek. They are capable of anything. If you escape, will I ever get to see you again?" she asked hesitantly.

"Yes, I promise," he said, "and I promised Junot and Cherga that I'd do everything in my power to get them out of there too, but I've got to save myself first and get myself into a position where I have the ability to make things right."

"How are you going to do that?" she asked.

"I have some ideas, but we don't have time to go into them now."

She said, "Maybe you could come up, and we could hide you in the girls' area for a while. I think you'd be safe there."

"No," he said, "they are going to start searching for me in earnest shortly, and this is one of the first places they'll likely look. Cahooshek's parasites are already lurking out in the courtyard keeping an eye on things. My plan is time critical, and I've got to go. It may be a while before I can contact you again, maybe even several moondats. Junot is working on a secure comm system that may pan out for us shortly, but I don't know if or when that will happen. Just remember that I'll do everything in my power to get back here and set things right. Just be careful. Watch out for these lower-than-dirt lowlifes. Move your credits around too. Don't give them a chance to try and grab your winnings because they will if they can."

"OK, I will," she said. "You just be careful, very careful, please, won't you?" She grabbed him and held him tight and kissed him, while she closed her eyes and just let the feel of his body next to her engulf her. He wanted nothing else but to hold her and love her.

"I have to go now," he said.

"I know, I know," she said. "I love you, Jack. I really love you," she said as she held him and looked at him with her amazing eyes.

He held her and said, "I love you too, Zshutana. I do truly love you too."

Just then, Li-ialah showed up with a bag full of food like Jack had asked her for. "What's this?" asked Zshutana.

"Just some food for my adventure," Jack answered for her. "I asked her to grab some things for me after she told you I was here. Thanks, Li-ialah. That should help quite a bit." Jack and Zshutana looked at each other for a few more moments. Then he kissed her briefly one more time and ducked out the back of the store and fell in behind a couple of shoppers as they passed by.

Jack looked back a few times and couldn't see Cahooshek's crew or anyone else that might be tailing him. Just to be sure, he took a couple of quick side jaunts and circled around but couldn't see anyone that might be following him. He headed toward the big parking garage and kept to the shadows and off the main traffic areas as much as possible. Lugging the bag of food, which weighed about fifteen pounds, and carrying his tightly wrapped katanas, he looked like he was going on an overnight camping trip, which was basically what he was planning. A lot of the other aliens in the mine were also carrying various things, so he didn't really look too conspicuous, but he felt like he was for some reason. *I guess it's just the fact that I haven't spent much time eluding the authorities as a fugitive that makes it all seem pretty strange and clandestine,* he thought. In some ways, it reminded him of his escape and evasion training that he'd done in the Air Force, except this was in an underground mine complex with lots of people around and not out in the woods after a simulated aircraft ejection.

Skenek Ipto Eh, the vehicle parking depot attendant; that was the name he'd filed away for future reference, Jack thought to himself. *I hope he's on duty today so I can pick up where I left off with him.* Geyu was the name of the other attendant, but he hadn't been on duty then, so Jack hadn't met him. Jack had never given the attendant his own name, so he didn't have to worry about how he would address the alien.

He finally entered the garage depot about ten mentus later. He looked around some, expecting to see one of the attendants. He didn't want to look like he was prowling around, so he strolled purposefully through the garage as if he was inspecting various things again. In less than a mentu, almost out of nowhere, the little attendant he'd seen before appeared. "Can I help you, sir?" asked the little attendant.

"Ah, yes, it's Skenek Ipto Eh, isn't it?" said Jack enthusiastically to him. The attendant was surprised that someone would actually remember his name, so a flash of concern went across his face as he realized that. "Nothing to be concerned with," said Jack. "I just recalled that you were on duty and very helpful when we were inspecting here previously for the geminute parasites. Do you recall?"

"Oh, uh, yes, you were with the Zilrhani when they were looking for those nasty little geminutes. I think that's what I remember," said the attendant hesitantly.

"Yes, yes, that's it," replied Jack. "It seems that I remember that you were doing a splendid job answering my questions and staying alert in the search for the geminutes." The attendant looked visibly relieved when Jack gave him a compliment on his actions. "Yes, in fact, I put in a word with the mine management staff about your good work here," said Jack. The little alien remembered now that this management person, or whoever he was, seemed like a decent type and had been nice to him and had complimented him on his work. "Well, I'm just doing a little follow-up from before," said Jack. "You can never be too careful with something as potentially devastating as these horrible geminutes. So have you seen any?" asked Jack.

"I, uh, well, no, I haven't seen any. I haven't seen any at all," replied the attendant.

"You have been looking and have remained vigilant, haven't you? This is a very serious matter here," Jack said to the attendant.

"I, oh, yes, no—I mean, yes, of course, I've been very vigilant, and I, uh, have been looking for them, uh, almost every daiyus," said the attendant, knowing that he hadn't taken a second glance around since the last time this geminute manager, or whatever he is, had been here.

"Oh, good, excellent work, then," Jack complimenting him again. "How about the maintenance and fueling crews? Do you know if they've seen any geminutes, or do you know if they've been keeping an eye out for the parasites?"

"Uh, no—I mean, I guess they've probably been watching out for them, but I don't know if they've really actually been watching for them," replied the attendant.

"Maybe we should go check with them and see if they've seen anything of the parasite types. Can you show me to the maintenance area?" said Jack.

"Um, yes, of course," said the attendant, kind of hoping that this geminute searcher manager person would actually leave him alone once he took him to the maintenance area. He wasn't too bad of a person, but he just didn't like officials showing up here and making him nervous.

The attendant led Jack down a ramp to the next lower level at the back of the large parking garage. There, he introduced him to the two maintenance workers that were on duty. Jack gave them a quick lecture on watching out for geminutes and where they might hide and to report them to their superiors if they found any. Neither of them seemed too impressed, as this is probably what they would have done anyway. Jack didn't actually care because his goal was to get their transponder IDs and learn as much as he could about the maintenance status of the vehicles and where they were put after they were serviced and ready to be driven again. After about ten mentus, he'd gotten all the information he could without starting to make them suspicious. "Thank you for your cooperation, and remember to keep a sharp lookout for geminutes or any other parasites. We'll be sending you some more information on them as soon as we update our files on their possible whereabouts."

One important thing Jack had learned was that the mine company vehicles were taken back to a large area closer to the attendant's office, but the private vehicles that were under contract maintenance were taken to reserved spots farther from the maintenance area and closer to the contract workers' mine entrance and living areas on the far side of the underground storage area, which was basically in a separate garage area. Jack thanked them and feigned going on about the business of inspecting and questioning about the geminutes.

He worked his way toward the private vehicle area and eventually to the entrance to the mine contract workers' area. He went inside and kept a low profile for a few mentus. Then after switching his jacket inside out again and changing his appearance slightly, he went back out to the vehicle storage area for private vehicles. The attendant's area was a good distance away now and virtually out of sight. He casually tried using the electronic access code on several vehicles using his translator transponder codes for the two maintenance workers IDs that he had just hijacked.

On the eighth vehicle, a slight hiss and quiet whistle noise beeped, and the door popped to the slightly open position. A little thrill went through him as he surveyed the vehicle. *Not too big and probably not too much range,* he thought. It also looked as if it was used daily and would be missed within a few hours if it disappeared. *I'll use it if I have to, but let's keep looking around for a few mentus.* His biggest concern was being busted by some attendant he didn't want to have to put down if he didn't have to.

A few mentus later and multiple more tries and he found two more similar vehicles. He was just about to concede and settle for one of the smaller vehicles when a bigger midsize vehicle somewhat like an SUV responded, and the door popped ajar. I didn't look like it had been used for at least a few daiyus or maybe even a couple of weneks from the dust on it. He pulled the door open and slid inside after looking around briefly and not seeing anyone that might be watching him. The vehicles that responded must be the ones that were under contract for fuel and maintenance by the maintenance garage he reasoned.

He closed the door and looked at the controls. He'd only seen the inside of the vehicle that Cahooshek's henchmen had brought him to the mine in, and that was from the backseat. He had studied up as best he could when he had access to the core data system. Most of the vehicles had a fuel system similar to a fuel cell system back on Earth but considerably more efficient and easier to service from what he'd read. They ran on some sort of highly refined fuel they called DiHydraxanathane. He hadn't gotten around, had the chance really, to find out exactly what that was other than it was abbreviated as DHd in his English translation. From the basic translation of it to English through the translator, it almost sounded like some sort of concentrated or enhanced H_2O_2, hydrogen peroxide, as in maybe an oxidizer or base for extracting hydrogen for some sort of highly efficient fuel cell.

He wasn't sure, but it didn't sound that far-fetched based on some of the fringe energy extraction technologies that were being developed on Earth but that were vehemently opposed by the big oil energy conglomerates. He'd even read some

Internet accounts of developers of various high-efficiency energy extraction systems either being bought out for their inventions or murdered if they refused to sell out and play the game.

From what he'd read, the various Nishdan vehicles could have a range of between 250 up to 1,000 miles or more, if he had converted that right, depending on the vehicle and its capacity. He wasn't sure of this particular vehicle's capabilities or range, but it looked to be one of the more capable units in the parking garage here, and the best part was it had opened on the command of the mechanic's ID that he had "borrowed."

From what he'd read, there was supposed to be a submenu in his translator that would link to a vehicle that he had authorization to drive. He hadn't been able to pull it up earlier to look at it because it would only be a viable menu item if you were in or near a vehicle you were authorized for. He hoped his translator had that option, since his whole gambit depended on being able to fire this baby up. Menu, Select, Bring Forward, List Items, from a list of various functions Jack saw transport, and then an Authorize Link. The mechanic's ID had gotten him in, but he wasn't yet authorized for the vehicle control through his translator. Suddenly, there were two aliens approaching from the right now as Jack looked up. He prayed they weren't planning on taking the one he was in. He guessed he could say he was doing maintenance if he was cornered. They kept coming and took a casual glance at him and continued on by. He pretended to be having a conversation with someone on a comm link so as not to seem too conspicuous.

They continued on past and eventually got into another vehicle farther down the row from him. Within about a half a mentu, they pulled out of their space and headed the other way toward the garage exit. *OK, OK, back to the task at hand,* he said to himself. Transport, Authorize, Select, Current Sandurah Vimar, Other-Select, Options. *Vimar, that's what this was called?* he remembered. *Well, one way to find out.* He selected Current Vimar. A separate HUD screen popped into view in his field of vision. "Initiate Vimar Link" flashed slowly in a small blue box. He selected that. The vimar and its displays came to life, and a similar display illuminated in his HUD field of vision. They seemed to overlay nicely. There were steering and navigation commands as well as situational readouts on both.

There were more options and data available on the vimar's panel than the translator HUD, which appeared to be a scaled-down version of the vimar's panel. *Nice, really very nice,* he thought. He liked the symmetry of it and the way it looked and the interlinked displays. *It looked user-friendly, and, well, why shouldn't it be?* he thought.

There were options for programming routing, time and distance readouts, and much more, as well as manual and automatic steering and several navigation modes. On the navigation options list was a map overlay function. He selected that, and a map appeared. There was a small blue diamond near the center of the display, which he guessed was his position. The map scale was too large, though. It appeared as though he was looking at about a tenth of the entire planet's surface. He could see the city of Wanana near the bottom left of the display and the Corodune mine town where he was in the center with the blue diamond. He looked at the option on the right and saw the command Scale.

Yep, there were in and out arrows, range, and auto just like you'd expect, he thought. Jack selected Auto, and the map scale jumped to what looked like several hundred feet, or in this case mu-uts. He could now see the parking facility as well as a small portion of the side of the mine complex he was on. He scaled the map to one range then two range clicks smaller. Now he could see the entire western two-thirds of the Corodune complex. There's what he was looking for. The entire mine complex had one main entrance, which was located on the south west side of the complex. The mine was essentially constructed like a fortress, and everything that came in or out had to go through the main gate. *Well, that's my only option out of here,* he thought to himself. *I don't know if there are any restrictions on getting out or not. Worst-case scenario is I'll have to run the gate, but hopefully not,* as various thoughts and options kept running through his head. Well. *There's only one way to find out,* he told himself.

He looked at the illuminated control console and selected the Engage Drive option. The vehicle made a minor clicking and humming sound. Then in the back, he could hear a quiet deep whining sound, and the vehicle gave a small unsettling lurch and slowly rose about two feet off the ground. The display changed to a command screen with driving functions. The basics were left, right, forward, and reverse. There were various sliding ranges for those as well as other functions including selections for manual, which was highlighted, as well as auto, speed, navigation, heading, course, planned, direct, and other options. *It all looks pretty self-explanatory,* he thought to himself.

Fuel, how much fuel do I have? He'd been too engrossed in the other functions and fascinating display and had forgotten about fuel. It wouldn't do much good to pull out of the garage and run out of fuel at the exit gate. He looked and saw at the top right "DHd 84.7 / 88.0," with a digital readout and a blue-colored scale showing a nearly full bar. Below that was what his translator showed as "Range 2344 Kk." He understood that to mean kahtak, which was something similar to a kilometer, or roughly fourteen hundred miles is what he came up with in his head. *Not the full ride but a good start,* he thought to himself. *Time to rock and roll.*

He eased out of the space with the forward arrow command, and using the HUD, he "thought" himself left as he pulled out. The vehicle responded nicely. It seemed pretty strange to him in that this manual mode was more like some of the more advanced aircraft autopilot modes that he'd ever flown in the past. As he maneuvered out of the garage, he saw the little attendant alien looking over another vehicle. He only half glanced up for a second and went back to whatever he was doing. "Thanks for your help, guy. I'll put in a good word for you with your supervisor." He laughed to himself as he moved up the ramp and out into the open of the huge mine complex. *Stay sharp now,* he thought. *You're light-years from being out of here yet.*

As he moved about fifty feet along what looked like a designated traffic lane, another slightly smaller vehicle whizzed by him on his left, and a shrill little whistle went off inside his own vehicle. It faded as soon as the other smaller vimar "car" was a few hundred feet ahead. Another larger utility-looking vehicle or truck passed him too with the same result. He was about three or four kahtaks, or kilometers, from the main gate from what he could tell by the map, and there was an inner and outer perimeter road inside the walled area as well as a smaller one outside and around the wall. The walled-in area of the mine looked to be about eight or nine kahtaks across.

The main population and building complex area was to the south and a little bit east with the rest of the area appearing to be mining areas with various mining structures all around. He could see this both on the map and visually. Another two cars, or vimars, passed him and then another. They were all going the same direction, and apparently, he was going too slow. No point in being too conspicuous, so he picked up his speed to almost match the other traffic. In the distance, he could see the wall, and he saw some vehicles going in the opposite direction. It appeared that the inner road was going clockwise; and the outer, the other way. There were a dozen or more connecting points between the inner and outer roads on this side of the mine complex as well as parking areas or other facilities in other locations.

He was torn between wanting to get a better feel for the vehicle's handling and going directly for the gate. He didn't know if there was any special protocol for exiting the complex or if you just drove on out. He knew there was a security detail there from when they'd originally entered. They'd had to stop, but it was just a cursory stop with no actual inspection. He decided to split the difference and decided to drive on past the main entrance road to the next connector road and then drive past the main gate going in the other direction much closer to the entrance. He wanted to get as much information on the exit process as he could but do it in as little time as he could. He couldn't spend any more time here in a stolen vehicle without risking getting caught. If they discovered the vehicle missing, they might even be able to shut it down remotely, or worse yet shut it down and lock it with him inside.

There was one larger vehicle coming toward him on the main road as he passed by the main entrance road. He didn't know if it had come in from outside the wall or was just transiting from the outer direction traffic. Most of the traffic seemed to be inside the wall going to various places in the mine complex as far as he could tell. The complex was large enough that you apparently needed "wheels" to get around if you had business or perhaps pleasure on the other side of the walled mine city.

It appeared that there was a lot more infrastructure to support the place than he would have initially guessed. Well, it was also considerably larger than he'd initially thought it would be because he'd seen such a limited area of the place since he'd arrived. The conzone and the retail area by Zshutana's place were about the extent of it. As he came up to the next transition road where he planned to make a turn, he could see some housing and other buildings in the next section before the next transition road. It looked like a residential community of some sort, a town within a town. He couldn't tell for sure as he made his turn and headed toward the wall road, but it looked pretty shabby much like a lot of the mining towns he's seen growing up. Well, this probably wasn't the vacation destination of Nishda, if Nishda had a vacation destination, which he somehow doubted.

He came to a near stop as he approached the wall road with the opposite direction traffic. Two vehicles went whizzing by him from right to left, and he pulled out and accelerated rapidly to match the traffic speed. The vehicle was quiet and responsive and he hoped reliable enough for the expedition he was about to undertake with it. The two vehicles in front of him came to a stop at the main gate road, which was probably the only place they stopped on this outer road. The first one turned out of the gate and stopped as a sentry approached the vehicle. The second vehicle, which was in front of him, continued on straight. He watched for a second as the guard said something brief to the driver and then waved him on.

Should he turn out now or go on for another pass around the complex? He didn't think he could learn much more about the exit situation than what he'd just seen. It was now or maybe never if they shut him down. Jack turned and headed out the gate. The guard was almost back to a small security hut but turned around as Jack pulled up. The guard waved a smaller version of the security wand that Jack was familiar with.

"Maintenance worker Trillmeer, what's brings you out this way in this nice Sandu transport?" queried the guard as he read Jack's hijacked data.

"High-speed maintenance test run," replied Jack. "The owner reported intermittent acceleration and occasional power loss at cruise speed."

"That would be somewhat unusual, wouldn't it?" asked the guard, trying to sound as if he knew what he was talking about.

"Of course," replied Jack, "but we found evidence of some geminute parasite infestation in the power distribution electronics section," hoping the guard didn't know squat about vehicle mechanics. Most of the rent-a-cops he'd ever known didn't know much about anything. "You heard about the geminute parasite infestation we had here, didn't you?" he queried the guard back.

"Oh, yes," replied the guard as he'd actually been somewhat briefed on the situation. "I didn't think they'd do anything to a vehicle like a Sandu transport, though."

"Oh, yes," said Jack, "they were into everything chewing on any power lead with more than point five milliamps going through it. This is the fourth one we've fixed so far, and there will probably be more. We repaired all the damage we found in this sweet transport, but we don't know for sure if we got it all or if what we fixed was the actual cause of the problem, since the report said it was mostly at high-speed cruise."

"Wow," said the guard, "I sure wish I could go with you for a test ride in that beauty, but I'm on duty for another four horuns," said the guard, practically inviting himself along for a future ride.

"Well, maybe next time," said Jack. "I've got to get this unit fixed and ready for the owner tonight, and I won't know if it's fixed unless I give it a good hard test run right now, so I've got to get going. I'll look you up the next time I go. What's your name?" asked Jack, humoring the eager young guard.

"Jogota," replied the guard, "Jogota 274GFU."

"OK, Jogota 274GFU, I'll look you up on my next test run, although it may not be in this nice Sandurah unit. I'm sure there will be more sometime soon. Gotta get this one done now, though," said Jack as he started to ease away from the guard and down the road.

"OK, thanks. Don't forget," said the guard as Jack pulled away.

"Don't worry, I won't," said Jack as he drove away and waved at the guard. *Well, I would if I could,* thought Jack as he started to accelerate, *but I don't think I'll be back this way for a while, and when I do come back, it won't be for a social call.*

* * * * *

"Why haven't your guards located the errant Varaci yet?" the senior mine boss belched at the number three mine boss in the room. The other minor bosses either cringed or tried to avoid being sucked into the conversation altogether.

"Why are they my guards?" asked the number three boss somewhat hesitantly.

"Because I assigned you the task of bringing the Varaci to the pit so we could finally get our losses back and be rid of this onerous creature!" roared the senior boss. "Does anyone know where this Varan is!" he bellowed.

Number three boss answered, "We all know the same facts. Our best guards were sent to detain him and bring him to the pit. They were instructed to incapacitate him so they could control him. Something must have gone wrong. He somehow jumped them and disabled them all before they could neutralize him and bring him in. We all know he is an extremely capable fighter. There were multiple witnesses at the scene that were questioned, and they all corroborated that information. Several of the guards were injured somewhat severely. The last the Varan was seen and tracked, he was heading for the deeper mine shafts in his assigned conzone sector. After he disappeared into the deep shafts, we haven't gotten a tracking signal at all. The coverage is quite sparse down there, so that means nothing, but the area is vast and has many levels. He could be anywhere down there. We have all the off-duty guards pulled in searching the area. It will only be a matter of time before we have him. There is no way out of there for him, but there are plenty of places he could hide."

The senior boss grumbled and spat, "Get me Cahooshek again. I want to question him again about this devil Varan. Never have I heard of any Varaci act like this or any other race for that matter. Cahooshek must know something more than he isn't telling us, or maybe his addled corrupt brain has just forgotten."

* * * * *

He was almost out of sight of the walled mine complex known as Corodune. The feeling he had was almost like he felt when they'd first achieved orbit in *Victory*. It was exhilarating, strange, and somewhat terrifying all at the same time. They always said you never forgot your first experience in zero g and being free of Earth's gravity. He knew he would never forget the feeling of being free of the stifling incarceration of the Corodune mine penal system. Nothing they could do would ever get him back there, even if it meant fighting them to his last breath. He relaxed a second and chuckled. *For God's sake, they didn't even have any beer there,* at least in the conzone side. That had to be the true definition of real incarceration and of cruel and unusual punishment.

Checking for any traffic in either direction, he left the very slightly visible main road, which was nothing more than a boulder-free trail. He turned and headed in a northwesterly direction that showed a 335 heading on his HUD readout. He drove and looked for traffic for about five mentus until he was sure he was completely out of view of any traffic that might be passing on the main road about twelve kahtaks to the southeast now.

He stopped behind a small double rise about ten feet high and watched and waited a few mentus to make sure he wasn't being followed. He then shut the vehicle off and took out one of his short-bladed kaiken knives. He looked at the roof of the car and saw the three small bumps that he'd noticed on most of the other vehicles. He went to the rear seating area and jammed the kaiken into the ceiling liner about six inches off center from the bumps. The liner seemed to be pretty tough, but it was no match for the extreme capabilities of the Burun-Rioc alloy he'd created. In fact, yep, he discovered he'd actually penetrated through the vehicles roof to the outside.

Amazing, he thought, *I forgot how utterly amazing this alloy is.* A bit more carefully, he cut away about a foot square section where the outside bumps were. He could see a single-sheathed line coming back to where it split and went into three small nodules that he guessed correctly were antennas. What each one was for was the million-dollar question right now. He couldn't see any labeling or other markings on them. He didn't want to cut the wrong one or ones. They were color coded, though—orange, blue, and a twisted sheathed wire that was yellow. That didn't tell him anything except that they were color coded.

Hmmm, he thought to himself. He went back to the console and scrolled through the display. Looking through the menus, he was looking for something useful. *I wonder, I just wonder,* he said to himself. There it was, a Maintenance prompt. He selected Maintenance. A pop-up warned, "Owner or Maintenance access only, authentication required."

As Jack wondered how to proceed for a few seconds, another pop-up announced, "Maintenance Access Authorized." *Of course,* he thought, *my mechanic's borrowed ID, it must have recognized that and granted me access.* This would all be useful and interesting in understanding the vehicle's drive system, but he didn't have time for that right now. Fuel System, Propulsion, Environmental, Driver Interface, Electrical, and Remote Access. He selected Electrical and found more options. Systems Schematics, External Link Systems. Yes, there it was, a schematic of the antennas.

This made sense. Since all vehicles most likely weren't the same, it would only make sense that the mechanics would need information for any of the vehicles they might be working on. He traced the antennae schematic with a cursor to the back. There they were listed by color code. Orange was the navigation antenna, blue was the comm link antennae, and yellow was tracking and remote access. *Hmm, the prior prompt was Remote Access.* He backed up one link and selected Remote Access. Several options were listed. There was tracking, which showed enabled; remote access showed enabled, and remote system override showed enabled. *Crap,* thought Jack, *they can most likely not only monitor the vehicle's position but also control it to some extent remotely.*

That's all I need is for it to snitch on me and then lock me out of the car. He tried to select or deselect each of these options. For some reason, they wouldn't change like a grayed-out screen prompt on a regular Earth computer. Must be a factory-only setting or something. Well, he knew which antenna was associated with that. He went back to where the three antennas were exposed, grabbed the yellow wire, and cut it with his kaiken knife. He went back and looked at the display. A warning message flashed at the bottom of the screen, "Communication error - select options. Select Degraded Mode, Display Status, Call for Help on Comm Link." He selected the Display Status prompt. The previous three selections were listed. Tracking, Remote Access, and Remote System Override all showed an inoperative antennae fault. *Yes, that did it,* he said to himself triumphantly. *And I won't be dialing Triple A for outside help either.* He went back and cut out a six-inch section of the yellow wire just to make sure that it couldn't touch and connect or maybe bleed through some small amount of signal to the antennae.

He scanned the sky and the horizon. Just a cool blue-yellowish sky with a few clouds farther to the west. This place was an extreme desert except for the amazing green terraformed zones he'd seen a few moondats ago before he'd first arrived at the mine. The sky, ah, yes, the sky, he hadn't seen the sky in moondats. It wasn't Earth's sky, but damned if it wasn't truly good to be outside under the sky and out of that hole called Corodune. It felt good, really, really good. He'd be happy if he never went back there, but he had a mission to complete, and nothing short of his being killed would stop him, nothing.

He got back in his nice new vimar car and studied the display again. He selected the navigation prompt and scrolled around a bit. He scrolled to the Select Destination prompt then selected Input Destination. Various options popped up as far as ways to list or search for places. One prompt said Say Destination. "Se-ahlaalú," he said out loud. "Verify Se-ahlaalú" popped up on the display with the prompt Navigate below the city name. "Yes, navigate," said Jack. A blue line appeared, and the readout showed "Se-ahlaalú - Heading 332, Distance 23,487.6 Kk. Current Range 4634 Kk. Arrive xx:xx." *Close enough,* said Jack to himself, *that's better than 10 percent of the way there. The rest will be easy. What was that old saying,* he thought, *something about a thousand-mile journey still started with but a single step.* Well, he'd have close to fifteen thousand miles, and 90 percent of it might be on foot. *Better get going, then. Time's a wasting.*

He engaged the drive on his new vimar "wheels" then floated about two feet higher than the landing gear legs. He did a small circle to make sure he wasn't being followed and then turned to a heading of 332 on the blue navigation display line and opened her up. The car accelerated nicely to about 200 Kk per horun. He was moving along pretty good, and he had to pay close attention, as there was no shortage of small hills, big rocks, and other potentially hazardous obstacles. He was moving close to 125 miles per hour, much faster than his ride to Corodune from Wanana with Cahooshek's flunkies.

He was sure this vehicle could go faster, but he wasn't sure if he could miss the obstacles successfully this close to the ground. If he'd been on a designated road, he might have been able to go faster. This was just as challenging as flying a fighter at the nap of the earth for radar avoidance. Even at six hundred knots, you still had better obstacle avoidance ability at two hundred feet than this. At least in a fighter, you could always pull up to avoid a collision.

He drove in a direct line for Se-ahlaalú. Periodically, he would slow and do a quick circle to check his six and make sure no one was tracking him visually. He settled into a routine of checking the fuel, the air and terrain around him, and the navigation readouts. At his current speed, it would take him about twenty-one hours to exhaust his fuel supply. Then what? He was able to scroll the map ahead and look around. There wasn't anything out in this direction for a long, long way. He couldn't risk going to Wanana because that's the first place they'd look for him once they discovered the missing vimar and put two and two together.

The government in Wanana was too closely linked to the mine and all the other small settlements or mines or farming operations anywhere near the vicinity of the city. If they put out an alert to Wanana and the surrounding areas, they would just try to grab him if he showed up at any of them. His best chance was to get as far from this area as possible and take his chances in Se-ahlaalú if he could make it that far. It was a long shot, but the reward would likely justify the risk.

Se-ahlaalú, from everything he'd been able to garner about it, was a bit of a rogue city with regard to the Trading Alliance. Neither did it have ties with nor did it want direct oversight by the Alliance. Though still technically a part of the Alliance, they did everything they could to disassociate themselves from the GTA. Jack didn't really know to what degree his information was true, but he figured he'd have a better chance there than in Wanana. He hoped so, and he'd surely find out if he managed to make it there. There wasn't much on the map, but there was always the chance he might come across some outpost that wasn't shown on the map where they hadn't been alerted about him, and he could beg, borrow, or steal some more DiHydraxanathane fuel.

There were at least a dozen greenbelt areas somewhat along his route between his current position and Se-ahlaalú but only three that he would come close to on his direct track to Nishda's other main city. The first one was about 210 kahtaks at his ten o'clock position. He would get to within about five kahtaks of it but wouldn't have to detour around it. The second one was maybe 4,600 kahtaks to his two o'clock position, but he would only get to within about 120 kahtaks to that one. The third one was about twenty thousand kahtaks at his eleven-thirty position, and he would have to detour around that one about twenty kahtaks.

The rest along the route would be several hundred or so kahtaks off his direct track to Se-ahlaalú, so he couldn't afford to go exploring those, since he wouldn't be able to make them anyway unless he could find more fuel. His plan was to keep driving to get as far away from Corodune as possible. He would drive straight through and try to make it to the perimeter of the second greenbelt and hole up there and rest for a while and then try to decide his next move. Right now, his best course of action was distance, so that's what he was going for.

Forty-five mentus later, Jack could see the first greenbelt starting to come into view off his distant left. He adjusted his course about three degrees left so that his track would come right up to the edge of the greenbelt. He wanted to get a close-up look at another greenbelt to see if it was the same as the previous one he'd witnessed. He'd studied up a bit and asked Junot and Cherga about them. Everything he'd heard was that they were built to generate oxygen for terraforming Nishda.

What didn't make sense was the ferocity of the wildlife he'd seen the last time they'd gotten near one in the vehicle that had taken him to Corodune. Supposedly, the symbiotic relationship of the flora and fauna system created the highest output level for the terraforming operation, but it still didn't make sense that they imported the types of animals he'd seen. There had to be more to it than that. Maybe they were establishing some sort of wildlife preserve for endangered carnivores or something. Whatever the reason, they had some seriously large and ravenous creatures wandering around out there.

About five kahtaks from the greenbelt, Jack started slowing and veered over next to the edge of the beautiful green jungle expanse off to his left. He wanted to get right up next to it and see what it was like compared to the other one. Were they all the same, or did the transplanted plant and wildlife vary from belt to belt? The vimar was very quiet, so it shouldn't disturb any of the wildlife unless they saw it visually. As he neared to within a little less than a quarter of a mile, he could see a few flying critters above and around the boundary of the forest. The trees were magnificent, probably topping out at 250 feet or more.

Up close now, he could see a variety of colorful birds as well as a wealth of insect life buzzing everywhere. With the vimar's side windows open, he could hear a cacophony of bird and other sounds. They were different from any sounds he'd heard on Earth but were in many ways similar. It was an amazing isolated greenbelt zone with an incredible profusion of life. He was close enough now that he could smell the jungle. It was the sweet yet musty smell of plant life and everything organic, both living and decaying. It was a real treat after the smell of the underground mine and all the alien bodies in close proximity for months. He wanted to get out and walk through the forest for a ways, but he knew it wouldn't be a rational thing to do. Maybe this area was different from the last, but he had no way of knowing that for now.

He had let the vimar coast to a stop about fifty feet from the edge of the jungle. He just sat and listened to the sounds, trying to learn whatever he could from observing the jungle. He was ready to goose the vimar if he needed to, but he wanted to listen for a while. It was starting to get dark, and night wasn't too far off. He heard some distant howling or whooping sounds as well as some high-pitched repetitive wailing, somewhat between a high-pitched frog calling and a cicada locust sound.

He listened for another mentu. Then suddenly, the symphony of noise exploded then abruptly ceased. Now there was total silence except for the distant sound of something crashing through the brush and then a screaming chirp and then another longer animal scream. Then silence. It sounded as if it had been a couple of hundred mu-uts away, but it was hard to tell with the density of the jungle. Jack had his HUD set and was ready to engage the drive and bolt. Cleary something had made a kill, but no further sounds of the drama came forth. Slowly, the bird, insect, and smaller animal sounds started up again. Whatever it was that had caused the excitement was over, and the other animals began to go back to their routine.

Yes, there was definitely some sort or predation going on out in the jungle. Jack cruised the perimeter of the jungle slowly for the next three to four kahtaks listening to the bird sounds and other wildlife. He then slowly eased away from the beautiful greenery and increased his speed as he headed once again directly toward Se-ahlaalú.

It was now nearly dark outside, but from inside the vimar, it almost looked like daylight. Apparently, the vimar had adjusted its night vision windows automatically. The range of the night vision seemed to be very good, but you did lose some visual acuity the farther out you looked. Jack slowed to about 150 kahtaks, or about eighty miles per hour. As a professional machine operator, he wanted to spend some more time learning about the operation of the vimar, but he thought it was more important to put distance between him and Corodune. That being said, there were probably more helpful options the vehicle had that he wasn't utilizing because he didn't have the time to read all the information that was in the vehicles database.

He planned on driving straight through to the second greenbelt. He hoped he could keep the adrenaline pumped up enough to stay awake for the 4,600-kahtak trip. He could sleep when he got there. He'd already been up for twenty stressful horuns, which wasn't a real problem; it was the next twenty that would be the hardest. Drive, just drive. He kept going, and after a while, he slowed and pulled the pack apart that Zshutana's girl Li-ialah had gathered for him. She'd gotten him a nice assortment of various packaged snacks and other food. Rummaging through it, he grabbed some cracker-type snacks and a couple of long meat-looking sticks of which there were about ten. He guessed roughly that if he took it easy, he could go for four or five daiyus on what he had.

* * * * *

"Your guards have been through every tunnel, mine shaft, side drift, and corridor in the area where the Varaci was last tracked, yet they can find no trace of him—is that what you are telling me?" the senior boss said as he simmered to just below boiling.

"Yes, Worthy Jondakav"—which meant "greatest or superior leader"—"they have been over it multiple times and can find no sign of him," said the number three mine boss. "Perhaps it is somehow possible that he escaped the tunnels and backtracked to somewhere else," added the third boss.

"Yes, it seems probable at this point unless your guards are completely incompetent, which would not surprise me at all from what I've seen," said the senior boss, who added, "This now changes the question to how would this Varan accomplish this without being spotted or tracked somewhere else in the mine? Does anyone have any ideas on this?"

The second boss, who had been silent and thinking, asked, "If he was able to escape the mine tunnels, where would he go, and what would he try to do?"

"We don't know that answer, but the Varaci seems to be quite clever and resourceful as well as being an accomplished pit fighter. This would make him even more dangerous than we'd previously thought," said the senior boss.

The fifth boss, who was assigned to monitor the guards' transmissions and progress, piped in, "I just received word from the reserve guards that were called up. One of their squad was missing for about four horuns. They thought he had just gone off duty again, but they reported that they found him about three horuns ago in a side corridor, number 23R8 off the main entrance corridor 4B."

"They found him three horuns ago and they are just reporting it now?" bellowed the senior boss. "What do they mean they found him? What happened to him, and what is his condition?"

"Well, that's just it," replied the fifth boss. "They said he was tied up and hidden in a maintenance access area where anyone rarely goes. He was tied very securely so he could not walk or even move, and he was gagged."

"Well, why on Nishda didn't he just signal for help if he was tied up for all that time?" said the second boss.

The fifth boss replied, "They reported that his translator had been smashed into many pieces and he had no way to call for help."

"Smashed? How did his translator get smashed and become inoperative?" asked the querulous senior boss.

"We don't know for sure," replied the fifth boss, "but it seems likely that whoever bound and gagged the guard somehow was able to smash the translator so the guard couldn't call anyone."

"Whoever bound and gagged the guard?" said the senior boss, now becoming somewhat weary of the whole situation. "We know who it was. What else do we know? We know, we know that this Varaci somehow escaped the mine tunnel and ended up far away in corridor 4B where he attacked and incapacitated a guard. How did he get up there without being spotted and tracked, and where is he going? If we can figure out where he is trying to run, then perhaps we can intercept him somewhere along his escape route."

"Escape route?" said the third boss with a questioning look.

"Yes, escape route. Is it not apparent that this Varaci is trying to escape from the mine altogether?" said the senior boss. "What have the guards at the conzone exit checkpoints said? Has there been any attempt by anyone not authorized to leave the conzone?" queried the senior boss.

"No, none reported," said the third boss.

"Then he must still be inside the conzone somewhere perhaps planning or waiting to escape. Place a full contingency of guards at all exits points and begin searching the entire conzone. He is no longer in the mine shafts but somewhere else, unless he has discovered some other way out of the conzone to the outside that we are missing."

"I don't see how that could be possible," said the second mine boss. "All the exits are guarded, and he would be tracked the instant he passed any scanning point. I believe it will be only a short time before he is sighted or tracked, and we will be able to capture him and deal with him then."

The senior bosses replied in an irritated voice, "You seem to forget that he already incapacitated and eluded an entire contingent of well-trained guards when this situation began. He is obviously quite intelligent and resourceful as well as highly trained in some sort of combat skills. The Varaci could pose a significant threat to our operation here if he isn't apprehended and dealt with. Where is that depraved reprobate Cahooshek? I sent for him quite a while ago."

* * * * *

Another horun of driving, and the terrain started changing from the fairly flat desert with rocks and debris to rolling hills with some short scrub brush and a few rock outcropping. It was somewhat of a pleasant change from the monotony of the desert expanse, thought Jack. It wasn't anything great, but it was at least different. As he drove on, it became more hilly and rougher in various places. He had to slow to about seventy kahtaks to keep from running into all the ravines and fallen rock along the route. He decided to stop and look at the maps and zoom in to see what was ahead, since it seemed to be getting worse instead of improving.

Jack stopped under a rock outcropping that would shield him from view from at least three directions plus overhead in case they were doing any satellite or drone-based searching for him. He couldn't imagine that he'd be a big-enough fish for them to task a satellite, if they had them, to his search, but you never knew. He just didn't really have much information on what their capabilities were. They seemed to keep a lot of that sort of information under their hat, or maybe they just didn't utilize satellite or other space-based surveillance. Maybe they didn't generally have a need for it.

The map showed a small hilly region about forty kahtaks long running diagonally to his direction of travel. He was about two-thirds of the way to the east of it in the direction it pointed. It looked like it might have a creek or ravine at the bottom of it and maybe some sparse vegetation growing along the inside slopes of the little valley. Well, without knowing the full capabilities of this vimar, he figured he'd better come back out and detour around the entire area. It wouldn't be that far, and he didn't want to get stuck or break down in some inaccessible location. *Better safe than sorry. There wasn't any Triple A Auto out here for sure.*

He'd been up for, what, close to twenty-three hours now. He decided that he wouldn't be accomplishing much if he kept pushing on at night in unfamiliar terrain even with the night vision windshield. His location seemed to be a pretty secure, so he decided to call it a daiyus and hole up and get some sleep instead of driving straight through. He got out and stretched his legs then took care of a little business. He got back in the vimar, ate another little snack, and stretched out with his katana next to him. He closed his eyes and was out in a couple of mentus.

* * * * *

The senior mine boss, Yuramah the Jondakav, was not happy, and he made sure everyone else around him knew it and that they were not happy also. There was little in the way of explanations and answers as to the whereabouts and location of the missing conscript. All they knew was they had another guard that had been attacked and incapacitated and that somewhere in the mine, the dangerous escaped Varan was hiding and couldn't be tracked or found. None of this made sense, and he was at a loss to explain it like everyone else.

Suddenly, a small commotion at the entrance to the room got everyone's attention. "You are not authorized to enter here, 5RetQ guard. Go to your supervisor if you want to ask permission for an audience with a mine boss," barked the bosses' attendant at the corner of the room.

"I did that," replied the lowly 5RetQ guard, "but he was afraid to bring this to your attention. It is most important if you'll only let me tell a boss. I'm certain they will want to know."

"What in Nishda's relben is going on there!" yelled the senior boss.

The attendant answered, "Great pardon, Worthy Jondakav, but some low 5RetQ guard is trying to see a mine boss for an audience. I told him to go to his supervisor, but he said he already tried that. Shall I call the Two Squad guards and have him removed?"

"Perhaps, but what does he want? Oh, sward, just bring him in here."

The attendant brought the low 5RetQ guard in. "This had better be important or they may have you neutered," he said to the low guard as he brought him to the senior boss.

"What is it you want that brings you here in violation of standard protocol?" said the senior boss sternly to the young low guard.

"Forgive my intrusion. I wouldn't have bothered . . ."

"Yes, I know that. Get on with what you have to say," said the senior boss.

"Oh, uh, yes, sir," said the low guard, slightly stammering, "I heard through the alert system about the missing conscript. Uh, so I looked up the alert and saw his image. I'm certain, uh, well, mostly certain that I saw him exit through my post at the main gate earlier in a very nice vimar."

"You saw him exit the mine entrance in a vimar earlier!" said the senior boss loudly and incredulously.

"Yes, yes, I had a short talk with him. He said he was taking it out for a maintenance check. He said he had to test it at high speed to see if it had been fixed correctly, uh, from a geminute infestation."

"Are you sure? How can you be certain it was the escaped Varaci?"

"I'm, I'm almost certain. I, uh, looked at the monitoring vido, and I could see the vimar's ID number. I checked it, and it belongs to a female manager in the supplies procurement department. I checked with maintenance, and the vimar wasn't scheduled for any maintenance. I checked with the female manager. Her name is Mynarrah, uh, uh, Zemanae Pe. She said she wasn't using it and hadn't loaned it to anyone. She said she only uses it about once a moondat to visit her family in Wanana. I think this Varaci you are looking for took it somehow."

"Great Genda!" bellowed Jondakav. Everyone cowered. "He's escaped the conzone and has stolen a vimar and gotten out through the main gate horuns ago. This is unbelievably beyond reason." The Jondakav looked at the young guard. "And you just let him drive through your post and didn't report it until now? Should I have you stripped and castrated?"

"Uh, uh, no, thank you," replied the low guard feebly. "We didn't get any information about an escapee until a couple of horuns ago. I, I even checked his ID, and it showed he was a maintenance worker. I did all, all of the required protocols for my job, I'm sure I did."

"Yes, you did," said the Jondakav Boss loudly, "and a whole lot more. Finally, someone that is actually doing something and giving us some answers to this bizarre mystery of the escaped Varaci. Very good job. You are to be commended for your vigilance. What is your name, 5RetQ guard?"

Visibly relieved, the young guard answered, "Worthy Jondakav, my name is Jogota 274GFU. I'm glad I was able to be of some help for you."

"Yes, so are we. You can go back to your post and then take a wenek off with pay. But before you go, tell us everything this escapee Varan said and did."

The guard told the bosses what he'd seen and what Jack had said about the test drive and other stuff about their brief conversation. "So you don't know where he was going other than for this test drive?"

"No, Worthy Jondakav, that is all he said. Then he drove straight out the main road that would lead to Wanana. That is the last I saw of him."

"All right, you can go now. Number Two, alert Wanana that an escapee conscript may be heading their way. Give them a full description of the Varaci and the vimar and warn them of his fight pit skills. Perhaps they will do our work for us and end this annoyance," said the senior boss. "We know that he is out of Corodune now. Let's see if we can get the Nishda S and D to task us a little orbital surveillance and scan all the area that would be in range of that vimar. I have an old acquaintance at Security and Defense that I can contact if they aren't cooperative up front."

* * * * *

Jack woke up about six hours later. It wasn't light yet, and he could have used some more sleep. For some reason, he felt uneasy. He switched on the vimar power and looked around using the night vision windows. He had a clear view all around for the most part except for near the base of the outcropping he was parked under. He kept watching and looking for any signs of movement. He didn't see anything. After about five mentus, he thought he might try to catch a few more z's. Then over at the vimar's ten o'clock position, he caught a glimpse of movement. It was something big, probably bigger than a man. He only saw it for a septu, but it looked like it was moving on all fours, a loping gait, but fast and low behind a nearby ridgeline. It disappeared behind a small rise with some sparse shrubs around it. He didn't know what it was, but it didn't look like a mine guard or other standard alien, if there was such a thing.

Was this something random, or was it something they'd sent after him? Whatever it was, it wasn't showing itself at the moment. He decided it might be a good time to go for a drive. He could see just a slight lightening of the sky to the west as a precursor to the sunrise. He set his katana next to him on the seat and prepared to engage the drive mode after a few seconds of checking the sync of his translator to the vimar again. "Brammmm," there was a huge crashing sound as something hit the vimar. The vimar rocked slightly. Then there was a loud thud and more rocking and the sound of something banging repeatedly on the roof of the vehicle. Jack saw something swinging over the right side of the roof and then for a split second over the windshield. Whatever it was, it was flailing loudly and angrily on top of the vimar. Something was pounding and scratching with a vengeance. A loud hissing screech filled the air as the top of the vimar continued to be pounded.

He didn't know what it was, but he was sure he didn't want any part of it. He engaged the drive mode, and the vimar started to rise. It rocked more but with a cushioned feeling, as whatever it was jumped up and down on the roof. Suddenly, it jumped off the roof to his side of the vimar and stood looking at him from about six feet away. "What the hell are you?" he said to himself out loud. The mostly hairless creature stood about seven feet tall on two sets of legs. It was a sickening pale yellowish and pink-colored flesh with medium to dark green around its extremities. The rearmost set of legs had an upward then downward configuration like a huge grasshopper, while the front back legs extended straight to the ground just in front of the rear set of legs. It was mostly hairless and quite repulsive looking with a small waist and broad muscular shoulders. It had long front arms that easily reached the ground and a flat broad head that looked something like a, well, there really wasn't a comparison; it was just ugly. It also seemed to have a ridge of muscle running down its back that continued down to a tail that rested on the ground and looked like it was used to balance with.

"Aren't you a lovely aberration?" he said to it as it stared and growled at the vimar. It picked up a good-sized rock then jumped onto the front of the vimar. It began pounding the roof and windshield then jumped to the side and started to pound the side window where Jack was sitting. The vimar seemed to be pretty tough, but he didn't know how much of this it could take without breaking a window or something else. The creature was hanging on securely and beating the vimar relentlessly. The noise was horrifically loud, and Jack was getting seriously pissed. "Get the hell off my vimar, you damned freak!" he yelled at it. His voice seemed to make it madder. He engaged the drive and started moving out, but he could go no more than a few kahtaks an horun here because of the terrain.

The animal, or whatever it was, started banging the large eight-inch rock against driver's side window again. This window was tough too, but it didn't look like it had the resilience of the front window. The rock was scratching and gouging the side window, and it was flexing considerably with the impacts. Jack grabbed the katana and unsheathed it in a half second. The animal was beating the window and was obviously trying to get directly at him.

He hit the button and rolled the window down about half an inch. He thought that would be safe, but the creature got the tips of its long bony front fingers in the opening and start jerking on the window. The window flexed even more and looked like it might let go. Jack leaned far over to the right and put the tip of the katana out the small gap he'd made. He jammed the katana into the upper torso of the creature once and then twice.

The creature screamed a deafening screech and grabbed the katana blade. It tried to rip the blade away from Jack, but when it grabbed the blade and pulled, it instead cut through all the fingers on its right hand, leaving nothing but a bloody blue dripping and fingerless hand with one smaller finger hanging by a thread of skin. The creature lunged at the vimar and screamed, trying to smash the window with its one good hand and a half of a hand on the other. Jack aimed the katana again and jabbed straight at its throat. Two more quick puncture stabs and it fell away, landing on the ground and convulsing in a heap on the ground. It was flailing and spraying its bluish blood everywhere from its throat wounds and hand. He must have hit a main artery or something, as it looked like it was bleeding out fast all the while it was still screeching and convulsing on the ground. "Damn, that was a bizarre wake-up call," Jack said out loud as he started to drive off.

Well, so much for getting any more sleep, he thought. *No sense in hanging around this neighborhood where this hideous creature might have a few friends and relatives nearby. I guess there are some other forms of wildlife here other than the ones I've seen in the greenbelt areas. That's probably the reason the towns and mines are all walled. There are definitely some unfriendlies out here in paradise.*

* * * * *

"Yes, Jondakav, this just came in from the S and D a few mentus ago," reported the duty officer for the mine's communication branch of the security detachment that employed and controlled the guard forces at the mine.

The senior boss looked at the report brought in by the duty officer. "This is all that they could come up with from the orbital surveillance division? Nothing from Wanana or any of the outposts reporting any sightings?"

"No, Jondakav, this is all they have. One possible vehicle movement spotted eight hundred kahtaks northwest heading northwest. There is no ID signal or transponder plot showing anything in that area, and no known mining research or other activities are shown as active in that area," replied the duty officer whose name was Jelzshinu.

"What is out there that would be of any interest to anyone?" asked the senior boss.

"Um, nothing, sir, there's literally nothing out there. There is a green zone in another sixteen hundred kahtaks from the vehicle's position and another that it may have passed, but other than that, there's really nothing."

The senior boss mused, "A vimar or some vehicle, eight hundred kahtaks away, with no ID or transponder heading directly away from us. It could be our escapee Varaci, but it would be a long shot, except that there is nothing else that indicates he is anywhere else. I do not wish to risk sending a squad of Provost Air Guards out there without more proof, but the lack of proof or information is almost as compelling as actual proof. All right, go ahead and request a Provost Air Guard squad from Wanana to investigate the potential target. I'll have to file an official request with the Wanana Provost's office, but they can get one of their crews going for now. This is going to cost us plenty. I think it's time to invoke the derelict conscript clause and confiscate our Varaci's credit account. We were, after all, the ones that staked him in his fight pit career. Now that he is missing or possibly deceased, we are entitled to seek compensation for our investment losses against his account as well as any outstanding debt he owes for his crimes.

"Pouvarnu," said the senior boss to the number four boss, "that is your area. File the appropriate request with the GTA financial office in Wanana. The sooner we can access any credits the Varaci may have, the sooner we can start to balance our own accounts. If he bet on himself, which he likely would knowing his own fighting skills, then he should have a sizeable balance in his account for us to impound."

* * * * *

Jack had worked his way around the valley that had blocked his progress the night before. It was about forty kahtaks long, but the terrain was so broken and full of dead-end paths that Jack had ended up going another thirty kahtaks to the northeast to get around the impassable areas. He wondered what had caused the valley and its terrain when everything else he'd see so far was more or less flat and dry. The travel was slow, and it had cost him another hour of probing before he'd found a route that was safe to navigate. The onboard mapping system was somewhat adequate, but it lacked detail out here in no man's land. There might be more detailed map sets available for anyone that intentionally planned on being out here, but Jack's nice new vimar didn't have them.

Finally, he was back on track and headed directly toward Se-ahlaalú again. This new route with the diversion around the valley would take him a little bit farther east, but he would still graze the east end of the second greenbelt that was within his vimar's range. Back out in the open and without anything showing on the map, Jack was able to open the vimar up to two hundred kahtaks again. The bad part was he still wasn't sure what he was going to do when he ran out of fuel. At this point, he was still just running. It was all he could really do under the circumstances. Any other destination would have surely put him at risk of running into some sort of capture situation. He usually prided himself of his well-thought-out and executed tactical planning skills, but here again he'd been totally limited in what he could do as far as prepping for this situation. Even when you know something is coming, sometimes you just can't prepare for it the way you wanted to. Well, he would just keep going until he couldn't go anymore. There was no other alternative, none.

* * * * *

"How could the Varaci only have 420 credits in its account?" the senior boss asked the number four boss when he'd reported the Varaci's GTA account credits as ordered. "We staked him so that he could make his own wagers when we made the unfortunate agreement to have him fight for us in the pit. He should have a considerable sum if he was betting on himself on his own fights with the odds we set. Something is not right about this."

"Perhaps he's just not smart enough to know to wager or didn't think that he could win. Maybe he doesn't even know how," said the number four boss, trying to somewhat assuage his senior boss.

The senior boss scowled angrily and replied, "Now let's see, you say this not-so-bright Varaci who manipulated us into sponsoring and fronting him credits to fight for us is not smart enough to wager? You say this Varaci who was the star employee of the foundry that Za-arvak was ready to go to war with us over is not so bright? This Varaci who eluded us in the mines, escaped without being detected, and stole a vimar and may be a tenth of the way across the planet and was nearly not detected except for our vigilant gate guard wasn't smart enough to wager on his own exceptional combat fighting skills? Is that what you are actually suggesting, Number Four?"

Number Four boss sat silently and only stared at the floor in response. "Perhaps you might wish to rethink that last statement and then tell us about the capabilities and intelligence of this Varan."

"Yes, Senior Boss, I am sorry I was only trying to, uh, suggest, uh, uh . . ."

"Never mind," said the senior boss brusquely. "We are up against a worthy and intelligent adversary. I suggest you consider that if and when you manage to come up with any viable thoughts as to how to deal with this situation. In the meantime, we can hope that this sighting is in fact our lost Varaci and that the Provost Air Guards will deal with him properly if it is in fact him.

"Pouvarnu, if you want to maintain your position as number four boss, I would suggest that you get busy and find out what happened to this Varaci's GTA account and all his credits," said the senior boss.

"Yes, Jondakav, I will get that as soon as possible. We will have to go through the GTA monetary office in Wanana to get full access to his account. That could take as long as a wenek or more and possibly longer if they require we file a request with the Central GTA Monetary Headquarters," replied the number four mine boss Pouvarnu.

"Yes, I'm aware of all that, so get on it now so that we can resolve this as soon as possible," barked the Jondakav boss, the senior mine boss.

* * * * *

Jack continued directly toward Se-ahlaalú as planned with an occasional zig or zag and check six behind him to see if he was being followed. It looked like he was a little more than two horuns from the last greenbelt and less than another horun after that before he'd be out of fuel. His prospects didn't look good, but maybe he'd run into some explorers or survey crews or someone out here in the wastelands that he could beg borrow or steal a ride from; if not, he'd be in for a pretty good hike. In the meantime, it sure would be nice to have some good ol' rock and roll to drive by. He really missed the sights, sounds, and smells of Earth. He took a few mentus to think about his situation and try to put it into perspective. Yes, you couldn't even begin to buy entertainment, even virtual reality entertainment at this level, but with that, you could always pull your goggles and headset off and come back to Earth and real reality. This had been one hell of a ride, but you couldn't turn it off when you were tired of it. Even some good old southern blues rock would be a great sound to accompany him here for this remote little ride. He began to hum and sing after a bit. "Sweet home Alabama, where the skies are so blue, sweet home Alabama, Lord, I'm coming home to you . . ." That seemed to fit his current mood.

He could just barely start to pick it up out in the distance at his ten o'clock position. The second greenbelt was just coming into view. It was down in a slight depression according to the topo relief of the map. They probably put it there to help hold the irrigation moisture in to some extent, thought Jack. Either way, he could see it now, and it was still a good eighty kahtaks out. He remembered what Zshutana had told him about the underground oceans and how they had tapped them to irrigate and transform the surface. It was still an ongoing process, and they were still setting up greenbelts in various places as well as agricultural zones.

He'd also found some additional information on Nishda when he'd been researching his escape options. What he'd found verified what Zshutana had told him about the vast underground oceans and how they could only slowly tap a limited amount of the water or the trapped energy might release and flood the entire planet. It said something about the trapped ocean being supersaturated and compressed at 1.2 million goulteps, or 60,000 psi if his conversion was correct at that time. Either way, it was fascinating.

He wished he knew more, but he hadn't had the time or the access to do any more research. He continued on and watched the greenbelt slowly grow in size. He wondered again if it had the same flora and fauna as the previous ones he'd seen. Hopefully, it didn't have anything like the creature he'd experienced last night or anything worse. He had decided he would have to stop and explore the greenbelt because he didn't really have any other choice. Since it was an alien-manufactured irrigated area, it might be possible that there would be a control or monitoring station there, maybe even some remote monitoring outpost manned by some lonely aliens. Maybe they'd be happy to have some unexpected company drop in. Even if there wasn't such an outpost, there would have to be somewhere that he could get some water and other supplies to continue his journey.

After another forty-five mentus and he was nearly to the edge of the greenbelt. He stopped about a hundred mu-uts from the jungle edge and put his side window down and listened. Birds and insects again, what a welcome sound even if they were alien in nature.

He'd originally had enough fuel to go maybe a hundred kahtaks beyond the far side of the greenbelt, but he was going to use some of it to explore maybe eighty or a hundred kahtaks of the perimeter of the greenbelt for any signs of an outpost or other facility. He'd also used some fuel on his earlier detour around the ravine. He wondered but had no idea where the well tap for the subterranean sea might be that irrigates the greenbelt. He reasoned that it might be near the center so as to be centrally located, but then that would involve a lot of jungle travel to access it. It also seemed plausible that it might be near the perimeter for faster and easier access.

He didn't actually have enough fuel to patrol the entire perimeter, so he hoped it would be somewhere within his range capability. Every kahtak he spent exploring was one less he could drive toward Se-ahlaalú, but at this point, it would be more important to find some sort of shelter, water, supplies, and hopefully, fuel.

The big question was, where would they most likely base an outpost or storage facility? Would it be closest to the nearest population center or more likely be based on terrain and accessibility? The nearest population center probably wouldn't matter this far from anywhere, so it would definitely be terrain, access to the underground sea and access to the facility from the perimeter. Jack studied the map on the vimar display for a few minutes, zooming in and out while scrolling and looking for anything that might be a sign of some sort of technology. It looked like there could possibly be three or four good areas to locate some sort of large well head and associated buildings if there were any.

He couldn't really see anything that stood out on the map that looked promising as that type of facility. Maybe the entire complex, if there was one, was underground. He zoomed in all the way and scrolled around the perimeter of the greenbelt. Maybe the map just didn't show it even if it was there. He kept scrolling. The greenbelt was the largest of the three along his route up until this point anyway. It was about 440 kahtaks long and about 130 kahtaks across at the widest point.

That was a pretty big chunk of real estate to keep irrigated, but with an entire underground ocean, you'd have plenty of water. He had no idea if the underground sea was fresh or salt water. If it was salt, did they desalinate it somehow or did they use salt tolerant plants in the jungles? That was another mystery he'd be interested in finding out about. When he scrolled to the southwest side of the greenbelt, he thought he saw what looked like a tiny straight diagonal cut into the jungle greenery. It was so small it barely showed up on the vimar's map. *Could that be something,* he asked himself, *or is it just a terrain feature or map glitch of some sort?* He marked the spot on the map and continued to scroll around the remainder of the perimeter of the greenbelt, but he didn't see anything else.

He went back and studied the tiny straight gash on the map. He measured the distance, and it was just under 110 kahtaks from his current position. He would barely have enough fuel to get there if the gauges and range estimate were accurate on the vimar. He centered the map cursor over the tiny gash and selected the navigate function. The thin blue line followed the perimeter of the greenbelt jungle to the spot. Well, that was his best shot considering the other dead-end options he had already weighed. He set up a nice comfortable speed of about a hundred kahtaks, or about fifty five miles per hour. With the quiet operation of the vimar, he could still hear the wildlife and he could now smell the beautiful green jungle. With his current speed, the wind noise didn't drown out the jungle sounds completely.

A little over half an horun later, the display of the vimar flashed a low fuel warning, which he had to acknowledge to get it to stop flashing. The orange warning stayed lit, but at least it wasn't flashing now. The fuel range display showed 96 kahtaks of remaining range, and his destination was showing 112. *Well, I might be a little short,* he thought, but hopefully there would be a few extra kahtaks hiding in the tank like his Jeep Wrangler back home on Earth. Well, all he could do was press on now, and if he ran short, it wouldn't be too long of a hike. Eventually, he got to the fuel range limit shown on the vimar's display and yet he was still going. Maybe he would make it to the suspected gash in the jungle. It wasn't like there were any other options at this point.

Just as he was beginning to think he'd make it all the way, the motive power of the vimar quit, and he quickly came to a stop. The vimar settled as the landing gear legs extended just before it bumped slightly to the ground. *Wow, only 4.7 kahtaks from the destination,* thought Jack. *It could have been a whole lot worse. That would be a quick two-and-a-half-mile hike, well, maybe not so quick.*

Just for the fun of it, he tried to get the vimar to power up again. A power cell meter was now showing on the display at 98 percent, now 97. The vimar lifted and drifted forty or fifty feet, but it was sluggish and minimally responsive. He set it down, and the power meter now showed 77 percent. He wouldn't be going very far on cell power. He was only about thirty feet from the edge of the jungle. He thought, *I think I'd better try to hide the vimar just in case they are looking for me out here.* He powered up the vimar and drifted slowly about fifteen feet into the jungle greenery and then set down. The power cells showed 51 percent. *The power cells definitely aren't meant to be a reserve power system,* he thought. *Well, at least they got me off the open desert and into the jungle.*

The only option he had at this point was to go and explore and see if he could find something that he could use. He gathered everything he thought he might need for his short hike including his katanas and tantos and the rest of the food from

Zshutana in case he had to climb a tree or hole up somewhere along the way. He shut the power down on the vimar then cut a bunch of greenery and camouflaged the vimar. If he couldn't find anything where the jungle gash was up ahead, he would have to come back and use the vimar as a shelter. He didn't want the vimar to be without power and not be able to get into it if he needed to.

He headed out for the gash in the jungle and went southwest along the edge of the jungle. His translator HUD still functioned normally, and his heading and speed readout confirmed that he was heading in the right direction. He zeroed out the trip measurement on his translator before he moved out. He didn't have very far to go, but knowing what sort of predators might be out there, he didn't really want to make a lot of noise or do anything that would alert any predators of his presence.

The boundary between the jungle and the desert was quite stark. It was almost as if a line had been drawn with very little overflow past the boundary into the desert. He thought that was pretty strange. It definitely made it look like an engineered bio system to see the stark contrast between the two biomes. He could hear a fair amount of animal activity in the forest, although it was mostly bird-type noises. It didn't seem nearly as chaotic as the other greenbelts he'd seen. The thought occurred to him that it may just be siesta time in the jungle and the real excitement wouldn't start until everyone had their afternoon beauty nap.

He pressed on to the southwest listening and watching carefully. He kept a constant eye on the sky in case there were any huge airborne predators and listened carefully to the jungle for any change of pitch to the background noise. If an attack came from the air, he could dive in and seek cover in the heavy foliage, and if something came from the jungle, he could move to the open desert where he would have room to maneuver with the katana. He kept his katana at the ready in case he needed it in a hurry. In the distance in the jungle, he heard a minor commotion and a few bird squawks. There was a half a mentu of quiet. Then the sounds returned to normal.

He liked being this close to the sights, sounds, and smells of nature again. It wasn't the safest environment, but it sure beat living as a conscript prisoner in an underground mine. He saw a huge variety of plants, flowers, and growing things of every size and shape. He wondered if any of it was edible and even if there might be carnivorous plants in addition to the animal carnivores that might be dangerous to animal life. He would keep an eye out for any man-eating Venus flytraps.

Something rushed away from him in the underbrush. Then some small creature made a series of high-pitched squeaks and squeals a little farther away. Was it just sounding a warning about his presence, or was it now an afternoon snack for another jungle dweller? In another hundred mu-uts, a large brown and iridescent

399

green insect-looking thing shot out and tried to either crawl up his pants leg or attack him. He wasn't sure what it was trying to do, but he kicked it away pretty hard, and it scurried away from him after his initial encounter.

It wasn't quite an insect and it wasn't quite a rodent, but whatever it was, he didn't want to get bit by it or have it attach itself like some oversized leech. If it was an insect, it was a rather large one at about six inches. Even if it was some rodent critter, it was still pretty good sized. The air was filled with every size and shape of buzzing and fluttering flying insects. So far, they seemed pretty innocuous. Hopefully, the terraforming engineers hadn't imported any three-foot-long mosquitos, wasps, scorpions, or their contemporaries.

He kept going, and nothing else exciting happened for the next few mentus. It was a little nerve racking having to stay this totally tuned in to his surrounding, knowing that some oversized predator might be lurking nearby waiting for some unsuspecting Varaci to wander into its area. Well, he didn't have any choice because he had to find an outpost with some fuel or something to get the vimar back in service, or he was going to have a long difficult stay or a short terrifying one.

This reminded him of fighter maneuvers in some ways. He'd had about eight hundred hours of air combat maneuvers training, and this was sort of what it felt like when you were being hunted by the Red Flag aggressors. The big difference here, though, was he didn't have an F-22 or F-35 wrapped around him and an ejection seat to punch out if things went to hell. Whatever was in the jungle would be hunting you for keeps instead of just for training. Well, the good news was that all the fighter training and watching your six did kind of crossover to his current situation. Staying alert and under control would be the two things that saved him if he got his butt in a jam out here with some sort of predator.

He remembered the old movie series about the dinosaur island and zoo—what was it, oh, yes, *Jurassic Park*. He hoped there weren't any packs of those really nasty killer raptors with their pack hunting ability and high intelligence. What he'd seen in the first greenbelt was bad enough, but he didn't need a pack of something like that hunting him. He hoped this whole greenbelt setup wasn't some mad alien scientist's personal amusement park of prehistoric carnivores.

He kept working his way carefully to the southwest, and after no further wildlife incidents, he finally came to the gash in the jungle foliage he'd seen on the map. He carefully slipped into the underbrush and worked his way to an opening in the tree line just ahead. He knelt down and watched the long clearing from behind the cover of undergrowth. The gash in the jungle appeared to be maybe 150 mu-uts, or about 500 feet, across and ran back into the jungle at least a kahtak or more. It was hard to tell beyond that distance because the trees and undergrowth and the gash all blended into one green mass beyond that.

In the distance, he heard a very mild rumble. It didn't quite sound like thunder but did sound like it might be in the air. The long clearing definitely appeared to be manufactured, but for what reason, he didn't know yet. There were no trees or jungle undergrowth, just some thin grasses and a few less-than-knee-high shrubs. It kind of reminded him of a runway cut into the jungle on Earth like he'd seen pictures of, except there were no tire tracks or anything similar, and it wouldn't make sense to cut a runway into the jungle when the flat desert was right at the end of the jungle gash. *Just another mystery, at least for now,* he thought to himself.

Jack estimated that he had about six hours of daylight left, so he could explore for about two and a half hours down and allow the same for getting back. He didn't want to cut it any closer than that. If he ran into any trouble, like maybe he was treed by a carnivore for a while, he would need the extra hour to get back to the vimar. He didn't want to try to find it in the dark. For all he knew, the predators here might have some sort or natural night vision capability like many Earth animals did. That was an advantage he didn't have, and he didn't want to go up against something that did.

He didn't see any activity of any sort while he watched the clearing for the next ten mentus. Only the random mostly birdlike animal sounds from the jungle stirred the air. The air itself was still full of a large number of insects that floated, fluttered, and buzzed everywhere. So far, he hadn't been swarmed by anything like mosquitos or killer bees. If he was going to terraform a planet, that's one thing he would leave out for sure. There were plenty of little tiny bugs and bigger bugs and then even bigger bugs. They all seemed to be interacting with each other.

They all seemed to be attacking each other and feeding on every other bug in sight. Not just big bugs feeding on smaller bugs, but he also saw a swarm of small little bugs attack and bring down a much larger bug. *Pack hunting insects, fascinating,* he thought. He stayed out of the clearing because he didn't like the idea of walking in the open where he would be a sitting duck and visible from both sides as well as the air. He worked his way into the greenbelt carefully along the edge of the clearing while staying hidden from the open area to his left. He'd gone about two hundred mu-uts in ten mentus when he heard a series of loud double screeches ending in a strange short "ahhkehh" sound, which came from the jungle on the other side of the open area. It was immediately followed by an equally strange ascending "whoop, whoop, whoop" call a little further to the right. *They must be having singing auditions today,* he said to himself.

Suddenly, up above him, he heard rustling and barking yelps in the jungle canopy. Near the top of the canopy, a troop of some sort of primates or maybe rodent-like creatures about thirty inches long were jumping and flinging themselves from tree to tree. Jack sat half concealed under some low overhanging type of palm fronds and watched them. They were babbling and screeching and seemed to be agitated. They formed an inner and outer circle high in the branches and then proceeded to circle in opposite directions. It had a somewhat mesmerizing effect as they went around in opposite directions.

They continued to screech and babble when suddenly from above the jungle canopy, first one, then another and then a third large bird predator swooped down and attacked the circling bands of primate creatures. The primate creatures all scattered in a coordinated starburst, and the flying predators jinked, janked, and banked, trying to catch the scattering pray. It looked like all the primate creatures had escaped when one of the bird predators banked hard and headed off one of the fleeing creatures as it jumped from one tree to the next.

Wow, what a show, Jack said to himself. *That's some serious aerial maneuvering if ever I've seen any.* The other two predator birds, which appeared to be slightly smaller than the successful one, made a couple of swooping circles beneath the canopy, deftly avoiding the trees, and then formed up on the larger bird. Jack wondered if he'd just watched a mother predator teaching its offspring how to hunt.

They all landed in an old barren tree about four hundred feet from Jack. They all began pulling on the dead prey and tearing it apart. It didn't look like it would make a very big meal for all three predators, as they were fairly large and appeared to have six- or seven-foot wing spans. The larger one squawked and seemed to be reluctant to share its meal. In the end, though, it relented and shared with the smaller ones. *That was an amazing show,* Jack thought to himself again. The bird predators looked like they might be a little larger than an eagle. They appeared to have feathers and also what looked like fur. They had brown wings with a speckled underside with a blue head and red tail feathers along with some type of streamer appendage or feathers that came out behind their tail. The streamer feathers were probably six feet in length and seemed to fly to the outside of their turns and maybe helped them maneuver, almost like a counterbalance during their sharp turns. They had a healthy set of claws and the head of a predatory bird, but they didn't appear to be as heavily beaked as an eagle. Their beaks seemed almost serrated and scissorlike without the downturn of an eagle's beak. From the way they were tearing into their prey and eviscerating it, it looked like they had pretty efficient eating utensils.

Jack decided to move out again and go further down the clearing. He was likely visible to the sharp-eyed predator birds, but they didn't seem to pay any attention to him. They probably did all their shopping in the forest canopy and paid scant attention to the forest floor activities, at least he hoped so. One would be easy enough to defend against, but three might be a little sporty. Checking his time, Jack realized he'd already burned an horun of his two-and-a-half-horun bingo, or return-to-base time allotment.

Maybe he'd just drop the last thirty mentus and call it a two-horun-out-and-two-horun-back mission. It was taking a bit longer to navigate this little mission with all the excitement along the way anyway. He headed further along in the edge of the jungle to see what he could find out about the long straight clearing. There had to be something technology-wise associated with it. Why else would it be there? The lack of vegetation in a perfectly straight line for a kahtak or more certainly wasn't a natural phenomenon. The key was to find whatever it was, and hopefully, it wasn't too well hidden or totally inaccessible. *On the other hand,* he thought, *maybe it's just a broken section of irrigation system that isn't watering the greenbelt.*

He could hear little creatures scurrying here and there in the underbrush. He caught a glimpse of a small mouse or vole-like animal. It was longer and skinnier than a normal mouse, almost weasel-like, and its coloring matched the jungle floor with brown and green lengthwise stripes along its body. He also came across a brightly colored pink and radiant blue slithering sluglike creature about a foot and a half long. It made a full S-shaped motion as it slithered away from him as fast as it could, which wasn't all that fast but was somewhat entertaining. He kept going for another horun, pausing, watching, and being as quiet and cautious as possible. He saw a variety of other small creatures in the underbrush as he stealthily crept along.

There was a complete cornucopia of crawling insects and other small creatures that looked half mammalian but had six, eight, or even a dozen legs. It was hard to take in the incredible variety of creatures and stay alert to what he was trying to do on his reconnaissance hike. If he were a prey animal here, which essentially he was, it would be hard to concentrate on watching for predators with the cacophony of activity that was continually going on around you. Two more times in the distance he heard the sound of something larger and fiercer trying to take down some other prey. So far, his luck had held as far as encountering anything big enough to attack him. Maybe his scent was foreign enough that he couldn't be detected or considered as prey, he hoped so.

He still couldn't see the end of the deforested gash in the jungle, and he was running out of time. From the map in the vimar, it looked like it could be as much as three or four kahtaks long, but the map scale was too large to tell for sure. With nothing to see in the clearing, he decided to call it quits and head back to the vimar and get a fresh start in the morning. He sure didn't want to meet anything like he

403

had on last night's stop out here in the jungle in the dark. Maybe night was when the big predators came out, and it wouldn't be too wise to be out here tripping around in the dark at feeding time if that was the case.

He turned back and started to retrace his route back to the vimar. Though it was still a couple of horuns until sunset, he noticed that the lighting in the forest was starting to fade a bit as the angle of the sun got lower to the jungle canopy. He now realized that it would probably be dark in the jungle at least a half an horun before the actual sunset. He decided it had been a good decision to turn back sooner rather than later. He'd plan that info into tomorrow's recon trip.

The rest of the hike back was pretty quiet. Things had seemed to settle down in the jungle somewhat as night approached. He laughed to himself and thought it was probably the calm before the storm. The light continued to fade, and he pushed himself to get back without making any undue noise. He made it back to where the forest gash met the open desert. He checked the desert side then moved onto the barren ground of the desert so he could walk easily again but stayed close to the forest so he could dive in for cover if he needed to.

As he got to within a half a kahtak of the vimar, he got down into the vegetation of the forest and listened and watched. Something didn't seem quite right; maybe it was just a feeling, but he still felt like something was out of place. Was it an animal or a flying predator? He scanned the sky and the desert and the jungle as best he could. The light was still a lot better here than along the forest gash under the jungle canopy. Nishda's retrograde rotation made the sun set to the east, and it illuminated the southeast-facing jungle edge he was traveling on. He still felt wary even though he didn't see or hear anything, and he decided to stay in the jungle cover as he worked his way back the last quarter kahtak, or eight miles. He was almost to where he would be able to see the vimar when he stopped and waited and listened again. He could almost see the area where the vimar was hidden but wasn't close enough to see the camouflaged vimar with the tree fronds and other camouflaging foliage he had piled on it. He waited and watched. It was deathly still without any birds or other sounds nearby.

Suddenly, a squawking, screeching flock of small white and blue birds burst from the foliage not too far past where the vimar was hidden. Jack crouched silently and motionless and waited. It was getting darker now as the sun was starting to edge below the horizon. He had to get back to the vimar or he would be finding his way back in the dark. It was still deathly quiet, and he didn't like the feeling he was getting, but he had to get closer and try to get to the vimar. He moved slightly deeper into the forest and worked his way toward the vimar as slowly and soundlessly as possible.

Every nerve in his body was wired, and his senses were on full alert. Breathe, step silently, listen, repeat; it was agonizingly slow going. He crept closer until he could finally just see the vimar covered with foliage. Did it look the same, or was there something about it that was different? When he'd placed the branches and fronds, he'd placed them all naturally lighter side down. It was hard to tell from where he was, but it looked as if some were now lighter side up. Had a gust of wind shuffled them around a bit, or was it something else?

Clack, tink came a slight sound out past the vimar in the jungle. Jack froze. What was it? Was something out there waiting, or was it a branch or a seed pod or something falling? No, it sounded too solid and metallic. *Patience,* he told himself. *So what if it's getting dark?* He waited another five mentus, and nothing; maybe it had been his imagination. No, the feeling he was getting wasn't his imagination even if the sound had been, which it wasn't. Something or someone was waiting for him, he could feel it. His whole subconscious and body screamed it. *Listen to your instincts,* he found himself saying to himself.

He decided to work his way around the far side of the vimar and farther into the jungle and try to flank whatever or whoever it was. If it was a hungry predator, it was a damned patient one. So what was it? Slowly, he moved out and around the position of the vimar. Soundlessly and low, he moved and crept. The light was nearly gone, but his eyes adjusted to the darkness and he could see fairly well. Nishda had no moon, so there was no reflective illumination, yet the jungle seemed to have a slight iridescence of its own. The stars were starting to come out brightly, and there were now thousands of luminous insects floating and buzzing in the air. The combined light of their glow gave just enough background light to see the major shapes and trees of the forest.

Twunk, click. The slightest nonforest sound registered at Jack's eleven o'clock position about a hundred feet between him and the vimar. A soft shruff and scrape at his two o'clock between the vimar and the edge of the jungle. Something was out there waiting, waiting to ambush him. He could definitely sense it, and now he could hear it. Then he heard it, something, just a dozen feet or so in front of him, a voice that was barely audible like he was hearing someone's earbud comm link.

He was that close. Someone was there waiting to ambush him, no question now. He'd gotten in close, too close. He could hear them but not see them. Where the hell were they? He started easing back slowly and as soundlessly as he could. A muffled snap as his foot crunched an old dry twig that he hadn't felt or seen because he was backing up. He froze.

Slowly, the prone, nearly invisible shape of a person rose up slightly out of the clutter of the forest floor and half turned to look in his direction. For a few seconds, nothing happened, but Jack could see the miniscule internal light on the inside of night vision goggles. The light illuminated the face of the alien person wearing them. Motionless, Jack probably wouldn't have been seen, but with the night vision, he knew he would stand out like a sore thumb, especially if it was combined with some sort of infrared or thermal capability. They'd been waiting for him, but they were expecting him to come from the desert side toward the vimar. They'd probably seen his tracks going out and expected him to come back in the same way.

He didn't wait for the camoed alien to move and attack. He bolted into the darkest and densest area of the jungle behind him before the ambusher could completely rise and turn. He heard the yell of someone giving a warning to his fellow ambushers. Then he heard the multiple small supersonic sound blasts of their energy beam weapons and saw blue dull light pulses flashing to his right where he'd first disappeared into the cover of the jungle. Their shots seemed to go high as well as he heard the sound of the beam weapons tearing into the foliage of the forest. It sounded like little thunderclaps as the energy beams vaporized the air molecules on their way past him. He jinked further left and kept moving but at a slower quieter pace. He figured it would take a few septus for them to get their act together and follow him.

How did they get here? Where did they come from? Do they have an airborne support platform or drones? He didn't know, but he had to put some distance between them and him. He could see well enough to keep moving, but he was afraid he would stumble into a hole or something that he couldn't see or into something that could see him that he didn't want to meet.

He stopped for a few seconds to listen and calm his breathing. Off to his right in the distance, he heard the sound of something fairly large running on four feet. It seemed to be moving off at a diagonal angle. Good, that was the direction he original had run; maybe they'd follow whatever it was initially. He came to a ravine that was shallow but got deeper and steeper to the left. He was able to cross it and get to the far side with no problem. He headed left and parallel to it on the other side. He didn't want to go down into it even though it looked like it had good cover, as there might not be a way out and he'd be trapped with his pursuers above him with the advantage to them.

So obviously, they did have some type of beam weapons that were good at a distance, and they were apparently trying to kill him and not capture him. By the sounds of the beams tearing through the jungle, he guessed it wasn't any kind of stun weapon. Well, that certainly changed the equation on how he would have to deal with them. Behind him in the distance, he heard more muffled firing and the scream of some unknown animal. More firing and more animal screams, and then he heard the scream of agony that wasn't animal. He turned and heard and saw a half-dozen blue streaks shoot skyward followed by the sounds of more multiple shots and screaming of animal and nonanimal. Then silence. It sounded like they were a good three hundred, maybe four hundred mu-uts behind him now. Hopefully, that was a score for the wildebeest or whatever it was.

Think, think, and keep moving, he said to himself. They had the technology, but he had been able to sneak up on them somehow. That didn't make sense. How did that happen? How did he get so lucky? They were here for him; there could be no other alternative. Somehow, they'd tracked the vimar and found him and set up an ambush, but they didn't see him coming into it. They were coming for him, for him specifically, that's why. They had his translator profile, and they were zeroed in on Jack of Vara, not the mechanic profile he had bootlegged into his translator and had later turned off.

If they were looking for his ID or anyone else's, they wouldn't have one to track. He needed every advantage he could get. They had the advantage at night with their night vision. He might just have the advantage of at least being electrically blind to them, which they didn't realize, at least yet. He would have to wait until the daylight if he wanted to engage them on a more even playing field. He had to go to ground and stay hidden until daylight. He could hear them searching about a quarter kahtak away. They were yelling and making a huge amount of noise in their effort to locate him. They had set an ambush using their technology, but their field craft skills sucked. From the sounds of it, they'd be lucky if they didn't shoot each other.

At his two o'clock, he could see a darkened rise. Maybe a kahtak further, there was a hill with about a hundred-foot rise covered in dense trees and undergrowth. He worked his way there then went up the side of it and listened for their search progress. They seemed to fade farther away for a while. Then they seemed to be working their way back toward him, but not directly. They were spread out and searching. How many were there now, he couldn't tell, but he could hear at least four distinct voices, maybe five. He knew they had secure comms because he'd heard one earlier. Why weren't they using them? These guys obviously weren't SEAL Team Six. Maybe they were just overconfident that they could track him down and find him and kill him. Well, he'd always been taught that it's mandatory to have a plan and a backup, but he also knew that most plans fell apart the instant you engaged the enemy. Hopefully, they weren't versed in that strategy and he could use that to his advantage.

The brush on the side of the hill was dense and nearly impenetrable. He could tell there were several game trials in and around it. He tried to step only on soft grass or bare rock where he'd leave minimal footprints. He wondered if any of them had any tracking skills. He hoped not and doubted it based on what he'd seen so far.

The cardinal rule in war, though, was never under estimate your enemy. So far, they'd failed miserably at that axiom, but you had to account for a steep learning curve in situations like this. *Stay sharp,* he told himself.

The stars seemed brighter now, and he could see reasonably well. He heard a sound off in the general direction of his enemy but farther ahead of them. It was a humming noise with some wind interference noise mixed in. Yes, it was a ship or a drone of some sort, and it was out ahead of them searching for him, probably with infrared or some other technology. He stayed as low as he could and out of the direct line of sight of whatever was up there looking for him. The hill was probably a pretty good choice. With all the wildlife around, it might be somewhat challenging for them to pick him out from all the other heat signatures.

He didn't know how sophisticated their equipment was. Did they have any actual experience or ever have to do this sort of thing on a regular basis? Doubtful, he thought, from the level of subservience he'd seen here on Nishda so far. The government seemed to rule with impunity, and they were hopefully too far out on the rim to warrant top-level equipment. He imagined the military forces on Earth might have better search capabilities than they did here, but then again, he'd better not bet on it.

He heard something up ahead moving in a shuffling gate and coming toward him in an unhurried manner. It didn't sound too large, but it was hard to tell. He moved off the side of the trail and had his katana facing toward the potential threat. Whatever it was, it was still coming closer. It was snuffling and snooting as it came nearer as if it were foraging for food, which it probably was. He was about four feet off the trail and could see its dark silhouette rambling along. It stopped about six feet from him and turned its head in his direction and continued to sniff the air. He couldn't see it clearly, but it looked somewhat like a medium-sized bear cub or a way overgrown monstrous raccoon.

He could see the shape of its elongated snout sniffing the air and trying to figure out what he was. It came a little closer and kept sniffing the air. It made a strange quiet "weeahah, weeahh" noise and started closing the range to him when it began snorting and breathing heavy. He held the katana, blade pointed right at it. It didn't seem aggressive, but then maybe it planned on feeding on him leisurely. He imagined it as always being hungry for some reason. As it came to within about four feet of him, he gave it a little poke with the tip of the katana, just enough to discourage it. It let out a scream and reared up and spun on its heels and down the trail, screaming all the way.

It ran away so fast it sprayed him with dirt from its frantically flailing feet. What was that smell? Oh, man, the thing must have sprayed a trail of dung as it hightailed it out of there. Wow, that was pretty nasty. Maybe that might help keep the searchers away too. He'd kept his blade up and ready in case it got angry and charged him. He would have cut it down if he had to. He listened for a minute and didn't hear anything. The searchers might have heard that. Did they think it was related to him? Probably not. He didn't think they knew that he was armed, so maybe they thought it was just another beast of the forest to avoid.

He continued up the trail the shambling beast had come down. After a while, he heard the searchers off in the distance. They seemed to be paralleling him or moving off slightly. *Good,* he thought, *just keep going.* He found a side trail that branched off to the right and went further up the hill. He decided to try and hole up for the night. It looked like there might be some rock outcroppings and other debris up there. Staying low and out of their view and hopefully out of view of their ship's sensors, he managed to find a small cave associated with some rock outcroppings. It had just enough top cover and was recessed enough that there would be no direct line of sight from above or from the direction of the searchers. It wasn't ideally suited for defense, but he could always go farther up the trail if he needed to.

He crawled into the little cave and decided to take inventory of everything he had with him. Just as he was settling in, he felt a very low-frequency vibration. It was very low, probably in the four-hundred-hertz range or lower, but it was steady and you could feel it reverberate right through your body. It was strange but not unpleasant. It wasn't the ship searching for him from above; it was actually in the ground itself. Then he heard a strange low hissing and rumbling noise way out to the west from where he'd been earlier, probably as far away as the jungle gash he'd been exploring earlier.

The noise grew in intensity, and it seemed to be getting closer. In the distance to the west where a minute ago he could see stars down to the horizon from up on the hill, he could now see what looked like an obscured roiling fog bank rolling toward him. The low tone seemed to diminish somewhat, but the low hissing sound seemed to envelope everything. As the fog bank got closer, the ground all around him started to give off a rising cloud of mist. Pretty soon, a solid blanket of saturated fog and mist was rising above his knees and rapidly climbing higher. In twenty septus, he was enveloped in the warm damp mist, and then he felt and heard the wave of rolling roiling fog pass over him.

His body was suddenly saturated with dripping moisture, and his senses were completely inundated in the gentle hissing, dripping, and whirling mist. What an amazing and strange sensation to be so completely enveloped, saturated, surrounded, and encapsulated in this totally permeating mist. Well, he had wondered how they irrigated these vast dense forest greenbelts, and now he knew. He didn't know exactly how they did it, but he knew what they did. He also knew that no one could be searching for him right now either, at least on foot. Maybe a drone or a ship flying overhead could look for a heat signature, but he was sure that the searchers were just as frozen in place with this as he was.

He couldn't see more than three feet in front of his face. He felt his way back to his little cave, but before he crawled inside, he stripped down and took a swirling mist shower. The tepid water ran off of his body like being in a shower, and it was both refreshing and rejuvenating. He was saturated completely through, but it wasn't cold, and it felt good. When he was done, he dressed in his wet clothes and crawled back into the cave. He decided it was safe to get some sleep, so he curled up in the corner of the tiny cave. *Man, what a day,* he thought. Then he was out in a matter of mentus.

He awoke with a start not sure where he was for a few seconds. He heard something rustling in the underbrush outside his little hidey hole of a cave. He listened carefully for a minute and decided it was probably some small scavenger looking for its morning meal. When he moved to get up, whatever it was scurried away as fast as it could. Now he was hungry, so he looked in his bag of goodies and found some snacks to nibble on. The big question now was, where were his pursuers, and what technology were they using to try to find him?

Looking out of his new temporary digs, he could see that the forest was still shrouded in fog and mist but not like last night's mist storm. He could see a good hundred feet, and the fog was wafting through the trees and brush in long twisted tendrils as a light breeze stirred it all around the hill he was on. His clothes were about half dry now, so they weren't too bad either. He heard something coming from the east, the low whine of some sort of engines and the high whishing sound of air being displaced over a ship's hull. He ducked back into his cave and kept the solid rock between him and the ship as a shield against any thermal imaging type of search they might be using.

The sound came and went overhead where the far side of the hill would be. Well, he hadn't had to wait too long to figure out what they were doing. The next question, which he wouldn't likely be able to answer was, were they searching for his specific ID, any translator ID in general or heat signatures, or some other form of search technology he wasn't aware of, or maybe all of the above?

Well, he wasn't sure what they were trying to do as far as finding him, but he was sure about what he had to do. He would have to take them out somehow because unless he found some sort of food and fuel cache hidden here by the greenbelt architects, then the only alternative was to take them out and take their ship. Since they had come here to take him out, then the only equation that worked would be to return the favor.

Another question, would they expect him to keep running, or would they expect him to try and return to the vimar? Since they surely knew the vimar was out of fuel, they would probably expect him to keep running, and they are also probably used to being feared and not used to having anyone turn the tables on them. He would go on the offensive as hard and fast as he could against them and eliminate as many of them as he could as fast as he could. He took a mentu to fix his mind-set so he could consign himself to the task at hand. They were trying to kill him; they weren't human, and eliminating them was his only way out of here. *That would work. OK, game on.*

He found a small bare spot with some damp muddy black dirt in it and grabbed a handful. He then found a puddle of water and made the mud more viscous until he had a nice black mud pie. Then he proceeded to cover his face, arms, and other bare skin with his homemade camo paste. He streaked his clothes and everything else he was carrying. He gathered his stuff and headed down the hill and back toward the vimar using his translator HUD. He heard the ship out in the distance again and went to ground under a heavy pile of deadfall. It passed on by and kept going. He was beginning to think they were looking for translator IDs, but he didn't want to bet on that. He wondered if they'd left anyone to guard the vimar. For all he knew, they could have fueled it and driven it away. Of course, if they did that, they could just leave and he would be stranded. That would be bad, but maybe they knew if there was some sort of depot or supplies or something he could use here. Maybe they were just following orders to hunt him down and kill him.

He had been cautious all the way, and now he was within about a half of a kahtak of where he'd left the vimar. He went to the opposite side so he could approach from a different direction. Now, he wondered if they would have some sort of surveillance equipment set up to warn them. Too many damned variables. He would just have to go for it, be careful, and hope for the best. His uncle Garret had been a Marine sniper in Vietnam and had actually written a book about his time there. There had been a lot of valuable information in that book about how they had survived all the booby traps and other horrors of that miserable war.

The VC obviously hadn't had any of the technology of Jack's pursuers, but they used what they had against the superior technology of the Americans very successfully. He would have to do the same. About two hundred mu-uts out, he started a slow sniper crawl toward the vimar's last known position. Crawl, pause, listen, repeat, just like before. Then he heard it, voices quietly talking, slightly guarded and cautious but not overly concerned about being attacked. For some reason, he involuntarily smiled. He placed most of his gear in a shallow hole and covered it then crept closer as soundlessly as possible with just a katana and a tanto in his back belt.

411

A little closer in, he could see some sort of a short black metal spike or post sticking out of the ground and another about sixty mu-uts further into the jungle. If he had to guess, he would say it was some sort of sensor to alert them if he tried to come back. They obviously didn't actually expect him to; otherwise, they wouldn't be sitting there having a chat about the latest baseball score or whatever. He didn't know how sensitive the sensors were, so he kept his distance. He worked his way to the left toward the open desert and saw another spike close to the edge of the jungle. The vimar was only about thirty feet into the forest, and he could just see the edge of it from where he was. The guards were on the other side, and he couldn't see them yet. The first two spikes he had been able to see and this third one were all in line of sight to each other. The one closest to the desert didn't have another one to the left or down the edge of the desert in sight from what he could see. They apparently didn't expect him to come from the desert side. Either they were careless and underestimating their enemy, or they didn't have enough spikes to create a full perimeter so they had left the least likely side unguarded. Since he'd come from the jungle side the last time maybe they didn't expect him to come from the open desert. He guessed it was more sloppiness than lack of spikes. *Too bad for you.* He hoped he was right.

He crept to the edge of the jungle and reconned up and down the edge. It looked clear. He didn't want to get too close to the last spike in case it had some sensor capability on the desert side. He also didn't want to get too far out into the barren desert side where he would be exposed for longer than he wanted to be. He could still hear them talking. It sounded like they were grousing about being left to guard the stolen vimar when they should be out on the search for the con where the action was. *Don't worry, boys, you'll get plenty of action in a few mentus,* he said to himself.

He worked his way closer to the edge of the greenbelt forest and watched and listened to make sure no one else was watching for him. He wanted to keep the vimar between him and the guards and get as close to them as possible with the vimar between them. He cut some leafy green fronds from the shrub in front of him to further break up his outline in case they looked his way. Then slowly and quietly and going as low as possible, he worked his way about ten feet around the last spike and out onto the bare ground of the desert. He could just barely see the guard or whoever these guys were sitting on the front of the vimar. The other one was to the left of the one he could see and was also on the vimar. He was pretty sure there were only two.

Jack moved slightly left so that he couldn't see either one. If you can see them, they can see you. He crawled cautiously forward, staying as low as possible with the fronds in front of him to break up his silhouette. When he got next to the line of the spike, he gently threw one of the fronds across the line to make sure it wasn't armed across his attack path. Nothing happened, and the guards were still talking. He made it back into the foliage of the forest and continued creeping forward. The vimar was now about twenty-five feet in front of him, and he was next to some low shrubs.

The guards stopped talking, and the leftmost guard got up and went around to the vimar's left side and opened it. The guard took out some provisions of some sort that they had apparently stashed in the vimar and went back to the front with the other guard. The guard had looked briefly in Jack's direction, but Jack was both camouflaged and frozen with his eyes down. The guard didn't have anything to cue him in that there was someone less than forty feet away ready to attack him.

The guard went back and picked up the conversation with his fellow guard. Jack crept closer until he was on the backside of the vimar. He was committed now and wanted a quick peek to see which way had the lowest visibility for the guards for his attack. He decided to go down the right side so that he would have a better swing with his right-handed attack. He thought he could get the first one easily enough with sheer surprise, but he didn't want any delay on his attack on the second one that would allow it to raise a weapon and get a lucky shot off in his direction. He didn't even know for sure if they had weapons but assumed they had to, and he didn't know what state of readiness they were in. He guessed they had a fair degree of professionalism, but that could be their undoing if they were overconfident in their attitude.

He looked all around briefly and cleared his surroundings to make sure no other guards were inbound. Then he pinned himself low and tight next to the right side of the vimar and moved slowly forward until he was almost at an angle to see them. He took three quiet deep breaths then took two fast steps around the corner and swung at the shape of the nearest guard sitting on the front of the vimar. His blade caught the guard between the neck and shoulder and cut clean through him and into the vimar. A look of utter surprise crossed the guard's face for an instant then turned to horror where it froze.

The blade went a good foot into the front structure and window of the vimar and stuck there monetarily. Jack tried for an instant to back it out in the opposite direction of his swing, but it wouldn't move backward. He pulled on it straight out, and it stuck for a fraction of a second and then came out. The other guard on the far side of the vimar was just as surprised but realized in a second that he was being attacked. He reached for his weapon, which was lying on the vimar to his right. He fumbled it for a half second then got his right hand on it and started to bring it up.

The weapon, a pulsed ion plasma rifle, was facing forward toward the forest, and the guard started swinging it back to the right toward Jack with one hand while at the same time reaching for the rifle with his other hand. Jack had now managed to pull the katana straight back and clear and started to raise it for a strike at the guard but realized he wouldn't have enough time for a full swing.

From a height of only about ten inches above the guard's right arm, Jack made a short quick downward swing. The blade caught the guard's right arm about three inches below the elbow and sliced through it like a hot knife through butter. The ion rifle and the guard's lower arm tumbled away to the right before the guard's left hand could grab the gun. The guard wasn't sure what had happened to him. He hadn't felt much of anything, but something wasn't working right and something didn't look right to him.

It took him about four long confused seconds to comprehend what had happened. The sight of his missing lower arm instantly terrified him. He saw some crazy person or thing with a very long knife. Where was his arm? Where was his rifle? The full realization of his situation then hit him. The guard screamed and rolled off the vimar to the left before Jack could start another attack. Jack didn't realize what had happened for a second either. The guard was gone, and Jack didn't know if he had another weapon or not. Jack reversed and went around the back of the vimar as fast as he could, ready with the katana to finish the guard. As Jack came around the back of the vimar, the guard was up and running and screaming straight for the jungle while holding the severed bloody stump of his right arm with his left hand.

Crap, thought Jack instantly, *I can't let him get away or call for help.* Jack bolted after the guard as fast as he could. The guard was about thirty feet in front of him as Jack raced after him. The guard now suddenly started to conceptualize the thought that he should call for help, and just as he was thinking to call, he thought of something else, a nagging realization of something important. What was it? he wondered. He heard a buzzer tone in his ears and saw a warning or something flash on his HUD as he ran at full speed for his life.

Jack charged after the guard when suddenly a loud buzz and pop filled the air and a large shower of sparks filled his field of vision in front of him. He thought they were shooting at him, so he hit the dirt and tried to figure out where it was coming from. There was nothing else, just a few secondary fizzling buzzes and a small cloud of rising smoke in front of him. An acrid smell filled the air. The smell of burning flesh and cloth suddenly became apparent. The spikes, thought Jack, they were a perimeter antipersonnel system. That's why they were so casual about their security. They thought if anyone or anything tried to come in, the intruder would get fried on the spike barrier. *Well, it looks like you fell for your own bag of tricks,* Jack said to himself.

Jack looked around quickly to see if anyone else was nearby or coming his way. He didn't see anything. He looked at the dead guard lying on the ground. The charge from the spike perimeter had thrown the guard back a good eight feet. Jack cut a nearby tree branch and threw it on the guard; nothing happened. He was out of range of the spikes. He grabbed and pulled the guard farther away from the spike line. He then pulled him farther down into a small gully to his left. He pushed the guard flat and cut some shrubs and hid the guard as best he could. They might find the guard, but if he could make them think he had just wandered off somewhere for a while, it would keep them less alert than if they knew they were being targeted. He checked the guard's translator output to see if there was an ID he could bootleg, but it appeared to be dead from the spike discharge.

He then went back to the vimar and the other guard. *Well, wow, you couldn't get much deader than that,* thought Jack as he looked at the gruesome sight of the guard. He had never killed anyone before and wasn't sure how or what he should feel about it. It wasn't something he liked or was even comfortable with, but he didn't see that he had any choice under the circumstances. It was either him or them, so the decision was already made for him. He would just have to live with it and understand that it was a justified and warranted action no different from any other combat situation that he had trained for over the years. And his pursuers, well, they would just have to die with it if he was to survive and come out on top.

It's true, they weren't human, which might have helped a little, but in the end, it was a kill-or-be-killed self-defense situation, and there was only one way to play that game as far as he was concerned. If you are acting as a paid assassin, or whatever these guys were, and you're going out to try to kill someone for fun or profit, you'd better realize that your intended victim isn't going to cooperate and is going to do whatever they have to do to survive. *Sorry, buddy, but if you think it's just a one-way situation, you've made your first and last fatal mistake.*

He grabbed the dead guard and dragged him off a distance from the vimar. There had been a lot of bluish-red blood initially, but the corpse had bled out completely in about twenty feet. He picked up the dead guard again and changed the direction about ninety degrees from the initial direction he'd dragged the corpse off. He was afraid that the upper and lower parts of the guard's body would separate and he would have to make two trips, but the unsevered remaining portion of the body held it together with the help of the guard's uniform. He hid the remains of the guard even better than the first one and erased any signs of the body dragging. Wow, he felt a little light-headed and nauseous, but he had to keep going. He imagined for a moment what it must have been like in the Iron Age or Bronze Age when the great battles were fought by thousands of warriors bearing swords, axes, and other blade weapons. It must have been a gruesome sight.

These aliens were different from any of the aliens he'd seen before. They weren't very big, maybe five feet five, but they were lean and muscular looking. Their heads were almost crescent shaped and not too wide but wider at the top than the bottom. Their coloring was a dark reddish-yellow with a hint of blue around the eyes, mouth, and ears. Their eyes were almond shaped and turned down slightly on the outside. Their mouths were small with thin downturned lips, and they had a small sharp nose. There were some faint striations of darker red across much of their body, and it looked like there was a slight raised texture where the striations were. He had no idea what race they were.

Jack checked the dead guard for an ID, which read "Neppin Fuuniam, Wanana Provost Enforcement Unit, Rating 4A. JGH28475." *This might come in handy if they don't find the bodies right off,* Jack thought as he proceeded to download the dead guard's ID. The last thing Jack did was cut the translator off the dead provost and then jam the katana through its core and short it out. He then carefully looked around to make sure he was still unobserved then went back to the vimar and gathered the guard's ion rifles and some of their provisions.

Both rifles were identical, and he decided he didn't want to carry two of them. He wanted to know if either or both of them were functional, though. He tried to fire the first one, but he couldn't make it fire. Maybe it had been damaged, or maybe he just didn't know how it worked. It looked pretty straightforward, but since it was alien technology, it could just be operator error. There was a safety on it somewhat like a conventional rifle, but it was labeled "Off–On–Rapid," with just those three positions. He tried the other one with the same result. He must be missing something. The guard with the severed arm had been reaching for the weapon, so it must have a quick access capability like any other weapon.

He thought for a minute about the first guard he'd just killed whose ID he now had. *Hmm, maybe.* He selected the dead guard's ID from the ID library he was building. He then tried the dead guard's ion rifle. A holographic display popped up in front of his face. A long, thin, narrow blue inverted V hung in the air somewhat like a holo sight on Earth. He pushed a small switch near the trigger mechanism, and a small light turned from blue to orange. He aimed at a tree about two hundred mu-uts out and squeezed the trigger. About halfway through the trigger pull, an orange circle popped up and locked onto the tree where he'd targeted. He squeezed the trigger further, and a blue pulse of light left the gun and struck the tree instantaneously, leaving a burning half-inch hole.

The orange circle was still on the tree and remained unwavering. He moved the rifle from side to side, and the circle stayed locked on the tree. He squeezed the trigger again, and the circle locked onto a bush where the V had been aimed. He moved the rifle off-line while watching the sight picture. The orange circle stayed locked on the target until he was about twenty degrees off the line of sight from it. As he moved the rifle sight back, the circle appeared again and locked on the same bush. While still twenty degrees off the target line, he squeezed the trigger again, and the gun shot out its blue pulse and hit the bush dead center. A couple of small birds launched from the bush squawking loudly and vanishing into the forest.

Interesting, thought Jack, *it locks on target until you retarget it and will hit the locked target even if you're twenty degrees off-line from it. Talk about easy targeting.* He saw a small number 198 in the tiny holo HUD. It had changed from 200 to 198. That must be the magazine capacity and counter. Looking at the rifle, he could see a rectangular indent on the bottom with a finger depression above it on both sides. He pushed the indent, but nothing happened. Then he put his thumb and middle finger on the opposing indent, and still nothing happened. He held his fingers on the indents and still nothing. Then he squeezed the indents rapidly twice, and the rectangular shape released and dropped into his hand.

Ah, that makes sense, something you wouldn't do naturally or inadvertently, but it was something that was fast and easy to release the, what was it, power cartridge or battery of some sort. He took the other rifle and did the same thing, and the rectangle-shaped box dropped into his hand. *Looks like I have two hundred more rounds,* he thought. The dead guards probably had some spare power mags on them somewhere, but he wasn't going to go back and check them now. He looked around over the vimar where the guards had been seated. They'd been eating and drinking when he'd attacked them. He grabbed a couple of more packaged food items that were still intact and stuffed them in his own bag.

He wondered for second what else he could do to improve this scenario. Then he decided to add another little twist of a diversion. He couldn't hide the fact that the guards or provosts, whatever they are, were now missing and probably dead, but he could deflect the suspicion off of him for a while. He went to the vimar and looked at the bloody mess and then took his tanto and poked four holes in a semicircle in the body panel where the blood was. He then drew parallel scratch marks back from the four holes so that it looked like a huge claw had penetrated the vimar and scratched it across the blood stained area. He guessed that this crew was probably a bunch of city boys that didn't have much of a clue about the wildlife out here in the bush.

He knew they'd already had one run-in with some sort of predator, and they may be already spooked by that threat. Maybe he could get them so freaked out that they'd be shooting at their own shadows. He added a couple of more quick scratch sets to the vimar and a couple on the ground. *That ought to do it,* he thought. Now all he had to do was exfiltrate and sit back and watch what happens. He moved to the open ground and headed out around the spikes. Just to see what would happen, he left the dead provost guard's ID in his translator and went around the last spike.

To his surprise, a warning tone went off in his ears and an orange warning flashed in his HUD view. "Danger Approaching Perimeter Kill Zone" flashed brightly in his HUD view. *Wow,* thought Jack, *the guard totally missed his warning cue in his haste to escape the attacking crazed mystery creature.* The warning must be keyed to the guard's ID and directly to the spikes. That would make sense so that only the friendlies that had laid the spike trap would be warned.

Below the warning message, he saw there was an options list; Power Level 1–10 with color coding that showed an orange range of 7–10, yellow 4–6, and white 1–3. There was also Disarm, Arm, and Power Off. He selected Disarm, and the HUD warning changed to "Perimeter Zone Disarmed." He then selected Power Off, but it came back with a warning that showed "Select Power Off at Sentry Units."

He approached the end spike and looked at it. He then tentatively reached down and grabbed it and pulled it out of the ground. On the spike, there was a Power On and Off switch. He selected the off position. He looked around and saw the next spike about sixty mu-uts away. He quickly moved it closer in to the vimar and set the spike but left the power off. Then he moved to the next one and moved it closer and then the next. He reduced the radius of the spike field by about two-thirds of the original by the time he got to the other side. He now had two spare spikes leftover. He switched the power of those two off and stashed them in his bag and then crossed to the outside of the spike field.

He set the power of the end spike next to the desert to off then stood back and selected Arm on the HUD and watched the warning appear again for the spike line. Hopefully, the two dead guards he'd sent on their way had set up the perimeter line and their buddies didn't even know how many spikes were set out. Now maybe they'll think the end one was set to off and some forest beast came in that way and attacked them. It may not be a perfect plan, but it's plausible and will give them something to ponder and hopefully confuse them. *These just might come in handy,* he said to himself as he patted his bag of goodies.

Jack moved out and retrieved his other bag that he had stashed on the way in and then carefully worked his way through the forest while stopping and listening every fifty mu-uts. He wondered how many more of these provost guards he would have to deal with. They were down two and possibly three from their original force if the earlier animal encounter had resulted in an injured or killed guard. He hadn't heard the ship fly over since his earlier encounter. Either they were conserving fuel for their return trip or it had medevaced out the possibly wounded guard or maybe they'd just given up, since they hadn't had any hits on his ID. Hopefully, they hadn't sent for reinforcements. He left the dead guard's ID on his translator for now in case they had some automatic fire control ID system set up for the field. That would possibly buy him some time and keep them from firing on him if he stumbled into an ambush. His biggest concern was, how would he find their ship or get the ship to come to him? If he could improve his odds by taking out more of their ground force, that might help bring the ship down. He began kicking around some ideas that he thought might work.

He came to the ravine he had skirted before and went down the left side of it this time. He didn't know where the hunting party was, but it made sense that they might be working a large search pattern back toward the area they hadn't covered before. When he came to the end of the ravine, he would work his way carefully back to the hill where he'd spent the night. He might have a little bit of a search advantage on them from up there if it wasn't already occupied by his new "friends."

As he worked his way southwest along the ravine, he heard a raucous from down below him in the heavy cover of the ravine. Suddenly, several four-legged large dog-size creatures burst from cover, screaming and crying as they ran up both sides of the ravine about five hundred feet ahead of him. A loud angry roar followed, and a large ferocious half-canine, half-feline-looking predator about the size of a very large Bengal tiger shot out of the heavy brush and locked its sites onto one of the smaller fleeing creatures.

The smaller creature ran up the side of the ravine, but near the top, it became too steep, and it had to change directions and came tearing back down to try and run up Jack's side of the ravine. The larger predator was faster but not as agile as its intended prey, but it knew how to play this game and turned back toward the ravine and used cutoff angle to close the distance to its prey. The predator closed the distance from an initial forty feet to about five feet in about four seconds. The prey animal went straight up the opposite ravine wall but didn't have enough momentum or traction to take it over the nearly vertical rim of the ravine.

In desperation, it flailed insanely trying to gain some foothold near the top of the ravine, but gravity won out, and the hapless creature tumbled backward down the wall of the ravine into the waiting jaws of the large cat canine predator. A growl and a terrified squeal and then a quick headshake by the predator was all it took to end the life of the smaller creature. The predator then held its prey against the ground and jammed its jaws further onto its victim to ensure that it couldn't escape if it was somehow still alive. After about ten septus of securing its prey, the predator picked it up and shook it one more time just to be sure it was dead. It picked it up in its mouth and looked up and around both sides of the ravine. Jack crouched motionless behind a rock and some bushes as it sauntered another four hundred feet further down the ravine and then bounded up over the rim with its dinner in its mouth. *Wow,* Jack said to himself, *looks like it was a good idea not to go through the ravine earlier.* He supposed that any of those predators could likely be hunting anywhere.

He had no idea what their official name here on Nishda was, but he decided to call the big predator a viper cat. They were big, fast, and deadly and would probably be all too happy to make a meal out of him or any of his provost pursuers if given the chance. He estimated that the viper cat must weigh in at close to 700 pounds and that its prey was probably close to 150 pounds or more, no light snack by any means. The other three or four prey creatures had escaped unharmed and were nowhere to be seen. He wondered if they were carnivorous or herbivores or omnivores. They didn't look like herd animals so were possibly a smaller predator of some sort that the larger predator would feed on like wolves on coyotes, only bigger. Maybe it was a food competition issue like wolves and coyotes, or coyotes and foxes.

He would have to watch out for them if they were in any way carnivorous. They might not be overaggressive, but even a single 150-pound animal would be somewhat dangerous. A pack would be even more so. Jack wasn't fully comfortable with his commandeered rifle as a defense weapon yet. He had no actual training on it, so he didn't know its limitations or reliability. It might even be able to be disabled remotely by his adversaries if they suspected he might have it. He would stick with his blades for now until he could verify the reliability and capabilities of the rifle.

He watched for a couple of more mentus, and the jungle remained quiet, so he decided to move out again for the hill. He stayed next to the ravine and watched for any kinds of predators. He could now see a small stream at the bottom of the ravine, which had appeared somewhere back by where he'd seen the predator attack. He saw a small armored four-legged animal foraging next to the stream in the dirt. It looked like it could roll into a ball if it were attacked. It was green and blue, and it looked like it had some sort of flattened spikes sticking out between the plates of armor all across its back. It looked like it would be a formidable nut to crack if it were rolled up in a defensive ball and the spikes were sticking out.

In another kahtak, he came to the end of the ravine and turned north toward the hill. He caught a glimpse of movement off to his left and froze. It was some sort of a herd animal that looked remotely deerlike, actually four or five—no, now at least a dozen now that he saw more ears twitching and more eyes looking at him.

They appeared to be more like a large antelope or something that resembled some of the African herd animals he'd seen. They had dark yellow and green alternating stripes on their legs and across the top of the backs, but their midsections were mottled gray and brown with lighter green spots. The overall effect was to nearly take away the shape and outline of the animal. They had narrow faces with a swept-back head and three short, pointed horns eight to ten inches long that followed the sweep of their heads. They had typical big deer ears—the better to hear you with—on the outside of their heads just below their horns. Their mouths were wide and looked like they would be equally at home foraging in the water for aquatic plants as they would be grazing in a meadow.

They were acting nervous like deer, but they hadn't bolted yet. Maybe they'd never seen a human or other bipedal hunter before. *They might be pretty tasty cooked over an open fire,* thought Jack. He still had enough food for several daiyus, so he couldn't really risk cooking anything right now. He would keep that option open for the future, though. Jack took a few more steps, and they all took a couple of quick bounds into the brush and instantly vanished.

In the few breaks of the canopy, he could see the hill in the distance. His HUD showed 2.3 kahtaks, so just over a mile to go. It wasn't all that far, but it was slow going between the thick jungle and staying stealthy and healthy. He began the trek toward his goal and settled into a steady routine of walk, listen, navigate, listen, repeat. You had to pace yourself and force yourself to be careful and diligent, or you could get dead pretty fast out here. Being hunted by two-legged and four-legged adversaries was a new adrenaline-saturated experience for Jack. It was most definitely exhilarating, but he was quite sure he didn't like being on the prey end of the equation.

If he knew more about the wildlife and other dangers in this alien jungle, he would have felt more comfortable, but there were just too many unknowns. Then he heard it again, the sound of the ship in the distance. *Maybe they were just reducing their number of patrols to save fuel,* he thought. He went to turn off his translator with the dead provost guard's ID broadcast, but then he decided to wait a bit and see what happened. He listened to the faint whine and wind sound as it passed off in the distance. Then he heard the Doppler effect sound change of the pitch getting higher as the ship changed direction and headed toward him. It had been cloudy with a low overcast all morning, but the clouds were just starting to thin and break up as the sun started to burn them off.

He waited until the ship sounded like it was about a mile away then switched his transponder off. He ran about a hundred mu-uts then went to ground in some heavy brush under some fallen trees that made a fair rendition of a cave. The ship flew just slightly off-line from where he was and then made a wide circle back toward his previous position, while he ran another hundred plus mu-uts before it circled back. It seemed to go back to the point where he'd switched his bogus translator ID off. He stayed low and behind cover as the ship slowed and flew past again. It went out another half kahtak and came back on the original line it had made on the first pass.

It seemed apparent now that they were more likely tracking transponder IDs rather than IR or any other type of bio signatures. Jack could only guess if they knew that the vimar guards were missing or dead, but they would know soon enough if they'd picked up Mr. Neppin Fuuniam's, Wanana Provost Enforcement officer, now deceased guard, ID and then started paging him. They now knew from the short ID hit they'd just captured that their guard was a long way from where he was supposed to be. There could only logically be a couple of reasons their guard was out here, and those reasons were that he was hunting the fugitive Varaci, most likely against orders and without contacting the rest of his team, or possibly taken prisoner, or he was in the process of being eaten by some jungle animal that was carrying its prize away. Jack hoped they wouldn't spend too much time investigating the vimar site and would instead mount up like a good posse should and charge over here for a rescue attempt.

The ship seemed to make one last slow pass. Then it sounded as if it made a high climbing turn to the northeast and headed away. *Off to round up the posse most likely,* he said to himself. As soon as he could no longer hear the ship, he headed toward the hill again. He didn't know how far the posse was, but it wouldn't take more than about five mentus each way to bring them back. He was hoping they would go to check in on the vimar site and find the little disaster he'd left for them to contemplate there. Hopefully they'd ponder that for another ten mentus, which would give him a good thirty to maybe forty mentus to get on down the road.

* * * * *

At the vimar site, the seven remaining Provost Enforcement agents didn't quite know what to make of the scene. Something violent had obviously occurred here, but they didn't know what. One of the automated perimeter guard spikes was off-line but only because it wasn't powered on. Something had obviously gotten inside the protected area and attacked the two junior provosts on guard duty at the stolen vimar. It was a total mess, and a quick inspection showed that there was no sign of either of the provosts. Now the pilot of their ship said he'd just gotten a twenty-septu hit on one of the missing provosts a good four kahtaks to the northwest. What on Nishda was happening here? Apparently, the new provosts had needed some additional training on the setup of perimeter defense systems, but they probably wouldn't be getting that now. Well, they'd better get to where that ID hit was and go from there.

* * * * *

Jack was nearing the base of the hill when he heard the sound of the ship out in the distance. It seemed to stop for about five mentus. Then he heard it start to move again. They must have stopped to investigate the last transponder hit he'd given them, and now they were moving again. The ship was making slow back-and-forth sweeps trying to reacquire the earlier ID hit they'd had. He guessed now there was a team on the ground and they were doing an aerial search while that team was down. *Good, that will give me a little more time,* he thought.

From his vantage point on the side of the hill, he could see a long shallow ravine on the southeast side of the hill. That would be his exit point. He pulled the small pack of decoys out of his pocket and took out two with timers. He programmed them to the provost's ID then preset them both for five mentus then continued to the top of the hill where he'd spent the night. He reconned the area and picked some heavy cover about three hundred mu-uts below the small cave at the top and about two hundred mu-uts from where the shallow ravine started below that.

The cover was good but not too cluttered from his hide down to the ravine. He went back to the cave and turned the time on the first timer up to six mentus, which was his best guess, then turned it on and hid it just outside the cave under some loose rubble. He then ran down the hill to his hide and set up his ambush position. He'd really wanted more time to recon the ravine because it looked promising, but he would have to go with what he had.

Less than a minute after he was hidden, the ship flew overhead the cave then circled back fast to the position where it had dropped the search team. There was a slight break in the clouds, and Jack got a quick glimpse of the ship as it passed overhead. It looked to be about ninety or a hundred feet long and was basically a dark shape that could be described as a flattened cylinder but much wider in the back than the front. It had two flattened ovals incorporated into the wider rear fuselage that might have been engines, but there was no turbine noise, just a medium whine with a deeper hum and the air rush that could be heard when it flew over. There appeared to be a cockpit or bridge area, but he'd only gotten a partial two-second look at, it so he hadn't seen very much detail.

The ship flew away fast, and Jack ran down the hill to the ravine and did a quick recon of the terrain. There, that's what he was looking for, a narrow passage through the ravine with piled-up debris on both sides that was the natural path down the hill. It looked fairly well used as a game trail. As long as some animal didn't trip his trap, this might work. He picked a spot where they would most likely pursue him, and it would be difficult to pass on the outside because of the brush on one side and the piled debris on the other. He took out his two perimeter spikes and planted them across the path and concealed them from the uphill side. He made sure he had just enough room to pass on the outside of the concealed brushy side.

He armed the spikes on high and moved back up the hill. He couldn't see the spikes at all and took a good sight picture of where they were located so he wouldn't screw up his approach to them. Two rocks and a fallen tree on the right, and a line of smaller rocks and a batch of red flowering succulent looking plants to the left. Once, twice, three times he framed that image in his brain then looked at it as he moved up hill to get the approach picture set in stone. Everything else pretty much blended together, and he didn't want to overrun the spikes in a mad dash down the hill. That would not be good. He made it back to his hide spot and went to ground under the heavy pile of debris there and waited. He hoped they didn't switch to some other form or search technology that might be able to pick him out from under his cool, damp brush-covered hide.

He didn't have to wait long as he heard the sound of the ship coming up the hill off to his right. He stayed very low and out of any direct line of sight from the direction the ship was coming from. The ship completely circled the hill, apparently trying to get a visual on what might be there or maybe looking for a place to land. He wished he had a way to remotely activate the decoy, but, oh, well, you couldn't have everything.

The north side of the hill had a somewhat open area about three-quarters of a kahtak from where the cave was. They probably didn't expect the Varaci to be armed and didn't know if he was there anyway. All they knew was they'd gotten an ID hit on one of their missing provosts. "Prepare for assault landing in one mentu," commanded the head provost officer.

Jack could hear the ship circling but only got a half-second glimpse of it as the clouds seemed to have settled back over the forest especially around the top of the hill. Then as he heard it circle to the north side of the hill, he saw the ship emerge from the clouds and settle over the open space north of the cave. It came to within about fifty feet of the ground then hovered. He could hear the sound of the whine diminish and the hum increase substantially as it went into a hover mode. It sounded as if it were using a considerable amount of power to maintain its hover once it was stationary.

As Jack watched, he saw four faint lines shoot from the side of the ship. The lines looked taught, but he could only see the top one-third or so because he was too low on the hill. He watched intently then saw four figures shoot down the line toward the ground. A couple of seconds later three more followed. He expected more, but the lines went back into the ship, and the ship rose into the clouds and climbed to a high circling watch position. Jack checked the rifle, and it seemed to be working properly. He had very briefly played with the holo targeting sight a few more times and felt pretty comfortable with it now. He would not target them until the last second in case they had some type of warning system that told them when they were being targeted.

It took the provosts a good five mentus to form up after their assault landing and then work their way cautiously up the hill to the cave where they found nothing except some tracks that may or may not have been made by a person. Jack could see them intermittently near the top of the hill, but there was too much foliage between him and the cave. His best line of fire was from just about a hundred feet this side of the cave then lower down the hill toward him.

He turned on his fake provost ID for five septus then turned it off and waited. It only took about twenty septus, and then he could see them form up and head down the hill in a leapfrog-type tactical mode. Jack turned on the prior provost owner's ID, and the gun came to life. He carefully lined up the blue inverted V on where he knew one of the provosts would be emerging from behind a large brush pile. He squeezed the trigger partway, and the blue V turned to orange.

As the provost sprinted out of cover, the orange circle locked on him, and Jack squeezed the trigger, sending the blue pulse on its way and into the center mass of the provost. A flash of white light illuminated the provost as the pulsed energy beam cut through the provost's uniform and flared brightly. The provost guard was punched back by the velocity of the energy pulse that had hit him.

To the provost, it had felt like he'd been hit in the stomach by a huge ramrod. He didn't realize he'd been hit by an ion rifle pulse that completely burned a two-centimeter hole through his body while cauterizing the outer holes as it had passed through but not the internal passage. He went down then half sat, half laid on the ground, trying to figure out what had happened. The energy pulse hadn't hit his spine or other vital organs or he would have been down and out instantly. The pulse had gone through a lung and missed his offset heart by less than a quarter inch. He was fatally wounded from the dead center shot, but he didn't realize it yet.

Just as the first provost went down, another came running from cover in their leapfrog advancement tactic. He realized too late that they were being targeted by someone with an ion rifle and tried to dive headfirst behind a clump of undergrowth. Jack instantly targeted the moving target, and the pulse caught the provost through the side of the hip and lower abdomen where the ion beam scattered off his hip bone, which dissipated the energy into his body. He was dead twenty septus after he'd hit the ground with the lower eviscerated portion of his body still lying on the open trail.

The others knew they'd been targeted and shot at, but they didn't know by who or exactly where it was from. They immediately started to return random fire from their concealed positions, while Jack peeked through the tiniest opening in his covered area. He knew he couldn't stay here long because his uncle had told him the secret to surviving as a sniper was to shoot, move, get concealed, possibly shoot again or not, then move again. He'd hoped to get another clear shot before moving, but they were at least trained well enough to maintain their concealment. He heard one of them yelling and something about move left and right off the trail. Why weren't they using their secure comms? Jack wondered. At this point, it didn't matter, as Jack figured they were going to try and flank him now.

He backed out of his hide and checked that the provost guard's ID was still on. Maybe they would hesitate shooting at him if they thought one of theirs was down there with him. He jumped up and ran, keeping his head low with as much cover between him and them as he could. About halfway to the spikes, he started yelling help requests as he imagined a guard might. He had to get at least some of them to funnel into the ravine and not try to flank him from the outside. A few random shots flew over his head then ceased as they got an update from their ship that one of their provosts was down there.

They tried to decide who or what they were dealing with, but they didn't have any answers. Jack didn't want to spook them too badly yet or they wouldn't try to advance on him. He'd already taken out two and now had to think of something to make them want to rush him. He fired off a couple of rounds in their direction and yelled for them to save him, that he was being taken by the Varaci fugitive. He raced to the spike area, saw his sight picture for his ambush and slipped through the safe area to the side of the spikes, and headed down the game trail. About a hundred mu-uts past the spikes, he went to ground in some heavy cover and started yelling, "I've got him! I've got him! Hurry up, I've got him! He fell, I hit him with a rock. Hurry, hurry, he's coming around, and my hands are tied up."

Jack had no idea if that's what a provost might yell, but it's all he could conjure up. What he was really hoping was that it sounded plausible enough and urgent enough that at least one or two would respond by rushing to their fellow provost's aid and that with the noise and confusion would keep them from noticing any warning that his spike trap might give them in their translator HUD.

He screamed louder and more desperately for their help. A couple of the pursuers weren't sure about what they were hearing, and another two were just too confused from the combat situation they were suddenly in to even know what they were hearing. The other one who was out front heard it clear enough, and it sounded frantic enough that he responded by jumping up and running to his comrade's aid. He bolted down the trail toward his desperate comrade and was almost to the spike trap when the head provost began yelling at all of them to hold up and reform. The rearmost guard heard the command and put on the brakes and yelled something about stopping to the other junior provost out in front just as the provost in front of him hit the spike line sensors and tripped it. A terrific bolt of light and sparks and a blast of smoke and debris sprayed the trail as the unfortunate rescuer wannabe met the same drastic but instantaneous end as the wounded one that tried to escape Jack's attack back at the vimar.

Jack wanted to grab the spikes, but the remaining four provosts opened fire in his general direction when they saw what had happened to their comrade. It was still maybe four against one or worse as far as Jack could discern, so there was nothing else he could do but turn tail and run. *I'd better put some fast distance between myself and them,* he said to himself as he raced down the trail and dove into the heavy cover of the jungle two hundred mu-uts further down the trail.

A hundred feet off the trail in the dense cover, he switched to stealth mode by going slow and quiet again and verifying that his transponder ID was off. *Crap,* he admonished himself; he'd forgotten to turn off his fake ID in the heat of the battle and still had the provost's credentials broadcasting. It was now switched off as he picked up the pace to put more distance between his last broadcast position and his pursuers. "Hit and move" was the only way he'd stayed alive as a sniper, his uncle had told him of his exploits in 'Nam. "Never let the enemy pin you down. Always take the war to them, don't let them bring the war to you." *Right, easier said than done, Uncle Garret. Wish you were here right now,* Jack thought to himself.

In the ship orbiting above, the pilot and copilot had tracked the junior provost's ID as it moved down the trail and then taken a hard left into the jungle. The pilot had been planning an aerial attack on the fugitive Varaci if he was given the word from the ground troops, but they didn't know the actual situation with their missing provost, and they didn't have a fix on the Varaci. The only ID signal they were receiving was that of their own team member, and now there was none. The pilot called the ground leader for a confirmation of the situation. "We have no verification on the Varaci or either of our missing provosts," reported the ground leader. He then quickly verified their tactical situation and the loss of the three provosts.

"Three hundred mu-uts from your current position and seventy mu-uts into the jungle to the northeast was the last position I showed for Provost Neppin Fuuniam 4A, but I have nothing on the Varaci. State your intentions, Ground Leader," said the pilot.

"We've had no confirmed communications from Neppin Fuuniam 4A or visual sightings. I suspect that maybe he is dead and the Varaci may have removed his translator and may be somehow manipulating it and using it to make it appear that Neppin Fuuniam 4A is in his control. I don't know how the signal would come and go, but it must somehow be compromised. I am hereby authorizing you to fire on the position of Neppin Fuuniam 4A," said the ground leader.

"Verify you want us to fire on the ID position of Neppin Fuuniam 4A?" queried the pilot incredulously.

"Yes, verified, fire on the position of Neppin Fuuniam 4A," replied the ground leader.

"Verified, will fire on Neppin Fuuniam," replied the pilot, "but we have no signal currently."

"Understood, no signal currently," replied the ground leader. "Fire on the last plotted position and any future positions plotted."

"Will comply," replied the pilot, not liking the authorization order. *Well, Provost Leader, it's your team member, not mine,* thought the pilot.

The pilot descended to a low ground attack altitude and told the first pilot to target the last plotted position of the Provost Officer Neppin Fuuniam 4A. "Yes, Captain Pilot," replied the first pilot as he armed and targeted the plasma cannons. He had also heard the provost leader's order and didn't like it any better than the pilot. The plasma cannon only took about two septus to charge and about the same to target the desired coordinates.

"Fire when ready," said the captain pilot.

"Will comply," responded the first pilot as he engaged the fire command for optimum range auto fire. One septu later, the plasma cannon unleashed a battery of superheated pulsed plasma bursts that streaked instantly with bright bluish-orange pulses toward the targeted position.

Jack heard the whine and ascending pitch change of the air noise of the ship as it accelerated and descended to its ground targeting altitude. He saw a flash of blue-and-orange light beneath the clouds as the plasma cannons pounded the position he had been in only about a mentu ago. Fortunately, he'd picked up his pace considerably after he'd discovered he'd left the phony ID broadcasting on longer than he'd planned. He was now a good three hundred mu-uts from where the plasma cannons obliterated the jungle. Even at three hundred mu-uts, he could feel a fair pressure pulse and shock wave as the forest yielded to the energy of the plasma beam devastation. He'd seen the flashes first and then heard the sound of the cannons firing, not the actual cannons but the sound of the near light speed plasma jets as they vaporized the surrounding atmosphere and made moderate sonic booms as the vaporized air cracked under the onslaught of the energy beam weapon.

He went to ground again to evade any search technology they might be using to try and find him. He'd heard the impact of the plasma beams themselves as they pounded and annihilated everything within a ten-mentu circle of where he'd been just a mentu ago. *Well,* he thought, *I guess they're not buying my captured provost hostage ruse anymore, or they just don't care enough about their provost boy that they are willing to sacrifice him for their mission or bonus or whatever has brought them out here.* That news would definitely call for a change in tactics. *No more provost deceptions. It was now strictly a game of hunter and hunted, but who was who in this new game?* he thought wryly.

His biggest question now was, how big of an ego did these hunters have? Would they keep on going thinking that they could wrap him up, or would they bag it and head in to regroup or call in reinforcements? They were down to four on the ground, and how many in the ship? How badass and sure of themselves were they right now, and how could he get them to stay the course? He didn't like the reply he gave to himself. Crap, he didn't have to like it; he just had to do it. He really wanted more time to analyze his situation and come up with another decent plan of attack. What he had to do now was turn the tables on them, backtrack, and attack. No different from a one versus four dogfight engagement like he'd trained for in the past except that he was out of his element here and he was outgunned and outnumbered and the bad guys had some serious air superiority to boot.

Jack listened to the sound of the ship and could tell that it had pulled up and was headed back to a higher altitude where it could fly overwatch and intervene if it had the opportunity, which he was going to give it. He cautiously worked his way back to the site that had just been attacked. He took out a decoy and programmed it to his own transponder ID. He listened carefully as the sound of the ship faded out in the far distance. He guessed it had reached its orbiting altitude and had throttled back to conserve fuel or just to loiter at a slow controlled speed where they could monitor for any transponder IDs. How long would it take to acquire his decoy and target his position? Without the luxury of a delay timer, he would have to find out personally in very short order. Once again, he listened to make sure the ground force wasn't closing in on him. He checked his exfil route then flipped the switch on the decoy and threw it as far as he could. Then he ran.

It only took two and a half septus for the ship's search protocol to analyze and locate the decoy signal. It was remarkably close to the spot they'd just targeted, so they must have missed him because his transponder was now showing up. The pilot double-checked the location of the ground team and confirmed that they were still at their previous position getting ready to initiate a search for the Varaci again. The pilot called the ground leader and ordered, "Varaci target acquired. Hold your present position. We will commence attack now."

"Holding our position. Clear to engage," responded the ground team leader. The ship didn't have to get to its optimum ground attack altitude to engage the target, but it did have to get within a twenty-one-degree attack cone to properly target the coordinates of the transponder with its plasma cannons, which had to be more or less aligned with the target. This took about eight more septus, and the communication with the ground crew had taken another sixteen septus plus some additional time to finalize the attack.

Jack had just at twenty-seven septus to clear the target zone. He couldn't run flat out, as the terrain was too treacherous and he had the potential of falling, so he had to use enough caution to make sure he didn't end up on the ground in the target area. He made it just short of 130 mu-uts before the plasma beams impacted the decoy, which he managed to throw another 34 mu-uts despite its light weight. He took a pretty good hit from the shock wave and felt the heat coming off the blast zone. Fortunately, it wasn't like the concussion from a bomb blast, or he might have been severely injured at that range if it had been something like a five-hundred-pounder Mark 82 GBU or JDAM bomb. He went to ground under some wet overhanging foliage and debris in case they were looking for him with a thermal targeting device of some sort. He figured that the residual thermal aura from the energy beam impact would blank out his and any other thermal images in the ship's sensors in the nearby area for the few septus it took him to go to ground.

The ship pulled up from the targeting run, and the pilot noted that the target's ID was no longer being transmitted. "Provost Ground Leader, we are showing the target as destroyed. We had a solid ID before the attack, and it has now stopped. The plasma impact zone shows a direct hit on the target," reported the pilot to the ground leader.

"I hear your report," replied the ground team leader. "Transmit the impact coordinates, and we will investigate the target zone. Hold further aerial attacks unless advised," said the ground leader.

"Will hold further aerial attacks," replied the pilot. "I am transmitting the target zone coordinates now."

The ground team wasted no time getting to the last impact zone of the plasma cannon, which was just under a kahtak. It took them four mentus along the jungle path and then partly through the denser part of the forest with no path. When they got there, they didn't find much except a blasted-out clearing and smoldering debris and churned-up ground from the devastation caused by the plasma cannons. They'd hoped to find some sort of confirmation of the terminated fugitive, but they couldn't find anything. The ground team leader estimated that there would be less than 50 percent chance of finding any remains, but he'd hoped for something considering what this mission had cost them in trained personnel so far. He wanted to believe that his mission had been completed, but he wasn't 100 percent convinced.

Jack had heard the team pass him about eighty mu-uts from where he was paralleling the trail back to the place where he'd set the spike ambush. He thought there was a chance that they might have set the trap for him but didn't think they would under the fast-moving circumstance. Without the provost's ID broadcasting through his transponder, he wouldn't be able to pick up a warning signal. After he was sure they were well past, he moved back to the trail and up the hill to where he'd started this gambit. It didn't take him too long to get back to where he'd first ambushed them on the hill.

He carefully searched the hill where he shot the first provost. He knew they hadn't evaced the wounded or dead provosts yet, but he couldn't see any sign of his ill-fated victims. He was more worried about another possible guard provost attending to what might be a wounded provost. Checking both directions, he couldn't see or hear anything. He moved up the hill quietly but fast, ready to attack anything that moved against him. As he passed the spot where he thought he'd shot the two provosts, he heard a strange snuffling, snorting sound off the side of the trail up ahead. As he came around the large boulder that one of the provosts had used for cover earlier, he saw a horrific sight as four of the smaller predator-looking beasts he'd seen fleeing the larger predator earlier were feeding on the three corpses of the now extremely dead provosts.

The animals yelped and growled not knowing what had interrupted their feeding frenzy. Two of the animals bolted in panic, but the other two that were facing him snarled and lunged at him. Jack instantly switched on the dead provost's ID and was already targeting the closer one and fired, hitting it on the lower pelvis as it tried to launch itself at him. It screamed and collapsed from its destroyed rear quarters, while the other one had launched itself through the air at Jack's midsection. He couldn't get the rifle targeted on the attacking animal fast enough. When he fired, he missed the creature, which hit the rifle with its gaping jaws between Jack's two hands as he tried to block the animal's attack using the rifle.

The momentum and weight of the animal attacking on the uneven ground knocked Jack backward and off his feet as the enraged creature ripped the rifle form Jack's hands. The beast tried to shred the rifle for a couple of seconds until it realized it didn't have its intended prey in its mouth. Jack rolled backward and sprang to his feet just as the creature reacquired its intended target and launched itself at Jack again. The creature was a blur as it shot toward its prey, but it was just slightly too fast to change its direction as Jack sidestepped its attack. Jack sidestepped just enough to avoid being slammed by the beast, and instinct caused him to pull the katana from its scabbard just as the animal landed and turned to attack again.

The creature leapt as Jack swung the blade up through its chest and neck, completely severing the animal's front half from its back half. The major back half slammed into Jack's right leg, half spinning him around, while the head and jaws of the upper half continued to snap ravenously while the four legs of the lower half clawed spastically as it spasmed on the ground. Jack saw the other two creatures watching from the cover of the undergrowth not forty feet away. They looked like they were about ready to join in the fray, but they could clearly see the results of the attack by their bolder pack mates and decided to bolt instead.

The screams of the wild beasts attacking Jack had set off a chain reaction in the jungle, and every creature within a half of a kahtak either screeched, scrambled, took flight, or bolted from whatever was causing the terrifying raucous. The air and underbrush was a cacophony of fleeing animal sounds and utter discord. *Nothing like setting off all the alarm bells,* Jack thought to himself. The total chaos up on the hill didn't go unnoticed by the hunting party, which was already back on the game trail having found no signs of their intended victim at the bombardment site. The four remaining hunters double-timed it up the trail heading for the hill as fast as they could.

Keeping his katana at the ready, Jack looked in every direction for any signs of lurking predators but didn't see any. He went over to the rifle on the ground and picked it up to examine it. The power magazine had been fairly well crushed by the powerful jaws of the angry beast. He checked that the safety was in the off position and test-fired the rifle, but nothing happened. In the ship, the pilot's observed the provost's ID that Jack was broadcasting, but they were under orders to not fire now.

Jack switched the provost's ID off then switched the safety from off to on and then back off. With the damage to the rifle but no way to test it without giving up his position, he had no way of knowing if it would work or not again. He went over and looked at the remains of the half-devoured provosts and pulled the deceased provost's transponder IDs just in case he might need them. He looked around for fifteen septus to see if they'd stashed any of the dead provost's rifles nearby, but he didn't find any. They must have taken the rifles with them, which would be the smart thing to do.

He kept the damaged rifle not knowing if it was any good and headed back up the hill to set up an ambush position if it looked good for that. He knew from before that he had another good exfil route out the east side of the area where he'd camped last night. Just as he made it to the top of the hill, a blue light and nearly simultaneous blasts exploded behind him and off his right side. The first blast shattered a large rock and sent fragments spraying in every direction, and the other blast hit a clump of small dead trees directly behind him as he cut to the right on the trail. The blast into the clump of dense trees shattered them into a thousand fragments and dissipated the ion pulse in a huge shower of hissing ionized sparks all around him, knocking him to the ground and sending him rolling and tumbling into the small ravine to the right of the trail.

"I hit him, I hit him," said the ground team leader to the other two provosts. Two of them had fired, and the other two had watched while the others fired. What they hadn't realized was that both their rifles were still in the transponder ID targeting mode because they'd anticipated their target would be transmitting a standard ID like any other fugitive. Since there was no ID lock, they'd targeted on the nearest medium to high-density object closest to where they were aimed when the targeting command was initiated by the trigger pull. Those targets were a large rock and a thick clump of trees. This would have been the proper mode at the long range that the provosts had fired if there had been an ID to target, but without an ID, they merely picked the next best object.

Jack hadn't taken a direct hit from either of the ion rifles, but the blast that had hit the tree clump directly behind him had dispersed the energy blast in a small supersonic shock wave and ionized a major portion of the tree clump, which had rocked him completely through his body and completely jarred his senses into a short-circuited blackout. He lay at the bottom of the shallow ravine for several mentus without moving.

The provosts made their way up the hill as fast as they dared while still being cautious about approaching this treacherous enemy's position. They passed the place where their former team members had been desecrated by the Neebuu beasts and saw that two of the beasts had been killed, obviously by the Varaci fugitive. "It appears that the Neebuus almost saved us the trouble," the leader said to the other two provosts. They cautiously approached the position where they'd seen the fugitive go down but didn't see anything until they made it to the top and saw the Varaci lying in the ravine unconscious.

They covered the unconscious fugitive with their rifles while they climbed down to look at him. "Is he dead?" the junior provost asked the leader.

"No, I can see him breathing," said the leader as he got to within about three mu-uts of the Varaci.

"Should we shoot him a few more times just to make certain?" asked the other provost.

"No, no, do not shoot him," ordered the leader. "Our orders were just to eliminate him, but we may be able to get a bonus if we can bring him in alive and relatively unhurt."

The ground leader called the ship and advised the pilots of their situation and told them to contact the Wanana command center to see if they wanted the captured

Varaci brought back alive or just eradicated. After a couple of mentus, they came back with an affirmative answer for the alive condition. When the provost command post consulted the mine bosses, they thought they might be able to learn something about how he had escaped and wanted to know more about what else he'd done. Since the mine bosses had already invoked the confiscation clause on their escaped conscript, they weren't worried about not being able to access his accounts. With the proper persuasion, it might be easier to get the information about the whereabouts of any of his assets directly from the Varaci himself. Back at Corodune, the bosses were ecstatic about bringing this debacle to a close. It had cost them plenty of credits, but it should at least even out in the end.

A few mentus later, Jack began to awaken when he felt himself being dragged up the embankment of the ravine. He wasn't really coherent yet, but he realized that his wrists were bound, and it felt like his feet might be also. He kept his eyes closed and tried to figure out what had happened to him. He was still alive, and except for feeling like he'd been seriously body-slammed. He didn't think that he was badly hurt anywhere. He took a few squinting peeks and could see that all his limbs were still attached, and he couldn't see any blood. They laid him on his side at the top of the ravine, and he rolled slightly so that he could feel his legs when they put him down.

Yes, it felt as if his legs were bound but not too tightly, as if he had some sort of walking shackles on so that he couldn't run. He heard them talking about how they had shot at him and thought they'd hit him dead center, but somehow, the trees had absorbed the blast and he'd only been hit by the ion pulse blast wave. At some point, they discovered they'd had their rifles on the wrong targeting setting and realized they hadn't actually targeted their target. They harangued each other for a couple of mentus over that. They sounded like victorious combatants anywhere, thought Jack, embellishing and reliving their victory over and over for each other. Nothing was mentioned about the ones he'd killed, so either they weren't too worried about it or they just didn't want to bring up the issue. Then there was talk about getting a bonus for bringing him back alive. Either they're mercs, thought Jack, or they're some sort of special police ops group that works for bonuses or other incentives. Same crap, different daiyus, as everywhere else that has their kind.

He didn't like having his wrists bound, or his legs for that matter. He snuck another sliver of a peek at his wrists and could see that they were restrained much the same way as the last time. That meant that one or more of these guys had to have a control disk of some sort. Well, he wanted to get aboard their ship somehow, and he'd even thought of letting himself be taken prisoner as an option, but he'd discarded that because he thought they were more likely to kill him than capture him.

He would just have to figure out how to get free before they got back to Corodune or wherever they were planning on taking him. He wanted to keep up the façade of being unconscious for as long as possible because he thought they would be a little more careless with him that way. If they forced him to wake up, he would play incoherent for them. The four of them were standing in a tight circle comparing notes and speculating on what amount of bonus they might get for bringing him in alive. He'd heard them call for the ship, and they'd acknowledged that it would be twenty plus mentus before it could land on the accessible side of the hill and get over there with a gurney. The pilots would have to bring a gurney over so they wouldn't have to carry their prisoner. That would take a few more mentus to put together than just a standard pickup operation.

It was completely overcast again, and the cloud ceiling had come down to about three hundred feet. All the noise and excitement had gotten the attention of a lot of the greenbelt wildlife.

They didn't see it coming because it came in low and fast, and it didn't make a sound. The huge brown-and-blue raptor hit the four standing provost agents at somewhere close to eighty miles per hour. Two of the provosts were killed instantly as the raptor's talons nearly tore them in half. The third provost, the ground leader, didn't fare much better as he had a huge gash cut across his shoulder and back, and his clavicle was both broken and shoulder dislocated at the same time.

The fourth provost was hit by the edge of the raptor's foot but only by the meaty part and not the deadly sharp talons. Still, the hit sent him tumbling headfirst and hard into the ravine behind Jack's back. Jack squirmed to his knees and twisted so he could see exactly what had happened and where the huge raptor had gone. It had considerable momentum when it struck, so it ended up a good three hundred mu-uts past where Jack was as it decelerated and started flapping its ten-mu-ut wingspan to make a turn back.

There were two rifles on the ground along with the two dead and one severely wounded provost within three mu-uts. Jack hastily grabbed the translator ID from the dead provost, the closest one to him, and rolled to the nearest rifle. He could get his right hand on the grip and trigger, but his left wrist was over his right wrist, and they were bound together. He tried to arm the rifle, but it didn't seem to respond. He looked back toward the direction of the monstrous raptor, and it was halfway back and accelerating toward him.

His bag of supplies and katana were lying on the ground next to a squat boulder about the size of a small car about four mu-uts away. He lunged and rolled headfirst toward the katana and came up just short and shuffled the rest of the way there in about two seconds. He grabbed the hilt of the katana and swung the saya, or scabbard, between his feet and pulled the blade free. He held his legs up with the shackles between them and swung the blade at the high-strength material that bound his legs. The blade cut cleanly through, and he'd known better this time not to swing it too hard. He saw a huge shadow cross over him, so he rolled closer to the large rock to give himself a backstop and hopefully a harder access from the monstrous bird.

The raptor had aimed to land right on top of him, but Jack had rolled just out of its talon's reach. The raptor skidded to a halt about five mu-uts beyond and flapped its two huge four mu-ut wings to help it spin around. Jack was up and moving behind the large boulder, which didn't seem all that large now that the bird was on the ground. The rock was the only cover here. He'd have to go across or down the ravine to get away on that side or straight out into the open toward the bird to make it to cover twenty mu-uts away on the other side.

The huge bird flapped its wings and hopped toward Jack on its huge mu-ut-long five-taloned feet. Jack shrunk completely behind the rock to avoid the flapping wings that the bird was now drumming down on him from above. He ducked to the ground as low as he could, but the long wings just reached all the way around the rock. As the bird got closer, it looked like it was going to hop up on the rock where it could then pounce down on him from above. He couldn't let it get to that position. As the bird raised its wings to try and beat him, he sprang forward and swung the katana from behind his head forward and over the top. The blade cut through the trailing edge of the bird's wing and cut two feet of its wing flesh near the back of the fuzzy-feathered wing.

The bird didn't realize it at first but saw the pink blood spraying through the air as it flapped its wings. Its predator brain thought for a second that it had killed or wounded its prey until it saw Jack dodge to its right and swing something at it then dodge again. This time, Jack took out another mu-ut of its trailing edge feathers, and the bird could see that it was losing parts of its plumage. It screeched a horrific blast of rotting carrion breath and tried to flap and spin towards Jack, but he kept dodging faster than the bird could turn. Each time he dodged, he took a swing at the bird's wing with his katana. If he could stay ahead of its rotation rate and whittle it down and not take a direct hit from a solid part of its wing, he might come out ahead.

The bird's frustration kept increasing along with its screeching. Its wing feathers kept decreasing, and it wasn't sure where its prey was, but it kept getting glimpses of it attacking its wing. It could already feel the imbalance caused by the loss of its feathers and lift as it flapped its wings. It had never experienced anything like this. It had never been attacked by its prey before. It had no way to deal with this, and it realized it might be in danger. It suddenly had had enough. It flipped around toward one of the already dead prey creatures, took three hopping steps, snatched the one writhing creature on the ground, and launched itself into the air.

Its takeoff didn't go quite as planned because as it tried to climb away, the lost lift on its left wing caused by the missing feathers and the cut wing caused it to turn left and careen toward the rising terrain. It flapped harder and harder, but it was still not climbing fast enough or in the direction it wanted to go. It screeched again and dropped its prey to try and lighten its load. It was just enough to give it the extra lift it needed, and it cleared the trees on the ridgeline and headed down the hill where it was able to gain enough speed and lift to control its flight. Still, it was having to compensate for its uneven lift that caused it to continuously turn left. It didn't know exactly what had happened, but it knew it was angry and didn't want anything to do with whatever kind of prey it had just encountered ever again. Jack could hear the huge raptor screeching angrily as it flew off laboriously into the distance.

Jack continued to watch it fly away down the hill. He was pretty sure that it wouldn't be able to fly back up anytime soon, but still, he would keep a lookout for anything else that might be in the air or on the ground. He moved back to the dead provosts and searched them both briefly. He didn't find any control disk and hoped it wasn't on the dead provost that the bird had carried over the jungle and had just dropped a half a kahtak away. The way things were around this place, something was probably already feeding on the dropped provost corpse; manna delivered directly from heaven.

He went over to the edge of the ravine and saw the crumpled body of the other provost. He shimmied down the ravine to check him out. When he got there, the injured but still alive provost was breathing and unconscious. It looked like the provost had taken a pretty good beating from being slammed down the ravine. Jack then grabbed the provost's translator ID and started searching him. *There, got it,* he said to himself as he found the control disk in the provost's uniform pocket. It took him a few seconds to figure it out, but then he released his wrist and leg restraints and pocketed the small control disk. That saved trying to cut the restraints with his katana. *Wow, can you believe that,* thought Jack, *saved by a huge carnivorous raptor. If that was some sort of divine intervention, I guess I'll take it.*

He left the unconscious provost in the ravine and went back up. He didn't see anyone coming yet. He grabbed a rifle and went over to the dead provost. He grabbed the other rifle and a power magazine out of the one that hadn't worked. He bent down over the dead provost and turned on the dead provost's ID on his own translator. Suddenly, he could hear the transmission from the ship. His translator comm must have paired with the matching provost's ID right next to him. The pilot reported, "On the ground. Will be at your position in estimate six mentus. Verify your position still on far slope. We are getting an erroneous reading showing your ground leader 0.62 kahtaks southeast of your last reported position."

Trying to sound as much like a provost as he could but also trying to sound scared and injured, Jack replied into the dead provost's translator, "Help, help us. Attacked by large raptors. One coming back at us now. Raptors took ground leader and Varaci. Hurry, help us." He then scanned the sky to make sure there really weren't any inbound raptors, turned off the provost's ID, grabbed his bag of supplies, and headed toward the ship but away from the pilots and around the far side of the hilltop from the direct line to the ship.

He stayed low and in cover as best he could, making sure that the ship's crew wasn't coming on this less direct route to the injured ground team. He came up the hill where he thought he would have good cover between him and where the pilots might be. He saw them working their way toward the dead and wounded provost, which would be another half a kahtak. They were leading a floating gurney of some type, and it seemed to not be going very fast. *Good, that would slow them down in both directions,* he thought to himself.

Jack stayed below the sightline of the pilots and headed toward the ship and hoped there wasn't anyone else on board the ship. In another two hundred mu-uts, he came over a small rise and could see the ship sitting on a level area another three hundred mu-uts out. He put as much blocking terrain between himself and the ship as he could. He stopped behind a small rise and checked out the other rifle. He turned on the dead provost's ID, and the rifle and its holo sight came to life. He turned the ID back off but had it cued up in case he needed the rifle.

He worked to within about a hundred mu-uts of the ship, and there was still no hostile indications from it. When he got to about fifty mu-uts, he was suddenly illuminated by a blue laser turret from the top of the ship. He dove behind some cover of rocks and bushes, but the blue light was still illuminating the other side of the rock pile. It hadn't fired, but it knew he was there and it was tracking him. *Now what?* he thought. He didn't dare go any closer. The ship was impressive looking. It looked very well-built and functional. It was a little less sleek than it had looked in the air, but then it was sitting on four large retractable skid-type feet that made it look somewhat ungainly, almost like an angry giant beetle

Either the ship was in an autonomous defensive mode or someone was still aboard the ship. He didn't hear any more comm transmission from the provosts that might have indicated that he'd been spotted, so he hoped that it was an autonomous mode and no one else was aboard the ship. He was far enough away from the pilots and their gurney, so he flipped the provost's ID on again. The blue targeting light from the ship went out. He decided it was an automatic defense system and would only allow authorized crew members near the ship. He hoped that's what he was up against; otherwise, he would have to wait for the pilots and take them out and try to figure it out from there.

He got up and moved away from the ship just to make sure it didn't think he was hostile. Nothing happened, so he moved toward the ship again. It didn't seem to pay any attention to him now. He moved closer, thirty, twenty, ten mu-uts. Then he was at the ship. There was a wide ramp from the side of the ship to the ground, but there was a closed access door at the top of the ramp. He went up the ramp and looked at the door controls. The door was big enough for personnel or cargo at about three mu-uts square.

With the provost's ID active, his HUD showed a new command function in the center with options for open, close, and lock with a miniature image of the ship's door. *Thank you, Junot, for figuring out this translator and all its command functions,* he said to himself. He pulled his katana and commanded the door to open, while he moved to the outside of the doorframe. He peeked into the ship and saw no one. He ducked low, slipped into the ship, and moved left into a small semicircular corridor and what appeared to be a staging area.

He waited to see if he could hear anyone coming and then looked around to see what he could figure out. There was a manual locking handle on the door, so he closed the door then pushed it down and into a locking detent. *Well, no one is coming in until I check this out,* he hoped. He moved forward cautiously with his rifle to clear the ship. The short corridor opened into a moderate-size main service room with equipment storage and an area for lashing down cargo. On the far side, there was a small arms storage area with six rifles still in their racks and about ten empty spaces. There were several smaller storage rooms of some sort to the left of the arms locker going toward the rear of the ship. To the right at the center was a short stairway of about six steps leading to the front of the ship with a wide transparent door that was braced open. It was all very utilitarian and military looking.

Jack approached the stairway and cleared his way up to the bridge of the ship. There were two side-by-side seats with a center instrumentation console between them where the crew would sit to fly the ship. Behind the pilot seats were another six passenger seats in a semicircle. There was no one on the bridge. To the right of the stairs was another short stairway going up, so he continued to the upper deck. He went up the stairs and found two small bunk rooms with their doors open and a bathroom between them.

The upper deck was a little smaller with a slightly lower ceiling than the lower deck. To the back was another bunk area that would accommodate at least a dozen more troops and another larger bathroom that had two commodes and four small sinks. To the right of that, up against the stairway and a bulkhead at the front of the room, was a small functional-looking galley designed to accommodate the crew. The ship was obviously designed for a small squad of armed troops for maybe a week or more deployment. The ship itself was obviously well armed as Jack had seen when they had obliterated the area in the jungle where he'd tossed the decoy.

He cleared the room quickly and decided the pilots must have been the only ones aboard other than the ground team that had tried to kill him. He hadn't seen any other main access doors to the ship other than the one he had come in on. He went back to the flight deck and checked out the equipment and crew accommodations. There were the two pilot seats with the six observer seats behind them. There was at least a dozen embedded display screens in front of and to the sides of the pilot seat as well a host of other controls and instrumentation. It looked fairly similar in a lot of ways to the shuttle *Victory* or any other advanced transport-type aircraft.

It was arranged similarly, although a lot of the instruments were unfamiliar. There was an overhead console with an array of communications controls and the center console with a layout of the armament and weapons systems. On either side of both of the pilot seats, there was a slightly raised armrest with a hand-shaped grip that would fit the pilot's hand. It was tilted up at a thirty-degree angle with about the right amount of angle for his wrists. The grips were contoured and ergonomic for a hand like his or any opposable-thumb person.

He sat in the pilot seat, and a full HUD display instantly came on in front of windshield. A list of options was shown on the HUD for operating the ship. A voice suddenly spoke from above his head. It startled him slightly for a second, but he instantly recognized it as the modulated voice of some sort of radio transmission. "Provost Janntaka One with report," said the voice on the comm.

"Go with report, Janntaka One," replied another voice.

"Janntaka One crew returning to ship with one badly wounded provost. Two additional killed and one missing, killed by Sabrav raptor, we believe. Ground leader is missing, and Varaci target killed or missing, reported by the provost ground team."

"Understand all dead or missing and also Varaci and one badly injured provost. Verify your target is dead or missing. Do you have visual or other confirmation?"

"Negative visual confirmation," replied the pilot's voice, "only reported from now dead or wounded provost about twenty mentus ago before we went to collect captured target and recover ground team."

"We copy, report airborne for return to Seema base."

"Janntaka One will report airborne," replied the pilot's voice. Jack understood instantly that the pilots were relaying their voice comms through the ship to an uplink communications connection, maybe a satellite. What that meant was that the pilots or other ground crew probably couldn't communicate directly with their base. They would have to relay everything through their ship if they were outside on patrol or for some other reason.

Jack estimated that he would have ten to twelve mentus before the crew got back to the ship. He looked at the options on the ship's HUD and selected Start Sequence. An orange warning flashed across the display, "UNAUTHORIZED." *Crapola,* he thought. He tried several other things including placing his hands on the controls and buckling into the seat and got the same warning. He knew what it was. He was going to have to get the pilot's, one or both, translator ID to get the ship to give him authorization to operate it. He studied the overhead comm panel for a minute and saw that there were two control heads to external communications links and another separate console with individual separate channels for ship to crew linked communications. There was also a ship-to-ship link unit and another separate unit for scrambling and decoding selected comm units. One of the external comms was off and another one in the on position that was being used by the ship's pilots to talk to their base. He switched the unit off. He didn't want the pilots calling for reinforcements if he could prevent it.

He went to the lower deck and checked out his rifle to make sure it was working. He knew the pilots were still a good ways off, so he opened the main access door slightly, drew a bead on a nearby tree, locked the targeting system on, and fired. Yep, the rifle seemed to work as expected. He closed the door and watched through the portal in the door for the returning pilots. It took them another twelve mentus, but then he saw them coming over the hill to the south. They had the wounded provost on the floating gurney. They weren't going very fast, probably because of the gurney, and when they got closer, he could see that they were looking nervously around at the sky. It was apparent they were afraid of another raptor attack—what had they called it? Oh, yes, a Sabrav raptor.

When they got to about a hundred mu-uts, Jack gently slid the door open about a foot and took aim at the pilots. One had a hand on the gurney and was somehow controlling it while his rifle was slung across his front. The other one was carrying his rifle at the ready while looking skyward and in as many directions as he could as fast as he could. They didn't look comfortable outside the safety of their ship. It was going to get a lot more uncomfortable for them in the next few septus, he thought. They were so busy watching for raptors and steering the gurney that they hadn't noticed the ship's door was now partially open.

At fifty mu-uts, he slid the door all the way open and yelled, "Freeze in your position and drop your weapons or I'll shoot!" The startled crew looked around for a second, and the pilot carrying his rifle aimed it all around, looking for the source of the voice. "Drop your weapons or I will fire!" yelled Jack again. The pilot guiding the gurney had stopped and was frozen in position, but the other one zeroed in on the direction of the voice coming from the ship. It started to swing it's rifle toward the ship's door that it now saw was open. Jack didn't have any choice as he fired at the already targeted pilot that was trying to draw a bead on him. The ion pulse hit dead center on the pilot's upper torso, sending him sprawling backward. The other pilot took off running to Jack's right as fast as he could. Jack put three rounds into the dirt just in front of him as he yelled, "Freeze and drop your weapon or the next one is on you!"

The running pilot suddenly stopped, froze, and then turned to face Jack. "Now lift the sling over your head with your right hand and drop your weapon on the ground and walk toward me with your hands on your head!" yelled Jack again. The pilot did as he was instructed. Jack checked the other pilot to make sure he wasn't moving. When the walking pilot got to about twenty mu-uts, Jack yelled, "Now turn around. Keep your hands in the air and kneel on the ground. Don't move or I will shoot you!" The pilot again did as he was told but kept trying to link his comm to the comm relay on the ship and then back to their ship's base. For some reason it wouldn't show a comm link lock. Jack came out of the door and moved toward the pilot while he looked him over and checked again on the pilot he'd shot. He circled around the kneeling pilot at a distance of eight mu-uts, watching him and checking the other pilot. "Stay just like that and don't move or you'll be dead," said Jack as he moved past the pilot and picked up the pilot's rifle.

Jack checked the other pilot and verified he was dead and uploaded the dead pilot's translator ID. As Jack came back to the kneeling pilot, the pilot shouted to him, "Who are you, and what do you want!"

"You know who I am," replied Jack. "I'm the Varaci you came all the way out here to kill. Now who are you, and what's your crew position on the ship?" said Jack.

"How did you get on our ship, and how did you get that ion pulsar to work for you?" asked the pilot.

Jack replied, "That's not your concern. I'm asking the questions and you're answering them, or your personal little outing for the daiyus will suddenly end in tragedy." Jack moved to within about four mu-uts of the pilot while keeping him covered with the ion rifle. "Now sit on the ground with your legs crossed," said Jack. As the pilot was shuffling his position, Jack copied the pilot's translator ID and read all his stats. He thought he had all he needed but decided to see if he could get any more information from the pilot. He backed up and scanned the sky down to the horizon for any signs of the Sabrav raptor. He definitely felt exposed here on the top of the nearly barren hill. "Now what's your name, pilot?" Jack said again, already knowing the answer as he pointed the ion rifle at his captive.

The pilot hesitated for a few septus then replied,"Bennon Colhanak."

"OK, Pilot Bennon Colhanak, we're going to have a friendly little conversation now, so pay attention if you don't want to start losing parts of your body that you consider important to you." Jack started a short interrogation of his prisoner. "What sort of range does your ship have?" he asked the pilot. The pilot just stared at him but didn't answer as if he was protecting some sort of secret information. Jack moved the rifle a couple of feet off the pilot and fired a round into the ground, which sprayed the pilot with wet dirt. The pilot almost jumped up, but Jack put the rifle back on him dead center.

"Who do you think you are!" yelled the pilot.

"I'll tell you who I am," said Jack. "I'm the guy you tried to obliterate with your aerial bombardment a while ago when you thought you had my position fixed in the jungle, and I'm the guy that took out your entire ground squad that was sent out to kill me, except for the last few that were killed by the big raptor. You're next if you give me one more incorrect, incomplete, or reluctant answer."

"You'll just kill me then anyhow," said the pilot.

"No, I give you my word. I won't kill you if you cooperate and answer my questions. The only reason your friends are all dead is because they tried to kill me. What I did was in self-defense, the same as you would have done." Jack went on, "The only reason you're still alive, even though you tried to kill me, is you have some information I want, and I'm willing to trade your life for it."

The pilot weighed that all for a moment and decided that in all fairness, it was basically true, what this Varaci had said. Maybe the Varaci would spare him if he answered the questions; it couldn't really hurt anything and sounded better than the alternative at the moment anyway. "The range of the ship is just under fourteen thousand kahtaks fully fueled, which is what we had when we left."

"How much range does it have now after all your recon or search flights over the area?" asked Jack.

"We still have around seven thousand kahtaks, more than enough to get back to our base. Why? Do you want me to fly you there?" asked the pilot somewhat snidely.

"Not likely," replied Jack, trying to decide if he should just shoot him and get it over with.

"I'm guessing you want me to fly you somewhere else, then," said the pilot, thinking that this may be his bargaining chip to save his life.

Jack let that hang without answering it. "So the ship is pilotable with a crew of just one, then?" asked Jack just to verify what the pilot had just divulged.

"Yes, two is better so that one can handle communication and other duties, but it can be flown with just one. Where do you want to go?" replied the pilot.

Jack responded, "Are you the captain or first officer on this ship?"

The pilot replied, "I am the first crew pilot. You killed the captain over there."

"I killed your captain because he didn't comply and was swinging his rifle to aim at me. He was warned twice and didn't comply," said Jack. That was also true, thought the pilot; so far, this Varaci hadn't lied to him or tried to trick him. Maybe, maybe he would keep his word.

The last thing Jack needed was to have to be watching over this pilot while he attempted to make him fly him somewhere. The pilot would also know the ship systems completely, something Jack didn't have the luxury of. Even if he did fly Jack where he was told, Jack still didn't want the pilot trying to set up clandestine comms with his base, and he could possibly enable some sort of tracking device. "Where's your base?" asked Jack, already knowing part of the answer.

"The ship is based near Wanana," replied the pilot cautiously.

"How far from Wanana—what's it called?" asked Jack.

"It's sixteen kahtaks east of Wanana. It's, uh, called Kahaluku," said the pilot, thinking that maybe he could get to the provost post where they could overwhelm the Varaci if he could somehow warn them.

Nice try, but no cigar, thought Jack. "All right, Pilot Bennon Colhanak, here's what we're going to do," said Jack. "You're going to walk two hundred mu-uts out in front of the ship while I watch you from the entrance door. Then you're going to sit on the ground and wait."

"Why? What!" said the pilot.

"Shut up," said Jack. "You already tried to kill me, and you just lied to me. By our agreement, I should just shoot you now." The pilot suddenly didn't look too well, thought Jack. "You're going to sit on the ground and wait," said Jack. "Then I'm going to spend about ten mentus getting the ship ready to fly while you sit there. If you sit there and behave the whole time while I'm getting the ship ready I will toss your rifle out the door just before I launch. When I'm gone, you can come get your rifle and go your own way."

"What, what the, you can't just jump in and fly this ship. It takes yenets of experience and moondats of training. You'll just kill yourself, and I'll be stranded here with no way out," said the pilot in an angry yet pleading voice.

"Don't bet on it, but if I do, that's the too bad so sad for you. At least you'll have a rifle," said Jack. "That's my only offer in light of the fact that you just lied to me about your Seema base."

The pilot looked incredulous. "How, how the, did you— What, what about the wounded provost we just brought back?"

"Shut up," said Jack. "the provost isn't my problem. If you don't stay put, you won't get your rifle, and you'll get dead much sooner rather than possibly living somewhat longer. I'll give you another two hundred or more power rounds from your dead captain's rifle. I don't know if you can use his rifle or not, and I don't care. Stay put or lose your rifle. I've been out here for a few daiyus, and I just now got a rifle at the vimar when I killed your clueless guards. Did your team think you were dealing with some criminal half-wit pickpocket or something?" said Jack as he badgered the pilot.

"They just told us that we would be hunting some Varaci escapee from the Corodune mine," replied the pilot.

"Well, then you got screwed by your boss or whoever sent you out here to play. Maybe if you're lucky, you'll have a next time to contemplate your situation a little better," said Jack.

"How am I supposed to survive out here? Where am I supposed to go?" said the pilot dejectedly.

"I don't know," said Jack. "You probably know what's out there better than I do. There's that bare strip near where the vimar ran out of fuel. I think it has something to do with the irrigation system for this greenbelt. There may be an entrance to an underground maintenance complex or something. I don't know because I didn't get to explore it very well before you and your provost ship came calling. Maybe there is a secure area with food and comms there. Maybe there's some vimar fuel so you can drive home. I guess you'll have to go exploring and find out. I would suggest staying under cover of the forest canopy and watching overhead for those huge raptors as well as several types of ground predators that I've encountered. Good luck, you'll need it. Now go and find yourself a comfortable spot out in front of the ship while I get the ship ready to fly. You only get one chance, so don't screw it up. You'd better hope that something hungry doesn't come out of the jungle before you get your rifle back. Now go," said Jack as he pointed the rifle at the pilot.

The pilot reluctantly went to where he'd been told under the threat of being shot. He truly did hope that nothing big and carnivorous came out of the jungle. He hunkered down low where he'd been told to and kept his eyes on the sky and the jungle. He wondered how long it would take the Varaci to figure out that the ship couldn't be flown by anyone but the designated crew members. He wondered how dumb the Varaci might be to think that he could actually fly the ship even if it wasn't locked to only the two assigned pilots. He could wait out the Varaci as long as he wasn't attacked by some jungle animal. Even if he was, the Varaci would be stuck here too, which would mean that his crew had actually more or less completed their mission. Maybe they would give a death bonus to his wife and two kindren.

Jack manually locked the door and set both the pilots' rifles over to the side after removing the power magazines and taking them with him to the flight deck. He checked that the pilot was where he was supposed to be. He loaded the captain pilot's ID in his translator and pulled up the preflight menu. He again selected Start Sequence, and the HUD came alive and displayed a checklist of required preflight items. It was basically like any other checklist he'd seen, only he didn't recognize some of the items. "Initiate Sub-systems Power Up," was the first command. He selected it, and all the other monitors and subsystems powered up. Next was "Engines Self-Test and Prestart Sequence," which he selected. The engine monitor display came to life and showed a series of self-test functions being completed. The self-testing sequence completed and then displayed "Ready for Engine Start."

He smiled as he went through the list of systems tests. Everything showed ready—, "Maneuvering Controls, Navigation, Communications, Weapons System Targeting and Fire Controls, Pressurization and Life Support, and Ship Damage Control System." When all the system checks were complete, the HUD display showed the command "Initiate Engine Start." Jack selected the icon, and the sound of two low-pitched vibrations, which grew in loudness and pitch, started. There were various mechanical and electrical sounds that started all around the ship as all the mechanical systems came to life as the engines spooled up.

He didn't know exactly what technology he was controlling as far as the propulsion system, but he knew the sound of starting engines on jet fighter airplanes. They didn't really sound like turbines, but they didn't sound purely electronic either. He wished he'd had time to study a manual, but he'd save that for later.

The pilot, sitting near the edge of the jungle, wondered why it was taking so long for the Varaci to figure out he wasn't going anywhere with the ship because he was locked out of the ship's systems. Maybe he was just desperate and scrambling around trying everything he could think of to make the ship work. Hopefully, he wouldn't do any damage to the ship. Pilot Bennon Colhanak really felt naked sitting out in the open with no weapon while the Varaci played around in the ship trying to figure out that it would never work for him.

What? What! He couldn't believe what he was hearing. It couldn't be. There was no possible way. It just couldn't be. It couldn't be what he was hearing. But he knew that sound better than just about anything else except maybe his own breathing. The sound of Kershavah crew assault ship starting its engines, there was no other similar sound here on Nishda. *How, how did this mine conscript Varaci get the engines started? How did he break into the ship's security system and override it? That's not possible, just not possible.*

But it was. The ship was now powered up and ready for takeoff. He could see the Varaci in the pilot seat and the shimmering heat rising off the rear of the engine pods. He wanted to run up and break down the door, but he knew he couldn't. He knew if he left this spot, the wretched Varaci would leave him with nothing because the Varaci had kept his word and done everything he'd said he would do so far. He also knew he couldn't get in the door if it was manually locked. Maybe, maybe the Varaci hadn't locked it. No, shimit, he knew the Varaci had locked it. Who was he fooling to think otherwise?

The engines were running, and the HUD checklist switched to "Takeoff Checks." Jack ran through the remaining items, all of which were system checks prior to takeoff. He checked again to make sure the pilot was still there. Jack thought, *All right, I'll keep my part of the bargain now even though you lied to me. He is, after all, a pilot, and he won't last an hour out here without a weapon.* He pointed to the pilot and yelled, "Stay put!" as if the pilot could hear him. He jumped up and ran to the door. He looked through the portal to make sure the pilot wasn't there then opened the door and threw out the pilot's rifles and tossed the power mags a good twenty feet out onto the ground. Then he locked the door. He bolted back up to the flight deck and saw that the pilot was still where he was supposed to be, glaring at him now in disbelief from what he could tell.

"Good boy, you've done one smart thing today," he said out loud. Jack strapped himself into the pilot seat. "OK, here we go," he said as he put his hands on the controls and felt a tingling as the flight control system read his tactile impulses. The display on the HUD switched to a flight parameters display. On the side, there were readouts for altitude, both relative and absolute, speed, vertical rate, heading, as well as a full array of navigation readouts for distance to destination, time to destination, and a variety of other information including weapons systems status and targeting. There was no displayed data for the navigation or route, since he hadn't input anything because for now, he was just going northwest to the north side of this greenbelt, at least for now.

Chapter 10: Renegade

The input to the controls on each side seemed to be duplicates, so Jack could use either hand. Maybe they had right- and left-handed pilots here too. He eased up on the right-side hand grip and felt the ship shudder as the engines spooled up to power. The engines were surprisingly quiet, but he could still hear and feel their immense power seething throughout the ship. He wondered how they could be so quiet yet so powerful. Active noise cancellation came to mind; he wondered if that had something to do with it. The whole ship began to wobble slightly as the weight of the ship lifted off its landing gear. The ship rose slowly then more rapidly into the air as Jack moved the control grip forward. The ship started to accelerate as it climbed skyward.

He looked down and saw the pilot briefly as he started running to where the rifle would be. A message flashed on the surround HUD saying "Landing Legs Retracted." It must be an automatic function, he realized. When he'd gained enough altitude, he moved the control stick to the right and banked until he was headed to the northwest. He kept his speed slow and controlled. He didn't know the limitations or operational parameters of the ship, although he was sure he was nowhere near any of its limits. Still, until he got a good feel for the handling of the ship, then he would stay in the "better safe than sorry mode." Also, if he was somehow being tracked by some command post or sensor array somewhere, he didn't want it to look like he was trying to escape. It would look better if the ship looked like it was performing another slow search pattern.

He headed northwest toward the edge of the greenbelt on the north side. He threw in a few casual turns in both directions as if the ship was searching for something. It only took a few mentus to reach the edge of the jungle. He didn't want to waste a lot of fuel, but he did one complete turn around the area to recon potential landing sites. There was a group of tall trees right on the edge of the desert boundary that he thought looked like a promising site. He could land on the open desert next to the trees yet still be partially covered by the trees, if . . . if he didn't screw up the landing.

Jack slowed his approach speed and circled around as he approached parallel to the tree line over the desert. The ship responded nicely to his inputs, and he slowed even more as he came up alongside the trees. The nose of the ship started to sink as he slowed. "Whoa, whoa," he said to himself as the nose started to drop even more. He added power and pulled the nose up. This stopped the nose sinking, but now the pitch attitude was too nose up for landing, and he was now accelerating and climbing. He added more power and pulled the nose up for a go around. He circled out and climbed back up to think about what had just happened. He looked at the ship's HUD display and saw an Approach/Landing menu. He hadn't noticed that a few mentus ago when he was busy looking outside for a landing spot and circling for the approach. He selected the Approach/Landing menu and saw a short checklist of landing items. One of them was Arm Landing Thrusters and Landing Legs. *Well, that might explain it and would obviously help considerably,* he thought as he admonished himself for not seeing the inputs on his first landing attempt.

The ship could hover with just control inputs, but for landing, it needed to arm separate thrusters to keep it level for landing as it reduced thrust to descend to land. He probably could have screwed the pooch trying to land without the thrusters. "All right, let's try this again," as he descended to come in for another landing attempt. He did basically the same approach but kept his nose a little higher this time. With the landing thrusters showing armed on the HUD readout, it now also displayed "Height Above Touchdown in Mu-uts."

He watched the display readout as he descended and slowed. When the display showed "80 Mu," he felt and heard the thrusters kick in. The attitude display of the ship settled to level as shown on the HUD. He continued his descent with the vertical rate slowly decreasing as he descended. He watched the height above touchdown count down seventy, sixty, all the way to twenty. Then it switched to single digits. Just after passing one, he felt the left rear and then the right rear and then the two front landing feet touch down. The ship eased onto the struts and settled nicely. "Not too bad for my first solo landing in a new ship, well, except for the part where I almost crashed and burned in a huge fireball on the first try," he said aloud to himself as he laughed. He somewhat hoped the pilot Bennon Colhanak he'd left stranded was having as much good luck as he was.

He ran through the shutdown check that appeared and then shut down and secured the ship. He would spend the night here and try to learn as much about the ship as he could in the next few horuns. After taking a few mentus to contemplate his situation, Jack started going through all the available menus on the HUD and found a complete section on systems and an operations manual. There was too much information to absorb everything, but with a little bit of selective reading, he managed to get a basic understanding and working knowledge of the ship and its systems. He ran through the navigation setup and programming functions and was able to set up a direct course to Se-ahlaalu. The display showed "Distance to Next/Destination" as "18186/18186." *Well, that would be a stretch,* he thought. He'd already come nearly 4,800 kahtaks. He had a lot farther to go; the display showed "Range 7658k." He would be a little shy, but it was what it was.

He was used to learning everything he could about systems and theory, but he didn't have time for anything more than a crash course to help avoid a crash. He learned that the ship was a Kershavah crew assault ship and was designed for short- to medium-range policing actions for a standard crew of up to eighteen provosts for a two-wenek period. The ship itself was armed with standard paired pulsed plasma cannons that could be targeted in either the air-to-air or air-to-ground modes.

The ship also had the capability to add on other modular weapon systems if needed. All he needed to really know right now was how to operate the ship. He could tell he wouldn't likely be able to functionally operate the weapons systems without another crew member, so he was hoping he wouldn't need them. The engines were some sort of a magnetic flux-shielded linear acceleration drive units contained in an ion plasma field containment system. They were nothing like he'd ever read about even in theory. He had a general idea of how they might work, but he didn't have time to get into the theory of the propulsion system. The fuel the ship used was called Pentricominate, but that's all the ship's data said about it that he could easily find.

There was something written about a huge entropy change and a large energy output caused by the bombardment of the fuel with high-energy plasma and the stripping away of the electrons to create an ionized state in a contained magnetic flux field. This then generated large amounts of directed thrust and was controlled by the ship's flux shielding containment system. Well, he'd have to take the builder's word for it because all he needed to do for now was to fly this baby.

He delved into the ship's communication system. The ship did have an ID system that was programmable with a discrete code for monitoring of the ship by a command vessel or traffic control system. He found the control head for the ID system and verified that the ID unit was off so that someone couldn't be inadvertently tracking him. He also found the ship's autonomous defense system input interface and programmed in all the bootlegged IDs he had just in case he needed to enter or exit under an alias ID.

As he sat studying, the sun had set and the light faded to the east and night had set in. He felt a slight tremble in the ship, and outside in the jungle, the mist began to congeal and swirl around the ship. Soon, the ship was completely enveloped, and the mist got denser until it began a continuous light drizzle. The ship was just barely outside the forest area in the desert zone, but it was still completely shrouded in Nishda's engineered precipitation.

He wondered what made the jungle grow where it did and why it didn't grow out on the bare desert even with the daily rain that it received that overlapped to the jungle. He checked the ship's self-defense systems and found that the blue lights he'd seen when he'd first approached the ship were both a detection and targeting system that could operate autonomously just as he'd suspected. It could be programmed in various modes with regard to outside intrusions. He saw that it was previously armed to target anything without the required crew ID at thirty mu-uts but would warn everything else at fifty mu-uts. Now he was truly glad that he hadn't gotten inside of that thirty-mu-ut range when he'd first approached the ship. He now set the auto defense to target anything, with or without the proper ID at fifty mu-uts.

It had been a harrowing wenek. He went to the galley, and after some exploring, he found some decent snacks to munch on. He snooped around some more and found the refrigerated and frozen storage coolers directly behind the galley. They weren't all that big, but they were well organized. He snooped through all the stored food and beverages. He found several small cases of well-packaged liquid. He looked at the label on the containers; it said Fennor Neekan Qalalé. *Seriously,* he said to himself, *qalalé, that's what Cherga said was their equivalent of beer.*

He pulled the seal off the corner of the rectangular bottle-like container. It popped slightly, so he smelled it as it bubbled up somewhat. Yep, it really was, that's surely what it was by the smell. He couldn't believe it. He tasted it, and it actually was some sort of brewed beer-type beverage. Not too bad; it was certainly a little different, somewhat musty and sweeter. It almost had a primitive taste to it. It reminded him of something, but he didn't know what. They were probably saving this for some sort of self-congratulatory mission-accomplished celebration.

Well, too bad, best-laid plans of mice and provosts. He wished that Cherga and Junot were here to share this, but he didn't think they would have liked the route he had to take to get here. *I will get to share one of these with you eventually, I promise you that.* He was almost too tired to eat anything, but he needed to keep his strength up. After eating something and drinking the rest of the container of qalalé, he took a rifle and his katana and other possessions and went and picked one of the pilot's cabins. He flopped onto the bed and was soon fast asleep.

451

He awoke with a start when he heard something screeching somewhere outside the ship. He grabbed his weapons and then listened to see if he could tell what it was. It had stopped for a minute then started again. He heard the sound of the defense system firing. It was kind of a rapid mid frequency zweeup, zweeup, zweeup. Something or someone was being fired on by the ship. He got up and went to the flight deck and peered carefully through the windows but couldn't see anything. Zweeup, zweeup, zweeup, he heard and saw the blue pulses of the ship's defense system shooting toward the jungle.

It was already getting light out, but the mist and fog were still swirling around the ship. It wasn't as heavy as when it first started. He could just barely see the outline of the trees in the jungle twenty mu-uts away. A sheet of mist moved past the trees, and a clear spot appeared for a few seconds. Jack could see the forms of some type of primates jumping through the upper branches of the forest canopy. There were a dozen or more creatures in the farther trees but none close in. They seemed to be highly agitated and were screaming and running about in frenzy. One of them hopped to the closer tree and tried to make it to the center of the tree and then down. Zweeup went the ship's defense system. *Crap,* he thought, *it was frying the local wildlife that got too close.*

He went and turned the system off then went back to see what happened. The primates were still in the far tree, and several of them threw some seed pods or something at the ship. One of them hit the ship and banged across the top of the hull. "Nice toss," said Jack. "Hmmm, sorry about that, little guys. It wasn't my intention to take out the neighborhood semi-indigenous primate group," he said aloud. It wasn't like he could actually apologize to them.

Aside from the early wake-up call, he felt pretty rested. He went and got something to drink and another snack of some type of cookie-like things that were in wrappers. He went to the pilot seat and checked everything out again then went back to the crew area. He discovered two small cabinets off the toilet area were actually tiny shower stalls. Well, he couldn't turn that down. He went back and turned the defense system back on but dialed the range and power down so that only something coming inside of ten mu-uts would be targeted but not killed. That was the closest range it could be set to. Back in the shower, he discovered that the showers had a small restricted flow rate, probably to conserve water, but, hey, there was only one of him instead of an entire crew, so he indulged himself and spent a good ten mentus soaking in the shower. He hadn't felt this great since the luxurious shower accommodation in Zshutana's apartment.

He had now had a hot shower in actual privacy, and he'd had an actual qalalé with dinner last night. It practically didn't get any better than this. The only thing that would have been better is if Zshutana was there with him. *Soon, hopefully,* he thought; yes, hopefully, he could make that happen sometime soon. He went through the pilot's storage cabinets in the room and actually found some clean clothes that came pretty close to fitting him. The provosts were some type of different alien he wasn't familiar with, and they were a little too small, but the pilots were different and larger, and the first pilot's clothing would do well enough. He hadn't felt this good in quite a while.

Back on the flight deck, he programmed the navigation computer for a direct route to Se-ahlaalu. It was still close to eighteen thousand kahtaks to Se-ahlaalu. *Well, no one said it was going to be a cakewalk,* he said to himself. After checking everything from the inside and verifying all the systems were operational, he decided to do a preflight exterior inspection. He wanted to get a better look at the outside of the ship and also make sure there weren't any spare provost pilots clinging to the ship somewhere outside. He turned off the ship's perimeter defense system and grabbed the rifle and his katana. After checking visually from the inside, he went down to the cargo deck and opened the door and cautiously stepped out. The primates were still throwing a bit of a tantrum about the ship's presence, but it had mostly died down now that the ship wasn't toasting them. Just in case, even with the perimeter defense system off, he double-checked to make sure he was broadcasting the pilot's ID so he didn't get the same treatment as the primates. He didn't quite trust his understanding of their systems yet.

The first time he'd seen the ship, it was in and out of the clouds. It had been hard to tell how large it was, since he hadn't had a reference. The next time he'd seen it, he was taking cover from it, and he was moving too fast to really get a good look at it then too. He came down the access ramp and jumped down to the ground. He estimated it was about a hundred ten feet, or somewhere in the thirty-five-mu-ut range in length, and maybe two-thirds as wide at the widest part near the back. The retractable boarding ramp entrance was about six feet off the ground where it went into the side and bottom of the ship. The ship was basically a cranked delta shape like many of Earth's military fighters, only much larger and thicker. It had large overhead semi-delta-shaped triangular wing that were probably seven feet thick. They looked like wings, but they didn't look like they served any aerodynamic function because they were too thick. Jack thought it sort of looked like an upside space shuttle.

Having seen the inside of the ship, it was apparent that the upper deck crew quarters were pushed out into the wing area internally. The engine pods were completely incorporated in the outer portion of the wing area. They didn't look as bulbous as they had appeared the first time he'd seen the ship. The engine pods were shaped somewhere between oval and rectangular. The rear opening of the engine bays had an array of about two dozen raised burnt ceramic-looking circles that seemed to have a dirty gold metallic mesh covering most of the raised ceramic area.

The front of the engine bay was a single slightly concaved surface with dozens of flat blue, green, and gold glass-like reflective bumps about two inches in diameter. Other than what he'd read last night, he had no idea what he was looking at as far as an engine technology was concerned. He had never seen anything remotely like it before. Outside of the engine bay area was an oblong rounded protrusion. There was a separate cover or housing on the top of the ship that looked like black obsidian, but it was crisscrossed with thousands of tiny parallel lines that gave it a shimmering but semitranslucent appearance. It almost reminded him of a gigantic black diamond that had somehow been scored with thousands of microscopic geometric lines. He knew from reading the manual that he was looking at the ship's pulsed plasma cannons.

He continued walking around the ship and inspecting all of the various aspects of it. There were numerous raised bumps and markings here and there on the skin, which he guessed were sensors of some type. It was in many ways similar to a large Earth aircraft but more advanced with technologies he had never heard of. It was strictly an atmospheric ship from what the manual had said. It didn't have any orbital maneuvering capability and no way of docking with another ship or space station. Still, it was a nice piece of technology that he would have liked to have been able to take back to Earth and tear into from an engineering standpoint. The boys and girls at the Skunk Works at Lockheed would have fun reverse engineering this little toy.

Jack completed the walk-around inspection of the exterior of the ship and found no discrepancies, although he wasn't really sure what he would be looking for on this alien ship other than obvious physical damage. Everything seemed to be in good order as far as he could tell.

He was at the left rear landing leg just ready to head back to the entrance ramp when he heard a loud high-pitched screech and the sound of something or multiple somethings crashing through the jungle very close by. A small brown or mottled creature shot out of the low thick brush and went right past him faster than he could react. He started to draw a bead on it, but it went by too fast and up the ramp and into the ship. That wasn't the main problem, though, as his attention was drawn to much larger crashing sounds out of the jungle sixty feet behind the small animal.

A much larger creature was in pursuit of the first one, and it came blasting out of the brush not fifty feet from Jack, practically straight at him. Jack swung the rifle up just as the larger predator saw him and changed its direction slightly more toward him. Jack pulled the trigger as he moved the aim of the rifle across the path of the charging predator and caught it once in the leg and across the top of it back. The creature stumbled and cartwheeled past Jack as it collapsed from its damaged leg and back wound. Jack followed it with the rifle and was going to give it some follow-up shots just as he heard more running and crashing sounds from the same direction as the first larger predator had come from.

A second later, another predator crashed out of the jungle directly at Jack, and he fired several more shots and barely dodged the animal's vicious slashing teeth as it lurched at him and tried to turn and attack at the same time. The creature went past him by five mu-uts from its momentum then scrambled to launch itself at him. The animal leapt and Jack's katana blade flashed across the middle of it, cutting it cleanly in two from front to back. It was dead before it hit the ground, but its jaws were still snapping and slashing while the rest of it convulsed for another ten septus.

The first one was still down and struggling to get up, but the grazing back wound had cut too many muscles and it was merely spinning in circles snarling and growling. Jack turned back toward the jungle to make sure there weren't any more crazed predators charging out of the brush at him. Nothing happened for thirty septus, so he turned his attention back to the wounded animal and put another couple of shots into it to finish it off. The creature kicked and jerked a few times and then was still. *Crap, this place is insane,* he thought. *Welcome to the Wild, Wild West. Well, now I've got some sort of critter inside the ship to deal with.* Fortunately, he was just off a direct line of the creature he'd killed with the katana, or he would have gotten a serious shower of blood and gore on him as the animal was turned into two smaller animals by his blade.

He looked at the dead predators briefly and decided they looked a lot like the ones he'd seen in the ravine earlier. If they weren't the same, they were close enough. Either way, he'd had his fill of these things over the last couple of daiyus.

He went to the ship and closed the door behind him. He thought it would be easier to kill whatever had run inside rather than try to chase it out and leave the door open and hope that something else didn't stray in. Whatever it was didn't look all that ferocious anyway, so maybe he could capture or kill it then toss it out if he could corner it in the lower cargo level. He didn't want to shoot inside the ship, so he started searching the cargo level by poking and prodding with his katana. About halfway through his search, he heard something hit the floor and scrape above him.

He went up the stairs and briefly checked the flight deck then went into the crew quarters. He turned on all the lights when he went in and watched carefully in case something charged him. He peeked in the pilot's berths as he went by then closed the doors. He went into the bunk area and stood quietly and watched and waited to see if it showed itself. He heard a slight shuffling on the far side of the room. He worked his way closer to it but still didn't see anything yet. He heard some shallow fast panting and another shuffling noise. There under one of the folded down bunks against the wall, he could see a small foot sticking out the back side of the low bunk near the wall.

The foot pulled itself in then slid out again on the smooth floor as it was trying to gain some traction. Jack moved to an open spot in front of the bunk about ten feet away and squatted down while keeping the katana between the animal and him. There under the bunk as far back against the wall as it could get was the cowering animal. It was locked onto him with its two large dark eyes. It looked like a cross between a dog and maybe a large very short-haired fox or maybe a very sleek-looking cat from what he could see. It was similar to some of the larger predators he had seen but smaller, sleeker, and less aggressive looking. It had a long thin muzzle and strange long ears folded or rolled up like a tube and flattened completely against its head.

"Hi, what are you doing under there, little critter?" he said, talking to it like he might talk to a stray scared dog. It responded with a high-pitched wavering growl that sent a cold shiver up the back of his neck. "OK, OK, I don't want to hurt you, but maybe you'd like to go back outside where you belong?" The animal just stared at him. *Now what am I supposed to do?* he said to himself. *Maybe I can lure it outside with some food.* Jack got up and went to the galley storage area and unwrapped a couple of different food items, one meat and one cookie-looking thing. He went back to the same spot and checked on the animal. It was still there, so he tore off a little piece of each and tossed it under the bunk from a distance.

The animal just stared at him and uttered another small growl as it pressed itself harder against the rear wall. He thought about shooting it or attacking it with the katana but didn't really want to do that. It had only run into the ship because it was running for its life. "Well, I took care of your big friends out there, so you can go back outside now if you want, and they won't be bothering you anymore," he said to it. The creature just stared at him and twitched its ears slightly. Just to see what its reaction might be, he whistled a few bars of "Home on the Range." The animal stared at him but cocked its head slightly and then seemed to notice that the piece of meat was not too far from its nose. It twitched its nose several times then glanced at the piece of meat for a second before it switched its eyes instantly back to Jack.

"That's OK, you can eat that if you want," he said and then whistled a few more bars. He took another piece of meat and tossed it across the floor where it actually slid up against the front leg of the animal. It jumped back a little farther into the corner and stared. Then it twitched its nose and sniffed the meat that was right next to it. It glanced at the meat, then at Jack, then at the meat and then back at Jack. It must have been hungry because the smell of the meat was garnering more and more of its attention. Finally, after a few more seconds of stare down, it snapped up the meat so fast that Jack could hardly see it move. Jack had seen a short-tailed weasel attack a mouse once, and this reminded him of that. It was so fast that it was just a blur. "There you go. How was that?" he said to it. It looked at him, and he whistled "Yankee Doodle Dandy" for it. He tossed it a couple of more pieces of meat, which it grabbed after a few seconds, and it also grabbed the original piece he had tossed to it.

"OK, I don't think you're going to attack me," as he sat down on the floor where he could get a more comfortable look at it. It got nervous and scrunched back into the corner when he moved, but he tossed it a few more morsels of food, which it snatched up and ate. Well, he had a well-fed visitor now, but he wasn't any closer to getting it out of the ship. *Maybe if I leave it a trail of food, I can coax it out* was Jack's next idea. He tossed it some more crumbs of food but stopped them sort of going under the bunk. The animal was reluctant at first, but after a few mentus, it crept out and grabbed the food then dove back under the bunk.

Well, that was a little progress, but I could spend all daiyus doing this and not make any progress, and I've got to get going soon. He next built a trail of crumbs all the way out to the flight deck to see if he could get the animal out of the crew quarters. All the while, he talked and whistled and even hummed to it. He managed to get it right up to the door. Then it ran back. He started again, but after a couple of more pieces, it stopped eating and went back under the bunk and lay down. Jack thought, *Apparently, you're full now, and if I had to guess, I'm thinking you're going to take a nap.* The animal curled up under the bunk and watched him. "OK, I guess you're not hurting anything. Maybe you'll decide to want to leave on your own in a little while. Don't you have a family you need to get back to or something?" he said to it.

Jack went to the pilot seat and ran through all the checks and set up again just to refresh his memory on what he'd learned earlier. It wasn't like he was even remotely trained on this ship, so anything he could do would surely help. He went and checked on the animal in the crew quarters. When he went in, it was up on the bunk curled up asleep. When he came in, it jumped down and scurried back under the bunk. "Hi, how you doing? Just checking in on you. Is there anything else I can get you?" he said to it just for it to hear his voice. He whistled another little tune for it. It peeked out from under the bunk a little and followed him with its eyes.

At least he'd gotten a better look at it. It was a little bigger than it looked hiding under the bed. It probably weighed forty or so pounds. It was very lean and sleek. It looked more like a dog or a hairless fox, but it moved like a cat. It was very lithe and agile and had a long slender tail that twisted and curled more like a cat's tail than a dog's. He walked around a little in the room, and it watched him from under the bunk. "Look, if you don't leave now, you're going to be stuck going for a ride, and I'm not even sure where we're going. If you don't go back outside now, there's no telling where you might end up." The animal just stared at him and sniffed the air a few times with its twitching nose.

He decided on one last try. He laid a small trial of food all the way out and went down the stairs and opened the door to the outside. After he opened the door, he went to the far side of the cargo deck and sat quietly against the wall. His visitor snuck out of the crew quarters and peeked around the corner from the flight deck and down the stairs. Jack was hoping that it would see the open doorway and bolt for its freedom. It stood watching from the top of the stairs. He talked to it and whistled "Oh Give Me a Home."

"Don't you have to go outside and pee or something?" he said to it in a nonaggressive voice. It lay down where it was and watched him. Ten mentus later, it hadn't ventured any further. "All right, let's play follow the leader." He dropped a few more tidbits and went out the door to the outside. He waited a few mentus and peeked back inside. He didn't see the animal, but at the bottom of the stairs was a pile of nice fresh poo and a puddle of pee to compliment it. "Oh, crap, literally. You've got to be kidding me," he said out loud. The animal stuck its head around the corner and looked at him then disappeared back into the flight deck.

Unbelievable, he said to himself, then laughed and thought, *Well, maybe you shouldn't have fed it so much.* He turned around and locked the door then went back to the crew's bathroom and found some towels and cleaning stuff that he used to clean up the mess. He went to the lower level then opened the door and tossed the soiled towels out, locked the door, and went back up to the flight deck. He strapped himself in and ran through the prestart checks and started the engines. As he ran through all the pretakeoff checks and made sure everything seemed ready, he yelled back to the creature, "OK, that was nasty! No, no, bad dog. Thanks very little. Don't do that again, OK? Oh, and by the way, we're leaving now. You missed your chance to deplane. I hope you'll like our destination, wherever that might end up being."

He grasped the flight controls and watched all the HUD data change again. Then he ran the engines up and slowly eased the ship off the ground. The ship trembled and wallowed for a few seconds as before, and then he eased forward as he started a slow climbing turn out to the northwest directly toward Se-ahlaalu. "Here we go. Hope you don't get airsick!" he yelled back just to have someone or something to talk to.

From the crew quarters behind him, Jack heard a high-pitched yip that sounded like a coyote. He thought, *Well, I'm not sure where we're going, but it looks like it's going to be the two of us for right now.* Jack climbed the ship to three thousand mu-uts and set a cruise speed of 0.86 Mach, or 0.86 the speed of sound as shown on the ship's speed indicator. This was just far enough under the Mach one speed shown on the HUD of 1,560 kahtaks per horun to keep the drag minimized and obtain the best range. The HUD readout showed that the ship could easily double that speed, but it would use about 200 percent more fuel. His goal on this flight was maximum range, not speed, and he didn't want the ship to look like it was fleeing if there was some way they might still be tracking him. Jack had gotten a basic understanding of the auto flight function of the ship and had figured out how to set the autopilot to maintain altitude and then programmed a course to Se-ahlaalu.

He spent some time scrolling ahead on the navigation display to get a better feeling for what was out there along his route of flight. The greenbelts, as well as the featureless inland seas, seemed to be somewhat evenly spaced, but they were irregularly shaped, although generally oblong. Like he'd thought before, they seemed to be located in areas of slight depressions on the map. If he had to guess, he would say that they had been located where they would have the best access to the underground water aquifers and where the topography was more conducive to terraforming and holding in the moisture locally.

There weren't any settlements or other signs of civilization this far out from Wanana. Most of those, including the Corodune mine, had been within the first couple of hundred kahtaks from the city. Though Nishda was now a habitable planet, it was apparently quite a ways off the beaten path and likely not particularly desirable as far as a place to live, so it lacked a large population base. Jack guessed that you could probably consider it sparsely populated by galactic standards.

Scrolling and zooming ahead, Jack looked at the map at a closer rage level. He noticed a small hatched area located on the map at about 4,200 kahtaks along his route and about 100 kahtaks northeast of his current flight track. It was labeled "Caution - Possible Pirate Activity This Area. No Plotted Position Known." He moved the map curser over the hatched area, and a pop-up data block appeared. It read, "This area may have illegal pirate trade activity. No specific location plot is known. Avoid transiting this area unless accompanied by armed escort."

Zooming in on the map range, Jack saw that there was an area of rugged hills and higher terrain mixed in with a possible tiny bit of green. It almost looked like a tiny oasis, but it was hard to tell without more map detail. If there was some sort of inhabited activity, it would probably be somewhere around the green area. His only other option was another greenbelt about three hundred kahtaks further to the northwest but considerably off his direct Se-ahlaalu flight path. He figured that his best bet for fuel or anything else would be with the possible pirate activity area. He plotted a course to about twenty kahtaks to the west of the grid and would come in low, slow, and quiet to recon the area. The HUD showed a total range of 6,188 kahtaks with a remaining time en route to the pirate zone of 3.94 horuns.

He checked the autopilot settings and went back to use the head and get something to eat and drink. He got a couple of things from the cooler and sat down on the floor. A head peeked out from under the bunk and looked at him somewhat expectantly. "Oh, so you think you might want something for lunch already. You just ate not that long ago." The animal made a little snuffling sound. "Oh, all right, if I'm going to win your trust, I'd better keep up the propaganda." He broke off a piece of his snack bar and tossed it to the creature. It snatched the piece of food the second it slid into range. He tossed another piece right to it, and it snatched it out of the air in a blur so fast he could barely see it.

"Very impressive," said Jack. "Since you seem to prefer the meat and are very fast at grabbing food and have those nice sharp teeth I can sometimes just barely see, then I'd guess that you're definitely in the carnivore family. I'd guess probably on the bottom rung based on the fact that you were almost someone's breakfast earlier today. Since you're stuck here, and remember I offered you the chance to deplane, I guess I'll have to give you a name. Let's see, I don't even know if you're a boy or a girl, so a nongender name might have to do.

"Umm, what was the name of the base the pilot was really from? Oh, yes, I believe it was Seema. That might be a decent-sounding name with no gender bias attached. How do you like that?" The animal looked at him and squeaked three little high-pitched notes. "Oh, you can talk, I see. OK, Seema, it is, then. I now pronounce you Seema." He tossed Seema some more bites of food, which it easily caught and devoured hungrily. He repeated the name every time he tossed it a bite so that it would get used to it and learn it.

Jack went back to the flight deck and went through the information on the HUD and the ship's database. He learned a few more things but still didn't feel comfortable with his basic knowledge of the ship. He watched the terrain and the map for any signs of habitation or anything that wasn't plotted on the map. At one point, he looked back, and Seema was sitting in the doorway to the crew quarters. She," he'd decided on female, since he couldn't see any indication otherwise. She was just watching him and checking things out in general. "Hi, uh, Seema, I see you decided to come out for a little snoop, but lets not hope poop," he said to her.

She dove back into the room but came back out a mentu later and took up the same spot in the doorway. "Well, we're about an horun and a half out, and I have no idea what we'll find when we get there. Hopefully, it will be an entire tanker of the Pentricominate fuel we need and all they'll want in exchange for it is one small tasty forest carnivore with funny ears." Seema looked down at the floor and then back up. "I'm just kidding, don't worry," said Jack, "but I do hope there's something we can use for fuel there, and hopefully, we do have something we can trade for it, since I don't have anything in my credit account at the moment." Seema suddenly made a series of about a dozen clicking sounds that varied in pitch then turned around and went back into the crew room. "OK, if you say so," replied Jack. He looked out the flight deck window. He could see an inland sea far off to the right in the distance. There was nothing around it on the map as far as settlements or other habitable features.

Thirty mentus out from the map's indicated pirate area, Jack started a descent to get down low next to the planet's surface. He could see the rugged hills farther to the northeast as he came in from the southwest side. If there was a small greenbelt somewhere up ahead, he couldn't see it yet. He was still about eighty kahtaks out from the hills, and he was slowing his speed initially to four hundred kahtaks. As he dropped down to less than three hundred mu-uts, he slowed to a leisurely two hundred kahtaks. He's figured out some of the ship's aerial detection technology from reading the manual, but getting it all working together with just himself at the controls would be challenging.

He had one display set to the thermal imaging scan and another to anything broadcasting a translator ID. The thermal scan showed numerous ground targets in the hills below him, but he had no idea if they were aliens or wild dogs or fresh hot oven-baked rolls. If there was a way to filter the search display data, he hadn't found it yet. A proximity display suddenly lit up and showed first one and then two more small ships racing away from the same location at Jack's one thirty position and twenty-eight kahtaks. One ship was staying low and looked like it was trying to use the terrain to mask its escape. The second one had launched and was headed straight away in the opposite direction at about eight hundred kahtaks per horun or probably as fast as it could go.

Well, someone's out here, and some of them just hightailed it by the looks of it, Jack thought to himself. They must have some sort of detection capability and saw me coming. They're obviously not stupid and probably recognize this ship as a Kershavah combat ship. The less of them there are, the better, whoever "they" may be. He started a slow turn toward the location where the two ships had just launched from. Another ship launched from the same location and ducked over the nearest hill to the north and made a fast escape in that direction. *Not much of a welcoming party,* said Jack to himself.

He continued his slow turn toward whatever was down there. He didn't want to arrive like a ship that was on a hostile mission or raid. He didn't know if they were armed or if they might fire on him. When he got to about five kahtaks out, he could see a large clearing and what looked like some type of complex up against or actually built into the side of the steep hills. There was also a variety of ground equipment and two smaller ships that hadn't escaped during his approach. He circled around the front and then the backside of the hill and complex.

He then went out a ways and came back in after having set up for a landing and armed the landing thrusters. He would have hailed them if he had known what frequency they were on, assuming they monitored a frequency. He didn't know what that might be, and he didn't want any chance of the provosts hearing him and tracking his position, so he maintained radio silence. He came in slowly and watched the HUD display count down his height above ground level while also watching for any signs of hostility from the locals.

The landing was uneventful, so he shut down the engines and watched for any signs of life. He checked the setting on the ship's defense system and programmed it to the closest distance with a nonlethal stun setting just in case he had to make a run for the ship while he was being pursued. He checked his rifle and katana and made sure everything was set. He saw Seema's face peeking out from under the bunk. "You have to stay here for a while. I'm not sure what we're up against. Wish me luck," as he tossed her a couple of more cookies.

He went to the cargo deck and looked out the portal and opened the door. He opened it a little further and waited for a minute. Then he yelled. "Hello! Is anyone here? I'm not a provost or any type of government enforcement agent. I've borrowed this ship, and I'm looking for some fuel." He repeated this again then saw a door crack open in one of the buildings built into the hill.

"Who are you, and what do you want?" came a voice from inside the door.

"My name is Jack Spartan, and I'm trying to buy some fuel. I'm not a provost. I borrowed this ship, but I'm low on fuel now," replied Jack.

"Come out of the ship and show yourself!" yelled the voice.

"You come out and show yourself too!" yelled Jack.

"How do we know you won't attack!" yelled the voice.

Jack replied back, "Because this ship has a lot of serious firepower. If I wanted to attack, the three escaping ships would be burning hulks and your building would be a smoking hole in the ground."

"Oh, uh, OK" came the reply.

"That's why I came in slow and easy, to show you I meant no harm," added Jack.

The door opened, and a weathered-looking older alien came out along with another younger alien that was carrying some sort of short weapon in his hands. Jack slung his rifle over his back and stepped out. Jack raised his hand and said, "I'm just looking for some fuel. Do you have any Pentricominate fuel that this ship uses?"

The older alien replied, "Pentrico, I'm not sure, maybe we can look and see. Who else do you have on the ship?" asked the alien.

"Just me," replied Jack.

"Just you in a provost Kershavah ship? I don't know if I believe that," replied the alien.

"Well, don't believe it, then," said Jack, "but I still need fuel."

"If it's just you, then where did you get a Kershavah ship?" said the alien suspiciously.

"I borrowed it from some provosts that didn't need it anymore. No sense in letting it just sit there and go to waste when I had somewhere to go," said Jack.

The two aliens looked at each other. Then the older alien asked, "And how exactly did you get the ship from the provosts that didn't need it?"

Jack replied, "I killed them all, except for the one pilot I left stranded. They came out to hunt me down after I escaped from the Corodune mine. They didn't leave me any choice."

"I suppose not, they rarely do," replied the alien suspiciously. The two aliens just stared at him for a minute, while the younger armed one was talking into a thin headset mic of some sort. The alien yelled back to Jack, "OK, come on down, and we'll see if we can find something that will work for your borrowed ship!"

Jack came down and walked toward the alien, glancing around carefully to make sure he wasn't being ambushed. As he walked out past the set range of the defense system, his translator beeped and flashed "Security Perimeter – Stun Level 2" in his HUD. As he came up to the two aliens, he said, "I appreciate your efforts. Just don't let anyone approach the ship unless I'm with you."

"Why not?" asked the older alien.

Jack replied, "Because it's not a very friendly ship, and it doesn't appreciate uninvited guests. I wouldn't want anyone to get hurt just because they didn't understand how a Kershavah ship defends itself. By the way, I didn't catch your name," said Jack.

"I'm Fregga Kitzu, and this is Korwas," he said, nodding at the younger alien.

"How are you doing, Korwas?" said Jack. The younger alien just nodded at Jack. "So what exactly do you do way out here so far from anywhere?" asked Jack. "You're a long way from anywhere on the map."

Fregga Kitzu weighed his words carefully. "We are a sort of, ummm, a remote trading post. We call our little operation here Uruku-bar," replied Fregga, who then added, "Come with me, and we will discuss you fuel requirements. So, Jack Spartan, what exactly are you going to do with the provost ship you borrowed? It seems that it would be a dangerous thing to have."

"Yes, that's true, but I just borrowed it yesterday, and I'm not sure that they even know that it's missing. I've also made sure that it's not transmitting any position or tracking information to the provosts' base. Right now, I'm a fugitive from Corodune and now also the provosts, so I need the ship to get to Se-ahlaalu," replied Jack as this strange character of an alien led him to the next building in the hill.

"So suppose we have the fuel that you need for your ship, what do you have to offer in exchange?" asked Fregga Kitzu as they stopped outside the building entrance.

"Well, what do you want?" asked Jack.

"We are open to galactic credits, and it would take quite a few to supply a Kershavah combat ship with fuel," replied Fregga Kitzu.

Jack replied back, "I have considerable resources as far as credits, but I can't get access to them until I get to Se-ahlaalu or possibly back to Corodune or Wanana after that."

"Haf," snorted Fregga Kitzu, "you ask me to give credit to a fugitive with a stolen provost ship that may not be alive tomorrow. This does not sound like a wise investment for our little operation here."

"No, I didn't say it was, but I will get the credits when I get to Se-ahlaalu, and I'm only asking for, perhaps, partial credit. I can trade for any of the ship's stores that might be of interest to you," said Jack.

"Hmmm," replied Fregga Kitzu, "what do you have in the ship that would be of value to us here?"

"Well, I'm not sure what you would consider as valuable to you, but I have all the remaining ship's stores that the provosts would have used plus anything else that's not attached or part of the ship."

Fregga Kitzu replied, "That doesn't sound like very much unless you have some sort of cargo we could use. What about the equipment for the crew? Do you have any of their provost combat gear?"

"Not much of a personal nature," said Jack. "They mostly died out in the field wearing their gear."

"I see," replied Fregga Kitzu.

"They were wearing or using most of it when they died about four flight hours south of here in one of the greenbelts where they were hunting me," explained Jack.

Fregga Kitzu said somewhat suspiciously, "Please tell me, if you would, how many of these provosts were hunting you, and why?"

Jack replied, "There were nine or ten provosts by my count and the two pilots from their ship. I'm not sure how they came to be hunting me except that I guess the mine bosses from Corodune contracted them somehow to come after me. All I know is that I escaped from the mine bosses who were trying to kill me, and then the provosts showed up. I stole a vimar from Corodune and went as far as I could until I ran out of fuel. Then the provosts caught up with me. It's been an interesting wenek as you might imagine."

"Interesting wenek indeed," replied Fregga Kitzu. "Come inside now," he said as he opened the door to the "in the hill building" and went in. "I have never heard of such a story. I find it difficult to believe that it is not, let us say, embellished that you somehow killed nine or ten provosts and their pilots."

"Yet here I am with a provost ship," said Jack.

"Yes, here you are," replied Fregga Kitzu, wondering if this whole situation was some sort of a trap or setup. He didn't know what to think at this point. It just seemed too implausible.

Inside, there was an open area in what looked like a small warehouse with a couple of small offices off to the right. As they came in, several aliens that looked as if they might work in the warehouse approached from different directions. "What about your provost ion rifle? Would you wish to part with that?" said Fregga Kitzu as four of the warehouse workers plus the quiet Korwas surrounded Jack.

"No, I don't wish to part with my rifle, but if you're interested in weapons, there are six more ion rifles in the ship that I would be willing to trade for the fuel," said Jack.

"Six more rifles, you say," replied Fregga Kitzu, trying to decide on his next move.

"Yes," replied Jack, "but you'll never get them without my consent. Even if I'm dead, the ship won't let you in. It will kill anyone that tries to get in except for me, even if I'm with them. Then it will sit there until it finally attracts the provosts that will be searching for it." Fregga Kitzu pondered his next move.

"I know him, I know who he is," said one of the warehouse workers excitedly who was standing to Jack's side.

"Lodak, what do you mean you know him?" said Fregga Kitzu, ready to give the attack command.

"I recognize him now, from when I was working at the Corodune mine as a contract machine operator, before my brother Veedav talked me into coming back out here last wenek. I told you about the fight pit and the Varaci fighter that had fought every one of the best fighters and beat them. He even fought a druga and won. This is him, this is that Varaci, Ja-ak of Vara, that's who he is."

"Are you sure? How do you know this is the same one?" said Fregga Kitzu.

"Oh, I'm sure, completely sure, yes, I lost over three hundred credits betting on him, well, betting he would lose, but he never lost," replied Lodak.

Jack said, "And I bet on myself to win every time, and the odds were highly rigged against me. That's why the bosses wanted to kill me and why I've got plenty of credits when I get to Se-ahlaalu. It's your move, Fregga Kitzu," added Jack.

Fregga Kitzu blinked. "I, uh, I was just finding your tale much too much to believe, but, uh, this clears it up considerably. Yes, this clears it up quite a lot. So six ion rifles, you say, that you are willing to trade?"

"Yes," said Jack, "but not mine. It stays with me."

"No, of course not, we wouldn't even think of that," replied Fregga Kitzu. "So you are a Varaci, then. I have never seen a Varaci, only heard of them. They are sort of, of in the same business as us, only off planet."

"Some daiyus I'm a Varaci and other daiyus not," said Jack, "whatever it takes to get through the wenek."

"Yes, yes, of course," replied Fregga Kitzu, "I completely understand what you are saying." Fregga Kitzu dismissed the warehouse workers and continued on with Jack.

Fregga Kitzu asked, "Now how much Pentrico fuel will you need for your ship?"

"Well, I'm not actually sure," replied Jack. "It has a range of 14,000 kahtaks, and I still have a reserve of 3,400. Se-ahlaalu is still 14,500 kahtaks, so I would need basically full tanks of fuel if I could get that much."

"Well, we don't actually have any Pentrico fuel," said Fregga Kitzu, "but we do have plenty of Tritrico." Jack looked at him incredulously. "No, no," said Fregga Kitzu, "the Pentrico is just higher density, nearly 40 percent higher in density, with an equally higher output than normal Tritrico. Your provost ship would naturally have a need for a higher energy, higher density, higher output fuel. I'm sure the Tritrico will work for you. It just won't have the higher performance, probably in acceleration and top speed. And you wouldn't have the same range as the higher-density Pentrico for the same volume of fuel. Does that make sense to you?" asked Fregga Kitzu.

"Yes, perfect sense," replied Jack. "Can the two be mixed?"

"No, no, they are the same molecular base structure, but they won't mix. They will stay separated which would likely cause power surges or other more damaging problems. I would guess that a ship like that would have the ability to use anything with the same heptane base structure, but it can probably only use a pure state of any one kind in order to focus the plasma ionization output. I've never heard of any process that would allow proper plasma ionization from different mixed input fuels."

"OK," said Jack, "then we'll have to drain the fuel that's in there and refill it with the Tritrico. Can you do that, and do you have any use for the Pentrico?" asked Jack.

"Well, probably," replied Fregga Kitzu, "someone will likely want it to add a reserve reservoir to switch tanks for a boost for, uh, should we say, emergency runs."

"Like the three ships that lit out of here when I showed up in the Kershavah?" asked Jack.

"Lit out of here? Oh, yes, yes, I know what you mean," replied Fregga Kitzu. "Yes, that is exactly what they would want it for. The Pentrico is not available anywhere except to the provosts or other government operations, so, yes, it would be plenty valuable enough to those that could use it."

"OK, then," said Jack, "I'll trade you equally, the same volume of Pentrico for Tritrico, and you'll come out ahead on that, but I'll still need enough extra Tritrico to get me to Se-ahlaalu."

Fregga Kitzu replied, "Well, we may not have quite enough for you to make it the entire distance to Se-ahlaalu. We generally keep just enough on hand in case some of our, uh, entrepreneurs need a little extra to return to Wanana or sometimes Se-ahlaalu. Usually, they have to tanker around enough of their own fuel to get where they are going. If they don't, then we gouge them nicely to get enough Tritrico to get back."

"I see," said Jack, "so why so far away from anywhere? Wouldn't somewhere closer make a little more sense?"

"Yes, we could probably be closer from a simple security sense, but the main reason is it increases the expense and trouble factor considerably for anyone to want to come all the way out here to bother us. It is just not worth their effort for our little operation, so we have remained unbothered for a long time. Your provost ship, though, it could cause problems for us if you were to stay here very long. Once they discover it is missing, they may come here looking for it. They might even task an orbital drone flyover to check on things here. It would be best for all if we fueled you and you were on your way fairly soon."

"Yes, I understand," said Jack. "I appreciate your help with that. Let's go get your ion rifles and anything else you might want from the ship's stores."

When they got to the ship, Jack told Fregga Kitzu to wait and not get any closer to the ship. He grabbed Fregga Kitzu's ID from his translator and went inside the ship and up to the flight deck. He plugged Fregga Kitzu's ID into the ship's security system so it wouldn't zap him when he crossed the security threshold. He then went back out and brought Fregga Kitzu inside the ship. Jack showed him around the ship, but when they got to the crew area, he said, "Wait here a minute."

He went in and found Seema sleeping on the bunk, and she immediately jumped down and hid under the bunk. He tossed her a cookie, and she grabbed it and happily ate it. Then he brought Fregga Kitzu and showed him the crew area. "What is that?" said Fregga Kitzu, pointing toward the bunk when he saw Seema poke her head out from under the bunk and heard her growl.

"Just a new friend of mine I picked up at the last greenbelt. Some larger predators attacked her, and she ran in here and doesn't seem to want to leave."

"Why, it looks like a tu-urak," said Fregga Kitzu. "I have never seen a real one, only on vidos. I like to see the many kinds of creatures they've terraformed with here. Some are quite large and dangerous."

"Yes, I've encountered several myself," replied Jack. "It can get very interesting out in the greenbelts for anyone outside their ship or not properly prepared. Now let me show you the ion rifles you're interested in, and we can go from there."

Jack took him back to the lower deck and showed him the ion rifles. There were six rifles, twenty-two spare power mags, and eight chargers. "It looks like the chargers are somewhat portable," said Jack. "You can have seven of them, but I'd need to keep two for myself. The rifles are programmed to the provosts' translator IDs, but I'm guessing that with a little tinkering, you can bypass that security issue."

"Yes," replied Fregga Kitzu, "I believe we may have some people that could handle that. It would probably just be necessary to remove the security ID function altogether. We have had to do similar things when trying to survive in our line of work. The rifles are hard to come by, so they are a fair trade for the extra fuel you will need, especially with the additional power magazines and the chargers and the Pentrico. These are all highly controlled by the government in Wanana, so it will serve our cause well."

"Let's see what else we have in here," said Jack. "I haven't even had time to inventory what's here."

They went through the weapons storage lockers and discovered several optical monoculars and seven more of the perimeter spikes that Jack had used against the provosts. They also found four ion pulse handguns in unopened containers that were stored vertically in a tall locker where two surveillance drones were also stored. "That's really interesting," said Jack. "You can have two of the handguns, and I'll keep two. I wonder why none of the provosts carried any sidearms and why they didn't deploy the drones against me when they were trying to track me in the greenbelt."

Fregga Kitzu replied, "You said there were nine provosts and the ship's pilots. I have dealt with them before, although not in such a situation as you. They are arrogant and above the law in many respects. If I had to make a guess as to the answer to your question, I would say that they didn't believe they needed the drones. That would not be as sporting to them. I would almost bet that they had a contest or perhaps a bonus for who would bring down the Varaci they were hunting. The drones would make it an unequal contest among themselves and would shorten their adventure of hunting you. Does this make sense to you?"

"Yes," said Jack, "and based on what I've observed of their behavior, I would say that you are probably right about what they were doing. They must have never heard of the doctrine of never underestimate your enemy, but, first, you must know your enemy and yourself before you know how to engage him."

"That sounds like a wise assessment of the situation," replied Fregga Kitzu.

"Yes, it is a wise doctrine written by a wise general twenty-five hundred yenets ago," replied Jack.

They explored some more of the storage area and found some comm gear and other assorted hardware. "What's this?" said Jack as he came across a moderate-size locked container. It was labeled "Detainment System" on the top of the container. "Open with Control Disk or Access Code" was printed on the side. There was a small flat keypad next to the label. Jack searched his pocket and found the control disk he'd found on the provost after the raptor attack. He scrolled through the tiny projected menu and selected a command that was labeled "Open

Storage Case 164." The container latch popped open, and Jack opened it to find five collars with one empty space for a collar or wrist restraints. There were four more control disks and a larger empty space where the leg restraints had been.

A small display screen was embedded in the top cover side that showed a list of programming and operating instructions. "Sync to Ship Defense System" was one the commands. Jack took one of the collars out and selected the icon on the screen. A "Choose Restraint" option popped up with a six-digit list displayed. One showed "In Use," but the other five were open. Jack looked on the restrain and saw a five-digit number that matched one of the open units on the display. He selected the matching number, and the screen flashed a "Programming Restraint" message for a couple of septus and then a "Restraint R26T3 Programmed."

The display changed back to the main screen and now showed the third unit in the list as "In Use." The display menu also showed a "Restraint Options" choice. Jack selected that, and a list of two synced restraints was displayed. One was the Restraint R26T3 he'd just programmed and the other was Restraint R26T1. *That must have been the one they had on me,* he realized. He looked at the options for the R26T3 restraint that showed "Perimeter Open" or "Perimeter Secured." He selected "Open," and a list popped up showing "Full Open" or "Escorted Only." Then he selected the "Secured" option, and then another list appeared that showed "Warn," "Stun," or "Kill." He went back to the "Full Open" and selected that.

From the top of the stairs, there came a plaintive oscillating whine and a short yip. Jack and Fregga Kitzu both looked up to see Seema peeking around the corner. "It seems to want something," said Fregga Kitzu.

"Yes, I think I know what. Stay here," said Jack as he bounded upstairs to the flight deck. Seema jumped back into the bunk area for a moment then came out to Jack when he whistled and called her name. He took the thin light restraint collar and put it around her neck, selected the Lock command on the control disk, and the collar locked lightly in place where he held it. Seema backed up and shook a couple of times and then looked plaintively at Jack. "Sorry, baby, but that will keep you from getting zapped. Trust me, it's for your own good," he said to her.

Jack went back down to the lower deck and asked Fregga Kitzu if he had any use for the remaining restraints. "Yes, most likely I can sell them to some smuggler—I mean, entrepreneur that would want to keep them for their ship," he replied.

"OK, take them, they're all yours," said Jack. "Now come on outside, Fregga Kitzu, for a minute while Seema takes care of her business." Jack and Fregga Kitzu went outside, and Seema followed, where she went under the ship's belly and did a nice little pile and puddle. As soon as she was done, she darted back into the ship as fast as she could. "That's what I thought," said Jack. "She seems to be a very smart animal. She did that inside the first time, but I told her not to, and she just let us know that she wanted to go outside. Predators are usually pretty intelligent. She seems to be on the smaller scale of predators that I've seen in the greenbelt. She may make up for her smaller size by being more intelligent."

Fregga Kitzu replied, "She does seem quite intelligent, and she is a sleek and appealing creature too. Perhaps I should go to the greenbelt and capture one for myself."

"Well, you could give it a try, but they—you called her a tu-urak—are probably pretty hard to find and catch, and, of course, you'd have to make sure you weren't eaten by the two larger predators that were stalking her or the next size above that and, of course, the giant flying raptors that swoop down for a light provost snack."

"I think perhaps you are right. Maybe it would be best if I just viewed them on the vido display," laughed Fregga Kitzu.

"Well, let's get this ship fueled, and I will be out of here. The sooner I leave, the better for the both of us. Go ahead and bring a couple of your guys in and take the rifles and other stuff." Everything went as planned, and the ship was fueled with all the Tritrico fuel the pirate traders had on hand. The ship gauges showed just under full. The rifles, power mags, and two of the ion handguns and the drones were all taken by Fregga Kitzu's personnel. "Thanks for your help, Fregga Kitzu. I couldn't have gotten much farther without your help and your fuel," said Jack as he was getting ready to leave.

"It was most interesting to make your acquaintance. It is unusual to meet anyone even more crazy than us, but I think you meet that requirement. Now here, here is the name of a Norian I know who is in Se-ahlaalu. His name is Talaka Vamava. You will find him at the location shown here on Ashongad EW. He may be able to help you with the disposition of this ship, but I can't guarantee anything.

"Your ship will be a dangerous commodity to deal with, much more dangerous than the small contraband that we deal with here. If not, then perhaps he may know someone that can. It might be better if you just disposed of it somehow, but there may be some other useful equipment that can be salvaged from this ship. It is unheard of for anyone to have access to a provost ship. Use caution in your dealings with everyone. They will not trust you, and you should not trust them. That is just the way it is in Se-ahlaalu. Se-ahlaalu is a remote outpost of a city on a remote outpost of a terraformed mining planet. No one goes there for a holiday, well, a legitimate holiday, if you know what I mean. I will message him and let him know that you are coming."

Jack replied, "OK, that's much appreciated. I will find him and see what he can do. Again I am in your debt for your help. Perhaps I can repay you some daiyus for your troubles."

"Perhaps," replied Fregga Kitzu, "but if you drop in for a visit again, it would be better if you didn't bring a borrowed provost ship. As nice as they are, I think they would tend to gather too much interest from those we wish to avoid if possible."

"I understand," said Jack. "It's definitely in my plans to ditch this little toy as fast as I can. Hopefully, I'll see you again sometime."

"Good luck, then, on your journey," said Fregga Kitzu.

"Thanks," replied Jack. "I'll take all the good luck or divine oversight that I can get."

Jack boarded the provost ship and prepped it for takeoff. Seema stuck her head out of the crew area and watched him while he worked. "Well, you made a bit of an impression back there," he said to her. "I thought about leaving you here for safekeeping, but I don't think you're ready for that yet, so you're stuck with me until one of us decides otherwise. Don't worry, we're not going all the way to Se-ahlaalu tonight. We'll make a little camping expedition at another greenbelt somewhere while I do a little more research on Se-ahlaalu and figure out a plan of attack. If you want out at the greenbelt, you'll be free to go on your way."

Jack finished the preflight checklist and was ready to fire up the engines. He had found a menu item for selecting alternate fuels and selected Tritrico. A warning popped up saying that non-provost-approved fuels could vary significantly and may not perform as expected as shown in the standard specifications data. Hmm, he wondered about the quality of the pirate's fuel and how far out of standard specs it might be.

He finished the checklist and started the engines. He then ran the takeoff checks and was ready to launch. "Here we go, Seema. Remember, just sit back, relax, and enjoy the flight." She looked at him curiously and ran back and jumped onto the bunk. Jack added takeoff thrust and felt the ship start to lighten on its landing feet. Once again, the ship wavered slightly at liftoff, and he did a slow climb out straight ahead then turned to the northwest once again and headed toward Se-ahlaalu.

As he started to increase his speed and altitude, Seema came out of the crew room and crept up to the front of the flight deck and looked out of the front windshield as the ship climbed out. She made a kind of a trilling sound followed by a melodic whining noise that varied in frequency from high to low. "Yep, we're going for a little flight again. I'll get us some dinner after we get up to cruise altitude," he said to her. She was a pretty animal, he thought, long and sleek and lithe as a cat but somehow very canine like too.

He went to four thousand mu-uts for a cruise altitude this time. They were high enough to see everything well but not too high to have to worry about oxygen if they lost pressurization. He wasn't too worried about that, but there was always the potential of being attacked and losing pressurization from a hull breach. Hopefully, they would also be less conspicuous at this lower altitude than if they went high. He'd plugged a higher altitude into the navigation computer, but it hadn't changed the fuel burn by going higher like it would have in any turbine-powered airplane on Earth.

The navigation computer showed that they would just be able to make Se-ahlaalu with an extra 118 kahtaks to spare. Not a great amount of reserve, but it would do. He'd taken all the pirate's fuel, so that was the best they could do. The ship would probably burn a little more for takeoff and landing, but he would still be on the plus side with the fuel. The total flight time to Se-ahlaalu would be 18.34 horuns according to the navigation readout with a total distance of 14,300 kahtaks. Jack started scrolling ahead on the map route to see where he would stop for the night. There were eleven greenbelt areas en route to Se-ahlaalu but only two that were close enough along his route so that it wouldn't cost him any extra fuel to detour there. The eleventh greenbelt, the last one, was directly along his route. He didn't want to get too close to Se-ahlaalu without more information about it, so he decided to stop at the fourth greenbelt, which would be just under seven horuns.

Well, they had quite a long flight even to the greenbelt, so after everything checked out and the ship was on autopilot, Jack decided it was time for a little dinner. He didn't like leaving the flight deck, but since Seema wasn't trained as a flight attendant, he didn't have any choice if he wanted to get something or if he had to go to the head. Seema watched Jack and followed him to the galley area where she knew the goodies were stored. She sat back at a safe distance and watched him get the food out and start to prepare it. Jack talked to her while he worked and threw in a few oddball whistling songs to keep her curiosity up.

She returned the favor by adding various random patterns of whines, whistles, squeaks, and trills to the conversation. Jack soon had the meal separated from its packaging. The label read, "Jiguuta with sennatap and tahteh," whatever that was. "So how do you like your Jiguuta prepared?" he said to her. "I usually like mine barbecued, but I guess I'll settle for it nuked tonight. I hope none of this is toxic to a tu-urak. I think that's what Fregga Kitzu called you, assuming he's actually correct." Seema let out a long plaintive oscillating whine. "Yes, I'm hungry too. We'll be eating in just a few mentus," said Jack.

He put the meal in the oven and hit the "Cook pre-prepped meal number 4" command. He wondered if it was microwave-type heating oven or some other technology he hadn't heard of yet. It looked and acted like a microwave oven, but it wasn't labeled. *Oh, well, no sense in worrying about that as long as it worked,* he thought. In less than an Earth minute, it beeped, and he pulled out the ready-to-eat provost dinner. It didn't look too bad, and it smelled OK. He tasted a couple of bites and decided it was pretty decent. Not exactly Kansas City BBQ beef ribs, but it would do. "I guess the provosts get some halfway decent rations even on their assault ship," he said to Seema. "It's probably too hot for you, I didn't think of that," he said to Seema. She whined and jumped around a little in anticipation.

He got out another meal and opened it up for her but only heated it enough to defrost it. "Here you go," he said as he started tossing her some small bites. She caught them in midair, and she was as fast and agile as anything he'd ever seen even as she was slipping around on the smooth floor. He took both meals to the flight deck and tossed Seema pieces as he ate his own dinner of Jiguuta with tahteh and whatever.

She came right up next to him now and waited with anticipation for each bite. It was only a half a dozen bites later that he was able to get her to take it from his hand. She started to get a little overzealous and grabbed his hand, but he told her "no" and "easy" until she learned to take it more gently. "You catch on pretty quickly, don't you?" he said to her. She looked at him and made a little vibrating or humming sound. "And you have no shortage of interesting noises either," as he laughed at her funny antics.

He looked at her more closely now that she wasn't hiding under the bunk or running in and out of the ship quickly. Her face was slender with a pointed snout. Her head looked kind of like a generic brown bird dog but with a more pointed muzzle with darker brown and grayish dark blue streaks from head to tail. She would be perfectly camouflaged for the underbrush of the greenbelt areas. Looking closer, he could see that her ears were considerably different in that they looked like delicate rolled-up tubes that streamed back from her head like a decorative hollow ponytail. They were rolled tight, and they actually fit tightly against a slight indentation that went backward on her head.

She had short smooth fur, which he wanted to stroke like a dog's, but he was afraid she'd spook at this stage. He continued to talk to her, and in a few more rounds, he had her feeding directly out of his hand so that he was touching her a little each time she ate. They finished their meals, and with a full belly, Seema decided it was time for a nap and headed back to sleep it off.

Jack continued to monitor the flight parameters and watch the changing terrain. Nishda was naturally a barren desert planet that might have had some localized green areas, but for the most part, it was in an arid landscape except for the engineered greenbelts. Wanana was located at forty-two degrees north latitude, and Se-ahlaalu was located at fifty-four north, so it was somewhat cooler and had some natural-looking vegetation surrounding it. The terrain he was flying over between the two cities was mostly north of either of them on the great circle or direct route between the cities.

The greenbelts were still more or less equally spaced along Jack's route, but there was a narrow band of sparse native green forested area between the sixty-five and seventy north latitude zone. Jack didn't know if these areas were native vegetation or just something that had migrated from the terraformed greenbelts to an area where they could grow. As he passed the highest latitude along his route of seventy-seven degrees north, he thought he could see a very small polar cap off in the distance to his right. It may have been an illusion or a mirage. At this relatively low altitude, it was too far away to tell if he was actually seeing an ice cap, and he didn't have any fuel to waste for sightseeing.

Jack couldn't tell from the altitude they were flying at what was below him, but he wondered if some of the creatures he'd encountered in the greenbelt areas might be native to the planet or if they were all imported for the terraforming like he'd been told. If there was some native wildlife, then they might have spread to the irrigated greenbelt areas, which were much more lush and established themselves there as well.

For all he knew, the part about the terraforming might be some sort of political propaganda used to establish control over an otherwise autonomous planet. Anything was possible when companies, alliances, or empires were involved and colluding with each other. Based on the corrupt governance of the planet that he'd seen so far, he wouldn't doubt it for a minute. He still wondered what the violent creature was that had attacked him the first night after he'd stolen the vimar. It didn't seem to fit into the rest of the equation as far as the rest of the wildlife he'd seen. Maybe it was the only native creature he'd seen so far and the others were all imports. Maybe it was a failed engineered creature they'd created when they were trying to create the drugas and gorroks that had somehow escaped or perhaps even been released. Maybe it was someone's lab pet that they couldn't bear to dispose of. All Jack knew was that he didn't know.

A warning flashed twice on the HUD display then showed "Fuel Range Estimation Error." That didn't sound good, he thought. He selected the prompt on the HUD next to the warning. Fuel Energy Density Error (-2.48%) Range 13,389Kk. *Crap,* he thought, *there goes my reserve range of 118 kahtaks and then some. That will put me short of Se-ahlaalu about 90 kahtaks, and that will be without any adjustment for the landing and takeoff at the interim greenbelt,* Jack reasoned. Either way, he would be short, but he would still have to land at the greenbelt for the night. If he didn't land at the greenbelt, he would end up trying to land somewhere short of Se-ahlaalu in the dark with minimum fuel. Better safe than sorry, especially since he didn't know even now if the fuel readings were accurate considering the error message he'd received. It must be the Tritrico that he'd gotten from Fregga Kitzu. It was apparently a lower density than normal, which resulted in less range. He didn't imagine the pirate operation stressed a great deal of quality control oversight in an operation like theirs. He would just have to deal with it.

Originally, in the vimar, his direct track to Se-ahlaalu hadn't been lined up with this greenbelt, but his side trip to the pirate operation had brought him far enough off his direct route so that he would now pass over the edge of this greenbelt. They were now eighty-four kahtaks out from the greenbelt destination. The sun would set to the east in another seven mentus, so he had just enough time to find the greenbelt and a safe landing spot with a short, minimum fuel recon pass. It would just be adequate time-wise if everything worked as advertised.

The near edge of the greenbelt was already in sight, and the sun was just touching the horizon to the east. He continued the descent and passed over the western edge of the north-south-running greenbelt. Though still flying the same course track that he had been all daiyus, he was now heading in a southerly direction instead of north. The greenbelt looked the same from the air as he came in lower on the far side of it. The one thing he was sure of was there wouldn't be any provost party hunting him here, well, he hoped not anyway. The edge of the greenbelt had a little more rough-looking terrain than the previous ones he'd seen. He slowed his approach speed and came in low to parallel the edge of the greenbelt. There was a flatter area right next to the edge of the greenbelt, and there was a small body of water inside the greenbelt not more than a kahtak from the edge. That could be good or bad, but it made it worth snooping a bit.

He circled once and armed the ship's thrusters for landing. The flat spot wasn't perfect, but it would do. The sun was halfway below the horizon, and the light was fading fast now. He'd discovered the landing lights in the ship's operating menu, but he wouldn't be comfortable operating the ship at night yet. For some reason, a lot of the information he was looking for wasn't easily accessed or organized like he thought it should be.

He selected Approach Lights from the HUD menu, and the area beneath and in front to the ship illuminated brightly. *Excellent landing lights,* he said to himself now that he saw them operating. The ship touched and settled with a slight tremor. The tremor continued as the engines spooled down. *What the hell,* he thought as he was ready to add power and go around. The tremor subsided, and just as he decided it seemed OK to stay, the entire area around him erupted in a curtain of mist and swirling moisture. His visibility went from unlimited to less than ten feet in just a few septus. *Whoa, just made that by a hair,* he thought as he shut the engines down and ran through the postflight checks. "A few minutes later, and we would have been landing farther out in the desert. Timing is everything, and I squeaked that in by good grace. Thanks again," he said out loud. Fuff, he felt a breath of warm moist air next to his hand and got a little nudge from Seema against his leg as he was completing the shutdown.

"Well, hi there, I guess either you're still hungry or you need to go out again. Hang on while I finish here and grab my weapons. We don't know what's out there, and right now, we can't see anything either." Jack unstrapped and grabbed his rifle and katana. *Let's see now,* he thought. He turned on the perimeter defense system then set it to stun then set the range all the way into its shortest range again. He then moved it out slowly at first to a range of one hundred mu-uts then further out to two hundred mu-uts or a little over six hundred feet. As he did, he heard a couple of varied squawks and muffled screams outside the ship.

"There, that should have cleared us a fair little space of real estate around the ship to snoop and poop. Come on, let's go see what's out there," he said to the little tu-urak. He went down to the ship's door and peered outside. "Fog and swirling mist is about all I can see," he said to Seema. He opened the door about a foot and peered out. Though it wasn't likely, he thought there was always a chance that something could have already been inside the minimum range of ten mu-uts of the defense system when he turned it on. Maybe not something big but still something potentially nasty.

The cool moist mist swirled all around him as he stepped out. He breathed in the clean moist air of the greenbelt, which felt good in his lungs and smelled better than the interior of the ship with its odors of machinery and its previous and current inhabitants. "Ahhh, now that's nice," he said as he took a few more steps out onto the ground beneath the ship. The sound of the ship cooling and clicking and popping was overriding the sound of the forest, but he could still hear the background noise of the forest life and all its ongoing dramas in the distance. He could just barely make out the shapes of the trees and other foliage at the edge of the swirling mist.

Seema slipped out behind him and followed him out onto the open ground where she began sniffing and snooping. The jungle was only about thirty feet, or ten mu-uts, from the ship. Seema stopped and froze about ten feet ahead of Jack. He watched her to see what she would do. She cocked her head to listen to the jungle, and then surprisingly, her ears came up and unrolled from their normal tube shape and turned into little parabolic-shaped sound collection dishes. *Well, I'll be,* Jack said to himself as he watched her steer her now six-inch sound collection dishes as she intently analyzed the sounds of the jungle. A low-frequency rumble emanated from her as she listened. She suddenly turned and bolted behind Jack and continued to growl. "I don't know what it is, but I'll take your word for it," said Jack as he covered the area toward the jungle with his rifle and backed toward the ship.

Suddenly, the swirling mist was lit all around by the blue flashes of the defense system firing several bursts as screams and yowls came from two separate directions out of sight in the fog. He could hear crashing and screaming as whatever had been out there ran from the painful torment of the defense system attack. Seema stood between Jack's legs and listened and growled for another twenty septus until she was convinced there was nothing more out there.

477

"That was interesting," said Jack. "You picked up on whatever was out there even before the defense system did. Those radar dishes you have for ears must be amazingly sensitive, so sensitive I bet that's the reason you keep them folded up most of the time. They also look to be a bit fragile. You probably don't want them flopping around all the time when they're not in use or they might get shredded." Jack reached down and stroked her on her neck and back. She jumped and shook a little, but after a couple of septus, she stood there and seemed to enjoy it as she continued to listen to the jungle.

"Come on, you'd better do your thing out here. Then we can go in and call it a daiyus," he added. A few mentus later, with that mission accomplished, they were back in the ship, and Jack dialed the defense system down to fifty mu-uts so it wouldn't be frying everything that walked by all night long. With everything secure, he decided to grab another quick shower after the daiyus's stressful intensity. *Hard to say how long it will be before I get another depending on whatever tomorrow brings,* he thought.

He grabbed a bottle of qalalé and kicked back on what was now, at least temporarily, his bunk. He lay there and unwound and thought about all the crazy stuff that had happened in the last wenek and moondats. He thought about Zshutana and Junot and Cherga. He wished there was a way to get a message to them and check on them and let them know he was OK. Maybe when he got to Se-ahlaalu, he could tap into their comm system and connect with Junot. He hoped they were all OK and that they weren't catching any heat because of his escape. There was no way for him to know right now.

He heard something then felt something nudge him from below the bunk. Seema peered up at him and gave a little vibrating whine. "Hi again," he said, "I just fed you a while ago and you were just outside. What is it you want?" She just looked at him with her big brown eyes and gave him a low vibrating whine and then put a paw up on the bed and kept looking at him. "You want to come up here with me?" he said. "OK, come on up here," he said as he patted the bunk. She jumped up on the edge of the bunk and wedged herself against him then gave a long sigh as she seemed to relax and closed her eyes. *Isn't that something?* he said to himself as he reached over and gently stroked the top of her head. She snuggled down a little closer and was fast asleep in a matter of seconds. *Well, it looks like I've got a new bed partner,* he thought as he closed his eyes and drifted off to sleep himself.

The next morning dawned with the ship still enveloped in fog. Seema was still snuggled up against him when he awoke, but she was awake and alert the instant he moved. The fog had thinned a bit, and the constant drizzle that had gone on all night had ceased. The moisture had permeated the ship overnight, since it wasn't pressurized on the ground, and all the interior view ports were fogged over, making it look foggier than it actually was. Jack wiped some of the moisture from the windshield and viewports on the flight deck with a towel from the crew area. He could at least see the jungle this morning in the dim light that filtered through the fog and overcast.

He wondered how often the fog and drizzle program ran for the greenbelts. Was it every night or two or three times a wenek, or was there some sort of sensors that ran the system when it needed more moisture? Did they all come on at the same time planetwide, or was each greenbelt programmed or monitored individually? Interesting questions, but he wouldn't be getting any answers to them today, he thought. "Should we get a little breakfast now, or do you need to go outside first?" he said to Seema as she sat looking at him. She didn't seem to be making any noise about it either way, so he decided to eat something first. After they finished their breakfast of various packaged food mysteries, he said, "OK, let's go outside for a few mentus and see if anything is lurking out there for us."

He set the perimeter defense out to three hundred mu-uts, but a warning popped up on the HUD stating, "Line of Sight Defense Only." That would make sense, he reasoned, since pushing out the defense range would likely encompass terrain that the ship's sensors and defenses couldn't see through or defend. If he still had the drones, he might have been able to deploy them, but that wasn't an option, since he'd traded them for fuel. After hearing a couple of minor squawks outside the ship as he moved the range outward, he said, "Come on, Seema, let's go check it out." She looked at him then followed him down the stairs and out as she had the previous night. The air was cooler than the previous night, and there was almost a slight chill in the air. They were about twenty degrees further north than the greenbelt where he'd picked up Seema, and he could definitely feel the difference in the temperature in the morning air.

Jack checked around the ship and made sure everything looked to be in good shape. Seema snooped around some and listened in every direction with her ears unfolded but stayed close to Jack. Jack walked to the edge of the jungle and spent some time looking at the flora. It was in many ways similar to the previous greenbelt, but there did seem to be some differences in a lot of the plants. They looked a bit less tropical and in some ways seemed more primitive looking. They looked simpler, and there was less undergrowth here, at least in this area. Out in the jungle, he could hear a cacophony of animal activity of every sort. Again, it was similar but not quite the same as he'd remembered from the other greenbelt.

He heard several strange animal and birdcalls that he hadn't heard before. The thought occurred to him that since the greenbelts were four hundred miles or more apart that maybe each one was a different biodiversity zone or biome that was separated by distance to keep the wildlife and flora isolated. Except maybe for the birds; it would be an impossible trek for any creature to reach the next nearest greenbelt. Each greenbelt could be a completely isolated island of flora and fauna habitat. Maybe the planet had been set up as a big game preserve or zoo for various types of wildlife from different planets, each with its own bio zone. He wondered what variety of sea creatures existed in the different isolated inland seas that covered the planet. There might be some seriously good deep-sea fishing opportunities there, or there might be some seriously big bad sea monsters lurking under the waves too.

He wanted to go exploring a little and see what the nearby lake might be harboring, but he didn't want to get too far from the ship on the off chance that they had tracked him this far. "Maybe another time," he said to Seema, "and besides, I didn't bring my fishing pole," he said to her. "Hurry up and do your thing. We're going to be launching shortly." She snooped and pooped around for a few mentus, and then they were ready to go. She was very wary and didn't seem to like being out in the open, so she stayed close to Jack the entire time. "Come on, let's get back inside," he said to her as he headed back in. Just before she hopped inside, she watched and listened to the jungle intently and let out a low resonating growl. "Something's out there again, isn't it? I'm thinking this greenbelt might be a little more dangerous than the last one, and that one was bad enough."

They went inside, and Jack locked the door and headed up to the flight deck. Just as he was settling into the pilot seat to look at his flight planning issues, the perimeter defense fired several times, and the sound of a mad screaming animal could be heard outside the ship. Looking toward the jungle on the ship's monitor, he got a glimpse of something fairly large and powerful thrashing behind the foliage and running away at the edge of the forest. "Maybe I'd better turn that up from stun to barbeque," he said to himself as he reset the perimeter defense to Kill All and moved it back into a hundred mu-uts so that it wouldn't have any potentially blocked zones. "I don't think this is a very friendly neighborhood," he said to Seema as she peered out the viewport at the jungle as a soft whine and growl reverberated from her throat.

Jack input Se-ahlaalu into the navigation computer again and confirmed what he already knew. He didn't have enough fuel by about ninety kahtaks, and it might be even more than that based on the fuel error calculation from the lower-density Tritrico. Well, he couldn't make it all the way, but he could get pretty close, close enough to hoof it if he had to if he was well supplied for a long hike. The one thing he couldn't do was burn the remainder of his fuel down to zero trying to stretch it as far as he could. He would have to stop short of running out so that he could make a controlled landing. Stretching it to the last drop of fuel would only result in a catastrophic crash landing. Without an ejection seat, like in the F-35, that would surely result in a dead pilot and a dead Seema.

Jack was scrolling ahead on the map to get an idea of the terrain and approach to Se-ahlaalu. He wanted to see what was between him and the destination. Se-ahlaalu wasn't that large of a city compared to Wanana. The info block on the map showed a population of 240,000, which was about a fourth of Wanana. Nishda wasn't exactly what you would call a teeming metropolis of a planet with only two main cities.

There was another greenbelt on this side of Se-ahlaalu, and it appeared to be about sixty or sixty-five kahtaks across at the point he would have crossed it. The far side of the greenbelt was about 120 miles from Se-ahlaalu. That was considerably closer to any city than he'd seen any of the other greenbelts. That seems a bit too close for the kind of vicious wildlife that he'd seen in the last two greenbelts. He zoomed in on the greenbelt, and it appeared to be displayed in a lighter color than the others he'd seen. Zooming in further, a text box appeared and showed the greenbelt as an agri zone with a warning that showed, "Caution Low Flying Autonomous Agri Vehicles." Is that what he thought it might be? It definitely looked that way by what it said. It looked like a warning about pilotless ag sprayers or crop dusters.

Well, that was interesting and definitely something to shoot for. He could probably make the closer edge of the greenbelt with just enough fuel reserve to make a safe landing. What was actually there was still a mystery, but it sounded like a better situation than the current greenbelt. Either way, he still didn't have a choice, but this looked better than what he thought he was up against a little while ago.

He programmed the nav computer for the close side of the greenbelt. The fuel calculations popped up almost instantly and showed him arriving there with less than ten mentus of fuel remaining. That wasn't a lot, but it might be enough. He could land short and walk to the greenbelt if the fuel use rate was higher, but hopefully, he would make it to the greenbelt. He also didn't know if the fuel calculations took into account any forecast or reported headwinds or tailwinds. Did the ship's nav computer even take that into account, and was there any sort of weather reporting or forecasting here like there was on Earth? Maybe they just discounted that factor altogether, since all of their operations were normally close to Wanana, and stretching your fuel reserves never really came into play. Well, they also didn't have much in the way of weather systems here except for what was manufactured locally in the greenbelts, so it probably was likely that weather didn't factor into flight planning here on Nishda at all. On Earth, weather dictated just about every aspect and phase of flight planning for aviation and space launches.

"OK, Seema, we're ready to rock 'n' roll," he said to her. Jack ran through the preflight checks, started the engines, and completed the pretakeoff checks and was airborne in about four mentus. As he lifted off, he saw several large carnivores scatter from behind the wall of jungle trees. What was left of another large animal on the ground was visible where they had scattered from, and it looked like they had all been feeding on the carcass of the animal. "I guess we missed the breakfast buffet this morning. I'm glad we weren't on the menu," he said to Seema as they climbed out and headed southwest.

Jack climbed to an altitude of four thousand mu-uts again and set the auto flight system for cruise. He could see a blue streak far out on the horizon to the right that correlated with an inland sea on the map that was labeled as Bantirri LF17DL. Maybe someday he'd get a chance to learn what all the designations were for on the various terrain features shown on the map. When they were established in cruise, Jack cut the cruise speed to a leisurely 0.72 mach. That was generally a good low-end minimum drag, best range speed for most transport-type jets.

This ship wasn't really an aerodynamic vehicle with a best lift over drag coefficient, but its fuel efficiency would still be affected by aerodynamic drag. The faster the speed, the more parasitic drag there was regardless of the type of vehicle. If he could find a good low drag, low power setting, he might be able to eek a little more range out of it. After a few septus, the ship's nav computer calculated a new burn for the reduced speed. It showed an increase of just under forty kahtaks. Not too bad but not enough to get to Se-ahlaalu. It might get him to the far side of the ag belt instead of the near side. It all depended on how efficiently the ship was burning the Tritrico fuel.

He played with the speed up and down a few decimal points, but each time the computer recalculated the range, it seemed to be slightly less than the 0.72. He'd hit it pretty close on his first guess and only had to modify it up a tiny fraction. Well, drag was drag wherever you were. He was showing a max range increase of 38.4 kahtaks with a flight time of six horuns and four mentus.

That best range speed was somewhat off from what he had calculated earlier when the ship showed 0.86 Mach as the best range cruise speed. The ship was a lot lighter now than previously, since he'd burned off over a third of the ship's weight in fuel. That must be what the difference was. Just like on Earth with all aerodynamic airplanes, the heavier the weight of a given airplane, the faster the best range speed would be. That wasn't something you worried much about in fighters, but apparently, it was a considerable variable here on larger craft like it was on Earth.

Seema was getting a bit more inquisitive now and spent the next thirty mentus snooping into every nook and cranny on the ship that she could get her nose into. "Are you really exploring, or are you just looking for anything that might look like food?" Jack said to her. She looked at him and twitched her long almost prehensile tail several times. Jack kept a close eye on the fuel burn rate versus the estimated burn and could see that they were burning more than the nav computer had estimated. *There goes my extra thirty-eight kahtaks we gained from our leisurely cruise speed,* he said to himself. There was no way to tell for sure without an accurate burn rate in the computer, but he still thought they could make the near side of the ag belt with enough reserve for a safe landing.

He wondered for a minute what sort of propulsion systems they had in their orbital and light-speed-capable transports. He had a lot to learn, and he didn't even know what he was going to do when he got to Se-ahlaalu other than look up the probably untrustworthy Talaka Vamava name he'd gotten from Fregga Kitzu. One of his first priorities would be to set up a new fake ID with a new banking ID. Then he would have to see if it was possible to contact Junot and see if he could get his credits transferred to his new account so that he wouldn't be an indigent Varaci living on the streets of Se-ahlaalu with his new tu-urak friend, Seema. He wondered if they had a fight pit or something similar. In a worst-case scenario, he could always start over on the fight pit circuit and hope for a second round of success.

He scrolled the map around Se-ahlaalu and got a feel for the layout of the city. There wasn't a high level of detail, but he could see the streets and tell where the city center was and the industrial area. The spaceport was located on the northwest corner of the city in a flat area next to a small river that ran through the center of the city. That was probably the reason the city was located here and so far from everything else on the planet. He wondered what the source of the river might be, since there was any falling precipitation on Nishda. He reasoned that it could be engineered like the greenbelts or possibly natural from a subterranean source like the underground seas. There was also a moderate area of higher terrain to the southwest that appeared to have some natural vegetation and what looked like a natural watershed that drained toward where the city was located. Hopefully, he'd get to see it all in a couple of daiyus.

Thirty mentus out from the near edge of the greenbelt, Jack started a slow descent. The fuel issue wasn't looking good, but it looked like they would be able to get to the near edge of the greenbelt. He could see the greenbelt clearly now at a distance of 180 kahtaks, or just over 90 miles. This greenbelt was visibly lighter that the jungle greenbelts, and as they got closer, he could see the splotchy patterns of the ag operation spread over most of the extent of the greenbelt. As he got closer, he could also see that the perimeter had a darker edge that was taller than the rest of the ag area. The greenbelt looked like it was surrounded by a barrier of high trees all the way around it as well as a grid of lower trees crisscrossing the entire greenbelt. At sixty kahtaks out, he could better see the trees and grids as well as some sort of center islands of taller trees and a couple of buildings or some type of structures. He couldn't tell what they were, but there was definitely something there.

The fuel situation was getting critical, and the HUD was giving him a continuous low-fuel status alert. It looked like he had another eight mentus of fuel with three mentus to his destination at the near edge of the greenbelt if the remaining estimate was accurate. He kept his speed up as he descended faster now, going slower than his best range speed would actually burn more fuel than keeping his speed up in a descent. He dropped down to not much higher than treetop level so that if he had any indication of fuel exhaustion, he could immediately initiate a landing sequence. He was still moving at four hundred kahtaks an horun at six kahtaks from the greenbelt. Six kahtaks plus thirty to the island in the middle of the greenbelt. That would be another four and a half mentus of his six advertised remaining mentus. That would be cutting it too close. What if there was no place to land in the island greenbelt? Well, he would just land on the crop area. Those were his only two choices.

He pulled the speed all the way back and held his altitude at sixty mu-uts. The ship decelerated rapidly and pushed him forward in the seat, and Seema skidded a few inches forward before she braced herself next to Jack on the floor. She looked through the forward viewport and twitched her tail. There in the middle of the tree island was a clearing. No time to do a flyby recon. The approach check was done, and the landing thrusters were armed. Slow it down, don't even overshoot the landing zone. The HUD was blaring at him, "FUEL STATUS CRITICAL LAND NOW."

His speed was slowed to a crawl. The height above ground counted down sixty, forty, twenty, ten, nine, eight, . . . three, two, one. He felt the back landing leg touch and then the other and now the front legs. He was down. He heaved a sigh of relief and began to run the shutdown checklist. "Damn, that was the closest I've ever come to running out of fuel in anything," he said out loud to himself and Seema.

He ran that last fuel calculation through his head again. Crap, that was five mentus and fifty septus, not five and a half mentus. That was too close, just way too close. He sat back in the chair and closed his eyes for a minute. Seema came over to him and nudged his hand. "Hey," he said to her, "I'm glad you're OK with that. I'm not sure that was worth the risk to save us thirty kahtaks of walking. I guess sometimes you just have to go for it, but I'm not sure this was one of those times." She nudged his hand again. "OK, I think I know what you're trying to tell me," he said.

Jack looked outside to see if he could see any kind of wildlife or other activity. It all looked pretty placid out there as far as he could see. He wished he'd had enough fuel to do a flyover and at least scan for life forms, but he hadn't had that luxury. He set the perimeter defense on stun and out to three hundred mu-uts. It gave him the same line-of-sight warning as last time.

He grabbed his weapons and gave a little whistle. Seema jumped down from the viewport and followed him down to the entrance. He cleared the area outside the viewport, and they went out. Seema ran a few steps ahead and stopped. She unfurled her ears and turned and listened in every direction. The popping and cooling of the ship probably didn't help her any, but the directional capability of her ears probably negated some of the sounds that were behind her quite a bit. After thirty septus of scanning, Seema was satisfied that there wasn't anything dangerous lurking nearby. She folded her ears and set about exploring. Jack did the same and found the area to be pleasant and peaceful.

There were some small birds and other minor wildlife but no larger creatures or predators that he could see. He went out to near the limits of where the defense perimeter was set and still didn't find any tracks or other signs of anything significant. He saw a few small rodent-looking critters scurrying around and mounds of dirt here and there from their digging. He watched Seema sneak up on a mound that had bits of dirt flying from it from some creature's digging. Her ears were peaked forward, and she moved with a smooth gliding slow-motion precision. She would freeze each time the digging stopped, and the little ground squirrel creature peeked out and moved again when it started digging.

When she was a mu-ut from the mound, she froze and waited. The squirrel critter looked around and then went back to digging. Seema's ears were now folded back and flat against her head now. One second, she was there, and then she was a blur. She was now on the squirrel's mound with a squirrel in her mouth. She shook it a couple of times to make sure it was dead then tossed it into the air and caught it and swallowed it in one quick motion. "Very impressive," Jack said to her. "It didn't have a chance, did it?" She looked at him with a look of satisfaction on her face then went on to stalk her next victim. "I'm guessing that's a lot more to your liking and better for you than the prepped junk I've been feeding you for the last couple of daiyus," said Jack.

Jack weighed his options now that he had some time to contemplate his next move. He was thirty kahtaks from the far edge of the greenbelt and then another eighty or ninety to Se-ahlaalu. That was doable in a couple of daiyus if he packed up a good supply of food and water. The other option was to check out the next greenbelt island about twenty kahtaks to the west, the one that looked like it might have some type of buildings or commercial operation on it, the one he didn't have enough fuel to fly to. It wasn't that far out of the way, and it would be a better option than the 110 kahtaks straight to Se-ahlaalu. All right, he'd give that a shot; all it would cost him is a little time, something he had plenty of at the moment.

He called Seema back and went back to the ship. She came running up to him with something in her mouth. "Got another one, eh? Did you get your fill of fresh squirrel? They do look pretty tasty," he said to her. She stopped in front of him and dropped the squirrel at his feet. "Seriously," he said, "that's for me?" She wiggled and made a little "hupf weep" noise and a short vibration trill. He knelt down to look at it and patted her on the head and stroked her back. "Well, that's very generous. Thank you so very, very much," he said. "That does look quite tasty, but I think I'll pass on that today, although that does look a lot like something I ate in survival school a few years back. I'll tell you what. You go ahead and eat it now, and if we run out of the preprepped stuff, then you catch another one or five, and we'll roast them over a nice campfire." He picked up the squirrel, patted her again, and handed it back to her. She seemed to understand and took the squirrel, flipped it in the air, and gulped it down in one swallow. "You're something else. What's not to like about you?" he said as they headed back into the ship.

Jack packed everything he thought he would need and that he could carry. Water would probably be OK as long as they were in the greenbelt, but once out on the desert, he'd need all he could carry. He checked the available settings on the ship to see what sort of a shutdown mode he could put it in. He didn't know how long the ship could power itself with the minuscule amount of fuel remaining in the tanks.

The ship had a small auxiliary power unit, or APU, in the aft of the ship that used a very small amount of fuel. It powered what the manual showed as a carbon plasma ion generator, which was displayed in the HUD manual. It somehow generated a direct stream of ions that were captured and funneled into a variable wave ablation regulator that then generated the required electrical power for the ship. It had something to do with the stable state of the carbon and the phase shift differential of the focused energy beam stripped ions. Jack didn't quite follow the technology, but it sounded interesting, and it apparently worked with great efficiency. As usual in this operation, all he was concerned with was, if he flipped the switch, would it work?

There was also a storage bank of power cells that were used to initiate the reaction in the ion generator that then powered the ship until the engine came online. It was all somewhat similar but with different technology from the turbine aircraft that he was familiar with. The technology was more advanced, but the structure and schematics of the systems were arranged in a similar fashion now that he'd found them.

The thought occurred to him that it might be possible that some of the newer technologies he'd heard about back on Earth might be some sort of reverse engineered technology from the alien spacecraft that had been rumored to have been acquired years back. He'd heard all the Roswell and Area 51 stuff since he was a kid but had never seen any evidence that it was true. Now that he was learning something about real alien technologies, it certainly seemed somewhat probable. If it were true, it would make sense that it had taken years to reverse engineer this type of technology. It probably took them years just to understand what they were looking at if they really had an actual alien ship to tear into. They knew they would have to go slow so they wouldn't destroy what they were researching, and without the language translator like he had, they might as well be trying to decipher hieroglyphics.

The Kershavah ship's APU appeared to be much more fuel efficient than any turbine-powered APU and had the definite advantage of having no moving parts to wear out or break. What it came down to was that he thought the ship would have power for at least a wenek or maybe more once he shut everything down except the perimeter defense system, which basically ran in a passive monitoring mode. As a precaution, Jack took his katana and cut a bunch of brush and small trees and placed them over and around the ship to try and break up its outline and give it a fair bit of camouflage. An horun later when everything was set and to his liking, he loaded up all of his gear and supplies and said, "Come on, Seema, time to head out and do a little exploratory hike about." With the ship closed up and powered down, they headed out in the direction toward the next greenbelt island.

* * * * *

The senior mine boss had just ended the comm link with the provost base. He sat for a mentu not sure how to evaluate what he had just heard. "What is it, Worthy Jondakav?" said the number three mine boss that had just witnessed the comm link call.

"The provost ship and its crew that were sent to eliminate the Varaci problem is now missing. They haven't heard from it in nearly twenty horuns, and there is no location signal or transmissions of any kind indicating its presence. The last report they received from the pilot was that they had captured the Varaci and they were bringing him back. Then there was a report that the provost team had been attacked by a Sabrav or maybe a Rannik raptor. The provost leader and two others were killed, and the Varaci was reported to have been carried off by the raptor."

"Oh, that would be good, then, the Varaci taken and eaten by a Sabrav raptor," replied the number three boss.

"Yes, I suppose that part is good, but that wouldn't explain the ship no longer being in communication and no position transmission from it. They will be sending another provost team to search for the ship in a couple of daiyus when they can assemble the crew that is on leave and get the other ship from its maintenance depot work. That was the primary on-duty team, and they will have to get the off-duty team and crew put together for a search effort. I hope the provosts do not try to bill us for their lost ship and crew or their search efforts. They were under contract for a specific fee and set performance."

"Yes, yes, I'm sure," piped up the number two boss, trying to add something useful to the conversation. "Maybe, maybe they just lost their position transmitter or something."

"Yes, or something," replied the senior boss, "I'm sure that's what it is, they just lost their transmitter," he said as he shook his head in disbelief.

* * * * *

The treed island was only about five kahtaks long. At the end of it was a row of tall trees that went straight in the direction toward the next tree island. The trees were maybe two hundred feet tall and planted in a line about four hundred feet in width. In the distance in all directions, Jack could see vast acres of various types of growing crops. Off in the distance, he saw a ship flying right near the horizon. He could see as it dipped lower that it was leaving a trail of light blue mist behind it. It disappeared below the next line of trees, and thirty septus later, it popped up farther to the left. It then made a tight turn and dropped down below the tree line again, heading the opposite direction. "Well, what do you know," he said, "it is some type of crop dusting operation. I guess, it's still the most efficient way to manage crops even on another planet. Who would have thought?"

He was a couple of kahtaks away from the crop duster, but he couldn't smell any of the chemical smells usually associated with that type of operation. He didn't think it too likely that they'd be using anything like the chemicals they used back on Earth that could be so overwhelming from an odor and health standpoint. He watched it make several more passes as he and Seema walked parallel to the tree line. It eventually pulled up and made a wide circle coming closer to them but was still a good kahtak away. It looked like a fairly large ship, but it didn't look like any crop dusting plane he'd ever seen.

It looked more like a flying tanker car than an airplane, but it did have short stubby wings on both the front and back. They didn't look like they were really for providing lift like on an airplane but maybe more for added aerodynamic maneuvering or stability. It was certainly a strange-looking machine, kind of a big flattened tank with a pointed nose and short steep front with rear wings but no tail. It was quiet too. At a kahtak, any airplane that size would have been loud enough to easily hear, but all he could hear was a faint humming whisper-like sound. He watched it head in the same general direction that he and Seema were going and then disappear below the tree line and horizon twenty septus later.

The hike was pleasant and relaxing, especially compared to the last weeks of insanity he'd been through. It felt good to be outside and just hiking along and working up a little sweat in the warm sun. He didn't know for sure, but he didn't think there would be any large predatory animals here in the ag greenbelt like there were in the others. Still, he kept an eye on the sky in case there might be any aerial predators. They could be anywhere because of their mobility, but he thought it would be less likely to find them here unless there was some larger prey for them, which there didn't seem to be. Spotting flying predators was something he had been trained to do for many years as a fighter pilot; the difference being was that the predators would be other fighter aircraft that could shoot you down but not living airborne predators large enough to kill and carry a man off.

Seema seemed to be enjoying herself considerably. She was running and stalking with her large ears unfurled. Then she would fold them and be chasing and running in circles just to burn off energy. She must be fairly young to have that much energy just to burn and have fun. She'd race out ahead several hundred feet then come tearing back in a broad circle, weaving and zigzagging through the underbrush and trees. Then she'd stop and freeze utterly frozen and listen for a minute to everything ahead and around her. Twice he saw her stop, stalk, and catch a small rodent that would be instantly flipped into the air and then swallowed whole. *At least she's not trying to share them with me now,* he thought.

After about an horun, Jack decided to take a break and have some lunch. He found a nice little spot with a small fallen tree and a pile of boulders that made a good place to sit and relax. The undergrowth was sparse, and he could see in all directions around him. The crops next to the tree line had varied little. One batch had looked like just a smaller, less mature planting of the previous one. With this much arable land, it would probably be a while before they switched crops. The ones he could see in the distance were different in color and shape than the near ones, but he wasn't going to hike several kahtaks out of his way just to see what they were. He also had no intention of being that exposed in the open where something undesirable could see him. He fed Seema a few tidbits of his own provisions, but she seemed less interested in them, since she'd been feeding on the available squirrel delicacies. Jack leaned back and closed his eyes and in a few mentus faded off for a quickie nap. It had been a long stressful wenek.

Suddenly, he awoke to the sound of shrieking and yelping and high-pitched growling. He opened his eyes and tried to assess the situation before he made any sudden moves. Off to his left, Seema was tearing through the underbrush with two large owl-sized birds diving and harassing her. She was alternately running and trying to hide from the onslaught of the two flying creatures that seemed to have her outnumbered and outmaneuvered. He grabbed his katana with the saya still on it and bolted toward her, yelling and swinging the katana above his head. He got to within about five mu-uts of her when the birds realized that they were now under attack themselves from another direction. They scattered upward and flew out and circled around and squawked and made a fuss. The larger one made a half-hearted dive at Jack but flew off when Jack swung the katana at it. They squawked and circled for another twenty septus and then headed back down the tree line.

Seema came running to him and dove under him and cowered in a little heap at his feet. "Hey, hey, are you OK?" he said to her. She seemed to come around in a few septus and seemed glad to see him, and she made a little fuss over being back with him. Jack looked her over and found two little cuts on her head and back. "I think you'll survive those," he said to her, "but you might want to stick a little closer to me, since we're both strangers in a strange land here. I think this might be a little different from your own greenbelt home but hopefully not as dangerous. Come on, let's get our stuff and get back on our little trek," he said to her. "I think you just met the local competition for your tasty little ground squirrels. I bet they didn't like you moving in on their food source and decided to tell you about it." She looked at him and gave him a plaintive little trill and fell in next to him as he went back and collected the rest of his gear.

Walking along the edge of the cultivated fields, Jack saw another tanker crop duster pass overhead on its way to or from a field. It seemed to be going in the same direction toward the next treed island where he'd seen the buildings on the ship's map. Out in the crop areas, he saw a couple of the ground rodents running around chasing each other. A shadow passed overhead, and another raptor dove down and pounced on one of the hapless creatures. "It looks like dinner is served again and not just for a tu-urak," he said to Seema.

A few mentus later, another crop duster flew over, this time directly overhead the tree line. Jack got a much closer look at it as it went over quite low. It mildly vibrated the surrounding area. A few smaller birds and animals squawked and flew for cover from its presence. Jack seemed to sense a static or magnetic tingling on his exposed skin and head as the ship passed overhead. It was quite low and seemed to be slowing. They couldn't have been more than a couple of kahtaks from the next tree island now. It was apparent that this was the destination of the crop duster ships, since they slowed considerably as they approached the island. It seemed as if the arrivals were fairly evenly spaced based on the time showing in his translator HUD. *Maybe they are sequenced in at specific intervals for servicing after their runs,* he thought.

As they got closer, they could hear the faint sound of other machinery in the distance. They came to the edge of the tree island where the tree line spread out and approached the crop duster operation cautiously. Jack took up a position from cover where he could watch and survey the operation with the monocular he'd gotten from the ship. He could see several support personnel working on or checking the equipment that serviced the big ag ships.

The ag ships looked to be about the same length and width as the Kershavah assault ship, but they were bulkier looking, basically more storage tank than anything else. They had short stubby wings that folded upward on the ground and looked like they were more for supporting what looked like retractable spray bars. They weren't very aesthetic looking, but then they didn't need to be, since they were strictly a functional design. Jack watched the ships being serviced with some kind of liquid being pumped into its hopper tank from an automated service vehicle. The vehicle pulled up and appeared to fuel the ship from underground hoses with whatever chemicals they used for their aerial application process. The workers seemed more interested in the service vehicles than they did the ship.

From a distance, the ship appeared to have a small crew door on the left side of its fuselage as well as some type of small cockpit on the front of the ship. He could see the windscreen that wrapped around the narrow front of the ship, but he hadn't seen any pilots go in or out of the ship. The map had said something about using caution for autonomous aerial application activities, so he was guessing that the ships were self-piloted. He wondered if the ship had a cockpit for manual operations for when the ship couldn't fly itself or maybe for maintenance or ferry operations. That would make sense for this kind of operation. His dilemma now was, should he go say hi to the maintenance people and try to bum a ride to town or see if it might be possible to borrow some sort of transport like perhaps the ag ship he was watching?

The problem with making contact now was it was possible that these maintenance types may have been alerted to watch out for a Kershavah ship and its renegade fugitive pilot. He didn't know if the provost pilot he'd spared had survived and then told them he'd stolen their ship or not. It probably would have been wiser to just kill the Kershavah pilot, since then he wouldn't have to be worrying about it now. Walking up and introducing himself might be tantamount to surrendering and walking back into to the Corodune prison. He was in no real hurry; he decided it would be better to wait and get a better feel for this operation and see what happened over a full daiyus of observation.

Jack watched the service crew for a while as the first ship finished its servicing and took off and left. He wondered if they were using Tritrico fuel or something else. From the strange electromagnetic feeling he'd experienced when the ship had flown over, he wondered if it was a different type of propulsion system altogether. Maybe it was some type of system that could carry a lot of weight, liquid weight, and was more accurate but not very fast. Jack moved farther around from his initial spot and could now see that there was another smaller ship on the other side of the large building. *That could be their service crew transport,* he thought. He had now seen four of the service team crew. After the ag ship left, a couple of them went into the service building, and the other two stayed outside and seemed to be just messing around. Twenty mentus later, another ag ship arrived for servicing, and the maintainers watched the entire process with very little involvement. They must have been tweaking the servicing system, and now they were just watching to make sure it worked. It appeared that everything had checked out. After the second ship had been serviced and sent on its way, the four maintainers got into their service ship and prepared to leave. Jack watched as they took off vertically and headed in the general direction of Se-ahlaalu.

Jack now had a fair idea of the ag operation's routine. He wanted to get into a ship and see how it was arranged as far as a manual override possibility. He would wait a while and see what the next ship did. It would be getting dark soon, so he thought the best thing to do would be to wait until it was dark and then do some closer recon. Jack kept Seema close, and she could tell by his body language that he was being cautious and stealthy, so she did the same. He didn't know if the maintenance team would be back, but from the looks of the operation, everything appeared to run autonomously.

He waited for the next ship. He didn't know if they ran all night of if they just worked during the daiyus. He would find out shortly. The shadows were now growing long as the sun touched the horizon to the east. He heard the first one a few mentus later as it came in and flared and then settled onto the ground near the large service building. A few mentus later, a second one arrived and landed behind the first. In the next fifteen mentus, six more had landed, and the area around the service building was crowded with ag ships. *I guess they don't work at night,* thought Jack. *Apparently, they all work right up until dark, and then they all head to the barn for their overnight rendezvous. That was pretty interesting,* thought Jack. They were so highly automated that he wondered why they didn't work 28/8. Ten mentus later, he had his answer.

From the side of the larger service building, dozens of small drones began streaming out into the air. With his monocular in night vision mode, Jack could see that most of them turned out fast and headed away from the nearby area. A couple of them seemed to linger, and one went out right over the nearest crop field. From an altitude of about a hundred feet above the field, the drone started periodically shooting a small pulsed energy beam. Jack wondered what it was shooting at for a second then remembered seeing a couple of the ground squirrels that Seema had been catching that were out in the field. *Now that's an interesting method of pest control,* thought Jack. *At least they aren't using poison.* Maybe that's why the raptor birds attacked Seema, because a lot of their prey is killed by the drones. There probably just aren't enough natural predators to control all those ground squirrel rodents out there. *Well, hopefully, they won't come into the forest here and start shooting at random Varacis and semidomesticated pet, a tu-urak,* said Jack to himself.

Jack waited until a couple of horuns after dark before he made his move. He'd reconned up and down the edge of the tree line surrounding the ag servicing operation and could see no further signs of any live attendants. He didn't know if the operation had a security defense system or not, but he couldn't spot any. That didn't mean that a spare drone might not come flying out of the hangar with its guns blazing if he approached. Jack didn't think there would be much of a defense system in place but you never knew. *Who would want to steal an ag ship for a joy ride anyway, well, besides me?* he thought.

There was a chance that there could be a defense system set up for stray predators or other creatures that might wander in from the forest. The dilemma now—there was always a dilemma it seemed—was, should he wait twenty-eight horuns and do a more thorough surveillance of the ag operation or try and go for it tonight? Going for it tonight added a higher risk factor because of the lack of additional intel, but waiting also added additional risk, as there was always a chance that they could track the Kershavah ship to its current position and, by simple deduction, track him to the ag operation. *In any combat situation, always go with your first best option,* he thought to himself.

OK, he would do a close-in recon of the operation. If everything seemed good, he would recon a ship and try to determine how or if he could override it to take manual control of it. His other dilemma was what to do with Seema. He didn't have anything to tie her up with, and she might throw a fit even if he did. He doubted if she would stay, and he was afraid she might get zapped by a security system designed to keep out pests. He would just have to risk taking her along, and besides, her incredible hearing could always be a benefit to him for detecting danger.

"All right, Seema, you're in. Come on, let's go snoop," he said to her as he readied to move in for the evening's recon venture. They approached stealthily from an area that offered the most cover until they were within about forty mu-uts of the nearest parked ship. *So far so good,* Jack said to himself. Seema seemed to grasp the concept that they were stalking something and fell in with Jack in his slow recon approach. Her ears scanned and twitched, but she didn't seem to give any indication of a threat. Jack could still occasionally see the drones way out in the distance hunting the crop-eating critters, but other than that, everything was still. Jack watched and waited in the cover of the brush for a good twenty mentus before he was ready to make a move any closer to the nearest ship.

He was just ready to start his approach to the ship when he saw Seema crouch low and utter the faintest deep growl. Something moved out of the corner of his eye. A dim blue-lit outline maybe fifty feet off the ground was approaching from his right. It was hard to make out what it was, but it seemed to be some sort of a drone. It was different from the rodent hunter drones, but there it was.

He froze but was ready to shoot it down with his ion rifle if he had to. If it attacked first, he probably wouldn't have a chance. He could barely make out the shape of it as it was just barely outlined in very dim blue light. If it wasn't for the glow of the blue light, he probably wouldn't have seen it at all. It coasted to a stop not twenty feet in front of him. *It must have some sort of heat-sensing technology or night vision optics,* he thought. Seema moved in behind him slowly with her ears twitching nervously. It seemed to shift position a couple of feet when she moved. He could just barely hear a slight background hum as it hovered there.

Jack slowly moved the muzzle of rifle toward the drone. It must have caught his movement, as it suddenly backed up about ten feet and then made a couple of quick half-circle flights back and forth on his position as if it was analyzing him. Jack kept the rifle aimed at it the whole time it was bracketing his position in case it tried something. Analyzing him must have been what it was doing, for as suddenly as it was interested in him, it suddenly became disinterested and resumed its previous track along the perimeter of the ag compound.

Jack breathed a sigh of relief. It must have recognized him as a worker or maintainer or something other than a threat and decided to go on its way. It had almost seemed more interested in Seema's movements than his. It must have been some sort of a sentinel drone, and it was probably looking for some specific types of animals that might be a threat to the ag operation. He hoped it worked autonomously like the other drones and didn't report in to anyone about a potential intruder. He could feel the adrenalin draining out of his body. He hated these kinds of situations. These are the kinds of situations where you just don't know what to do because there is nothing in your past experience or training to give you any idea about what the right or wrong response might be. There was definitely not much information to go on to base your reaction to something like that. "OK, Seema, let's keep going," he said quietly to her.

He made his way to the nearest ag ship with Seema close behind. The access door to the cockpit was near the ground and was less than a mu-ut square. It had a manual recessed latch, which he moved to the up and open position. The door swung open on a forward hinge, and he looked inside to see a short ladder leading to the higher level of the cockpit above. He slipped inside and called to Seema. She jumped up into the inside bay of the door, and Jack latched the door behind them. He bent down to lift her up the four feet to the higher deck level, but she crouched and leapt up before he could even bend over. "OK, I guess you don't need my help with that," he said to her.

He climbed the four short ladder stairs and got to a small space directly behind a single small and not-very-comfortable-looking pilot seat. Sitting in the seat, which was hard and definitely not comfortable, he looked at the dark cockpit with a minimal amount of instrumentation and controls. He looked around and found a switch labeled "Auxiliary Crew Power." When he flipped the switch to on, the instruments and HUD came to life. He looked at the instruments and saw that the ship hadn't been filled with whatever the ag tanks held for spraying. Seema came up next to him and looked out the nearly vertical front windshield in front of them. Jack patted her on the head and stroked her neck and back. She gave a little humming whine and curled up on the deck next to his chair and went to sleep.

There was a Manual Flight Control Override switch in the front console directly in front of him. He switched it on and watched as the HUD announced a warning with three beeps and flashed a "Crew Manual Control Engaged" message. Jack said to Seema, "Well, I have it figured out how to take manual control of the ship, but we don't have any fuel yet. Should we wait until we're fueled or try to take one of the other ships if they fuel those first?" She looked at him with her large brown eyes and made a plaintive little low trill sound. "Yeah, well, you're no help," he said to her. She trilled at him again and curled up in a little circle on the floor.

Thinking about the situation, Jack thought that if he took off with a ship before the others all left on their daily rounds, it might be much more noticeable than if he just left with the ag ship crowd and then sort of disappeared in the middle of the ship's mission. Since the ships didn't have pilots, and it didn't look like the maintainers would be back before morning, he decided the best thing to do would be to wait for morning and let the ships all launch themselves and just go along for the ride for the first few mentus of the flight.

He opened the ship's HUD display to the maintenance and operating section and set about learning as much about the ship's operation as he could. The ship would be easy enough to fly. It wasn't very fast but made up for that with its ability to precision track the spraying applications on the crop fields. Jack suddenly felt a slight rumble through the floor of the ship's cockpit.

He now knew what to expect when he felt that as he looked out the cockpit window toward the forest. He could see the heavy mist beginning to rise from the forested area while the outside of the ship's windshield began to fog over from the ultrahigh humidity. In a few mentus, the entire ag service area was shrouded in heavy swirling mist and fog. It started to drizzle, and the air was heavily saturated with moisture. Jack spent the next couple of horuns studying up on the ship's operation. It would be vaguely similar to the Kershavah but without all the bells and whistles. The navigation system was very basic, but it would do an adequate job of guiding him to Se-ahlaalu.

It was ninety-four kahtaks to Se-ahlaalu from his current position. He might be able to borrow this beauty and then put it back on auto, and they might never know what happened if it just returned to its programmed course. *Wishful thinking maybe, but it might be worth a try,* thought Jack. "Come on, Seema, we're going to take one more break and then hole up in the ship until morning," said Jack. She was passed out after a hard day of dealing with attacking raptors and other excitement, and she didn't seem too enthused to be going outside, but she hopped down and followed Jack anyway.

Jack spent a few mentus walking around the ship but didn't want to get more than a few feet from it for fear that he'd lose sight of it in the fog. With their chores finished, they went back up to the cockpit and settled in for the night. Jack made sure the ship was back under its own command before he curled up on the floor next to Seema with his bag of supplies for a pillow. She moved over next to him and wedged herself against him and under his arm. It wasn't comfortable, but it was better than the pilot seat, thought Jack as he drifted off to sleep. About four hours later, Jack awoke to the sound of machinery and the ship's systems powering up. He carefully peeked outside and saw that it was still dark. The fog had thinned a little from the drizzle, and he could see the automated fueling machine working on the ship. He watched for a few mentus then went back to his makeshift bed and back to sleep.

As the sun came up and started to thin the fog on the greenbelt, the ag ships started to come to life. In sequence, from the first to the last launched, they woke up and started their engines. The order was random and not in the order that they had parked on the ramp. Jack saw and slightly heard the first one start and then the second about the time the first one launched. He stayed low and out of sight in case there were some sort of maintenance personnel in the area that he wasn't aware of. He turned the cockpit power on but didn't take control of the ship. Seema sat in the back and watched the show. Jack's ship was the fifth to launch. It started its engines and went through a series of automated self-test functions. Jack could see it scrolling through a checklist on the display, and the items turned from orange to blue on the list as each item was completed. Two mentus after the ship had started its checks and engine start sequence, the engines changed pitch, and it lifted off. After climbing to a height of thirty mu-uts, it turned and headed north toward the edge of the greenbelt. As soon as they'd gone a few kahtaks out of sight from the ag operations base, Jack switched the ship over to "Crew Manual Control and turned the ship in the direction of Se-ahlaalu, which he'd already programmed into the nav computer. He climbed to three hundred mu-uts for the flight to Se-ahlaalu. The flight time showed twenty-three mentus to destination.

The ship wasn't very fast, but it would still be a short flight. Jack scrolled ahead on the map again and looked at the area to the southwest of the city with the higher terrain. There were several small valleys running parallel to the city between six to twelve kahtaks from the edge of the town. There didn't appear to be any activity of any sort there, but you could never tell. He didn't know how old the maps in this ag ship were, so they might not necessarily be current. He didn't know if it would be a big deal for an ag ship to show up at the spaceport, but he didn't want to find out. Maybe it was a routine thing and maybe not. Someone might recognize an ag ship and wonder what it was doing near the city. His best bet was to land somewhere undetected, abandon the ship, and send it back on its way if possible. If the ag operation was somehow tracking him, he wanted to get away from the ship as fast as possible once he'd gotten to his destination, preferably undetected.

He descended to a hundred mu-uts and aimed toward the hills that were now visible to the southwest of Se-ahlaalu. He slowed slightly to a hundred kahtaks, or about fifty miles per hour, and scanned the terrain of the hills as he flew over them low. There was a small overgrown building in the first valley that didn't appear to be inhabited. The next valley was empty, and the next had three small buildings clustered together at one end. There were no vehicles or ships, but they did look like they'd been occupied sometime recently. The next valley closest to the city didn't have any buildings or other signs of civilization. It was a little more rugged and inaccessible than the others, but there was a small meadow that might work for a landing zone.

Jack circled briefly but didn't see anything other than a couple of herd-type animals that ran as he flew over. "This looks like a good a place as any. Fasten your seat belt," he said to Seema. He'd already been through the prelanding checklist, and like the Kershavah ship, it had an "Arm Landing Thrusters" prompt, which he'd selected. *It likely did that on its own when it was flying autonomously,* thought Jack.

His landing went as planned, and he shut the ship down. He looked around but didn't see anything in his field of vision from the inside of the ship. He shut down the engines and everything else but left the crew power on and left the "Crew Manual Control on for now. He checked outside the ship and opened the door and jumped down with Seema and his supplies. He did a quick recon around the ship and let Seema listen for anything that might be around. She twitched and tilted a few times but didn't seem to find anything that concerned her. "You're quite the asset," he said to her as he patted her on the head. He said to her, "All right, you stay right here a second while I go and turn the ship's power off of manual override. You stay out here, OK?"

She wanted to jump back in the ship with him, but he wouldn't let her. She got very upset when he went into the ship without her, but being a forest predator as well as prey, she didn't make any noise or call attention to herself. Jack flipped the manual flight switch back to ship control and jumped down to the door and out of the ship. He latched the door and said to Seema, "Come on, come on, Seema, the ship will probably take a couple of mentus to get itself going." He ran for the nearest cover from the ship and headed into the underbrush thirty mu-uts up the side of the hill.

As soon as Jack switched the ship's control back to the ship, it powered itself up, thought for a mentu with its computer brain, then decided it wasn't on its programmed mission profile and commenced corrective action. It ran its self-checks and started its engines. Another mentu later, it had plotted a course back to the greenbelt and its assigned plot. It didn't really know or care that it wasn't where it was supposed to be; it just wanted to correct the error. Another half mentu later, it lifted off and headed back to where it was supposed to be. Later that daiyus, while applying the advanced natural growth stimulant to the crops, the ship would decide it didn't quite have enough fuel to complete its tasked mission and headed back to the ag operation base. It ran a series of self-tests but couldn't find any maintenance discrepancies or fuel leaks. It would just pick up tomorrow where it had left off today.

"There goes our ride," Jack said to Seema. "I hope we didn't need it anymore. Come on, Seema, let's get hoofin' and put some distance between us and here." Jack headed parallel to the valley floor but about halfway up the side of the hill so that they would be hidden from both the valley floor and anyone that might be up on the top of the hill. The cover wasn't heavy, but it was adequate enough as far as providing good concealment. If anyone had been in the valley, they would have seen the ship land, but maybe not his exit into the nearby cover. Hopefully, they would probably think that whoever was flying the ship had left in it also.

Twenty mentus of hiking put them near the end of the valley where the hill tapered off and they could easily cross to the other side. From the top of the hill, they could see the city in the distance not more than about eight kahtaks. Jack was looking at the southwestern edge of Se-ahlaalu, which was spread out before him. He could see the slightly raised area of the spaceport on the northwest part of the city in the far distance. He could just barely make out the river coming out of the hills farther to the northwest.

"Well, this should be an easy-enough hike," he said to Seema, "but what am I going to do with you when we get there? You know I didn't really bargain on having a friendly little a tu-urak tagging along. Not that I don't want you along, but it does complicate things a bit. I don't know how safe it will be for a tu-urak in the city. I don't even know if normal everyday people keep pets on this planet, since I've spent all my time here on Nishda in a prison. The only normal people I've met here were incarcerated in prison with me. Well, all we can do is give it a shot and see what happens, unless you'd like to wait here for me for a few daiyus until I can come back and get you." Seema just looked at him with her big eyes and gave a little rumbling trill. "No, I didn't think so," said Jack. "Now if something bad happens, don't say I didn't try to warn you. OK, then, let's go."

They proceeded down the hill and toward the city in the distance. A few mentus later, they came to a tall fence that was well hidden in the tall tree line at the base of the long hill. *Sure didn't see this from the air,* he said to himself. They walked the edge of the fence for a several hundred mu-uts, but nothing changed. There were signs attached to the fence, but they were on the other side, so he couldn't read them. The fence didn't appear to be electrified, but it was a good four mu-uts tall. There was no telling how far it went, and he didn't want to go much farther or it would start taking him away from the city. Moving farther down the fence line, they came across a pile of old wire and other assorted junk. Jack pulled several pieces of wire out of the pile and then went over to the fence and took out his Katana. "No sense in continuing with this scenario," he said to Seema. "Get back, go on, get back now," he said as he shooed her back.

He took an overhead swing stance and aimed for the middle of the fence. He took a hard downward swing and hit the fence about two mu-uts off the ground. The blade of the katana made a loud ching as it hit the fence and cut it all the way to the ground. "That was easy enough," he said aloud. He ran his finger gently across the blade edge to see if it had dulled it, but it was as perfect as when it was new. "Come on, Seema," he said as he pushed his gear through the gash in the fence. On the other side, he could read the sign. "Se-ahlaalu Kavekka Hunting Reserve. Stay

Out. Fines and Conscription for Unauthorized Entry," it had posted. "Well, great," said Jack, "that's all we need is to get conscripted in Se-ahlaalu for trespassing. No thanks, been there done that somewhere recently," he said. He quickly repaired the fence with the wire he'd found and headed away from the fence at a fast pace. "Whatever is in there, we probably don't want to let out. I guess that wouldn't have been a very good place to leave you after all," he said to Seema.

Thirty mentus later, they were approaching the edge of town. Jack wrapped the rifle in the bundle with the other katana as they worked their way around the edge of the partially walled city. There seemed to be some walled areas and some others where there appeared to be some houses or grungier-looking areas right at the edge of the city. He stopped at the edge of a wall and peered into the city. It looked like any other lower-rent semi-industrial neighborhood area he'd ever seen.

He wondered why the city wasn't fully walled like the Corodune mine complex. Maybe there wasn't the threat of the dangerous wildlife like the cities that were closer to the more southerly greenbelts. There were streets with houses and streets with businesses of some sort or another. Most of the houses and buildings looked like they were adobe or bricks made out of the locally available desert building materials. There were some metal structures and other miscellaneous buildings, but most were the tan or brown adobe-looking structures.

Seema peered in too and with her ears listened to the noise of the city in the distance. For some reason, Jack didn't think that she looked too impressed with what she was seeing. The area they were in looked more like low-rent residential, so he didn't know what to expect as far as any reception or confrontation. His goal was to remain as incognito as possible. He saw a few vimars and some commercial-type vehicles going about their business. None of them looked as fancy as the one he'd borrowed from Corodune. He saw several people going about their business along the street and by the houses.

There were a variety of several different types of aliens, although not as diverse as he'd seen in the mine. He guessed the mine had a higher density of different types of aliens because of the draw of employment there with the mine and being closer to the larger city of Wanana. It might be a little more homogenous here as far as Nishdans, but you never knew on a planet of all immigrants. Over there, yes, he saw some animals of some type in the backyard of a small house that had a mesh fence. They looked more like goats or some type of small herd animal, but still they had some domestic animals. Hopefully, Seema wouldn't cause too much of an issue.

The streets, at least right here, appeared to be fairly wide, although they weren't paved. The vimars and other vehicles floated a couple of feet above the ground, so there was no need for any pavement, just a throughway for the vehicles to pass. The task now will be to find this Talaka Vamava. He had the location from Fregga

Kitzu. His translator didn't seem to have the ability to find a specific address, even though it had the ability to find its way back to a previous location. It was more like a simple lat/long computer than a database navigation system. "Come on, Seema, let's go find out what we can find out. You stay close to me here. There's no telling what kind of a reception we'll get here," he said to her.

They went a couple of streets farther north until they came to a small business with an open door that looked like it might be selling food and maybe some clothing and other miscellaneous things. A sign over the door said, "Seeoot's - Eat in Here." A thin, strange-looking alien with long stringy looking red-and-brown feathery hair was inside behind a counter. There were two equally strange-looking aliens sitting at one of the four tables eating some sort of cold plate lunch.

Jack went in with Seema close on his heel and went to the counter. "Excuse me, I'm new here and I'm looking for a location that I have written here. Any chance you could point me in the right direction?" The alien looked up from behind the counter, while the other two patrons glanced his way.

"Do you want something to eat?" asked the thin alien behind the counter.

"Not right now, but maybe I can come back later with the wife and kids when I have some more time. I've got to meet someone in a little while, and I need to find this location," replied Jack.

"Well, we have some food, and there's some things to buy over there. That's what we have," said the thin alien.

"Yes, I understand, but I don't have the time right now," said Jack.

The two aliens at the table were both staring at Jack and Seema now. The one on the left jumped up with a small club in its hand and came menacingly toward Jack. "That's a tu-urak. Those things are dangerous," it said as it kept advancing toward Jack.

"This one's not, and it's mine, so back off and leave it alone," said Jack.

The alien took a couple of more steps toward Jack and said, "Those things should be killed so they don't hurt nothing."

"Not this one," said Jack, stepping between Seema and the alien. "Now go sit down and finish your lunch before I turn this into a very bad daiyus for you."

The alien stopped and hesitated and looked at Jack. "There's two of us and only one a you," said the alien.

"Well, you'd better get about six more friends if you want to even up the odds, and your friend over there doesn't look too thrilled about what you're planning," replied Jack.

500

The alien didn't look too sure about the situation himself. "You, you'd just better watch out around here with that tu-urak. Someone isn't going to like seeing a wild animal walking around here where people are."

"Thanks for the warning," said Jack, "but no one is going to mess with my tu-urak. That would be a serious mistake on their part." Keeping an eye on the situation, Jack now turned back to the alien behind the counter. "So you, do you know where this location is I just showed you?"

The alien looked at Jack and his tu-urak for a second then decided to answer, "Now, uh, I don't know exactly where, but that one name, Huunaj Ruj, next to the Ashongad EW name, is up by the spaceport, probably a couple of kahtaks north of it. Karveja spaceport is about eight kahtaks north, up that way," it said, pointing. "You'll have to ask someone up there. You sure you don't want something to eat?" it asked.

"Thanks," said Jack. "Maybe I'll be back later after my meeting," as he went out the open door while keeping his eye on the other two patrons.

"Well, that didn't go too well," he said to Seema once they were outside. "Apparently, they're not all that fond of wild and vicious man- or alien-eating forest tu-uraks." Seema paced back and forth around Jack but didn't seem too interested in Jack's declaration of her unpopularity. Jack could now see a raised area in the distance that had a fair amount of faster-moving traffic on it. It almost looked like a highway or interstate for the floating vehicles that were going in both directions. *That would make sense,* thought Jack, *as far as vehicles making better time near the surface without cross traffic issues.* They would need an unobstructed throughway just like surface vehicles would on Earth.

A mentu later, he saw a large ship making a wide arcing turn from the sky and descending in the direction of the spaceport. It looked more aerodynamic like an airplane and didn't look like it was designed for reentry, so it must have been an atmospheric ship. He guessed that there was no reason to differentiate between spaceports and airports here, since they were probably one and the same. Since Se-ahlaalu wasn't nearly as large as Wanana, he estimated that this main highway would be the one that would take him to the spaceport. If he just paralleled it, he should at least get to the general area of his destination.

Eight kahtaks to the spaceport and then another couple past it should be about ten kahtaks total, just an easy five-mile jog if he got to it. He decided not to run, though, as it might call too much attention to himself, especially if they didn't happen to jog around here for fitness, especially with tu-uraks. It reminded him of the time he'd stayed at a beautiful five-star hotel in Caracas on a technical liaison assignment, and the van driver told the occupants that if any of them were runners, not to run here because if the police saw you running, they figured you were running from something and might just shoot you. Yes, in some ways, this place did remind him of the beautiful outskirts of Caracas. Better save the running for emergencies only.

After several kahtaks, they left the semiresidential area and passed into an area of what looked like light industrial and warehousing. *That's usually what you find around airports or seaports,* he thought. There were more vimars and larger truck-size vehicles coming and going. He passed an area that looked like it was more of a convenience store and fast-food retail area for local workers. He avoided getting too close to it where he might draw any attention. He got a few stares from passersby, and one vimar stopped and watched him for a minute then moved on.

He'd seen a few more aerial ships come and go as well as one larger ship that came in high and hot. It was definitely an orbital capable ship from the look of it with its shielding and the shape of its hull. It looked more like a cargo rig that was designed for bringing cargo from a larger ship in orbit down to the surface like some of the ships he'd seen docked with the big trade ship *Yuanjejitt.* This one was about half that size and a little more aerodynamic looking. He'd heard a distant triple boom a few mentus before he saw the ship and recognized it as the sound of a ship reentering and slowing through the sound barrier during its descent.

An horun later, he was passing abeam the spaceport and heading toward another industrial zone on the northeast side of it. They stopped for a snack from Jack's pack and then headed across a small open field and under a small overpass on one of the smaller throughways heading into the spaceport. Just before crossing under the overpass, Seema froze with her ears open and twitching. A high resonating growl came from her throat as she focused her attention on the underpass.

"Something's there, isn't there, baby?" he said to her. "Let's find out what it is. I doubt that it's any of your forest predators, but there are plenty of other kinds of predators around." Jack pulled the katana and carefully eased up to the front side of the underpass. He could see some assorted garbage and recently trampled grass in the underpass, which stretched about forty mu-uts to the other side. The opposite end had more trees and cover visible on it than this side. He couldn't see anything all the way through, but that didn't mean anything especially with Seema's warning.

He didn't want to cross the throughway above with Seema because there was too much fast-moving traffic, and it looked like the next chance to cross was a long way off. Jack yelled, "I know you're down there! Come out and show yourself and you won't get hurt." There was no response. "I know you're down there. If you don't show yourself, I'll have to come down there, and you will get hurt." There was still no response. Seema growled again. "All right, you haven't given me any choice, I hope you are ready to die." He hoped that would shake them up a bit. He thought about putting a couple of rounds in the dirt at the end of the tunnel with the ion rifle, but he was afraid that might attract too much attention this close to the spaceport and freeway.

He flipped the katana so he would be striking with the dull edge, which could still make a nasty gash or bruise but wouldn't slice through limbs like soft butter. He wanted to tell Seema to stay, but he didn't know if she would, and if she did, she might run over the top of the overpass through the traffic. "Come on, Seema, but stay back a little and give me some maneuvering room," he said to her. He went down the tunnel with his back against one side and the katana at high ready. He had no idea who or what he was up against or how many. Just before the end of the tunnel, he gave a loud banzai yell and then jumped back twenty feet. Two aliens rushed from each side of the entrance, but there was no one to jump like they'd expected.

They looked to see where their quarry had gone and then saw Jack at the same time and rushed him. He caught the first one with a left-to-right moderate katana swing to the shoulder then pushed off the wall as three others came crashing through the first one that was now rolling on the ground clutching his shoulder and screaming. The next one came straight at him, and Jack popped him with a front kick to the face, which sent him crashing against the far wall with the sound of his head hitting the wall solidly. The next one spun to attack him and caught a fast hard toe kick to the liver area then a quick snap kick to the side of the head that dropped him instantly into a curled fetal position of clutching, writhing, moaning pain.

The last one turned and ran out the end of the overpass opening they had come from and disappeared. Jack sprinted after him. Something hit him hard from above and knocked him forward and down as he exited the overpass. The attacker was on top of him that had dropped from above. Jack used the momentum of the hit and kept his roll going, all the while the attacker was trying to hit him with something in his hand. Jack had kept the katana for a couple of seconds then let it go in the roll, afraid he would roll over it and get cut himself, since he was holding it backward.

First things first, he blocked then looped with his left arm and caught and locked the attacker's striking arm. He then hit the attacker with a short palm strike followed by a hard right elbow to the face as they rolled again. Jack rolled away once more then jumped up and placed a nice defensive front kick to the solar plexis of the new one that rushed him sending it sprawling back and into the embankment. The earlier attacker that had run out of the overpass had turned back and was scrambling for the katana on the ground. Before the alien could get his hands on it, Jack saw a brown flash and heard a snap and a tearing sound followed by a terrified scream. Jack was up and moving as he saw the second alien that had attacked him struggling to his feet. Jack grabbed the katana and turned to the first one that had dropped from above. Its face was pretty mangled from the elbow strike, and it was holding its face and bleeding nicely into its own hands from a broken nose and multiple broken teeth.

He turned back to the last one that had tried to attack him that was lying on the ground, writhing with its leg shredded and a nice set of bleeding lacerations in the shape of a tu-urak bite. "Nice try. I'll be sure to remember that one," said Jack. He went over to the least injured one and grabbed it by its stringy red-and-blue hair.

"No, no, don't kill me. Don't hit me with that long knife," it pleaded.

"Is that your natural color?" asked Jack.

"Wha-wha-what?" it replied.

"Shut up and listen," said Jack. "This location here," showing it Talaka Vamava's address, "where is this?"

"I, I, I'm not sure. That way, up that way a couple of kahtaks, I think. I've seen that up there somewhere before. Please don't hurt me. I didn't do anything. We just wanted to see what you had."

"Now you know," said Jack as he shoved the sad-looking alien back and down. "Consider yourself very lucky today. I could have easily killed you all, but it was a lot harder to go easy on you. I almost got myself hurt because I was being nice to you idiots."

"OK, I, OK—I mean, we appreciate that," whimpered the alien.

"You might want to consider a different line of work before someone ends this career venture for you permanently," said Jack as he collected his stuff and headed out with Seema. Just out of sight of the now injured aliens Jack stopped and gave Seema a big hug and looked her over really good for any injuries. "Thank you, Seema. That was wonderful, I'm glad you didn't get hurt. I bet they never expected to get chewed on by a wild killer attack tu-urak beast of the forest today, did they?" he said as he rubbed and patted her. "Very, very good girl, Seema. You're a very good girl in so many ways."

Keeping to the back ways, Jack worked his way in the direction of the throughway with Talaka Vamava's address on it. He came across two workers loading some type of containers onto a cargo vehicle and asked them if they knew where the address was. The shorter one answered that it was "three more endways along this throughway then on the left."

"Is that one of those forest carnivores like I've seen on the animal shows?"

"Yes," said Jack, "but this one is mostly tame."

"Is it dangerous at all?" asked the other alien.

"Only if you're a ground squirrel or you try to hurt her," replied Jack.

"Well, that's kind of nice. I've never seen one in real life. I've never heard of one being tamed like that before," said the shorter one.

"Yes, she's very intelligent," replied Jack, "and thanks for your help," he said as he waved to them and headed toward the direction they'd indicated. *Well, at least everyone's not a butthead in this city,* Jack said to himself. As he glanced back over his shoulder after a few moments, he saw the shorter worker talking into some sort of handheld device with his back half turned. *Hmmm, interesting time to call home to ask your wife about tonight's pork roast,* he thought.

Jack counted down the requisite number of endways and saw the marker that designated it as Ashongad EW. He turned down the end way and started looking at the various buildings. There were about ten to choose from, but only one had more than one or two vehicles at it. The third one on the left had four types of vimars and a larger cargo transport parked outside. It was one of the larger buildings on the throughway, and as he got closer, he could see it had two larger doors that would accommodate the larger transport vimars. A couple of the other buildings had some identifying signs on them advertising different products or services, but the larger one didn't. *That would be about right from the little bit I know about this Talaka Vamava,* thought Jack.

Jack went up to the main entrance that was on a small extension to the building and tried the door, but it was locked. There were several dark windows, but he couldn't see through them at all. He tried banging on the door and waited a minute, but nothing happened. He tried again with the same result. *One more try,* he said to himself, *and then I'll have to try something else.*

As Jack went to bang for the third time, the door popped open a crack, and a voice from inside rasped, "We're closed. What do you want?"

"I'm looking for Talaka Vamava," replied Jack.

"No one around here by that name" came the reply.

"Well, I must be pretty close," replied Jack, "because this is the address Fregga Kitzu sent me to."

After a ten-second pause came the reply, "Wait."

A mentu later, the voice said, "Who are you, and what's your business with Talaka Vamava?"

"I was sent here by Fregga Kitzu to meet with Talaka Vamava. My name is Jack Spartan. Fregga Kitzu was supposed to contact Talaka Vamava and let him know I was coming. I have something Talaka Vamava might be interested in."

"OK, then, where did you meet this Fregga Kitzu?"

"I met him when he supplied me with some fuel for my ship at his Uruku-bar trading post operation."

After another twenty-septu wait, the voice said, "OK, go around to the back of the building," and the door slammed shut.

Jack went around the side of the building through a fence opening and then toward the back. He wasn't quite sure what to expect, so he would be clandestinely ready with the katana if needed. He gave a wide berth to the corner of the building and came to a set of metal stairs that went to a raised platform with a set of double doors on another loading ramp. Just as he reached the top of the stairs, both doors opened, and three rough-looking aliens came out to size him up. "Nice weather we're having, isn't it?" said Jack.

"What? What are you talking about?" said the middle alien. "Weapons?" demanded the alien.

"Yes," replied Jack.

"Hand them over," said the alien.

"No," said Jack, "I don't hand my weapons over to anyone. Been there done that." The aliens looked at each other but weren't sure what to do. Apparently, they hadn't expected this response. They acted as if they were waiting for some sort of instructions.

"Fregga said you weren't afraid of confronting anyone," said a voice from the dark interior of the building. "That was the final test to make sure you were who you said you were," continued the voice of a svelte-looking, dark-skinned alien that was wearing some of the nicer-looking business attire that Jack had seen since he'd been on this grand adventure. The alien had nice clean features and a straight short nose with close-cropped brown, silver, and gold hair. His eyes were almost oriental but then not. He almost, but not quite, reminded Jack of Zshutana. His coloring was different, and he was definitely more swarthy. He was distinguished looking but also somewhat ruthless looking. Jack could imagine him living up to his appearance. Whereas Zshutana looked vulnerable yet wise, this Talaka Vamava looked like he could slit your throat while he served you afternoon high tea with crumpets. "Also your unique little pet, which he mentioned, is certainly a giveaway. Come in now, and we will discuss what it is you have to offer, and vice versa."

They went through a warehouse full of various goods, containers, and other unknown commodities to an office near the front of the building. "Please come in and have a seat. Can I get you something to drink?" offered Talaka Vamava.

"Yes, that would be nice," said Jack. "Just some ice water or a soft drink, anything actually."

"So please tell me of your most interesting journey from the conscript area at Corodune. I believe that is what Fregga conveyed to me." Jack gave him a quick rundown of the trip from leaving Corodune with the stolen vimar to knocking on Talaka's door.

"That is most incredible," said Talaka. "And you landed an ag ship in the hunting preserve and walked all the way here with your beautiful little tu-urak friend without encountering any problems?"

"Yes, we walked. It wasn't very far actually," replied Jack, "but I didn't say we didn't encounter any problems."

"I see," said Talaka. "It seems there are always problems, doesn't it?"

"Yes, it does. Apparently, that is the nature of things here," responded Jack.

Talaka nodded and smiled. "And so, if you don't mind my asking, what were you in the conscript system at the Corodune mine for that eventually required you to then escape?"

"Oh, I guess you could call it a case of mistaken identity. That would be the best way to describe it," said Jack.

Talaka smiled broadly. "Mistaken identity. Yes, I believe I've experienced that once or twice myself on occasion. Fair enough," said Talaka.

Chapter 11: Contract

"So what is it you wish me to do for you?" asked Talaka Vamava. "I am not really sure why you're here after your remarkable journey."

"Well, actually, neither am I," said Jack, "except that Fregga told me that you may be able to steer me in the right direction, and he said there is a chance you might be interested in the provost Kershavah ship in some capacity. Also, if needed, I should still have access to considerable credits if I can get access to them through my contacts."

"So you still have access to the provost ship at the greenbelt ag operation?"

"Yes," replied Jack, "unless they've found it, but I don't think they'll be able to find it for at least a few daiyus. I'm not really sure what it is that you do, but Fregga suggested that you might have some use for the ship," said Jack.

"I find it absolutely incredible that anyone would even be able to access a provost ship of any kind, but to do so and then pilot it undetected halfway around Nishda is nearly beyond comprehension," said Talaka. "This is very interesting. There might just be a way to turn this whole situation into a profitable venture. No one has ever had unrestricted access to a provost ship, and that in itself could be quite valuable. The problem would be of disposing of the ship and its associated evidence."

Talaka continued. "The provosts or anyone over on the Wanana side wouldn't believe that what you've done could happen either. That might be the key. If we could get to the ship and completely gut it, take everything out of it, then it would be a huge windfall for our side of this little planet. Would you be willing to accompany myself and a team of my people back to the provost ship while we spend probably two daiyus stripping it and hauling it away?" asked Talaka Vamava.

"Yes, of course," replied Jack, "it's the only way your crew would be able to access the ship. It's still powered in a low power state, and it will defend itself against any nonauthorized intruders."

"And how exactly were you able to access the ship if you're not in fact an authorized provost yourself?" asked Talaka.

"Well, that part is somewhat complicated," said Jack. "Basically, I was able to access the ship's security system and program my identity into the ship as an authorized crew member, more of that mistaken identity, so to speak." Jack didn't want him to know that he had the ability to bootleg anyone's translator ID and use it to access anything that they were authorized for.

"You were able to program yourself into the ship's security system," replied Talaka. "Now that would be a most useful talent, a very useful talent indeed. In case you are wondering, I don't always dress this well in my line of work. I've just now returned from a meeting regarding some upcoming business transactions," said Talaka.

"Actually, I hadn't thought about it, but I did note that you did have good taste in business attire," replied Jack.

"In fact, most of the time, my standard business attire is much more like what you are currently wearing," said Talaka.

"Really, that bad?" queried Jack, raising an eyebrow.

"Well, maybe not quite so, uh, underdistinguished," laughed Talaka.

"Umm, you should have seen me before I upgraded into some of the provost's leftover apparel," said Jack.

"Well, if that's an upgrade, perhaps I shouldn't try to imagine," said Talaka. "So I presume that you have no place to stay, since you've just arrived in Se-ahlaalu in such a unique manner," said Talaka.

"Yes, that would be a correct assumption," said Jack. "I can't say as I've had much of an opportunity to explore any of the nearby tourist attractions in the city."

"I imagine not," replied Talaka. "In that case, I think it would be appropriate of me to offer to put you up at my home as my guest for the duration of your tenure here—if you're so inclined, that is?"

"That would be most generous and most appreciated," replied Jack, "as long as it's not an inconvenience in any way."

"An inconvenience? No, not in any way at all," replied Talaka. "We would consider it an honor. How often does anyone get to have such a unique and interesting guest in their house?"

"Well, that would be greatly appreciated, then," said Jack. "You said *we?*"

"Oh, yes," replied Talaka, "my wives and kindren. We don't often find guests that we would consider entertaining. It is not always so easy in my line of work."

"Wives?" replied Jack.

"Yes, I've two wives and seven kindren. Not an unusual situation here on Nishda, an unincorporated planet, particularly on the Se-ahlaalu side," said Talaka.

"Yes, then I look forward to it," said Jack.

Talaka added, "Let me finish up some minor things around here and then we will leave for my humble home."

"That sounds good," replied Jack.

Talaka showed Jack around his warehouse, which was basically an import export business, at least as far as Jack could tell on the surface. After a few comm calls and other miscellaneous things, they were on their way to Talaka's home. It was only about fifteen mentus away and was in a nicer residential area of the city up on the side of the hills that overlooked the spaceport and the city. They arrived to find Talaka's two wives and seven children waiting at the entrance to greet them.

The house was a very nice two-level affair built partially into the side of the hill and designed to blend completely into the surrounding landscape. "These are my wives, Sensara and Sesjetta," said Talaka, introducing his two wives. "Sesjetta, we just found out, is expecting again, her third. Soon, we will have eight young ravenous mouths to feed," laughed Talaka. Talaka then introduced his seven children, ages three to fifteen. Jack didn't think he could even pronounce many of their names let alone keep them all straight.

"Now Jack has a strange and unique treat for the children," announced Talaka.

With that, Jack whistled and called Seema, who was still hiding in Talaka's vimar. She came timidly out and ran up behind Jack and hid behind his legs. The children all swooned and wanted to go pet her. "Wait, wait, wait," said Jack, "she is quite timid with strangers. You must let her get used to you. I don't really know what she'll do, but she must have a little time to get comfortable with you for a while. She has been known to bite, so don't antagonize her in any way or overwhelm her with too much attention. The best thing to do would be to just sit down and let her come to you when she's ready." The children and wives were both fascinated and a little frightened of her, which was good in a way, thought Jack. He didn't want anyone to get nipped or worse. In five mentus, Jack had her wiggling, whining, squeaking, trilling, and investigating all the children. Seema was just as curious about them as they were about her, and she seemed to have a strong affinity for the younger ones.

"Now you can pet her," said Jack, "but be very gentle with her. Don't pull her ears at all because they are very sensitive and fragile. Just pet her head and back, and she will be very fond of you and let you touch her." In just a few more mentus, the children and Seema were swarming over each other like they'd been raised together from the beginning.

"A most beautiful and unique animal. She seems quite intelligent and capable," said Talaka.

"Yes, she is," said Jack, "but I've had no experience with her or any like her until a few daiyus ago. I don't know anything about the species other than what I've learned from her myself. She does seem to understand that I saved her, and she is quite affectionate and adaptable to her surroundings."

"Come, let us prepare for the evening meal. I'm sure you would like to rejuvenate a bit after your travels," said Talaka. Jack looked at Seema, and she seemed to be perfectly happy playing with the children and receiving all their attention. Talaka showed Jack to a guest room toward the back of the house. The room was nicely appointed with its own bathroom off to the side. *Apparently, Talaka is doing quite well in the import export business,* thought Jack. "Take your time and enjoy your surroundings. Evening meal will be at 1900 horun, so you have nearly two horuns to relax and prepare."

"Thank you," replied Jack. "I'm looking forward to both relaxing and to dinner—I mean, evening meal."

"Dinner? Is that a Varan word for the evening meal?" asked Talaka.

"Uh, yes," said Jack, "*dinner* or *supper* is a word for evening meal on my home planet."

Jack went in and explored the bathroom and its amenities. It was well stocked, and he was soon enjoying a hot misting shower. He thought about Zshutana and wondered if he was getting any closer to being able to help her and Junot and Cherga. He hoped so. He peeked out into the bathroom a couple of times to check on his bag of possessions, and everything seemed well. He was just glad he'd had a shower recently on the provost ship, or he would have been considerably more ripe than he had been at his arrival here.

After his shower, he found a razor and other useful items and took advantage of them. When he came out an horun later, he found Talaka and his wives in the kitchen making big decisions about the evening meal. "Ah, did you enjoy your freshening?" asked Talaka.

"Oh, yes, very much indeed," replied Jack.

"Excellent, then," said Talaka. "So we were just discussing that as the guest, which would you prefer, a fine roast ganayet or possibly a baked benusenah?"

"Well, I'm not really sure," said Jack, "as I'm not sure that I've had either. If I have, I don't remember anything by those names."

"Hmmm, in that case, I believe we should have both, and then you will be able to give an honest opinion the next time someone asks," stated Talaka.

"Oh, no, that's not necessary," replied Jack. "I'm sure either one would be perfectly excellent."

"Nonsense, I insist," said Talaka. "It will make a nice contrast, and it sounds most appetizing to me now that I've thought of it."

"Well, if you insist, then there's nothing I can further say about the matter. We will just have to have both, and I'm sure I'll relish them both equally," replied Jack, playing along with his host's overtures.

"I'm sure you will find them both excellent, as Sensara is a master at one, and Sesjetta, the other. Now let us retire to my office for a while as the wives work their magic with the meal. Oh, and I checked on your lovely Seema a few mentus ago, and she is quite enjoying the company of the children. She is quite energetic and is giving them a good deal of entertainment."

"That's great," said Jack, "as long as she doesn't get carried away."

"I'm sure she will be fine. I further admonished them not to push her too hard or do anything that she might consider a threat. Now, can I offer you something to drink, a rupeeti perhaps or maybe a vetta-mina or a guinhali?"

"Well, I'm, not sure . . . uh, would you happen to have any qalalé?" asked Jack.

"Qalalé, yes, of course. Do you prefer the Lokaran bulatti type or the darker sumusta?"

"Hmm, probably the sumusta, as long as it's not too dark," replied Jack, not knowing what either of the types of qalalé these might be.

The qalalé was quite good, a little sweeter than anything Jack had previously had, but he certainly wasn't complaining. It was sweeter, but it also had an interesting little after-bite. Talaka began. "I have made a couple of comm calls while you were refreshing, and with some help, I think I have come up with a better alternative to the plan of stripping the Kershavah ship in the field. That might expose us to the provost teams if they are searching for the ship, which, of course, we know they will be."

Jack listened intently while Talaka continued. "If you are willing, I believe there is a place where we could fly the ship and dismantle it there discreetly. This would allow us more time to properly disassemble it and disburse the components, which would give us a much better security situation and also allow us to make a better profit with less risk."

"I'm all in," replied Jack. "We just need to ferry in enough Pentrico or Tritrico fuel to the ship to get it wherever you want to take it."

Talaka continued. "I have some business associates that are willing to take on this project for an even share in the profits. They can only offer you 20 percent of the estimated value of the ship due to the risk, the logistics, and their limited resources. Most of the components will likely have to be sold off Nishda, and it will take some time to fully disburse and receive payment for all the ship's components."

"That will be fine," said Jack. "What do they estimate the street value of the ship to be?"

"Street value?" said Talaka.

"Yes, uh, the value of what my percentage is based on?"

"Ah, yes, an interesting term. They say the ship is valued at approximately 12 million credits, so your percentage would, of course, be 2.4 million," replied Talaka.

"That's quite excellent," said Jack. "When do we go?"

"Sooner would be better," replied Talaka. "We will need a tech team to go through the ship and make sure it is not transmitting any distress beacons. We will have to disable or block any tracking the ship has so that they can't track it back to where it is being delivered. If you are fine with that, then tell me how much fuel do you estimate you will need?"

"Well, that, of course, depends on where we are going," said Jack, trying to contemplate any potential downside to the arrangement.

"Oh, yes, of course," replied Talaka. "It is only about twenty kahtaks to the east of Se-ahlaalu at a shipbuilding and maintenance facility run by an associate of mine."

Jack replied, "Well, in that case, I would make a rough estimate of about four hundred lektahs, which should give us enough with some reserve leftover. More would be fine too, but four hundred should do it."

"Yes, that will be easy enough. This will have to be done at night to minimize the risk of snooping eyes learning of our little operation," said Talaka.

"Of course, that will indeed be easy enough," said Jack, "but I will need 50 percent up front and 50 percent on delivery to ensure the integrity of the transaction. If you wish to confirm the validity of what I've told you about the ship, you could do a flyover to check it out, which I would recommend anyway. It is somewhat camouflaged to hopefully hide its presence."

Talaka replied, "That should not be a problem, the 50 percent up front. The flyover has actually already been accomplished by my associate. His name is Doronno Fiashcolo, and he took it upon himself to verify your information as soon as I told him about it."

"OK, good," said Jack, "one hurdle accomplished. Another thing I will need is a secure GTA account with my exclusive access that is not in my name, as I'm sure you can understand why. Do you know of any way to provide something like that or know of anyone that can?"

Talaka pondered that for a moment while he contemplated what an astute individual this Jack Spartan was. "Yes, we can do that, but it will take a couple of daiyus to set that up. Fabricating a fake GTA account is quite difficult because a deceased citizen's ID must be used that has not been deregistered from the GTA accounts list. In other words, they must find a deceased person that has not been reported as deceased and convert the account so that you will be able to access it as the deceased person that hasn't been reported as deceased and won't be."

"That does sound a little complicated," said Jack.

"It is," replied Talaka, "but it can be done. It is also a bit pricey. I believe the going price was around fifty thousand credits the last time I checked."

"I see," said Jack.

"The cost is not an issue in this case, though," said Talaka. "Under the circumstances, I will be most happy to cover the cost for you. We will all make a considerable profit on this venture. Consider it a gift for bringing me the opportunity to become involved in this little project myself."

"That is most generous," replied Jack. "I'm looking forward to getting started as soon as possible and working with you on this."

"Good, very good," said Talaka. "Doronno is assembling his crew and a ship with the ferry fuel right now and should be ready by middaiyus tomorrow."

Jack would be leaving himself a little bit open without the account right now, but that's the best he could hope for under the circumstances. He couldn't use any of the bootlegged IDs he had for various reasons, including the fact that the ones that were still alive would find themselves suddenly quite rich. He would just have to ride it out and hope for the best with Talaka and his associate Doronno. "I will call the people that I know that do the account manipulation right now. There is always a chance that they may have one ready to go and won't have to go searching for a candidate. Then we will go for the evening meal, which should be most excellent."

"That sounds good. I am truly looking forward to it," replied Jack.

As it turned out, the account manipulation people didn't have a GTA account readily available, but they thought they could have one in a few daiyus if they put the word out for a potential candidate to their own contacts. The evening meal was excellent. Jack hadn't had anything close to this since Zshutana's, and he was glad to be enjoying himself and relaxing after so many moondats of strife. Talaka's children were well behaved and still enjoying the company of Seema. She seemed to be getting a fair helping of table scraps, even though they had been admonished not to feed her during the meal.

After the meal, Talaka and Jack went back to Talaka's office and discussed some ideas and plans for tomorrow's mission. They would recon the area around the Kershavah ship and make sure that nothing was in the area that looked like provosts. Then they would land, and Jack would gain access to the ship, while Doronno Fiashcolo's tech crew fueled the ship and checked it for tracking devices. They would then finish prepping the ship for the short flight and wait for darkness. Jack would then fly it over to Doronno's disassembly hangar, which had been prepped for its arrival. Doronno and Talaka would accompany Jack in the Kershavah ship to help him navigate to Doronno's hangar and also because they knew it would be the only time they would actually ever get to fly in a Kershavah assault ship. That was the general plan laid out by Jack and Talaka with input from Doronno via comm link.

The next morning, they were up early. Talaka checked with Doronno Fiashcolo, and everything was going according to plan. The ship they would use also used Tritrico, so all they would need to do is transfer eight hundred lektahs of fuel to the Kershavah ship using hoses and pumps. It would take Doronno's tech crew several horuns to go through the entire Kershavah ship to search for and stop or remove any tracking devices on the ship. Doronno said they were very good techs, but the key, of course, was getting access to the ship. Normally, you couldn't get close to a provost ship, but Jack would make that possible. Everything would be checked and rechecked. The reception hangar was being prepped, and Doronno was setting up a broad spectrum local jamming transmitter in case they missed any hidden tracking transmitters. Talaka kissed his wives good-bye, and he and Jack left in a nondescript vimar at 0900 horun for the forty-mentu drive to Doronno's maintenance depot. Jack decided to leave Seema there with the children when they left. She seemed to understand when he told her to stay, although it was obvious that she wasn't happy with it.

On the drive there, Talaka said, "Well, my friend, if all goes well today, you will be a wealthy person by this time tomorrow. What do you propose to do with your newfound riches?"

Jack could tell it was a probing question, so he answered carefully. "Well, I'm already somewhat wealthy. I just need to figure out how to get access to my account. What we are doing here will improve my financial position considerably, though. As I'm sure you're aware, keeping a low profile is the best way to protect your assets, while flaunting your wealth is a sure way to lose it. So don't worry, there will be no moondat-long party binges for me. My primary goal is not to attain wealth but to use anything I attain to help some loyal friends that helped me more than I could ever repay them. Two of them are conscripted in the mine under a similar mistaken identity situation that I was conscripted under. My number-one priority will be to get them out, hopefully in a manner that won't leave them as fugitives on the run like my situation."

"Loyal friends," said Talaka, "that is a rare commodity in this age. I could count on one hand the number of people that I would completely trust, and even some of those would be conditional. It is just the nature of the business that I am in. It seems as if no matter how generous you are to people, they will try to take advantage of you for more. It seems as if everything must be handled as a business transaction rather than by a person's word. It is sad that things must be run that way."

"Yes, it is," said Jack. "That is why when you find a trustworthy friend, you must do everything you can to help them. How I will accomplish that, I don't yet know, but I will do whatever I need to make it happen."

"I believe you would," replied Talaka. "Your friends are in an envious position to have someone with your obvious talents willing to risk so much to help them."

"Well, they deserve nothing but a maximum effort attempt on my part," replied Jack.

Talaka was silent for a while then started reviewing the possible situations that might occur on their mission. Soon, they were out of the city, and ten mentus later, they were approaching a remote industrial site with several large hangars and a full perimeter fence. They were waved through the checkpoint entrance and headed toward a hangar at the rear of the complex. Talaka said, "Doronno's operation here does mostly legitimate ship repair and outfitting, but with the limited clientele this far out on the rim and with Se-ahlaalu being the smaller of the two cities on Nishda, he tends to service more of a specialty niche than do other larger operations. He will occasionally take on a more unique job like the one we are about to embark on, although I would guess that this is likely the most, should we say, adventurous to date."

"Well, I'm glad he was interested in this," said Jack, "and I'm grateful to you for getting it set up and for Fregga Kitzu for sending me your way."

"So am I," said Talaka. "It is good to find good people and explore new possibilities."

"Yes, yes, it is," replied Jack.

They came to the hangar, and they were met by Doronno Fiashcolo as soon as they parked. After the introductions were complete, Doronno said, "Ah, good, we are nearly ready. All of the crew's equipment is loaded, and the ship is serviced. The ship is in the hangar, and I'll have it pulled out as soon as everything and everyone is ready. Come on in now, and we will inspect everything and go over our plans."

An horun later, everyone was satisfied with their plan and ready to go. Doronno would fly the ship, and he introduced Talaka and Jack to his first pilot Forto Alerdac and the four tech crew members that would work on the Kershavah ship. The ship was towed from the hangar, and everyone boarded. The ship was about half the size of the Kershavah that it was going to retrieve but much more plushly appointed.

"This is one of our upgrade trade-in models we just received a wenek ago," explained Doronno. "The customer in Wanana wanted a bigger newer ship, and we gave him a better price than he could get over there. This trade-in is in very good condition, and it's just the right size for our little venture today. I topped it off, and it holds eighteen hundred lektahs of Tritrico, so we'll have plenty of fuel for this short flight. Also the ship's pumps will easily transfer the required fuel to the Kershavah with the transfer hoses we stored in the aft cargo hold. It would easily seat fourteen and the crew of two, but the owner had an executive seating configuration of eight. It will serve us just fine for today. It is also a very quiet ship, so that can only help us too."

Jack could tell that Doronno was an enthusiastic business owner and salesperson. He could always tell when someone was really interested in what they were involved in. Jack asked Doronno, "So what is your specific interest in the Kershavah other than the normal profit you'd make in a deal like this?"

"Well," replied Doronno, "the Kershavah, like any provost ship, will have systems, technology, and possibly weapons systems that are not available to regular people, civilians, and other interested parties. The engines are more advanced as well as all the integrated flight control and command systems. From what I've read, there should be a great deal of interesting things for us to get our hands on that we would otherwise never be able to access. There are many people that would like to incorporate these systems in their own ships, so that will be our market, our very hush, hush market, if you understand what I mean."

"Absolutely," said Jack. "Why settle for everyday technology when what you really want is the top of the line? And, yes, the Kershavah does have some pretty impressive weapons. It has twin plasma cannons, which I wanted to test-fire, but I couldn't easily run the weapons control system at the same time I was flying. It would have been possible in cruise with the autoflight system engaged, but I was also somewhat concerned that someone or some type of monitoring system might be able to detect the cannons firing and possibly find and track me because of that."

"Plasma cannons, yes, that's excellent," said Doronno. "I was hoping for something along that line, but I didn't know what to expect as a provost ship could be configured in various ways."

"I'm sure you'll be happy with your acquisition," said Jack. "All we have to do is get it back to your hangar for you."

They made a casual flyby of the greenbelt at a higher altitude where the Kershavah was hidden in case there were provosts or others near the ship. "It's at our two o'clock position, now two thirty," said Jack. "It's covered in cut trees and shrubs to camouflage its outline from casual observers."

"I'm not sure what you mean by a two o'clock position, but I am looking where you are pointing. That would be at about a 15 percent position by our understanding. Yes, it was difficult to spot earlier, and I can still barely see its outline," said Doronno. "Some of the trees are wilted and out of their normal shape, but overall, it's very hard to see."

"I still don't see it. Well, maybe I see it," said Talaka.

"That's OK," said Jack. "You're just not used to looking for things from the air. The important thing is that the camouflage is still there and there are no other ships or vehicle around. Let's descend and make another quick flyby just to make sure. We should probably leave it covered until we are ready to leave with it, and we should camouflage Doronno's ship too while we're parked, just in case."

Another flyby verified what they'd seen the first time, so they swung around and landed about forty mu-uts from the Kershavah, just outside its defense systems range. Jack got ready to jump out on landing and said, "I'll disarm the sentry system then call on your handheld comm link when it's clear. You can move your ship closer right next to those overhanging trees then get it at least partially camouflaged." Jack headed toward the Kershavah as soon as the door was open. As he passed the Kershavah's perimeter defense, he got the expected warning on his translator HUD as he moved toward the ship. He checked the area around the entry door and noted that there weren't any footprints or other disturbances that would indicate s possible provost ambush.

Jack opened the door and cautiously cleared the cargo deck then the flight deck and crew bunk area. Everything looked as he'd left it, including the small tamper tags he'd placed in various locations before he'd left. He brought the ship to normal power mode and shut down the perimeter defense system. The critical fuel alert was still flashing on the HUD. He called Doronno and Talaka to let them know it was safe to approach. Doronno's smaller ship lifted off and coasted to a stop about five mu-uts from the Kershavah. Doronno and the rest of them piled out and along with Jack set to work camouflaging the smaller ship. They were done in about ten mentus and set to work on the Kershavah.

"That's an amazing blade the way it cuts those small trees and brush," remarked Doronno, "as well as being most unique and attractive. I don't think I've ever seen anything like it before."

"Thanks," replied Jack. "I made it myself when I worked at the Corodune foundry. It's my own alloy I came up with. It's quite remarkable."

"Yes, and so is the Kershavah ship," said Doronno. "I didn't think I'd ever get this close to one, and I surely didn't think I'd get to fly in one and then get to take it apart. This venture is going to be most interesting." The tech crew set to work as soon as they accessed the ship. Two of them unrolled a long fueling hose and connected it from Doronno's ship to the Kershavah's fueling port. Doronno explained that it wouldn't transfer fuel at a very high rate, but since they didn't need that much, it wouldn't take too long.

Jack took the other two techs and Doronno and Talaka into the ship and got them going on the ship's systems. He showed them the tracking and transponder system he'd shut down then delved into the ship's maintenance and operating systems on the ship's HUD. The techs soon had a very good handle on the ship's systems and capabilities. "What an incredible find we've got here," said Doronno. "I haven't had this much fun since I was racing sand sleds in my youth. Now that I think back on it, I'd say that's a good way to get yourself killed if you don't have a fair amount of skill and luck to go with it. It's probably much like this current venture if you think about it. Perhaps it's best to just not think about it," said Doronno as he laughed out loud.

"That does sound like fun," said Jack.

"Yes, fun as well as very, very dirty and brutally exhausting," said Doronno. A few mentus later, one of the techs gave a whispered report to Doronno. "It seems we lucked out," said Doronno. "Andello says he found a reference to a self-powered emergency beacon that is designed to start transmitting if the ship loses complete power. Another ten to twelve horuns, and this ship would have started crying to its momma that nobody loves it anymore."

"Well, it's a good thing we got back to it as soon as we did, then, or none of this would be happening now," said Talaka.

"The techs are looking for the beacon now so they can totally disarm it. We can't take any chances like that. There could be other parameters programmed to trigger it also."

A half horun later, they were able to locate the beacon along with another standalone beacon that could be triggered from the flight deck by the pilots. The beacons were located against the upper skin of the ship toward the aft end of the main fuselage near the nexus of the other comm antennas. Everything had taken less time than they'd allowed, and they were now ready to fly, but they still had a good two and a half horuns until the sun set.

As they were finishing and standing around a bit admiring the ship, Doronno said, "It kind of seems like a waste to just fly the ship to the hangar and start tearing it apart. It's too bad we can't fly it around a while, maybe out over the open desert somewhere, and maybe even give those plasma cannons a little test-firing action."

"Haf, you sound like a little child with a new toy," chided Talaka, "but I admit that would be fun."

"Yes, well, I am just a simple person who likes impressive ships, so it is only natural for me to want to take it for a proper test drive," replied Doronno.

"Yes, it is pretty impressive," said Jack. "I'm with you on the ship appreciation aspect. I'd like to fire those guns myself, but I think the lower the profile we keep, the less likely something could go wrong, and we'd be less likely to be discovered. It's probably best if we sneak back to your hangar long after dark and as quietly as possible. It's even possible that the cannons being fired is one of the main signatures they are looking for to try and find the ship. Maybe you can sell those cannons to someone else for their ship and you'll get to test-fire them then."

"Yes, I must concur with Jack," said Talaka. "There is no sense in exposing ourselves any more than we have to. The consequences of getting caught would be, well, let's just say, less than optimal."

For the next two horuns, Doronno had his tech crew go over the ship and learn as much about it as possible. He had them complete a full radio frequency scan of the ship's emissions to make sure that there was nothing trackable by orbital or ground-based sensors. Even though the provosts had jurisdiction in this sector, they had little interest in policing around Se-ahlaalu so far from their home base. However, with one of their ships missing, they might be a little more vigilant in this area than usual.

Talaka asked, "Should we start the engines and make sure they are working like everything else?"

Jack responded, "No, I don't think that's necessary. They were working perfectly when I shut them down. We would have to completely decamouflage the ship to do that, which would leave us exposed for a while. I don't think the potential reward would be worth the risk. If for some reason there was a problem when we try to leave, we could shut it down and fix it and come back later if we need to." They all thought about it for a mentu and had to agree. Talaka really liked the way Jack's logic worked. He decided that Jack would be a good asset to have in any kind of operation.

They bided their time going over the arrival plan back at Doronno's and every other detail they could think of. Jack asked if they should wait until much later like maybe after midnight or new daiyus hour before they returned. Doronno didn't think so, as there was very little traffic at that time, so that might arouse suspicion. If they arrived a few horuns before new daiyus, they would blend in with the normal late night traffic that was till arriving or departing at that time, which would be mostly cargo ships that operated late into the evening.

Since Se-ahlaalu was so isolated from anywhere else, most of their goods were imported, some from Wanana and much from off planet by freighter ships that mostly ran at night. "I saw one arrive at the spaceport before I got to Talaka's," said Jack, "but that was during the daiyus."

"Yes, that could have been a freighter or a combination of freight and passengers, but the bulk, maybe 70 percent, run at night into Se-ahlaalu," said Doronno. He added, "I think about 2500 horun would be a good time. The freighter traffic is starting to taper off, and in my sector, it would just look like another test flight of one of our ships, which happens several times a wenek."

Finally, at 2345, Doronno instructed his pilot Forto Alerdac to be ready to depart with their executive ship. "Forto," instructed Doronno, "Talaka, Jack, and I will depart in the Kershavah. Have your engines started and follow us at a distance of about one kahtak just like a normal test flight observer ship. We will do a couple of small test flight patterns about ten kahtaks east of the base like we normally do on test flights. Then we will head to the hangar. After we are down, I want you to circle for about twenty mentus and make sure that no unusual ships are in the area or that nothing else out of the ordinary is around."

"Yes Doronno," replied Forto, who seemed slightly vexed by the present situation from the tone of his voice.

"Is there something you wish to add, perhaps a suggestion of some sort?" asked Doronno. "Please speak up."

"No, nothing at all, I was just thinking," replied Forto.

On the flight deck of the Kershavah, Jack went through the start checks and then brought the engines online. Looking at the ship's control options, Doronno, sitting in the first pilot seat, selected the DNV option prompt. The ship's windows and

HUD illuminated like the night vision windshield in the vimar that Jack had borrowed from Corodune. "Ah, very nice, full daiyus-at-night vision capable like I would expect in such a ship," said Doronno.

"I didn't realize it had that option," said Jack. "I flew it at dusk but used the landing lights, so I wasn't aware of that capability, but I did drive a vimar once that had that ability. This seems to be much more clear and luminous than what the vimar had, though."

"Yes, some of the newer vimars offer that as a pricey option," said Talaka. "You can retrofit the older vimars, but those systems are limited in viewing area, but they are better than nothing. This advanced Kershavah system encompasses the entire windshield and viewports area with the best optics." Everything checked out good as expected, and they lifted off and stayed low as they made their way to an area about ten kahtaks east of Doronno's base.

They could see Forto Alerdac in the distance in Doronno's ship with the tech crew shadowing them as instructed. When they got to the test flight area, Jack did several routine test flight maneuvers like Doronno instructed then headed toward the base. They came in and landed in front of the most remote of the hangars. As soon as the engines were shut down, a small ground crew brought out the tow dollies and began rigging the ship to be towed into the hangar. Forto landed beside the Kershavah and began to shut down. Doronno called him on the handheld comm. "Forto, what are you doing? You are supposed to be orbiting for twenty mentus to perform patrol sweeps like I instructed."

"Yes, Doronno," replied Forto. "I didn't see anything around, so I decided to come in and land."

Doronno barked at him, "Get back up there and fly the patrol sweeps like I said. That's a very important order."

"Yes, OK," replied Forto. "I just didn't think it was necessary," as the engines spooled up, and the ship took off again.

"Problem?" asked Jack.

Doronno replied, "Oh, no, I think he just wanted to be in on the Kershavah part of this a little more, but he didn't seem to grasp the importance of his role in this for some reason."

"OK," said Jack, thinking that these are the kinds of problems you could run into in a nonmilitary command environment where people weren't trained to or didn't think they needed to follow orders as instructed.

The Kershavah was towed into the hangar, and the doors securely closed. "Everyone involved here with the Kershavah will get a nice percentage of the profit for this. That keeps everyone happy, and no one likes the GTA and its local strong arm enforcers anyway. The daiyus shift is off-limits to this area, so they'll never know what goes on here," explained Doronno to Jack and Talaka. "We should have the ship completely cannibalized in about ten daiyus, so there won't be any evidence of it for very long."

They watched as the tech crew set to work on inspecting and analyzing the Kershavah before disassembling it. "There will be a lot to learn from this ship, and there will be a lot of very good salvage technology and systems from it. This will be quite a good windfall for us," said Doronno.

Jack replied, "Well, it was fun while it lasted, but it did cost a lot in lives to get it here, even though they were provost lives. The strange thing is if the provosts hadn't come after me, I might still be stuck in the greenbelt hunting wild animals to survive and living off the land. It's funny how things work out, isn't it?"

"Yes, you never know what will happen. All you can do is try to control the outcome of the things you are aware of and plan for contingencies. You just do the best you can," said Talaka.

"Well, let's go to my back office and celebrate with a few rounds of Kinsar or perhaps some Bulat or even some Meadar," said Doronno.

"I believe Jack is a qalalé drinker," said Talaka, "but perhaps we can get him to try some of our finer indulgences."

"Well, I might give it a go if you insist," said Jack.

"Give it a go?" replied Talaka. "Jack seems to have many interesting sayings for things from what I've seen."

Doronno then led them through the next adjoining hangar bay where a couple of smaller ships were just parked while awaiting their turn in the maintenance depot. As they entered the next bay, Jack was struck by the sight of a beautiful larger ship sitting by itself. "Wow, that's a beautiful ship!" he exclaimed to Doronno and Talaka.

"Ah, yes," replied Doronno, "the beautiful ship *Carratta*, with a sad tale but no resolution to her fate, I'm afraid."

"Sad tale? How so?" asked Jack. They stopped to admire the ship, which was maybe another six or seven mu-uts longer than the Kershavah ship but even more elegant and obviously built for space by her structure and various appliances.

Doronno began. "Well, *Carratta* was built as a luxury yacht, or should I say more correctly, as a luxury expedition exploration yacht for the wealthiest transportation entrepreneur here on Nishda. His name was Emnal Ramidew, but he died suddenly of some internal circulatory problem about, oh, what now, eighteen moondats ago. The ship is still owned by his family, but they don't wish to keep it, and the market for such a unique and expensive private vessel is nonexistent out here on the far rim sector. It will eventually have to be moved to some other location to sell it, but the family hasn't decided what to do with it yet. The ship was actually built on Paldamar in the Chardoran system and ferried here for its fit out and completion to Emnal Ramidew's specifications. It was only just partially competed when he died, so here it waits to be dealt with."

"What a shame never to have been able to get to use your dream ship and explore like you wanted to," said Jack.

"Yes, it is a very capable ship," said Doronno. "I believe his intent was to retire and explore as much of the galaxy as he could."

"So what would a ship like this cost?" asked Jack.

"I believe, and I'm not really sure, as I have no actual numbers other than what was planned for the fit out, that this ship would have cost somewhere close to thirty million credits plus the cost of outfitting it to his specifications, which was going to be another two plus million. I don't believe his family actually knows what the ship is worth, as they are only asking twenty-one million for it. Perhaps that is what he told them he paid for it, or perhaps he got it for an exceptional price, since he had many connections in the transport industry."

"Can we go inside and take a look?" asked Jack.

"Yes, certainly, everyone who sees it wants to look at it because it is such a unique and beautiful ship. There aren't any more like it on Nishda or anywhere close by. This just isn't the usual area for wealthy yacht owners, so the ship is a novelty around here. I could probably make a steady income by turning it into a museum and letting the wishful be wealthy snoop through it."

Doronno went to the side of the ship and palmed a code into the access panel. A clamshell pressure door with docking ring and stairs opened to the interior. They entered up the stairs and into a foyer entry room with a series of storage lockers and other gear. The room looked like it would hold six or seven comfortably and was obviously designed as a staging area for entering and exiting the ship.

Doronno explained. "This is the main crew or owner entrance, which is also designed as a docking bay. There is also a larger cargo hold door at the rear of the ship as well as another small orbital docking ring. The ship is fifty-four mu-uts long and has a usual crew and passenger compliment of ten or more if shared staterooms are used. In some ways, it is slightly similar to the Kershavah ship as far as layout, but that is about it. Come let us see," as he led them up a short stairwell and into the common area, which was also attached to the dining area. "There are two larger estate bedrooms at the front of the upper deck and four smaller estate rooms at the back of the upper deck. The flight deck bridge and the dining area as well as a common area are all located on the upper deck," explained Doronno as they proceeded toward those areas.

The ship was exceptionally well built and well designed, which Jack could tell as they went through the ship. "There are four smaller but very comfortable crew or estate rooms on the lower level with access from where we came in. You can also access them with a small lift just off the bridge. The main galley is off the bridge, which serves as a casual dining area for the bridge equally well. There is a small crew galley on the lower level and a toilet facility downstairs."

They went to the short front hall off the main dining area into the upper estate room area. "Here are the two main estate rooms on the upper deck. They are quite nice as you'll see," explained Doronno. "Here is the master's room," which they entered.

"This is really very nice," said Jack, "just absolutely beautiful," as he stood looking at the large master suite.

"The two larger upstairs suites each have their own toilet and shower facilities with a shared one for the four smaller suites," said Doronno. Jack and Talaka explored the master suite and its adjoining facilities.

"A person could get used to this if they had to," said Jack.

"Yes, they certainly could," said Talaka. They then looked at the other slightly smaller but no less luxurious staterooms and shared toilet room.

"Really nice, very, very impressive," said Jack.

"Yes, and now the bridge," said Doronno. He took them back the way they'd come and then to the front of the ship and the bridge flight deck. "As a pilot, I believe you'll find this to your liking also," said Doronno as he pointed out the flight deck before them.

It is truly a thing of beauty and perfect functionality, thought Jack. *What an amazing layout.*

"Here you have the two pilot seats and behind them six observer seats with two additional observer seats off to each side," said Doronno. "Everything on the ship is double redundant from the 4D navigation system to the life support, the drive engine controls, and maneuvering engine controllers, and imagine this, not just a self-sealing pressure hull, which is better than most ships, but a double self-sealing hull. Even the auxiliary power system is replicated as well as the iso-shielded energcell banks and the dual grav generators. Yes, Emnal Ramidew spared no expense, as he believed that safety was paramount for the ship's intended mission. The ship is truly designed and built to be self-sufficient for deep-space exploration where assistance from other ships may never be available. He could have gotten a larger ship for the same credits, but he went with quality and capability over quantity. It's too bad we weren't able to finish the full fit out and make it into the true luxury ship it was intended to be."

"Well, it certainly looks plenty luxurious the way it is," said Jack.

"Oh, it is," said Doronno, "but there were a lot of purely aesthetic upgrades slated for it as well as a full complement of appointments for the aft of the ship, which is essentially just an empty cargo bay now."

"What does the ship's name signify?" asked Talaka. "Is it the name of his wife or something?"

"No," replied Doronno, "it is the mythical Sherdawain language word for, uh, something like 'life blood' or 'life miracle' or 'mystical blood' or 'flow of life,' something approximating that."

How can a race be mythical but have a language?" asked Jack.

"Oh, I guess not really mythical, though many call it that," said Doronno. "There was a mysterious race that apparently actually existed at one time. They have records of the language and many tales of ancient daily life and a few other historical records, but there are no physical evidence, artifacts, or other things, as if the race never existed or just disappeared. Some think it was from a solar system that went nova or perhaps fell into a black hole."

"Interesting. How do they have the language then if there are no artifacts or other records?" asked Jack.

Doronno replied, "Well, the story goes somewhat like this. In the far quarter quadrant of the Hanzara sector, they periodically come across a very low-frequency analog radio frequency at the 406 frequency range that seems to bounce around the sector but never dissipates. Some say the signal is still being transmitted from whatever mysterious abyss the Sherdawain civilization disappeared into. Sometimes the signal is highly distorted and broken, but at other times, it is perfectly clear and fairly strong. They think it has something to do with the harmonics of the frequency that causes it to replicate or self-modulate back into space.

"They don't really know, and they've never been able to locate the source or the time frame of the transmissions, but the language of the transmission is the mysterious or mythical Sherdawain language. That's about all they know about it, but there's enough of it floating around out there that they were able to translate it and create a fairly extensive vocabulary. The mystery is that the transmissions are all just everyday run-of-the mill dialog such as everyday communication stuff with no signs of turmoil or other information about the fate of the civilization.

The theory is that whatever happened to this lost race must have happened instantaneously, since there is no indication that they ever experienced any type of distress. So it's become a bit of a mythical, mystical, ethereal, mystery language that people like to reference for various reasons, thus the ship's name, *Carratta*."

"It sounds fascinating especially with all the unsolved mystery part involved, but I do like the name of the ship and the meaning it alludes to," said Jack.

"Well, if nothing else, it's entertaining to speculate over," added Talaka.

On the bridge, Doronno powered up the main electrical buses and brought all the instrumentation online. They all fawned over the displays and information available from all the sources and systems on the ship. "This kind of puts the Kershavah to shame," said Jack. "I can't say I've ever even imagined anything this spectacular."

"Well, the Kershavah is a great ship in its own right," said Doronno. "You have to remember that they are two totally different creatures as far as what they were designed for to begin with."

After another fifteen mentus of looking and ogling, they decided to head to Doronno's office two more hangar bays down. "This is really my work office," said Doronno. "The front office is mostly for show and meetings with customers, while this office is where I do all the planning, scheduling, and real work of the business. I do keep an adequate supply of beverages here, though, for celebrating special occasions such as this."

They all three sat and enjoyed a few good drinks, while Doronno and Talaka regaled each other about their adventure of stealing the Kershavah and expounded on the good fortune of the profit they would be making from it. Jack tried some of their other drinks but decided to stick to the qalalé, since he liked that the best.

"I will have your agreed-upon payment transferred to your new account in a daiyus or two as soon as we can confirm that it has been set up properly and we can get the ID information programmed into the ID generator that we will have for you to use to access your account."

"That will be fine," said Jack, knowing that he would copy it into his own translator ID library as soon as he got it from them.

"So what are you going to do now that our mission is complete and now that you will have a substantial fortune at your disposal?" asked Doronno. "I could probably use someone around here with your talents if you're considering looking for some type of position somewhere. Of course, we would have to do something to help you keep a low profile with your recent history and all."

"Well, thank you for the offer," replied Jack, "but I'm not sure that would be the best thing for you with my status as a fugitive. I believe the provosts think I am dead, but there is the question of their missing ship, which they may try to investigate further. You never know who may let something slip as far as what's happening in your hangar with the Kershavah ship. You know how people like to talk. They just can't keep a secret if there's something interesting to talk about."

"Yes, this is true," said Doronno, "which is why the remnants of the ship need to disappear as soon as possible. If not sold, we will move them off-site somewhere so that they can be well hidden. I'm sure we could work something out as far as finding you a position, though."

"Yes, the same goes for me," said Talaka. "You would be a most valuable asset in any position."

"Thanks also, I appreciate that, and I would consider working with both or either of you, but as you know, I have another more urgent agenda that I must deal with first."

"Yes, I understand," said Talaka. "A burden such as that must weigh heavily on your mind."

"Yes, it does, and I have to do something about it as soon as possible," replied Jack.

"What do you plan to do? Perhaps I can help in some way," said Talaka.

"Well, it depends," said Jack, "on whether Doronno will accept my proposal, not so much Doronno but his clients to be exact."

"A proposal, you say?" said Doronno. "What kind of a proposal do you speak of?"

Jack replied, "The ship *Carratta*, you say there is little prospect of selling it to anyone here on Nishda and that it would have to be moved to somewhere with a better market?"

"Yes, that is the case," answered Doronno. "I've sent word to the builders on Paldamar about its availability six moondats after the owner's death, but I've heard nothing back from them. They are not as likely to be willing to deal with a previously sold ship as they are with building new ones. They would want a substantial commission from the family if they were to broker it plus the cost of moving the ship and whatever the crew must be paid to deliver it and return. It would be quite a complicated and expensive process by any standards."

"OK," said Jack, "then here is my proposal. I would like you to approach Emnal Ramidew's family with an offer of eighteen million credits." Talaka and Doronno looked at each other then back at Jack. "Yes," said Jack, "eighteen million credits with a deposit of two million up front with the balance of sixteen million due over a five-yenet period. I will need to keep four hundred thousand of my Kershavah, uh, 'commission,' for operating expenses."

Doronno and Talaka looked at each other again. Doronno asked, "Are you truly serious?"

"Yes, quite serious," replied Jack, "but you would have to sell them on the eighteen million as a serious offer in light of the fact that they won't be getting any other offers and it will cost them quite a lot to move and market *Carratta*. You will need to convince them that it is likely their only and best deal. They may take a loss, but something tells me they aren't hurting anyway, so maybe they'll just be glad to unload it and be done with it, especially if you are charging them storage or other fees. Also you have to talk them into carrying it as an interest free loan for it to work for me, and you will have to help me crunch the numbers as far as what I can generate using the ship as a go-anywhere, carry-anything cargo transport and fast messenger service. That's actually is the real question—can I generate enough income with the ship to make the payments on it?"

Doronno sat there for a mentu contemplating what Jack had just laid out for him. "So you want the owners, the family of Emnal Ramidew, to give you the ship for two million credits and then you will pay the rest over time?"

"Yes," said Jack, "but only if you, both you and Talaka, think I can make enough to make the payments on the ship."

"I have never heard of such a thing, at least not on the sale or purchase of a ship. That is a most unusual concept. I have heard of certain governments funding building projects that must be paid back over time but never anything such as this," said Doronno.

"Well, there's nothing illegal about it, is there?" asked Jack.

"No, not that I've ever heard of. I've just never heard of such an arrangement," said Doronno.

"That is a very unique proposal. I've never heard of anything like that either," said Talaka.

"Do you think I could make enough to make the payments?" asked Jack.

"Well, I'm not sure, but I believe you could," said Talaka. "You would have to, well, probably carry some contraband items more often than not, to, uh, should we say, less-than-desirable destinations, but it probably could be done."

"Well, present company excluded, it couldn't be any worse than the places and people I've had to deal with since coming to Nishda," said Jack.

"Well, at least you wouldn't have provosts shooting at you. Well, actually maybe you still would depending on where you went," said Doronno.

Jack laughed. "That's true, but at least I'd be getting paid for my efforts this time." They all got a good laugh out of that. "And there's one more part that involves you, Doronno," added Jack.

"Now I'm beginning to be a little bit afraid of what you might propose," said Doronno with a chuckle.

"You probably should be," replied Jack with his own little chuckle.

"OK, then, what is it?" asked Doronno.

"The guns, the plasma cannons," said Jack, "I would like the plasma cannons for *Carratta*. Could they be mounted in a low-profile turret on the ship and the targeting and fire control system wired into *Carratta*?" Doronno blinked and looked at Talaka again.

"Makes sense to me," said Talaka. "Anyone in that type of business that is unarmed would be in a somewhat precarious position."

"Yes, it could be done, but this type of ship is, well, rarely if ever armed, especially with something of that nature," said Doronno.

"Won't they be surprised, then, if they ever try to hijack or rob us?" said Jack.

"Very surely they would be," replied Doronno, "yes, very surely they would."

"How much for the guns and the installation and maybe the provost ship's perimeter self-defense system too? Can I still afford the ship and make the payments with those add-ons?" asked Jack.

"You want the perimeter self-defense system too?" said Doronno.

"Well, it sort of goes along with the defense and offense capabilities of the provost ship, I would like to think," replied Jack.

"I, well, hadn't really thought about that yet," said Doronno. "The guns, as you call them, are probably the most expensive item on the Kershavah next to the engines, but in reality, there probably isn't that much of a market for them around here. It would probably take me considerable time to sell them, just like *Carratta*. I would like to get perhaps two million for them if I could plus the install—"

"I'll let you test-fire them all you want on our proving runs," said Jack.

Doronno smiled. "Hmmmm, you drive a very hard—no, an easy bargain, Jack. All right, for you, I will let you have them for one million, installation included, and I'll throw in the perimeter defense system too. I would at least break even on that portion of the Kershavah salvage, then. Of course, this is all contingent on whether I can get Emnal Ramidew's family to accept your unique, uh, unusual, actually plainly bizarre proposal to begin with."

"I'm sure you'll have no problem. We're in like Flynn," said Jack.

"In like what, who?" said Doronno.

"Oh, just a saying," replied Jack.

"And what of me? How can I help?" asked Talaka.

"Well, you've helped immensely already," said Jack. "Like they always say, it's not always what you know, it's who you know, and you definitely knew the right person to make this all happen."

"Well, as you say 'well' often, it's been interesting and profitable, so the pleasure has been mine."

"Well, then, there is one more favor I ask," said Jack.

"Yes, anything," said Talaka.

"I will need a place to stay for a moondat or however long it takes to fully outfit *Carratta*. I would also use that time to learn all I can about piloting the ship as well as every aspect of navigation and how I'm going to earn a living for myself and the ship in my brave new world of clandestine cargo and information transportation. If it isn't too much of an imposition, I would like to stay at or possibly rent a room from you during this time period."

"Rent a room? No, I have no rooms for rent. That would be absurd. You are welcome to stay as long as you please. It will be an interesting time for all of us. A person could not normally even find such interesting times to pay for even if he wanted to. If need be, I could also give a good reference and vouch for your honorable intentions of payment for *Carratta* to Emnal Ramidew's family."

"That would be greatly appreciated," replied Jack, "however, I'm not sure you would want to vouch for a fugitive smuggler with dubious intentions for the use of their ship."

Talaka answered, "That would not be a problem, as my own reputation is somewhat nefarious, and anyway, I think the only concern for Emnal Ramidew's family would be recovering as much of his investment in *Carratta* as possible."

"One more question for now," asked Jack. "How, physically, do I make the payments on *Carratta* if I am zipping all over the galaxy with contraband and other interesting deliveries?"

"Oh, that is fairly easy," replied Doronno. "The GTA monetary system data is carried from system to system by certified sealed courier data packets on just about every transport ship transiting the galaxy. In worst-case situations, it sometimes takes several moondats for all the transaction data to make it into the central monetary system, though usually it would take just two to three weneks. It worked much better and was much more efficient when each world or system had its own monetary system. The only downside was the conversion rates between the different systems. Because all transactions were of a local nature, it was difficult if not impossible for the GTA to tax or regulate many transactions. For this reason, the GTA took over the galactic monetary system and centralized it on their core planet system of Azhmana-amah.

"The answer to your question, though, is that anytime you would make a payment, you would just pay at the local planetary system that you are in to the account you wish to credit, and the data would be forwarded to the GTA central monetary system and back to Emnal Ramidew's family here on Nishda."

Jack asked, "Would that be a problem as far as the payment being late and not being credited on time?"

"No, not really. The payment time stamp would always accompany the payment. Under the circumstances of this unusual arrangement, I'm sure we could make a provision to allow for slow processing due to the nature of your business," replied Doronno.

"Would it be possible to add a grace period in case I run into credit flow problems of my own?" added Jack.

Doronno replied, "Well, that would be up to Ramidew's family. If they aren't really hurting for the credits, which I doubt, then they would probably agree to something like that. Since they've probably never heard of anything like this proposed arrangement prior to now, we could easily propose any allowances or conditions that you would think you'd need. I'm guessing their biggest concern is ridding themselves of a ship they don't want or know what to do with. They probably don't want it back and would just be happy as long as they get their full credits in the long run."

"OK, that all sounds pretty encouraging. I guess I'll drink to that," said Jack.

"Me too, and Talaka too, I would say," said Doronno. "This certainly has turned into an interesting evening after a truly interesting daiyus. I can't remember the last time I've had this much high-level entertainment in one daiyus," added Doronno.

"I will second that," said Talaka.

Chapter 12: Carratta

The next morning, Jack woke up with a bit of a hangover, the price of a successful business transaction, he reasoned. Even with his head pounding slightly, he felt totally elated. If Doronno could pull off the contract negotiations with Emnal Ramidew's family, his entire life and, umm, he guessed, he'd call it his current career track, would be taking a drastic change for the better. He had certainly bitten off a lot as far as what he'd have to train for, and he would have to learn a ton of new skills if it all came to fruition. Navigating his own starship around the Milky Way Galaxy was a bit beyond even his comprehension and imagination, yet here was an opportunity he could not have even fathomed a few moondats ago or even a few daiyus ago. Just grasping that concept was challenging to get his head around.

Something wiggled at the foot of the bed as he started to move a bit himself. A brown mottled head popped up from the side of the covers. "Well, good morning, Seema. I almost forgot about you this morning with all the excitement last night. I think I remember you wiggling your way in here when you figured out I'd gotten back." She jumped up next to him and obviously wanted his attention as she wedged herself up against him so that he would pet her and show her some attention. "I guess you've been getting along with all those children. You seem to be even more domesticated than ever." She made a pest of herself for a few mentus as Jack rubbed her and petted her while she ate up every bit of his affection. "Come on, let's get up and see what's going on today. I have a feeling there will be a lot happening," he said to her.

In the kitchen, Jack found Talaka's wife Sensara with a couple of the children. While she found something for Jack and Seema to eat, she informed him that Talaka had gone to his office already and that Jack could use the blue vimar in the back courtyard to go to Doronno's if he wished. He thanked her for her hospitality. Then after a quick shower, he and Seema hopped in the vimar and headed to Doronno's complex where Jack could hardly wait to see his hopefully soon-to-be ship *Carratta*. He sure hoped that Emnal Ramidew's family would seriously consider his offer. It sort of seemed like a long shot now that he thought about it, but as they say, no guts no glory. He just hated this kind of waiting game, though, and nothing had even been initiated yet as far as he knew. What he did know was that it was going to be agonizing waiting for a decision. "Seema, if everything works out here, as it possibly might, we are in for some interesting times ahead. I hope you're up for them, or would you rather stay here with Talaka's family?" Seema tucked her head under his arm and then curled up next to him on the seat.

After being waved into Doronno's facility, he went straight back to the office near *Carratta*. He passed several different ships in different levels of refurbishment or repair on the way back to the hangar office. He went up and knocked on the door. "Yes, Jack, come in" came the voice from inside. "The gate watch said you were on your way back. Please sit down. I see you brought your interesting little friend. I hope we didn't ply you with too much qalalé last night. It was a grand adventure we had yesterday, and my crew is working fast to salvage the Kershavah ship."

Jack replied, "Yes, it was a good daiyus yesterday and, fortunately, not too precarious as far as getting the Kershavah ship from where we salvaged it from yesterday."

"Yes, indeed, and only a fraction of your original exploit for certain," said Doronno.

"Your proposal for *Carratta* was quite the intriguing surprise yesterday, but now that I've had time to think about it, there are a lot of excellent arguments for it."

"I'm glad you think so," said Jack. "It seems like a bit of a long shot to me because I don't really know much about the logistics of the markets and intricacies of dealing with the various people, governments, local authorities, or others. I'm not even aware of what a lot of the intricacies of that type of trading operation might involve. I may be completely out of my league as far as even knowing where to start or how to function in that type of environment."

"Well, I'm sure we can get you a considerable amount of information and training with regard to those issues. I think it would be most advantageous for you to get the right crew for your operation. A few good crew members that have experience in all the aspects involved with that type operation would be essential."

"I absolutely agree," said Jack. "I would have an immense amount of new things to learn in addition to the ship itself. Do you know if there are experienced crews available that would be willing to be involved in that type of operation?"

"Oh, yes, I'm sure there are always plenty of privateer adventure types willing to ply themselves to that type of operation. The biggest concern would be verifying their experience and abilities. Those types usually live on the edge, and trying to verify their actual experience would be difficult at best. We can come back to that later. Right now, we need to see what the outcome of the offer you made will be. I went ahead and contacted Emnal Ramidew's family with your proposal. The good news is they didn't reject it outright, but they said they would need some time to consider all the ramifications of the offer as they've never heard of such a scenario before. I agreed with them but mentioned to them that they should not take too long, as the potential buyer was also considering some other possible ships even though he liked *Carratta*."

"OK, great, that sounds like a good strategy, and thanks," said Jack. "You're the expert on how to make these deals come together, so I'll leave it up to you. Are there actually any other ships available?"

"No, not really," said Doronno, "not in *Carratta*'s class that would be available at anywhere near that price range or even anything else anywhere near Nishda. I just don't want them languishing too long on a decision, and a little pressure never hurts. Even if they aren't willing initially, it will force them to make a decision or a counteroffer. If I don't hear from them in a couple of daiyus, I will contact them and add a little more fuel to the fire under their feet."

"I'm glad you are the one dealing with them on this. I'm sure I'm a little too close to the situation, and I wouldn't know the right tactics to use to get the best results."

"Yes, that's what I do. Even more than repairing the ships, I make the contracts happen, and I like to believe that I give everyone involved a fair agreement. So while we wait for a response, would you like to begin your indoctrination to the ship's systems?"

"Yes, that's exactly what I'd like to do," replied Jack, "as long as you think there's at least some chance of the offer being accepted or at least countered."

"Oh, yes, I believe there is at least a 40 or 50 percent chance of them liking the offer. Like I said yesterday, they haven't gotten any offers since Emnal died, and they are aware that they won't likely get any around here or anywhere else on Nishda. I'm sure they're quite realistic about their position. It just depends on how low they are willing to go to rid themselves of the situation they're stuck in. Well, let's go take a look at *Carratta* and let you get a little experience with some of the systems," said Doronno.

Back on *Carratta,* Jack was even more ecstatic as he looked more closely at the beautiful ship he'd first seen yesterday. Even if he didn't have much of a chance of his offer being accepted, he would still have wanted to learn everything he could about *Carratta* and the systems and technology of this amazing starship. Doronno logged him into the ship's security system and gave him full access to all the ship's technical information.

"Who was Emnal Ramidew going to use as a crew for his exploration missions?" asked Jack.

Doronno replied, "He wanted to get his family members involved and trained, which they'd agreed to, but they lost interest after he died, or possibly they just weren't all that interested to begin with. I believe they might have been humoring him to some degree so as to stay in good standing for his estate. As well planned out as the ship was from a technical standpoint, I don't think he put as much thought into how he was actually going to carry out his dream of exploring with his own ship. I guess he thought his family members had the same enthusiasm for his desired adventures as he did. That's another reason why it's possible that they will consider your offer. They didn't have much if any interest in using the ship themselves, and they are likely to want the proceeds from the ship for their own agendas, whatever those might be."

That gave Jack a bit more optimism knowing they didn't have any interest in the ship themselves. Seema had followed behind them and cautiously snooped here and there as they talked about the ship. "I will wait until we find out if we've got a contract before I start any installation plans for the plasma cannons and perimeter defense system as well as any fitting out the ship will require," said Doronno. "We'll have both of them off the Kershavah in a couple of daiyus, but there's no sense tapping into *Carratta*'s hull and systems before we know anything from Emnal's people."

"OK, that makes perfect sense to me," replied Jack.

Doronno left Jack with the ship and went back to his office. "What do you think, Seema? This could be our new home if everything comes together." She unfurled her ears and listened in every direction inside the ship as if getting a feel for the way the ship was supposed to sound. "Go ahead and check it out, Seema. You'll want to get as familiar with *Carratta* as you can. She'll sound a lot different, though, once we're up and flying," he said to her. Jack walked through the ship again and let Seema snoop anywhere she wanted. He checked out the big open cargo bay and took a cursory look at all the storage and equipment stations in the bay. Then he went back up to the flight deck and sat down at the pilot seat and started going through all the systems on the ship's big HUD display.

The ship had two main star drive engines buried in the nonpressurized outer hull at the lower edge of the ship. The engines were phase paralleled at the quantum level to work fully synced with each other. They were each a hybrid linear grav field compression generator that would encapsulate the ship in a quantum field effect bubble or shell that isolated the ship from surrounding space. The nearly infinitely highly polarized phase shift points between the front and back of the quantum field were steerable, variable, and fully controllable. The phase shift quantum point energy levels are so highly oppositely polarized that they would instantly vaporize anything between them down to the atomic level because of the unimaginable forces just outside the quantum bubble. That would also happen to the ship except that the ship is isolated in a quantum field effect bubble, which keeps the massively polarized points in space from ever touching and also creates an acceleration force between the points that was nearly beyond comprehension. The ship, isolated in its quantum field effect bubble, remains unaffected by the gargantuan physical forces occurring less than a mu-ut to the front and rear of its hull. The ship could be steered in hyperspace by modulating the polarized phase shift points independently at the front and back of the ship.

Carratta also has two sublight maneuvering engines and sixteen ion maneuvering thrusters that can operate with *Carratta* either in or out of the quantum field effect bubble. The quantum field effect bubble is essentially an inwardly impenetrable quantum shield that can be manipulated to allow the thrust output from *Carratta*'s stripped-plasma-ion sublight engines and maneuvering thrusters to penetrate the shield. The quantum field is permeable from the inside out but not from the outside in because of the directional phase alignment of the quantum energy field. This allowed using the ion maneuvering thrusters while *Carratta* was in the quantum bubble.

The force generated by the sublight engines and thrusters could penetrate outward through the bubble, while no force could penetrate inward through the nearly infinite polarity shift of the quantum bubble. The two main sublight engines were at the aft of the ship with four each top and bottom maneuvering thrusters, two lateral thrusters on each side, and two each fore and aft thrusters for a total of sixteen ion maneuvering thrusters. The stripped-plasma-ion sublight engines were fueled by pure force-stripped ions of variously available noble gases in an inertial electromagnetic confinement cell. The stripped noble gases were then recovered to their normal nonionized state and reused continuously. Only periodic refueling of the noble gases, usually argon but also neon and helium, with a lower output level was necessary, and this could be accomplished by using *Carratta*'s small but efficient gas scuppers and separation/distillation units in the rear upper wing housings or by direct fueling from an external source.

Jack was fascinated by the science and capabilities of the ship. Some of the technology sounded vaguely familiar from some of the hypothesized theoretical systems he'd read about back on Earth, but a lot of it was outside the realm of any of the conventional physics or propulsion system engineering he'd ever heard of. He knew he ended up here on Nishda in a starship, but the speeds they traveled were barely fathomable. From his understanding of what he was reading, *Carratta* was capable of speeds of a light-year in 5.2 mentus. He'd run all the calculations on his translator calculator, and it came out that *Carratta* could make it from Earth to the nearest star, Alpha Centauri, in just under twenty-two minutes, Earth time. He had to let that soak in for a couple of minutes. "That's crazy. My head can't even grasp a number that big velocity-wise," he said out loud.

He had always wondered what it would have been like to go back in time and tell someone from the eighteenth century that you could get from New York to

London in less than three hours on the Concorde and how utterly unbelievable that would have sounded to them. Now he knew how they would have felt hearing that supposedly absurd claim, yet here it was right at his fingertips, a ship that could make the Earth-to-Alpha-Centauri run in twenty-two minutes. Hot damn, he just couldn't get over it. Hot, hot crazy ridiculous damn!

Jack leaned back in the pilot seat and closed his eyes a minute and envisioned what it would be like piloting this amazing ship through the galaxy. He felt like a ten-year-old kid again wondering what it would be like to fly in an airplane for the first time. Something nudged his leg. He looked down and saw Seema looking at him. "Hi there, stealthy girl, did you finish snooping around for a while?" She nudged him again. "I'll bet you need to go out and snoop around outside for a few minutes. OK, come on, we'll go out back of the hangar. I guess that's a problem we'll have to address on *Carratta,* isn't it? We'll think of something."

Jack spent the next four daiyus studying everything he could about *Carratta*'s systems and her operation. He guessed it would take a couple of weneks of straight-up cramming to get a fair to good understanding of the ship's systems along with their theory and how to apply it to practical applications. There was a lot more to it than that, though. Not only did he need to understand the ship's systems and how they operated and how to apply them but also there was a vast amount of studying to be done on navigation, which included not only intergalactic navigation but also solar system and planetary navigation.

You didn't just point and go. For instance, he'd learned that approaching a solar system at high warp speed was not recommended because of the coronal outflow of the star all the way to the outer regions of the star's heliosphere. This could interfere with the navigation systems accuracy, and if it wasn't a system of known orbital periods for the system's planets, then the potential for a catastrophic collision event existed when coming out of hyperspace. This interference would also vary because of the current level of solar activity and the mass and the variable electromagnetic radiation emissions of the star, none of which was always predictable and often variable.

The point of the information was you needed to come out of light speed hyperspace a good safe distance from known solar systems and farther for unknown systems. That just included the physical and ship's aspects of it, and he hadn't even touched on the political ramifications of all the different planets and governments. Fortunately, there was a vast database in *Carratta*'s data cortex that contained most everything he would need in those respects. Still, this wasn't a simple atmospheric ship like the Kershavah that he'd picked up the operation of fairly easily. It was an entirely different environment that bore little resemblance to anything he'd ever encountered or contemplated before. Press on was all he could think of to do.

On the fifth daiyus, he was getting a little anxious about the possibility of his offer not being accepted. Doronno had assured him several times that it was nothing to worry about. Either Emnal's family was still considering the offer, which may have included a considerable amount of interfamily "discussion," or they may have been occupied with other issues in their private little world that actually placed Jack's situation at the bottom of their priority list.

"Great," said Jack, "my future is in the balance, and they're arguing about whether they want Italian sausage or pepperoni on their pizza tonight."

"Sausage, pepperoni, pizza?" asked Doronno.

"Ah, yes, a native dish of my home planet," replied Jack. "I'm sure you'd like it if you could try it. Boy, does that sound good about now. I wonder if Talaka's wives could conjure up some sort of facsimile of one."

"I don't know. You should ask. They are very good at cooking," said Doronno.

"Yes, indeed, they are," said Jack.

"All right, come back at 1400 horuns today, and I will call them and see what kind of pressure we can put on them. We mustn't act too enthusiastic or they may ask for much more in a counteroffer," said Doronno.

"OK, I'm leaving that aspect of it in your hands," said Jack. "I'm just anxious that all my studying will be for naught if they turn us down."

"You should not worry," said Doronno. "They will come around, maybe not at eighteen million but at something reasonable."

Back in Doronno's office at 1400 horuns, Jack asked, "So what will you ask them or pressure them with to try to get them to accept the offer?"

"I'm not going to call them now," said Doronno.

"Why not?" asked Jack. "Do you think they need to think about it longer, or are you afraid they'll think I'm, uh, we are too anxious and raise the price out of sight?"

"No, it just wouldn't make sense to call them now, there wouldn't be any point to it," said Doronno.

"What do you mean there wouldn't be any point to it? What's—I'm not sure what you're getting at," said Jack somewhat confusedly.

Doronno replied, "Well, it wouldn't make any sense to call them now—"

"Well, why not?" asked Jack, becoming more agitated with Doronno's attitude.

Doronno began to laugh and tried to stifle it. "Well, because Emnal's son Thalak called about a half horun ago and said they would accept the contract for eighteen million with your initial payment of two million under the condition that I would guarantee the safe return of the ship if you failed to make the payments after three moondats. Of course, I explained that—"

"Are you serious?" said Jack as he jumped up clapped his hands and yelled, "They accepted the offer? You're serious, right? I hope you're serious," as he jumped up and down excitedly.

"Yes, yes, I'm completely serious," said Doronno as he chuckled and smiled at seeing Jack's elation over the news.

"Yes, yes, yeahah!" shouted Jack as he did a little dance in front of Doronno's desk.

"I take it you are pleased with their answer, then?" asked Doronno.

"Oh, yes, oh, yes," said Jack, "wow, oh, man, I can't believe it. I was really starting to worry there for a while."

"'Well, good, I am quite pleased too," said Doronno. "In fact, I believe everyone is happy with the situation."

Doronno continued. "I did explain to him that I couldn't guarantee the return of the ship because of the nature of the business undertaking of the buyer. I told him that it would be a wise decision to keep the ship in his company's name and keep the insurance in force during the period that you are paying for the ship. This made sense to him, and he agreed that this would be the best thing for him to do. So even though there will be a sales contract on *Carratta* with you as the buyer, they will retain ownership until the ship is paid for in full. I said I would try to recover the ship if it were possible in case you, the buyer, failed to complete payments on it. Of course, if I had to recover the ship, there would be a charge for my services, but he would get his ship back."

"Oh, yes, that sounds quite, what, uh, sensible and reasonable to me. That's basically how any loan would work on my planet—the seller or bank retains ownership until the item is paid for," said Jack.

"Really?" said Doronno. "And I thought I was being so clever and innovative. Well, as long as all the parties agree, then it sounds like we will be signing a contract in a few daiyus. I will put together a draft of the contract for both parties to examine, and then we will schedule a meeting for contract signing."

"Great, that will be just great. Now I really want to get back to the ship and dive into the systems and other aspects of operating *Carratta*."

"I believe that *Carratta* will have an outstanding and enthusiastic new owner," said Doronno. "Yes, I believe that even *Carratta* will be pleased with this arrangement."

"I sure hope so," said Jack, "and I can't thank you enough for your help and expertise on this whole affair," said Jack. "Come on, Seema, let's go tell *Carratta* the good news," as he headed out the door with Seema in tow on their way back to *Carratta* once again.

Later that daiyus, Doronno came by the ship to find Jack hard at work deep in the HUD systems manual of the ship. "Hi Doronno, I'm really having a great time learning all of the magic *Carratta* has to offer. I can't wait until we get to take her up for her initial trails."

"Yes, I'm looking forward to that too," replied Doronno. "I had my engineers start planning the installation of the plasma cannons and perimeter defense system for *Carratta*. It is quite the capable and beautiful ship. I almost forgot to mention that I asked, insisted actually, that Thalak Ramidew give us a one moondat grace period from the time that the ship is put into service, not the contract date, before payments will start to become due. He agreed to this because I explained that the buyer would need to start generating income from the ship, which couldn't happen until the ship became operational."

"I didn't even think of that," said Jack. "I'm really glad you're the one putting this contract together."

"Yes, well, I'm just providing our standard functionary services," said Doronno. "If you hadn't thought of it and proposed it in the first place, I never would have even dreamed up a contract structured like this. I wouldn't even have known that you were interested in the ship, yet here we are. Isn't that truly fascinating?"

A few daiyus later after reviewing the contract, both parties agreed to the conditions of the contract, and they all got together on a Foursday morning and concluded the signing of the contract. One thing they'd changed during their negotiations was that Doronno was able to get the terms changed to an eight-yenet Nishda period from five. He convinced Thalad Ramidew that this was necessary based on what he calculated the buyer could generate by putting the ship into service. He also convinced him the slightly reduced payment would be much better than no payment at all. Jack was again very grateful to Doronno for this, since he didn't have any idea how much or even how he would generate the revenue he needed to make the payments.

With only four hundred thousand in operating capital, he wouldn't last long if he couldn't generate a sizeable cash flow to cover his operation. Fortunately, the Nishda month, or moondat, was sixty-four daiyus long, so he would have nearly double the time of an Earth month to generate the income each month. With the extra million added in for the plasma cannons and perimeter defense for a total of nineteen million, Jack would have to come up with 193,181 credits every moondat to make his payments for the balance on the loan of seventeen million. He would have to hustle. For some reason, that moondat number sounded bigger than the total of nineteen million to him. Thank God it was an interest-free loan or he'd never be able to make the payments on *Carratta*. His 400,000 credits would barely carry him for two moondats unless he could haul some serious cargo. He hoped it wouldn't be a short ride. The key would be getting access to his prior winnings as soon as possible and getting the bootlegged GTA account from Talaka.

A couple of daiyus after the contract was signed, and after two million of Jack's Kershavah commission was transferred to the Ramidew's for the sale of *Carratta*, Talaka told Jack the alias GTA account was finally set up. The remaining four hundred thousand was transferred to Jack's new alias account with the deceased but unreported as deceased citizen's name of Desdewah Annilar Ri. *Well, thanks, Des,* said Jack to himself. *Sorry about the inconvenience, but I appreciate your, uh, timing on this.* Talaka told Jack it had taken longer than they'd expected because they needed to find someone without a next of kin that wouldn't be looking into the deceased account holder's affairs.

The next daiyus on board *Carratta,* while studying more of the ship's systems, Jack said to Seema, "Well, Seema, it looks like we're on our way. I hope you're up for this kind of adventure. You've been a great asset and good company to me so far at every turn." Seema came up and sat next to Jack and leaned against him for a scratch. Watching her, Jack seemed to think that she grew more intelligent each daiyus. For an animal, she really seemed to have great insight as to what he was doing and what was going on around her.

She had explored the ship thoroughly, and it appeared she's made it her own. Jack had taken a little time and done some research on tu-uraks but hadn't been able to find much other than a few images with an explanation that they were omnivores that lived in Nishda's greenbelts with stats that showed their average size and weight. *Well,* thought Jack, *maybe in a space-faring culture, they didn't spend as much time studying every miniscule organism that lived on their planet to the nth degree like they did on Earth bound Earth.* He was pretty sure they weren't native to Nishda because Nishda had been terraformed, but there wasn't anything about where they may have come from.

The following daiyus, two of Doronno's engineers began evaluating *Carratta* for the installation of the plasma cannons. Jack met them that morning and started discussing the installation and how he thought it should work on *Carratta.* Unlike the Kershavah ship, he wanted the ability to target and control the guns by a single pilot from either the left pilot seat or the right, or copilot's position. He and the two engineers, Donser Zshillic and Esdahk Wivcahj Ne, agreed that since there was only one available targeting console that it would then have to be mounted between the pilot and first pilot seat or directly overhead between them. Jack opted for the overhead position so that he could better maintain visual contact with whatever was outside while operating the weapon system. They then decided that the turret should be mounted on top of the ship on the flat area that started about four mu-uts behind the flight deck windshield. It was high enough that the turret could rotate a full 360 degrees and could partially target something at *Carratta*'s six o'clock position.

The gimbal mounts on the actual cannons could swivel twenty-one degrees up or down and right or left of center. On the Kershavah, the ship had to be aligned within that forty-two-degree x and y axis envelope to lock onto a target. On *Carratta,* the cannons would have the same gimbal capability plus the full 360 turret rotation capability. If the targeting system would have allowed it, Jack would have mounted the two turrets with one gun above and one below the ship both to create redundancy through separation and to have a completely independent field of fire. This would have required two independent tracking and targeting computers to do that, which they unfortunately did not have.

They would need to take the four targeting sensors from the Kershavah and distribute them front and rear, top and bottom. They just wouldn't have redundancy in any given direction. Without the bottom sensors, *Carratta* would have been blind underneath from a target tracking scenario. Even though *Carratta* couldn't shoot in the bottom direction, she would still need to track and target an enemy. The ship's normal active and passive sensor systems could locate another ship from any direction, but the targeting system couldn't begin a targeting solution unless an enemy ship was in view of the targeting sensors. If Jack ever had to engage anything that approached from underneath, he would just have to roll *Carratta* over to a position from which he could target them with the top turret or pull up so that the top of *Carratta* was exposed downward toward the target. This was not unlike a fighter jet, thought Jack, but even better, since the turret rotated and there was no up or down or positive or negative G forces in space because of *Carratta*'s grid field grav system with dual grav generators and the quantum field effect bubble stasis effect.

The engineers and their installation crew began working on the turret platform construction and housing as well as the cannon gimbal mounts for the through-hull targeting controls. Hardwired optics and telemetry feedback was more difficult and expensive to install, but it was always more reliable for critical systems control in an installation like this. The rest of the outfitting was fairly routine and not that involved, since *Carratta* wouldn't be getting any of the additional luxury upgrades she was originally slated for. One thing Jack did opt for was a not new but nicely functional vimar and the two rovsleds that were originally slated to be installed at the back cargo ramp at the aft of the ship.

The vimar was on one side of the bay, and the rovsleds, the other. They were all angled in toward the cargo bay door with a cargo door width passage between them on the deck. Jack and Talaka both agreed that ground transportation would likely be required in Jack's operation. Doronno also suggested that some lightweight cargo sleds might be appropriate in the future if Jack's upcoming experience showed that he might need that capability. The initial ship's stores for food and other provisions would also be included by Doronno's company, since these were obviously essential and that was part of the services his company normally provided at the completion of a ship's refurbishment or initial fit out.

The next item on the fit-out list would be the crew that Jack would need to operate *Carratta*. An experienced pilot could probably get *Carratta* up and down from orbit if no comm works or other collateral duties were required, but it was really a minimum two-pilot job, and a crew of three would be better for actual missions. Jack obviously wasn't an experienced pilot in this environment, so he would definitely require at least a very minimum of one other experienced crew member.

Doronno came up with what appeared to be a workable solution a few daiyus later when he told Jack and Talaka that his company pilot Forto Alerdac, who had acted as Doronno's first pilot on the Kershavah mission, and another of his employees named Wehsh Hevedu, who was a former maintenance officer on a Dellak class transport, had offered to help crew *Carratta* when Doronno had announced that the new owner of *Carratta* was looking for a working crew for his new ship. He told them it would likely just be temporary and that they wouldn't receive any pay until the completion of a revenue run. Doronno's shop was steady enough at the moment that he could afford to loan a couple of his employees to Jack at least for the short term if they wanted to take a break from their routine and go fly some actual cargo runs for a moondat or two.

Jack met with them both along with Doronno and expressed his appreciation for their interest in helping him crew his ship. He explained his situation of being new to this type of venture and his need of a good crew to help him get up to speed on *Carratta*'s operation. He asked them about their motivations and why they wanted to leave their current jobs, though probably only for a few moondats or so.

They both gave the same general answer about just wanting a little break and to do something different for a short time. Forto Alerdac also stated that *Carratta* was such a beautiful and unique ship that he really wanted a chance to serve on her for a while. He said he had really dreamt about being able to operate *Carratta* all the while he'd seen her stored in the hangar for the last eighteen moondats. Jack said, "I certainly understand and agree with you on that." *Carratta* really was one of the nicest ship's he'd ever seen too and couldn't wait to get to fly her and put her to work. Of course, except for the few cargo ships Jack had seen during his initial entry to Nishda, he had really never seen any other real starships other than in sci-fi novels and movies, but he didn't mention that to any of those around him now.

They both seemed like legitimate types that would be willing to put forth some good effort in helping Jack learn *Carratta* and all the operations associated with her. He'd originally been a little concerned about Forto Alerdac because of the previous issue of him not following Doronno's orders during the Kershavah recovery, but he seemed like a genuine-enough type now. Doronno vouched for him, so it seemed that he should give him a chance. Also he was the only pilot qualified volunteer that had come forward, so he would have to take him based on that alone.

After the interview, Jack asked Doronno if either of the applicants knew anything about the details of the purchase and finance details regarding *Carratta*. "No," replied Doronno. "All they know is that you're the new owner of *Carratta* and purchased her to use as a fast courier and special cargo ship. Of course, Forto Alerdac is aware of the Kershavah recovery, since he was involved and is somewhat actually implicated in it, but he doesn't know the details of how you came to be in possession of it. Wehsh Hevedu wasn't involved in the Kershavah recovery, but I'm sure he's heard the employee gossip in house, and he's been working on the demolition crew on the Kershavah for the last couple of weneks."

"OK, that's good," said Jack. "Let's just go ahead and keep it that way. No sense in feeding the fish more than they should eat."

"Um, yes, I believe I know what you mean," replied Doronno. "That's how we would do it unless otherwise advised by the owner or captain."

"I would have guessed that," said Jack, "but I'm just verifying that for general security reasons."

The following daiyus, Jack started going over the ship's operation with his soon-to-be new crew members. Both Forto Alerdac and Wehsh Hevedu had a fair amount of experience on multi-crew-member ships, so Jack would be striving to learn as much from their experience as he could. They went over systems, normal and emergency operations, comm protocol, and checklist usage and content, as well as deciding what other subjects they needed to address. Jack was actually ahead of them from a systems standpoint because he'd been into the ship's systems manuals for a couple of weneks. They both had a better understanding and working knowledge of how the systems actually operated than Jack did but just because of their previous experience in the operation of various ships in their past.

That night, Jack asked Talaka for a favor. "Yes, I'm sure it won't be a problem, whatever it is," said Talaka.

"Well," replied Jack, "I was wondering if your wives could make me up several different disguises to use in my semiclandestine trade business so that I could change my appearance in different ways. That might come in handy for me in certain circumstances, if you know what I mean."

"I don't see why not, but I'm not sure what good that will do," said Talaka. "You can't really fool anyone that you would be dealing with in an official capacity, since your translator ID will give away your identity to anyone that you would have dealings with. They would simply check it and know who you are."

"Yes, that's true," said Jack, "but they wouldn't have a visual picture of what I look like if I could alter my appearance."

"But that is the point of a translator ID," said Talaka. "It doesn't matter what or who you appear to be—you are always who you are as identified by your translator."

Jack stared at Talaka for a good thirty septus trying to decide. "What is it you are contemplating, my friend?" asked Talaka.

"Your absolute level of trustworthiness," replied Jack honestly.

Now it was Talaka's turn to contemplate for a few moments. "I must be honest and say that it depends," replied Talaka. "If it is something that would endanger my family and business, perhaps more than you actually have already, then I would have to take careful consideration of the situation."

"Well, this does push that boundary, perhaps considerably, I'm not even sure how much," said Jack. "Maybe it's better if I don't go any further with an explanation. I'll leave it up to you to decide," Jack added.

Talaka watched Jack then laughed out loud as he further contemplated the situation. "It's not likely that I would be able to stand it very long if I didn't know because whatever it is, coming from you, I'm sure it will be absolute ecstasy based on the things I've already known you to do so far."

"OK," said Jack, "but don't say I didn't offer to spare you. One of the friends I mentioned back at the mine, he's a convict that was falsely convicted as a scapegoat for his employer." Talaka continued to listen. "He figured out how to bypass and hack into any translator. Something that's apparently never been done before. He's quite talented at those sorts of things."

"Are you serious?" asked Talaka, half smiling and half laughing.

"Absolutely deadly serious," said Jack. "Not only can I turn off my translator and have no transponder but I can transmit anyone else's ID that I can bootleg or steal just from being in reception range of their transponder. I can capture it and store it in a library of stolen IDs that I store right in my own translator. Then I can broadcast any ID I have and essentially be anyone I want to be that I've previously borrowed an ID from."

Now completely serious, Talaka asked, "And you know this works—you've somehow tested it and know that it works?"

"Oh, yes," said Jack, "it's how I escaped from the mine. I just walked out with a guard's ID. It's also how I escaped from the provosts, because they couldn't get a lock on my real ID because it was off. I also stole some of the IDs from the provosts I killed and used them to trick them into thinking I was one of their own while they searched for me from the air with the Kershavah. It's also how I stole the Kershavah ship, by using the dead captain's ID to gain access to the ship's security system. The first pilot I left stranded at the greenbelt thought I was crazy or stupid for trying to steal their ship. He was wrong, probably dead wrong."

Talaka sat dumbfounded for a mentu. "Halashatau," he said, "do you understand the repercussions of this, of what you just told me? Maybe you shouldn't have told me about this, but it does answer all the unanswered questions I had about how you got here and the Kershavah ship. Even I couldn't have imagined anything such as this. This is most astounding. You must tell no one else about this. Do you know the trouble this could cause you?"

"Probably," said Jack.

Talaka went on, "Not only would they kill you for knowing this but they would want to know how it was done so they could try to stop it. This has never been done and would totally, as in totally, completely undermine their control of every citizen of the GTA. Anyone that knew you could do this might try to turn you in to the provosts or any other agents of the GTA for a huge reward."

"Yes, I suppose so," said Jack.

"You, my intriguing friend, have made yourself a target, a very, very big and potentially profitable target with this knowledge and ability. Do they know you can do this?"

"No, at least I don't believe so," replied Jack. "It's not likely they would suspect such a thing, and I've used it very judiciously as I will continue to do so. The only ones that might be able to directly testify about it are dead, except for the Kershavah first pilot who is also likely dead, unless he was very lucky. They might be able to speculate, but it's more likely they just think I'm somehow particularly devious."

Talaka added, "The closest anyone has ever come to this is the situation where we can hack into a dead person's GTA credit account using a somewhat simple copy of the deceased's ID. That doesn't really involve their translator. The only reason that works is because the person is assumed to still be alive, and we just use their account and ID and keep them 'alive' by blocking their end of life signal by disappearing their translator. I thought this trick was somewhat sophisticated, but it is nothing compared to what you say you can do."

"Well, I hope it's not more than you want to deal with," said Jack.

"It's quite a revelation," said Talaka. "I will have to think about the implications of this for a while. Oh, and don't worry, I'm not interested in turning you in for a reward, but there are plenty of others that would."

"Thanks, I appreciate that," said Jack.

* * * * *

Doronno's engineers had fabricated a low-profile turret housing for the plasma cannons with double actuator servos that ran off the same power and frequency inputs as the Kershavah targeting gimbals so that it could all be tied seamlessly to the Kershavah targeting and fire control system now being installed on *Carratta*'s flight deck. All that was then needed was to remove the original forty-two-degree lateral tracking limits that were programmed in the Kershavah software, since the guns could now track a full 360 degrees in rotational direction. The shape of the ship's hull limited the rear downward deflection angle of the guns to negative eighteen degrees aft but allowed the full twenty-one degrees down in the forward direction until they were seventy-eighty degrees left and right.

This all had to be programmed as well as physically limited on the gimbals so that the guns wouldn't be able to deflect downward and hit *Carratta* as the turret was firing and swiveling from front to aft. A simple interference beam detector, which could be overridden in an emergency, would serve as a backup to both systems. If the low-power sensing beam, set a half a degree below the gun's maximum depression angle but one degree above the ship's hull, ever sensed the ship's hull, it would instantly cut power to the fire control computer, and the plasma cannons would stop firing but continue to track. Doronno's engineers were rightly adamant about not wanting the plasma cannons to be able to hit *Carratta*. Since both the cannons and *Carratta* were inside the quantum bubble, this would afford *Carratta* no quantum protection from her own weapons system. With a triple redundancy safety system to prevent that, they seemed satisfied that their project would be safe.

The perimeter defense system involved installing the four Kershavah overlapping sensors and electronically phase steered and autonomous monitoring/targeting ion pulse beam weapons similar to the ion pulse rifles Jack had gotten from the Kershavah ship. One 100-degree overlapping field of fire, combination unit for each quadrant of the ship, would give them a full 360-degree coverage for the ship. The control and programming module was then installed on *Carratta*'s flight deck, and the systems status output was incorporated into *Carratta*'s avionics suite and HUD display.

548

Five daiyus later, the engineers and their installation crew had both systems up and running. They couldn't target actual targets in the hangar, but all the simulation and calibration models built into the targeting systems passed all the self-test and simulation function tests. The way the plasma cannon system worked was by charging an electrostatic containment field capacitance bank directly on both sides of each cannon. With the capacitance banks fully charged, the cannons could rapid fire eighteen fast bursts from each gun, which could be fired together or separately. These could be selected at any grouped rate of two or three or more, including continuous bursts until the eighteen rapid bursts were depleted. Those bursts were at a continuous rate of 2.3 per septu, or they could be set to two pulsed shots at a rate of two every two seconds. Once the eighteen precharged bursts were expended, the cannons could then continue to fire at a sustained rate of one shot every 2.41 seconds, which was the rate that the cannons could charge from the ship's electrical system under normal conditions.

"Why do you believe that you will need the plasma cannons on *Carratta?* Do you think that we will encounter hostile ships or some other situation on our cargo or messenger runs?" Forto Alerdac asked Jack as they were going over the plasma cannon installation and operations.

Jack replied, "Well, I'm not really sure, since I have little experience in this type of operation. Talaka seemed to think it was a good idea when I proposed it to Doronno, so I can't be too far off in my thinking. I'm not sure where we are going or who we might run into, so like some other things in life, it is better to be prepared and have them and not need them than to need them and not have them. There is another saying on my planet, 'walk softly and carry a big stick'. If we have to operate clandestinely it would be wise to carry a big stick. Hopefully, we will never need to fire them in anger at anyone or anything."

"I suppose that makes sense," said Forto. "It just seems a bit unnecessary and I'm guessing costly to add them. In my experience, we never needed any type of weapons on a cargo ship. It almost seems like *Carratta* is being turned into more of a combat ship to me."

"No, I hope she does not need to be a combat ship but just a ship capable of defending herself if need be," said Jack. He added, "In my own previous experience, I always found that having the ability to stand your ground and bring possible destruction to a hostile enemy was the best way to avoid ever having to actually engage that enemy. Think of it as peace through strength."

"Well, it is your ship, so you must do what you are comfortable with," said Forto Alerdac.

"Exactly," said Jack, "and while we're at it, let's just call the cannons the 'guns' from now on. That is shorter and will make for an easier command if needed."

"Yes, OK, 'guns,' as you say, Captain," replied Forto.

The fitting out of the ship continued over the next week, and all the systems were tested, updated, and run through various simulations. Doronno, Jack, and the rest of the crew agreed that two months of provisions would be a good starting point as far as provisioning *Carratta*. They decided that the average mission length would probably run around two weneks for the types of contracts Jack was likely to get with a ship of *Carratta*'s size and speed. It could also easily go over that by a wenek or two if time was of the essence. They wouldn't want to be stopping for provisions on every trip leg if they could avoid it. There might even be some destinations where it wouldn't be possible to reprovision because of local political issues or other reasons. *Carratta* could hold another moondat or more of provisions in her normal storage and pantry areas, but for the type of mission they were contemplating, this should be adequate.

The fit out was going well, and Jack could tell that Doronno's crews were well versed in their trade. The previously empty cargo area was now a well-appointed cargo bay with every type of hold-down and securing device imaginable. A small cargo lift that could attach to a multitude of various-shaped containers was now secured at the rear of the bay in its own tie-down gantry. Though maintenance officer was Wehsh Hevedu's primary job, he would also be the ship's loadmaster in charge of checking and securing all cargo.

Jack was fascinated by the little cargo lift, since it was somewhat like the larger cargo movement system he'd seen on the huge Lokar trade ship *Yuanjejitt*. What was fascinating is that it could lift and simply float the cargo on and off the ship like they had done on *Yuanjejitt*. Wehsh explained that it was just a small antigrav lift gen that was attitude stabilized to carry various loads and various shapes of cargo containers. It wasn't fast, but it could get the loading job done. *Maybe so,* thought Jack, *but it was still cool and fun to play with,* as he drove it around and in and out of the cargo bay, while Wehsh and the others laughed at him. It charged itself in its storage gantry and should have enough capacity to load and unload just about any job they would come across, explained Wehsh.

A full fire suppression system had been plumbed around the cargo bay in case there was ever any hazardous cargo that suddenly needed extinguishing. "This is awesome," Jack said to Doronno. "I wouldn't have thought of that until I needed it."

"Better to have it and not need it," said Doronno.

"Exactly," said Jack, "exactly."

"I believe we are now ready for a test run tomorrow," said Doronno.

"OK," said Jack. "I've been anxiously awaiting this day, and I'll really be looking forward to tomorrow."

The next morning, Jack, along with Seema and his crew of two, were there, plus Doronno and Talaka and Doronno's engineers. "I wouldn't have missed this for anything," said Talaka.

"I'm not expecting any real problems at all," said Doronno, "maybe a few adjustments and alignments at the most. *Carratta*'s already an excellent proven ship. All we are doing is testing all of her fit-out additions and the rest of her normal systems. We may or may not fully test the plasma cannons, but we'll test the targeting and tracking system. If everything works as expected, we may test-fire the cannons."

"Guns," said Jack, "I'm calling them guns from now on."

Doronno's ground team had already hooked up a large tug to *Carratta* to maneuver her out of the hangar. The auxiliary power units were online and supplying the ship's power. When they were ready, they engaged the landing foot antigrav generators that were used to raise the ship for towing and slow taxi operations. With Jack in the captain's seat and Doronno in the first pilot seat, they gave the ground crew the OK to commence towing the ship from the hangar. *Carratta*'s overall length was 54 mu-uts with a height of 6.7 mu-uts and a total overall width of 33 mu-uts. The width of the crew and cargo section of the ship varied from 4 at the front to 14 mu-uts at the rear. She was a very sleek and fast ship, and *Carratta* looked the part. Forto and Wehsh occupied the observer seats and checked the various ships systems as they were slowly towed out. Once they were well clear of the hangar and onto one of the three launch and landing pads for Doronno's complex, they gave the ground crew the OK to disconnect.

"Just run through the prestart checklists like you've been simulating for the last few weneks, and we'll go through a normal start sequence then run all the system checks with the engines running and all the systems online," said Doronno.

"Yeah, this is great. I feel just like a kid in a candy store," said Jack with a big grin on his face. "Prestart checks," Jack called as Doronno pulled it up on the bright colorful interactive HUD.

"Prestart checks," responded Doronno. Jack watched as the HUD display began running through the checks automatically or waiting for a crew response where required. The HUD prestart displayed "Aux Power I and 2 – Online. Electrical and Telemetry Busses - Primary, backup Secondary, Core Hot Control Linked and Switched Primary Synced from Aux, Primary 1, Primary 2, Standby 1, Standby 2 – Online All - Complete. Crew – Acknowledge, Complete."

All the system checks ran through their respective self-test sequences. The engines, both sublight ion drives and the main linear grav field compression generator engines, life support, grav field, communications, navigation, telemetry, cloaking generator, hull integrity and instrumentation, passive and active sensor systems, and the plasma cannons, "the guns," targeting and tracking system both primary and aux, all passed and were online or ready standby. Everything checked and came online automatically as the systems completed their alignment and self-test function. "All Systems Pre-Start Checks – PASS 'Ready for: 1. Ion Drive – Start. 2. Main Grav Field Generators – Start" displayed the HUD in bright blue letters.

"Start and bring the ion drives online first," said Doronno. "That will give you the ability to launch and climb to orbit if you're in a hurry for some reason. You can always bring the main engines online later when you need them—that is, unless you need to establish a quantum state for asteroid or other hazard protection and, of course, for reentry to any planet or moon with an atmosphere or surrounding debris field. For today's test run, we wouldn't really need them outbound, but we'll go ahead and bring the main engines online just to test their functionality in preparation for later when we go to light speed. We would also need them for any acceleration above four G's."

Doronno continued. "The max sustained acceleration of the ion drive is four G's, which is quite good, but it can surge to eight G's for a little over five mentus. *Carratta*'s own grav field will compensate for the G forces induced by the ion drive acceleration up to the first four G's. Above that, the crew will experience the associated amount of G forces. The grav field is primarily for the crews functioning and comfort while *Carratta* is operating outside of the quantum field, and it can compensate for the ion drive acceleration quite well, but it's functionally limited to four G's. Above that, the grav field starts to distort, and you can get some interesting effects and you'll feel it. Four G's of instantaneous and continuous acceleration is really highly adequate for anything inside most sol systems and most destination planets. You will need the main engine quantum stasis field generators online and inducing the quantum field to accelerate above that and for the near infinite G forces for light speed plus. Without that, we would just be a smear of ionized plasma spread across space."

"Good safety tip, I'll try remember that," said Jack.

"Don't worry, *Carratta* will remember it for you," said Doronno. Jack selected the Start icon for the ion drive, and he could hear and feel a slight shudder in the ship as all the ion drives and thrusters came online. A mid tone whine and a faint electrical hiss could be heard in the background throughout the ship. It sounded like pent-up energy that was eager to be released. "As you've probably read, the ion drives run continuously when they are online," said Doronno. "They have to be kept minimally powered in a constant static state until needed, so they will cycle continuously at a low power balanced stasis field containment level until they're needed. At this point, their greatly reduced output is recycled back to a stored charged state in each engine thruster drive core. When you call for acceleration, they ramp up to whatever rate you call for within their limits and we're on our way. You should have a readout on the ion drive panel of both engines and all thrusters as well as a smaller minimized readout showing their status on the HUD. You can see all the blue status readouts here," as Doronno pointed to the ion drive screen and HUD.

"Now we can start the main engines. Then we'll run the preflight checks," said Doronno. Jack selected the main engine start icon. The HUD readout ran through a series of sequenced steps that showed all the start sequence functions of the start. Again, Jack could hear some of the sounds as the mechanical and electrical actuators cycled during the engine start sequence. There was a series or strange sounds that were totally alien to Jack as far as engine start sounds. There were a dozen clicking sounds that were moderately loud followed by a high-pitched, almost grinding, and then lower pulsing sounds. "Electrostatic field couplings aligning and field integrity self-test," said Doronno.

"I've read and reread all the operating manual on this and run through all the sims, but it didn't say anything or simulate any of the sounds," said Jack.

"Yes, I know," said Doronno, "that's why I am giving you a running verbal dialog on the start sequence so you'll know what the normal start sequence sounds like. Every ship is unique in its systems in that regard, so it's good to know what's normal or not."

"So if I hear a large boom, that's not normal or good, and it's time to bail out?" Jack said as he laughed.

"Yes, if you hear a large boom, you might what to start thinking about your next career choice," chided Doronno in response to Jack.

The noises settled down and were replaced by the sound of the two main engine quantum stasis field generators powering up. It only took them about twelve septus to reach full operational level, which showed on the HUD as "Main Engine 1 – Ready, Main Engine 2 – Ready." "Both main engines are up and ready to be engaged," said Doronno. "They can be engaged for just the quantum stasis field or for both the field and drive, but, of course, not the drive by itself and not the drive in close proximity to anything like a planetary body or a sun. *Carratta* won't let you turn her into an ionized plasma smear."

"That's good to know," said Jack. "Is there any way that can be overridden either by accident or intentionally, as in what things not to accidently do that would ruin your daiyus?"

"No, not the drive and field requirement anyway, but the celestial body proximity part, yes. The one electromechanical function in the main engines is to engage the drive, which has to be coupled through the stasis field actuator first. If the stasis field isn't actuated physically and sensed by the core logic as engaged, it won't engage the drive field," answered Doronno.

"That's good," said Jack. "How about the stasis field dropping off-line while the ship is in transit?" asked Jack.

"Theoretically, that's not possible," replied Doronno. "The quantum stasis field state is hyperstable. Once it's established, it actually takes a pretty good jolt from the main engine disruptor circuit to destabilize and collapse it. This can only be done internally from the ship inside the stasis field. Ships have been known to be stuck in an active stasis field until they could induce a stasis disruption pulse, but they have never accidently come out of stasis as far as we know. Ships have gone missing, of course, but we don't have any way of knowing what caused their disappearance, since they've never been found. The most logical best-guess theory for the missing-ship problem is a navigation error that put them into a celestial body, but there are other more exotic hypotheses also.

"Now let's run through the full systems tests on the maintenance page. You wouldn't normally need to do that, since you're getting full-time telemetry feeds from every system on the ship, but since we did some invasive maintenance to the electrical system and hull, we should run a full systems scan of the ship. It will only take about five mentus," said Doronno. They proceeded to run a full diagnostics scan on the ship. Everything came back as good except a single hull breach sensor error at station 1286U. "Well, we know that we didn't do any hull penetration in that area for the gun turret mounts, but we did run some sensor and control wiring through that area. Most likely just a breach sensor knocked out of position. Can you check on that, Wehsh?"

"Yes, standby a mentu while I check it out," replied Wehsh Hevedu.

"We can run through the prelaunch checks while he's working on that," said Doronno.

"Roger that," replied Jack.

"Roger that?" said Doronno.

"That means, uh, yes, I copy—I mean, understand and will comply," said Jack.

"Roger that, OK?" said Doronno. "Don't worry about your comm right now. I will handle the comms and clearance from Se-ahlaalu arrival and departure as well as orbital clearance. It's really just a formality on Nishda because of the light traffic, but on more populated planets, it will be considerably more important. Orbital arrivals are somewhat standardized on most planets, but there will be local variations. Most of the time, you will just follow the instructions of the orbital arrival and departure control directors. If you find yourself requiring a more clandestine arrival or departure, then you will be operating in a totally different situation. We'll talk about that later.

"Go ahead and program a level off at three thousand mu-uts. If there are any hull integrity issues, we will be OK at the altitude. We can run through a series of preorbital tests there also," added Doronno.

Wehsh returned from inspecting the section with the hull integrity error. "That was it, Captain," he said to Jack, "just a loose sensor connector that must have gotten knocked when they were installing the new wiring in that area. It probably came loose from the engine start vibration we just induced. It should show good in the diagnostics now unless there's something wrong with the sensor."

Jack went back to the page that had showed the bad sensor, and it now showed no error or sensor issues. "Looks good now. It looks like you fixed it. Good job," said Jack.

"Roger that," replied Wehsh, and they all got a little laugh from that. "Well, let's get this beautiful ship going now," said Wehsh.

"Everyone set? All systems blue?" inquired Doronno of the crew.

"All set," replied Wehsh.

"Set here," responded Forto Alerdac.

"As set as I'll ever be," replied Talaka.

"OK, then, here we go," said Doronno. "Just ease up on the control stick then gently increase the accel grip to about an eighth, which will be maybe a tenth G as we clear the surface area. Make a turn to a heading of 020 and intercept the course line you've set." Jack pulled back on the climb and descent control, and *Carratta* gave a very slight shudder as the ion drive thrusters on the landing feet and the attitude thrusters all engaged to lift *Carratta* of the ground. *Carratta* climbed nimbly to an altitude of fifty mu-uts. Then Jack called for landing pad retraction and carefully nudged the acceleration control.

Carratta started to move slowly in the forward direction, and as she did, Jack banked slightly to make a left 160-degree turn to a heading of 020. As they climbed higher, he nudged the accel control, and the ship rapidly sped up again. The ship climbed more, and Jack accelerated more. The readout on the HUD showed he'd stabilized at a speed of 860 kahtaks. "That didn't take long, and I didn't even feel the acceleration forces. Yeeha, and, hot damn, I'm flying a light speed starship, my, as in mine, light speed starship. Who would have ever thought it in this lifetime or the next!" Jack said somewhat quietly to himself.

"You're approaching your level off altitude, and the auto flight is not armed to capture, so you will have to level off manually," Doronno pointed out to Jack.

"Yes, that came up rather fast," said Jack as he struggled to level off gently but overshot the planned level off by six hundred mu-uts.

Doronno added, "No need to be gentle if you are trying to stop a climb or descent. *Carratta*'s grav field will compensate for it."

"Of course," said Jack. "I'm used to being careful to not overstress the ship and the people in it."

"No need to think about that here," said Doronno. "*Carratta* will limit the G acceleration to a max of eight G's and a max felt acceleration of four G's when not in the quantum stasis field."

After Jack had leveled, Doronno talked Jack through engaging the auto flight modes of the ship. They ran through various integrity tests of *Carratta*'s systems and then practiced a series of manual flight maneuvers for Jack to get a good feel for *Carratta*'s handling characteristics. "You're doing extremely well," said Doronno, "considering you said you've never flown anything like this type of ship before. You seem to have a natural ability for it, which doesn't surprise me considering your other recent exploits."

"Yes, I have some considerable experience but definitely not in anything like *Carratta*," said Jack.

Doronno continued. "OK, let's program your next climb to a hundred thousand mu-uts. I'll get us a clearance, and then you can program the assigned orbital track."

Doronno got a clearance to the requested altitude then told Jack, "Now program in the orbital track 486P-R that the controller just assigned us. That will tell *Carratta* the programmed track as well as the course direction and orbital grade of the track. At that low of an orbit, we can get just about anything we want, so I requested a polar retrograde orbit on published track 486." After Jack had programmed the orbit as instructed, Doronno showed him how it displayed both pictorially on the HUD and in the nav data readout. "When you've confirmed it in both areas and you have your clearance, you can execute it on the auto flight command control. If you don't specify any particular rate, speed, or route, *Carratta* will pick the most advantageous. That doesn't mean fastest or most direct but the most like you've previously flown during the rest of the flight. You can always adjust or override your previous profile parameters here," said Doronno, pointing to the input for flight parameters selector, "or you can disengage auto and fly the ship manually, but it's better to stay in auto flight when you're adhering to a clearance so you don't miss something and bust your clearance."

It all made sense to Jack, especially since he'd spent so much time learning the switch-ology and other functions, but like any new airplane he'd ever flown, it was initially overwhelming trying to put it all together from theory to the real deal. It was even more challenging, since *Carratta*'s speed was so amazing, and it seemed strange to only feel the slight vibrations and mechanical feedback from *Carratta* but without any of the G forces that Jack had felt his whole life in airplanes. It was a little bit disconcerting in that respect.

Once they had their clearance, Jack hit the execute command, and *Carratta* accelerated and pitched up while turning in the shortest direction toward the 486P-R route programmed in the nav core. *Carratta* climbed and turned to intercept the course at an amazing rate. She was now accelerating through three thousand kahtaks an horun at a rate of sixty thousand mu-uts a mentu. That was nearly twice as fast as any fighter Jack had ever flown in full afterburner, and *Carratta*'s deck angle was only a moderate twenty-two degrees. If they had gone vertical, they would have been climbing at nearly four times their current rate. Doronno pointed to the selection input command. "You can set your speed and rate here if you need to meet any specific requirements that a controller requires. When you get comfortable with *Carratta* at these nice docile speeds and rates, we will move up to something a little closer to normal. We're only doing about a third or less of what you might be required for sequencing into or out of a busy spaceport on another planet besides Nishda."

Criminy, thought Jack, *it seems borderline insane, but apparently, it's no big deal for a ship like* Carratta *or probably any other starship.* They were at a hundred thousand mu-uts in under three mentus. *Carratta* had continued to accelerate to low orbital velocity, and they were now at an orbital velocity of 7.8465 kahtaks per second with an orbital period of 1.4326 horuns according to the HUD readout. "Wow, this is simply amazing," said Jack.

"Yes, *Carratta* is a very capable ship, and she does it with great elegance."

"I can certainly see and appreciate that," said Jack.

Jack looked out on the planet Nishda. He'd seen a little of it on the vido display from the air during his descent from the huge cargo ship and then much lower in the Kershavah, but it took on a whole new aspect now as he gazed at it through *Carratta*'s windshield. The planet was a dusky tan and red dotted everywhere with patches of greenbelts and bodies of water as well as a faint green band at around sixty degrees north and south latitudes. From their current altitude, he could see very little of any signs of habitation. He did see something he hadn't seen previously, and that was two greenbelt zones that were actually touching bodies of water. Previously, he'd only seen them isolated from each other.

Jack asked Doronno, "Are the lakes or seas fresh or salt water?"

"Yes," replied Doronno.

Talaka piped up, "What Doronno means is both—some are saline and some are fresh. Actually, around 70 percent are fresh, and the others are saline. I know that the saline seas have different life types in them than the fresh ones and also that they distill directly at the deep aquifer taps and convert the saline water to fresh. The fresh taps are produced for the irrigation they need, but some produce both saline for seas and fresh for irrigation."

"That's quite interesting," said Jack. "I had been wondering about that. They must have to do this on a huge scale to produce that much fresh water."

He thought, *Wouldn't that be handy on Earth for countries that were surrounded by salt water but had very little fresh water?* "Now I saw some weather systems when I first arrived, but I didn't see much of anything on my flight in the Kershavah, and I don't see anything now," said Jack.

"You must have arrived in the wetter season," said Talaka. "There is quite a bit more precipitation now on Nishda than there ever was previously. There didn't used to be any except a tiny amount for less than two moondats of the yenet. A couple of dakuns ago, there was only that and the locally engineered greenbelt rain, but now the planet is developing its own weather systems because of the higher water vapor content of the atmosphere."

Doronno said, "Now let's program an orbital altitude of seven hundred kahtaks with a track of 348E-P, and I'll get us a clearance." Jack now figured out that this designation would mean track 348 with an equatorial prograde orbit. Once again, *Carratta* climbed to the programmed orbit in less than four mentus. They'd climbed from a one hundred thousand mu-uts low altitude orbit to a seven hundred kahtaks orbit in nine mentus, thought Jack, and *Carratta* was just loafing. They were now at an orbital velocity of 7.50802 kahtaks per second and an orbital period of 1.64274 horuns. Doronno had them switch orbit four more times both up and down and then finally descend back to three thousand mu-uts. He ran Jack through two more climb and descent profiles with more track changes as well as a couple of emergency level offs. "We'll start working on some more emergency procedures tomorrow. I'll switch seats over to your side and you can take a little rest while I let Forto get some *Carratta* practice from the first pilot seat," said Doronno.

The next daiyus, they went over much of the same plus a good amount of low altitude manual flight maneuvering. They found a few little squawks that needed adjusting, but for the most part, everything worked perfectly. The fun part came when they ran the targeting tests for the guns, and after everything checked out, they decided to test-fire them on the desert. They fired a few single test shots at some hapless desert rocks that instantly disappeared in a blast of ionized plasma and dust. "I like 'em, I like 'em a lot," said Jack. Everything on the plasma cannons worked as advertised with no overheating or other issues, so they soon graduated to rapid fire bursts and combinations. They were having a good time tearing up the rocks and desert landscape. *Carratta* could be maneuvered to fly nose down with her thrusters while still maintaining a level flight vector so she could actually achieve a very good depressed targeting angle. The minus twenty-one degrees of the guns plus another thirty-five degrees nose low would allow her to target something that was fifty-six degrees below level flight attitude.

That would be plenty adequate by Jack's estimation, much better than an F-35 or F-22. Even Forto was having a good time. He'd never had any experience operating an armed ship before. "Yes, the shooting stuff in practice is always fun," said Jack, "but when you're shooting it up for real and the other guy is shooting back, it becomes a whole different ball ga— a whole different situation."

"You have been in a situation where other ships have been shooting at you?" asked Forto.

"Oh, yes," said Jack.

"Another ship was shooting at you?" asked Talaka. "Who was it? Was it the GTA or maybe pirates?

"No, oh, no," said Jack, "just a fighter, uh, ship, and enemy ground forces with missiles."

"Who were these that were shooting at you?" asked Forto. Jack was trying to figure out how to explain it but hadn't yet found anyone since this adventure had started that grasped nations fighting against other nations.

"Just, uh, bad people from other countries on my planet that wanted to harm the nation that I lived in, so our military, our soldiers, had to fight back."

"Vara is like this?" asked Doronno. "They fight among themselves on your planet? I've never heard of such a thing. Why would they do that?"

"No, not Vara," said Jack, "another planet, a planet called Earth. Nations have always fought against other nations for lots of different, usually stupid reasons, such as territory, religions, resources, sometimes misunderstandings and even for the ego of some of the nation's leaders, and a myriad of other usually senseless reasons."

"That is a very strange thing to even consider," said Doronno.

"Yes, I suppose it is," replied Jack, "but that's the way it is. Hopefully, someday, all the fighting will stop, but I doubt that it will in my lifetime."

"And you say your planet is called Irth?" said Talaka. "I don't believe I've ever heard of it."

"Me neither," said Forto.

"Nor I," said Doronno.

"And how did you come to be on Nishda?" asked Forto.

"It's a very long story," said Jack. "I'll tell you some other time when we're not engaged in training as we are right now."

After a couple of more horuns, they finished their training maneuvers for the daiyus and headed back toward Se-ahlaalu and Doronno's hangar. "We will cut it a little short today," said Doronno. "There are some business things I must attend to later, and this will give you more time to review for tomorrow's light drive exercise. Go over the procedures for programming and executing the light drive engines and for plotting and navigation with *Carratta*'s nav systems as well as the limitations for light drive transit in or near sol systems and other large gravitational and electromagnetic fields."

Later, Jack asked Forto if he wanted to go over the procedures for light speed flight, but he declined, saying he had some other things he had to attend to and that he was already familiar with it. *Maybe so,* thought Jack, *but I'm not and you're not as far as* Carratta *is concerned.* Jack could have ordered him to, but he decided to let it go for now and see what transpired. Jack dove into the light drive engines systems and operations manuals again to try and get a better grasp of his understanding of the technology and its operation. He ran some simulations, but he was sure the real operation would be much more intensive than the fairly simple steps in the ship's sim mode.

Seema had been very tolerant of being cooped up the last few daiyus, and she was starting to act a bit antsy. "OK, time for a break. Let's go out back of the hangar and let you run around some. You're probably getting hungry too, so we'll knock it off in a bit too." Seema managed to catch a couple of small ground rodents of some type out in the field behind the hangar. "You're a hoot to watch," Jack told her. She was fast and graceful, and her total concentration when hunting was a marvel to watch. With her radar-like ears unfurled, she must have been able to hear the most minute sounds. Jack still wondered if they furled to protect them just physically or also because of how sound sensitive they must be. Either way, it was fun to watch her in her element.

The next morning, they all arrived at the ship except Talaka. He'd told Jack that he wanted to go but had to meet with some business clients that had arrived from Tenaloo and Dimtoo, two of the Nishda system's outer planet outposts where they were doing some exploratory mining.

* * * * *

The next day, Doronno asked, "Well, are you ready for some high-speed trial runs in light drive?"

Jack liked Doronno's direct approach and personality. He didn't waste much time on formalities and expected others to know what they were supposed to be doing. "As ready as I'll be with just flying sims and reviewing the manuals," said Jack.

"Good, I'm sure you'll find this entertaining if you've never run an actual light drive ship in hyperspace before."

"No, only sublight ships," said Jack, not wanting to say just how far below light speed anything on Earth would actually be.

"Well, of course, the most important thing is to know exactly where you are at all times. It's extremely important to know your exact position in relation to all the local system planets and other bodies. This isn't normally a problem, but if you were to try and plot a course to another system and you were off, you could theoretically attempt to transit through a solid object, like a planet or moon or even a star, if your plot was off due to a position error. The quantum bubble is nearly impenetrable, but it isn't capable of penetrating something as large and dense as a planet, at least very far. Also if it were an inhabited planet, the inhabitants wouldn't be very appreciative of that amount of kinetic energy transfer to their planet—that is, if any of them were still alive to complain."

"Another important safety tip, thanks," said Jack.

Doronno replied, "It's not a likely scenario, since you are always well clear of most systems' heliospheres and the influence of the magnetospheres of the system's planets. In a worst-case scenario, if you're not entirely sure of where you are because of a minor quantum shift error or other anomaly, then you should make only short jumps well away from the current system. I'm talking about a ten or at most twenty light minutes at most in a projected clear direction so that *Carratta*'s nav system can reorient itself and be able to plot a safe course for your next transit.

"If you are even less sure of your situation and you don't know what's around you because you're in uncharted space, then you may need to spend a few horuns in sublight drive until you can get yourself into an area where the nav system can see and plot your position and you are sufficiently oriented. That might be tedious, but it may be the only safe option you have in some cases, unless, of course, you like high stakes gambling."

"Ummm, better safe than sorry," replied Jack.

"Yes," replied Doronno, "in uncharted or poorly charted space, it's quite easy for a projected track to look clear, but there are an infinite number of poorly detectable objects that could interfere with your navigation besides something as obvious as a star or planet."

"So you're saying if you're positionally lost, then you may have to make short jumps or sublight transits visually, away from whatever body or system you're near?" asked Jack.

"Not totally visually," replied Doronno, "although that could be required and at least helpful as far as verifying your track. You would use whatever resources you had available with *Carratta*'s systems, but if the nav system says you're here or there and there's not supposed to be this big planet sitting there, then it would behoove you to be skeptical and not transit through something you can obviously see."

"Sort of a trust but verify and use your best instincts," said Jack.

"Exactly," replied Doronno.

"The biggest error a ship's crew can make is trying to get too far into a system in light drive, even at minimum light speed. This may not be too much of an issue for a short transit jump, but the farther away the jump originated, the less reliable the estimated termination point will be. Since everything in space is constantly changing position in relation to everything else, then a calculated arrival point may not be where it was a few moondats or yenets ago as predicted by the nav computers, especially if the data is from a third-party source and has never been verified by *Carratta*'s nav system. It's much better to stop short of your destination on a long jump and then recalculate and make another jump closer to or just barely into the system if the area is clear. Yes, you can steer in light drive, but since you can't get a highly accurate position fix in the quantum bubble, you can only make general direction changes but not really accurate termination point plots. The more course changes you make in light drive, the more error there will be at the new adjusted termination point. Better safe than vaporized into a plasma smear, I always say."

"Good point," said Jack. "What do you mean by third-party data?" asked Jack.

Doronno replied, "Most of the nav data in *Carratta*'s database, as in nearly all of it really, since *Carratta* is new, is from other sources and hasn't been verified by *Carratta*'s own nav system except for Nishda's position and the system she originally came from where she was built. All the nav databases of the galaxy that are programmed into every ship are accumulated data from many thousands of ships that have all been accrued over time and sent to the GTA Navigation Data Bureau. There, it is analyzed and disseminated to navigation databases throughout the galaxy. It is all collected, collated, and distributed third-party data. Most of it is fairly accurate, but a lot of it hasn't been officially verified."

Doronno added, "There is also the issue that many ships and navigation systems are built by different races on different planets. Even though the data is required to be standardized, there may be differences in it due to less than perfectly standardized equipment or programming errors. You will likely see some minor errors when you cross-check *Carratta*'s verified data against the third-party data when you get to any new destination. If available, always use your own verified data or GTA verified data, but that will likely only be about 10 to 15 percent of the time especially out here in the far rim areas. There is a lot of uncharted space out there."

"I can just imagine. It is a big galaxy," said Jack.

"The nav data will display as verified or unverified anytime you plot a course with the navigation system. Heed that wisely. If a ship's nav data was corrupted or not completely accurate in some way and was then sent to the GTA Navigation Data Bureau, it could be sent on with the data error if it wasn't caught by the verification process. All that being said, what it really means is, don't jump too close to a system inbound especially if you've never been there in *Carratta* and verified the nav data personally."

"OK, that's also very good to know. I guess there are a lot of variables to consider out there in the Milky Way Galaxy," said Jack.

"Milky Way Galaxy?" said Doronno.

"Yes," said Jack, "that's what we call the galaxy on my planet Earth."

"Most interesting," replied Doronno. "Everyone just calls it the galaxy or wheel, or from the ancient language, it was called Unradda Agga Cirg, which means 'great silver wheel.'"

"Now that is interesting," said Jack, wondering what ancient language Doronno was referring to. He would have to come back to that later.

"What about changing destinations when you're already in light drive?" asked Jack.

"Yes, you can change your destination, but you don't want to do much tight maneuvering. Even in a quantum bubble at the speed you're transiting, you could end up someplace you weren't planning on being. If you're in an open area, you can change your destination but stop even further short of your new destination and recalculate. Better yet, just stop, recalculate, and execute a new course unless time is of an absolute essence."

"Whenever you change course in a quantum bubble in light drive, a small error will be induced because of the errors inherent within the quantum state itself. In reality, the quantum state is a different state of existence than normal space and it can sometimes shift or have displacement errors from the normal fixed or known coordinates of normal space. And of course normal space isn't stationary either so the accumulated errors between normal and quantum space are always cumulative and increasing. Those errors are even more cumulative if you change course multiple times while in the quantum state. Also since star plots are based on past positions, whether by moondats or yenets or more, the course calculation plots aren't that accurate to begin with."

Doronno continued once again. "Since the average star is transiting the galaxy from fifty thousand to over a million kahtaks an horun, then known positions will change constantly relative to every other galactic body. And don't forget, the galaxy is also traveling through space at a velocity of 2.7 million kahtaks per hour. Also since you are not really in known space but kind of close by but actually somewhere else, when you're in a quantum field, you can't get an accurate fix from a place where you really aren't. A lot of that is corrected in *Carratta*'s predictive database, especially in known systems, but then again, it is still just a predictive estimate. Just think of long-range navigation over vast distances in space as general destination locations and not absolute. I suppose you could think of it as driving to Wanana. You would stop at the edge of the city to locate an address deep inside the city. You wouldn't just blast through the entrance gate at two hundred kahtaks an horun without slowing to navigate the smaller side throughways and vimar passes."

"Hmmm, yes, that sounds like a very good analogy," replied Jack.

The theory discussion went on for a while longer. Then Doronno said, "OK, here's a list of five coordinates we'll practice plotting and jumping to today." Doronno gave both Jack and Forto the list of destinations they were to plot a course to. These are well clear of the Nishdan system and were in the middle of interstellar space or a moderately far destination system. No point in actually going anywhere other than locally, since the nearest system, Suufak, which isn't inhabited, is 3.2 horuns away. "We can plot some other destinations, though, for practice. Nishda is a bit remote, but it does have Burun-Rioc ore, which is essentially why we are all there."

"Yes, it does," said Jack, thinking of his amazing katanas, tantos, two ion handguns, and the ion plasma rifle he had stashed in one of his locked captain's cabin storage cabinets.

An horun later, they were landing feet up and heading to a geosynchronous orbit of 45,700 kahtaks above Nishda. "That will get us initially clear of any local Nishda traffic, and we can run multiple different plots while we head out of Nishda's system to where we can go to light drive," said Doronno. "It will take us 3.8 horuns to clear the heliosphere if we go tangent to the orbital plane of the system's planets."

They had already gone quantum as they were departing Nishda. Jack couldn't see much more than a slight shimmering with minimal distortion as they gazed down at the dusty-looking planet with the green and blue splotches all over it. "*Carratta*'s quantum field generator is very clean. There is almost no visual distortion as you can see," said Doronno.

"It's just amazing to me," said Jack. "You couldn't even pay for a view like this on my home planet."

"OK, now let's run through some plots," said Doronno to Jack and Forto. Doronno watched them as they each took turns entering and running the various plots. After two horuns of practice with lots of different variable and coordinates from all quadrants both near and far, Doronno said, "OK, I think you've both got that down quite well. We'll work on some systems knowledge for the next 1.8 horuns while we clear the heliosphere."

Not quite three horuns later, Doronno pointed out the display that verified they were just leaving Nishda's system and could go to light speed. Jack had watched earlier as Nishda had almost disappeared from the aft view display in about an horun and a half as they headed away from the planet and away from the Nishdan system. "OK, we're ready to try some actual light speed runs. We'll let Forto go first, since he's had some experience at this, and Jack can watch." Forto plotted a 2.4 light-year outbound run and established a proposed course, checked the core data for any known anomalies in the sector, and accelerated *Carratta* with the ion drive until a verified track was established.

"I read about establishing a track," said Jack, "but it didn't clarify why, which I thought was kind of strange that it didn't actually specify a reason."

"Go ahead," Doronno said to Forto.

"Well, it's best to establish a good track in sublight drive," explained Forto a little smugly. "You don't absolutely have to, but if you have a good track already established, you won't have to try and correct it while you're in light drive. There will be less possible induced error, and you will be less likely to have a termination point Coriolis drift error if you start out true. The error may be tiny to begin with, but it can be multiplied considerably on a long light drive run."

"That's correct," said Doronno. "And you won't get the unpleasant visual effect of the instantaneous heading change if *Carratta* isn't pointed in the direction of the light drive course when it's initiated as she attempts to correct for a larger error. It's quite unique in that you don't feel it but your eyes see it, and it will make your head spin if you're not anticipating it."

"It still makes me want to puke even if I know it's coming," said Forto. "It is much better to be tracking true to your planned course when you engage the drive."

As Doronno had previously explained, they'd gone perpendicular from the orbital plane of the system's planets to get away from the planets and sun's magnetic influence as rapidly as possible. It was also important that you exited any system in the direction of your desired course; otherwise, the system would still be between you and your destination. You could always do a short light speed hop away from the system to address that issue, but that wasn't the most efficient or safest way to navigate.

Jack could see the Nishdan sun dimming rapidly as it shrank in the display by the minute. They went over more theory and various techniques during the time outbound from Nishda in addition to their navigation exercises and systems review. "See the course line there," said Doronno.

"Yes, it changed from orange to blue," replied Jack.

"Yes," replied Doronno. "When it's blue, the display shows 'Light Drive Capable,' so we will be safe as far as interference from Nishda's system. We are also scanning for any unknown objects, ships, unknown anomalies, or stray tu-uraks," said Doronno. "It is more accurate because it takes into account more factors than just the distance from Nishda's sun and its heliosphere."

"Well, if there are actually any stray tu-uraks out here, they will likely hear us coming," laughed Jack.

"OK, Forto, if you're ready, go ahead and execute," said Doronno. Forto engaged the quantum light drive and . . .

Jack wasn't sure what to expect, but it wasn't like any of the *Star Wars* movies or other sci-fi flicks where the stars all suddenly blurred into long streaks that went blasting past you. Even at two thousand plus times the speed of light, you wouldn't get that effect with thousands of stars zipping by. What he saw was a slight pulling away of the visual star field and a momentary ten-septu intermittent flickering blanking of everything visual as *Carratta* transited from present time visual to quantum transit time visual. There was now a shimmering ethereal clear shell of energy encapsulating the ship. It looked somewhat rigid and fluid at the same time with fields of strangely colored, jerking, swirling, and arcing with patches and streamers semiopaque energy cascading over it. It had a slow overall flow from back to front, and the stars could still be seen through the shell. The stars were no longer points of light but slightly jiggling smears and swirls and oscillating mirages in varying places. They were beautiful but also slightly terrifying because Jack knew how unbelievably fast they were traveling. Just outside, the quantum bubble space was going by so fast that he couldn't think of a number to quantify it.

"It's somehow a bit mesmerizing, isn't it?" said Doronno.

"Very. It's quite amazing to think what's going on outside of it," replied Jack.

"Yes, it is nearly incomprehensible," replied Doronno. Their first termination point was twenty-eight mentus away, but there was no point in going all the way there, so Doronno had Forto terminate the run after another five mentus. There was actually a little more visual excitement coming out of light drive than going in. The quantum bubble was so stable once established that it took a bit of a destabilizing energy phase disruption jolt to come out of it. As Forto executed the light drive termination, there was a series of flashes and pulses outside the quantum bubble as the light drive engine generators transitioned from quantum space to normal space.

When they came out of quantum light speed hyperspace, they were still moving at a velocity of five hundred thousand mu-uts per second, or just over a million miles per Earth hour. "Now if we were entering a system and fairly far from our destination planet, we would just keep this velocity or maybe even increase it if we had a considerable distance to go," said Doronno.

"From our current speed, it would take just about three horuns to slow to an orbital speed with the constant four G deceleration of the main ion drive engines. We could do it in less time, but anything above a four G decel would be felt in a direct ratio above that—that is, if you wanted to decel or accel at six G's, you would have to endure a felt acceleration of two G's if you weren't using the quantum field. Since we are still in the quantum field but not in light drive, we can accelerate or decelerate at the limits of the sublight drive, which is a continuous 9.7G's. That is the thrust acceleration limit that *Carratta*'s sublight engines can generate to accelerate or decelerate. We took it easy on the way out so that you would have plenty of time to assimilate everything we were learning. The most important thing to remember, though, is to establish your precise position after terminating your light drive run. You can see that *Carratta* already has a solid position fix on the nav display but that she is now fine-tuning it in all three axes. When all nine readouts are less than 0.10 and within 0.02 of each other, then you've got a good reliable position fix."

"Why nine readouts for three axes?" asked Jack.

Doronno replied, "*Carratta* is using multiple inputs for each axis point and plots each point itself in a three-dimensional axis. Even out here in the middle of nothing, your position plot will be within less than about fifty thousand kahtaks. In any charted system, you will be within a thousand kahtaks within half a million kahtaks of a known charted planet or moon, and the error will continue to decrease the closer you get to a known fix. That is very accurate indeed."

"So it sounds," replied Jack.

"Of course, we are quite close to Nishda by galactic navigation standards," said Doronno. "If we were planning a two hundred light-year run, the accuracy would be considerably lower at the termination point for several reasons. The farther you plot and the less recent a system's position was updated, the less accurate the termination point solution will be. If you plot a course to a system that has never been accurately charted and logged in *Carratta*'s or the core's database, then it's more of a guess than an accurate plot. Stay well outside that system's heliosphere on your initial plot by a factor of at least ten. It's much better to sneak up on an uncharted or not well-known system than to come blazing in and hope for a safe arrival. You can always make another short jump to the edge of the system's heliosphere once you established an accurate fix from outside the system."

"Why would you ever want to accel or decel without the quantum field?" asked Jack.

"Well, you normally wouldn't, but I'm giving you hypothetical situations in case you run into a situation where you'd need maximum acceleration and you didn't have the quantum field established yet or perhaps some type of interference or malfunction was preventing it. Considering the line of work you are going into, it's good to know all of your available options."

"OK, that's very good information to know," said Jack.

"Yes, it could be important to you at some time," replied Doronno.

"Go ahead and plot a course to your next waypoint, then decel to orbital entry speed, then execute the new light drive course without establishing a new track vector for the course," said Doronno.

"Oh, do we have to do that?" pleaded Forto.

"Yes," said Doronno. "Jack should get at least one exposure to changing course without establishing a good matching track so that if he ever experiences it, he'll know what it is. You can take a break if you want and not watch it. Go back and tell Wehsh what we're doing," he said to Forto.

"OK, I believe I will," replied Forto as he got up and headed back to the galley area.

"It's not a very pleasant sensation," said Doronno, "but it's better to see it now than experience it later unexpectedly without any prior exposure."

"Well, OK, then, let's do it," replied Jack. "Is there any physical danger to the ship?" he added.

Doronno replied, "No, not really, but you will feel it as well as see it. Wehsh and Forto will feel it slightly, but without the visual disturbance anomaly, it will be mostly negligible. Even in the quantum bubble, the grav field doesn't compensate as well in rotational acceleration as it does in straight line linear acceleration, but the worst part is the visual aspect of it."

Jack plotted the new course while slowing as Doronno had said. "OK," said Jack, "ready when you are after you check my plot."

"Your plot looks good. Go ahead and execute." Jack executed the new course without the track matching it.

He felt a mild gut-wrenching twist as *Carratta*'s ion drive attempted to compensate and align with the new quantum course, which was independent of the ship's physical track. After pulling lots of G's in fighters, which was never an issue for him, this sensation was completely different and not good, not good at all. On the other hand, the visual aspect was really incredibly startling. He hadn't expected anything drastic from a mere heading change, but what he saw and what was added to the physical feeling was downright disturbing. It wasn't just a spinning sensation or a twisting of your head rapidly like a twirling ice-skater might experience; it was much worse.

Now his whole head felt like it was suddenly attached to some major league pitcher's high fast curve ball. *How long could this last?* he thought as his head, the view of the ship, and the outside suddenly melted into a multicolored blur of disassociated shimmering unreality. *What the hell,* he thought. *How could this all be correlated to a simple directional change of the ship in its quantum field?*

Oh, crap, he felt really nauseous; it felt like his mind had unwillingly left his body. Suddenly, it stopped as fast as it had started. His head was still spinning, but at least it was now attached to his body and in one place, more or less. *What, what the hell was that?* he thought again.

"We're back on track and aligned with our light drive course track," said Doronno. "That is a bit of a thrill, isn't it?"

"I'm not sure I'd exactly call it a thrill," replied Jack, "more like my soul was ripped from my body and put in a centrifuge to separate out the good from the evil."

"Hmmm, that's a good description," said Doronno, "maybe one of the better ones I've ever heard. Anyway, you can see why you want to avoid that error if you can."

"Yes, absolutely if you can. What's so strange is that with all the visual sensations, there is not that much felt acceleration, just a bit of unpleasant rotational force," said Jack.

"Well, it's a good thing that *Carratta* is shielded in a quantum field effect bubble because if you felt the actual forces outside of the bubble, well, you wouldn't likely feel it for very long because it would certainly make an instant mess of *Carratta* and all of her contents," said Doronno.

"Yes, that's the truly freakish part of the whole equation," replied Jack. He then asked, "Why do we get the bizarre effects like we just experienced, and why do you seem to tolerate it? Are you just used to it?"

Doronno replied, "It has to do with everything inside the quantum field having to be in the same alignment. If the quantum field bubble is generated without the contents of the field, in this case *Carratta* and everything in her being in the same phase alignment with the predicted quantum field vector, then everything within the field will try to align with the predicted field to comply with the unique physical laws within the quantum field. After the field has been established, then it becomes isolated from the outside influences and it behaves normally within in its own isolated environment. That is really what makes light speed drive possible. I did not actually experience the disorientation that you just did for a fairly simple reason," added Doronno.

"OK, and why is that?" replied Jack.

"Well, I closed my eyes just as you executed the jump, so my mind didn't have to try and comprehend what my eyes would have been seeing."

"OK, wow, I guess that would be one way to minimize the effect," said Jack.

"Yes, but it's not always that easy to do because you know what's coming. It would sort of be like closing your eyes when you know you are being attacked by one of those large predators in the greenbelt," said Doronno.

"Yes, well, I suppose that would be another very good analogy," replied Jack.

After several more nav plots and light speed jumps by both Jack and Forto, Doronno had them plot a course back to Nishda. They each made one run to the systems edge and then headed back to Nishda at sublight speed after their second approach run. As they settled in for the last part of the run into Nishda, Forto said, "Jack, uh, Captain, I, uh, tried to look up your home planet of Urth, just to see what it was like, since I, uh, we had never heard of it. I believe that's what you said it was—Urth, wasn't it? Well, I couldn't find anything on it, not even a planet called Urth. I was just curious as to what kind of a place my new captain had come from."

"Well, I really don't know why you couldn't find anything on it," said Jack. "Maybe there just isn't any information on it, or maybe you didn't look in the right places. Maybe it hasn't been discovered yet."

"What do you mean discovered?" said Forto. "Any world under GTA oversight would be in the data core, so there should at least be something on it."

Jack replied, "Well, as far as I know, no one on Earth has ever heard of the GTA either, so it's unlikely that Earth would have any association with the GTA or be under its oversight."

"Well, how can that be?" said Forto. "Every planet is under GTA oversight. I've never heard of any known planet that wasn't."

"Well, maybe Earth isn't a known planet. Don't worry about it for now. Just pay attention to our mission here and what we're doing right now. I'll explain it all later," said Jack.

After two uneventful approaches to the Nishdan system, they entered Nishda's arrival zone. Doronno went over the communications arrival requirements with Jack and explained the comm procedures and setting the assigned arrival code in *Carratta*'s transponder. "That's almost the identical arrival procedures for most installations back on Earth," commented Jack. "The equipment is just a little different."

"Nishda's arrival sensors are all passive," said Doronno. "You have to call them, get an arrival code, and then they can track you. Most planets are like that. Some planets have active tracking and can see you without calling them. They won't initially know who you are, so you will still need to call them and get an arrival code before you penetrate any of their published access zone boundaries."

"Is that part of their defense system?" asked Jack.

"Not necessarily, but it could be. It's more likely a traffic flow requirement at busier planets and their spaceports, monitoring for import violations, quarantines of specific contraband, or just general government arrival procedures and monitoring, and the usual government-approved harassment.

"Of course, there have been some contraband runners that have been known to skirt the legal entry process from time to time," said Doronno.

"And how exactly would they do that?" asked Jack.

Doronno replied, "Well, it would technically be illegal, of course—that is, if the planet had specific entry regulations, which they all do if they are under GTA control. These contraband runners would use a stealth mode of entry to the planet. They would use their cloaking capability like *Carratta* has and enter quietly in a less-inhabited area where they would be less likely be detected or reported. Then they would have to make a clandestine meeting with whomever they were dealing with or perhaps come in under some false pretense in an area that would likely not be monitored by the local authorities."

"And why would a ship like *Carratta* or any other ship have a cloaking capability if they are just going about their normal everyday commerce?" asked Jack.

"Oh, there are various legitimate reasons to run cloaked," replied Doronno.

"First of all, though, *Carratta* is not an ordinary ship. She's a bit of an anomaly in that she was really built as a high-end exploration yacht of which there aren't all that many constructed. There are a few pirates lurking around out on the fringes, and that is sort of where *Carratta* was designed to explore, so for safety reasons, Emnal Ramidew spared no expense and gave *Carratta* full cloaking capability. Pirates, and possibly others, would like nothing better than to get their hands on a fast and capable ship like *Carratta*. It would be a real windfall for them. Also as an exploratory ship, *Carratta* might want to sit quietly and observe some primitive culture or wildlife without drawing any attention to herself. Then also knowing that *Carratta* is a somewhat rare type of high-end luxury ship, Emnal Ramidew might have wanted to just enjoy his privacy and not have strangers snooping around her all the time for whatever reasons."

"That all makes sense," replied Jack. "So you're saying the cloaking works on the ground while *Carratta* is docked?"

"Partially, yes, the visual cloaking can be utilized but not the full electromagnetic spectrum, as this would cause blanking and possible shorting interference with any electronic systems in the vicinity of *Carratta*."

"What if there is nothing else around, just *Carratta* in the wilderness parked somewhere?" asked Jack.

"Yes, you could do that, but there would be a slight risk of *Carratta* blanking her own sensors due to feedback from the cloaking system, which is designed and tuned for use in space and atmospheric flight," said Doronno.

Doronno explained. "The visual cloaking works by restructuring refracted light pixels from around the ship back into a projected image of the surrounding environment somewhat like a giant HUD display. *Carratta* isn't invisible or doesn't disappear. It's just that the surrounding environment is projected around the ship. This effect can be accomplished from infinite angles by focusing a dynamic center point perspective from any point on the generated image's projected surface as viewed from any given point outside of the ship. That's about the extent of what I understand of it," said Doronno, "but it works quite well. From a distance of a hundred or so mu-uts, *Carratta* is nearly impossible to see visually. Up closer, you can begin to make out some shifting anomalies as the image overlap is updated toward all viewing points."

"I'll take your word for it," replied Jack. "Just show me the on/off button."

"You can program a remote control function into your translator when you leave the ship. You can then turn it off or on if you can't see the ship. That's a good feature. Hopefully, you'll be close, though, by marking your position in your translator HUD, but it would be good to have that backup option."

"What about approaching the ship with the visual cloaking armed?" said Jack.

"That isn't a problem," replied Doronno. "You can walk through the projected image in either direction. With *Carratta*'s perimeter defense system from the Kershavah ship, you will have both passive visual and active perimeter defense capabilities. It would be best to leave it at the lowest end of the nonlethal setting, though, as you don't want to fry any stray citizens that might wander into *Carratta*'s protected zone. It would be best to just gently leave any intruder wishing they hadn't attempted to breach the perimeter. Most any operational ship will have a similar but less capable system for security reasons. There is a warning mode that you can set to broadcast to anyone wearing a translator that they are entering a protected secure zone of a starship so that they don't get zapped first. Think of it as a courtesy warning to strangers."

"OK," said Jack. "I learned about inadvertently toasting the locals when I parked the Kershavah next to one of the greenbelts on the way to Se-ahlaalu. I accidently fried some type of small primates, and they weren't happy about it."

After an uneventful reentry and approach and landing, they headed up to Doronno's office for a little debrief and rehash of the flight. "So where is your planet Urth in relation to Nishda or any other charted nearby planets?" asked Forto when they were nearly finished.

"Well, I honestly couldn't tell you, since I didn't have access to any navigation instrumentation on the flight that brought me to Nishda," said Jack.

"Well, where is your Urth in relation to other planets we would know?" retorted Forto.

"Forto, I honestly don't know. Earth is outside of any influence of the GTA, and we were not aware of any of the planets I've learned about since coming to Nishda," replied Jack, trying to remain diplomatic.

"Well, that does seem sort of implausible, don't you think?" said Forto.

"Implausible or not, that's the truth," replied Jack. "What do you want me to do—make up some imaginary position? I have no idea where my home planet Earth is located in relation to Nishda or any other GTA planet. That's too bad, so sad for me, but entirely true."

"So then you just show up here in Se-ahlaalu with a stolen Kershavah provost ship and then turn around and buy *Carratta,* one of the most expensive and beautiful ships I've ever seen. That sounds beyond belief to me. I've never heard of such a thing."

Jack contemplated the conversation for a moment and then replied, "Well, there's plenty of things you've never heard of and plenty I've never heard of. That's what keeps things interesting. All this just seems to be the way things have worked out, and I'm very grateful that they did. In fact, I never would have imagined that things would have worked out for me the way they did either, but, hey, here I am, and, hey, here you are, and you get the chance to crew on the beautiful *Carratta,* and I get the chance to captain the beautiful *Carratta.* Shouldn't we just be grateful and thrilled by that prospect too?"

"I didn't say that I wasn't pleased to be on *Carratta.* It all just seems, seems, way too, I don't know what, unlikely," said Forto.

"Well, it surely does to me too, but I'm just going to go with the flow and see what happens. That's about all we can hope for sometimes," replied Jack. Then he added, "Why don't you just take the rest of the night off and we'll see you back tomorrow for some more light drive runs tomorrow? I know I need all the practice I can get."

After Forto had left, Jack said to Doronno, "What's your feeling on Forto? He seems a little disconcerted about the whole situation, and he doesn't seem happy with the information I've given him about Earth. Truthfully, that is all I know except for the mechanics of how I got here and the mine."

Doronno replied, "Forto's a good first pilot. He's a little high strung, but he's a bit of a detail person, so I guess he's not happy not having all the details. As far as having someone watch your back and keep track of details, he's very good at that."

"Somehow I feel like he's watching my back a little too closely for some reason," said Jack.

"I think it's just his way of reconciling his surroundings. I'm sure you'll get used to it," said Doronno.

"Well, if I wanted someone watching my every move that closely, I could have just stayed in the mine," replied Jack.

"Perhaps Forto is just a little nervous himself about having an inexperienced starship captain," said Doronno.

"Maybe," said Jack, "but you told him the conditions when he signed up for this position."

"I think he really just wants the chance to be on the crew of *Carratta* because he is so enamored with the ship," said Doronno.

"That may be the case," said Jack, "and I don't mind being questioned about my technical competency on the operation of *Carratta,* but that isn't really where his questions were leading."

"Just give him some time," said Doronno. "I'm sure he'll turn out to be a good first pilot once he is fully immersed in your operation."

"Let's hope so," replied Jack.

"Is that really true what you said earlier about your Earth not being under the GTA's oversight?" asked Doronno.

"Yes," said Jack, "we have never heard of anything like the GTA."

"That's amazing," said Doronno. "I haven't heard of any worlds not under GTA control. There must be a few pockets of remote worlds that haven't been polluted by the GTA. Now if you're not in the Trading Alliance, who does your Earth normally trade with? Are there other worlds that are not GTA controlled too?"

"No one," replied Jack. "Earth is a standalone planet, I guess that's what you would call it, and plenty polluted of its own accord. We are not even aware of any other inhabited worlds. Although we have suspected it for over a hundred years, we do not officially acknowledge the presence of life other than on Earth. Our Earth is the only planet in our solar system that supports life as far as we know."

Doronno stared at him for a minute trying to comprehend the information that Jack had just given him. "You are absolutely serious as far as what you're telling me?" asked Doronno. "Your Earth is an unknown planet not in the GTA, and it's isolated and trades with no one?"

"Yes, that's exactly what I'm telling you," replied Jack.

"Amazing, unbelievable, truly amazing," said Doronno. "How did you get here, then, on Nishda?" asked Doronno. Jack gave him the condensed version of his story including not being able to communicate and being accused of being a stowaway and being sold to the mine as a conscript. He left out the part about Zshutana, Junot, and being able to hack the translators.

Doronno thought about it for a bit and then said, "That is amazing. There might be a reason why your planet isn't under the GTA control. I will have to do some quiet research on it, but I'm guessing that your planet is not known by the name of Earth by the GTA. More than likely it has a different name, identification, and classification as possibly a primitive inhabited planet. It is unlikely that the GTA wouldn't know of a planet such as your Earth. It's strange, though, from what you've described, your Earth isn't really a primitive planet to be left alone for self-development. You've already done a considerable job of that based on what you've told me."

Doronno continued. "Planets must self-develop on their own up to a certain point, but then they are brought into the GTA and given advanced development help in exchange for resources and allegiance to the GTA. For some reason, your Earth has been bypassed. That is quite perplexing. I have never heard of an actual situation like this. I will look into it. One thing is for certain and that is that your Earth is not a developmentally stagnated world. If one of its inhabitants, who has never seen our level of technology, has landed in the middle the GTA-controlled galaxy and not only mastered it but also totally excelled at it in every respect, then you are not technologically or intellectually primitive in any way. That too is somewhat disconcerting. I wasn't really sure who or what you are, but Talaka vouched for you, and everything he's said has been proven. Now, however, you've added a truly strange and unknown enigma to a question that I didn't even know existed."

Doronno went on. "You've suddenly made my life considerably more interesting and added a great deal of intrigue to it."

"Well, I hope I haven't caused you any trouble by any of this," said Jack, not sure of his status with Doronno at this point. "Hopefully, this won't cause any problems with the acquisition of *Carratta,*" said Jack.

"No, no, not to worry at all. This merely heightens the level of intrigue and fascination with this situation and my involvement to an even higher level than I imagined. I thought I was merely involving myself in an interesting and dangerous but profitable illegal salvage operation, but I believe it goes far, yes, far beyond that now. I never would have guessed that this venture could become this thought-provoking and intriguing. I believe I have been blessed with a truly unique and potentially rewarding opportunity. For this, I actually thank you," said Doronno.

"Well, yes, I hope it will be too," said Jack, "and I hope it doesn't turn into a situation you would regret in the long term."

"No, that isn't how things work," said Doronno. "Rare opportunities like this seldom come but a few times in a lifetime, maybe only once or not at all for many if not most. We should be thankful for them regardless of whether they meet our own preconceived expectations or not."

"Thanks for understanding that," replied Jack. "I didn't ask to be put into these circumstances either, but they are what have been dealt to me, and I will do whatever I can to survive and, if possible, rectify my situation to the best of my ability. Frankly, there is nothing else I can do other than that."

Jack left Doronno's feeling like they had come to a good understanding of the situation that was acceptable to both of them. When he got back to Talaka's that night, he was informed by Talaka's wives that they would have additional guests for dinner. A while later, Talaka arrived with his two off-world guests whom he introduced to Jack. "This is Jack Spartan of Vara, a client of Doronno Fiashcolo. Jack Spartan is staying here while Doronno prepares a ship that he is having fitted out by Doronno's facility. Jack Spartan, this is Jeedah Teldor and Senefreh Ka Landas. They visit us from Tenaloo and Dimtoo, respectively, Nishda's two outer planet satellite exploration outposts. They are both assigned there as remote oversight agents of the GTA mining and exploration division. They've come here because we—the Se-ahlaalu Commerce Association, that is—are one of their support resources. This is both a boon for us and hopefully a great benefit for them as we seek to provide the best resources available for our GTA benefactors."

"It's a pleasure. Please just call me Jack. I hope you are enjoying your time here while you pursue your business here on Nishda," said Jack in a semiformal greeting.

"Yes, we are, and we hope to enjoy it in greater depth," said the one named Senefreh. "It is always a relief to get away from both of the outposts and onto a fully, well somewhat fully, inhabited and developed planet where one can indulge one's self in some of the more refined and entertaining activities similar to one's home world."

"I believe I understand exactly what you're saying in that respect," replied Jack in his best sympathetic tone. "I'm guessing, then, that the outposts leave a little to be desired as far as the finer indulgences one would occasionally desire?"

"Yes, an excellent deduction," replied the one named Jeedah Teldor. "Talaka here has helped us on several occasions to endure the rigors of our somewhat desolate but otherwise excellent career-enhancing positions at Tenaloo and Dimtoo. He always seems to know the best people to put us in contact with whenever we visit. It's much better than the time we went to Wanana for a holiday. Fortunately, we have enough seniority to take full advantage of our off time and get away for a few daiyus of, uh, relaxation on Nishda."

"Yes, and I'm sure you've well-earned that relaxation time here," said Jack.

"Indeed, we have, and time is of the essence," replied Jeedah.

"Well, as soon as my wives have treated you to one of the fine dinners they prepare, I will whisk you both off to the engagements we have arranged for you," said Talaka.

"Yes, as always, we are looking forward to both," said Senefreh Ka. "Perhaps Jack of Vara would care to join us on our adventures over the next several daiyus. I'm sure you would find it quite entertaining," said Senefreh Ka to Jack.

"I'm very sure I would, and I would love to if I wasn't scheduled for more early proving runs over the next two or three daiyus. I thank you for the consideration of the invite. However, duty calls, so I must pass," replied Jack.

After the fine dinner, Talaka delivered his off-planet guests to their appointed engagements and returned back home. "Very nicely played," he said to Jack. "I didn't get much warning of their arrival, and I wrongly assumed from their messages that they would want to go directly to their entertainment, which I had to arrange for them. I didn't get to tell you anything about them and their impending visit. Apparently, they enjoyed their dining experience here last time and expected more of the same."

"No problem at all," replied Jack. "So they are GTA functionaries that are assigned to the outposts of Tenaloo and Dimtoo as some sort of oversight monitors from what I gathered?"

"Yes, they're harmless enough, basically just low-level GTA snoops that watch over some of the low-priority exploratory operations for mining and research. They are able to get a few daiyus off every six moondats or so. They come here with the excuse that that they're on a resource and support mission. All they're really interested in is getting together with some of the local talent from the entertainment district that provides those activities in the old section of Se-ahlaalu."

"Well, that's no different from anywhere else I've ever been," said Jack. "Cooped-up workers of any sort need to blow off some steam every now and then."

Talaka started to ask, "So did you, uh . . ."

"Copy their translator IDs?" replied Jack. "Yes, it's very simple. If I'm within about ten mu-uts, I can read and copy anyone's complete ID profile and store it in a library bank for later usage."

"Well, be very careful with that capability," said Talaka. "It's not something you'd want the provosts or any GTA agents to know you have."

"Don't worry, I'll be as careful as possible," replied Jack.

"That would be a very interesting capability to have," mused Talaka, "very interesting but dangerous."

"Well, if everything I plan to do works out and I can get back here, I will have my genius friend modify your translator like mine, and then you can do the same thing," said Jack.

"That would be interesting, but I would have to think about that. It sounds interesting, but it might also be one of those 'don't touch or you might burn your fingers from the fire' type of things that one should just leave alone. I'll have to consider that to some extent," said Talaka.

"There's now another favor I would ask of you, since you've been so good with all the others," said Jack.

"Go ahead, I know it will only be something fascinating for me to ponder," said Talaka.

"The credit account that you were able to set up for me under the name of Desdewah Annilar Ri, would it be possible to get possibly two or three more accounts like it with different names?"

"Well, yes, the people I know that do that can always come up with more, since that's what they do. It is just a matter of time, timing, and credits to get them set up. Why do you believe you will need more accounts?" asked Talaka.

Jack answered, "I'm going to go make a concerted effort to recover all my fight pit winnings along with my friends and their considerable winnings. I'm not sure what I'll have to do to get some or all of them back, but it may not be exactly conventional, if you understand what I'm saying. If I am able to recover these credits, I want to spread them around, as in move them around to keep them from being encumbered by the mine bosses or their GTA associates. What I need to do is be able to move and hide the funds as much as possible within their own system so they can't easily track them. Of course, the problem I have is I don't have much up front credits other than my four hundred thousand for operating expenses. I can use those funds to pay for the accounts, or if you can loan me that amount, I will pay you back with interest," said Jack.

"With interest? Hmm, now there's that interesting concept again," said Talaka. "That sounds like a whole new business concept to investigate. Yes, I can loan you the credits for that. It would probably be the same fee, I would say, the same 50,000 credits for each. If you want three, it would be 150,000 credits, of course."

"That would be fine," said Jack. "Perhaps you can negotiate them down to maybe 120,000 for a quantity discount."

"Now that's an idea too. I will have to give that a try," replied Talaka.

The next three daiyus were spent practicing approaches and departures and light drive runs with *Carratta*. "I don't think there's much else I can teach you operationally about *Carratta* other than refinements and smaller details," said Doronno. "You've got all the systems down better than I do, and everything I've shown you seems to come second nature to you. All the techniques you've learned can be used at any arrival and departure destination with what is in the data core for most anywhere you would go. Forto will be able to help you considerably, and everything else, you'll have to learn by experience."

"I'm not sure I feel as ready to graduate as you think I am," replied Jack. "There is an amazing amount of things out there in the galaxy that I have no experience with at all."

Doronno replied, "Well, most of the things you might run into are going to be in *Carratta*'s stored data core, so you won't be without guidance. Still, it will be a challenging environment because you won't always be doing easy cargo runs from planet A to outpost B. Still, there's no doubt you'll run into some situations that aren't in the data core."

"I guess if I run into something I can't figure out, I can just phone home," chuckled Jack.

"Phone home?" said Doronno.

"Forget it," said Jack, "I'm just laughing at myself."

"Now for the fun part," said Doronno.

"And that would be what?" said Jack.

"The legalities and requirements of being a certified courier and licensed transit carrier who is authorized to operate at any of the GTA sanctioned spaceports out there. We will need to register *Carratta* in that category so that the GTA can get its fair share of any of the usage fees you'll be assessed anytime you use a spaceport that is under the GTA's jurisdiction."

Jack winced at the thought of more bureaucratic paperwork nonsense. "Is that all really necessary for what I'll be doing?" he asked.

"For the most part, yes," said Doronno, "you'll probably enter and access most of your commercial transactions through any of the main spaceports on most planets probably 90 percent of the time. Only if you're making a clandestine transaction would you ever avoid a spaceport with GTA oversight. Don't worry, they aren't that pervasive as far as monitoring what any given ship might be doing. Most of the GTA observers will be like our two love-enamored friends that were just here and are only interested in their own little agendas. As long as you pay the landing or other assessment fees, they will generally leave you alone. As long as the customs and oversight functionaries don't have to get off their lazy lower sides and investigate someone that hasn't paid their fee or use tax, then they won't likely bother you.

"Their job is simply to collect fees for the GTA. As long as they are accomplishing their job and getting paid, they won't care too much about anything else unless it's a totally blatant issue of some sort. You might get an occasional young enthusiast who thinks they are doing some vital duty, but that would be rare. Most of these types of jobs go to politically connected or other favoritism or nepotism types that have little motivation to do anything but collect their pay. Most of the time, they would rather watch something they deem entertaining on their desk vido display. Your best approach is to just play the GTA game and keep the lazy functionaries from having to get out of their chair. If you do run into a more intrusive type, it's usually that they are looking for a small, shall we call it gratuity of perhaps fifty credits or so that you can buy them off with."

"OK, I get it," replied Jack. "So how much does the rest cost, and how do I pay it?"

"Well, that will depend on where you go and what facility you use. On average, I would say the GTA access fee will vary from five hundred to a thousand credits. Then you will have to pay the use fee to whatever the company or local government is that runs the spaceport. You will also have various services available at any of the places you'll go, and it's probably wise, for protocol reasons, to get at least some token servicing or provisions anyplace that you stop, especially if it's for more than just a quick cargo pickup or some sort of quick turnaround like that. On average, I would say you will have to spend around a thousand to fifteen hundred credits at any place you stop long enough to look for contracts or spend a daiyus or two reprovisioning.

"Generally, the daily fees aren't too bad because they'll get most of their payments up front when you dock. Anytime you arrive in a system, you will contact the spaceport for a dock assignment. Based on what you'll be trying to get for contracts, you won't need to go to any of the higher fee docks. Something in the lower class D or E cargo zones would most likely work for you, but stay away from the F and G docks unless they're the only thing available. Those, especially the Gs, are usually just off-loading locks for shuttle to orbit cargo transfers. *Carratta* wouldn't fit in there too well with the container shuttles and would likely draw too much attention there. You may need to venture in that direction, though, if you're looking for a more clandestine cargo run. The A and B docks are generally pure passenger docks for dignitaries and the rare private yacht like *Carratta*. She would easily blend in there, especially on the B docks if she were configured purely for passenger or executive carriage. Most of the time, you'll want to be in the C or D docks, but you could go up or down a grade without drawing any undue attention to yourself."

"That all sounds pretty straightforward," said Jack, "but how do I go about finding contracts and getting paid for *Carratta*'s services?"

"That will vary according to your situation," said Doronno. "Some clients will pay 50 percent up front with the balance paid on delivery. Some won't want to pay anything until you deliver. In both cases, you won't release the cargo until they've paid in full at the destination. They may want to inspect the cargo on arrival to make sure it isn't damaged or hasn't been tampered with. Passenger and courier service would normally be paid up front with a stipulation for time and condition of anyone or anything transported. Failure to meet the conditions stipulated would result in a partial or total refund to the client based upon the conditions of the contract. If a courier message or client has to be somewhere in a specific time frame, which is normally based on coordinated galactic time, then you'll have to meet the conditions for the full fee stipulation."

"OK, I don't like dealing with this sort of stuff, but I suppose I'll get used to it or I'll pawn it off to one of the crew members if I can," said Jack. What happens if I complete a contract and the client doesn't want to pay at the end?"

"Well, that's up to you. You can file a complaint with the GTA Trade Commission Office, but if you don't think the client will be able to pay, then there wouldn't be much point to that and you may just have to write it off or possibly take the cargo somewhere else and try to sell it if you think it has some value. This would put you in a gray area as far as legalities, so you would want to get a declaration from a port official that states that the recipient has refused to pay for the shipment. Of course, that may not be available depending on the type of operation you are running at the time. Hopefully, that won't happen, but it could. As you can see, there are many variables involved. Now, if you decide to take some less than, let's call them reputable contracts, then, of course, anything is possible, and you'll have to deal with the situation in whatever manner you think will give you the best outcome. One thing is for certain, though."

"What's that?" said Jack.

"You're going to have some interesting times. I almost wish I could go along to see what type of interesting exploits you might find yourself in," laughed Doronno.

"Well, you're certainly welcome to accompany us especially as we're just starting out all wet behind the ears now," said Jack.

"Wet behind the ears . . . hmfmm," laughed Doronno. "Thanks for the invitation, but the key word in my statement was *almost.* I really wouldn't mind a little adventure, but I have too much going on here and too many schedules to meet. You are taking my first pilot and an excellent tech too, which isn't really going to hurt me but isn't going to help things around here schedule-wise either."

"OK, and I do very much appreciate that, but if you change your mind, the offer stands, and I do appreciate all you've done to help me out in this venture," replied Jack.

The next two daiyus, Jack spent going over the fit out and provisions with his crew of two. Doronno had *Carratta* registered as he'd said, so the bulk of the paperwork was now complete. Talaka let Jack know that he had two more bootlegged GTA credit accounts in the works for Jack and that it would probably take another two to three weneks to get them set up and to find another one. Talaka also had some connections in the shipping business and put out word that he had some high-speed discreet transport available for hire. Jack also registered *Carratta* with the local space transport board and listed *Carratta* as available for hire and posted a suggested but negotiable fee schedule based on information Doronno researched on the current fee postings for similar services.

"Now I wouldn't really try to undercut any of your potential competition out there," said Doronno. "That might get you some clients but probably not very good ones, and you might not be able to make enough to meet your payment schedule. Your selling point will be what a great ship *Carratta* is. *Carratta* is new and fast, and anyone would love to ride on her. You will have a unique market niche, so you might as well try to exploit it. There are some fast transit ships but not many that can carry a decent cargo load. There are plenty of cargo hulls floating around out there but none as fast and attractive as *Carratta*. Most of them are much larger and are on scheduled runs that need to be contracted in advance.

"I don't think you will find much competition for on-demand charter with a fair cargo capability. What you are trying to do is somewhat unique, so you should be able to command a premium fee. The only time you might consider taking a lower fee is if you are offering to depart from a location you are currently at after completing a contract and don't have anything arranged for another run. Also if you just happen to be going somewhere with another contract and someone wants to just happen to want to go that way or at least in the general direction, you could offer them a discount. Then you also might be able to offer up some fast transportation to someone that better fits their schedule than the scheduled transports that they would have to wait another wenek or more to catch. Then you could offer a discount price on a chartered ship they wouldn't otherwise be able to afford but not less than what they would pay for a bulk transport. These would just be side contracts to whatever your main contract would be, bonuses basically to help your profits. Some of your best possibilities will be when some cargo or person has to be somewhere as soon as possible, but there is no direct service or no scheduled service to that destination for daiyus or weneks. That will definitely command a premium fee depending on the client."

Jack was just beginning to think he had this somewhat figured out, at least in theory, which, of course, was usually enough to get you in some serious trouble by his estimation. Jack decided it was now time to go out solo with just his crew for a couple of half-daiyus runs to practice on their own. They repeated some of the inbound and outbound arrivals and departures just to refine what they'd previously done. He also plotted runs to various other destinations for the practice of researching the destination's arrival procedures and the programming of the navigation coordinates. They even initiated a couple of the runs and then terminated them after a short time just to practice aborting a run and then recalculating an amended return to Nishda and other destinations. Forto seemed somewhat bored by the exercises but agreed with Jack that Jack needed all the practice he could get. Wehsh Hevedu was just happy to be away from the daily grind of production schedules at Doronno's shipyard.

The next daiyus, Doronno told Jack that *Carratta*'s previous owners wanted to know when *Carratta* was expected to be deemed operational so that they might anticipate when their payments might start arriving for *Carratta*. "Well, I suppose we could say anytime," said Jack, "but maybe you could convince them that we need to wait until we get our first contract run. I don't know if they'll buy into that, but we could try."

"I will suggest that to them and see what they say, but I can't guarantee anything," replied Doronno.

"OK, that's all I can ask," said Jack. "In the meantime, I'm going to try and recover some of my winnings I told you about earlier."

"How are you planning on doing that?" asked Doronno.

"I'm not exactly sure," replied Jack, "but I have a few ideas forming in my head."

"OK, but I would caution you about doing anything drastic that would get us all in trouble. We didn't help you get set up with all this just to watch you get taken down for doing something, uh, something rash."

"Believe me, I understand," said Jack. "I have no intention of doing anything that would endanger anyone here after all the effort and help you've so generously given me." Jack spent the next daiyus mulling over the plan he'd been running through his head for the last week then decided it was time to act even if it was something that might be deemed a bit risky.

The next daiyus, Jack went to Doronno and laid it out for him. "How exactly is any particular ship identified when it enters a system and approaches a planet to request a dock assignment? I know you will call and ID yourself, but are there other ID functions that the ship provides on arrival?"

"Yes, of course," replied Doronno. "In addition to your call sign and the transponder code you are assigned for, the arrival the ship will broadcast a unique discrete code assigned to it by the builder or facility that assigns the ownership documentation."

"So *Carratta* was assigned a discrete number by her builder before she arrived here?" asked Jack.

"Well, no, *Carratta* hadn't been assigned a discrete code yet, since she hadn't been finished and assigned to her new owner yet. We actually just assigned *Carratta* a new discrete code when we did the contract with Emnal Ramidew's family for the sale to you and registered it with the contract GTA documents recorder in Se-ahlaalu."

"So you can program the discrete code here?" asked Jack.

"Yes, we would do that with any new or sometimes a used ship we register to a new owner," replied Doronno, sounding a little apprehensive of Jack's questions.

"So are these discrete codes all in some big database that every spaceport has access to?" asked Jack.

"Eventually, they are as the list is updated and disbursed to the various planets through courier-updated data dumps."

"So a new ship that originates from some remote planet might show up here at Nishda and not be in the database of the local spaceport as far as who it's registered to?" asked Jack again.

"Yes, that's highly possible, not necessarily probable but possible," replied Doronno.

"OK, here's what I want to do," said Jack as he ran his idea past Doronno, "and I want you to run it by Talaka to see what he thinks so that you don't think I'm crazy."

"I already think you are crazy," said Doronno, "kind of frighteningly crazy, but I think I like it, and it will keep us from being implicated if it doesn't work, at least I think it will. What about Forto and Wehsh Hevedu?"

"I won't let them in on it. I know that doesn't sound fair, but if they don't know, they can't really be implicated," said Jack.

"OK, that sounds slightly reasonable. You have a devious mind but in a good way, I would say," said Doronno. "One thing is for sure—things have sure taken a turn toward the improbable since you showed up here, Jack Spartan of Earth."

Jack replied, "Well, I aim to please, I do aim to please. And one other thing," said Jack, "I want the ship's security system access locked to me and me alone, except maybe to yourself as a backup. I'm not saying I don't trust other potential crew members, but I don't necessarily trust the other potential crew members, if you know what I mean, at least for now and until they've proven themselves. No one gets access to *Carratta* unless I authorize it directly through her security system. I don't want any secondary authorization access capability through other crew members, but I do want the ability to alter anyone's access myself if need be."

"That's easy enough. I'll have that programmed by tomorrow. I guess you can't be too certain under the circumstances," replied Doronno.

"No, there is just too much at stake under our current situation to leave anything to chance," said Jack.

"I will also set the access for you to program the discrete registration number for you on *Carratta* so you can change that when necessary," added Doronno. "I won't bother warning you about the implications of getting caught doing that."

"Thanks, I understand," said Jack. "Also, are there any specific discrete code series that are for specific types of ships, let's say freighters, yachts, dignitaries, military ships, GTA ships, or are the discrete codes just randomly assigned numbers?"

Doronno looked at Jack for a minute, knowing to some degree what he was contemplating now. "Yes, there are certain prefixes and designations associated with certain types of ships that are assigned when a ship is registered or commissioned. Somehow, this is getting more convoluted by the mentu. I'll get you a list of the various designators for ship types tomorrow also," replied Doronno, thinking about what a crazy situation he was now involved in.

Chapter 13: Deception

"Take tomorrow off," Jack told Forto and Wehsh. "Then on Trisday, we're going to make another local practice run or two to work out some new procedures I've been thinking about."

"What kind of procedures?" asked Forto.

"Some possible discreet arrival and departure procedures that may help us with our upcoming operations," said Jack, knowing he had to give Forto something or Forto would keep prying until he did get something.

The next daiyus, *Carratta*'s security access was programmed as Jack had requested, and Jack now had the access code to get into *Carratta*'s discreet registration program and list of prefixes for the various ship and mission types assigned throughout GTA space. Jack thanked both Doronno and Talaka that night for all their help. Talaka told Jack the other credit accounts were in the works, but he didn't think they'd be set up before Jack left on his first run. "That's not a problem. I probably won't need them for a while," said Jack.

"Make sure you get back to us and let us know what happens as soon as you can just in case we need to take some evasive action on our part," said Doronno.

"Don't worry," said Jack, "I'll be on it as soon as possible. If you don't hear from me by twenty-two horuns on Foursday, you can assume that I have run into some sort of trouble. I probably won't be able to contact you discreetly, but I can get a signal to you through the standard Nishda comm links." They then proceeded to work out several code words that meant different things other than the benign chatter that they sounded like.

"Your mind works in unique ways that seems accustomed to this type of activity," said Doronno.

"I have some experience in clandestine communications procedures and intel ops," said Jack. "Also since I've been on Nishda, it's almost been a full-time job thinking of ways to outsmart the mine bosses and their GTA accomplices." Doronno and Talaka wished Jack a safe and successful venture, and Jack thanked them for making it possible.

The next morning, Jack and his crew of two along with Seema had preflighted *Carratta*, boarded, and were ready to launch at 0800 horun, Se-ahlaalu time. "Where are we going today?" asked Forto as they were prepping *Carratta* for takeoff.

"Just an out and back training mission, but I've got some twists to add to it today to make it interesting," replied Jack.

"What kind of twists? What do you mean?" said Forto.

"Well, it'll be a surprise," said Jack. "It wouldn't be as interesting if I didn't make a surprise out of it. The more realistic the training, the more we will learn from it. Just go along with whatever I come up with, and it will be more fun than the straight old plotting and basic nav exercises we've been doing that you've been bored with up until now."

Just for the fun of it, they initially plotted and executed a run to the Benuvah system, a system over thirty thousand light-years away that Jack had certainly never heard of and none of the others were familiar with either. After a fifteen-mentu run with some course changes in hyperspace, they plotted a run back to Nishda. On their way in, Jack gave a new order to Forto. "Let's set a course for the spaceport at Wanana for something different for today's arrival."

"Wanana? You want to go to Wanana?" asked Forto somewhat surprised but more as a confirmation.

"Not necessarily, but we can set up an arrival just for practice, since it's something different from what we've been doing at Se-ahlaalu," replied Jack.

"Yes, Captain, new coordinates after Nishda system entry and position update plotted. Ready to execute run to Wanana when position update is verified," responded Forto.

"Very good, Forto," replied Jack. "Ship status update, Wehsh?" added Jack.

"All systems optimal, Captain. Nothing but perfection coming out of *Carratta*'s systems, as expected," replied Wehsh.

"Very good, Wehsh, continue as planned," replied Jack. Jack had already switched *Carratta*'s discrete registration code during the midflight navigation exercise to Nishda.

"OK, gentlemen, we are going to attempt a clandestine entry to Nishda for our exercise. Since we may have to attempt something like this during our cargo operations, we might as well give it a try here on Nishda and see how it works out for us. Now Wanana doesn't know *Carratta* or who we are, so we are going to try our entry under a different call sign and see if we can pull off this little deception."

Forto spoke up first. "That's probably not a good idea. What if they try and, uh, make us verify who we are? What if they board us for an inspection and find out who we really are? I don't think—"

"Relax, Forto," said Jack, "this is just a partial trial run. We'll be OK, and besides, you knew that some of the missions we might be making would possibly be a little more than routine cargo runs."

Forto replied, "Yes, but entering a spaceport under a false ID, we probably can't fool anyone that—"

"It's OK, Forto. Just follow my orders and it will work itself out just fine, I promise. If for some reason things don't seem right, we can just disappear back to space and come back on the other side of Nishda to Se-ahlaalu. People are always more perfectly willing to believe you than disbelieve you so they won't have any reason to doubt who we are unless we give them a reason to. We need to test this type of approach to see how well it works, so we might as well give it a shot here where we know how things work. Just do as I say and we'll learn how to cope with these types of situations," said Jack. "How about you, Wehsh? Any concerns?" said Jack.

"No, this sounds kind of interesting. Maybe they'll have some Hunarnar food near the dock we get. I haven't had any Rimpalé or Kimba in a couple of yenets since I was on the trader *Gehnnaka*. Oh, and what do you mean by *gentlemen?*" added Wehsh.

"Oh, just an Earth language word for formally addressing your entire crew," replied Jack. "It sort of means like an upstanding or good crew, whereas if I said, 'Heave to you scurvy swabs,' that would be a less than complimentary way to address a crew."

"OK, well, I guess we'll take the first one, then," replied Wehsh.

"Good choice. You'll be picking up my Earth sayings in no time," said Jack. "You can have the landing, and I'll handle the comms," Jack said to Forto. As they approached the designated comm point, Jack keyed the mic and transmitted the interrogation request to Wanana spaceport arrival. "Wanana arrival, Cenzar ship *Tentah-eh* requesting arrival code and class A dock assignment, estimated arrival in sixty-eight mentus."

"Cenzar ship, that's a GTA dignitary call sign," blurted Forto.

"Yes, I know that," replied Jack. "Remember you're supposed to relax and watch and learn how we're going to be making clandestine arrivals."

"Yes, but a GTA dignitary call sign, that's not very clandestine. You're going to get us in some real trouble," moaned Forto.

"Welcome, *Tentah-eh,* squawk code 11387. We'll have a dock assignment for you shortly" came the reply on the main comm link.

"Thank you, Wanana. *Tentah-eh* squawking 11387, standing by dock assignment."

"See, easy, nothing to it," said Jack to Forto. "Maybe we'll be having some of that Rimpalé and Kimba shortly."

"Easy, well, well, easy until they find out we're a cargo yacht out of Se-ahlaalu five mentus after landing," said Forto.

"Relax and watch, Forto. You're making it hard to concentrate on my acting career here," said Jack. Jack keyed the mic link again. "Wanana arrival, *Tentah-eh* will be dropping low on entry to observe the local terrain. We may be below comm link altitude for a short time."

"Understand, *Tentah-eh,* call arrival control before entering the arrival for Bandu corridor at designated point Jolba."

"Understand, we will report before point Jolba for the arrival," replied Jack.

"Now what are you doing?" asked Forto.

"I'm executing my plan. Watch and learn, Forto," replied Jack, hoping that Forto would ease off and get with the program.

They dropped down to 200 mu-uts, nearly 1,100 kahtaks from Wanana. Jack headed close to the Corodune mine complex but not directly at it. About a hundred kahtaks from the mine, Jack called Wanana arrival again. "Wanana arrival, this is *Tentah-eh,* do you hear us?"

"Yes, *Tentah-eh,* we hear you, go ahead," replied the Wanana arrival controller.

"We are having a problem with our number three ion drive maneuvering module overheating. We may have shaken something loose during the reentry with all the turbulence. We are going to shut it down and land and inspect it. We want to try to avoid doing any serious damage. We see a mining complex about eighty kahtaks out. We will land there just in case we need any assistance. Can you call them and advise them of our status and our intention to land there? We are not, repeat not requesting any assistance at this time. Do you hear us?" said Jack.

"Yes, we hear you. We will advise Corodune that you will be landing there and may need assistance but not currently at this time," replied the Wanana controller.

"There, now Corodune will be getting official word from Wanana approach that a GTA dignitary or some type of official ship will be landing near the mine complex so we don't have to convince anyone of who we are," explained Jack. "Also they probably don't really want to have to deal with us anyway, and since we have not requested assistance, they will be happy to comply and leave us well enough alone."

"Yes, but why are we landing at a mining complex? What's the point of that?" asked Forto.

"It's just part of the exercise," said Jack. "We don't really want to go into some busy place like Wanana until we get a little practice on some less strict places like a mine complex town. We need to find out what sort of inspections or tactics the various spaceports and other places may have. We probably won't be able to find enough easy straight-up totally legitimate contracts for *Carratta,* so we have to push the envelope as far as the kinds of cargo and operations we are willing to take on. The only way to get more of those types of potentially lucrative contracts is to learn how to operate in an environment where we're likely to find them. I also don't want to pay a class A dock fee in Wanana, so we'll just skip that altogether for now. I told you earlier that I was going to throw some twists into this exercise, so we all need to play the part and handle this situation as best we can. Got it?" asked Jack.

"Yes, OK, it just seems a bit excessive if we are not really getting anything to transport," said Forto.

"Practice, remember practice makes perfect," said Jack. "How about you, Wehsh?"

"Sounds good to me. I haven't done anything this interesting in, well, maybe ever," he replied.

"Don't worry, I guarantee I'll keep it plenty interesting enough for you," said Jack. "OK, Forto, you've got *Carratta* for the landing. The main entrance to the mining complex is to the west of the completely walled mine and town operation. Let's set down about two kahtaks outside the wall. That will keep all but the most curious from snooping around us and give us time to react if we see anyone coming. If they think we're a GTA ship, they'll keep their distance." Forto seemed to be a little more enthusiastic now that he was going to get the next landing. "Don't worry, Wehsh, we'll get you some takeoffs and landings sometime soon too," said Jack.

They made their approach and landing as Jack had specified and went through their shutdown checklist. The Corodune security operations office called them on a local standard comm frequency to verify that they didn't need any assistance. Jack thanked them and told they were OK and that they would be there for a while checking on their damaged maneuvering module and that they would give them a call if there was anything they needed. "We may come in for some supplies or food later if we get the ion drive problem under control," Jack advised them.

"Thank you, and please check in at the entrance gate if you do" was all the security ops replied.

"See, that wasn't so bad, was it?" Jack said to his crew as he excused himself from the flight deck.

Fifteen mentus later, he came back to the flight deck wearing one of the disguises Talaka's wives had made up for him. "Who, what, who are you?" said a startled Wehsh when Jack appeared. Jack was decked out in colorful long robes with an official uniform look to it. Under the robes, he had a short tanto sword and one of the ion pistols from the Kershavah ship. He hoped he wouldn't need either, but, well, it was better to have it and not need it . . . His hair was now white and long, and he sported various mottled stripes and circles on his now dull orange-and-red complexion.

"It's just me," said Jack. "How do you like my Dunorian look?"

"How, what, why are you dressed like that for?" said Forto with some disbelief.

"Talaka's wives made this up for me. I don't want to go strolling in there just looking like myself. If I look more like a GTA dignitary, then it will be just that much more convincing. If we ever have any issues with our presence here, then this appearance will be the description or images they have to go by instead of the real me. They'll have nothing else to go on. The only thing they have is what *Carratta* looks like, and there could be several ships that are similar to her out there somewhere too. No sense in giving away anything we don't have to."

Jack continued. "Now I want you two to stay here with the ship. Someone, take Seema out around the ship for a few mentus for a short walk—that'll add to our mystique. Forto, run the pretakeoff checks and keep the ship ready to launch. I'm going to go into the mine complex in the vimar and snoop around some. Maybe I'll find some of that Hunarnar food for takeout, but don't bet on it. I'll probably be in there for about three horuns, give or take. I'll call you in three horuns to update you or possibly sooner. If you don't hear from me in that amount of time, you can assume something may have happened. If a security contingent comes out to the ship, be ready to launch, but don't until you find out what they want. Don't let them get *Carratta*. I'll find a way to get back to you if anything goes bad. Got all that, swabbies?" said Jack. Both Wehsh and Forto answered in the affirmative.

Jack headed into Corodune in the blue vimar from Talaka. It wasn't quite dignitary quality, but the guards at the mine had probably never seen a GTA dignitary, so that wouldn't matter. He checked in at the main security gate and asked directions to the main parking area for the mine even though he knew where it was. Three mentus later, he parked the vimar and headed straight to the Dirga level retail area and to Zshutana's apartment. He reconned the stores and establishments around her place but didn't see any sign of Cahooshek's crew or anyone else that looked like they might be surveilling her place. Well, if there was anyone there, they wouldn't recognize him, so he would just be another caller to anyone that was watching. He went casually up the steps and buzzed her door. He wondered if she would recognize him without him telling her. Maybe she was watching him on the monitor and didn't want to answer. He buzzed again.

"Coming, coming. What do you want?" came a gravely male voice from inside. Jack was suddenly on the alert and looked around, but there was no sign of anyone around or watching him. The door opened, and an older long-faced small alien looked out. "Can I help you? What is it you want?" said the alien.

"I'm looking for Zshutana, the female who lives here," said Jack.

"Oh, that business isn't here anymore. You'll have to go somewhere else for that sort of entertainment. Good-bye," said the alien as it tried to close the door in Jack's face.

Jack jammed the door open with his foot and pushed his way into the room. The small alien fell back against the wall and then tried to get up and run, but Jack grabbed him and said, "Wait, what do you mean she's not here anymore? She's a friend of mine, and she was just here a little over a moondat ago. Who are you?"

The little alien was obviously shaken but didn't seem overly afraid. "I'm Deljen Voyla and I live here now and I run the clothing and outfitting shop down below. I assumed you were just another client looking for the girls that were here. I didn't realize you knew the girl."

"Where is she, and what are you doing in her apartment?" said Jack.

"Well, I don't honestly know where she is. I just know that she moved out and this apartment became available. I've been wanting a place much closer to my store, and this is perfect."

"When did it become available, and you say you don't know where she went?" asked Jack.

"Almost four weneks now is when I moved in. I believe it was empty a couple of daiyus before I snapped it up, and I'm sorry I don't know where she might have gone."

"What else can you tell me? Anything you can think of, maybe where her girls might have gone? Maybe they would know," said Jack.

"No, no. There were several other, uh, former clients that came by looking for the girls, but I couldn't tell them anything either. I thought maybe on the other side where they, umm, worked, but they'd already been there, and there was nothing over there now but storage. So I'm sorry I can't tell you anything more."

"All right," replied Jack. "I'm sorry to have interrupted and barged in. Say, who did you rent this place from? Who is the landlord?" asked Jack.

"The landlord," said Deljen Voyla, "he's a somewhat, uh, unpleasant type that goes by the name of Cahooshek. I believe he has something to do with the mine, a rather pungent, disagreeable creature that floats around in a mobile chair. Do you know him?"

"I know of him," said Jack, trying to keep from openly seething and giving away anything else. "Well, thank you for your help, and I'm sorry to have come in uninvited, but it's quite important that I find her."

Jack left and went downstairs and got something to drink, some sort of fruit concoction, while he rearranged his plans and tried to think what to do. He checked his translator time and saw that he'd only been gone for forty-two mentus. OK, directly to the next step, then, is all he could think of. *Get your act together and move on for now,* he thought. He headed straight for the mine manager's office outside the guard shack near the entrance to the conzone side of the mine.

At the manager's office, there was an outer office with a male alien clerk. Jack strutted in trying to act like how he thought a GTA dignitary might act. The clerk didn't bother to look up and said, "Yes? What is it you want?" in a somewhat bothered tone.

"I am Senefreh Ka Landas of Dunoria. I was told you might have some technical experts in your conscript zone that might be capable of assisting us with our damaged ship. I am the Chief GTA Oversight Administrator for the Octal Ondor galactic sector. I need to speak to your manager."

The clerk jumped up with sudden newfound enthusiasm. "Oh, yes, right away. We had no idea you were coming. You must be the one from the GTA ship that just landed outside the wall. I saw it on the display. It's really a nice, uh, err, beautiful ship."

"Yes, thank you. Your manager now, if you don't mind," said Jack.

"Yes, yes, I'll be right back. I'll get him right now," said the frazzled clerk.

The clerk ducked into the inner office, and after a few muffled words that Jack could hear from inside the office, the manager appeared with the clerk in tow. "Arpek Ansarvu at your service, GTA Administrator, uh, uh . . ."

"Senefreh Ka Landas of Dunoria," replied Jack, "you may address me as Ka Landas."

"Yes, yes, Ka Landas, what may we do for you?"

"As your clerk might have informed you, we've had a slight engine problem aboard *Tentah-eh*. I was told that you had reasonably good techs in your conscript section that might be useful for our purposes. I would like to see a list of the mine maintenance techs and their qualifications as fast as you can, please," said Jack.

"Well, yes, we can provide that for you, but, why, uh, wouldn't you be better off using a contract tech instead of a conscript or convict?" asked the manager.

"No, we would not," replied Jack bluntly. "We have full authority to commandeer any conscript or convict that is under GTA oversight, which this mine is. Contract workers are costly workers and would have to be hired under contract, and it would take time to find and negotiate with such techs. Also they would likely want to return here, which we are not likely to do for some time. We often use conscript techs, as it is much more efficient to acquire them, and they are generally as good or better quality than the contract types anyway. Now a list, if you please, as soon as possible."

Ten mentus later, Jack was sitting at the manager's desk going through a list of conscripts and their qualifications. He was looking for Junot's bio but had to go through all the mine's conscripts and convicts, since the manager's office didn't have a way to discriminate the inmates with their technical skills. He had to act like he was looking at all of them as the manager and clerk kept fawning over him even though he'd told them they could go about their own business. He checked his time and saw that he had been gone from the ship for an horun and forty-eight mentus. He'd planned on taking Zshutana back to the ship first if she'd been willing to come and then coming back for Junot and Cherga. There it was; he'd found Junot's convict record. He pulled Junot's record aside along with several others so that it appeared that he was shopping for the best candidate.

Ten mentus later, he came across Cherga's record and set it aside along with the dozen others he pulled. He went through another five mentus worth and then said to the manager that he thought he had enough candidates to choose one or two that he could use. He went through the candidate finalists again and asked the manager what he knew about several of them, which was basically nothing, since the only information was what was in the conscript's records. Jack quickly studied the candidates more thoroughly then narrowed it down to five. He asked the manager to check on the remaining sentences of the five candidates then studied the records a little more. "I think this one will do," handing Junot's record to the manager. "He has good and varied technical skills and has no record of any violence. He appears to be incarcerated for attempted fraud and records manipulation. That shouldn't present any problem for our needs."

He then looked at several candidates for a couple of mentus as if he couldn't decide. "This one too," he said to the manager as he handed him Cherga's file. "The first one appears to be somewhat small, so he would be of little use for physical labor, which we need from time to time in our official GTA capacity. This one looks capable, and it says that he is serving a sentence in lieu of his sibling. That seems quite generous of him. I'm sure he would not mind being released into our service, which is surely much better than the mining complex duties, I would imagine. Now, do you have a figure for these two convicts for their societal incarceration debt? We don't wish to encumber your operation with any undue financial stress from the monetary compensation you are obtaining from the work debt of these convicts."

"Um, yes, let me find out from the accounts office," said the manager, wondering if there was any way he could pocket some of the payoff himself.

A couple of mentus later, the manager was back. "It looks like the convict Junot has a balance of 32,700 credits and the convict Cherga's payoff is currently 44,180 credits."

"Yes, well, very good," replied Jack. "Can you give me the transfer account information and prepare a release for me? I would like to get back to the ship and check on the repair status."

"Yes, yes, of course," replied the manager. "Just give me a few mentus to draw that up. It will be just like a standard release, only it will show an early termination."

"That will be fine," said Jack. "Please have that prepared for me."

"Yes, just give me a few mentus. I have to clear this with the mine bosses for final authorization. That shouldn't be a problem. It will just take a few mentus," said the manager.

"Yes, thank you, please hurry," said Jack. *Crap,* thought Jack; he was hoping to avoid any interaction with the bosses, but it now appeared to be a risk he would have to take.

"Yes, Your Excellency," the manager said to the number three boss when asked why he was calling. "The chief GTA oversight administrator from the GTA ship outside the wall has requested to commandeer two of our mine convicts for use aboard the GTA ship. He is making full restitution for the convicts' payoff balance."

"How much is the balance due for the convicts?" asked the number three mine boss, wondering how much the bosses would pocket from this tidy little payoff.

"That's very good. Yes, just take care of the GTA administrator with all the assistance you can give him," said the number three boss. *Number one will be quite pleased with this. We need as much revenue as we can get after the losses we took on that Varaci debacle. Number one will be very pleased with my handling of this,* thought the number three boss to himself.

A short while later, the manager got back with Jack again. "Here are your releases for the two convicts and the account transfer information you requested."

"Most excellent work," said Jack to the manager. "I will be sure to note the excellent assistance and cooperation of your office here," said Jack to the manager.

The manager now had a look of ecstatic gratitude on his face. "Oh, thank you, we, I, that is much appreciated. We are truly happy to serve you here in your, uh, uh . . ."

"Time of technical need," said Jack.

"Yes, yes, that's it," said the manager.

Jack ran the transfer through from his assumed account name of Desdewah Annilar Ri to the account information provided by the manager. "There, the transfer is complete. You may check your balance to verify it," said Jack, hoping the manager wouldn't notice that the account name differed from his alleged GTA name of Senefreh Ka Landas. He guessed that the only thing the manager would be interested in was that the transfer amount turned out to be correct, but he would make up something about the name being his financial distribution account if he needed to.

"Splendid, splendid, there it is, the transfer is complete. We thank you for stopping by so that we could assist you today," said the manager, somewhat hoping that the GTA administrator would hurry and leave now so he could get back to his own interests.

"Yes, and thank you for your assistance," said Jack. "If you could please have the two convicts escorted to my ship, that should conclude my business here." Jack didn't want Junot or Cherga to see him. They may or may not recognize him. Cherga would likely understand and play along, but Junot, if he recognized Jack, would probably get so excited he might blow Jack's cover. He had at least one more stop to make and hopefully two, and he wanted to cut his time here as short as possible.

"Yes, oh, yes, we would be happy to get that taken care of for you right away," said the manager.

Jack left the office and headed to his next stop. A few mentus later, he stopped and called *Carratta* on their discreet channel. After two pages, Wehsh answered, "This is Wehsh, go ahead."

Jack replied, "Wehsh, this is Jack. Where's Forto?"

"Uh, um, he left about forty mentus ago. He said he'd be back in a little while. He said he was going to go take care of something and would have some good news when he got back and that I needed to do what he told me if I wanted to be part of his plan."

"What? I told him specifically to stay on board and be ready to launch. Did he say exactly what he was doing?" said Jack.

"No, that's all he said, but he was acting kind of funny, like he was all hyped up about something. I know that's kind of a normal state for him, but this was, uh, uh, different. I was just stewing about it and I was going to call you, but I was afraid I'd maybe interrupt you or something."

"Son of a, son of a, damn, damn it," said Jack. "All right, Wehsh, here's what I want you to do. There will be a security detachment showing up at *Carratta,* but they are from me. They will be escorting two mine workers that are named Junot and Cherga. They are delivering them to *Carratta* and they are both friends of mine, so treat them well and get them on board. You, Wehsh, are now in charge of *Carratta* until I get back, not Forto. Do you understand?"

"Uh, yes, I understand," said Wehsh somewhat hesitantly.

"Wehsh, I think Forto is going off the reservation, which you probably don't understand, but I'll explain it when I get back. Now listen, if Forto shows back up and anyone is with him but me and me alone, I want you to launch *Carratta* and return to Se-ahlaalu just like we did coming over here but in reverse. Do you think you can do that?" asked Jack.

"Yes, yes, it won't be graceful, but I'm pretty sure I can do that," replied Wehsh.

"OK, good," said Jack. "Don't let Forto on *Carratta* if anyone is with him. I have some more business to take care of here. I'll be back as soon as I can, and I'll check in with you if I can. Call me if anything happens, OK?"

"Yes, Jack, I'll do it."

"OK, Jack out, and stay alert, Wehsh. Don't let Forto try to pull anything else on you."

"OK, OK, I won't," replied Wehsh.

Jack headed down as fast as he could go without drawing attention to himself, down toward the bowels of the mine and toward the one place where the most despicable alien he'd met so far was, down to Cahooshek's miserable lair.

* * * * *

"You, come with me," the guard said to Junot, while at the same time another guard was ordering Cherga, who was in the common area, to do the same.

"What is it you want?" said Cherga to the guard.

"I don't know, and you don't need to know. Just come with me as ordered," as the guard slapped wrist restraints on Cherga faster than he realized what was happening.

"What the, what are you doing?" said Cherga.

"Precautions. Just come with me," said the guard. Cherga had no idea what was happening. Why was he being restrained, and if this was something dangerous or serious, why was there only one guard? This didn't make sense; it didn't really make any sense at all. Two mentus later, they met up with another guard who had Junot restrained the same way.

"Cherga, what's happening? What's going on?" said Junot somewhat desperately.

"I don't know," said Cherga. "They're taking us somewhere, but they won't say anything else."

"Be quiet now, no talking. Now let's go you two cons. We have orders to escort you," said one of the guards.

* * * * *

Jack went to the central core and down the lift to Cahooshek's level. He headed down the corridor to where Cahooshek held sway over his demented little kingdom. As he got closer, he noticed that it smelled just as bad as it had the first time he was there. He went in cautiously and went to the wall where the stairs were and looked in. In the far corner of the room, he could see one of Cahooshek's flunkies, one of the Dumb and Dumber brothers. *What was his name?* thought Jack. *Either Kreshku or Ruggal, whatever, it didn't matter.* Where was Cahooshek? *Only one way to find out,* thought Jack. He walked into the room and straight back to the counter where Cahooshek had formerly been, which was now occupied by the flunky. The flunky looked up somewhat puzzled as he wasn't used to getting dignified-looking visitors down here in Cahooshek's area. "I'm looking for the one they call Cahooshek," said Jack in an official sounding, he hoped, GTA manner.

"And who are you?" said the flunky, who was actually Ruggal, in a belligerent tone, which was the only way he knew how to talk to anyone.

"I am Chief GTA Oversight Administrator Senefreh Ka Landas, and I have official business with Cahooshek. Do you know where he is?"

Ruggal the flunky, who had never even seen let alone spoken to a GTA official, blinked for a moment and then tried to form an answer. "I, uh, he, Cahooshek, he's not here, Direc— I mean, Ad, Adamin."

"You may address me as Administrator Ka Landas," said Jack in an authoritative tone.

"Yes, uh, Directator La Kannis," stammered Ruggal the flunky.

"That's Administrator Ka Landas," repeated Jack tersely. "Enough," said Jack. "Where is Cahooshek? I wish to deal with him immediately." Jack had a strong desire to deliver some retroactive justice to this clown of Cahooshek's, but he knew it wouldn't serve any purpose and would only complicate matters. He wanted to beat the information out of him about Zshutana, but he didn't know if this flunky even knew anything about her.

"Cahoo, Cahooshek went back, back to Sumtoka for the mating ritual," stammered Ruggal. "He'll be gone for three moondats, so he left me and Kreshku in charge of everything here."

"Cahooshek is in considerable arrears to the GTA. He has taken payment for his assignment here and failed to deliver the required information for his assigned task. Where on Sumtoka is he, and when did he leave?" demanded Jack.

"He left ten—no, twelve daiyus ago on the scheduled Koruanum transport. I have the location here on the writings from Sumtoka," answered Ruggal as he handed Jack a data card. "He'd been pleading with them to hold his spot for the last two yenets, and now he was finally able to go."

"And how did Cahooshek, who is so far in arrears to the GTA, manage the fee to Sumtoka?" asked Jack just slightly less vehemently.

"I'm not sure," replied Ruggal, "maybe something to do with the mine bosses."

"What did Cahooshek do with the mine bosses that allowed him to go to Sumtoka?" growled Jack, trying to pressure Ruggal into divulging anything else he might know.

"I don't know, I really don't," said Ruggal. "All we do is run his errands and do stuff like watch people or watch for people."

"What do you mean by watch people or watch for people?" barked Jack.

"Well, well, we just watched for an escaped conscript for a while, and we watched some female's apartment over on the Dirga level, a female that had a business that had female workers, you know, for males that wanted females for, you, you know, and we got supplies and brought in some workers and things, just that kind of stuff is what we did."

Yes, Jack knew exactly what kind of stuff these lackeys did, but he was now pretty certain that this one likely didn't know anything about what had happened to Zshutana, though apparently they'd been tasked to watch her, which he knew from firsthand experience. "All right, I'm sure that's all you know," said Jack, "but if I find out later during my investigation that you've withheld anything from me, you'll answer to the full extent of the GTA enforcement system."

"No, no, I swear it, I don't know anything else. I've told you all I know about it," whined a thoroughly intimidated Ruggal.

"I'd better not find out otherwise, or I'll be back to deal with you personally. Now go about your business and don't tell anyone about this questioning—this is still an ongoing investigation—and I mean anyone. Do you understand?" demanded Jack.

"Yes, yes, no, I won't," stammered Ruggal. Jack spun and exited like he owned the place. He realized how much he hated this acting charade he was having to perform, but he realized it was just going to be part of the new business enterprise he was involved in.

* * * * *

"And why do you want to see a director or administrator?" said the main gate guard to Forto, who'd asked him where he could find someone in charge when he'd come from the ship to enter the mine complex.

"I'm from the, the, uh, GTA ship out there, and I have something important to tell someone in authority. I need to talk to someone, a director or administrator or someone," he'd told the guard.

"You say you're from the GTA ship. Someone has already come from the ship in a vimar," stated the guard.

"Yes, I know. I'm from the, the GTA ship too, but I walked over because the vimar is already here. I need to talk to someone in charge. It's very important," implored Forto. An agonizingly slow horun later, Forto was sitting outside the mine guard command office waiting for the chief of guards to return from wherever he was to see him.

* * * * *

"You two get into the back of the vimar and wait here while I check out with the transport agent," said one of the guards escorting Cherga and Junot. The other guard stood outside, while Junot and Cherga sat in the back of the utility vimar. "What's the matter, Junot? You do not look too well," said Cherga.

"I think I know what's going on," moaned Junot. "I think they're going to take us somewhere and kill us. I think we're going to have an accident so they can get our credits from all our winnings and the other's too."

"Perhaps," said Cherga as Junot looked even more distraught, "but it wouldn't make sense that they would take us out in a vimar somewhere in daylight, at least I don't think so. I think if they wanted us dead, they would create an accident in the mine or maybe just shoot us as we were supposedly trying to escape. They haven't really treated us too badly other than binding our wrists so we can't cause any trouble."

"Do you really think so—I mean, that they aren't going to kill us?" appealed Junot.

"Yes, so you can relax a bit. Let's just see what this interesting situation brings. Maybe it won't be so bad after all," said Cherga.

* * * * *

Finally, the chief of guards returned, and Forto was nearly paralyzed with anxiety wanting to see him. The other guard said, "You'll just have to wait a few minutes.

The chief just got back, and he knows you're waiting. He'll be with you shortly." Fifteen mentus later, Forto was ushered into the chief of guard's office.

"So I understand you are supposedly from the GTA ship outside the complex and you wish to speak to an administrator regarding something important," the chief said to Forto.

"Yes," explained Forto, trying to convey the importance of speaking to someone higher up that could negotiate with him for the important information he had.

"Perhaps if you could give me some of the details, I may be able to direct you on a course that would be more helpful," said the chief.

"Look, this is very time critical. If I can't see someone of importance in the next few mentus, I'll just have to leave and go back to the ship," said Forto in a slightly threatening voice in hopes that he could get this chief of whatever to get him to someone important.

"Well, I'm not sure that would be possible right now," said the chief, "at least until we get to the bottom of this situation. You say you're from the GTA ship, yet your ID has no link to any GTA identification," the chief began to say.

"That's what I'm trying to tell you," blurted Forto. "It's not a GTA ship, and we're not with the GTA. The captain is here on some, some sort of unknown mission, I don't know what, but neither the ship nor the captain is with the GTA."

"And what is this captain's name?" asked the chief.

"His name, he claims his name is Jack Spartun of Urth, at least that's what he says," offered Forto.

"Hmm, wait a mentu, hmmm, OK, replied the chief, "we don't seem to have anyone logged into the mine by that name or anything close to it."

"Well, uh, well, maybe he used a different name or something," appealed Forto.

"Now how would he do that?" asked the chief. "We are a high security facility. Everyone in and out is scanned by translator ID. We do have a GTA administrator logged in by the name of, of . . . surely now you must happen to know his name?" asked the chief.

"No, how would I know his name?" asked Forto.

"Because he's from the GTA ship, which you are also allegedly from. Oh, and by the way, *your ship* has a confirmed GTA discrete code and was verified by Wanana control as an arriving GTA ship under distress. Now, the GTA official's name is Chief GTA Oversight Administrator Senefreh Ka Landas, which was verified by translator ID also."

Forto felt his face burning, and he didn't know what to do. "I'm telling you that this is all fabricated or something. I don't know how or why, but I need to talk to someone important and let them know what's going on," raged Forto on the verge of tears.

"All right, we will pass on your story—the, uh, information, that is—up the chain of command," said the chief. "As soon as we hear something back from the administrators, we'll let you know what your disposition will be."

"My disposition?" said Forto. The chief just stared at him and watched him.

Twenty mentus later, the chief came over to Forto, who was now being guarded by two of the chief's own special detachment guards in a side room that looked a lot like a holding cell. "The mine bosses in their great wisdom have elected to hear your story," said the chief.

"Oh, thanks be, thank you," said Forto.

"You'd better hope it's a good story and that they're in the mood for a good story, which they are probably not, since it's getting close to eating time, which they don't like to be delayed to or interrupted from," said the chief. "You'll be escorted up by my guards, but, first, you'll be searched. I hope you don't thoroughly upset them, as that might come back on me for pushing this report up to them. That would not be good . . . for you," said the chief.

Forto wasn't feeling too well as his escorts searched him and then herded him up to the mine bosses' office. Outside the office, he was searched again by the mine bosses' guards then ushered into an outer waiting room with his escorts still present. A new young assistant to the bosses named Jogota came out to assess the visitor. "Now please give me your information so that I can pass it onto the bosses," said the assistant. Forto started in with his plea for urgency and gave a quick synopsis and that he wanted to trade something for the information.

"Trade something? You want something from the bosses in exchange for this information?" asked the assistant.

"Yes, but it won't cost the bosses or the mine or anyone anything," beseeched Forto.

"Shouldn't your duty to the Corodune complex come before your own personal desire for gain as far as giving us this information?" queried the assistant.

"Yes, no, but I'm not from the Corodune mine. I'm from Se-ahlaalu, but the information is about the mine," answered Forto more frustrated than ever.

"Stay here. I'll be back shortly," said the assistant Jogota.

What kind of stupid place is this? thought Forto to himself. *I'm trying to give these idiots timely, valuable, even critical information, and they act like a bunch of herd grass eaters chewing their grass.*

* * * * *

After Jack strode out of Cahooshek's dingy, smelly lair, he called Wehsh. "Have you heard from Forto?" he asked Wehsh.

"No, nothing yet," replied Wehsh.

"OK, if you do, just tell him that I will be another two or three horuns, that I got hung up a bit and will check in later but I'm running late, all right?"

"Yes, I'll do that just as you say, Jack," replied Wehsh.

"And, Wehsh, my friends should be there with their escort shortly if you haven't seen them already. I'll be there very shortly myself, OK?" said Jack. "And, Wehsh, don't tell my friends who the captain is. Don't tell them my name. I don't want them getting crazy and trying to come back inside and find me if something goes wrong."

"Yes, OK, got it like you said," replied Wehsh.

"OK, see you in a bit, Jack out," said Jack.

The number four boss said to Forto, "So you are saying that this Jack Spartun of Urth is not a GTA administrator and that you want us to confiscate the GTA ship and give it to you. And you are a pilot on this GTA ship and that you walked in from the ship but you have no GTA ID."

"Yes, that's it exactly. I don't know what he's doing here, but it's apparent that he came here for a reason. There's nothing wrong with the ship, and he lied to the Wanana controller so we could land here for whatever his reasons," said Forto in his best imploring voice.

"You realize that the GTA ship has been verified as well as the GTA administrator according to Wanana control and our own chief of guards?" said the number four boss.

"Yes, and I don't know how. That is all fabricated too somehow. He's not a GTA administrator," said Forto.

"Wait here," said number four, "I'll be back in a few mentus."

* * * * *

The utility vimar left the garage and headed out of the mine complex through the main gate. "Do you realize how long it's been since we've seen the outside of the mine?" said Cherga quietly to Junot. "Even if they kill us, at least we got to go outside and see the planet and the sky once again."

"But you said they weren't going to kill us," said Junot.

"No, I don't believe they are," said Cherga reassuredly to Junot. They drove out but really didn't go very far; in fact, they only went out the main gate and drove a short two kahtaks right up to one of the most beautiful ships either of them had ever seen.

They both stared in awe at the spectacular ship. The guards in the front seat did the same. "It's even more beautiful up close than from a distance or on the vido," said one of the guards.

"What are we doing?" Cherga asked the guards in the front seat.

"We don't know really," said the guard. "We were just told to deliver you both carefully to the GTA ship and come back as soon as we were done."

"G . . . GTA ship?" asked Junot.

"Yes," replied the guard. "Apparently, it had some sort of maintenance problem and landed here this morning. Now we are delivering you here for some reason. That's all we know," said the guard in the right seat. "They don't pay us to know much, just to do what we're told," added the guard. Cherga and Junot just looked at each other not knowing what to say.

Wehsh verified that it wasn't Forto and that two people were being delivered by a guard escort. He opened *Carratta*'s entry door and went out to meet them. "Here are your conscripts that you purchased along with their restraint controls per our orders," said the guards as they handed over the control disk to the person that had come out meet them.

"Thank you for delivering them. That should be all we need for now," said Wehsh to the guards.

The guards got back in their vimar and proceeded to drive off after admiring the ship for another mentu. Cherga and Junot stood looking at the person with the restraint control. Wehsh fiddled with it for a second, and the restraints dropped off the new arrivals' wrists onto the ground. "Hi, my name's Wehsh Hevedu. I'm the maintenance officer on *Carratta*. Welcome aboard," as he motioned them to come aboard the ship.

"It's, uh, nice to meet you," said Cherga, somewhat at a loss for words. "Who are you, and what are we doing here?"

"Well, I'm Wehsh Hevedu, like I said, and I'm not entirely sure myself what we are all doing here, but apparently, one of the things we're doing is getting you out of the mine and onto our ship."

"Our ship?" asked Cherga. "Whose ship?"

"Well, not my ship. I'm just the maintenance and load officer. I just said *our* because I'm on the crew."

"Whose ship, then?" said Junot, finally coming out of his state of shock enough to start asking questions.

"I can't really say that right now," replied Wehsh. "Just come in and help me keep watch. We're not really out of danger yet, and we may have to launch on a moment's notice."

Junot and Cherga just looked at each other again, too far out of their recent element to even know what to ask. Just then, they heard a whine and a sharp chirp as Seema peeked around the corner and let out an alert that there were strangers aboard. "What was that?" asked Junot, who was startled by the strange noise.

"That's just Seema. She's the captain's, or I guess the ship's tu-urak. She just let me know that there is someone new on the ship that she hasn't seen before," said Wehsh.

"That's a tu-urak?" asked Junot. "And the ship has one?"

"Yes, and she's a good one too. Now come up to the flight deck and help me watch for vimars or anyone approaching the ship. Hurry now, this is important," said Wehsh.

Junot and Cherga were awestruck by the incredible view of *Carratta*'s interior. "What kind of a ship is this?" asked Cherga. "It is quite remarkable."

"*Carratta* was built as a luxury exploration yacht but that didn't work out, so she's been converted into a fast cargo courier specialty ship," answered Wehsh.

"It's really beautiful," said Junot. "I've never seen a ship like this even from a distance, only in pictures."

"Well, now you're on one. Welcome aboard. I can get you something to drink if you'd like if you promise to watch out the front and yell if you see any kind of activity."

"Yes, we can do that," said Cherga.

"Good, I'll be right back," said Wehsh as he headed to the galley to grab some refreshments.

Junot looked sad for a minute. "Now what's the matter?" said Cherga.

"I think I know what happened. I think they did kill us," he said to Cherga.

"What, what are you talking about? That's crazy," said Cherga.

"No, I think they killed us and we went up to the great eternity, or at least they are taking us there in this unbelievable ship," said Junot as he smiled at Cherga.

Cherga laughed out loud then patted his friend Junot on the back. "You could be very well right, my friend, you could be very well right."

* * * * *

Jack headed back up the central core and out to where the vimar was parked. He kept alert in case the situation had changed and they were now looking for him. He made it out of the inner security checkpoint with no problem. Was that a security contingent over there? No, just some off-duty guards going about their usual business, it looked like. Finally, he made it to the vimar. The attendant asked him if he needed anything as he approached the vimar to leave. "No, no, thank you," he said to the attendant. "I believe I've accomplished everything I can today, so I'll be leaving now."

"Well, thank you, GTA Administrator. If there's anything else you need while you're here, please let us know."

"Yes, thank you, I will," said Jack as he looked around while getting in the vimar. He tried to look relaxed or in charge or something, but for some reason, it had felt like a trap. *I must be getting paranoid in this old age,* he thought to himself.

Jack left the garage and drove out to the main gate, where he was checked through with no problems. "Wehsh, come in, it's the captain," Jack said in case someone was listening.

"Wehsh here, uh, Ja—Captain," almost saying "Jack" by mistake.

"I'm outside the gate and I'll be there in about two mentus. Be ready on the loading ramp and ready to stow the vimar."

"Roger that," said Wehsh, using the new term Jack had given him for acknowledging an order a few daiyus ago.

"Are my friends aboard yet?" asked Jack.

"Yes, Captain, they're aboard and helping me watch for security patrols and other less than desirables," replied Wehsh, thinking of Forto now.

"Excellent, excellent job, Wehsh. I'll be aboard in one mentu."

"I'll be standing by, Captain," said Wehsh. "You two stay here and watch for anything while I go open the loading ramp for the captain," Wehsh told Junot and Cherga.

"We will do exactly as you say," said Cherga. "I have no explanation for this," said Cherga to Junot.

"Me neither, I have no idea. This is, is truly, uh, truly crazy," replied Junot.

* * * * *

"Why have you wasted our time with this bizarre tale when you have nothing to prove it with?" said the number one boss to the Forto.

"I have the proof on the ship, I swear it. I've been trying to get someone's attention for horuns, but they just now brought me up here," pleaded Forto to this new and frightening boss.

"And what sort of proof do you offer about this GTA ship that you claim is not?" asked the number one boss.

"There's nothing on the ship that has anything to do with the GTA. The ship is called *Carratta*. It's a luxury yacht converted for fast messenger and cargo service for this Jack Spartun of Urth," explained Forto, hoping to convince this gruesome-looking boss in a last-ditch effort.

"The only name similar to that I've ever heard is the Varaci Ja-ak that was confirmed dead over a moondat ago by the now missing provost crew." Forto had been afraid to bring up the provost Kershavah for fear of being implicated in its disappearance, but now it seemed like his only hope. "That's him, he's the one that brought the provost ship, the provost Kershavah ship, to Se-ahlaalu. He's the one that—"

"You are telling me that a Varaci brought a provost Kershavah ship to Se-ahlaalu a moondat ago and his name was Ja-ak?"

"Yes, yes," stammered Forto. "I don't know about him being a Varaci, but he could have been. He said he was from a planet called Urth. I couldn't find anything on it when I looked it up. He just showed up, and we—they went and got the Kershavah ship and salvaged all the parts from it. They even took the ion plasma guns—I mean, cannons from it and put them on the ship *Carratta*."

The number one mine boss just stood there and shook his head incredulously for a few septus. "So if we sent the provosts to Se-ahlaalu, they would find their ship there stripped of its cannons," said the mine boss.

"No, no," answered Forto, "they've probably taken everything now. It's completely disposed of or hidden somewhere. There wouldn't be anything of the provost's ship left."

"So it would be a waste of time for anyone to try to recover anything there," said the boss more as a matter of fact than a question.

"Yes," replied Forto, "but you could get this Varaci or Urthun Jack, and then the ship *Carratta* you could turn over to me and—" A slight roar was heard in the distance through the walls on the upper level of the mine complex where the number one boss held sway over the operations of the mine.

"What, what was that?" asked Forto, fearing that he already knew the answer.

"I believe it was the sound of your GTA or *Carratta* or whatever ship launching without one of its pilots," said the number one boss to the room.

"I tried, I tried all daiyus to get someone to listen to me. You could have gotten this Jack Spartan person if, if you'd—"

"Silence!" roared the number one boss. *How, how had the Varaci survived after he was reported dead? How did he get back here and back into the mine? What was he doing here?* thought the boss to himself.

"Find out what the GTA administrator was doing here!" he barked at boss number four and the new assistant.

"Well, we already know," said number four. "He was looking for a couple of convicts to commandeer for service on the GTA ship. The conscript mine manager called to verify the authorization to release the two convicts. The GTA administrator paid off their service debt balance and had them delivered to the ship. It was all according to regulation, Your Excellency."

"Yes, I'm sure it was," replied the number one boss, staring off into space trying to analyze the entire scenario.

"Now I can't even get back to Se-ahlaalu," complained Forto in an angry yet plaintive voice.

"Get back to Se-ahlaalu?" said the number one boss.

"Yes, that's where I live," said Forto. "You or your people wouldn't listen, and now they just left with the ship I should have gotten. Now all I can do is go home and back to work in the shipyard."

"No, I am quite sure you are mistaken. That definitely won't be possible," snorted the mine boss. "I somehow believe you were trying to commandeer a GTA administrator's ship through false pretenses. We just lost two valuable mine workers to an escaped criminal that you brought here, and possibly you are also involved in the hijacking and destruction of a Provost ship not to mention what might have happened to the crew. You are hereby convicted of fraud and conspiracy and attempted piracy of a possible GTA ship."

Forto couldn't believe what he was hearing. "What, what are you talking about? Are you crazy!" screamed Forto.

"I believe that would constitute a sentence of, umm, thirty—no, forty yenets for this criminal. Take him away, guards. Take him to the conzone side and get him properly incarcerated."

"No, no, no, you can't do this. I tried to help you. No, no . . ." cried Forto as the guards grabbed him and hauled him away. "You can't do this. This is some kind of a joke or something. Nooo, no, stop, no!" screamed Forto as the guards hauled him off to the conzone.

* * * * *

"Ready to launch, Wehsh?" asked Jack as they locked down the vimar.

"Yes, all set, Jack. Your friends are on the flight deck watching for me. But what about Forto?" asked Wehsh.

"He tried to sell us out to the mine bosses. I'll explain it all later," said Jack. Jack and Wehsh bolted up to the flight deck, and there they were, Junot and Cherga, looking none the worse for wear since the last time he'd seen them.

"Captain, we have no idea what is a happening to us here, but we believe we owe you a huge gratitude for whatever it is you are doing for us," offered Cherga. "We just have no idea exactly what it is that is happening."

Jack disguised his voice to keep up that charade until they were away from the mine. "Don't worry, you will. Right now, we must clear this area as fast as possible."

"The prestart is complete, uh, Captain. Ready for the start and launch checklist," said Wehsh. "Please take a seat and strap in," Wehsh said to the new guests. "All systems check but no destination is entered into the nav system," said Wehsh.

"Just get us into space, and we'll worry about that later," said Jack.

"Wanana departure control, GTA ship *Tentah-eh* on the ground at Corodune ready for departure to transit gate Bandor One."

"Wanana control, we understand. Do you not wish to continue your previous arrival to Wanana?"

"Negative, Wanana. Our repairs are complete, but we have had a change of plans and need to depart to Dunoria now," replied Jack. Junot just continued to stare at the strangely dressed GTA administrator that reminded him of someone.

"You are cleared to transit point Bandor One as requested. Have a pleasant run, GTA *Tentah-eh*."

"Yes, and thank you for your assistance," replied Jack as he spooled up the ion drive, and *Carratta* lifted off the ground and turned spaceward with a pleasant roar that everyone at Corodune could hear, at least those anywhere above ground level.

"Approaching Bandor One," announced Wehsh when they were about a mentu out.

"Good," replied Jack. "Plot a course to Dunoria to keep up our ruse. Then check for inbound conflicts and plot a nav entry to Nishda from the other side of the planet."

"Roger, and, and what was it?" asked Wehsh.

"Wilco," said Jack, "but without the 'and,' just 'roger' and then 'wilco,' which means 'will comply.'"

"Roger wilco," replied Wehsh as he plotted and executed the initial sublight portion of the run to Dunoria. "Now in five mentus, go to cloaked mode then steer us clear of the direct track, and then after a few mentus, we will have disappeared," said Jack.

After a few mentus on a divergent course to the other side of Nishda, *Carratta* went into cloaked mode and drifted along at 0.002 light speed toward one of the Se-ahlaalu arrival fixes. Jack got up and turned to Cherga and Junot. "As I was saying previously . . ." said Cherga.

"Jack?" said Junot tentatively.

"What?" said Cherga.

Jack smiled and pulled off part of his disguise hair. "Hello, Junot. Hello, Cherga. How are my good con friends doing?"

"Holy Creator of the eternal reaches!" exclaimed Cherga.

Jack stood up and took a couple of steps toward his friends and embraced them. "Hi guys, hey, I missed you two. Glad to see you are all well and holding up since my recent exit."

"Jack, Jack, I can't believe it, I can't, I can't, I can't believe it!" shrieked Junot. "We thought, well, we thought!"

"Maybe that you were dead," said Cherga. "By the Great Being of the farthest reaches, I can't believe it!" bellowed Cherga.

"Yep, I made it, but I can tell you it's been a harrowing, what, six weneks."

"I've got a lot to tell you, but that can all wait until later," said Jack then went on. "What do you know about Zshutana? I went to her apartment, and there was some older male merchant living in her place. He didn't know much, but he knew that Cahooshek had something to do with the rent he was paying for the place. I went to Cahooshek's office under the mine central core and grilled one of his flunkies who told me that Cahooshek had gone back to his home planet Sumtoka for his mating ritual. That's about all I could find out and still have time to get you guys out before we had to leave."

"We don't know either," said Junot. "I went to see her three daiyus after you escaped, and I was able to upgrade her translator like we wanted to with the call capability and discreet comm functions. I called her two daiyus later to tell her that they were going to stop allowing any cons to work outside the conzone. I think that was directed mostly at me but maybe because of you, I'm not sure. But when I called her, she didn't answer, so I tried her on the discreet piggyback line from the maintenance depot, and her direct line had no signal. I asked Za-arvak if I could go out to the Dirga level for mid meal the next daiyus, since I wasn't going to be able to do that anymore. When I got to Zshutana's, she wasn't there, and the place was empty and the girls were all gone. There were a couple of workers in her apartment, and they were just cleaning it up a little even though it didn't need much. I haven't been able to find out anything else. I'm really sorry about that Jack. That's the best I could do," said Junot regretfully.

"That's OK, Junot. I appreciate your trying, and you've given me more information than I had before. Now we have to get back to Se-ahlaalu and let some friends know that they could potentially have some trouble., Wehsh can you plot a course for reentry to Se-ahlaalu? We need to warn Doronno that Forto may be spilling the beans to the bosses or maybe the GTA about the provost ship and *Carratta*."

"Well, I can do that, but what are 'spilling the beans,' Captain?"

"Probably just one of his stupid sayings," said Junot.

Jack looked at Junot, and they burst out laughing. "You got that right, buddy, you sure got that right," said Jack as they all laughed out loud.

Jack reset *Carratta*'s discrete ID code back to *Carratta*'s code, while Wehsh plotted their position and executed their course and arrival back to Se-ahlaalu. "Jack, you must tell us about this ship. You are the captain. Is it yours? This is the most unbelievable thing I've ever seen. I couldn't begin to imagine this outcome in my best imaginings," said Cherga.

"It's a long story, but we've got a few, uh, looks like about twenty mentus to kill on our approach to Nishda," said Jack. "Let's grab a snack from the galley, and I'll bring you up to speed. You're not going to believe the journey I've had getting here, but it's really going to captivate you, of that I guarantee."

Cherga and Junot sat mesmerized for the next fifteen mentus as Jack told them of his remarkable journey. They asked question after question whenever he came to a dangerous or critical part. "Well, believe it or not, that's just a glossed-over version of the whole ordeal," said Jack. "Here's the big question for you both," said Jack. "We were a little short on crew for *Carratta* with just Wehsh and Forto. Now with Forto gone, I'm at a bare minimum for even ferrying the ship, and I certainly can't run a profitable cargo or courier service with just Wehsh and I. What I'm saying is that there are two crew positions open if you're interested in joining us on *Carratta*. I can't guarantee a specified income right now, just a percentage of whatever we clear after we make the expenses for *Carratta*, which are considerable, oh, and all the qalalé you can drink.

"Also as you might have guessed from our first little adventure today that not all of our operations will be, let's say, 100 percent GTA approved. There's always a chance that we could be boarded and maybe even end up back in the mine or someplace like it if we run into bad luck. As of now, you are both legally released from the mine, so I would understand if you just wanted to go to Se-ahlaalu and get back to some sort of normal life. There's a good chance that there would even be some employment openings available at Doronno's shipyard or maybe working for Talaka. It's completely up to you, but I'll need to know by tomorrow because we're going to do a quick turnaround and head out tomorrow. If you want to stay on in Se-ahlaalu for now and maybe reconsider later, that would be OK too."

"Where are you going tomorrow so fast?" asked Cherga.

"We're going to Sumtoka to find Cahooshek and find out what he did to Zshutana. If she's not alive and well somewhere, he's going to have the shortest mating ritual in Sumtokan history, and he'll never be mating with anything else ever again. You can think it over for a while or talk it over, whatever you want to do, but we are on a tight schedule. I just need to warn Doronno and Talaka about Forto so they can deal with that however they need to."

"Well, the 'all you can drink qalalé' sounds good to me, I am in," said Cherga.

"Are you serious?" asked Junot excitedly. "I have always dreamed of being on a starship as part of the crew. I only imagined something like that in my greatest fantasies. You couldn't keep me off this amazing ship if you tried," chirped Junot, "I mean, if that's OK," Junot added.

"I'm glad to hear it. Here's your chance, then," replied Jack. "Welcome aboard, swabbies. We'll figure out your exact duties later, but I'm thinking Junot will assist Wehsh, who may or may not be with us permanently. He's just on loan from the shipyard right now. That's right along Junot's specialty anyway."

"Cherga, you're good at organizing and executing things. As *Carratta*'s operations officer, you'll be in charge of cargo scheduling and coordinating, on and off-loading, securing, storing, etc., and also assist me in security as well as everyone else. There will be a lot more to it, but that's a general description of what needs to be done to make *Carratta* work. I'm sure you'll have lots of questions, but we'll get to them later," said Jack.

"Just one question," said Junot.

"What's that?" replied Jack.

"What's a swabbies?" said Junot.

"Don't worry, you'll find out soon enough," said Jack as he laughed at Junot's question.

"We'll be entering Nishda orbit in four mentus," said Wehsh over his shoulder to the others.

Jack came back to the captain's seat. "Very good, Wehsh. You're now promoted to first pilot in addition to your maintenance officer position. You'll be training Junot as our backup or replacement maintenance officer depending on your final disposition as far as going back to Doronno's. As you can see, this operation isn't going to be your everyday routine cargo or fast messenger operation. You may want to reconsider whether you want to be part of *Carratta*'s adventures, or more likely I'd say misadventures. It's strictly up to you. We can sure use you as a valued crew member, but I would understand if you didn't want to get involved in this undertaking," offered Jack.

Wehsh thought for a mentu then replied, "Well, it seems like a little out of the ordinary, but this has been the most exciting amusement I've enjoyed in a long time. I'll stay around for a while. If I decide I don't like it, I can always jump off somewhere along the way or whenever we get back to Nishda. A chance like this doesn't come along all that often, so I might as well jump at it while I can."

"That's good news, then," said Jack. "Wehsh, you have the landing. I'll take the comms and get a clearance. Just in case, watch for any unusual activity at the shipyard, like possibly provost ships or other government vehicles. I don't think they would have had time to put together a posse yet, but we'll be on the alert just in case."

"Roger and wilco—I mean, roger wilco," replied Wehsh.

"Jack, what's a posse?" asked Wehsh.

"That would be anyone we don't want to see," replied Jack.

Their entry and landing went as planned with no unexpected problems. Jack talked Wehsh through the landing and taxied in next to Doronno's big hangar.

Once on the ground, Jack gave Doronno a rundown of the situation at Wanana. "Are you certain that Forto was trying to ruin your mission and turn you in or cause you some kind of trouble?" asked Doronno.

"Yes," said Jack. "I gave him specific orders to remain on the ship and have it ready to launch on a moment's notice. I couldn't have been any more explicit that that. He disobeyed that order and told Wehsh that he had some big plan and that Wehsh needed to do what he, Forto, told him to do if he wanted to be part of it. I would think if it was some kind of misunderstanding that you would have heard from him calling for help by now. I don't know exactly what he was up to, but he can't follow orders, and obviously, this isn't the first time. If he went in and tried to make some kind of deal with the mine bosses or anyone else in there, then he screwed himself very royally. If those vermin at the mine could get away with it, they would steal *Carratta* and put everyone involved with her to work in the mine for twenty years of hard labor. Forto made a seriously bad choice, and now it looks like he's going to have to pay for it."

"You can make an inquiry to the mine about him if you want, but I don't know what, if any, information you'll get from them. Believe me, Doronno, if I thought there was even the slightest chance that I was wrong about this, I wouldn't have launched *Carratta* until I knew for sure. I didn't risk everything to go get my friends out of the mine without knowing exactly what I was doing and how to go about it. Forto and his little game almost ruined everything I've been planning. I'm sorry he pulled this, but I had to do what I had to do to salvage the situation," lamented Jack.

"Yes, I understand completely, and based on what you've told me, I can't come to any other conclusion either. That's just too bad for Forto," said Doronno.

Jack had contacted Talaka to let him know about his friends' rescue and their addition to the crew of *Carratta*. Talaka insisted on having them over to stay as he wanted to meet the friends that someone like Jack would risk everything for. Knowing that Jack's friends had just gotten out of several years of incarceration, with the fine cuisine that accompanies such situations, he elected to throw Junot and Cherga a get-out-of-incarceration celebration. Doronno was invited and brought his wife along for the occasion as well as Wehsh and his girlfriend. The dinner was fabulous as expected, and Junot and Cherga nearly ate themselves into a stupor.

They couldn't talk much business with the wives and girlfriends present, but they did delve into the false pretenses that the mine had used to imprison Cherga and Junot. It didn't come as a big surprise to anyone that had any knowledge of how things operated over in Wanana and with the GTA and its cohorts in general. "We may have to skirt some of the GTA legalities to operate a successful and profitable business here in Se-ahlaalu, but we don't do anything like that," said Talaka.

"Treating innocent citizens like that will come back to bite them sometime," said Doronno.

"Yes, you are right, I'm almost sure of that," replied Jack.

After dinner, they all retired to the Talaka's office, while Wehsh went home with his girlfriend and Doronno's wife chatted with Talaka's wives. "Junot, Cherga," said Jack, "were you able to keep my winnings from the fight pit in your accounts without the mine bosses stealing it from you? I told Talaka and Doronno that I had substantial credits banked from my winnings and I'm hoping that's still the case." asked Jack.

"Yes," replied Cherga. "We were afraid that the bosses would do something to steal it from us, but so far, they haven't. Either they didn't know you had transferred your winnings to us or they haven't gotten around to tracking it down yet. It does take some time to access or track down credits in an account from what I've heard."

"Jack, Jack, that's what I haven't told you yet," said Junot. "Right after you left, Zshutana told me that Cahooshek's goons were watching her, so she transferred your winnings that you'd left with her over to my account. She left me a message and said she was afraid they would do something to her, and she didn't want your winnings to get stolen or tied up with her account if something happened. She said she thought there was a better chance of saving them if she could get them out of her account and into mine or Cherga's. I'm sorry I forgot to tell you that."

Jack sat solemnly and thought for a mentu and then said, "She must have suspected that they were going to try and pull something on her. I don't know if the mine bosses knew if I had escaped Corodune yet, but they had it figured out shortly or those provosts wouldn't have shown up at the greenbelt that fast. I'd still like to know how they found me and tracked me. I want to know just for future reference. I didn't think to question any of the provosts to find out, and maybe they didn't even know themselves," said Jack. "Talaka, I have yet another request," said Jack. "I'd like to get a couple more of those discreet accounts for Cherga and Junot. They may be up against some of the same problems I could be having."

"Ah, yes, I have good news on your previous request," replied Talaka. "My, uh, consultants were able to come up with two more of those accounts because of a couple of unrelated accidents, one in Bacdirra, just outside of Wanana, and another one in the Xellamur zone, right here by Se-ahlaalu. For one of them, they had to pay the wife of the deceased, but she was happy to get the credits."

"That's great, well, at least for us," said Jack. "You can set those up for Cherga and Junot, and I can take care of everything I owe you now. Cherga and Junot can transfer my winnings to my new account, and everyone will be squared up on this issue. Guys, you can transfer my chunk over to this account for Desdewah

Annilar Ri, and as soon as Talaka gets them assigned, you'll have your own separate counterfeit accounts that aren't under your names so the mine bosses and the GTA won't be able to mess with you very easily. You should be able to remain completely anonymous this way."

Cherga started laughing and couldn't stop for half a mentu. "What on earth—I mean, Nishda is so funny? I don't think I've ever seen you laugh that hard before Cherga." said Jack.

"Jack, Jack, here we were worried that you had been killed or captured, maybe lost or possibly eaten by wild creatures, and instead, you were out conquering the entire planet of Nishda single-handedly," replied Cherga as he continued laughing.

"Yes, well, far, far from that," said Jack. "You're not too far away from your guess on those other possibilities, though. I think I came pretty close to buying it numerous times, but there must have been some sort of divine guardian watching over me or I never would have made it to here where I'm sitting with all of you enjoying a great tankard of qalalé. We can't stop, though. Tomorrow we go after Zshutana, and we don't quit until we find her, one way or another, by any means possible."

"A pact, then," said Cherga. "No rest until we find Zshutana. Whatever it takes, we will not stop." They all raised their glasses and swore an oath; nothing else mattered until they found Zshutana, one way or another.

After the good-byes, good-lucks, and thank-yous, they were ready to launch at 0700 the next morning. "Your course plot to Sumtoka looks good after transit point Keltar One. Good job," said Jack to Wehsh. "Did you guys follow that?" said Jack to Cherga and Junot as he wanted everyone at least partially cross-trained on all aspects of *Carratta*'s operations.

"I, I mostly understood what you were doing," said Junot.

"Me too, sort of mostly," replied Cherga.

"Don't worry," said Jack, "you'll get a lot more training and practice shortly, but for today, we just need to get on down the road," said Jack as he looked at Junot and mouthed the words "stupid saying."

They ran the full prestart and launch checks, and fifteen mentus later, they lifted off and were heading for transit point Keltar One. "Quantum field established, and main engine generators are fully online and ready for light drive run in hyperspace," announced Wehsh as 3.7 horuns later, they approached their transit point for Sumtoka. Jack had worked the departure clearance and transit authorization from Se-ahlaalu control.

"*Carratta*, you are cleared for transit from Keltar One," said the controller.

"Understand we are cleared for transit from Keltar One," repeated Jack. "Thanks for your assistance."

"Have a good run, *Carratta*," said the controller.

Jack announced, "That's calculating out at about 4.2 daiyus transit time to the published outer Sumtokan entry transit point, then another short fourteen-mentu jump and then about three and a half horuns to orbit," said Jack.

"I confirm that," said Wehsh.

"Execute when ready," ordered Jack. As Wehsh executed the light drive command, the quantum field bubble made the star field pull back slightly and then flicker and black out as the jump to hyperspace in the quantum field caused the ship to overrun the visible light waves and temporarily render *Carratta* in a zero null state.

All four of the crew watched in amazement as the strange shimmering ethereal shell of energy encapsulated the ship. The swirling jerking colors and the slow pulsating flow of the quantum energy field flowed toward the front of the ship, mesmerizing the observers. "Oh, oh, that's, that's amazing," said Junot excitedly. "I've seen vidos of it, but I've never seen it for real. Look at all the, the stuff, I don't even know what it is."

"It's just the quantum energy field," said Wehsh. "We're encapsulated in a quantum energy field, a bubble, or some call it a shell. A pure quantum energy state exists between the ship and normal space right on the outside of that bubble. They say that what you're seeing visually doesn't actually exist, but since it's there and we're seeing it, then it seems to me that it exists. We just don't know what it really is, since there is no way to sample it. Me, I'm just glad it's there or we would just be a smear of plasma ions spread across space."

"Can it crash or collapse or fail or anything like that?" asked Junot.

"No, not really, at least hypothetically," said Wehsh. "The quantum field is so stable once it's established that it takes a deliberate disruption to shut it down and exit it. It's almost as if it likes being in existence between the two different types of energy states and you have to force it to leave."

"I guess you'd say it's sort of self-sustaining in some ways," said Wehsh. "Some have theorized that it's a transition zone to another dimension or state of existence and that we are skirting or transiting the unreality between parallel but completely dissimilar realities. I'm not sure if that's correct or even makes sense, but it's another of several theories."

"Well, it's good news that it works," said Cherga, laughing. "Just imagine how long it would take to get your parts together if you were spread out over a light-year or more as plasma ions."

"Oh, right, just great, thanks a lot," said Junot. "That's all I needed to think about."

"Hey, you don't have to worry about it, Junot. If that ever happened, all that would be left of you would be a few stray ions fizzling around in interstellar space. Just think, though, how big you would be—you'd be the longest Riinan in the history of the galaxy."

Everyone laughed but Junot. "Hey, Junot," said Cherga, "maybe Jack's got a game of farakal stashed on the ship somewhere."

"No, sorry, I don't have any games," said Jack. "I would have gotten one if I'd thought about it, but I didn't. Maybe we can find one at one of our stops."

"Do you two play farakal?" asked Wehsh.

"Yes, do you?" said Junot.

"No, but I've wanted to learn it sometime. Maybe you guys could teach me."

"Sure, yes, of course," said Cherga. "All we need is a game set, but you'll have to watch out for Junot."

"Why is that?" asked Wehsh.

"Because he cheats," replied Cherga.

"He cheats?" said Wehsh.

"Yes, I do," replied Junot, "and Cherga taught me how, and now I'm getting really good at it, but don't worry, we'll teach you how to cheat too." Wehsh looked at them suspiciously then smiled, not knowing if he should take them seriously or not.

The next four daiyus in transit were spent with everyone learning the ship and their assignments. This was just like back on Earth where Jack had a couple of friends in the Navy. They spent their long transit times on ships and submarines studying everything there was to know about their ship. On *Carratta,* they practiced dealing with simulated hull breaches, system repairs, and other mock drills. They divvied up housekeeping duties and discussed whether they should have a rotation schedule or just have each person take a chore that was somewhat agreeable to them. In the end, Jack decided on a two-wenek rotation period, since no one could decide which job they did or didn't want to do.

Jack figured it was better that way anyway, since it was more opportunity for each crew member to learn more about the ship and each other's duties, even the mundane ones. The ship was big enough and comfortable enough, but with four people and a tu-urak on board, things could get pretty messy in short order. Seema really liked skulking around the ship and spying on everyone. You would not always know where she was, but she always knew where you were, and you would see her peeking out from various places while she stalked everyone and tried to climb onto every lap she could as often as possible.

Carratta's galley was very nicely functional and capable of preparing just about anything, but it was manually operated for the most part. It was nothing at all like the fully automated large-capacity galley system that Jack remembered from the big cargo ship that had hit *Victory*. He'd wondered about that from time to time when he had the time to think about it. Had that big ship just not seen the shuttle, or were they just totally disinterested in *Victory*'s existence? What were they doing in Earth orbit and Earth's atmosphere? He wondered if anyone had seen or known what happened to *Victory*. The size and mass of the cargo ship was almost incomprehensible, but he knew now that with the stealth capabilities of most starships that there was a good chance that no one had even seen that monster in Earth's atmosphere.

Jack told Junot that after he'd gotten familiar with *Carratta* that he wanted him to start working on more of the translator's comm system upgrades. Junot had told him that he'd already worked out a paging or call system that could locate and ping whatever specific translator was stored in their database. This would allow them to utilize just about any local comm system without having to go through the formal sign-in protocols of whatever system they were bootlegging onto. Because their system used roving random frequencies, there was no way they could be traced. If they were within line of site of another translator, they could completely bypass the local comm system and comm directly.

"Also, Junot," said Jack, "how hard would it be to set up a program that would allow us to modify any of the IDs that I've bootlegged from various people? I'd like to go in and amend certain aspects of an ID like their work history, qualifications, planet of origin, even their name. For that matter, would it be possible to fabricate a completely counterfeit ID on someone?"

"Yes, I was sort of thinking along those lines myself a few daiyus ago," said Junot. "I haven't figured out a way to break directly into our own IDs yet, but since we have the ability to capture other people's ID, it would be easy enough to modify them, since our copy of them wouldn't be hard encrypted like ours are in our own translators. I don't think you could completely fabricate an ID from scratch very well, though. You would really need a legitimate registered encrypted discrete ID number to start with. Then you could build it with whatever data you would want to put in it."

"That all sounds interesting," replied Jack. "Start putting something like that together as soon as you can get to it between learning all of *Carratta*'s systems and other stuff."

"OK, I'll get right on it soon," said Junot.

An horun out from their first arrival point approaching Sumtoka, Jack and Wehsh were double-checking their navigational fixes against their predicted plot. Jack briefed them all on the arrival. "Our actual position looks pretty good compared to our predicted arrival point," said Jack. "We won't be able to get a really accurate fix until we're out of hyperspace, but it looks like we're well within the 0.02 deviation tolerance data established for the Sumtokan system. That should put us at three Sumtoka system radii, or r, outside the system. That's a little closer than our initial plot but still plenty safe as far as nav tolerance allowance. Another short hop to the near side orbit of their farthest planet, Nahjeehee, will put us about 3.4 horuns out of Sumtoka at sublight speed."

"I thought I just read yesterday that you weren't supposed to get that close to a system's outer orbit," said Junot.

"Well, that's true especially for our initial arrival fix," said Jack, "but *Carratta*'s predictive plot shows that the outer Sumtokan planet Nahjeehee will be on the far side of the system from our arrival fix. Sumtoka is a verified GTA nav system, so we should be good there. We'll verify that when we come out of hyperspace and get an accurate fix on all the Sumtokan system bodies. Once we do that and it looks good, we can jump to the edge of Nahjeehee's orbit and then proceed at sublight from there. That will save us a couple of horuns of transit time. If this weren't a verified system or Nahjeehee was on our arrival side, we'd stay at sublight all the way in or at least make a much shorter approach jump. Sumtoka is the fifth planet in of seven planets, or the third one out from their sun Ruanah. The next planet out from Sumtoka is Jor. It's got some underground mining complexes but is pretty close to being uninhabited." Jack pulled up an image of Sumtoka on the overhead display that showed a rust-red-and-blue planet that was mostly shrouded in clouds of the same color.

"The red clouds you see are a type of aerial bacteria that produces most of Sumtoka's oxygen as a byproduct of their biosynthesis functions. The blue clouds are another type of bacteria that feeds on the oxygen-producing bacteria and produces nitrogen as a byproduct. They balance each other out by shifting the pH levels of the atmosphere one way or the other as one organism becomes more predominant than the other, causing the slightly out-of-balance atmosphere to rebalance toward the correct levels. Sometimes, stronger local bacteria imbalances occur, which then create convection currents, which cause storms, which cause mixing of the bacteria, which then cures the imbalance.

"The planet surface coverage is about 22 percent saline oceans and 10 percent fresh water. There's a similar biologic function that occurs in the saline oceans as in the atmosphere, but the fresh water remains mostly bacteria-free because of its acidity levels. Sumtoka's population density is fairly high and is listed at 22.6 percent on the GTA index as compared to Nishda's 0.87. One of the unique attributes of Sumtoka is that the natives can't mate, or more accurately can't produce offspring off their planet. Their physiology is tied to and requires the presence of the bacteria in their atmosphere in order to ovulate and conceive. They haven't been able to replicate the required conditions off of Sumtoka. Their mating ritual takes that into consideration, and it's staged at specific times within the mating period season to coincide with the highest bacterial concentration levels of their summer moondats. That is why Cahooshek is here now. The start of the mating season is in three daiyus, and apparently, he's on his last legs of opportunity to sire an offspring before he's deemed ineligible. If he doesn't mate now, he'll never have any little Cahoosheks to carry on his genetic line."

"Does Sumtoka or the galaxy really need any more little Cahoosheks running around?" said Cherga.

"Well, not as far as I'm concerned," replied Jack.

"We'll need preorbital entry authorization before we get to Sumtoka's outer orbital limit. Once we're in orbit, we'll need to request entry to the spaceport at Duccadu, and we'll need a dock reservation before we're allowed entry and arrival to Duccadu's Dacarus spaceport. According to Cahooshek's flunky Ruggal, Cahooshek will be in the nearby town of Tanuah where he's apparently been assigned a mating timetable for the three moondats that he thinks he's going to be here mating. *Carratta*'s arrival data shows that we'll need the T-Ra, or terahertz virtual system, to penetrate the thick clouds of bacteria and precip to have a good visual for our approach and landing. The precip percentage in the Duccadu area is on average 71 percent of the time, and it pretty much rains all night every night in the winter moondats.

"Sumtoka's demographics show a total planet population of around 911 million in seven major population centers. Their economic structure is some agrarian, light industry, some heavy industry, a little mining, and basically no tourism. Apparently, it's not anyone's idea of a garden spot for holidays," said Jack.

"Yes, but I think it's Cahooshek's holiday destination right now," said Junot.

"I almost feel sorry for him if you're planning on terminating his mating ritual, almost but not quite," said Cherga.

"He's lucky that I just don't just terminate him," said Jack, "but we need him alive at least until we find Zshutana. He's more than earned whatever he's got coming from us, but finding Zshutana is more important than any retribution."

They came out of hyperspace an horun later and recalculated their present position. They plotted for the short jump to the systems outer planetary orbit and then made that quick run in under a mentu. From there, it was nearly a three-and-a-half horun sublight transit to Sumtoka, where they obtained their orbital entry authorization and then a reservation for the Dacarus spaceport dock 28B. They received an orbital arrival track routing and entry time, which they initiated fourteen mentus after they entered orbit at their assigned orbital entry point and time.

"OK, here we go," said Jack as they started down.

"Entry checks complete and all systems optimal for Sumtoka entry," confirmed Wehsh. They descended through the upper atmosphere and then hit the tops of the bacteria-stained clouds. Even in the quantum field, they could feel the turbulence as they descended through the multiple layers of dense swirling bacterial cumulous precipitation. The clouds and bacteria-laden moisture couldn't get to *Carratta,* but the buffeting on the quantum bubble could still be felt as the field pushed its way through the thick atmosphere. They followed their assigned track toward the spaceport at Duccadu and then slowed their approach to eight hundred kahtaks as directed, about eighty kahtaks out to blend into the traffic flow around Duccadu.

Once they were aligned with the spaceport arrival corridor, they were vectored toward their final approach sequence point. "You are cleared for final approach to Dacarus spaceport," said the controller as they arrived at the final approach point on the arrival.

"Understand *Carratta* cleared for the final approach to Dacarus," said Wehsh as Jack piloted the ship on its arrival course. They knew they were completely enveloped in the dense clouds above Sumtoka, but the cloud penetrating T-Ra system visual made the approach to the spaceport almost as clear as if there were no clouds.

The city spread out ahead of them, and the spaceport lay below them in the mash of the city sprawl. As they got lower and slowed further, they could see the spaceport with its collection of ships in different spots. Jack told Wehsh to secure the quantum field for landing as they lined up for their final approach to the spaceport and dock. "Your assigned dock will be straight ahead and two kahtaks," said the controller. "Just follow your lateral and vertical arrival guidance to touch down *Carratta.* You are cleared to land at dock 28B."

"*Carratta* is cleared to land at dock 28B," replied Wehsh to the controller. The landing zone was marked with 28B on the surface with a perimeter of dim green lights around the landing zone. Jack eased *Carratta* slowly down, and they touched the landing zone and settled onto the landing feet.

A few mentus later, *Carratta* was shut down, and a transient inspector showed up with a crew manifest and declaration form for the crew to fill out. "Any regulated or prohibited freight on your ship or manifest?" asked the inspector.

"No," replied Jack. "Feel free to inspect the ship. We are running empty inbound, but we are looking for an outbound cargo or fast courier consignment for any destination. We are a freelance runner for hire. We'll also combine shipments if the customers agree."

"Very good," replied the inspector. "Please fill out this crew manifest and file it with the Transient Registration Office in the main terminal. You will need to file your manifest before you or your crew can leave the spaceport and go into the city."

"Thank you," replied Jack. "We'll get that taken care of in just a few mentus."

The inspector, who only looked vaguely like Cahooshek and didn't use a floating gurney and was considerably younger than Cahooshek, then made a quick tour of the ship. "This is a very nice ship for a fast cargo and courier service. It appears to be quite new. You can register with the travel authority over in the main terminal, and they will give you several sources for possible contracts. There are usually some executive types looking for something nicer than the scheduled bulk transfer ships if your price is reasonable."

"Thanks," said Jack. "We appreciate the information."

"Will you be needing any supplies while you're docked?" asked the inspector.

"Possibly," replied Jack. "We'll need to do an inventory and see what we need first."

"OK, if you do you can put in an order for any supplies or other items with the supply depot office at the end of maintenance building over there," the inspector said while pointing to a row of dark green buildings, "they're open 26/7 if you need anything," added the inspector.

"We'll do our inventory and get with them shortly," said Jack. "Thanks for your help."

"Have a pleasurable stay," said the inspector as he walked off toward the main terminal.

"I didn't know what to expect," said Jack, "but this inspector fellow was quite pleasant, nothing at all like the miserable Cahooshek. I guess that just goes to show that you can't judge an entire race and its planet by its one miserable Cahooshek."

"If they were all like Cahooshek, it might be better to just plasma ionize the entire planet from the air," said Cherga.

"Well, let's hope there aren't too many Cahoosheks around," said Jack. "Let me see that crew manifest the inspector gave us," said Jack to Wehsh. Jack looked at the manifest. "OK," said Jack, "because of our specialized mission here, we're going to list Wehsh as the captain, and I'm going to be Noorovii Nevevgev," said Jack, "which is just an ID I picked up along the way from one of the goons that attacked me under a bridge on the way into Se-ahlaalu. His ID just shows him as a laborer, so that's what I'll be on this layover. If I'm going to go pay Cahooshek a visit, I don't want my real name associated with *Carratta*, where they could easily track me back here. It's going to be a real surprise for him to see me, and I if let him live for some reason, I don't want them tracking me back to *Carratta*.

"Cherga and I will leave together, while, Wehsh and Junot, stay on *Carratta* and keep her ready to launch. While I'm gone dealing with Cahooshek, Junot will go to the supply depot office and pick up a few token items that we can use in the galley or something. Cherga and I will go register with the travel authority and go through the motions of looking for a consignment. If we were to get one, all the better, but for now, our real objective is to get to Cahooshek and find out what happened to Zshutana. I'll check in periodically, but I'll stay on the encrypted line of sight system and off the local comm nets just in case they have a way of tracking any comm transmissions. Everyone got that?" asked Jack. Jack headed to his room and came back a few mentus later and was ready to roll.

Jack and Cherga filed the crew manifest as instructed by the inspector and headed into the city. They found a vimar for hire and had the driver take them to the nearby town of Tanuah. "Say, isn't Tanuah where they are having the mating rituals or something like that on Sumtoka?" Jack asked the driver.

"Oh, yes, well, every town has a mating ritual district. But honestly, you don't look like you'd be heading there for that, since you're not Sumtokan," replied the driver.

"Oh, no, of course not," said Jack. "I just heard about it from someone a while back. I got the impression that it was just in certain towns."

"No, it's in every town, but, of course, it's seasonal and only for designated breeders. My first chance will be coming up in two yenets, but I'll have to pass the genetics backgrounds and come up with the entry fee for my level by then. I've got about two-thirds of the twenty thousand credits saved up," said the driver proudly. "So what are you here for?" asked the driver.

"Oh, we're just freelance mine workers looking for a contract. We just got into the city, but the same person told us there was a very good place to eat local Duccadu food near the city center of Tanuah."

"Well, I can take you there if you want," said the driver.

"Well, that would be great, but I don't remember the name of the eating place," said Jack, hoping it wasn't too much of a stretch.

"Well, there are several good places at the center there," said the driver. "There is Hahatey's, Nilwokos, and the Barbahaddah."

"It could have been Nilwokos," said Jack, "but it's been a while, so I don't remember. You can just drop us in the center, and we'll go and look around until we find something that looks good." A few mentus later, Jack paid the driver his eight-credit fare and gave him a two-credit tip, which he seemed pleased with.

"Come on, Cherga, let's go get us bite to add to our cover story. Then we'll do some snooping around." Jack picked a crowded stand-up restaurant near the center of the town where the workers and customers would be too busy to scrutinize them closely. They ordered some fast food, and while they were waiting, Jack grabbed one of the passing workers and asked, "Do you know where this hotel is?" showing the worker the address for Cahooshek's mating appointment.

"Yes, that's about a kahtak east on Fardenem, which is one vimarway over, but I don't think there's a hotel there. I think that's where the mating house is," she said to him.

"Oh, OK, maybe someone gave me the wrong location," replied Jack. "Do you know where there is a decent hotel?"

"Oh, yes, there are two on the north end by the river and one on the south end, but it's not as nice, much less costing, but definitely not as nice," she said.

"OK, well, thanks for your help," he said to her.

"You have a devious mind," said Cherga. "You've gotten all the information we need and never said anything about what we're really doing or where we're going."

"Well, the less real information we leave behind us, the harder it will be for anyone to add up what we're doing and track us back to the ship," said Jack.

"Yes, but my head is spinning just trying to keep track of what you're saying to people."

"Don't worry," said Jack, "just play along and you'll get the feel for it after a while."

After their quick bite of Sumtokan fast food, Jack and Cherga headed over to the vimarway that the mating house was located on. The first time, they just walked by it and did a casual recon of it as well as checking out the other buildings and businesses nearby. The mating house, as the food worker had called it, was just an ordinary two-story building with some parking on the side. Jack's translator translated the small sign on the front of the building as Tanuah Mating House - Level Four Reproduction Authority. "How romantic," said Jack to Cherga, "it looks like a dental office for having a root canal or something as equally enthralling."

"Yes, I don't believe the Sumtokans put a lot of, uh, personal expression into their mating ritual," said Cherga. "I believe it is mostly functional and more of a status symbol and desire to have your offspring carry your genetics on from what I've read. I believe they have more of a desire to meet their reproductive goals for lineage status rather than anything else. Something about each generation wanting to upgrade it social status by producing hopefully better offspring. Some are totally excluded, and I'm not the slightest bit sure how Cahooshek was able to attain a spot, but I guess there can be some corruption and payoffs involved in the process from what I've heard."

"That doesn't surprise me," said Jack, "which, of course, makes me wonder how he managed to get the required credits to bribe his way into the process when it would appear that he wouldn't be eligible in the first place."

"That's a very good question, but I think we both might know the answer," said Cherga.

"Yes, I think that's the most likely explanation," replied Jack.

As they had passed by, Jack had taken inventory of nearby businesses, which included some sort of a bakery or snack shop that was closed for the daiyus, a place selling clothing and footwear, some sort of an arcade where there seemed to be a mixed crowd of people playing various electronic games, as well as some sort of table games that he didn't recognize. There was also a mom-and-pop-looking eatery that advertised something called Hojono Belnz and Lenamec, neither of which he'd heard of.

He was trying to find a place to hang out for a while and watch the mating house for a glimpse of Cahooshek. According to the information he'd gotten from Ruggal, Cahooshek wasn't due there until tomorrow. He decided to try the arcade and see how long he could drag that out. He and Cherga hung out for a couple of horuns playing some of the games while keeping an eye on the mating clinic, as Jack was now thinking of it. After a while, he said to Cherga, "I think we're going to have to rent a vimar and come back tomorrow. There hasn't been much activity at the mating house except possibly staff workers leaving at the end of the daiyus."

They went back to the place where they'd eaten and found a vimar for hire and got a ride back to the spaceport terminal. They checked with the spaceport travel authority and discovered they could rent a vimar right there, which they did under Jack's fake bootlegged name. Jack didn't want to use *Carratta*'s vimar because he didn't want to risk it being seen or recorded anywhere near the mating house.

The next morning, Jack and Cherga went back with their rented vimar and parked off the side street where they could see both the parking area and front door to the mating clinic. Jack had worn a few features of his disguises from Talaka's wives to change his and also Cherga's appearance from the previous night so that they couldn't be easily recognized by anyone. Jack said to Cherga, "I did some research on Sumtoka's local mating house requirements, and it looks like daiyus one is usually spent in final interviews and medical exams, or in Cahoosheks case probably paying off bribes. So if he shows up today as scheduled, it will most likely be a daiyus of just bureaucratic paperwork but no real action for him. What an enjoyable way to get ready for the mating ritual you've been waiting for all these yenets."

Cherga replied, "Well, there are many different mating methods throughout the galaxy that I've heard of, but this one certainly is the most uninspiring, I would say. Sumtokans are bipedal, but they are a different major genus and are too different physically, genetically, and ritually to make mating possible with most of the main types of genera in the galaxy that are known to be able to cross-mate."

"What are the, uh, what would you call them," asked Jack, "rules or laws or maybe restrictions regarding that?" asked Jack.

"Well, there are really no laws or restriction," said Cherga. "It would be just biological and genetic makeup that determines that. The closer two species are together genetically and physically, the more likely they would be able to interbreed. The genetics are able to work themselves out. Some species may be close enough physically to mate but could never produce offspring, but others are too different and cannot mate physically or reproduce. There is not likely to be any physical interaction between those types of species, since there is no common physicality or attraction. Some species might be able to physically mate but not reproduce, but then some, but not many, can mate and also produce a hybrid offspring."

"Is that common, either of the last two?" asked Jack.

"Well, it's not common, but it's not uncommon either," replied Cherga. "For some reason, it seems that the more closely related species are genetically, the farther they are apart location-wise in the galaxy. This is one of the great mysteries of science. You would think they would be closer to each other and that they would then be likely to crossbreed, but for some reason, the more closely related species seem to be scattered farther across the stars from their nearest genetic relatives. No one seems to know why."

"That's very interesting," said Jack, wondering where he and Zshutana fell into that equation. He wondered if anything he was doing would do any good in helping find her, and he wondered if he was actually doing everything he could to find her. He prayed that the answer was a yes to both of those questions.

Jack and Cherga had seen several vimars park and several more hired ones come and go that morning at the mating clinic. Finally, at around 1120, a van-type utility vimar pulled up in the parking area, and the driver opened the side door, and a grossly too-familiar Cahooshek floated out in his portable chair and into the front door of the mating clinic. "Yes, I saw him," said Cherga. "Now what do we do?"

"We wait," replied Jack. "Let the others know we'll be waiting and tell them to keep going about their normal business. Why don't you go grab us some food at the little place around the corner while I watch for our friend and we'll see what happens?"

After their lunch on the stakeout, Jack made a quick trip to the small food place called Jemra's for a quick break. "Any change?" he asked Cherga when he got back.

"No, but this is a boring way to spend the daiyus, but I would sit here for a yenet if it would help you find Zshutana," said Cherga.

"Thanks, I truly appreciate that," replied Jack.

Finally, at 1540, the same van vimar pulled up and waited outside the mating house. "I'm guessing that's for Cahooshek, unless there's some other floating chair mutant utilizing the mating facility today," said Jack. A few mentus later, Cahooshek floated out of the building accompanied by an attendant of some sort. The driver opened the side door again, and Cahooshek, the soon-to-be mated abysmal Sumtokan, floated into the vimar. "Here we go," said Jack.

The vimar pulled out of the parking area and headed west, while Jack and Cherga followed from two hundred mu-uts back. "They'll be easy to follow if the traffic is light," said Jack, "but it gets a lot more challenging when it gets busy, so help me keep a good lock on them," he said to Cherga.

"I'm not sure what you mean by a 'lock on,' but I will keep them in my sight at all times," replied Cherga.

"Same thing, it means the same thing," said Jack.

They followed the van for about eight kahtaks until it pulled into an upscale-looking eating establishment with a lot of expensive exterior décor and a few attendants standing around outside to wait on people. Cahooshek got out and floated into the building, while Jack and Cherga watched from across the vimarway. "It looks like he is treating himself to an expensive meal after his grueling daiyus of interviewing and bribes," commented Cherga.

"Yes, so it seems," replied Jack, "and I have a pretty good idea of how he's managing to finance his entire extravagant adventure. Zshutana told me he's been trying to save for many yenets to finance this mating expedition and that he was a long way from ever being able to accomplish this. Now all of a sudden, he's rolling in dough and buying his way into his mating adventure and fancy restaurants."

"Rolling in dough, restaurants?" said Cherga.

"Yes, uh, rolling in credits, and restaurant is a food or eating store," said Jack.

"Hmm, OK," replied Cherga, "it is challenging to understand many of your crazy sayings. Many don't seem to translate at first, but I believe I know what you are saying about his suddenly newfound wealth."

An horun and a half later, the van vimar pulled up, and Cahooshek floated out of the expensive restaurant to get in it. Jack noticed that he didn't seem to be navigating his chair to the best of his abilities as it bounced off a post and the wall on the way to the van. "It looks like he has enjoyed himself a bit too much," commented Cherga as the floating chair struggled to find its way into the van. "I hope he enjoyed himself because I think that it will be the last time he does for a while," said Jack. The van vimar pulled away from the restaurant, and Jack and Cherga fell in behind it. They followed Cahooshek's van through several kahtaks of light traffic until it came to a place that looked like a fairly grungy motor hotel. There was a main office and four short rows of ground floor rooms off a main corridor.

The motel was on the dingier side of town, and it wasn't much to look at. It didn't look like it was overly popular, but then it was early in the daiyus and could possibly fill up later. It had no amenities such as a pool or restaurant or other things that Jack would have expected back on Earth. Of course, Jack didn't really know what sort of things inns or motels had as amenities on a planet like Sumtoka or any other alien world for that matter. Mostly it just looked like some rows of rooms for travelers to sleep, and that was about it.

"It looks like he's saving his credits for fine dining and the time at the mating house," said Cherga.

"It kind of looks that way," agreed Jack. "He should have plenty of credits to spend but not as many as he would have if Zshutana hadn't sent my share over to Junot. I don't have any idea how much this multi-moondat mating adventure is costing him either, but it's probably not cheap considering the condition he's in. Maybe he's planning on retiring afterward and he's smart enough not to blow all his credits on fancy lodging. If you're not entertaining someone in your room, then there's no point in wasting the money. Of course, his lair back on Nishda was pretty grungy too, so maybe he just feels at home in a dump like this. This is probably a step up from his digs on Nishda anyway."

"Digs?" said Cherga.

"Living arrangements," replied Jack.

"Ah, yes, that is probably close to the truth," agreed Cherga.

The van vimar had dropped Cahooshek at a room farthest from the office and on the cross street side of the motel. After guiding Cahooshek and his floating chair into the room, the driver left and was likely not expected back until tomorrow, based on Jack's estimation. The place looked pretty quiet with only three or four other customers, at least ones with vimars, and they were all closer to the office.

Jack was trying to decide where to confront Cahooshek. Inside Cahooshek's room would be the least likely to attract attention, at least versus kidnapping him, but that posed a problem too if he made too much noise and alerted someone nearby. The alternative was to drag him out of the room and into their rented vimar, but that posed the problem of being spotted and possibly forensics left in the vehicle if there was ever an investigation of any sort. He decided that inside Cahooshek's room would be better especially in light of the lack of other motel customers.

"All right, Cherga, here's what I want you to do," said Jack. "I'm going to go pay our friend Mr. Cahooshek a little visit in his room. I want you to stay right here, actually even farther back behind that dark building there," as Jack motioned to the empty-looking place across from where they were. "You'll be able to see in almost all directions approaching the motel as well as Cahooshek's room. I'll go visit him on foot and have a little chat with him. If you see anyone coming or notice anything that might be a giveaway, then call me, and I'll sprint right back here as casually as possible."

"OK, I'll be right over there, then," replied Cherga. "If you need any help, just call me, and I'll be right there."

"Thanks," said Jack, "but I think I've got this covered, for Zshutana."

Cherga replied, "Just let me know if you do. What are you going to do to him, or should I ask?"

"I'm going to make him talk, and if he won't talk, it won't be a good daiyus for him," said Jack.

Cherga just shook his head in agreement and said, "That is good."

"Actually, it's not going to be a good daiyus for him anyway," added Jack.

"Even more good," said Cherga.

Jack got out of the vimar and crossed the vimarway at the corner in an unhurried manner with his head down and his hood covering his head. He passed by Cahooshek's room and did a little recon as he went around the corner at the end of the building. He hadn't seen or heard anything, and after a couple of mentus, he came back along the building toward Cahooshek's room. A vimar went down the vimarway but didn't even bother to slow. He searched, but he hadn't noticed any surveillance equipment of any kind, although he didn't really have any idea of what Sumtokan surveillance equipment might look like. He got to Cahooshek's door and looked up to check that Cherga could see him and gave him a discreet thumbs-up. He listened through the door and could hear a vido or news display talking, so maybe Cahooshek hadn't passed out yet and was still getting ready for his big daiyus tomorrow.

Jack took a couple of deep breaths, readied himself, then banged on the door. "Sir, Mr. Cahooshek, this is your driver. You left something in the vimar." There wasn't a peephole, but Cahooshek might not have been able to look through one if there was. Jack could hear some shuffling and a couple of small banging noises. Jack had no idea what the driver sounded like, so he tried to muffle his voice but make it loud enough for Cahooshek to hear. "Sir, I have your article here that you left in the vimar. Can you hear me, sir? I thought you might need it," implored Jack.

Inside the room, Cahooshek was trying to clear his head and understand what the person at the door was saying. Was it the driver he'd hired? What was he saying, something about something he left in the vimar? What could he have left? "What is it? What did I leave?" he managed to mutter back.

"I don't know, sir, but it was there where you were sitting in your chair. Maybe it's something off your chair," said the voice from outside the door.

"All right, all right, I'm coming," groused Cahooshek as he climbed back in his chair. He could have made it to the door without it, but he didn't like people to see him struggling without his chair. Cahooshek snuck a peek out the side of the window and could see the person standing with his back to the door and partially hunched over. It sort of looked like the driver. He wasn't sure, as he hadn't really paid that close of attention, what with all the interviewing, arranging of payoffs actually, and all the other important things on his mind. "Yes, yes, just give me a mentu, just wait. You should have seen that I dropped something when you let me out," he admonished the driver through the door as he was unlatching it."

"Yes, sir, I'm sorry. I just didn't see it then. I just wanted to get it back to you tonight," said the voice.

Cahooshek opened the door partly to see what it was he'd dropped. Jack jammed his foot in the opening as soon as the door opened and shoved hard to overcome the chair that he knew might be there. The door flew open hard and hit Cahooshek's arm and pushed his chair back with him in it. It took Cahooshek a moment to realize that something was happening and that it wasn't good. Jack saw Cahooshek reaching up to rub his arm and trying to grasp what was happening. He lunged toward Cahooshek, grabbed him by his arm and the front to his tunic, and yanked him out of the chair and slammed him onto the bed. He didn't want to hurt him too badly, at least not until he got all the information out of him that he could.

Jack glanced behind him and looked out the door but didn't see anyone, so he kicked the door shut and turned his attention back to Cahooshek. He slapped Cahooshek a couple of times to get his attention as well as to put some serious scare into him. Cahooshek started squirming and started to scream. Jack grabbed a piece of clothing that was lying on the bed and jammed it in Cahooshek's mouth. "Shut up or I'll gut you like a pig, you miserable wretched puke," said Jack. Cahooshek was now fairly terrified. He didn't know what a pig was, but he didn't want to be gutted like one.

"Whah, what do you want?" Cahooshek tried to say through the cloth that was jammed in his mouth. He was trying to catch his breath from the exertion, and all that came out was a garbled mess of gasping gagging sounds.

"You don't look like you're in very good condition to engage in moondats of mating ritual," growled Jack in Cahooshek's face as he pulled the cloth out of Cahooshek's mouth.

How, what, how did this person know he was going to be mating? Was this the driver? thought Cahooshek.

"Look at me, look . . . at . . . me," said the person to Cahooshek. "Do you recognize me? Do you know who I am?" said the angry voice from the stranger that was holding him down.

"No, no," rasped Cahooshek as he shook his head, trying to clear it, though this attacker did seem to look somewhat familiar.

"Where is Zshutana? What have you done with Zshutana?" said the highly agitated and very serious, angry person looking at him from half an arm's length away.

Zshutana? What was this person talking about? What did Zshutana back on Nishda have to do with anything here on Sumtoka? "I don't know what you're talking about Zshutana," somehow Cahooshek managed to sputter.

"Zshutana from the Dirga level back at the Corodune mine," said Jack as he gave Cahooshek's arm a good twist. "Look at me closely," said Jack. "My friend, my girlfriend, is Zshutana. You did something with her, and you stole her winnings from my fight pit matches. Yes, that Zshutana."

Cahooshek just stared; his mind was trying to comprehend. *It couldn't, not possible.* His head was spinning; he felt dizzy. His mouth was very dry. He moved his lips, but nothing came out.

"That's right. You're starting to get the idea," encouraged Jack.

"You are, you're, you're dead. They said, the bosses, they said you were dead," Cahooshek barely managed to squeak out.

"They were wrong, very seriously wrong," replied Jack. The color was completely gone from Cahooshek's already horrid face now. "I've come here for one reason and one reason only. You are going to tell me what happened to Zshutana. If you don't tell me, I will kill you here and now," said Jack as he stared ruthlessly into Cahooshek's eyes.

"But we're, this, this is Sumtoka, how, how—"

"Shut up," growled Jack, "but think about that fact for a second. I came all the way from Nishda, something you've been saving up for since you got there. I came all the way from Nishda to find out what happened to Zshutana. If you think for a septu that I am leaving here without the answers I want from you, then you are thinking wrong, dead wrong." Cahooshek's head was still spinning. This crazy pit fighter, the one he bought to work in the mine, his name was, was Ja-ck, a Varaci, that was it. He was twisting, pushing; it hurt. He tried to squirm.

Jack slapped him again, hard enough to bring him back to the topic at hand. "Where is Zshutana? You'd better start talking now, or things will go from bad to worse and then more worse for you," said Jack in a measured even voice.

"I don't know, I don't know where she is," stammered Cahooshek. *Oh, shnepsa saph, that hurt, is that his knee in my side?* thought Cahooshek.

"Bullshit," growled Jack, "the new tenant in her apartment told me you are the landlord and that you pulled her out of there. Your idiot flunky Ruggal told me you stole her credits so you could come here for your mating ritual," said Jack, slightly embellishing the information he'd gotten.

"But, but Ruggal didn't know that I forced her—" said Cahooshek, stopping in midsentence.

"Tell me now where she is or you'll pay in pieces, very important pieces," said Jack.

For a second, Cahooshek thought, *What is he talking about? What is he going to do? He can't kill me or he won't get an answer. Maybe I can convince him to leave with some story and he'll be gone, and I can get back to my mating ritual. Then I can get back to Nishda.* Jack could see the wheels turning in Cahooshek's demented brain. He pulled his short katana knife from under his tunic, grabbed Cahooshek's hand and smashed it flat on the bed, then brought the blade straight down, severing the two smallest fingers on the outside of Cahooshek's left hand.

He let Cahooshek's hand go, and Cahooshek stared at it in horror as he opened his mouth to scream. Jack stuffed the clothing back in Cahooshek's mouth as he tried to scream, only to be stifled into a muffled groan as he flailed around trying to free himself. Jack held him tight and kept the cloth stuffed in Cahooshek's mouth. Jack pinned the wounded hand down again as it was spraying the bluish-red blood around everywhere as Cahooshek flailed helplessly.

"Shut up or I'll kill you now," said Jack, meaning it. Cahooshek was heaving but was settling down under the threat of being killed and Jack's weight pressing on him. Jack took the piece of clothing and wrapped it around Cahooshek's bleeding hand and then allowed him to use his other hand to hold it. "That's your one and only warning. Where is Zshutana?" said Jack in a clear, calm, calculating voice. Cahooshek could barely comprehend what was happening to him now, but he knew he had to tell the truth now or he would be dead in a mentu and would never mate.

"I, I sold her, I sold her to a Santaran ship, a Santaran ship in Wanana."

"What do you mean you sold her to a Santaran ship in Wanana?" snarled Jack.

"A Santaran ship, slavers, slave traders, where we get some of the convicts for the mines. I sold her to the Santaran ship," groveled the now pathetically whining Cahooshek.

Jack wanted to strangle the life out of this wretched piece of vermin excrement, but he had to get the information out of him. "For how much?"

"Uh, uh," stammered Cahooshek as Jack could see him start to think. Jack lifted the knife and started to grab Cahooshek's arm. "Fif-fifty thousand, fifty thousand credits," said Cahooshek, feeling relieved that the knife hadn't come down on his hand again.

"And where did they take her?" asked Jack more resolute than ever.

"I don't, I don't know, I swear I don't know," pleaded Cahooshek in a whimpering voice.

"Where was the Santaran ship headed?" demanded Jack.

"Coravu, I think. I think they were going to Coravu, but you never can know if that's where they're really going," offered Cahooshek.

"Then where?" said Jack.

"I don't, I don't know, not for sure. I think I heard them mention Ranara." Jack could have grilled him more, but he didn't want to spend any more time on Cahooshek; he could do his own research on those planets. In the back of his mind, Cahooshek thought, maybe, maybe there was a chance he would leave now that he had the information.

"Zshutana had at least 2.4 million credits from her winnings on the fight pit matches," said Jack. "She also had," Jack took a wag, "another hundred thousand credits of her own, and you sold her for fifty thousand credits. That's easy math. You owe her 2.6 million credits." Cahooshek's eyes got even wider than they had when Jack came through the door and pinned him to the bed. Jack took his knife and grabbed Cahooshek by his translator. Cahooshek started to struggle and wail. "Shut up or I'll kill you right now," he said again to the worm Cahooshek. Cahooshek thought Jack was going to kill him but maybe not now, maybe he, maybe he didn't know anymore.

Jack turned the blade and sliced through the translator band and pulled the translator from Cahooshek. He copied and transmitted Cahooshek's ID from the severed translator. He could see all of Cahooshek's files and commands now. He scrolled to his credits account. The translator display showed a 2,614,328.38 credit balance. "So you don't have much more than what you stole from Zshutana. I guess you've spent some on your trip here and other expenses. Not much to show for all your corruption back at Corodune," said Jack.

Cahooshek was now making guttural burbling noises and assorted grunts and snorts, but he was close enough to his translator that it was coming through translated to Jack. "I had another 104,000, but I lost it betting on you. The mine bosses told me to bet on you, and I lost it all," whined Cahooshek.

"You mean they told you to bet against me because the fights were supposedly rigged and they undercut the percentages on the odds and were going to rake in a nice profit, but I kept winning every time and you lost. Guess you bet on the wrong fighter. Too bad, so sad," said Jack. "Now you're going to pay Zshutana back for what you stole from her. Transfer 2.6 million credits to my name in my account right now. I should take the rest for interest and the cost of tracking you down, but I'll leave you your fourteen thousand," said Jack.

Cahooshek's head was spinning again. Now he felt hot like he was going to puke. Now he was mad. "No, no, no, you can't do that. You can't take all, all my, that. I need it for mating. I have to pay the mating house tomorrow. No, I won't do it. I'd rather be dead, I'd rather be dead," cried Cahooshek.

"All right, I can arrange for that right now," said Jack, actually wondering if he could make the transfer himself using Cahooshek's translator as he lifted his knife again and grabbed Cahooshek's good hand while he stuffed the bloody clothing in Cahooshek's mouth again.

"Wha, wha ah u doung?" came the muffled cry partially through the translator as Jack stretched out Cahooshek's arm.

"I'm going to kill you now like you said you preferred, but it's not going to be quick or nearly painless like your two fingers. I'm going to drag this out for horuns and skin you piece by piece. In fact, I have all night. I'm going to remove nonessential parts of your body one piece at a time. Now just remember, this is your preferred choice." Cahooshek writhed and fought and tried to scream. "Why are you making such a big fuss? This is what you chose," said Jack.

He'd already cut off his fingers; Cahooshek knew this insane Varaci or whatever he was would do it just like he said he would. "No, na, thtop. Ul do-ot. I'll ranthsfer it. Thsop, pleasve don't, lease," Cahooshek pleaded as Jack let off the pressure of the blood-soaked cloth.

"Well, all right, if that's what you want," said Jack. "I'm perfectly happy to give you whatever choice you prefer."

"No, no," gasped the sobbing Cahooshek, "I'll transfer the credits."

"Then do it," said Jack, "and don't make me wait because I don't care either way at this point. I was really looking forward to it, really, I was."

"You'll let me live, then?" pleaded Cahooshek.

"Yes, I'll let you live, not that you deserve to, but I'm a man of my word," replied Jack.

"A man? What's a man?" asked Cahooshek, tentatively afraid of the answer.

"That's what we are on my planet, humans, not Varans or Varacis. Now get busy and transfer."

What the shirba was a humuns? thought Cahooshek as he complied and transferred the 2.6 million credits to Jack's account.

The transfer looked good. It had cleared the local Sumtokan banking system. A minute after it cleared, Jack transferred it to his ghost account under the bootlegged account name he had paid for. In a little while, he would move it to Cherga's and Junot's bootlegged accounts for further safekeeping.

Cahooshek lay on the bed whimpering and curled in a fetal position looking utterly beaten and nearly dead. Everything he'd worked for, stolen for, colluded for, conspired for, and cheated for was gone. He wouldn't have the hundred thousand credit mating fee he needed tomorrow to carry on his lineage. What did he really have to live for now? Fortunately, he had paid for a round-trip fare from Nishda. Maybe he could get back to his lair and try and start over. He didn't know, he just didn't know, as he lay there in a heap of utter misery.

"Listen up, Cahooshek, I'm only going to say this once." Cahooshek looked up at Jack; how he hated this humuns or Varaci or whatever it was. "I traveled all the way here to find out what happened to Zshutana. You'd better hope that I find her alive and well. If I don't find her alive and well or I find out that you've lied to me about anything, and I mean anything, I will make it my sole objective and singular quest to hunt you down and finish what I started a few mentus ago except that I'll string it out over a wenek. Do you understand what I'm telling you? Well, do you?" growled Jack.

"Yes, yes, I, I . . ." whined Cahooshek.

"Is there anything else you want to add or change? Now is your only chance to not be held accountable for any errors or omissions. Any changes, Cahooshek?"

"No, no, nothing," stammered Cahooshek.

"OK, then," said Jack, "I have forewarned you. If I find out that you lied or left anything out or if I find that anything has happened to Zshutana, I will hunt you down no matter where you are and no matter how long it takes me to find you. There is no place you can run, there is no place you can hide, and there is no place in this galaxy where you will be safe. You'd better hope that what you've told me leads me to Zshutana and that she is alive and well." Cahooshek just stared at Jack in horror and shook his head.

"Now you may be wondering why I've let you live, and here's why. I want you to think about our little meeting here today for every moment of the rest of your miserable life.

I don't want a daiyus to go by that you don't dwell on the fact that I'll be coming for you if things don't work out my way. There is nothing that can stop me, and I won't rest until my own personal version of justice is complete. I could have let it go as far as you putting me in the mine because you didn't know what or who you were dealing with, and you were probably misled somewhat even though your intentions were to enslave me for your own monetary gain. Now the mentu you brought Zshutana into the equation, it changed everything. You knew exactly what you were doing with her, and for that, I would simply kill you, but I'm going to leave you alive for one reason, and that is if I don't find Zshutana, I will exact total retribution on you in a manner so horrifying that you can't even begin to fathom it. I hope you have a good and sickeningly demented imagination and that you are capable of comprehending exactly what I'm telling you down to the very core of your aberrant perverted soul because that is what I will do to you, only it will be ten times worse. Don't worry, though, because if you can't imagine anything that horrifying, I assure you that I can."

"If I find out you've told the provosts about our little meeting here today, which could possibly interfere with my mission to find Zshutana, then the same retribution will apply. The one thing you can do, though, is this—if you make it back to Nishda somehow, you can tell those reprobate mine bosses that I'll be coming back for them too and that I will take down their fraudulent criminal mine conscript operation and that it will be them spending the next thirty yenets working in the mines and not the conscripts or convicts that have been fraudulently incarcerated there as slave labor. Have you got all that?" said Jack as he seethed at Cahooshek.

"Yes, I, I, do understand," gurgled Cahooshek partially through his nearby translator while shaking his head.

Jack grabbed Cahooshek's translator where it lay next to him on the bed and stuck it in his coat pocket. He took a quick look at the floating chair then took out his katana and with one quick swing literally cut it in half. It crashed to the floor in a heap of sparks and smoke. "You won't be going anywhere fast tonight. I guess you can tell them that you were robbed if it comes to that, but it had better not lead back to me, and you had better believe me that I will know the instant it does. You have no idea who I am or what I'm capable of. Always think twice, Cahooshek. You'd better always think twice before you try to interfere with anything or anyone I'm involved with," said Jack as he stared venomously at the sickening heap of misery called Cahooshek. He then sheathed his katana, spun around, and slammed the door closed on his way out.

Jack looked both ways and couldn't see anyone or anything watching him except for Cherga, who was nearly hidden behind the far building across the street. Jack walked casually across the street, taking up the same nonchalant gait that he had coming over. Damn, damn, he couldn't believe what he'd just done and what had transpired as he headed toward Cherga and the rented vimar. He got in the passenger side and told Cherga to drive and head back to the spaceport. Cherga could tell Jack was wired high on adrenalin.

"Should I ask if he's still alive?" said Cherga.

"Yeah, yes, he's still alive, but he's not in very good shape and he's not going anywhere for a while and he's not going to be doing any mating, at least not in this lifetime. He sold Zshutana to some kind of slaver ship called Santarans, but he's not sure where they were headed next. He thinks they might have been going to a couple of planets called Coravu and Ranara. What do you know about them?" said Jack.

"Nothing good," said Cherga. "Santara and its race of Santarans are involved in all sorts of activities that are illegal on most other GTA-controlled planets, including slaving and slave trading. No one knows how this is possible, but most suspect that the Santarans are actually quietly sanctioned by the GTA to do the dirty work that the GTA overtly prohibits in their normal trade system. Basically, they are the go-to planet for when the GTA wants to accomplish something that they might otherwise be questioned on. Appearance is everything in this GTA arrangement. The GTA gets to look clean while they allow illegal activities in the background, and the Santarans are one of the races that do their dirty work."

"Maybe I should have killed him," sighed Jack.

"Yes, I would have easily voted for that," said Cherga.

"What about the two planets Coravu and Ranara?" asked Jack.

"They are just two planets that are less than reputable," replied Cherga. "Most planets or systems have some degree of corruption just like you've seen on Nishda. Some are worse than others. Coravu and Ranara would fall far into that category, as they deal with both the supposedly reputable GTA as well as with the Santarans."

"OK," said Jack, just shaking his head.

"What are you thinking?" asked Cherga.

"Just thinking, just, just thinking," sighed Jack.

Chapter 14: Runners

Jack and Cherga got back to the spaceport terminal forty mentus later and turned in their rented vimar. Back on *Carratta,* Jack checked to make sure everyone was present and accounted for. "All right, let's get *Carratta* ready to launch as soon as we can. Are we all settled up with the local supply depot and everything else here?" Wehsh and Junot confirmed they were all set in that respect.

Less than ten mentus later, they were ready to launch. Jack remembered to transfer Zshutana's funds over to Cherga's and Junot's ghost accounts so that it was registered before they left Sumtoka. "I'll brief you all later. Just get us in the air and headed to the nearest Sumtoka departure point." They got their clearance and finished their checklists, and *Carratta* was on her way to orbit. They filed for Lokar just to have something on the Sumtokan records. Three and a half horuns later, they hit their transit point and went to light drive headed toward Lokar. Five mentus later and with a short course alteration, they came out of hyperspace and drifted at 0.48 light speed.

"OK, guys, here's what went down," announced Jack. He gave them a short synopsis of his meeting with Cahooshek without all the gory details. "This isn't going to be the cargo mission I advertised to you when you signed on, at least not yet. My primary mission is to find Zshutana, which I know you have all agreed to already. The situation is becoming a little more demanding than I had originally hoped for," explained Jack as he continued to explain to them what Cherga had told him about the Santaran ship and Coravu and Ranara. "So I've got plenty of credits now to continue the search for Zshutana for a yenet or more if needed. It's just going to be a lot more challenging than I originally expected. I'm sure I can tap Zshutana's funds also, as I'm sure she won't mind me spending them looking for her.

"I can pay you all the promised rate that I initially advertised to Wehsh, but again, the priority is going to be finding Zshutana and doing whatever is required to make that happen. So I need to know who is still in and if you're up for whatever this might entail."

"Wait," said Cherga, "you said you paid to buy us out of the mine, is that not correct? How much did that cost you?"

"Uh, well, that's nothing," said Jack.

"No, it's not. I wish to know," said Cherga.

"Me too," said Junot.

"All right, then," as Jack told them the ransom he'd had to pay for their release.

"We can't thank you enough. I would have asked sooner, but this last wenek has been the craziest in my life," said Cherga.

"I am just so totally thankful that I was able to get you guys out of there. That was my only concern," said Jack.

"Yes, and you risked everything to do it," said Junot.

"Yes, and Forto almost crashed the whole plan," said Wehsh.

"Well, forget Forto. He's paying the ultimate price for his duplicity and stupidity now," said Jack.

Cherga began. "Jack, I don't want any pay for our services on your crew. We have plenty of earnings from our foray into the fight pit gambling world, so until I've paid back what you paid to get us out, don't even think about paying us."

"The same for me," said Junot. "I'm doing something I only fantasized about my whole life and never would have been able to do if it wasn't for you. I'd work here for you for free forever."

"Thanks, guys. You don't know how much I appreciate that," replied Jack.

"No, it is us that are the appreciative ones," said Cherga.

Jack said to Wehsh, "I'll pay you as I advertised, and I'll throw in a 20 percent hazardous duty bonus if you're willing to stay on."

"That sounds good to me," he replied. "It sounds like it's just starting to get interesting. If you can pay me, that's great. If you can't, that's OK too. Either way, I don't think I'm going to die of boredom."

Jack laughed. "No, no, I don't think you will die of boredom, but the prognosis of dying from something else is still somewhat likely."

"Well, I guess there's only one way to find out," replied Wehsh.

"That is a very true statement, Mr. Hevedu. That is a very true statement indeed."

"Plot our position, then, Mr. Hevedu, and have Junot verify it for you then plot and execute a course to Coravu."

"Roger wilco, Captain. Our course is now plotted for Coravu, executing your command."

"Thank you, Wehsh," said Jack. "Now let's go Santaran hunting," said Jack to them all. The star field pulled back and then blanked as *Carratta* was enveloped in the strange and eerie glow of the quantum field in light drive hyperspace. *Be with us, just be with us and let us find Zshutana,* Jack said to himself. They were on their way . . .